A.C. DONAUBAUER
Commitments – Book 2

I0656327

Commitments - The Order: Book 2

A.C. Donaubauer

First published as ebook in February 2016
Paperback
2nd edition

Copyright © 2019
        Astrid Donaubauer-Grobner
        Waltenhofengasse 3/3/3302
        1100 Vienna, Austria

The author online:
        www.ac-donaubauer.com
        www.facebook.com/acdonaubauer

Cover: Biserka Design

Editing: Jürgen Donaubauer, Hannes Ohrlinger
Proofreading: Philip Scott

Print: CreateSpace, an Amazon.com enterprise
February 2019

ISBN 978-3-904142-06-9

For Maria. Nature made us sisters, but your big heart made us mother and daughter for a while.

Thank you.

CHAPTER 1

Plans

Tyront looked at the younger man opposite him and shook his head indulgently, causing his full, slightly greying hair to dance with the movement. "You have been in a very good mood these last few days. This doesn't happen to have anything to do with a certain ambassador having left the city, does it?" he chuckled.

There was a glint in Enric's clear blue eyes when he smiled weakly and stretched out his long legs, crossing his ankles over each other. "Are you suggesting that I do not appreciate the great chances for the Kingdom the delegation's visit has opened up? That would be implying that my disposition is somewhat unpatriotic."

"No, my boy, I am suggesting that you are relieved that he can no longer try to charm your companion away from you."

The younger man looked somewhat disapproving, his piercing blue eyes slightly narrowed. "Are you saying that I was afraid that he would have succeeded eventually?"

"Maybe not succeeded in charming her, but probably in taking her away from here somehow. I doubt that she would have gone voluntarily. You seem to have grown on her, after all. I have noticed that she is more relaxed now when you touch her."

"Yes, that she is. And that was hard work. Basically, I have been wearing her down," Enric replied with a lazy smile, glad that the conversation had moved away from the ambassador.

Tyront grinned. "Devious. What is she up to at the moment? The healers' building is not yet finished, so she can't really start any healing or teaching yet. Do you know if she has contacted young Rolan yet?"

"She mentioned thinking about an expedition of some sort to teach the herb gatherers which plants to look for, where to find them and how to treat them once they have found them. She will probably ask her assistant to take care of some organisational matters in connection with this."

"You don't seem too enthusiastic about that idea. I myself think it is a valid use of her time until she can start to use the building."

Enric sighed. "Yes, I know it is. It's just the thought of her leaving the city for several days with a bunch of strangers that doesn't sit well with me. I hinted at the chance of accompanying her, but she treated it like a put-on and laughed it off." He shook his head. "Could I make her stay with an official order? Would you back me up on that? It would mean neglecting her studies and combat training for quite some time, in fact."

Tyront looked incredulous. "You are not seriously asking me that, are you? I can't be seen backing you up on something like that. I'd say it's good for you to let her do something on her own for a change. She is rather a capable young woman and it's time for her to handle things without your being there to fix each little thing that goes wrong or even prevent its going wrong in the first place."

"I am not doing anything of that sort," Enric retorted, knowing fully well that he was.

"You aren't? Then how about your sending magicians to the construction site of her building to make sure it gets finished in time? And then you wanted to accompany her on her negotiations with the apothecaries." Tyront narrowed his eyes. "Is it possible that you are trying to show her that being with you increases her chances of success? You are not *that* desperate, are you?"

The younger magician looked slightly irritated. "Weren't you the one to preach that being a leader also means being a mentor?"

"What *you* are doing is not mentoring, though, as it is meant to serve *your* personal aims instead of your protégé's," the older man replied with raised eyebrows.

"This sounds as if you are in favour of her accomplishing something without my help and will thus grant her permission for her idea of a herb gathering expedition."

"Yes, if the details are halfway reasonable I will not put obstacles in her way," he said. "Even if being without her for a few days threatens to break your heart."

"That's nice. First you keep pestering me for years finally to settle down with a nice girl and when I do, you keep taunting me because I happen to become attached to her." Enric shook his head. "I should have known there would be no pleasing you."

Tyront smiled. "I am pleased, believe me. Very much so. Your falling in love with her was a lucky stroke for all of us. But it is comforting to see that she keeps you on your toes, so to speak. A man in your position has a great choice of compliant females, so the temptation to pick one that is willing to cater to your every whim is clearly there. But in the long run a less docile partner is more stimulating."

"Yes, I dare say that is something I will probably never lack: stimulation," Enric said with a lopsided grin. Then he turned serious. "How about the report on the results of the negotiations with the delegation? Has Marrin sent it yet? I am looking forward to reading it. I am curious what they have agreed on. Why again was the Order not included in the talks?"

"Because they mostly talked about trade, and this is not one of the Order's areas of expertise or responsibility."

"Of course - only invite the warriors when the trade talks have failed and we need to hit them on the head," Enric retorted with some sourness in his voice.

"Look at you... So, there is a little of your father in you, after all. Feeling the urge to get back to your roots, being a merchant, negotiating trade agreements?"

The younger man grimaced at the mention of his father. "Hardly. Don't tell me *you* are happy with being left out? There is valuable knowledge about magic in the Western Territories, so I don't see how we were not entitled to participate in the negotiations."

"I think you overestimate the progress and depth of the talks. It was mostly about establishing a preliminary trading and messenger structure, exchanging information about goods available for trade and determining an exchange rate for our currencies."

Enric gave a feeble grin. "So they haven't really managed to leave you out of it entirely, have they?" He leaned forward. "I wonder who your informer is. But of course you won't tell me."

Tyront shrugged. "Of course I won't. You go find your own able agents in useful positions."

They looked up when a knock sounded at the door and a servant delivered a folded message. The older man turned it to take a look at the seal.

"Ah yes, I see Eryn finally has her own seal." He studied the curved lines that formed an elegant ornament for several seconds. "Interesting. It does remind me of your own - which is hardly a coincidence, I dare say."

"No, not at all. I instructed Vern accordingly and he delivered a design in record time. Very useful, that boy. We really should keep an eye on him. I suppose she sent you the request for her expedition?"

Tyront opened the seal and nodded after a few moments. "Yes, indeed. She asks for provisions for herself plus one, and for fifteen herb gatherers for ten days."

"Plus one?"

"Yes. It seems she wants to take young Vern along with her. To make illustrations for documentation purposes. She mentions writing a book with instructions where they would be indispensable." He looked at the second piece of paper that was included and smiled. "She has even sent a signed letter of permission from Orrin where he agrees to entrust his son into her care for the duration of the expedition. I like these little touches of thoughtfulness." He read the letter again. "It's odd that she has not requested any servants for the journey. As I assume that she doesn't intend to cook and prepare camp every night for all these people, I will approve two more people to take care of this."

Enric smiled when an idea hit him. "Make one of them the orphan girl from the kitchen, young Plia, will you? Eryn hasn't really had much chance to spend time with her in these last weeks and I know she feels bad about it."

"Alright, Plia, the kitchen girl it is." Tyront made a note. "Any preference about the second one?"

"No, not really. But somebody who can do heavy lifting and has no problems taking orders from a woman would be good."

"Well, that second part would rule you out at any rate," Tyront said with a thin smile. "It took me years to get you to take orders from the King, after all. You see? Your accompanying her would be completely useless."

* * *

Eryn knocked at the door to Orrin's quarters and smiled when Junar opened it.

"Hello. I keep running into you more and more often these days. Why do you even bother returning to your home anymore?" she grinned at her friend.

"Because I am an independent woman with my own income and do not want to leech off my rich lover. That's why," Junar explained with mock haughtiness.

"*Lover.*" Eryn shook her head with a grimace, looking at the petite woman in front of her whose appearance with her nicely flowing dress was so much more female than Eryn's own preferred no-nonsense style with trousers and tunic and her hastily braided hair hanging down her back. "I still have problems connecting that term with Orrin."

"Good," the seamstress said. "I wouldn't want you to think of him that way."

"No danger there, sweetheart. He is all yours. Is my favourite sixteen-year old around? I have good news for him."

"In his room with his nose in a book; as always when he isn't drawing some part of the body no normal person can identify. Be careful of that monster you brought here. It has a nasty temper."

Eryn frowned. "Monster? You mean the cat I brought here for him to practise repairing soft tissue? It's still here? Why? He told me he just wanted to feed it and then set it free again. That was more than a week ago!"

Junar nodded gravely. "Yes, that was the initial plan. But somehow that beast has managed to brainwash Vern into keeping it. It sleeps on his bed, eats leftover meat and then pees on whatever looks expensive."

"Oh dear," Eryn said with a sympathetic grimace, feeling slightly guilty. "Do you want me to talk to him about it?"

Junar sighed. "No, that's Orrin's problem, let him handle it. His son, his quarters, his responsibility. Though one of these days he'll have no servant willing to clean his quarters any more, I am afraid. Removing stinking, wet, dripping items or being attacked by the cause of them is hardly an incentive to work here."

Eryn chewed her lip. "And the cat's in his room now? Where I am supposed to go?"

"You caught it, so you obviously know how to deal with it. And you can shield yourself. Where is the danger for *you*?"

"Well, catching it was not really a matter of great personal danger for me," she admitted. "I basically stunned it and slung it over my shoulder. It might remember that and take revenge on me."

Junar scoffed. "You stunned the cat with magic in order to catch it? That truly was a heroic act. It's not like you are several times the size of the poor creature."

"You go out there and try to catch one of these cunning beasts with your bare hands, then we can talk," Eryn shot back. "They have claws. And teeth. And they move like lightning. Have I mentioned the claws? Veritable daggers, I tell you. And suddenly it's a poor creature? A minute ago you called it a monster!"

"Says the woman who can heal herself instantly. I have not yet heard anything that would warrant your fear of going in there, so off you go. Don't make me drag you in there by your ear," the seamstress grinned.

Eryn straightened. "Alright. I am not afraid of a cat. *I am not afraid of a cat*. I can stun it again if need be..." She knocked at Vern's door and opened it when he grunted something unintelligible.

He was hunched over a book on his desk, the ends of his overlong fringe almost touching the paper. The enormous, red tomcat was curled up on his bed, opening one eye when she entered, flicking the tip of its tail in a gesture that, however miniscule, somehow managed to convey a promise of pain to the careless person who took any undue liberties, such as for example getting too close.

"Good news," she announced cheerfully. "The departure of the expedition has been cleared! We will be off for ten days of wilderness and herb gathering in no more than three weeks!"

Vern looked up, blinking a few times so as to leave the world of skin disorders behind him and concentrate on the here and now.

"That's brilliant," he then grinned. "I wouldn't have thought that Lord Enric would really have let you leave."

"What's that supposed to mean?" she huffed indignantly. "I am a grown woman and an important person in that bloody Order. Of course he let me go!" She didn't mention that Enric had tried to dissuade her several times, had hinted at wanting to accompany her and had very likely hired agents to keep an eye on her. This would kind of make Vern correct, and that would just *not* be right. Even though he basically was.

"When are we leaving again?" the boy asked and rubbed his hands.

"In three weeks. There is quite a bit of planning to be done before that and I suppose this is a good opportunity to get my new assistant started, even though he officially starts only in a few weeks. But I think it might be a good idea to have somebody here to take care of things while I am gone, so I am going to break it gently to him that he is supposed to start earlier than planned. He is going to be so thrilled," she added dryly.

Vern gave a broad grin. "Hey, if you don't kick him where it hurts most, you will be off to a better start than last time."

"Oh, great. Why exactly am I taking you with me to have you around me all day long?"

"Because you need somebody with very good drawing skills and it seems that mine are unparalleled in the city," he replied smugly.

"Yes, right. I knew there had to be some good reason for me to be willing to endure this."

"Would you rather take Rolan on the trip? He could double as your servant," the boy asked with a malicious grin.

"Shut up or I will make *you* double as my servant," she threatened mildly. "It would certainly make things easier for Plia."

"Plia is coming, too?" Vern smiled. "That's terrific. It will be good to have a *friendly* female face there as well."

"Are you telling me my face is not friendly?"

"Seriously - do you ever look into the mirror after you get up? I wonder how Lord Enric endures it."

She looked at him and sighed. "You know, I am starting to wonder how hard drawing can really be. Maybe I could learn it myself within the next three weeks."

"You go on and try that," he smirked. "It will make you return to me and go down on your knees to beg me to accompany you."

She sighed. "Yes, probably." When she made to sit on his bed, a low growl warned her to think better of it. "Why is that cat still here? I thought you just wanted to feed it once after it wakes up to calm your guilty conscience for using it and then get rid of it? It does look rather fierce. Has it eaten anybody yet?"

Vern looked hurt. "Ram'an, you wouldn't do that, would you?" he cooed and fondled the cat behind one ear without being bitten, scratched or otherwise harmed.

Eryn raised a brow. "You named the cat after the ambassador? Really? That is bizarre, even for you."

"Why? I like the ambassador. I know you had some kind of row with him, but that was taken care of, wasn't it? So it's not disloyal of me to use his name for the cat."

She sighed. "No, not really. I am just wondering why you kept him. I mean, he is a street cat and Junar mentioned that he keeps pissing everywhere."

"That's grossly exaggerated. That was just because Ram'an had no lavatory."

"And he has one now?"

"Yes, he has a box with sawdust. And he uses it. He only pees on father's shoes when he is upset."

She shook her head in exasperation. "I really need to be more careful with what I use to teach you. If I ask you to heal a horse, will that also end up in your bedroom? And who is supposed to take care of that beast while you are on the expedition? If it treats others in the same friendly way as it does me, nobody will want to go near it."

"Oh, that's not a problem," Vern waved her off. "He just needs his food twice a day and his box cleaned up once a day. The servants can easily do that. He mostly sleeps, so he won't bother anybody. It's a pity though, that we are on the first floor. He can't get in and out of the window that way."

"Have you tried it?"

"Have I tried what?"

"Leaving the window open, genius. There is a ledge under it that stretches around the whole building. He might figure out a way to get down and up again. You would be amazed what some of these little buggers can do."

Vern eyed the cat doubtfully. "I don't know. He might run away and never return."

Hardly, Eryn thought. Why give up two meals a day and a warm place to sleep? But what she said was, "You wouldn't want to keep him here if he doesn't want to stay, would you? I don't have to tell you how I feel about keeping prisoners, do I?"

He sighed. "Alright. I will give it a try, I promise."

Good, she thought. With a little luck the cat would not find its way back up and Orrin might in time forgive her for the feline assaults on his shoes.

"So, I need to be off now to find my new assistant," she pasted a big fake smile on her face. "That is going to be so much fun!"

*   *   *

She wondered what the best place to meet Rolan would be. In her quarters? Not good, she didn't really have a study there and using Enric's was not really an option. While she knew he would be more than willing to let her use it, it just didn't feel right. The parlour was too casual and the guest room was no more than a collection of books and papers; they would have to sit on the bed, something that was not at all appropriate.

7

What a nuisance that the healers' building was not yet ready for use. She would ask Lord Tyront if she could use one of the meeting rooms the Order had at its disposal, she decided. That was official - maybe a bit too much - but that couldn't be helped right now.

She took out a sheet of paper and a pen and scribbled a quick note, sealed it with her new stamp and ordered the messenger to wait for a reply after delivering it. If Lord Tyront was at home right now, it should only need a few minutes before she had her reply; their quarters were not that far apart.

Taking out another sheet, she started writing a note to Rolan to summon him and wondered about the appropriate way to do this. Phrasing it like an invitation would seem weak. An order might be a bit strong. A request? But that would leave the chance of his refusal open, wouldn't it? She finally decided to phrase it like the order it basically was.

A knock at the door brought Lord Tyront's answer in which he let her know that she was free to use each and every meeting room she deemed fit for whatever purpose now and in the future. That was convenient. She decided to use the one she knew from her negotiations with the apothecaries. At least it was easy enough to find.

She finished her note to Rolan, instructing him to meet her in one hour and bring a pen and notepad with him as this would be his very first day of work as her assistant.

It would be a relief to let him do most of the work in connection with the expedition. Enric had hinted none too subtly that he expected her to complete in advance some of the studying and combat training she would miss. That meant extra hours of reading and fighting, in addition to her healing lessons with Vern.

But she was willing to accept these conditions for the chance to escape the confines of the city for the first time in almost ten months. She had lived almost all her life amidst trees, gathering herbs, bathing in ponds and rivers, yet had for quite some time now been restricted to a place with no more than a meagre few trees and a river she would rather not risk having skin contact with, at least not the part of it within and downstream of the city. Feeling real soil under her feet again, hearing the rustling of the wind in the leaves above her... Then again... sleeping outside with sixteen men, without sanitation, being at the mercy of the elements - another part somewhere began to speak out and Eryn shut it up, angrily. It seemed she had become accustomed to the luxury of life in the city. Maybe it was about time to get reconnected with the outside world, to remind herself that life was not about soft beds, lavish breakfasts and long, hot baths.

* * *

She turned from her position in front of the high window when a loud knock at the door reverberated through the spacious meeting room with the domed ceiling and the oblong table surrounded by six uncomfortable looking chairs. A servant opened the tall door, bowed, then announced Rolan.

As she had expected, he did not look too thrilled to set eyes on her again. Whether it was due to being summoned unexpectedly or his new position in general, she wasn't able to say. But she hadn't chosen this, either, so they would both have to come to terms with it somehow. She was older, wiser and thus more mature, and higher in rank, so she was probably the one who was supposed to make this work.

When the servant had departed and left them alone he bowed and said formally, "Lady Eryn."

He was wearing the customary brown magician's robes. His blonde hair reached to his collar and was tucked back behind his ears, and perhaps because of his new role his bearing was stiff; he avoided eye contact with Eryn as far as he could. He didn't bother hiding the fact that meeting her gave him no pleasure at all but was instead a nuisance he knew he had to endure.

Twenty-two years old, she mused. Only six years older than Vern, but a lot further advanced than that when it came to cynicism and disapproval. Well, at least with regard to disapproval. Vern was pretty cynical and sarcastic for a teenage boy.

"Rolan." She nodded to him and walked closer, motioning for him to sit while she herself would remain standing for now. Was she supposed to thank him for coming? It was not as if he'd really had much of a choice in the matter. Thanking him would probably equal mocking him.

"I appreciate that you came here on such short notice," she said and decided that it sounded right. "You were informed that we would start working together in a few weeks, but something has turned up where I need your help now already. I hope this does not cause you any undue inconvenience."

"No," he replied stiffly, clearly finding it *hugely* inconvenient to sit there.

"Good," she smiled thinly. "I see you brought pen and paper." She pointed to her own sheets she had brought and pushed them towards him on the table. "The first task I need you to assist me with is planning an expedition that is scheduled for three weeks' time. Its purpose is to..."

"An expedition?" the young man interrupted her and frowned. "I have no idea how to plan an expedition! What am I supposed to do?"

"First of all, you are supposed to remain quiet and listen to me while I am talking," she replied sharply. "You might learn something useful, after all."

9

She saw him press his lips together into a thin line. Just brilliant. Telling him off was definitely not a good start.

"The purpose of the expedition, as I was trying to tell you before," she continued, "is to teach the herb gatherers where to find and how to handle plants for medicines and medical treatments. I have already talked to some of them to determine a ten-day-route." She bent down to pick up a sheet and push it towards him. "The blue line on this map is the route I have set. I want you to take this and put together a file with all necessary information for this trip. Have a copy made of everything, so that each of us has the complete version."

He pulled the sheet towards him and studied it, frowning. "This is complete nonsense."

"I beg your pardon?" she said icily, hands on her back and waited for him to look up.

"There is no accommodation near most of the sites you have marked. Where are you planning to sleep?"

"We are going to camp in the woods, city boy. What's more, we need to work on your way of phrasing your objections in a more respectful manner," she added and groaned inwardly. That had sounded an awful lot like somebody *she* had kept insulting. Was she turning into a female version of Lord Tyront? Surely not!

"Let me rephrase that," she said sweetly and bent down to him, bracing her palms on the smooth, polished wood of the table. "If you ever again call anything I did or said *nonsense*, I will kick your sorry butt from here to the sea - have I made myself clear?" She smiled when he nodded silently after a moment's hesitation. Good. That had felt a lot more like herself.

"Excellent. Now back to the matter of the camping. As we are not going to stay at any inns most of the time, we will need tents, food that stays edible for some time, and cooking utensils as well as sensible clothes for travelling through the woods. For the night we also need warm blankets. It is getting warmer already, but the winter is not entirely over yet. At least we shouldn't have any snow. I hope."

She watched him scribble the items she had named on his notepad and waited until he had finished before she continued. "Then we need equipment for treating and storing the herbs. I have a list of that prepared as well." He wordlessly took the second sheet she gave him, looked at it, then grimaced.

"What now? Do you not agree with my choice of items? Then I assume you must have had ample expertise in the treatment of herbs to be in a position to judge this?" she said cuttingly and folded her arms in front of her.

Rolan gave her an annoyed look. "I can't tell. Your handwriting is quite a challenge to decipher. Or is this the way people in the Western Territories write? Then I would kindly ask her Ladyship for a translation."

She narrowed her eyes at him. That had been witty, but she could hardly admit that. Shaking her head at him, she pursed her lips. "We will just have to get you accustomed to my handwriting." She gave him an evil smile. "Or if you prefer an approach that would be less taxing for your poor eyes, I always can dictate and you just follow me around all the time and take notes. Wouldn't that save you so much trouble?"

He swallowed, and she saw the unease at the image, clear on his face, of his trailing behind her with a notepad for everyone to see.

"I think I will give the list another shot," he assured her hurriedly.

"Good. That's what I was hoping for," Eryn nodded and then returned to the items for the expedition. "We need enough paper and ink for Vern to draw, and something to store his work afterwards without anything getting torn, wet or otherwise damaged. I have never travelled with books or papers, so you need to figure out something here."

She walked a few steps and then murmured more to herself, "Have I forgotten anything?"

"Weapons," Rolan prompted.

Frowning, she turned back to him. "What? This is not a raid, but an expedition for teaching herb gatherers! Or do you suggest we rob and burn down a few villages while we are at it?"

He showed impatience with his eye movements. "And what if you are waylaid or assaulted? Are you just going to raise a big, strong shield around all of you and wait until your attackers become exhausted from hitting it?"

"We are talking about herb gatherers, not battle-hardened warriors! They would very likely only hurt themselves with a sharp-edged blade that is longer and heavier than a herb gathering knife."

"And *your* weapons, Lady Eryn? Or do you intend to leave here without any armaments at all? And without anybody who knows how to use a sword? Will you alone be defending a group of seventeen if necessary? After a mere ten months of combat training?" He visibly fought for calm. "Well, that should make my position redundant soon enough."

"Hey!" she cried out in bewilderment, "I thank you very much for not prematurely arranging my untimely demise!"

"Wouldn't dream of it," he grumbled sullenly and pretended to write something down. "Is there anything else, or can I leave?"

"No, that's all from my side. For now. I expect regular updates on your progress. If I don't hear from you I will come and find you. Then I will make you talk." She smiled without humour. "Just take the easy route and keep me informed, will you?"

He stared at her for a few moments, then bowed and left hurriedly.

Eryn let herself fall onto a chair, feeling the tension drain out of her body now that Rolan was gone. That had not gone too badly, had it? She had not really expected a harmonic meeting, not when each side was clearly unwilling to work with the other and didn't bother hiding that fact; but at least he had left with a clear idea of what to do, hadn't he? She sighed. She earnestly hoped he would get at least some of the things done so she would not have to take care of everything herself.

* * *

"Good afternoon," Enric greeted her from one of the sofas and put aside his book when she entered the parlour. "How was your meeting with Rolan?"

She sighed. "How do you know about that? I wasn't even aware that you had anything scheduled with Lord Tyront today."

"I didn't really. At least nothing official. He told me that you needed a place to meet with your assistant when we had lunch together."

"So when you don't have a work-related reason to see each other, you eat together?" She shook her head.

"Don't change the topic. Tell me about Rolan. Did it go well?"

"Oh, yes. Fabulously well. He is a real sweetheart. I would so much love to adopt him. Can I please?" she begged with mock eagerness.

"Hardly," Enric chuckled. "He is only five years your junior, which means he is of age. People would think you just wanted a live-in lover."

She grimaced at the thought of Rolan in her bed. "Well, then maybe not."

"Yes, I agree. So it did not exactly go as you hoped?" he asked a third time, not giving up.

"I don't know." She sat next to him on the settee, let him kiss her on the temple and took a sip from his cup on the table. Enric played with a strand of her hair, content with the cosy, intimate situation between them and waiting for her to go on.

"I suppose it could have gone worse. He did not leave the room screaming but rather cursing under his breath. That is a good sign, isn't it? And I did not kick him even once, though there were several times when I really wanted to, so I feel I showed great restraint presented with my new challenge in the form of my very reluctant assistant."

"I am so proud," Enric smirked. "Only a short while ago *you* were the prisoner, now you are doing your own subduing."

She grinned. "What can I say? I must be a fast learner." Then she bit her lip and thought back to what Rolan had said. "Do you think I need to take weapons on the expedition?"

"Definitely," he answered immediately. "I would imagine you are pretty much the only one able to use them, so if there are any problems, you should be prepared."

12

"But I am a magician! Why would I use swords?"

Enric stared at her. "Because there are very strict laws to deal with magicians who use their powers against non-magicians."

"What? But healing is a form of doing just that," she pointed out matter-of-factly.

"You know what I meant. The rules apply when it comes to less amiable interactions. Such as fighting."

"Even if it is in mere defence?" she asked incredulously.

"That is what you would have to prove afterwards. If there is even the shadow of a doubt, you would be made accountable for whatever damage you'd caused. The King must be seen to be keeping us under control, and from your studies of the history books you should already be aware why. There were a few quite... unpleasant incidents in the past with rogue magicians." He cocked his head and frowned. "Why do you think it is we really practice sword fighting, Eryn? Hardly to defend ourselves against other magicians. It is our way of making sure that we can defend ourselves against non-magicians, because due to the laws we would otherwise be unable to stand our ground in a fight."

Eryn stared at him open-mouthed and then rose to pace the parlour. She threw her hands up in frustration and anger. "I am slowly going crazy from the lot of you! Why did nobody ever tell me this in all those months that you forced me to train fighting? I mean, I would have understood that reason!"

"What do you mean, nobody told you?"

She looked up at the ceiling. "Exactly what I said! Not a single one of you mighty warriors thought it worth your while to tell me *why* you were making me learn this! It would not have been so excruciating had I known that there was a valid reason for it! You are damned idiots, all of you!"

She looked down again and narrowed her eyes when she heard Enric laugh. "So, Tyront never told you? And neither did Orrin? But you trained with him almost every day for *months*! He never mentioned anything about why to you?"

"I am so glad you find this amusing! I honestly fail to see any humour in it. And don't blame Orrin! You have been training with me for about two months now, and have *you* ever bothered telling me? No, you haven't!" she exclaimed.

"I would have, if I'd known that nobody else had told you."

"We had discussions about this! I told you that I found all this fighting a waste of time and magic! Why didn't you tell me then?"

He shrugged. "I thought you just wanted to be difficult. Logical arguments hardly ever work when somebody just wants to let off steam."

She closed her eyes and shook her head. "I don't believe this. And I only found out by accident because I hadn't thought of bringing a sword to the expedition. Imagine if I had defended myself with magic during an attack! I might have been punished severely without even knowing that I was breaking a law at the time!"

Enric sobered again. "Yes, that is the one thing that would have been dangerous." She had only got away with stunning the guards at the gate during her flight attempt because she had still been considered a prisoner and was thus practically expected to violate the laws. And then nobody had really been harmed back then, so they had been more than willing to let her get away with it - especially as she had at that time not been bound to the Order and thus their rules.

"I see why you are upset. And you are right. Somebody should have told you. So you would have been less resistant had you been aware that we train sword fighting for the protection of non-magicians?"

"Of course! I wouldn't have hated you so much for making me learn how to cause harm, when my life's mission was healing, not injuring people. I would have accepted it as just another way of avoiding unnecessary damage."

He sighed. "It seems we have made life more difficult than necessary for all of us." Then he smiled. "Imagine - I could have got you back into bed with me so much sooner."

She sniffed at the suggestion. "Dream on, pretty boy. I wouldn't have hated you any less after your knocking me out constantly and your little trick with my father's shield. Without your little trick of locking me in your quarters after my flight attempt, you might have had to wait for the next Freedom Night to try again."

He grinned confidently. "No, I wouldn't have waited that long, believe me. Not after kissing you in the street that day. It was a very distinct reminder of what I was missing."

She stared at him in confusion. "How did we get to that topic? I am still mad at you for not telling me about your laws on the use of magic against non-magicians." Sighing, she fixed him with an annoyed look. "It is quite a challenge to talk to you about something you are not comfortable with. You get me off track every time."

"Not very effectively, as it seems," he remarked. "You keep finding your way back to scolding me."

"Yes, sure. As if that made any difference. What am I to do now? Single-handedly fend off hordes of attackers with a sword? Am I even allowed to shield myself?" She quickly thought back to the incident when she had met Plia and saved her from the stone-throwing bullies by raising a shield to protect her.

"Yes, shielding is fine. People can't get hurt by a magical shield." He frowned. "Unless..."

"Unless what?"

"Unless you trapped them inside an airtight barrier and suffocated them."

"Oh, come on!" she cried out. "Who would do a thing like that?"

"You would be surprised at what people do when they fear for their safety or want to protect the ones they love," he said calmly and thought back to when he had seen her lying on the ground unconsciously with the apothecaries huddling together in a corner. His own life had not been in any danger whatsoever, but he had been willing - no, eager - to hurt them, to send them to the floor cringing with pain. If Tyront hadn't stopped him right then and there, there was not telling what would have happened.

She perked up upon hearing this. "That sounds like you have some personal experience in that area."

"Let's just say I have once come pretty close to violating that particular law," he said and smiled without humour.

"So shielding myself without causing any harm to my attackers is alright? Then I should also be able to shield the rest of the expedition. If they are close enough together, that is."

"Basically, yes."

"What about magically enhancing my speed and strength when I fight a non-magician opponent? Is that allowed?"

"Yes, it is even advisable. Otherwise Orrin wouldn't have emphasised teaching you that skill. You are, however, supposed to use that very considerable advantage to just disarm your attackers and not kill them. In that case you would still have some explaining to do, though not as much as with a hole in someone's chest caused by a bolt."

She shrugged. "No problem there. I am not eager to kill anybody, neither magically nor manually."

"Good. The thought of my bloodthirsty companion roaming the woods for easy prey would have made me rather uneasy," he said and rose when somebody knocked at the door. "Judging from the knock, that is Tyront."

And true enough, the Order's leader came in moments later.

"Lady Eryn," he nodded and acknowledged her bow.

"Lord Tyront," she replied.

"How was the meeting with young Rolan?" he asked and took a seat.

She suppressed a smile. So he had come to see how well his revenge had worked. How charming.

"Unexpectedly productive," she replied seriously. "I have included him in the planning of my expedition, and he has accepted the tasks I have given him. Of course it remains to be seen how well he will carry them out."

Tyront studied her and then nodded. "That is good to hear. How is the planning going?"

"There is a thing or two to figure out yet," she shrugged. "But nothing insurmountable, I would say."

Enric handed his superior a steaming cup. "We have just discussed the laws on the use of magic against non-magicians. It seems Eryn has not been aware of them until now."

"I beg your pardon?" Tyront frowned. "How is this possible? She has been here for at least ten months."

"Yes, tell *me*," she murmured and folded her arms.

"Lord Orrin has never mentioned that to you?" the older man asked incredulously.

"No, and neither have you two," she pointed out, tired of having put the blame on Orrin yet again.

"Well, then I suppose we can consider ourselves lucky that you have shown restraint in ignoring at least that rule so far."

She gave him a look of annoyance, but kept her mouth shut. She suspected that he was provoking her deliberately. Maybe he was disappointed at her report of the meeting with Rolan and had hoped for desperation and mayhem instead, so he might be looking for another reason to punish her for something. Oh no, but not today.

Tyront smiled, as if something had been confirmed, when she remained silent and just glared at him.

Enric watched the two of them and hid a smile. She was learning. Good.

"We also talked about the matter of defending the expedition against attacks. As the only magician and very likely the only trained fighter, not taking young Vern into account here, keeping attackers off might be quite a challenge."

The older magician nodded. "Yes, I have been thinking about that as well. I will increase the number of participants to twenty-three. Four swordsmen should be sufficient in addition to you, Lady Eryn."

"Oh, no," Eryn moaned. "That would mean that he was right and I was wrong. And that I have to admit it openly."

"Yes, that's how it would seem, my love," Enric smirked and added, "I'd better talk to Rolan about that, as he is now doing the planning."

"No," she protested. "You won't tell him, *I* will. You said I could do my own subduing."

Tyront raised his brow at Enric and slowly shook his head. "You told her that? Really? So glad to see that you are being a commendable role model," he said.

"Oh, but Lord Tyront," Eryn remarked with controlled smugness, "Why would I need him for that, when you yourself are such a shining beacon of exemplary leadership?"

He looked over to her and pursed his lips, torn between amusement at her careful phrasing of the insult and surprise at her audacity at insulting him at all, however subtly.

Being in a good mood, he opted for humour and raised his cup at her with a thin smile.

CHAPTER 2

Preparations

"What's the matter? You look a bit glum," Enric said from his preferred position of observation, the door frame to his study.

Eryn glanced up at his tall figure and sighed. "I had been hoping for a few applications for the three positions for healer trainees, but none have come so far. It seems that Lord Poron, Vern and myself are the only ones interested in the profession. I am rather disappointed at that," she admitted. "But I suppose convincing people after a lifetime of thinking that warrior skills are the only way of being a genuinely useful member of society for a magician, my expectations might have been set a bit high. They probably only see a woman, an adolescent male and an old man and think that this is the kind of image that awaits a healer."

Enric remained silent. That was true enough, he knew, but he was reluctant to confirm it. And then he was already working on an idea to change that perception.

"We could make a public announcement for all magicians," he suggested. "Pointing out that only the most able and suitable candidates will be considered."

"I am afraid that will not make much of a difference when nobody wants to do it anyway. Not much competition to overcome there, I'd say," she said wearily.

He came closer and crouched before her, taking both her hands into his. "Come on. Tyront and I could say a few words as well, pointing out how important this new way of using our skills is, the honour it will bring."

She grinned despite herself. "Yes, I can see how this will make quite an impression, coming from two warriors. Why don't you add Orrin to the mix, just to make it really laughable for the audience?"

"Your lack of trust in the credibility of the Order's high command shocks me, my love."

"Good. I would have hated to think that I have lost the ability to surprise you after only such a short time of living with you."

"Hardly," he quipped. "You surprise me every morning when you manage to drag yourself out of bed in time for your appointments.

17

Though I should say that you seem even more reluctant than usual when you need to rise for fighting lessons. Or is that just my impression?"

She laughed as he had hoped and patted his cheek. "That's just your imagination, Enric. I don't hate rising for *our* appointments any more than I do for all the others."

"That's a relief. Well, I think it is." He snatched a bread bun from her breakfast tray, earning himself a withering look. "Don't be greedy, there are two more."

"I wanted to take the ones I don't eat now with me. I like to take a bite or two when I take a break."

"Don't tell me Lord Poron lets you eat in the library?"

"I don't know, I never dared to find out. I generally go outside for that. *One must show respect in the presence of books,*" she quoted her father.

He watched her take the half-eaten bread bun on her plate and dunk it into her drink before biting into it. He remembered how she had told him that it was a childhood habit she had held on to despite her father's attempts to make her give it up.

"What is on your schedule today? History? Battle strategy? Botanical studies?" He grinned when he said the last one.

She snickered. "Yes, quite right. I really need some lessons from you lot in botany. The Order distinguishes between two major characteristics in a plant: edible or inedible."

"Not anymore, my love. Now that we have you with us, we do so much more. You have not yet fully grasped the concept of including yourself in the Order, so it seems."

"What can I say? Whenever I see something completely idiotic and useless, I aim to distance myself from it."

"I see." He pursed his lips, none too happy with her assessment of the institution he had spent the greater part of his life in. "Shouldn't you rather try to change things you deem useless instead of trying to avoid being tainted by association?"

"Oh my - you are not kindling the revolutionary in me, are you? I wonder whether I should report you to Lord Tyront," she said.

He shivered. "I fear the day you and Tyront band together against me."

She guiltily remembered that they had more or less done that already by keeping the truth about the extent of her dispute with Ram'an from Enric. He was still not aware that Ram'an had first used a truth block on her to interrogate her and then tried to confine her inside his quarters.

"So, what tortures will you have to face today?" he rephrased his question.

"Political strategy or some such, I think. Lord Poron has prepared a new stack of books for me to read for the next few days."

"Good. That should be a fairly useful subject for you if you pay attention. When is your history test due, by the way?" he ventured further.

"In ten days. And five days after that I am to be tested in battle strategy. It seems they all want to have the exams taken care of before I head off with the herb gatherers," she said with a grimace. The schedule sounded gruelling when she repeated it.

"Lord Poron is the one who is supervising you in political strategy, isn't he? He might want to test you as well before you leave."

"Yes, he has told me as much. But I have agreed with him to split the load. I will learn only half of it now and the rest when I return. Have I mentioned that I like him?"

Enric smiled. "No, but it is obvious nevertheless. I find it quite interesting how you manage to make friends among the high ranks in the Order."

"Like Lord Tyront?" she asked, full of mischief.

"Not exactly, but you are joined with the second in command and are friends with numbers four and five in the ranking."

"Yes, absolutely. As if *I* were the one to have chosen my connection with you, Number Two."

He grinned. "I admit you had some help in making that decision. Don't tell me you are regretting it? You are still supposed to be in that blissful post-commitment phase after one month."

"Blissful post-commitment phase? Don't tell me that is what we have now? If so, I dread when grey and dull daily routine catches up with us. No more fights, manipulation, threats and other jolly events."

Pulling her into an embrace, he laughed. "Don't worry, there will always be fights and threats between us as long as I am your superior and you are meant to follow my orders."

"What a relief," she grinned and wriggled free from his arms. "I am afraid I need to leave now. My doubtless fascinating books describing how to make my enemies think they are my friends, while I am perfectly aware that the concept of a friend is no more than an enemy I have decided not to kill yet, are waiting for me."

"No, my love, that would be *diplomacy*. Political strategy is about how to lie to your enemies with a smile on your face while you quietly plot their annihilation."

She shook her head at him. "You know, that does sound immensely depressing. I really hope I will never be important enough to apply all that terrible knowledge." She smiled brightly. "But then maybe I wouldn't have to! Being a woman I always have the less complicated option of making people compliant by taking them to bed at my disposal, don't I? Classic female strategy."

Enric looked taken aback slightly, then smiled weakly. "That, dearest Lady Eryn, I would not recommend. You might otherwise find out that the people you intended to make compliant have a tendency to die under the most suspicious circumstances."

She frowned in mock confusion. "That does not sound like political strategy anymore. Too direct and obvious, not cunning and subtle at all."

"No," he agreed with a dark expression, "That is plain and simple jealousy. Not as complicated, but much more dangerous in my case."

*   *   *

Eryn rose to open the door for who she assumed had to be Plia knocking. And indeed, the girl stood there, beaming and obviously hardly able to contain her excitement, judging from the restless energy that radiated off her.

"Eryn!" she called out and hugged the magician warmly.

Eryn smiled and waited for those now happily less thin and feeble arms to release her again, so she could ask the girl to come in and close the door.

"Is it really true? I am to come to the expedition with you?" Plia's large green eyes were wide with excitement.

Eryn took her hand and nodded. "Yes. Enric suggested it, and I have to say that it was a fabulous idea. I was not really sure if you are comfortable with a ten-day trip through the wilderness, but from your reaction just now I see that I needn't have worried about that."

"I have never been outside the city before," the girl admitted. "I am a teeny bit nervous about that, but as long as you are there, I won't be afraid."

"That is a great proof of trust, but Vern will also be with us. And four armed men to protect us as well, so, there is no need to be afraid at all, even if I don't happen to be around for some reason," she smiled.

"Vern is coming, too?" Plia asked with what was clearly supposed to be a casual tone of voice.

Eryn watched the faint blush rise into Plia's cheeks and wondered if this crush on Vern was cute or if it might cause trouble later. It was probably harmless. Plia was thirteen years old, still more child than woman, and Vern had never treated her as anything else than a younger sister from what Eryn had seen.

"Yes, he will take the chance to learn more about botany and do the drawings I need for the herb gatherers' books so they can look up the plants later when we are back."

The girl looked suddenly uneasy. "Eryn, I have no idea what I need for the journey. I have saved a little money and..."

"Little flower, that is exactly why I have sent for you today. Junar will be here any moment, and she will take care of the clothes you need for the trip. And don't worry about the money. The Order will take care of that."

"The Order?" she whispered in awe. "But I am not a member!"

"But I am, and they are trying to keep me happy," Eryn smiled. "So don't feel guilty about it, they have more money than they need." She put an arm around the girl's shoulders and looked at her. "Have you grown in these last two months? I don't have to bend down so far any more to your shoulders, I think."

"A little," Plia smiled. "Cook says it's the regular food and proper work. Though I am a bit sceptical about the last part. I would have thought that heavy lifting would rather stop the growth as it pulls me down."

Eryn laughed and stepped away from her. "Let me have a proper look at you, then." And she did: less pale, not as thin, more muscles from working, clean, neatly combed hair, clothes that fitted. A much better picture than the one she remembered from the time when they had first met. She fondly remembered that Orrin was the one who had made the change possible by offering to her to get Plia the apprenticeship in the Palace kitchen in exchange for Eryn's participation in the fighting competition.

They heard another knock, and Plia went to answer the door, but Eryn held her back. "No, you are not here as my servant. At least not yet. You are my guest, and as such you don't have to answer the door."

Junar breezed in with a large black bag slung over her shoulder and slopped it down on the nearest available free surface. "Dear me, this is heavy!"

"New bag?" Eryn asked, eyeing the monstrosity. "What do you have in there? Your entire shop?"

"No, just what every upcoming sought-after seamstress requires to work professionally." She grinned. "Orrin had it made for me. I decided to allow him to present me with occasional gifts every now and then to keep him happy."

"To keep *him* happy? How very considerate of you," Eryn smirked.

"Plia, my dear girl!" Junar said and kissed the girl's cheeks. "Look at you, you have grown so much! And probably will continue to for another three or four years. I think we will have to take that into consideration and add extra length, so the new clothes will fit you for longer." Then she turned to her friend. "How about you? You haven't ordered anything for the expedition yet, either. Don't tell me you plan to stomp through the woods in those nice city clothes I made you? I would skin you alive for that!"

Eryn sighed. "Then I'd better not say it but order a bunch of trousers and shirts suitable for stomping, I suppose?"

"Good girl," the seamstress nodded, obviously satisfied, and turned back to Plia. "You are aware that you will have to wear trousers as well? I hope you are not too uncomfortable with that, but a dress is not really a good choice where you want to go."

"That is alright, I don't mind at all. Quite the opposite, I look forward to it. Trousers seem so much more practical, but they make us wear dresses all the time!"

Junar sighed. "Oh no. That is Eryn's bad influence. As a role model she is clearly not suitable, at least not from a fashion point of view."

"Says the woman who makes my clothes," the role model commented. "Not a very flattering assessment of your own skills, dearest friend."

"My skills are not the problem, Eryn, it's the resistance they encounter all the time," she retorted.

"Not all the time, surely? What about all the dresses you made me? I have worn every single one of them, haven't I?"

"True," Junar conceded, "but that was quite a fight. Plia, sweetheart, why don't you take off your shoes and dress and step on that chair here? I would like to take your measurements now."

Plia undressed as asked and stepped up on the chair in her undergarments. Junar queried her about her preferred colours and the kind of tasks she would have to take care of during the expedition to fit the cut and material to the challenges.

"Eryn, I suppose you will dig in the dirt for plants, kneel on the cold, hard ground, climb rocks and do a lot of other things that will rip, tear and strain whatever I make for you?"

"Absolutely right," she confirmed happily. "And I can't tell you how much I am looking forward to that."

"Yes, I imagine you are. If something is unladylike, I can depend on you to enjoy it. That means I have to make a few extra pairs of trousers for you to pack. Lord Enric wouldn't thank me for letting you run around among those men with torn clothes."

"Yes, let's focus on what Enric's needs for this expedition are, shall we?" Eryn lifted her eyes and shook her head.

"You'd better. He is very protective of you. I'll bet he is none too happy about your leaving him alone for such a long time to be off on an adventure with so many strangers."

The magician sighed. "Protective? Try *possessive* instead. He is a grown man. You don't need to pity him. He will somehow manage to keep himself occupied while I am gone."

Junar looked surprised. "You are incredibly insensitive! I wonder if you really don't care about how much he is going to miss you, or if you are just pretending."

"Oh, come on! I have lived with him for no more than a month! I dare say he will survive my absence somehow. And we are actually talking about ten *days*, not ten *months*!"

Plia's eyes darted from one woman to the other and back again, fascinated by the exchange.

The seamstress sighed and shook her head. "I really, really hope you will miss him a lot out there in the wilderness, benighted in your chilly camp, alone, with nobody to hold you in his arms and no more than a blanket to warm you. That could make you appreciate him more."

"Don't you think that freezing in the wilderness would rather make me appreciate his quarters than his person?" Eryn replied and ducked quickly when a rolled-up measuring tape was thrown her way.

*   *   *

Eryn picked up the sheets of paper that had been delivered for her during the day. Enric had made it a habit to put them on that chest of drawers next to the door, the one she had still not managed to get rid of after swearing to do just that when she had bumped her toe against it one tipsy night after vising Ram'an in his quarters.

It was the third of Rolan's reports she had received. He sent them regularly every second day, which was fine by her. He had started collecting the items she had told him to put together and kept them in one of the Order's storage rooms. They had in these last six days exchanged no more than brief notes, questions asked and answered. He kept updating her with copied sheets for her file, such as a list with the names of all participants, checklists with progress updates and suggestions on how to transport the paperwork safely. The available boxes and chests were intended for transport in a coach and were not suitable for horseback, as they were much too bulky and heavy. One option would be shielding the papers all the time, but that did seem rather impractical. Another idea was using oilskin cloth, which was definitely something to consider. Maybe Lord Poron could be of service in figuring out a feasible solution for this. She would instruct Rolan to contact him.

*   *   *

Eryn lifted one of the flat wooden boxes Rolan had brought to their second meeting, judging its weight with one hand.

"This is rather heavy," she commented. "You are aware that we are riding horses through the woods, I assume? And that we would need more than one as they are rather flat?"

The young man clenched his jaw. "It's either a little extra weight or wet papers. Make your choice."

Eryn found to her surprise that she felt devious joy in taunting her assistant and wondered if she was supposed to be contrite about it. No, she decided, surely not. But at least she knew now why Lord Tyront took such pleasure in teasing her. The privileges of leadership, she mused. Maybe she would get used to being a person of authority and importance in the Order after all...

"Hmm. Why is that box so heavy, anyway?"

He wordlessly took it out of her hands, opened a clasp and let another, even flatter box slide out.

Impressive, she thought. Two boxes that smoothly fitted into each other, making it less likely for water to enter through an opening. The surface was smooth, very likely treated with some kind of oil compound to keep water out.

"Interesting. What do you think how many sheets will fit inside one of them?"

Rolan shrugged. "I managed to squeeze in about twenty, but they don't look so good when you take them out again, a bit crumpled. Fifteen should be fine."

She bit her lip as she watched him put the two boxes together again. He had anticipated her question and tried it before. That was neat. Not what she would have expected from a person with such an obvious dislike of working with her.

"Then I think we will take four boxes. Even Vern won't be able to finish more than sixty drawings during our trip. And we will hardly find that many different plants, anyway."

He took out his notepad, a smaller one this time, and made a note.

"How is everything going with the planning? Any trouble so far?"

"No," he just said, and then shrugged. "Apart from your furniture. It does need quite a lot of extra pack animals and they are hard to obtain at this time of the year."

She blinked at him. "My what?"

"Your furniture. Table, chair..." His voice trailed off at her expression.

Watching him with narrowed eyes and a frown she wondered if he was making fun of her.

"What? You are a woman! And a wealthy one. You will be expected to travel in style."

Closing her eyes, she shook her head. "And you are an idiot, and a colossal one at that. What makes you think I would travel with a table and chairs through the woods and then complain about the weight of paper boxes? Use that brain of yours, dear boy!" She saw him flinch at the address and had to admit that it was maybe not entirely appropriate with her only being a little older.

"How was I to know that you want to sit on a log and sleep on the hard ground?"

"I did my own herb gathering only a year ago, how would I have carried a table with me? On my back?" She shook her head at the image.

"Fine," Rolan spat. "Then maybe her Ladyship would be so kind as to provide me with a packing list of what she intends to bring to the expedition?"

"No," she smiled sweetly, "her Ladyship will do no such thing. She is a big girl and will pack her own things. She deigns let you know, however, that one pack animal for herself and the servant girl will be sufficient. Unless you had planned to induce me to bring any other hard-to-carry, useless items?"

Rolan closed his eyes for a moment as if to collect himself and then looked at her with barely contained vexation. "Is that everything? Can I leave now?"

"Yes, unless you have any other questions?"

"No," he replied in a tone that suggested that he would rather gnaw off his own leg than talk to her any longer than was absolutely necessary. He bowed quickly without looking at her before closing the door of the meeting room behind him.

She grinned and shook her head when he had left. Why had she ever hesitated to ask for an assistant?

CHAPTER 3

The Gesture

Eryn yawned as she closed the last page of the book Lord Poron had given her the previous week. It was too long-winded, too stuffy, too boring. And yet she had to memorise a good part of it. She looked down at the page of notes she had made. There was hardly anything substantial, just plotting and killing. Was that really something they thought it wise to teach people? Why not make them learn about the merits of honesty and directness instead?

She saw Lord Poron come in through one of the large double doors, his pace unhurried and his steps quiet as befitted his surroundings. His sharp, intelligent eyes focussed on her and at her exaggerated sigh of discontent his wrinkly face twisted into a smile. "I see that your current reading material is not offering you any more pleasure than the other books, my dear. But at least you will have a short break from them now. Come, we need to leave for the announcement."

"What announcement? Are you sure I need be there for it?" she frowned in confusion. "I was not informed, after all."

"Oh yes, I think you should. It will be quite interesting, I imagine." The septuagenarian magician picked up the book in front of her and returned it to its spot on the shelf.

She shrugged. "Alright. Where is it?"

"Outside in the Palace square. Maybe we should make a little detour to pick up your robes. When so many of us are present, it doesn't hurt to remind people of your status, my dear. Go on - make haste. We don't want to be late," he urged her on and all but pushed her out the library.

"Yes, yes, I am on my way," she sighed. "What is this great announcement about?"

"You will learn about it soon enough. If you hurry, that is, and we manage to get there before it is over," he added, with concern showing on his face.

"You know what? Why don't I run to my quarters for my robes and meet you at the Palace gates in a few minutes?" she suggested. Having him urge her on all the way to her quarters and then to the

Palace square was not an encouraging prospect. "I promise, I will be quick."

When she had pulled the robes over her head not much later, she quickly went into Enric's study to look down at the square. There were indeed a great number of what looked like magicians assembled, and a few curious onlookers had also found their way there, keeping their distance to the all-powerful and venerated members of the Order.

Strange, she thought and turned back to meet Lord Poron downstairs as she had promised him. If this was important, Enric had surely known about it. Why hadn't he mentioned anything, especially as she was supposed to be there as well?

Lord Poron nodded when he saw her running towards him and gestured for her to walk out the Palace first. The magicians stood together, each of them clad in their brown, unadorned robes, talking casually. From the snippets of conversation she managed to catch, she figured that they, neither, knew what awaited them.

She saw Orrin standing to one side of the crowd with arms folded, his stance broad as usual, not part of the hubbub, but observing it. She approached him and stopped next to him. He acknowledged her with a brisk nod and continued observing his fellow magicians.

Orrin was neither unusually tall as Enric was, nor radiated the almost intrusive authority that surrounded Lord Tyront, but there was a kind of calm, commanding power and confidence that made him stand out. It was that and his penetrating green eyes that made people eager to avoid getting on his wrong side. And his fighting prowess, of course - which showed in his straight posture, as if he were in a continuous state of expecting an attack. The long, thin scar along one side of his face certainly did nothing to soften the hint of danger. He had to be about as old as Lord Tyront, in his early fifties, but his profession as warrior trainer had earned him the impressive, muscular body of a fighter. That and the lack of any grey in his full head of hair made him appear slightly younger.

"What is this all about? Do you have any idea?" she asked him and let her gaze wander over the assembled men. There had to be more than a hundred and fifty of them.

"Wait for it," he said with a knowing smile.

Eryn didn't try to make him reveal what he knew. She knew that such attempts would be futile. He was a stubborn person. "You know," she said rather amazed, "I was not really aware of how many magicians there are."

Orrin looked around. "Quite a few, yes. Though not all of them are here right now. The children with magical abilities are not around, and neither are most of the Council Members."

"How many magically gifted children are there?"

"About forty. Not all of us pass on the ability."

She then saw Enric emerge from the Palace gates and walk towards them, of course clad in his blue robes. They looked different, though, she noted. He obviously had found time to have Junar do some work on them. His broad shoulders and small waist were emphasised to his advantage, she mused while she watched him come closer and finally stop in front of the assembled magicians.

The murmuring around her died down little by little as everybody who had caught a glimpse of the blue robes fell silent. When finally the last of them had ceased talking, Enric nodded towards Orrin, who then stepped up next to him. He flashed Eryn a quick smile and raised his voice, increasing the volume with a little magic so everybody could understand him.

"Good morning, everyone. I assume you are wondering why I called for this assembly. I wish to address the matter of the three official openings for healers to be trained."

Eryn closed her eyes. No - please not, she thought with a groan within. No desperate attempt to find somebody who would take pity on his companion and do her the favour of working with her. Or use the opportunity to make a good impression on Enric without any serious interest in the healing profession as such.

She opened her eyes again when he continued. "I am here to warn you not to apply for them prematurely, as it is a commitment to hard work and requires not the strong magical powers required for fighting, but instead something much rarer: an above average intellect and willingness to put it to good use."

Eryn frowned in confusion. What was his plan? Why did he discourage people from applying when none of them seemed to be very eager to do so, anyway? Shouldn't he rather try it the other way round?

"Healing abilities are still rare in our Kingdom," he went on. "So those of you who decide to apply and are accepted will not only have to face the challenge of mastering a new set of skills and work as pioneers in a new field, but also be prepared to take over responsibilities in a leadership role in a few years."

She began to look more relaxed. Now, that sounded more like it. That argument would surely apply to magicians of lesser strength who had not much chance of rising up to the ranks of power in the traditional warrior hierarchy.

"Healing skills will make us stronger as a Kingdom, as warriors, as magicians, and as a society. Imagine being hurt or incapacitated and being able to heal yourself and others. Imagine a farmer with a broken leg who does not have to wait for several weeks until he can work again to feed his family. Think of your children, companions, friends in pain and being able to help them with the touch of your hand." He paused for effect and looked around, meeting as many eyes as he could. "People in the Western Territories hold the art of healing in such high esteem, that every single magician is taught the basic principles of it without even being a healer. We are in the very lucky position to have our very own healer here in the Order to teach us this skill, to share her knowledge with us. And we are going to make use of this chance."

He drew a dagger from his sleeve and dragged the sharp edge across his palm without showing any sign of pain. Then he lifted his hand high above his head for everyone to see. The cut had been rather deep and blood ran down his forearm in crimson braids.

What was he doing? Eryn wondered if he wanted her to step beside him to do a little healing demonstration for the crowd and waited for his sign to join him. But none came.

When he was sure that the attention of all present was focused on his bleeding palm, he closed his eyes, and Eryn stared at him open-mouthed. He would hardly... would he? No, that was impossible! He didn't know how!

She started breathing faster when she saw the cut close itself slowly, and the blood stopped oozing. He kept the hand lifted over his head and pulled a clean white cloth from a pocket with his other hand to wipe away the blood and reveal to the gaping crowd a perfectly unmarked palm.

Enric looked towards his companion and was immensely satisfied with the surprise and utter disbelieve he saw on her face. Orrin then pulled his own dagger from a sheath inside his boot and cut his hand the same way. He, too, held it up high for everyone to see and closed his eyes. Eryn covered her wide-open mouth with both hands and watched the warrior heal himself just like his colleague had done only moments before.

She only noted how completely silent it had been when the murmuring around her erupted, getting louder and more agitated with every second.

Enric was pleased with her reaction to his little demonstration, and he and Orrin walked over to her, both showing unmistakeable smugness at her stunned expression.

"But... how?" She shook her head at herself. How was pretty clear, wasn't it? There was only one other healer in the Kingdom who could have shown them. "I mean, when?" She gestured helplessly at Enric.

"I asked Vern to teach me a few basic things while you and Orrin had your dancing lessons, and I told him to keep it a secret. I wanted to surprise you." He smiled down at her. "It looks like I have succeeded."

She released her breath slowly, still shaking her head, only now considering the impact of what he had just done, of what both of them had done. They had just shown the entirety of magicianhood in the Kingdom, that the two most revered warriors in the Order did value the skill of healing highly enough that they considered it worthy their time and effort to master it.

Enric saw her restraints at showing affection in public fighting with the impulse of doing exactly that, and waited for a few moments to see if she would do anything. Then he sighed and pulled her into his arms, "Come here. And don't bother denying that this is what you were thinking of," he murmured before he pressed a kiss on her lips.

She hesitated for a moment, then slung her arms around him and hugged him firmly, her check resting on his shoulder.

"Thank you. So much."

"You are welcome. But we will have to see if this changes anything. Don't expect too much from it," he warned her.

She let go of him and smiled. "This doesn't make a difference. The gesture was an amazing one, whether any magicians act on it or not. I appreciate it very much." Turning to Orrin, she lifted her arms to hug him as well and groaned slightly when he squeezed her none too gently.

"Can't breathe," she gasped in exaggerated suffocation.

He chuckled. "You are still too soft. I would have thought that your combat training should have taken care of this by now, especially with your new training partner."

"If you hug Junar like that, you will need your new healing skills often enough," she laughed and kissed his cheek. When she then looked around, she saw Vern coming her way, a wide grin on his face.

"That was quite a show, wasn't it? Can you hear them talking? They are totally confused," he beamed as if happy about a trick well played. "And the look on your face was a sight to behold! Your wide-open mouth, the bulging eyes... Very elegant, *Lady* Eryn."

She flicked his earlobe with her fingers and grinned when he rubbed it. "Careful, boy. I might decide to punish you for giving unauthorised healing lessons."

"Unauthorised?" he sniffed. "You think Lord Enric is not authorised to authorise me? When I last checked, he still outranked you."

"Yes," Enric said, "that was also my impression. And whatever she decides to threaten you with, consider it nullified."

"Nice," she retorted, "so much for *my* authority."

* * *

"Nice show," Tyront commented and leaned back in his chair. "And effective, too. I have received a total of four applications since yesterday."

Enric raised his brows. "That is excellent news. Have you told Eryn yet?"

"No. I want to have a closer look at them first."

"Don't tell me you are going to preselect the candidates you don't approve of? She would never trust you again if she found out."

Tyront was quick to react. "No, of course not. What do you take me for? She is the one who has to work with whatever candidates she chooses, so what would be my benefit? I am just curious."

"Why don't you let her take over the selection process altogether, then?" Enric asked.

"Because I can't be seen to let her handle everything in connection with healing. And it also forces her to work with me occasionally. She needs to get used to that." He grinned evilly. "It seems that her new assistant will teach her a thing or two about leadership as well."

"Why? What have you heard?"

"Not so much heard as read," Tyront said and picked up two letters from his table. "Young Rolan is not too happy about working with her, I can tell you that."

"Reports?"

"No, better. Letters of complaint." He held up the first sheet and read aloud, "*Lady Eryn seems to find it appropriate to repeatedly address me with the insulting term 'idiot'. I do not consider this professional conduct, and neither do I think that this arrangement can work to our mutual satisfaction in the long run. I would be eternally grateful if you could see your way to considering a different position for me.*"

"Oh yes, that does sound like her," Enric remarked and sighed.

"Wait, there is another one. That's the first one, actually. He must have written it after their very first meeting," Tyront said and started reading again, "*Lady Eryn has today threatened me with physical violence in case I fail to comply with her demands. I quote, 'I will kick your sorry butt from here to the sea' and 'If I don't hear from you, I will come and find you. Then I will make you talk'. I am seriously concerned for my safety and urgently ask you to reconsider your choice for my assignment. She has furthermore threatened to act out her disdain for my person by making me carry out demeaning and embarrassing tasks in public.*"

He let both sheets sink. "Leadership potential if ever I saw it."

"What are you going to do about it?"

"Me?" Tyront shook his head and smiled broadly. "Not a thing. And why would I? I am looking forward to his messages, they amuse me. And he unintentionally keeps me informed about what she is up to. An unpaid agent, so to say. A very useful young man."

Enric grinned and shook his head. "You devious old scoundrel. Has Eryn, too, sent you any letters to make you reconsider your choice?"

"No, nothing. But I would be very interested in what she has to say. I suppose I will have to ask her for a progress report. Though reading it will take quite some time, I imagine. Her handwriting seems a bit... impatient, to put it mildly. And after regularly deciphering Orrin's scribbling, that is saying something. I gather she is not too enthusiastic about writing reports?"

"No, not really. If it wasn't for her tight schedule, I would suggest regular meetings instead."

"I will consider that. We can discuss this when she is back from her expedition." He looked at the younger man. "Have you got more used to the thought of her roaming the woods for ten days with a bunch of strangers yet? Only seven more days until she leaves, unless I am mistaken."

Enric sighed. "No, not really. I am still not happy about it, but she is determined to go, and I see why she must. She has been locked inside the city for quite some time now. After growing up in the country I can see that she wants to get out of here for a while."

"You are not worried that she won't come back, are you?"

"No," he frowned. "Why? Do you think I should?"

Tyront smirked. "How would I know? I don't have any secret intelligence from my agents in this regard, if that's what you were hinting at. No secret plans to flee the country that I am aware of. She has passed all her tests, by the way. At least the ones she has already had. There is still one in political strategy pending, I believe. Lord Poron wants to test her in the next few days about one part of the books."

"Good. She has even been taking books to bed these last weeks, so it's good to see her efforts were not wasted." Enric pursed his lips. "There is something I have been thinking about. Some of Vern's lessons have been rescheduled due to his healing training, and I was wondering if he could continue two or three of his subjects with Eryn instead of with the rest of his class. He is smart enough to handle learning at greater speed."

"And you are not thinking about your companion at all, but only of the benefits for the boy?" Tyront asked mildly.

Enric thought carefully before answering that. "*Not at all* would maybe not be wholly accurate, but as the boy would benefit from this arrangement considerably, I do not think that I am giving Eryn undue preference here."

"I see," Tyront replied slowly. "Then we'd better make sure and emphasise the advantage to the boy when we communicate this to his teachers. It might otherwise seem as if you are trying to rearrange the Order to make your companion happy. And we wouldn't want to create that impression, would we?"

Enric narrowed his eyes. "You think I am a love-struck fool, don't you?"

"Does it matter what I think?" he said with a thin smile. Then he became serious. "Enric, you have never made any demands or asked for favours in all this time since you rose to power. From where I stand, you are entitled to a little foolishness. I have waited for quite some time for you to find a companion, and as long as this doesn't stand in the way of your duties, I have no problem indulging you a little every now and then."

Enric nodded slowly, absorbing the import of Tyront's words. Generosity wrapped in a warning. That was just like Tyront.

*   *   *

Eryn sighed and shook her head at the note she had just received from the apothecaries. Only three days until the expedition was due to set off, and they thought that this was the perfect time to demand a teaching schedule for the training they had to do according to their agreement with the Order. She had no intention whatsoever of preparing one before her departure, especially as the healers' building was not yet finished anyway - and that was where the lessons would take place.

Then an idea brought a mischievous glint to her eyes. Why not let Rolan deal with the apothecaries? At least that would keep him busy for as long as she was gone. They were rather demanding and unpleasant people to talk to, and getting them used to dealing with her assistant couldn't hurt for the future anyway.

She looked back at the last of the books she had to go through for her exam with Lord Poron tomorrow. Ahead lay ten days without any books on whatever the Order deemed useful knowledge - no tests, nothing. That did seem like complete and utter luxury. Shaking her head at her rambling thoughts, she rose to refill her glass. They had successfully managed to make her, a woman who had revered and enjoyed books all her life, dread them now and dream of days without reading a single page. If that was what the Order considered effective education, she would have to have words with a few people here.

Looking at the box with several pairs of sturdy leather trousers that had been delivered earlier that day, she decided that she deserved a break from her book. Junar had been quite busy, too. She had made garments for Vern, Plia and Eryn in addition to her usual workload.

Rolan had informed her by messenger that all provisions, cooking and sleeping gear, paper boxes and accessories were almost complete and ready for packing. It looked like everything was going according to plan.

She looked over at the door behind which Enric was toiling in his study, and pondered. The closer the date of the departure came, the more restless she felt. First she had attributed it to excitement, but now she began suspecting that there might also be a part of her that was reluctant to leave him behind.

What he had done for her, the healing lessons with Vern, had touched her. He had never really made it a secret that he liked her very much, but this... It seemed that his attachment to her went deeper than she had expected. Love even, could it be?

She shuddered at the word. Her father had warned her about it more than once. He had loved her mother, and that had not exactly turned out to been a blessing for him. Fleeing to another country, hiding who he was all the time, that was what devotion to a loved one had brought him. He had told her that she, his daughter, was the only blessing that had come from his love.

In the years spent in her little village she had seen a few happy couples, but many were anything but. She had witnessed violence, infidelity, brooding dissatisfaction, disappointed hopes and frustration. And what those emotions could do to people in the long run... There were couples radiating happiness at the time of their commitment ceremony who were not even able or willing to look each other in the eyes a few years later. It was amazing how much could change between two people who had initially been dedicated to each other, connected in, well, love.

Abandoning a companion was not something that happened very often in the countryside. It was a matter of being seen to honour the commitment regardless of the discontent and resentment between the two people who were all but fettered to each other by an oath foolishly taken in a more optimistic mind. Ending it would have been cheating, and those who were caught up in an unhappy relationship themselves were the most severe guardians of virtue in order to make sure that others suffered just as much.

She had been determined never to get caught in that trap, as hiding her magical abilities would hardly have been possible any more when being so close to another person all the time, let alone avoiding the unhappiness she had seen.

But then there had been the King and Enric with their own ideas and schemes. Enric had told her at the evening of their commitment that he had planned to ask her to join him anyway, even without the King's interference, but had wanted to give her more time to come around to it. She wondered how he would have reacted if he had asked her one day and she would have rejected him for fear of future unhappiness.

Those, however, were futile thoughts now. She was caught in the very trap she had always wanted to avoid, and to her relief and surprise it had so far turned out to be less of a torture and more of a pleasure than she had ever dared hope.

But emotional attachment had its downsides. What if one of them one day started resenting the other or fell in love with somebody else? Or just got bored with the partnership?

She rubbed her face and tried to push these thoughts to a distance. There were no guarantees that this would work out, so why not enjoy it while it lasted? That's it, she thought, and sighed at her own foolishness; that was why she had already started missing him before she was even gone.

CHAPTER 4

Political Strategy

Eryn took a deep breath and indicated to the two guards with a nod to open the doors for the throne room. She straightened her shoulders and entered. Apart from the golden throne on the dais, the room was empty but for the single figure standing in front of the tall windows with his hands behind his back, seemingly savouring the rays of sunshine on his face with eyes closed. Seeing him like this, enjoying a relaxing moment, seemed oddly private. She remembered when she had first laid eyes on him several months ago when she had been brought to this very room for the Order to test her magical strength. He was a young man in his mid-twenties of average height and build with hard blue eyes and slightly curly hair tamed into a pony tail at the nape of his neck. But underestimating him due to his youth would be a capital error. She had come to know him as a formidable opponent and a savvy and ruthless politician.

"Your Majesty?" she said carefully and heard the doors being closed behind her. Only then did the King turn and smile at her.

"Lady Eryn. It is a pleasure to see you, as always."

She bowed to him and watched him stroll towards her. Being alone with him unsettled her still.

He seemed to be in a good mood today, though, she noted with some relief. The message had not said anything as to why he had summoned her, but usually being called to the King at short notice tended to turn into a rather unpleasant experience, judging from prior encounters with him.

"Walk with me," he said and offered her his arm. He smirked when she hesitated slightly before taking it.

"Not afraid of me, are you?" He chuckled. "You are a powerful magician, after all. If one of us has reason to be afraid, it should be *me*."

She swallowed and remained silent, unsure how to reply to such a statement. She could confirm his words, but that would seem like a threat. Or tell him that she would never ever use her magic against him. Which would frame her as a lot more zealous to please than she cared to appear.

The King started walking and put his hand on hers so she couldn't just let it slip from his arm, gently pulling her along.

"I propose a little walk through the gallery. It is delightfully warm and sunny at this time of day, and if you keep looking to the left where the windows are instead of the dull pictures of long dead monarchs on the wall to the right, it is quite pleasant."

He took her hand off his arm and held it in his own while he opened the door for her, as if afraid that she would withdraw it if he let go of her. After they had entered the gallery, he put her hand back on his arm and resumed their walk.

She looked around and decided that he had not promised too much. It was sunny and unexpectedly warm.

"I have been informed, my dear Lady, that your results in political strategy were not as promising as the ones in your previous exams. I admit that I am rather disappointed in your lack of interest in that subject. It is a fascinating topic you could greatly benefit from if you paid sufficient attention to it."

Eryn looked at him in surprise. That was the reason why she was here? Because one of her exam results had been below standard? That was the kind of issue he felt he needed to deal with personally?

He smiled his quiet smile as if reading her thoughts. How she hated that.

"Would you care to elaborate on the reasons for this rather poor showing, if you'll forgive me for putting it so bluntly?"

"I am not a great friend of manipulation, keeping secrets, cold-blooded calculation and using other people to my own advantage, Your Majesty. I feel that I've had my fair share of that already," she answered calmly.

His smile didn't vanish, only changed its quality slightly and now showed genuine bemusement.

"Indeed, that is true. Though I would not see this as a valid reason for discarding the field, but rather for embracing it all the more, even if only for reasons of defence. And I recall an occasion or two when you yourself have resorted to less open ways of action and thus employed what we would term *political strategies*."

She stopped and tried to pull her hand from his grip, but the King held on to it and made her resume walking.

"No false indignation, Lady Eryn, if you please. It is rather wasted on me, I fear."

"I have done no such thing," she huffed impatiently.

"I will elaborate, then, with your permission, as your memory does unfortunately seem to have failed you. There is the matter of Ambassador Ram'an's rather aggressive course of action in obtaining information from you, and your decision to keep this from Lord Enric to avoid what you would consider imprudent actions on his side. That is definitely a political strategy."

She forced herself to remain calm and walk on when stopping and staring at him would again have been her first impulse.

"Pardon me?" she asked with seemingly no more than polite interest.

"Lady Eryn," the King shook his head disappointedly. "I told you, no games right now. There is just you and me here."

She swallowed again. Feigning ignorance had not worked, she would have to try something else. "How might you have learned about this?"

"From Lord Tyront, of course."

Eryn looked at him in surprise. "He informed you of this?" That was unexpected.

"I would not phrase it quite like that. But why don't *you* work it out by using that capable brain of yours? I can tell you this much: it was another political strategy."

Frowning, she let her gaze wander along the high windows. Lord Tyront had informed the King of this. Why? The ambassador had left the Kingdom only days later, and there had been no actions to hold him accountable for his little deed. But the King had said that *informed* was not the correct term for what Lord Tyront did, hadn't he? Had he maybe not done it voluntarily, but been spied upon? She looked at the King.

"May I ask whether you learned about this when Lord Tyront made me tell him about the matter?"

The monarch smiled approvingly and nodded for her to go on.

"In the library." She sighed. He had not raised a soundproof barrier that day, she remembered. Had that been due to forgetfulness, or had he omitted it intentionally? Then it hit her.

"Lord Tyront chose the library to make it easier for your sp... agents," she corrected herself, "to overhear us. He decided to let you have this information without doing it directly, or there would have been the requirement for you somehow to react to the news, which would not have been in your interest."

"Not in the Kingdom's interest," he corrected her gently. "But well done. You have figured out the little puzzle. Let's move on to another one of your political manoeuvres. When you first started healing people in the city, you collected a small fee for your services, didn't you? I imagine your intention was to use the money to purchase the means for you to flee the city."

She looked straight ahead, not meeting his gaze, and remained silent. What could she say, after all? Admitting to him that she had indeed been planning to escape his custody with the money?

"What is more, the discovery of the money's disappearance from your box at the money lenders' was the result of another political strategy. But let us not go into too much detail here. There are so much more interesting ones we can talk about. Like the matter of your commitment to Lord Enric, for example."

She gave him a look of irritation that earned a low laugh. "Yes, definitely more interesting, isn't it? Why don't you try to put the picture together, Lady Eryn? I will supply the missing parts."

He is the King, you are his subject now and need to obey him, she reminded herself, and breathed in and out. But that didn't mean that she had to like it.

"At the ball you invited me to spend the night with you to force Lord Enric's hand," she said flatly. "He reacted the way you'd hoped he would by making me agree to a commitment to him, though I feel that this was a rather risky assumption on your side. Sharing a bed with another person is hardly a reliable sign for willingness to commit to them. You even joined us then and there to make sure I would be bound to the city and would thus no longer be able to resist the next logical step after agreeing to stay here anyway: joining the Order. As the arrival of the ambassador was scheduled for the next few days, you needed to make sure that he found me here neither as a prisoner, nor a free woman with the option to leave here at her own discretion, but a member of the governing magical institution bound to the Kingdom by a magical oath."

"Well summarised, splendid! I should add that there were quite a few more issues to take into consideration long before that. The idea of how to make you join us was first born when Lord Enric lied to me about your protective field. He made sure to impress on me that only he himself and Lord Tyront would be able to penetrate it, thus eliminating all other candidates."

Eryn forced herself to meet his gaze calmly, even though her stomach clenched at the thought that he was aware of Enric's lie. But he didn't seem to be holding any grudge. No hurt feelings, just another political strategy...

"That was when I first suspected his interest in you, though not necessarily any emotional one. That only occurred to me when I learned about him spending the Freedom Night with you as a lover."

She ground her teeth. So it really seemed like everybody but she herself had been aware of that juicy little morsel.

"His interest in you had been increasing steadily after that occurrence," he went on. "Until he had decided to act on it by making you fight and defeat Lord Orrin to be able to train you himself. Another political strategy. You see? They are everywhere." He smiled at her. "Your companion is rather skilled at using them himself. His next move was using your public insult at the competition as justification to make you fight, and of course, lose against him in the streets. And to give him a chance to finally kiss you again after such a long time, even though he seemed to have underestimated the effect it had on him if I am to believe the reports. I wonder if this was when he realised that he was in love with you."

She shook her head, wishing he would stop talking about this.

"Your almost successful attempt at flight not much later was quite a shock to all of us - and a danger to all the little manoeuvres around you. But it was lucky Lords Tyront and Enric were able to stop you when they did, because it was only then matters started developing at speed. Lord Enric's next political strategy was to persuade people - namely the Magic Council and myself - to place you in his custody, even though your powers were completely blocked by the manacles at that time and you didn't exactly pose any danger to anyone. And this was when he finally managed to make you..."

"Stop," she interrupted him and pulled her hand from his arm. "No more of this."

There was a glint of dark delight in his eyes. "Why ever not, Lady Eryn? This story is such an impressive study of how political strategy can be employed to make things happen, to steer them. In this case we have different players to make it even more interesting, each pursuing their own goal and finally achieving it." They had reached the end of the long gallery, and the king took her by her elbow and led her to a bench.

"Sit," he commanded, "and pay attention." His face became stony serious when she didn't comply. "That was an order."

She returned a pained look and sat. Being forced to look up at him was not pleasant, it made her feel trapped, vulnerable. Which was doubtlessly just what he had intended.

"Good. Where was I? Ah yes, Lord Enric finally managed to break your resistance. Or shall we say, make his *conquest*, because you had not really given up the resistance at that time - still haven't entirely, from what I hear. Lord Enric's goals had thus been achieved for that moment, but as I said, he was only one of the players, and my own goals and Lord Tyront's were far from being accomplished. We were already aware of the pending visit from the Western Territories at that time and were eager to make you join the Order. Lord Enric, however, was not in possession of this piece of information, which was due to another one of Lord Tyront's political manoeuvres. He was sure that pressuring Lord Enric to make you attach yourself to him for this reason alone would not have been crowned by success. Your companion is undoubtedly loyal to the Order, but this would have exceeded even his readiness to serve it and the Kingdom. He was too patient with you, content with having you close to him and giving you the time you needed, letting you sleep in his guest room, even though you were physically intimate with each other already at that point. Unfortunately, time was of the essence for the other players. And only here we reach the point where your narrative from before begins with my own little political strategy at the ball." He looked at her intently. "Do you now see why my assumption that he was willing to enter into a commitment with you was not as risky as you thought?"

She glared up at him standing above her, angry at his words. "Why are you telling me all this?"

He stared back into her eyes. "To make you understand. To show you that you can be at one moment the one steering the game just like Lord Enric did, only to be the one being played by others an instant later. Lord Tyront is a close friend of his, and yet this has not stopped him from manipulating Lord Enric. Learning this game, Lady Eryn, is key to surviving at the top, where you are bound. You either learn to play it or are the plaything yourself." His gaze became softer. "But you *are* learning, are you not? You kept the information about the ambassador's truth block and thus the proof of his very obvious personal interest from your companion. But Lord Enric is no fool, he had worked out the ambassador's intentions from the very beginning, when the rest of us were still smiling at his somewhat amusing jealousy, which has, in hindsight, turned out to be completely justified."

Shaking her head, she rose from the bench again. "I still don't understand why you wanted me to hear all this. How will you benefit from my playing the game better? Wouldn't I be more dangerous to you? Or are you counting on me never reaching a level of skill that would matter to you?"

"Very good questions, my Lady. And I will answer them honestly, as I enjoy not having to engage in any games with you right now. I want you to be a strong player in this game, as your goals do not run contrary to my own in most regards. You are not seeking power, but rather after being independent and not controlled by others. And you are a challenge I find most stimulating, one that will grow to be even more interesting in the years to come due to your considerable abilities. Most people around me attempt to diminish my power, thwart my plans or even kill me. But not you. Your goals have nothing to do with me other than not wanting to be controlled by me more than is unavoidable. This is why I see you not as an adversary in the game, but as someone close to an ally, even though not exactly that. Another consideration is that I would not want you to be played by others too easily to be used against me." He raised his eyebrows at her. "Does this answer your questions?"

She nodded slowly, her head reeling.

"Our character determines the nature of the political strategies we use," he then went on. "Look at Lord Orrin, for example. A man straight as an arrow, probably not a dishonourable thought in his head. What political strategies do you think *he* has used on you?"

So the quizzing had not yet finished, she thought wearily and let her mind wander, thinking back. Which one of his actions had first changed her behaviour, made her cooperate? Well, Vern had been a major factor. She looked up at the King, who observed her closely while waiting for her answer.

"He introduced me to his son," she said quietly.

"Indeed. A very powerful manoeuvre, and a brave one. Some would consider it heartless to use his own son like this, but if you really look at the man behind it, you see that it wasn't. His political strategy reflects his way of seeing you: a prisoner, but innocent, a victim of circumstances, fatherless since you were a young girl; and his own life as an only parent to a son exactly the age you were when you lost yours. But he was willing to risk something, willing to pay the price in case he was wrong in his judgement of you. Most of us will not take that gamble. We are only willing to make others pay."

She swallowed at the King's very accurate judgement of Orrin's character and wondered how well he was able to determine her own; and if she would care to hear it.

"People like Lord Orrin are not dangerous in the game," he went on. "Because they follow the simple wisdom of not doing to others what they would not appreciate having done to themselves. It is what I would call a *good person*." He smiled thinly. "Do not ever make the mistake of misjudging me for a good person, Lady Eryn. I am not. I may not be bad as such, but bad enough at times to be dangerous."

Eryn studied him for a while, thoughtful. "Yes, I think I have figured out that much." Then she asked, "You are so young, if you will forgive me for saying so. A year or two younger than me, I think. How can you be so good at this?"

The King chuckled and took both her hands in his. "Because I have been playing this game all my life, was raised to play it competently by a devious, manipulative master of his craft: my father."

He then lifted her hands to his lips and kissed first one, then the other. "You are aware that this is another little game I play, I assume? Would you care to hazard a guess as to its nature?"

She swallowed audibly and then shook her head.

"No need to be afraid. Your hesitation makes me assume that you are on the right track. Tell me," he ordered.

She looked away and tried to ignore the fact that he was still holding on to her hands.

"You first started casually touching me at the evening of the ball, the commitment."

He waited for a few moments before prompting her when she didn't continue. "Go on."

"I think you want to remind me of the order you gave me back then to make Lord Enric act. You probably enjoy making me uncomfortable that way."

"Well done," he smiled. "I dare say Lord Enric has impressed on you that I would very likely have found a way to spend the night with you one way or another. And I wouldn't have hesitated for a moment to take you to bed, in case you had been wondering. It would have been a triumphant night for me either way - a victory,

41

whether my plan had worked or not. This, Lady Eryn, is what I keep reminding you of, my little game I play with you. The beautiful thing about pointing this out to you is that it will now work even better in the future. And that, dearest Lady, is the master class: playing the game with open cards - and still winning."

He let go of her hands and watched with a smug smile when she took one step back, closing her eyes for a moment to collect herself.

"And thus, Lady Eryn, I must congratulate you. You have just passed your second exam in Political Strategy. I asked you to identify four political manoeuvres and you did, at least to a degree that was possible with the information that was at your disposal. I calculated that practical examples from your own experience might be more useful than what long dead kings got up to a hundred years ago. Fortunately, the last year of your life has been such a rich buffet of examples to choose from."

She stared at him in utter astonishment and then breathed in and out deeply several times. She leaned against the window behind her and started laughing to release the tension in inside her, the sound reverberating through the gallery.

"I wasn't aware that you had taken over part of my training, Your Majesty. And I am glad I wasn't, to be honest. It would have terrified me," she admitted.

"Good. I wouldn't like to think that the thought of being tested by me is a pleasant one," he remarked with a half-smile. "I will talk to Lord Poron about the second part of his teaching plan. My primary objective is to make sure that you can use the principles in practice rather than identify them in a book, and you have convinced me that you can do that easily enough. In fact, it seems that you even possess a certain talent yourself for the field that you seem to feel nothing but disdain for. In my opinion you will not profit very much from being made to read the rest of the books on the topic, rather the opposite. It might frustrate you even further. I will thus recommend considering my assessment as the final one here."

Recommend, she thought with wry amusement. As if Lord Poron would dare contradicting a Royal recommendation instead of treating it like the order it really was.

She bowed. "I am grateful. I was not too eager to get back to the subject after my return."

"And now you no longer have to. Consider it a little parting gift. I wish you a pleasant journey, Lady Eryn. Try to keep it an uneventful one for Lord Enric's sake."

CHAPTER 5

The Expedition Starts

Eryn sat up straight in their bed, her eyes wide open. The dawn was only starting to break, which was uncharacteristically early for her to wake without an outside prompt. She swung both legs out of the bed onto the thick carpet and took off her night gown to quickly slip into a pair of trousers and a tunic.

"What is the matter? Where are you going?" Enric yawned and shook his head at the unfamiliar sight of his companion full of energy at this time of day.

"I need to see Vern. I have thought of something, and he needs to take care of this today. I hope I'm not too late," she explained and hastily tied her hair together with a ribbon, without checking if it matched the colour of her tunic. She had other problems right now.

"He will still be asleep. Come back to bed." He lifted his blanket invitingly.

Smiling an apology, she backed out of the bedroom. "Sorry, I really can't. But I will be back in no time. I just need to instruct Vern, then I'll return." She laughed. "Hey, that rhymes! Does it count as a poem?"

Enric sighed and watched her turn and disappear from his field of vision. Moments later he heard the door to the Palace corridors shut.

Eryn fastened the cloak as she walked along the corridor towards the Palace gates. Though it was still early, she was of course not the only one around. She nodded to the servants she met carrying firewood and cleaning the windows, floors, pictures, ornaments and whatever other items that had collected dust and were not supposed to be seen being cleaned during the day.

She imagined that Plia would already be busy in the Palace kitchen, where the breakfast trays for all residents were probably in the process of being prepared right now.

Leaving the Palace, she quickly crossed the large square before it and entered the warriors' quarters. After spending so many months there, she could find her way through the maze of corridors blindfold. Reaching the stairs, she bounded, two steps at a time, and knocked on Orrin's door three times in quick succession. No reaction. She waited for a minute and then tried again, a bit more assertively. Another minute went by, then the door was opened with a jolt and Orrin glared at her with tousled hair and an unfriendly expression.

"You! What do you want? This better be important or I will slap you," he growled.

"Now, now, Orrin," she smiled. "There is no need to be grumpy. You can go right back to bed - I just need a quick word with Vern. I'll be gone in a matter of minutes."

"I am about to despatch you from here in a matter of seconds, right through the window, if you call me grumpy again," he said and shook his head at her.

Eryn just grinned and squeezed in when he didn't step aside to let her through. She went straight for Vern's bedroom, knocking gently and entering without waiting for an invitation.

Orrin smiled when he heard his son howl in frustration at being woken two hours too early.

Eryn chided him. "Come on - don't be such a baby! Are you awake enough to understand and remember what I am telling you, or do I need to empty a jug of water over your head?"

"Go away," he wailed desperately. "Is this what is awaiting me with you out in the wilderness?"

"The water jug was no empty threat, Vern," she warned him and watched his narrowed eyes focus on her.

"Speak then, wench. And then be gone."

"Wench?" She rolled her eyes.

"Evil spirit, if that's more to your liking - or just supply your own unflattering term of choice," he growled and folded his arms. "Would you like me to go on looking for an insult that is to your liking, or will you just tell me why you woke me practically in the middle of the night?"

"Colours," she said, deciding to ignore his irritation in favour of telling him why she had come. "I need you to bring colours. I thought of something important. Some of the plants can only be distinguished by the colouring of their blossoms, so this has to be visible on the drawings. I have only ever seen you drawing with a pen, never using coloured paints or inks. Do you even have any?"

He grimaced and shook his head. "No, I don't. Never needed them or felt the urge to be that creative. I don't even know how to use them properly. Are you telling me that I have one day to figure out how to properly use, mix and preserve them for a ten-day-trip?" He groaned even more loudly than before. "You are joking, aren't you? Why do you do this to me? I had everything finished, everything packed!"

She hid a grin. "To torment you, of course. As with everything else I do, my primary objective is to make you despair."

"Oh, shut up," he grumbled and got up to light a lamp and grab a pen and paper. "So, which colours do I need?"

When she re-emerged from Vern's room several minutes later, she noted that it had become considerably brighter outside. Orrin and Junar were sitting in the parlour fully dressed and had ordered four breakfast trays that now stood on the dinner table.

"Eryn," Junar sighed. "I don't mind telling you that the next ten days will probably be the most relaxing ones I have had in a while."

"And a bright good morning to you, too," Eryn replied sardonically and took a seat in front of one of the trays without invitation. "I assume that one is for me? Or has Vern's appetite increased that much? If so, I should probably pack more provisions for the expedition."

"It is for you," Orrin said. "But don't get used to being fed when you wake us at this hour. Next time it is a boot applied to your backside."

"Perfectly charming," Eryn commented and bit into a piece of sweet bread. "I can see what attracts you in him," she said to Junar.

Vern shuffled out of his bedroom. He had not bothered with getting dressed and looked at the three people at the table.

"Didn't you tell me you wanted to go back to sleep?" Eryn enquired.

"I smell food," he just said and took a seat next to her.

"Ah yes, one of the three needs a man has," she laughed. "Eating, sleeping and…" She fell silent at Orrin's very pointed clearing of his throat and warning look.

"And what? What's the third need?" the boy asked and looked at her.

Eryn swallowed. "You know, if you have to ask, you are probably too young for the answer."

"Ah," he nodded wisely. "Sex, then."

Junar hid her smile behind a napkin while Orrin cast his eyes to the ceiling. "A highly adequate conversation topic during breakfast. Thank you so much, Eryn. I must say that your title and your manners don't share any common ground presently."

Eryn raised her nose haughtily. "Is His Lordship implying that my table manners are not up to the standards of his sophisticated company, pray?"

Vern chuckled and almost choked on his bread.

"Are you going to survive that or can I have that bread bun?" Eryn asked with a greedy look at his tray.

He finished coughing and protectively pushed his tray out of her reach. "You take your greedy hands off my breakfast!"

Orrin buried his face in his hands and sighed. "Whatever came over me when I opened that bloody door?"

* * *

Eryn watched the bags, parcels, bundles and other items being strapped to the pack animals. It was one more hour until the scheduled time of departure, and the Palace square was a confusion with horses, servants, herb gatherers and family members who had come to say goodbye.

Rolan stood next to her, ticking off items on one of the many lists he had made in these last few weeks. "Yellow, green, purple, red, blue, black and white?" he said and Vern nodded.

"One hundred sheets of blank paper?" Another nod.

"Four water resistant paper transport boxes?"

"Yes," Vern confirmed again.

"Ten pens and five glasses of black ink?"

"Positive."

"Two bags of fine sand for blotting the ink?"

"Yes, everything here," Vern stated.

Rolan nodded and marked the last line on his paper with a flourish and an air of satisfaction. "Excellent. From my point of view you are ready to leave."

Eryn turned to him. "So eager to get rid of me, Rolan?" She laid her flat palm on her chest in mock devastation. "You are breaking my heart."

"That was not the impression I'd intended to make," he replied awkwardly and Vern grinned at his discomfort.

Rolan looked around, obviously desperate to find something to do that would give him an excuse to get away from her. "I better check if the food has been properly secured," he said.

"Yes, you do that," Eryn nodded with exaggerated seriousness. "We wouldn't want to leave a trail of food and then starve in the woods, would we?"

The look he flashed her before hurrying away told her clearly that this was not such an unattractive option from where he stood.

Vern laughed as soon as her assistant was out of earshot. "You tease the poor guy. One day he will snap like a twig and throw you out of a window."

"Little pleasures," she grinned. "It's not my fault that he doesn't let off steam."

Vern looked around and rubbed his hands in anticipation. "I can't wait to get started on this. I have never been outside the city for more than a few hours. This is going to be so brilliant!"

Eryn looked a little concerned. She had been out for days at a time alone in the woods with no comfort whatsoever before and she knew what awaited her, but Vern would probably face a rude awakening out in the wilderness. She should have talked to him about that before, she thought and started worrying a little.

"You know," she said carefully, "this might not be as romantic an adventure as you seem to expect. For the next ten days life will be a lot less comfortable. No city benefits out there in the woods."

He waved her off impatiently. "I know," he snorted dismissively. "I have read travel diaries about all and any possible catastrophes we may have to face: thunderstorms, landslides, floods, earthquakes..."

"I was thinking more of everyday inconveniences," she interrupted him. "Such as frosty nights, cold water for washing, sleeping on the hard ground. Things like that."

"I can handle that," Vern promised confidently. "I am a warrior's son after all, am I not? No challenge is too great for me."

She sighed and shook her head slowly. Suddenly he saw himself as a warrior's son when he usually lamented that other people's expectations of his fighting skills were much too high because of just that fact? But she decided to give up trying to warn him for now. He was intoxicated, excited and looking forward to his first adventure, free from parental supervision, teachers and whatever other plagues a teenage boy's life held. He was not open for anything that would dampen his mood right now. She would let him relish the spirit of optimism a bit longer. He would need reminding of it soon enough.

They stood next to each other, watching the lively bustle around them for a while.

"Hey, there's Plia," Vern said and pointed towards the Palace gates. He lifted a hand and waved to her. The girl smiled and changed direction to join them. She was wearing leather trousers of the same sandy colour and make as Eryn's own and a sturdy tunic that showed when she walked and her cloak billowed out.

"Everything packed and ready, little flower?" Eryn asked affectionately.

"Yes, I think." She shrugged. "Whatever I have not packed I will have to learn to do without."

"Good attitude," Vern said by way of a compliment and grinned.

Sure, if one grew up with owning practically nothing, that was a point of view that made life easier, Eryn supposed.

"Did you both eat a hearty breakfast that can sustain you for several hours? We will ride for quite a while until we take a rest stop."

Vern shrugged. "You know me, I never skip a meal. I am more likely to squeeze in an extra one, for that matter."

"I had breakfast several hours ago," Plia said.

Eryn chewed on her lower lip and thought for a moment. "Then I think it might be better to eat a little something before we leave. Vern, why don't you run to the bakery and fetch us a few bread buns? The sweet ones."

The boy nodded and trotted off towards Kingsway.

Plia watched the horses with slightly widened eyes.

"Don't worry, you will ride with me. I picked an extra docile one for us, so, there is no need to be afraid."

"I am not," the girl lied. "Just excited."

"Yes, right," Eryn smiled and saw Orrin come their way.

"Where is my boy?" he asked, and nodded to Eryn and Plia.

"Grabbing a little sweet pastry for us girls, so we don't faint from lack of strength and fall off our horse," Eryn told him.

The warrior nodded and looked around at the busy square. "You will take good care of him, won't you? Don't let him fall off a cliff, be bitten by anything poisonous or get lost, do you hear?"

"Well, I will see what I can do. But seeing that he's quite an accomplished healer already and my being not too bad at it as well, I would say his chances of survival are better than average."

"I know. I wouldn't have permitted your taking him with you into the wilderness otherwise."

"It's just for ten days, and we plan to spend only six of them actually gathering herbs in the woods. The rest is relatively boring and unspectacular travelling on roads and sleeping at inns. So don't worry. It's a herb gathering trip, after all, so what can really happen? We are not on a reconnaissance mission to scope out enemy positions or some such."

"That remains to be seen," he said and inclined his head towards the Palace gate. "It looks like your companion is on his way to say goodbye to you as well."

And true enough, Enric was walking towards them with an expression that was not exactly displeasure, but more resignation. He didn't bother hiding the fact that he was not at all thrilled about seeing her leave.

When he had reached them, he nodded to Orrin and Plia and put an arm around Eryn's shoulders to pull her against him.

"Still determined to go?" he asked in a feeble attempt to be humorous.

"Yes," she smiled. "Otherwise I would look pretty foolish, wouldn't I?"

"I could live with that."

She elbowed him in the ribs none too gently. "Of course *you* could live with that! You wouldn't be the one people would snigger at behind your back."

At that moment Vern returned with a paper bag full of bread buns and greeted his father before he bowed to Enric. Eryn's stomach grumbled when she smelled the sweet, warm pastries.

"Mmm!" Junar's voice came from behind her. "Something smells delicious here!"

"Sure," Eryn sighed in resignation, but stepped aside to make space for her. "Trust you to be around just in time to steal my last treats for the next ten days. Vulture."

"*My* treats," Vern pointed out and held out the bag to his father's lover. "And I am sharing them with her." He then offered the bag to Plia with slow deliberation.

"Traitor," Eryn mumbled and snatched one for herself from the bag. "But don't worry, I will make you pay for that. I have you at my mercy for some time, after all." She grinned wickedly and sank her teeth into the pastry, enjoying the rich, warm sweetness.

"Maybe I should stay here, after all," Vern mused. "I could ask Rolan to go in my stead."

"Splendid. Then I will probably end up in a fast-flowing river. With stones tied to my feet and around my neck."

"He would have to face my wrath, if that is any consolation," Enric smirked.

"Thank you, that does warm my heart."

"Glad to hear it. Where are your swords? You should carry one of them, at least," he frowned.

"While I am in the saddle? Seriously?"

Orrin gave her an astonished look. "Of course. Or would you prefer to start looking for it while you are already being attacked?"

"I thought you made me take four swordsmen so I don't have to take care of any trouble that might arise?"

"We did," Enric confirmed and then pointed out, "but that doesn't mean that you can forego all caution when it comes to defending yourself. I really wonder if it was a wise decision to let you out of my sight for that long."

"I'll have you know that I have managed to survive for quite some time before you came along. I dare say I will continue to do so for the next few days."

"Good. You would never hear the end of it if you didn't," he grinned and took a pastry from the bag Vern kept offering to all of them.

"I suppose I wouldn't hear very much anymore in that case," she retorted dryly and snatched the pastry out of his hand before he could bite into it. "That's mine. I ordered them."

"Greedy, single child," Junar muttered and reached into the bag to hand Enric another one.

They stood together companionably, munching their sweets and watching the other members of the expedition say their goodbyes to their loved ones.

"I suppose it's time for us to say our farewells, too," Eryn said and turned to her companion. "Be good and play nicely with the other magicians. No breaking of any noses or anything of that kind while I am gone."

He grinned and grabbed the collar of her cloak to pull her close. "With you gone I won't have any more reason to," he pointed out and kissed her.

She then freed herself from his firm embrace and hugged Orrin and Junar before mounting her horse and waiting for Orrin to help Plia into the saddle behind her.

One of the four swordsmen approached her on his horse and exchanged a few words with her before nodding and riding towards the city gates. Eryn rode over to the assembled herb gatherers, most of whom had already mounted their rides and waved a final salute to the ones they were leaving behind.

Eryn watched the large group set in motion towards the city gate and followed, casting a last glance behind her to her own little family.

* * *

Plia kept turning around in the saddle for the next hour until they were too far away to see the city any more. Vern steered his black horse next to theirs and said conspiratorially, "You see the swordsman with the black trousers on the red horse? The bearded one? I think that is an old friend of my father's and will very probably keep him informed about anything that happens."

"Alright, thanks for the warning," Eryn replied. "Though I suspect he is not the only informant near or among us."

She then concentrated for a moment and smiled when Plia gasped behind her.

"I had no idea you could to that! Wouldn't this have helped you to flee from the city?"

"Yes, very much actually. But I only learned it when the ambassador came here, and by then I had given up leaving here ever again."

"Why did you change your hair colour just now?" she asked and carefully touched the blonde tail that hung down Eryn's back as if afraid that the colour would rub off.

"I don't want to attract too much attention, and I could hardly avoid that with my original hair colour."

"Why not?" the girl asked. "It's not as if you can't defend yourself."

"True, but I would rather like to avoid situations that would make defending myself necessary. News doesn't travel as quickly to more remote areas, so people in some villages we pass may not have heard about the brown-haired, female Order magician yet and may try to capture me to take care of the foreign spy. Just like my own village did."

"Oh," Plia then said. "But you would be able to defend yourself this time, wouldn't you? And the men would protect you."

Eryn shrugged. "I dare say they would. But why not avoid trouble instead of walking into it?"

The girl looked up at the blonde braid for several seconds, then shook her head. "It looks strange. Really."

The woman chuckled. "I thought exactly the same when my colour changed back to brown last year. I'd had blonde hair since I was five years old, and after more than twenty years I had become so used to it that I had more or less forgotten that it was not my real colour. Looking into the mirror the first time was a real shock back then. I suppose it just depends what you are used to seeing."

She heard Plia giggle and looked to one side to Vern, who had changed his own hair to her shade of brown.

"Nice," she commented. "Now *you* can be the enemy spy to be captured and locked up."

"They would hardly manage to keep me locked up very long," he sneered. "Unlike poor, helpless you back then, I am trained in the arts of destruction and mayhem. I would turn whatever building they tried to keep me in into a pile of rubble."

"Destruction and mayhem? We have hardly left the city walls behind us, and already you have turned into a big, bad, savage warrior. It must be the fresh air. Now change your hair back, my lad. Some of the herb gatherers have started looking at us rather nervously."

"Which has, of course, nothing to do with your new hair colour, but must be due to *mine*," he snorted but did as she had told him.

"I didn't say that, but your little joke just doubled the strangeness of the situation. Let's not overtax them now right at the start of the journey."

$$* \quad * \quad *$$

It was almost completely dark when they reached the town Eryn had marked on her map as the first halt. It was large enough for two taverns, and all but a few members of the party would sleep in a warm bed tonight.

They had ridden for about ten hours with only a few short breaks in between and all but fell off their horses. Plia herself had dropped asleep against Eryn's back and nearly tumbled down when Eryn made to dismount.

"Careful, little flower," she warned and helped the girl out of the saddle after she herself had firm ground underneath her feet. She stretched and then unstrapped a leather bag with the things she needed for the night from the saddle to take with her to the inn.

"I hope they have decent food here," Vern yawned and shouldered a bundle. "I am starving."

"When are you not starving?" Eryn commented.

"I told you, it's because I am still growing."

"Judging from how much you eat you should be at least as tall as a house by now."

"Very funny," he growled. "Don't tease me when I am hungry." He took the bridle of his horse and looked around. "Have you seen any stables here?"

Eryn was tickled at his innocence. "Vern, this is a small town. Even if they had stables, they would hardly be big enough to accommodate all our horses. We will lead them to a meadow and leave them there."

"Overnight? Just like that? What if somebody steals them?" he exclaimed in horror.

"That's why some of the men will stay to watch them at night. They will do it in shifts so that everyone will have at least a few hours of sleep," she explained patiently.

"Oh," he then said sheepishly after considering her words. "That does make sense."

"Come. Take everything you need for the night, and the guards will take our horses to the meadow for us. Plia, do you have your things?"

The girl nodded and waited until both of them had handed over their horses' bridles to the swordsmen. They walked towards the entrance of the inn, and Vern opened the door for them to enter. The noise in the large room decreased for a few moments until the men at the tables and the counter had studied them, then it rose within seconds back to its previous level.

A few of the herb gatherers had managed to commandeer a large table for themselves and waved them over to sit with them.

"Ah," Vern sighed and leaned back against the wall behind him. "It's so good to sit on something that does hold still for a change."

The herb gatherers exchanged amused looks.

"Lady Eryn," a voice to her left said and she turned and looked at a familiar face. "It has been a while."

She grinned broadly. "Look at that, and I thought you were lost without a trace when I didn't see you in the morning at the square today." It was the gatherer who had sold herbs to her in back alleys and had later been beaten up for it by the League of Apothecaries.

"No, I wouldn't have missed this." He nodded to Vern. "Young man. I don't think I have ever thanked you sufficiently for healing me that time. I was rather dazed and don't remember much."

Vern grimaced. "You didn't look too good, either."

"Yes, I imagine I didn't. I was told it took you quite some time to fix me up again. Several hours."

The boy nodded. "But that was not so much because your injuries were so complicated, but due to my lack of practise. I was extra careful and slow to make sure I didn't make grow things together that were not supposed to be connected."

The man laughed. "And I thank you very much for that. I am greatly in debt to you. Should you ever need anything from a simple man such as myself, do not hesitate to ask, and I will grant it if it is in my powers."

"Can I ask you what you name is?" Eryn cut in. "You never told me for obvious reasons, but I venture these days are behind us."

"Garn. Happy to meet you officially, Lady Eryn."

She quickly took his hand when he made to bow and shook it. "Let's not bother with this here. And neither with calling me *Lady*. Titles are at times more of a hindrance than a help in these rural areas. I would be grateful if you could spread this among your colleagues."

Garn nodded. "Surely, no problem." After a moment's hesitation he added, "Eryn."

A waitress and what seemed to be the publican brought a large tray each to their table and started putting bowls with some kind of meaty stew in front them.

Plia shifted uncomfortably and smiled apologetically when Eryn gave her a questioning look. "Is everything alright with you?"

"Yes. Sure. Just a little sore from riding," she grimaced.

Eryn shook her head, annoyed at herself. She had been unconsciously healing away her own soreness bit by bit all day long without even thinking of the poor girl. Taking Plia's hand into her own, she closed her eyes for a moment and sent her magic to the sore areas on the inside of the girl's thighs.

Plia sighed with relief when the burning sensation ceased. "Thank you very much. That is a lot better."

The men at the table watched them in fascination. Eryn raised her brows and smiled.

"Does anybody else have any sore areas that require healing? If I pick up that spoon, you will have to wait until I am done eating."

Heads shook, some grinning, and they started eating.

Vern was the first to empty his bowl and kept looking around for someone he could order another helping from.

Eryn shook her head at him, her own bowl still half full. "Are you even chewing your food? How can you be done already?"

He shrugged. "Practice."

Plia put her spoon down and sighed contentedly. "That was not bad, but they watered it down a bit too much."

Of course, Eryn smiled, working in the kitchen would have made her observant of things like that.

Vern greedily eyed the girl's bowl. It was still half full. "Are you eating that, Plia?"

"No," she said and pushed the rest of her food towards him. "Enjoy it."

The boy grinned at her gratefully and started gobbling up the food as if he hadn't eaten anything in days instead of only a few minutes before.

"Be careful when you feed strays," Eryn commented dryly, "or you will never quite rid yourself of them afterwards."

Vern looked at her intently. "If you are referring to my cat, then let me tell you that I have no intention of getting rid of him."

"You have a cat?" Plia enquired curiously.

"Yes," Eryn answered before he could swallow, "a mean red monster from a back alley. I caught it to make him practice healing on it, and he decided to keep it. His father was not too happy about that, as you might imagine."

"He is not that bad," said Vern, defending his pet. "He just needs to get used to living inside now. A bit like Eryn," he added with a malicious grin. "It took them months to hammer her into shape for the city."

Some of the herb gatherers froze and watched for Eryn's reaction to a seemingly very disrespectful remark from a boy many years her junior to an influential Order magician.

Smiling broadly, she leaned back and felt the tension at the table relax almost instantly.

"That's because I am hard to tame. And you see where I am now? I have finally managed to get out of the city. And I didn't even have to break down any walls or overpower gate guards this time."

Garn smiled. "As long as you don't abandon us in the woods and run off to the west."

She shrugged. "Hardly. I have become rather used to the city. And there is this little matter of the Order binding its members with a magical oath. I wouldn't even have been able to leave the city without the intention of returning. So no need to be nervous on my behalf," she added with a smile and then yawned.

"Tired?" Vern asked and suppressed a yawn himself.

"Yes," she nodded. "I think I will retire for tonight. We are going to have an early start tomorrow, so I recommend you take it easy on the ale," she warned the herb gatherers and rose to summon the waitress to be shown to her room.

CHAPTER 6

Unwanted Attention

Eryn yawned and looked over to Vern, who was reading a book about medicinal herbs. His horse didn't require any particular attention from his side, it was used to following behind the others and thus made it possible for its rider to occupy his mind otherwise.

She herself had also tried to read while riding, but she quickly felt dizzy with the letters dancing up and down in front of her eyes due to the horse's motion. The party had started early and had now been on the road for about four hours. It would soon be time for a lunch break. According to her calculations, they should reach the next village in about half an hour. As long as there were inns along their way, there would be no need to camp or light a cooking fire with tables, benches and service available.

With Vern educating himself and Plia snoozing most of the time behind her, Eryn became rather bored and let her gaze wander to see if there was anybody around who might be in the mood to talk to her. It was a good opportunity to get to know the herb gatherers a little better, as, after all, she would be working with them in the future.

But her eyes instead caught one of the swordsmen, the one Vern had pointed out to her as his father's likely informant. She steered her horse next to his and smiled when he looked at her questioningly.

"Hello. I was told you are an old friend of Orrin's," she began.

The man nodded hesitantly. It seemed as if he would have preferred for that little detail to remain unknown. "You could say that. Why?"

"Just checking. I am trying to figure out how many spies I have around me, and you are the only one I have been able to identify so far."

"I am no spy," he said indignantly.

She grinned. "So you are telling me that Orrin has not casually asked you to send word to him every now and then of how things are going?"

He sighed. "I don't think I have to tell you this, do I?"

Eryn thought for a moment, then nodded apologetically. "I am afraid you do. You see, if you were Lord Tyront's or the King's or even Lord Enric's agent, I couldn't order you to tell me about it, as those three are higher up on the ladder of power. But I do happen to outrank Orrin, so his orders are somewhat voided when they contradict mine."

The swordsman looked at her sullenly. "So you are telling me I am not to send word to him?"

"No, that's not what I am telling you. I am asking you to admit to reporting to him, nothing more. Send him as many messages as you want, for all I care. Should there be something I need you to omit, though, I will let you know and you will have to comply."

The man nodded, clearly not all too happy about any of this.

She leaned a little closer to him and lowered her voice. "You don't happen to know who else sends reports to the city, do you?"

"No, sorry," he said and shook his head.

She straightened again and sighed. "It doesn't matter for now, I will make it a game to figure it out. What is your name, friend of Orrin?"

"Barul," he said.

"Happy to make your acquaintance, Barul," she said and smiled. "It was nice talking to you. Give my regards to Orrin when you next write to him." With this she fell back next to Vern again who looked up in surprise as he didn't seem to have noticed that she had even been gone.

* * *

"The other three swordsmen surely are agents as well," Vern said with conviction. "I bet they are."

"Probably," Eryn admitted. "Though that would be rather obvious, wouldn't it?"

"Maybe they think it is so plain that you'll discard the idea as too easy to see through. Then you wouldn't suspect them anymore, which would make them perfect spies," he pointed out.

"That thinking does sound a little twisted," Plia said and tried to catch a glimpse of the men without falling off the horse.

Twisted it was, Eryn thought, but that didn't mean that it was less likely - quite the opposite. But what did it really matter to them, if she worked out who their spies were? As she had told Barul, she couldn't order the others to withhold information and stop them from sending it back home when their clients were more important than her. She studied the one in the lead in front of the group. What she could do was to be careful who was around her in case she didn't want something to turn up in any of their reports.

"Do you think they have any other spies in the group? Some of the herb gatherers maybe?" she asked.

Vern shrugged. "Unlikely. They keep together mostly, and one of them occasionally stepping out for no apparent reason might be suspicious. It's easier for the guards, they can pretend to check the area for wild animals, robbers and the like and send off their little messages then."

"Always assuming that all spies were told to send regular messages instead of giving only one detailed report after we have returned," she pointed out. She wondered what exactly their instructions were. Sending regular reports back to the city while they were travelling would require a minor army of messengers - especially after entering the woods. But then the men who were most likely to send spies after her - among them Enric and the King - had deep pockets and could afford to pay for however many riders it took to follow the group for the mere purpose of keeping their clients informed.

"Yes," Vern admitted, "assuming that."

"I don't like this," she complained, "this is *my* trip, *my* project. They shouldn't be checking on me like that! It's as if they didn't trust me!"

"But," Plia ventured carefully, "isn't the Order paying for it?"

"Yes, it is," Eryn sighed unnerved, "hit me with logic, will you?"

* * *

"You know, today the soreness is not as bad as yesterday, I have to say. I think I am getting used to all that riding," Plia said happily once they had dismounted in the evening and were on their way into the public room of what would be their last inn for the next seven days.

Eryn chuckled. "Really? So you don't think it might have anything to do with me healing you every now and then while you were sleeping behind me?"

The girl's face fell. "Oh. And I thought I was turning into a travel-hardened woman with thighs of steel," she sighed.

"After only two days of travelling? That would have been very impressive," Vern sniggered and secured an empty table for them.

There were only a few men in the pub, the rush would probably start in an hour or so.

"How many in your party?" A stocky man emerged from behind the bar, wiping his hands on a grey apron.

"Twenty-three," Eryn said. "Can you feed that many?"

"Feed, yes," the barman said. "But not seat them for very long. They either eat quickly or do it standing up. Can't annoy the regular crowd."

"No problem," she assured him. "How many people can you accommodate for one night?"

"I got eight rooms. Some of you got to sleep on the floor, though. Not so many beds," he murmured. "You look important, you'll have a room to yourself, then? Got one that's too small for several men, but it should do for you."

"I'll share it with the girl," she said and pointed to Plia.

"Suit yourself," he muttered and sauntered off to the kitchen to arrange twenty-three meals.

"This is going to be the last night with a roof over your head for a while," Eryn pointed out. "So try to enjoy it. From tomorrow on it is going to be camp fires, cold, hard ground with occasional rain and wind." She rubbed her hands gleefully at their uneasy expressions.

Leaving their horses on the meadow where they had agreed the animals could spend the night, the herb gatherers began trickling in.

The publican returned with the first tray of food, a thick soup with generous bits of vegetables and meat.

"Better than yesterday evening," one of the herb gatherers said appreciatively.

"Yes," Plia nodded. "More sustenance, less water."

"Will you do the cooking for us when we are out in the woods?" one of the men enquired.

"Yes. Cook has shown me a few things that will warm you and fill your stomachs and are not too hard or complicated to make."

"Good," Eryn nodded. "We don't want to have a bunch of hungry men around us in the wilderness, trust me."

"When have you ever been alone with a bunch of hungry men in the wilderness?" Vern asked.

"Not in the wilderness, but I used to eat with the warriors three times a day, if you remember. That was bad enough, actually. And it will hardly be more pleasant out in the wilderness. You see? Experience in combination with logical deduction."

"I don't think you can compare hungry herb gatherers with hungry warriors," Vern said. That statement earned him a few raised eyebrows.

"Careful, boy," one of them said. "We all carry knives for our work. Just remember that unhappy in combination with a weapon is unhealthy, whether it is a sword or a herb gathering knife."

Vern swallowed and nodded. "Sorry, I didn't mean to imply..."

"Relax, he is only messing with you," another one said. "And it's not like we are much of a threat to a magician, eh?"

Tensions, Eryn realised wearily. Hardly avoidable in a situation like this, when grown men were supposed to show respect to a boy for no other reason than his being born a magician.

"No, not physically," she said with a smile, "but I bet he will return home less innocent than he left. I heard one of your songs yesterday, and my ears are still burning."

That made them laugh, and the mood was a lot less tense in an instant. Plia smiled at her with relief.

* * *

Eryn looked around the small room the publican had given them. He had not lied, it really was not very spacious.

"I will sleep over there," Plia said and let her blanket drop to the floor.

"What for? The bed is large enough for the both of us. I tend to be a bit possessive as regards blankets and the like, so if you find yourself on the verge of falling to the floor or freezing, just wake me up and we will redistribute the resources evenly."

"I don't know, it just doesn't feel right - your being forced to sleep in one bed with me," Plia frowned.

"Why? Don't tell me you are worried about my station and the strain sharing a bed with a servant must be for me?" Eryn laughed. "Really, Plia, after you have slept in the woods for one night, you will see that this is a wonderful equaliser. Cold feet and aching backs, whether you are born high, brought low or anywhere in between."

Plia shrugged. "Whatever you say. Who am I to contradict the mighty magician?"

"There's a good girl. Can you have a peek at the door for me? Does the lock look reliable?"

"Not really, no. Rusty and a bit loose I'd say."

"Then grab the chair and jam it under the door handle. No, not like that. The idea is to avoid the handle being pushed down from the outside. Like this." Eryn readjusted the position of the chair's backrest. "See? Useful knowledge for a girl on the road."

* * *

Plia barely managed to hold on to the bedspread before she nearly fell out of the bed. Eryn had successfully conquered about three quarters of the narrow bed.

Carefully trying to find a spot that would allow her to go back to sleep without facing the constant danger of being shoved off the bed, she quickly stilled and listened. There were noises outside their door. The moon was not bright enough to see clearly and was more hindrance than help, as it somehow seemed to be casting more shadows than light.

"Eryn?" the girl whispered as loud as she could when she saw the door handle being rattled cautiously. "Eryn!" she repeated and urgently shook the woman's shoulder to wake her. "Wake up! Eryn!"

"What?" Eryn whispered back sleepily. "Do you need more space?"

"I think somebody is trying to get into our room!" the girl told her hastily, never taking her eyes off the door. "The door handle is moving!"

Eryn was fully awake in an instant.

"Down on the floor and under the bed with you. Now," she instructed calmly.

"What? And leave you alone to fend off whoever is out there? No!" Plia protested in a horrified whisper.

Eryn's tone was reasonable, but steely, when she explained, "I am a magician, I can defend myself. You might be in the way and get hurt. Now hide under the bed. This is an order."

This time the girl obeyed, though reluctantly.

"What are you going to do? Won't you stop them now?" she whispered from under the bed.

"No, not yet. I want to make sure it's not Vern trying to play a trick on us. I wouldn't want to hurt him by accident because of a stupid prank."

"You think it might be Vern?" Plia asked hopefully.

"Sure, why not?" Eryn said reassuringly, bracing herself. She knew fully well that this was not Vern. He wouldn't play a tasteless trick like that on them.

She groped for the herb gathering knife on the night stand and closed her fingers around it. Using magic to defend herself was not allowed, so apart from shielding herself this was her only means of defence. Her sword was in the bag at the other end of the room, the handle sticking out. She briefly considered getting up and fetching it, but discarded the idea when the door yielded to their visitor's efforts. She quickly leaned back and pretended to be asleep, hiding the hand with the knife under her pillow.

Moments later she heard the chair quietly scrape over the wooden floor when it was pushed towards the wall and heard footsteps coming closer to the bed. She was about to create a shield, when she suddenly felt large hands at her throat choking her and keeping her from screaming.

Damn! He had moved too fast, she had counted on his being more careful. That was a stupid mistake, she realised through the haze of pain.

"What do you want?" she croaked and tried to pull her hand with the knife out from under the pillow, but he pressed her head onto it with enough force to hamper her efforts.

"A little fun, pretty lady," a deep, unpleasant voice answered and cackled. A nauseating gust of sour breath wafted her way. That alone would have sufficed to make her eyes water, but right now it paled in comparison with the pain his hands at her throat caused.

Finally managing to pull her hand free from behind her head, she fought through the daze the lack of air caused and magically enhanced the strength in her arm to drive the knife deep into the man's torso. She didn't really have time or enough light to aim properly, but wherever she had hit him would definitely cause him serious trouble. There were just too many important organs in that general vicinity, and not hitting a single one of them with the blade was practically impossible.

She heard him gasp - first in shock, then in pain - and felt his grip on her throat loosen. Fuelling the muscles of her arms with more magical strength, she pushed him off her and heard him land on the floor with a loud thud.

"Plia?" she croaked hoarsely. "Come out and make some light." She wanted the girl out of the man's reach while he was lying on the floor so close to the bed.

The girl shuffled out from under the bed, breathing heavily. "Are you hurt? Is he dead?"

"I don't think so, at least not yet. Be quick, I need light."

Plia quickly groped for matches on the small nightstand, her trembling fingers finally managing to strike a match so that it produced a flame and lit the single candle. Both of them looked down at the dirty, heavy man on the floor with the knife sticking out of the left side of his torso. They didn't really see much of him in the dim light, but neither of the women had any particular desire to study him in more detail.

Eryn swiftly grabbed his hand and made sure that he was unconscious with a quick surge of magic to his head; only then she examined the damage she had done.

"I have pierced his lung," she murmured and slowed down his heartbeat and thus breathing. Opening her eyes again, she instructed Plia, "Run and fetch Vern here quickly - I might as well use this as an opportunity to teach him something. And then go and wake the publican and send him up. Try to avoid our swordsmen. I don't want this to be in any of their reports. Enric wouldn't react well to it."

The girl nodded and scampered off to do as she was told.

Eryn closed her eyes again to monitor the status of her attacker and make sure he wouldn't die on her while she waited for her apprentice to arrive.

"What the..." Vern gasped when he arrived no more than two minutes later and saw Eryn kneeling on the floor next to a seemingly lifeless man who had obviously been stabbed.

"Come here," she said and grabbed his hand to pull him down to her when he was close enough. "What do you see?"

"What happened here?" he demanded with wide eyes.

"Later. First comes the healing, then the explaining. Assess the damage. Now."

He scowled at her but obediently closed his eyes and sent a surge of exploratory magic into the recumbent man's upper body.

"Right lung," he murmured. "The heartbeat is slow; did you do that?"

"Yes," she confirmed. "Proposed course of action?"

"You pull out the knife bit by bit and I heal the damage?"

"Alright. What problems will we face?"

He thought for a moment. "Blood in the lung."

"How can we deal with that?"

61

"A shield around the damaged area," he answered immediately.

"Good. Let's start with that."

She watched him create a small barrier to keep the blood from oozing where it shouldn't.

He breathed in and out several times before she heard him say, "I am ready. Pull it out a bit."

She did and stopped when he told her to. Watching him tease the tissue in the lung to knit together again, she felt pride rise inside her despite the dire situation. He was doing extremely well. Only sixteen years old, and yet a professional through and through. Somebody who was woken in the middle of the night to heal for the first time in his life a ruptured lung and who did it without panicking, would hardly be thrown off track by any other medical emergency anytime soon.

"A bit further," he instructed and brought her back to the matter at hand.

When she had removed the entire blade from his body, she put it aside and asked, "Are you finished?"

"No, there is liquid collecting in his lung. It needs to be taken care of."

"How can you do this?"

"By making the blood vessels more permeable in that area so they reabsorb the blood," he said after a few moments of consideration.

"Do it."

When both of them opened their eyes again, they looked up at several people. One was the publican in a too short nightgown that revealed hairy legs, then of course Plia, and behind them stood Garn, the herb gatherer and the second man Vern was sharing the room with.

"We are done now," Eryn announced and rose from the floor, pulling Vern with her. "We have made sure he will sleep for another few hours. That should give you enough time to do with him whatever you do here with people who attack women in their beds," she said grimly.

"What happened?" the publican asked and looked down at the unconscious figure.

"He broke into the room, tried to choke me and told me he was about to have a little fun with me. I stabbed him, and the young man here, a magician, healed him." She carefully omitted mentioning her own magical abilities.

"Healed him? I didn't know magicians can do that," the man frowned in confusion.

"Not all of them," Eryn shrugged.

She waited for some kind of reaction, and when none came, added, "Is there a chance we can have him out of here very soon? We are going to have a long day tomorrow, and a few more hours of sleep would be really helpful."

"You want to go back to sleep now? Just like that?" the pub owner asked incredulously. "That is cold-blooded if you don't mind me saying so. You must have nerves of steel!"

She shook her head. "No, not really. But my magician friend here will make sure I can find some sleep. A healer is a really useful thing to have around." Patting Vern's shoulder, she watched the three men drag out her attacker - to lock him up somewhere, she hoped.

"Garn?" she called after them, "Would the two of you come back here after you have disposed of him?"

After he had nodded to her in confirmation, she closed the door again.

"Vern, that was exceptional work under very stressful circumstances. You did well, immensely so. I am very proud of you." She pulled him close and hugged him.

He sighed and wrapped his arms around her. "Alright, that almost makes up for being dragged out of bed to take care of your victims."

He let go of her again and lifted her chin to look at the marks on her throat.

"You let him get very close," he said and she could detect a hint of suppressed anger in his voice. Only now that her mind was no longer focused on healing, she started feeling the pain at her throat again. She should have healed it away before his arrival to hide the marks, she thought. But she had been concentrating on keeping the brute on the floor alive.

She smiled when she felt warmth seep through his fingers at her chin into her skin, and the burning sensation in and around her throat ceased moments later.

"Thank you, dear lad."

"Next time we stay at an inn, you will share a room with *me*," he said grimly.

"That wouldn't have changed much. We are not allowed to attack them with magic, you remember? Most sacred law and all that?"

"I know that, thank you very much," he snapped at her. "But I wouldn't have let him approach that close. We are allowed to use protective barriers to keep them off us, after all!"

She swallowed her remark that this had been the initial plan and just nodded. They heard a knock at the door, and when Plia opened it, the two herb gatherers came in as she had asked them to.

Eryn looked at each of the four people around her. "I need you to promise me that you will keep this a secret. Don't tell anybody about what has happened here tonight; not your colleagues, and especially not the swordsmen. And nobody at home. This is an order. Have I made myself understood?"

Plia nodded and so did the herb gatherers, though with visible reluctance.

"Vern?" she asked when he just folded his arms and frowned at her.

"I don't like this one bit. This is not something you should keep to yourself, especially not when we have four guards here to protect us! How are they to know that they are needed when you treat them like enemies just because you don't want to face Lord Enric? This is not a wise move, Eryn."

"Vern, I am not going to discuss this with you right now," she glared at him. "I gave you an order, and I need you to confirm it to me."

"Yes, Lady Eryn," he said sullenly and then turned away with a last angry look at her to walk back to his room.

*　*　*

Eryn sighed when Vern came down the stairs of the inn giving her an angry look before going to another table to sit at for his breakfast.

Plia watched him with a frown. "Oh no, he is still angry at you. And we haven't even really started the proper expedition yet," she sighed.

"Yes, what a marvellous start," Eryn growled and took a hearty bite of the thick slice of bread the publican had cut for her. He seemed to be particularly eager to make up for last night's incident as well as he could and had insisted on not charging her anything for her own and Vern's room. Well, she thought, there were still six other rooms they had to pay for, so it was not that much of a loss for him.

They looked up when the door opened and two men came in, one of them tall and thin, clad in dark grey clothes that might at some point in time have been black, the other one smaller, stout and with first signs of baldness visible on the crown of his head. The publican met their gaze and pointed them towards Eryn.

The taller one of them cleared his throat.

"You would be Eryn, the one who was attacked last night?" When she nodded, he continued. "I am the local magistrate and need to ask you a few questions, if you don't mind. This here is my deputy, who will take notes."

And if she did mind, she wondered, would he just leave? Probably not. She took a gulp of her hot tea to wash down the dry bread and motioned for them to take a seat.

"I am at your disposal, gentlemen," she said.

"We appreciate that very much. Is the young magician you have with you, around? We would need to talk to him as well."

"Yes," Eryn replied, "he is at the table over there. Would you like me to ask him to come here now?"

"No," the magistrate shook his head. "I would prefer to talk to him separately. Regulations, you understand," he added apologetically and then looked at Plia. "This is the young lady you shared your room with, I assume?"

"Yes, her name is Plia."

The girl nodded in confirmation.

"Good. Would you please describe the happenings of last night now, Eryn?"

"May I suggest that Plia starts? She was the one who woke me before the attack."

The magistrate turned to the girl. "Alright, then. Tell us what happened."

Plia swallowed and took a deep breath before she started relating the reason for waking up and how she had heard the noises and thus woken Eryn. She continued with having been told to hide under the bed and then looked at Eryn to go on.

Both men listened to her narrative of her grabbing the herb gathering knife from her nightstand, hiding it under the pillow and stabbing the man when he was choking her. She then told them about sending Plia off to fetch the young healer and how she had sat with him when Vern had healed her attacker.

"Very impressive," the magistrate said and pursed his lips. "I would imagine that it is not easy for a woman of your build to push a man so much heavier off her."

"It wasn't," Eryn assured him. "But you know what they say: fear can lend us extra strength in dangerous situations."

"Yes, I have heard that, too. One more thing: the publican has told me that when he had entered the room he saw the young magician and *you* on the floor with closed eyes. Why?"

She thought quickly. "He instructed me to pull out the knife bit by bit so he could heal the man step by step." That part was still true. "I like to close my eyes because this helps me to better concentrate on the instructions and precise movements. And in this case my eyes wouldn't have helped me very much as the light was not very good with only one candle, and I couldn't have seen the blade inside the body anyway." That part was not so true anymore.

"So you are the young man's assistant?" the magistrate asked with raised brows.

She suppressed a chuckle and nodded honestly. "Yes, that I am. I have some medical training as well, so he finds me useful. He is a very talented young man, and it is an honour for me to work for him."

"Interesting," the magistrate mused. "From what the publican told me, I rather had the impression that you are the one to lead this group instead of assisting somebody else."

"Oh, that," she waved dismissively. "I just take over the administrative matters of this trip, so young Vern doesn't have to waste his time with such trivial things."

"What is the purpose of your trip, if I may ask?"

"We are off into the woods to gather herbs. The men with us are all professional herb gatherers."

"Herb gathering?" The magistrate frowned. "I had the impression that gathering herbs is something that is done alone or in pairs. I have never before encountered such a large party."

"That is because they are undergoing additional training as to the nature of the required herbs that are needed for new types of medication. Unfortunately, there is not really any reading material available, so they need to be shown. That is the purpose of this expedition."

"And the young man is the one to show them? Quite an accomplished young lad with both healing and botanical knowledge."

"Oh yes, he is the Order's child prodigy, so to say."

"I see." He looked at his deputy who nodded to confirm that he had written everything down. "Well, Eryn, that was all. Thank you very much for your time. If you could send over the young man now, please?"

"Of course, it is a duty and an honour to make sure justice is served," she purred and got up to walk over to Vern's table.

"That thin man in black is the local magistrate," she murmured. "He wants to talk to you about last night. I told him that you are the big healer and I your humble assistant. You lead this expedition, I only do administration. Got it?"

Vern nodded and rose wordlessly to make his way to the two men.

She watched him sit down and talk to the magistrate, adopting an air of calm superiority that was suitable for a young and yet so highly esteemed man with such great responsibilities.

After only a few minutes they rose, nodded at her once more and left again.

Vern returned to the table and looked down at her, shaking his head.

"My humble assistant with some medical training. I had real trouble keeping a straight face over there."

She grinned up at him, glad that he had obviously decided to put their disagreement behind him.

"You did fine - no sign of amusement discernible from here. I liked your slightly bored expression, as if doing things like healing injured lungs in the early morning hours was something you do every week, as if you didn't understand why people made such a fuss about a minor thing like that."

He grinned back. "I am getting better at lying. Must be your influence."

She snorted. "I certainly hope so. I wouldn't want to think that you have frequent contact with other liars, scammers and pretenders."

CHAPTER 7

Into the Woods

It was late morning when they finally reached the woods. The weather was grey and windy, and the relative protection of the trees around them was a relief. The path, however, was narrow and they had to ride behind one another, which made talking without resorting to shouting impossible. Thus the conversations between the travellers were limited to short exchanges only.

Plia clung to Eryn and looked around uncomfortably.

"So many trees," she murmured. "And they are so tall. And these roots look rather spooky. Are there any wild animals around? Anything big that could be dangerous for us? Do you hear those noises? What are they?"

Eryn laughed. "Relax, little flower. This is an ordinary forest, nothing much to be afraid of, especially when you are travelling with such a large party. And yes, there are a lot of wild animals around, though almost all of them are more afraid of you than you are of them. Most of them hide or run away as soon as they hear or smell us."

"So they will not attack us?" the girl enquired to be absolutely sure about this.

"Not very likely, no," Eryn reassured her. "And if they did, they would encounter a large number of ready knives and a few swords and end up roasting over the fire in no time."

Plia remained silent for a few minutes before she asked, "Do you think Lord Enric will find out about the attack?"

"I don't see how he could. The swordsmen were nowhere near when it happened, and I don't think they have seen us talk to the magistrate," Eryn shrugged.

"Why don't you want to tell him? What would happen if he learned about it?"

"He was worrying about something happening to me as soon as I was removed from his protection, and I don't want him to think that he was right."

"Which he basically was, wasn't he?" the girl asked slowly.

"Basically," Eryn agreed. "But not completely. He would use this incident to make me stop going on any other trips, which would not at all be right in my view."

"What if he does find out about the attack somehow and that you tried to keep it a secret?"

She sighed. "Why do you ask me all these questions? Are you thinking I should tell him as well?"

"I don't know. I just don't want him to be angry with you," Plia said.

"Neither do I," Eryn agreed. "But I think I am more likely to make him angry by telling him about it than by sparing him."

"So you are telling me that lying is better than telling the truth if the consequences are less unpleasant?"

She swallowed. Was that what she was saying? In that case she really was not suitable as a role model and should probably be spending less time with impressionable young people.

"Well, not exactly," she began hesitantly. "It's more like that protecting others by telling them a slightly changed version of the truth is sometimes kinder than worrying them with very blunt, unkind facts. It would in this case even be inconsiderate of me to do so." Yes, that did sound better.

"A slightly changed version of the truth? You mean a lie?" Plia asked pointedly then quickly lifted her arm to protect her face from a low hanging branch.

"Do you really want to discuss this, or are you just after telling me what a bad person I am?" Eryn shot back slightly irritated.

The girl shrugged. "At first I wanted to discuss it, but somehow the things you say don't feel right."

"What do they feel like, then, if you would care to say more?"

"Like you are working hard to make it sound right but are in fact just trying to justify your cowardice," Plia replied with uncharacteristic bluntness and flinched when Eryn growled something clearly not very friendly under her breath by way of a reply.

*   *   *

"How much further would you like to ride today before we make camp, Lady Eryn?" One of the swordsmen had approached her as soon as the path had become wide enough for two horses.

She handed him the reigns of her horse while she searched her pockets for the map she carried, then unfolded it. After studying the map for a minute, she pointed to a thin blue line.

"This here is the small stream next to us. We have been following it for about one hour now, so we should be about here." She pointed to a spot and then indicated another one that was marked red. "Here is the area where I want to make camp. I think we should reach it in about one or two hours, depending on how steep the path is."

The man nodded. "Alright. So it doesn't make sense to take a break for lunch right now."

Eryn shook her head. "No. Preparing the food, unpacking everything we need and then packing it again would cost us more time in the end." She thought for a moment, then asked, "Your name is Grend, isn't it?"

He looked surprised. "Yes, my Lady. Why do you ask?"

"In case I need to call for you to safe my life, I don't want to shout *Swordsman*," she smirked.

"I would come whatever you shouted," he retorted with a glint of humour in his eyes.

"That is good to know, thank you."

"At your service," he nodded to her and let himself fall back to the rear of the group.

"So two more hours at the most until we make camp for today?" Plia asked from behind her. "That is welcome news. I am starting to get bored with riding."

"You won't be bored any more as soon as we've stopped," Eryn promised. "Setting up camp and cooking will keep you busy enough."

"I don't mind that. I prefer doing something to doing nothing," the girl sighed. "Not that I regret coming along, mind you," she added hastily in case the complaint might seem ungrateful.

"Even if you did, there wouldn't be much choice for you now, I am afraid. Sending you back home is not an option."

Vern appeared beside them. "I am hungry. When are going to stop and eat something?"

"In about one hour, two at the most. And if you keep moaning until then, I will push you into the water over there." She pointed to their left where the stream could be seen through the trees.

He shrugged. "It doesn't look deep, and I can dry my clothes with magic afterwards."

"Oh dear," she sighed. "Threatening a magician really is a challenge. I can't hurt you, because you can heal it away. Leaving you behind would not sit well with your father. Gagging you wouldn't work, either if you have magic at your disposal. Knocking you out would just make it necessary for me to check on you all the time to make sure you didn't fall off your horse. I am wondering if I should have brought golden shackles for you."

"Right," he snorted, "like my father would have appreciated that very much, either: rendering me helpless in the middle of the great, big unknown."

"Great and big together are rather redundant, you know."

"So is bringing a magician to an expedition and then shackling him," he retorted.

"I did not bring you because you are a magician; I brought you because you are an artist," she pointed out. "So shackling you would be an excellent option."

"Great," he huffed, "so much for responsible leadership."

She grinned. "Out here in the woods I don't have to be a responsible leader. None of my leaders is here to scold me."

"Should the fact that no other leader is here not motivate you even more to be a shining light to us less sublime creatures?" Vern pointed out.

"No," she shook her head with conviction and winked at him. "That doesn't sound right."

*   *   *

When they had finally reached the clearing, they found it a suitable place for spending their first night out in the woods. Vern sighed with relief and got off his horse with a stiff, clumsy movement and then lifted his arms to help Plia down from Eryn's mount.

The second servant they had brought, a rather small but lean man, immediately commenced unloading the cooking supplies and building a fire in the centre of the clearing.

Plia sorted through the packages and bundles and selected the items she would need for cooking her first meal for them.

The herb gatherers and swordsmen dismounted as well and secured spots near the fire for themselves for later. The guards exchanged a few words and then split into two pairs for a quick sweep of the area surrounding the camp.

"How long will it take before we can eat?" Eryn enquired and watched Plia chopping root vegetables with a large, menacingly sharp looking knife that seemed oddly out of place in her small hand.

"About an hour," she replied without interrupting her work.

"Good." She turned to Vern. "That means we can get a bit of work done while we are waiting."

"How about resting a bit instead?" he grimaced.

She pretended to consider this for a moment, then shook her head. "No, I don't like it. Come on, city boy, collect your drawing supplies and follow me."

She let loose a loud whistle and all eyes turned towards her.

"Gentlemen, as there is another hour to kill before we can eat, I propose we use that time and have a look around. This is a very good place for our camp, as we are practically surrounded by quite a number of different species of useful herbs." She drew her herb gathering knife and turned to one side, facing the way they had come. "Follow me."

Only a few paces off the track she found one of the herbs she needed.

"Vern?" She waited for him to step next to her. "These are the first drawings I need from you: A detailed picture of the plant as a whole, then close-up details of the leaves, stem and blossoms. Don't forget the underside of the leaves, they are very characteristic in this case and help distinguishing it from others when it isn't blooming at the time of gathering."

She turned to the herb gatherers while Vern squatted down and started working on his assignment.

"This plant I am sure all of you know. It is commonly referred to as Bloodherb, as its most common use is to staunch the flow of blood from wounds." Several heads nodded in confirmation. "The usual way of harvesting it is cutting it off like this," she continued and bent down to a plant near the one Vern was currently drawing, and neatly severed the stem close to the ground with her knife.

"If you collect the herb close enough to the city and you can pass it on within a few hours, this is acceptable. Should you happen to be out here, however, with a two-day journey back ahead of you, this will not work. The plant will not be fresh enough anymore. And as per the agreement you signed with the Order, the quality of the herbs must be as agreed for us to pay you for them." She noted with amusement several glances dart towards Vern, who had negotiated the contract with them back then, but who was completely caught up in his task of drawing and thus oblivious to them. "I know this has in the past not been much of an issue, as the League of Apothecaries had less strict requirements, and I can assure you that this is not just something we thought up to make life as hard as possible for you, but to provide a high level of quality for our patients." She then squatted down next to another plant close by.

"So collecting the herbs in a way that keeps them fresh as long as possible is your best shot at delivering raw materials that are up to my standards. Watch..." she instructed and inserted the knife into the soil around the plant and cut a circle around it. "If you keep the roots attached to the plant, it will stay fresh for longer. And the great thing about this is," she smiled up at the men looking down at her, "that the roots are another useful part of the plant that is generally neglected and that I am willing to pay some extra if you bring them." She saw the sparks of interest kindle in their eyes.

"Vern?" She dangled the roots in front of him when he looked up. "A drawing of the roots as well, please."

He nodded and took the plant from her, placing it beside him for later use.

She turned back to her audience. "Then I would say you each collect a few of them, get a feeling how to cut them without damaging them and bring them to me. I will return to the camp and prepare my equipment for turning them into medicine. The less complicated potions I can prepare right here, and you are welcome to take those home for your families."

That earned her looks of surprise from the gatherers. Medicine being given away for free was definitely not something they had ever experienced with the apothecaries. She hid a smile. Little surprises like that which didn't really cost much more than the price of the glass vials would keep them on her side and ensure their cooperation in the future.

* * *

Eryn was carrying back a heavy leather bucket filled with water from their nearby stream and was stopped by a swordsman with a somewhat reproachful look on his face.

"Lady Eryn, I would prefer if you asked somebody else to do things like that," he said with mild reproof, then took the bucket from her hand unasked to carry it the rest of the way. She indulged him and followed.

"Grend? There is something I'd like to show you," she said sweetly when he had placed the bucket next to her things.

He frowned. "Yes?"

"Hold still for a moment, if you will."

She sent a surge of magic into her arm and leg muscles, stepped behind him and bent down to wrap her arms around his thighs to lift him up into the air without any apparent effort. He cursed and whirled around when he again felt steady ground under his feet.

Around them the others, both guards and herb gatherers, chuckled.

"I am a magician, Grend. I know you are not used to female ones, but thanks to my magic I am stronger and faster than any of you, even than all of you together if need be." She pinched his cheek and winked at him. "I can carry a simple bucket of water, trust me. But I do appreciate the chivalry, even though it is a little wasted on me in this case."

"Nice demonstration," Garn said behind her and grinned broadly. "We could have saved a lot of pack animals if you had carried our things instead."

She snorted. "Charming." Looking around, she then stated, "It looks like most of you are back. Good. Judging from the smell we should soon be getting something to eat."

"Yes, all but two have returned. Ah, and there they are," Garn said, pointing at two figures emerging from between the trees with a bundle of herbs in each hand. They let the plants fall onto the already impressive heap next to her equipment.

"My, my, that is a lot. I suppose I will be quite busy in the evening with it all. It is a pity they won't keep until we are back because they would have been useful material for training the apothecaries. But these also grow closer to home, so I can order them from you on shorter notice."

"No problem," Garn nodded. "They can be found only one riding hour from the city in the woods, so you can have them within one day." He looked at her thoughtfully. "You know that you didn't need to have paid us extra for bringing the roots as well, don't you? You could just have refused to accept the plants without them. Your young friend has pointed that out in the contract."

"Yes, I am aware of that. But bringing the roots is something we will profit from, and I believe in sharing profit with those who make it possible."

He nodded slowly and smiled at her. "I see. I suppose many would think this a stupid way of reducing your own profit, but it will ensure you our loyalty. Well done." He bowed.

"The food is ready!" Plia's voice announced. "Bring your bowls!"

A collective sigh of relief was audible throughout the camp, and the men eagerly hurried over to their bundles to retrieve their eating utensils.

* * *

Eryn plucked the small white blossoms from the stems and let them drop into a bowl at her side. Plia walked over and sat down next to her.

"Finished with cleaning everything up? Ready to sit back and relax?" she asked the girl and continued her work.

"Yes," Plia nodded and watched her for a while. "What exactly are you doing? I mean, I can see what you are doing, but why?"

"Different parts of the plant have different effects, or at least a different intensity. The blossoms, for example, can be simmered in water and used like tea. The drink is not so strong and can be used to prevent illnesses or stop them when you notice first signs of something. It also depends on whether dried or fresh blossoms were used of how strong it really is." She picked up one of the leaves. "The leaves of this plant have more oils in them than the blossoms, and that's what I need for the medicine. So I make two different kinds of medicine. There are powders, where the herbs are first dried and then ground. The advantage is that they stay active for a long time, and you can thus have a larger supply. The disadvantage is that the effect is not as strong and you need to administer it more often."

"And the second kind of medicine?" the girl enquired curiously.

"Potions. They are fresh and work best of all, but of course they dry out and become useless if you don't use them up in time. But there is one thing I learned from Ambassador Ram'an that will be of immense advantage. He showed me how to imbue medicines with magic to increase their effect. I have only ever practised it with kitchen herbs, but now that I have fresh herbs at my disposal for the first time in quite some while, I can try it on actual medicine."

"You practised with kitchen herbs? So you made magical kitchen herbs? What for?"

"I needed to experiment with enhancing their characteristics. If I can do it with cooking herbs, then I can also do it with medical ones. And the advantage is that I can test the success on myself and without any danger, because the way to see if it works is to see if there's an increase in the strength of taste."

"What plant is this?"

Eryn held up the herb. "It is called Bloodherb, because it helps to staunch loss of blood when you are wounded or, let's say, your nose bleeds. For this you would ideally use fresh leaves if you have them handy. But there are other uses as well. If you feel a burning sensation in your throat, you can use it. Basically for every tissue that needs help healing and can get into direct contact with it when you swallow it, such as your throat, stomach and intestines. Another use would be if you feel tired or unhappy. The oils can make you more alert, awake and active. Women often use it when they have menstrual disorders, and you can also use it to bring down fevers."

Plia stared at the plant and shook her head in disbelief. "And all this can be accomplished by *one* plant? How many other healing herbs are there?"

Eryn laughed. "I have no idea. I am sure my knowledge is sketchy at best. Thousands, probably. My father had many books about the medical use of herbs, but they are from the Western Territories and most of them don't grow anywhere near here so I have never encountered them. Others I have often used and sometimes even discovered new things that were not mentioned in the books."

"This is amazing," the girl whispered and then looked up. "Can I help you? I could pluck off the blossoms for you. Can we use some of them for a hot drink? I would love to see what it tastes like!"

"Sure, why not? But don't you want to rest a little? It has been a long day for all of us."

"It has been for you, too, and yet here you are, sitting and working," Plia shrugged. "I am not tired. And maybe you can tell me a bit more about the plant and what it can do. And how to turn it into medicine."

"Yes," Eryn said slowly and considered the girl thoughtfully. "I would like that very much."

* * *

Vern was very obviously not in a great mood when he stomped back from the stream where he had just washed himself the next morning.

"You don't look particularly happy. What's the matter?" Eryn enquired and sipped her hot drink from a metal cup.

"I hate washing myself with cold water," he murmured. "And sleeping on the hard ground last night was not exactly pleasant, either. Then there is finding somewhere to use as a toilet in the woods, always looking around if anybody is near to see you. I miss my privacy," he sighed.

Eryn grinned. "I tried to warn you, dear lad. The wilderness is no walk along Kingsway. But this will stand you in good stead, trust me. You will appreciate the comfort you have at home a lot more for a while, I promise you that."

"That's no great comfort right now," he said sullenly.

She sighed in exasperation. "Come now, pull yourself together! At least you can warm yourself quickly after your ice-cold bath. Look at the herb gatherers, they can't do that, and you don't hear them complaining."

"They are used to that, they do it all the time," he continued to grumble.

"Then look at Plia. She is not used to anything like it either, and not only does she not complain, but she's the first one up to prepare breakfast. And you don't catch her moaning about. See? She is even smiling at people as she goes about her chores."

That seemed to work. Vern watched Plia for a few moments and then sighed. "You are right. I suppose I'd better man up quickly."

She grinned. Of course, being forced to admit that a girl three years his junior was better able to deal with the discomforts than a trained magician was hardly good for his pride.

"How about your drawings of the Bloodherb? Are they finished?"

He nodded and pulled out one of the paper transport boxes from a sack behind him. She took a good look at the pictures he handed her, held them close to her eyes.

"Very good - amazing work as always. Blossoms, roots, leaves, stem... everything there. Very good. We can use information from the texts in my father's books with the pictures later and add instructions on how to harvest and transport them properly. Maybe we can even write something about what ailments to use them for and how to prepare medicines. That way we could use the same book for both herb gatherers *and* apothecaries."

"I don't think that is a good idea," Vern disagreed. "That would mean for each of them having a book with surplus information. I suppose the herb gatherers would probably like to take the book with them when they go into the woods, so keeping it thin by leaving out facts they don't need would make sense for them."

She thought for a moment and then nodded. "I see what you mean. Two different books, then. You know, maybe that's better, anyway. It could be a matter of pride for each group to have its own version." She rose and stretched. "If you would excuse me now, I need to go wash myself."

Vern frowned. "But surely not with all the men around?"

She rolled her eyes. "They would hardly be foolish enough to try anything on with me, would they? But I will walk a bit further upstream to wash, if it makes you happy."

"Yes, it does. Thank you."

* * *

She had decided not to break camp but stay in the area for another day, as there were a number of different plants around she wanted to teach the herb gatherers about and demonstrate their proper handling.

Vern was occupied drawing each and every type of plant as a whole and its single parts in detail. By the end of the day he had an impressive collection of about fifteen sheets.

Eryn sat down in the evening to take care of the herbs gathered during the day and made sure to have Plia around when she repeated to Vern the important information about the plants she had earlier relayed to the herb gatherers, when he had been busy drawing. The girl listened quietly but intently while her quick fingers disassembled the parts of the plants as per Eryn's instructions.

Plia kept experimenting with brewing different hot infusions with the blossoms and leaves, amusing herself by mixing different ones together to test new combinations of flavours and asking Eryn about the effect these combinations would have on the human body.

"Plia is really good with this herbal stuff," Vern remarked when she had returned to the fire to boil another pot of water for them.

"Yes, isn't she? I was wondering if she would be interested in ending her apprenticeship and working with herbs instead," Eryn mused.

"You mean as a herb gatherer?" the boy frowned. "I don't think this is such a good idea, her roaming the woods alone and defenceless."

"No, of course not." She shook her head. "I was thinking more along the lines of the profession of apothecary."

Vern remained silent for a while before he asked, "That would mean joining the League, wouldn't it? I am not sure I would be comfortable with that, either. The surviving members may not have participated in the attack on us, but they might have known about it. And they would have benefited from it as well had the assault been successful. I wouldn't want her to take orders from them. Or worse, maybe even become like them one day."

Eryn nodded, understanding his feelings well enough and sharing his sentiments. "Any other ideas, my lad?"

"Hm. Couldn't you hire her to work for the healers and thus the Order as an apothecary? They have signed their exclusivity to us, but not the other way round. We never agreed not to make our own medicines. I am rather proud of that bit, to be honest," he smiled.

"I don't know, that sounds a bit sneaky to me. I want to show the apothecaries that we can all work together and benefit from this arrangement without springing tricks on each other. Hiring and training our own apothecary doesn't really support that idea or convey my goodwill sufficiently. Quite the opposite."

"Then don't call her an apothecary," Vern shrugged. "Call her a medical herbalist or some such, and make her responsible for checking the quality of the stuff the League wants to sell to us. You could also make her take care of the herbs the herb gatherers deliver to us and then forward them to the apothecaries after making sure the quality is within what we said we would accept."

Eryn stared at him. "Boy, you are a genius," she whispered, awestruck.

He grinned broadly, pleased with himself and at the praise. "I know. And don't you forget it."

*　*　*

Tyront took the two envelopes from the servant and handed one to Enric.

"So these are the first reports about the expedition. I am curious," he said. "Though I suppose the journey to the woods will not have been too eventful. The group is too large to be attacked impulsively."

He opened the envelope and started reading. As he had expected, nothing of great interest seemed to have transpired. Good weather for travelling, uneventful stays at the inns and so on. He was about to say that when he looked up and frowned at the expression on Enric's face. It was tense, and his lips were pressed into a thin line.

"What's the matter? It seems that my report was less informative than yours."

The younger man looked up and wordlessly handed the letter to his superior. He held on to a second sheet that had been attached, and quickly let his eyes wander along the lines of writing.

Tyront whistled through his teeth, looked up at the man opposite him and nodded towards the other paper. "What else to do you have written there?"

"A report from the local magistrate," he growled. "It seems she posed as Vern's assistant and omitted the fact that she is a magician. She is travelling with blonde hair." He got to his feet, furious. "I bet she wouldn't have been attacked if she had not tried to blend in and hide who she is!"

"Relax, Enric," the older man said. "Everything has worked out fine. She even managed to defend herself without using magic and risking violating the law."

Enric was quick to reply, his voice increasing in volume. "Relax?" he said, "The letter says that the publican had seen strangulation marks on her throat! He got really close to her, had his hands around her *throat*! How can I relax with this picture in my head?" Enric roared and balled his hands into fists. "She didn't even have her sword handy and had to defend herself with a herb gathering knife! What if there are two of them next time, and one of them secures her hands? Why didn't she shield, damn it!"

Tyront waited and watched the younger man fight his agitation with several deep breaths until he was calm enough to sit again.

"Finished?"

Enric nodded.

"So I don't need to explicitly order you not to jump on the next horse to follow them?" Tyront said and gave a tight-lipped smile that did not hide the fact that the question was not meant as a joke.

Enric closed his eyes for a moment. "No. Though I admit that this was my first impulse."

"I guessed as much. But she has handled the situation alone and, considering the outcome, well enough to prove that she is not helpless. She would not welcome any interference from your side." His gaze wandered back to his own report.

"How come that my informant is less well informed than yours seems to be?"

Enric smiled without humour. "Because I have more than one. And the one to send me this letter has been following them with a distance of several hours. So whatever she manages to hide from the men that are with her, he will probably hear about later if he buys drinks for the right people."

Tyront nodded appreciatively. "I see you have been extra careful. You don't normally approve of the use of agents, and now you have even resorted to using one more than myself."

"Two more. I have three men to watch her."

CHAPTER 8

The Storm

"There is a storm brewing," Garn said as he looked up at the sky.

Eryn turned to him and followed his gaze. "It does smell a bit like rain, but a storm?" she said doubtfully and continued packing up her equipment.

"Didn't you see the sunrise?" the herb gatherer frowned. "A storm, definitely. Trust me on that."

"Alright," she shrugged, "if you say so. Then we'd better look for a well-protected spot for our next camp tonight." She had never been good a predicting the weather from whatever mysterious signs stars, sun, moon, clouds, insects and birds gave.

She nodded to Garn, and then walked over to where the four swordsmen stood together. They stopped talking and nodded to her when she stopped next to them.

"A storm is on the way," she informed them wisely.

"We know," Barul replied. "We saw the sunrise. And there is the dew, of course."

Of course, she thought; everyone here seemed to be some kind of weather prophet, except for herself.

"Good," she nodded, eager to hide her ignorance. "Then we really should find a sheltered spot for tonight. I don't want to stay here for another night, or we will not be able to get up high enough for the plants I need."

She strolled over to where Vern was lashing his paper transport boxes to his horse and leaned forward to whisper to him, "Do you have any idea what a sunrise looks like when a storm is coming? And about the dew? There isn't even any!"

Vern hesitated for a moment, then frowned. "I think if the sunrise is red it means that it's going to rain. I don't know about the dew."

"Alright, let's think. People keep telling me there is a storm, and there is no dew. So that's very likely the connection. Dew means no rain, no dew means rain."

"Why is this important right now? If you have people around you who know about this, just ask them," Vern pointed out.

"But I don't want to look like an idiot. It seems everybody else knows about this, and I am supposed to be leading this expedition. How will they trust me with their safety when they find out I know less than them?"

The boy sighed. "I don't believe we are having this conversation and I am the voice of reason here! Admitting that you don't know everything doesn't make you weak, but shows that you are strong enough to own up to it and willing to learn something new."

She grimaced. "No, I don't think so. Are you sure you understood that correctly?"

"If you don't want to listen to me then stop pestering me! Go away so I can finish my packing," he brushed her off. "And from what I can see, your stuff is not yet fully packed, either. Get on with it, or do you want to cause a delay, oh great omniscient leader?"

He winced when she smacked him on the back of his head before returning to pack the last of her things.

*   *   *

The clouds high up in the sky had become denser and were turning darker with every hour. Eryn led her horse next to Vern's and said, "Alright, are you interested in my new weather expertise? I have learned quite a few nice things."

"Out with it, then," he grinned. "Did you have to reveal your ignorance, or did you obtain that knowledge with stealth and cunning?"

"The latter, of course. I have a reputation to protect here. Do you want to hear it now or not?"

"Sure."

"Alright, listen and learn: When the birds fly low, there will be rain. And when the moon is hazy. Also when the night is windy. When the wind keeps changing its direction several times within a short time, there will be a storm. As for the dew, my logical deduction was right. If there is no dew, it means there will be rain. The sunset thing is interesting, though. It seems that a red sun*set* means good weather for the next day, but a blood red sun*rise* means rain," she concluded proudly.

"Well done," he complemented her. "So the woman who wants to show that we can all work together without tricks and dishonesty just tricked a bunch of herb gatherers into teaching her about the weather. Nice move."

"You should have stopped after the *Well done*," she sighed.

He pretended to think for a moment, then shook his head. "No. Where is the fun in that?"

*   *   *

It was mid-afternoon when the first heavy drops of rain started to fall. Eryn looked around and cursed. She had hoped for another hour in the dry to move on. But continuing in the rain was not a good idea. The area, however, was not exactly suitable for waiting for a storm to pass. There were no convenient rock walls nor caves anywhere to protect them from the elements.

She looked over to Vern, who wasn't looking very enthusiastic about the prospect of heavy rain, either.

"Vern? How long can you hold a shield?"

"What do you mean? That is not a very precise question. What kind of shield, how big, how strong?"

She thought for a moment. "A large one, big enough to protect an entire camp. Not particularly strong, only strong enough to keep off the rain."

He shrugged. "I don't know, I never had to hold a shield for more than an hour. But I suppose it's worth a try. I guess we can switch every one or two hours if necessary."

"Yes, that's what I was thinking." She stopped her horse and raised an arm. "Halt!" she called out and watched the horses in front and behind her come to a stop as well. "We will make camp here for the night."

She saw the concerned frowns on many of the faces and how their eyes swept the area, somewhere far too open and unsuitable for making camp even in fair weather. The rain had started becoming heavier in these last few minutes. Sighing, she dismounted and created a shield, letting it grow until it was wide enough to protect every single member of the group and pulling it to the ground so that they were within a dry dome. They looked up in surprise, marvelling at seeing the water fall towards them and then be stopped in mid-air as if hitting a pane of glass.

"I am aware that this is not the most suitable spot," she explained loudly, "but young Vern here and I will try to make sure that you have a safe and dry night nevertheless."

The herb gatherers had started talking agitatedly, clearly impressed by that trick - and a lot more relaxed than only a few moments ago.

"How long can you hold that shield?" Barul asked and led his horse next to her.

"I am not sure, but it is a rather weak one, so I think several hours should not be a problem. And we have another magician here, so we should manage to stay dry until morning at least."

Garn approached her with a broad smile. "I have to admit, this is quite unlike any other gathering trip I have made so far. Food being cooked, rain protection... I hope I don't get used to it, or I will never again venture out of the city without a magician."

"Don't tell her that," another herb gatherer cut in, "or she might let the shield collapse to avoid that."

"Can I make a fire, or will we choke on the smoke if I do?" Plia asked and critically eyed the magical barrier.

"No, go on, no imminent danger of that. It's not an airtight barrier, or we would all suffocate after a while," Eryn said.

She watched the men around her dismount and remove the saddles from the horses. Some of them offered Plia a hand in cutting vegetables and dried meat, and it soon started to smell very promising.

The four swordsmen had sat down close to her. She kept forgetting the names of the other two. Barul, Orrin's friend, was easy to remember, and also Grend.

Vern came over and let himself fall on the ground next to her. He held two leather pouches in his hand and shook both of them. One jingled with coins, the other rattled with what she assumed were dice.

"How about a little game to pass the time?" he asked and grinned.

Eryn shook her head. "Not me, dear lad. If I keep losing, I might become angry enough to forget that I have a barrier to maintain. And I don't really own any money, so I would just lose my companion's."

"How about you?" he asked and turned to the four swordsmen.

They looked at each other and shrugged. It didn't look like there was much else to do, and they had quite a few hours to kill until it was time to sleep.

"Why not?" Barul said and they used a wooden chopping board Plia relinquished to them to throw the dice on.

*   *   *

Eryn watched them play for about four hours, and even though Vern lost a coin here and there occasionally, his heap seemed to be the only one that kept growing. She watched him surreptitiously slip a coin or two into his pouch every now and then to avoid making his run of winning too obvious.

When the first of the swordsmen, Sebarn, had run out of money, he lifted both hands before him.

"I am out," he declared. "A man should not risk more than he can afford to lose, and as I don't want to return home naked and without my horse, I'd better stop right here."

Eryn studied him for a few moments, then moved closer to Vern and whispered something into his ear. The boy looked at her doubtfully.

"Alright, I'll ask." He turned to Sebarn. "There is another stake I would accept instead of money: information."

The man frowned suspiciously. "What information?"

"Whose agent you are."

"What?" he exclaimed, taken aback.

"Oh, don't be like that," Eryn cut in with a sneer. "I have no doubt that all of you send your little reports back to the city, I just want to know who reads them. I know which one of you reports to Orrin, now I would like to know who is paid by the King, Lord Tyront and Enric."

She watched their uneasy expressions. "No need to be afraid, gentlemen. I will not discriminate against you as a result of your client's identity. In fact, I will continue to hide all my secrets from you just like before," she grinned and raised her eyebrows. "Sebarn? Are you up to the challenge?"

She could see how he was in two minds about this, it showed on his face clearly enough. He was not supposed to reveal his client's name, but then he could hardly refuse a woman's challenge in front of all these men, could he? And it was not as if she wasn't aware that he was sending information back, anyway.

She smiled triumphantly when he sighed and nodded.

"Come on, Vern," she urged him and rubbed her hands. "Make him talk."

The boy shook the dice in one hand and rolled them. Sebarn swallowed.

"You need at least thirty to win that round," Grend pointed out and leaned back with a half-smile. He didn't seem to see much hope for his colleague.

The swordsman slowly picked up the dice and held them for a few moments before throwing them. Six pairs of eyes counted the eyes of the dice eagerly, then one groan and five laughs were audible from the small group.

Eryn leaned forward. "Out with it, man. Who pays you?"

He sighed in defeat. "Lord Tyront."

She smiled. "Thank you so much." Her gaze wandered to Grend and the last one, Torvig. "Then we have you two, one for Enric, one for the King."

Grend cleared his throat. "I think this is a good point to stop the gambling."

Torvig nodded in eager agreement.

"Pity," Eryn shrugged. "But at least I have narrowed it down."

They looked towards Barul when he released a loud sigh. "So it seems everybody here but me gets paid for sending information back home. I really need to talk to Orrin about that. Maybe I can convince him that his having the only unpaid informant makes him look greedy and is bad for his reputation."

Vern leaned back and laughed loudly. "Good luck with that!"

* * *

The storm reached its peak in the early morning hours, howling and attacking the barrier with gusts of wind, airborne tree branches and so much water that it seemed at times as if they were at the bottom of the sea.

Eryn felt the first signs of weariness after holding the large barrier for more than ten hours and shook Vern awake.

"Vern? Can you take over for a while? I can hardly keep my eyes open anymore."

The boy yawned and nodded before getting up and stretching languidly.

"Sure. Is anything left from Plia's latest brew?" he asked hopefully.

"No, sorry. I had the last cup. But I have enough herbs left for you to make another pot. Mix the Bloodherb with a few leaves of Bear's Ear. No, the one next to it. Does that look like a bear's ear to you?"

He looked at her in an amused sluggishness. "How would I know what a bear's ear looks like? We don't have many bears in the city. Go to sleep - you are getting irritable."

She looked around. "I don't know if I can with that roaring inferno around me."

He grinned in his wicked way. "Oh, no problem there. I would be more than happy to help you fall asleep. Really."

Yawning, she shook her head at him. "You know, if it wasn't for that grin, I would probably accept your offer. But I am worried because I think I wouldn't wake up again until we are back in the city."

"Have it your way," he shrugged, picked up the herbs and walked to the small metal pot next to the remainders of the fire to collect some rain water.

When he was back next to her after he had put the pot on the blaze in the fireplace and added a few logs of wood, he turned to her. "I have raised a shield, you can collapse yours now."

She concentrated and reduced her barrier in size instead of just removing it, making sure that Vern really had a strong enough protection in place.

"Where is your trust, I ask you?" he said with a shake of his head and a lopsided grin.

"Asleep already," she mumbled and turned away from the fire. She pulled her fur blanket up to her shoulders and was snoring quietly after a few minutes - despite the racket from the weather.

* * *

A loud crack made her sit bolt upright and her eyes darted around in confusion, taking in her hazy surroundings that swam into focus after a few seconds. It was dawning, and most of those around her didn't look as if they had been woken by the bang, but been up for a while already.

She felt a warm hand on her shoulder and looked up into Barul's face.

"Don't be alarmed, everything is alright. It was just a falling tree, and that was rather loud." He smiled and nodded at Vern. "But the boy's shield has held it off easily."

Eryn let her gaze wander along the shield's edges and soon found a long part of a trunk, about as high as a two-storey house and about as thick in diameter as the shoulder width of an athletic man. Her eyes widened slightly, and she whistled through her teeth. That tree hitting the camp would certainly have caused more than one death.

Barul nodded. "Yes, makes you think, eh? I bet that has earned young Vern a few bonus points with the herb gatherers."

He was right. She saw several of the men approach Vern and slap him on his back and shoulders, ruffle his hair and offer other signs of gratefulness and manly shows of affection.

She exhaled and smiled. "Yes, seems like it - it only required saving them from being crushed by a huge tree trunk. And there are people who say making friends is hard."

The swordsman nodded slowly. "I know he doesn't have many friends, neither does Orrin for that matter. They are both careful when it comes to letting people get close to them. It took Orrin and me years to become friends. But when they do, they hold on to you." He looked down at her. "It seems you have managed to capture them both. Orrin has told me to keep an eye on both his son *and* you."

"He did?" A slow smile spread across her face.

"Yes. He has a soft spot for you." He grinned. "And he met his girlfriend thanks to you, so I suppose you must be a good influence."

"Funny. He keeps telling me I am a bad one on his son," she chuckled.

They both watched Vern standing amidst the herb gatherers, awkwardly accepting their thanks and words of praise.

"Not from where I stand," Barul said thoughtfully.

* * *

It was late morning when the storm relented and rain finally ceased. Cautiously, Vern let the shield shrink. The tree trunk was looming over the campsite in an inconvenient angle, and he had to hold the barrier until everybody had packed their things and moved out of the way. When he finally let it dissolve from a safe distance, the huge trunk rolled to where the campfire had been, then came to a halt.

When they set off again, it didn't take long until the forest became more open and the path took on a noticeable slope. They had to stop occasionally to remove debris from the storm, and the slippery soil hampered their progress further, as they had to slow down and tread more carefully than would have been necessary on dry ground.

Eryn sighed when they stopped in front of yet another fallen tree blocking their way. She nodded to Vern, and both of them dismounted.

Having two magicians perform the heavy lifting was quite efficient, though the first time they had done so had not sat well with the men, as all they had seen were a woman and a boy doing what should have been their task. But after watching them lift a piece of wood the size of a large dinner table without any apparent effort, both herb gatherers and swordsmen had agreed that they would be more of a hindrance than a help if they tried to interfere in any way.

They lifted the thin, long trunk over their heads and threw it down the incline to their left. They watched as it crashed noisily through the undergrowth, then returned to their horses. Eryn was about to swing herself back into the saddle, when she frowned and stilled. Plia looked down at her, worried.

"What is it?"

"Shh." Eryn held up a hand to silence the people around her. There was a sound, a high-pitched one. It sounded a bit like a whining.

"Do you hear that?" she whispered to Plia.

The girl listened for a few moments, then shook her head. "No. Do I hear what?"

She looked at Vern. "You don't hear anything, either?"

The boy also listened intently and was about to reply that he hadn't heard anything, when his eyes widened. "Yes, there is something! It's coming from over there, behind that rock."

Eryn unfastened the sword from her saddle and unsheathed it.

"Stay here," she told the others and carefully moved towards the sound.

When she heard steps behind her, she whirled angrily and looked at Vern and Barul. "I told you to stay down there, that was an order!"

"No," Vern said simply. "You surely remember what happened last time I left you alone. I have decided to ignore that order."

"Vern!" she hissed, but he just raised a brow and shot her a cool look.

"Shut up and go on. And raise a shield this time."

Closing her eyes for a moment, she breathed out and then looked straight at Barul. "You don't have the excuse of youthful idiocy like him, so why don't *you* do what I tell you?"

"Orrin told me to keep an eye on you. So I would hardly stay behind while the two of you go tramping off into the woods unsupported, would I?"

Cursing their stubbornness, she turned back and moved slowly towards the sound. It became louder with every few steps and resembled more and more the wailing of a small animal. And where small animals were, big ones might be close as well. She gripped the sword tightly and carefully climbed over another fallen tree trunk. It had to be really close now.

"Shield!" Vern growled behind her, and she raised one around her and the two men behind her to shut him up.

"What is it? Can you see anything?"

She shook her head and carefully slipped down the trunk on the other side. Drawing in a sharp breath, she took a step back.

"What?" This time it was Barul's voice asking, and only moments later he landed right next to her, hand at the hilt of his own sword.

They found themselves looking down at the lower half of a dead mountain cat, its head and torso buried under the tree they had just climbed over. Next to it on the ground sat a dark brown kitten, the source of the wailing sounds.

Vern had in the meantime joined them and stared down at the sad sight.

"Oh, no," he sighed. "It must have been killed in the storm."

Eryn stared down at the kitten and swallowed hard. It could hardly be older than a few weeks. And with its mother dead, it was doomed. Barul sighed and unsheathed his sword.

"What are you doing?" Vern cried in outrage and stepped in front of the cub protectively.

"Step aside, boy," Barul said calmly. "It is the kindest thing we can do. It would not survive long out here alone. A quick death is better than being killed by a larger predator that likes to play around with its prey before eating it."

"Eryn!" Vern called out and grabbed her wrist to pull her beside him to stand against the swordsman. "Tell him to stop this! We can't let him kill it!"

She blinked and rocked her head trying to tune out the miserable sounds the tiny creature behind her made while sitting next to its dead mother.

Both men had their eyes on her, waiting for her decision. Why? Why her? What made her fit to decide between life or death for this small creature?

"It will die here, Vern," she whispered miserably. "I am so very sorry, but we can't save it."

"Why not?" he asked defiantly and made her look up into piercing eyes that demanded a justification, a good one.

"What do you want to do with it? Take it home with you? This is a wild animal!"

"Me? Don't be ridiculous! Father would kill me if I brought home another stray." He looked at her pointedly.

"What?" she shouted when she caught his meaning. "I can't take a mountain cat home with me! Have you seen how big the mother is?"

"Was."

"What?" she asked in confusion.

"Not is. *Was*. She's dead now," he corrected her and folded his arms. "Dead and leaving behind a helpless infant that is going to be killed either way if you don't do something. And soon."

"You can't be serious! Are you even listening to yourself? I can't bring home a wild animal!"

"Why not?"

"Because Enric would kill me, just like Orrin would kill you!"

Vern slowly raised a brow at her. "That is complete and utter nonsense, and you know it! That man is so crazy about you, he would do anything to make you happy."

"*You* are the crazy one here," she hissed.

Vern nodded slowly, then turned and grabbed the cub, lifting it up to her eyes. It was small enough to fit into the palm of one of his hands.

"Alright," the boy said and stared at her. "Kill it then, if you can."

"No," he said sharply when she made to step away to let Barul do it. "*You* do it. Your decision, your dirty deed!"

She breathed heavily, alternatingly looking into Vern's hard, unforgiving eyes and the round, yellow, terrified eyes of the small, furry creature on his palm.

"You are a bastard, Vern," she whispered, in vain trying to swallow the lump in her throat that threatened to choke her.

He smiled coldly. "No. I'm compassionate. I'm told that's a good thing in a healer."

The herb gatherers and the other three swordsmen had gathered around their horses when the two magicians and Barul returned. They frowned when all three wordlessly returned to their horses and mounted up.

"What was it?" Plia enquired.

"A mountain cat was killed and left a cub behind," Barul said with a resigned sigh.

"What about it, then?" Garn frowned and looked from one face to the others.

Then they heard a muffled wail, and all eyes darted towards Eryn.

Vern grinned broadly when she lifted the small feline bundle out of the inside pocket of her cloak.

"I am proud and happy to announce that it has been adopted," he explained and gleefully watched the shocked and unbelieving expressions around him. "Look at the dark brown fur, same colour as its new mum's hair. Isn't that so cute?"

"Oh, just shut it, will you?" Eryn growled and urged her horse into motion.

* * *

She was aware of the whispering behind her, had been for the last two hours. The kitten had been protesting, clearly not very comfortable in the folds of the dark fabric of Eryn's cloak. Plia had handed her a few slices of dried meat to feed to it, but it seemed that hunger was currently not its main problem.

Not hard to understand why, Eryn thought gloomily. She had not been particularly hungry for quite some time after her own father had died. Did cats even experience sadness? Probably. It certainly had to feel that something important was missing in its life.

She had finally given up and sent the cub off to sleep with a tiny and very carefully dosed surge of magic. Next time they made camp, she would have to work out how and what to feed it.

What would Enric say? The thought made her stomach churn. He would already have learned about it when she would return. Either Torvig or Grend, whoever was being paid by Enric, would send him a message soon enough.

Well, at least he would have got over his initial shock by the time she arrived at the city, she thought, but it somehow failed to cheer her up. How would he react to her bringing home a wild animal? What would she do in his place?

She reached into the pocket and carefully lifted out the sleeping ball of fur to look at it. It was so tiny, but wouldn't remain so for long. It was breathing evenly, all four paws and the comparatively large head drooping limply. Vern had been right, the fur had about the same colouring as her hair. Well, not now while she was blonde, obviously, but when she changed it back to its original colour.

She brushed off small bits of earth that had got stuck between the tiny toes and then hesitantly let a finger glide over the silky fur. It was soft, and the body underneath was warm to the touch. Sighing, she put the small creature back into the pocket when she heard another horse come closer. So somebody had finally worked up the courage to talk to her.

She saw Garn's horse draw even with her own and waited for him to speak.

He cleared his throat and then started, "We were wondering if you were fully aware of the consequences of a wild animal in the city..."

"Garn?" she interrupted him mildly with a tense smile.

"Yes?"

"Just belt up, will you?"

CHAPTER 9

The Cat

Eryn and Vern sat on the ground, surrounded by most of the herb gatherers who had just finished preparing their sleeping place for tonight, and two of the swordsmen. They all looked down at the sleeping fur bundle on Eryn's lap.

"There is no other way, we need to try and feed it some of our food as long as there is no milk available," Vern explained. "Have you checked what sex it is?"

She shook her head and lifted the cat carefully to check the spot between its hind legs. Frowning, she looked at Vern.

"Strange, I can't see anything."

"If nothing is obvious, that usually means it's a girl," Grend smirked.

Eryn looked at him seriously. "Not where I am from it doesn't." She watched the herb gatherers' grin at the swordsman's discomfort with her repartee.

"Well, there is another way to find out. We are healers, after all," she sighed, closed her eyes and let her magical senses infiltrate the small body.

"Ovaries," she murmured and opened her eyes again. "A female cat. That's good, isn't it? They are surely more compliant than males, right?"

Vern stared at her for a few moments, then started laughing loudly. The swordsmen were the first to join him, and several of the herb gatherers snickered as well. Even Plia smiled.

"What?" Eryn exclaimed. "Did I say something funny?"

Vern grinned and shook his head. "That theory about compliant females, does it result from your own experience or rather your perception of yourself? I would be very interested in Lord Enric's opinion on that. And Lord Tyront's, as he was for some reason seen lying unconsciously on the Palace square not too long ago."

She flashed him an annoyed look. "Idiot! And I'd thank you very much for not comparing me with a wild cat."

"Why not? I think it's oddly apt..." the boy retorted and ducked when she tried to smack his head.

"You do that a lot, have you noticed?" he complained.

"You give me cause to do it a lot, have you noticed *that*?"

He pretended to be thinking for a moment, then shook his head in conviction. "No. And thus we have disproved the theory of the compliant female. How long is she going to sleep? It must have been a while since she last ate anything. They need to be fed regularly while they are so small, don't they?"

Eryn nodded. "Yes, I think so. At least that's what I know from human cubs, um, babies." She looked up at Plia. "What will you cook today? Anything meaty?"

She nodded. "Yes, stew again. That should be fine if we chop up the meat into very small pieces. I need to get started anyway, or a hungry mountain cat won't be my greatest problem," she smiled with a quick sweep of the men around her.

"Cute as a new button," one of the herb gatherers said and looked thoughtfully on as Plia left. "And an able cook. Old enough for my son, I would say."

Vern sent him an annoyed look. "She is thirteen years old, that's too young for anyone's son! And she is not for sale!"

Eryn saw several of the men smiling at Vern. A few of them exchanged knowing looks.

"Of course not," the man said hastily. "That's not how I meant it."

So it seemed that Vern's standing really had improved after last night. Only a night ago, none of the men would have cared about placating him, Eryn mused, and turned her attention back to the cat.

"I wonder how to transport it. I mean, I can't have it in induced sleep all the time we are in the woods, can I?"

"How about a little cage made from twigs? We have enough string to bind some twigs together for that," Vern suggested.

"A cage?" She thought for a while, then nodded hesitantly. "I suppose we could try that. Can you hold her for a while? I can build one while Plia is preparing the food."

She didn't wait for a reply, but carefully laid the cat on Vern's lap. It wasn't as if he had much of a choice. It wouldn't do for him to refuse holding the cat for a few minutes after he had effectively blackmailed her into adopting it.

Unsheathing her herb gathering knife, she started collecting thin, flexible twigs that looked as if they could stand up to the attack of tiny claws and teeth for a while. When she had collected a bundle, she took a roll of string from one of her herb supply bags and returned to the boy to sit down next to him again.

"I have never made a cage, so this is going to be interesting," she murmured.

"Allow me," a resigned voice to her side said, and she looked up at Torvig. What? The swordsman wanted to make the cage for her?

He sighed and sat down next to her. "My father was a farmer. We had to build fences every spring to keep the fruit trees from being damaged by deer. They like to chew off the young, juicy bark. So I'd say I am rather handy with twigs and string."

Wordlessly, she placed the pieces she had collected in his large hands and watched in fascination as his fingers skilfully assembled a grid and bound it together. It took him no more than half an hour until he presented to her a small, round cage, tapered at the top.

Carefully taking it from him, she shook her head. "This is amazing! Can I come back to you for another one when the cat is fully grown?" she grinned.

"Sure," he chuckled. "But we would probably have to use tree trunks instead of twigs for that one." His tone became serious. "How did you plan to raise it in the city, if I may ask?"

Eryn grimaced. "I haven't really done a lot of planning yet. My primary objective for now is getting it back to the city alive. I suppose I need to start reading a few books on wild animals; my expertise is rather in the area of plants."

"This cat is very young. It's got to grow quite a bit yet," the swordsman pointed out.

She nodded gravely. "I know. I have seen the mother."

"You will have to start training it very soon. Otherwise it will be a danger to the people around you. Always provided you intend to keep it."

"I suppose I will have to wait for my companion's decision on that. I can't afford my own quarters yet."

Torvig looked taken aback. "You would move out of Lord Enric's quarters to keep the cat?"

"I think rather he would kick me out," she murmured.

Torvig studied the kitten for a few moments. "You know, a well-disciplined mountain cat could probably live in the city, if you took it on regular hunting trips in the forest. It is an animal of prey, after all. Never forget that, no matter how soft and furry they look. They are natural born killers."

She frowned. "Doesn't that statement rather negate your previous one about its being able to live in the city?"

He smiled thinly. "No, not at all. *Humans* are natural born killers as well. It doesn't keep us from living in the city, does it? It just requires discipline."

* * *

Eryn woke the cat with a weak infusion of magic and watched it stir and slowly open its round, yellow eyes, looking around in confusion. She pushed the plate with the chopped meat towards it and waited.

The tiny nostrils twitched in recognition of food, and the small head slowly turned towards the plate and sniffed.

She held her breath while the tiny triangular nose hovered over the food, obviously still deciding whether it smelled edible or not. Exhaling in relief, Eryn watched the pink tongue flip out between the furry jaws and taste the juicy meat.

Vern grinned next to her. "Good. I suppose we can keep her alive by sharing our food with her. Getting our hands on milk would have been quite a challenge up here. What are you going to do at night? She might try to run off."

Eryn sighed. Maybe that would be best, anyway. Wasn't it rather cruel to take a wild creature like this to a city where it would always be denied its true nature?

"Then I can't stop her, can I? I'm not a jail warder, Vern. I won't force any creature to stay with me against its will."

"Not that discussion again!" he exclaimed. "She is too small to know what's good for her! I mean, you wouldn't let your own child just run away from you like that?"

"But this is not my child, it's a wild animal," she explained patiently. "I will take care of her, but only if she permits me."

The boy folded his arms and just glared at Eryn wordlessly.

Eryn rubbed her face. Why was there so much discord between her and the boy lately?

When she looked back at the cat, she smiled. "Look, she has eaten up everything. Can you get some more from Plia?"

Vern nodded and rose to refill the plate. He even cut the meat into small crumbs when he had returned. The cat had in the meantime risen and cautiously started sniffing her surroundings. Eryn held her fingers close to her nose and smiled when the rough tongue rasped over it and small teeth bit into her fingers. They still smelled of the meat she had cut before. Lifting the cub with one hand, she sat it on her thigh and started feeding her the meat Vern had brought. After a few moments of hesitation she accepted the food from Eryn's hand and even used the small paws to hold on to the fingers that held the meat.

Eryn then poured a bit of water from her pouch onto her metal plate and put it before the cat. When the cub just stared at it, she moistened her finger. It took her several tries to have the raspy tongue lick it from her finger. Only then did the cat hesitantly lower its head to the plate and sniffed the water before the tiny pink tongue started lapping.

A few minutes later the cat's eyelids grew heavier and it fell asleep on Eryn's thighs, the head cosily snuggled against the crook of her arm.

"You know," she said and watched the cub's breathing deepening, "somehow I have the feeling that it's not going to run away for now."

* * *

The night was surprisingly uneventful. The cub had woken a few times and gobbled down another few bites of food they had placed close by. Every time she had returned to Eryn and curled up against her, taking advantage of the warmth her body provided.

The cage, though, was not at all well received, and the cub kept complaining by mewling loudly while sitting in it during the ride.

"Can't you send it back to sleep?" Grend frowned and steered his horse next to Eryn's. "It's making the horses more and more nervous. They can smell the predator, and hearing it as well doesn't make things better."

"I know, and I am sorry for that. But it does seem rather harsh to knock out the little cat because it is a nuisance. I mean, how would you feel if I did this with you?" She remembered perfectly well what it felt like, Enric had done it to her often enough.

Grend sighed. "But the cub looks stressed, doesn't it? Wouldn't it be better for it to sleep during the ride instead of sitting in the cage, howling away?"

Eryn felt her resolve waver and finally nodded. "Alright. But only as long as we are on horseback." She held a finger inside the cage and almost immediately felt a furry cheek press against it. Moments later the cub went limp.

* * *

The King took a seat at his desk and took the sealed envelope from his advisor. Marrin watched the monarch lean back and unfold the swordsman's letter. King Folrin's eyes followed the lines and suddenly his brows arched in surprise. His eyes ran down the lines of the sheet faster, and when he had reached the end, he let it drop to onto his desk and shook his head.

"Bad news, Your Majesty?" Marrin enquired carefully.

"Let's say it is *news*. Very interesting news at that. Hard to say if good or bad at the moment. Say, have the reports for Lords Tyront, Enric and Orrin arrived yet?"

"They have indeed, Your Majesty. They arrived with the same messenger as yours."

"I see. Then schedule a meeting with Lord Enric for about two hours' time. If he doesn't request one within the next hour, kindly suggest to him that seeing me would be wise."

"Yes, Your Majesty. Anything else?"

"Yes, one more thing: obtain for me a book on wild mountain cats. Lord Poron will surely be able to assist you here."

Marrin frowned in confusion. "Wild mountain cats?"

"Indeed." The King smiled thinly. "It seems as if Lord Enric will soon need to deal with two dark-haired females equipped with teeth and claws."

* * *

Tyront pinched the bridge of his nose and shook his head.

"Vyril?" he called out and looked up when she appeared in the doorway to his study.

"Yes?"

"I am expecting Enric to turn up here any minute. Send him to me directly, will you?"

His companion nodded and frowned. "Is everything alright, dear?" Her gaze fell on the piece of paper in his hand. "Not more bad news about Lady Eryn, is it?"

"Not as bad as the last one, no. But worrying news nevertheless. I begin to question the wisdom of ever letting that woman out of our sight," he sighed and shook his head.

Right at this moment an impatient series of knocks rattled the entrance door.

Vyril nodded and turned to open the door for Enric.

He nodded to her briefly and without a word strode into Tyront's study and closed the door behind him, clasping what looked like a letter.

"Please, please tell me that your report does not mention any fierce creatures she found in the woods and has decided to bring back with her?" he pressed out between clenched jaws and all but threw the paper on Tyront's desk.

The older man cleared his throat and shook his head in regret. "I am afraid I cannot comply with that request. Mountain cat, it says. Help me a bit here, will you? How big do they get?"

"Pretty big," Enric sighed and let his head sink into his hands. "Knee height, if we are lucky. And more than an arm's length in size, not including their tail."

Tyront whistled. "Sounds dangerous."

"They are. They eat *horses* when they are hungry!"

"Oh my," the older man grimaced. "Well, at least it won't starve in the city. We have plenty of those here."

Enric looked up incredulously. "Are you making fun of me? My companion, who hardly ever gives me the chance to do anything for her, is about to bring a fierce killer into the city, and I either need to tell her to get rid of what now looks like a small, harmless ball of fur or find a way to keep a bloody mountain cat in the city! A little compassion would be appreciated right now!"

"Sounds to me like you have made a decision already, or am I mistaken here?" Tyront asked mildly.

Enric stared at him for several moments, then closed his eyes. "So it would seem. I suppose I am going to see the King. I bet he is already expecting me."

"That is a valid assumption, yes," the older man nodded. "But you know what? There is always a bright side to everything."

"And what would that be, pray tell?"

"It wasn't *your* agent she unmasked publicly, but mine and Orrin's," Tyront remarked dryly.

* * *

Orrin leaned back in his chair and laughed aloud. Junar watched him for a while and waited for him to share with her what had put him in such a good mood. When he was still guffawing a minute later and brushed a tear from the corner of one eye, she sighed with some impatience.

"Come on now, what is the matter? Something to do with Eryn, isn't it? Out with it, or do I have to wrestle you to see that letter?"

The warrior grinned broadly. "That would doubtlessly be very entertaining for both of us, but to no avail. I am a trained fighter. And a magician."

She folded her arms and stared at him with a stern look on her face. He sighed and gave in.

"Vern has made Eryn adopt an orphaned mountain cat." He waited for her reaction.

Junar frowned. "What exactly does that mean? Why is that funny?"

"Because," he smirked, "a mountain cat is a pretty sizable and scary predator. Lord Enric will soon find himself living with a big, dangerous creature. And in addition to that he will have a fierce wild cat!"

She nodded her head indulgently while Orrin leaned back again and cackled.

"You are terrible! Considering your own battles with Vern's cat, I would have expected a bit more compassion from you."

"Don't you see the beauty in that? She brought a street cat to Vern that has turned out to be a real trial for me. And now Vern made *her* bring a mountain cat back to Enric! Junar," he leaned forward and took both her hands to kiss them, "there is justice, after all! Finally!"

He thought over the last two decades, the defiant boy who had made use of his position of power to take revenge, especially lately. Nothing great, just minor things that had been more of a nuisance than a real offence. Such as making him train Eryn immediately after he had tampered with her internal shield that day in the throne room. Or using him to convey to her that a delegation from the Western Territories would be arriving.

He rose to pour himself and Junar a generous glass of expensive wine. This warranted a minor celebration.

* * *

Vern sat in front of the fire, finishing the last drawings for the day. The cat kept pouncing on his moving pen and he gently shoved it aside every time it came close to tearing the paper or smudging his work.

Eryn sat with Plia beside him. Eryn reiterated details of the herbs of the day for both of them as she prepared the gathered plants that were awaiting being turned into medicine.

This would be their last night in the woods, and Eryn wanted to talk to the girl about Vern's idea.

"Plia, there is something I would like to ask you."

"Yes?" she answered and continued to pluck leaves carefully from stems.

"I have the impression that working with herbs and learning about them gives you pleasure. You keep asking a lot of questions about them, remember almost everything after my first description, and there are your experiments with the hot drinks every evening."

Plia looked up from her work and frowned. "Is there something wrong with that? I didn't want to cause you any extra effort. You should have told me to leave you alone." Her tone was worried.

Eryn sighed. "No, that's not what I wanted to say. I meant it as a compliment, in fact. Why wouldn't I wish you to be interested in a field that is clearly very important to me? Quite the opposite." She saw Plia breathe out in relief. "I was wondering whether you wouldn't prefer working with herbs to working in the Palace kitchen."

Vern smiled quietly and continued colouring the blossoms of his drawing.

"Me, working with herbs? How?"

"I thought that maybe you could be an apprentice somewhere else. I am in the middle of building up healing services in the city, so somebody with your interest and eagerness for the subject would be very welcome."

Plia drew in a quick breath. "You mean I could work with *you*?"

"That was my thought, yes. I can't promise you anything, I would have to talk to the Order first and ask for their permission. But as you are not a magician, I don't see much of a problem there. Also, apprentices don't cost that much. Of course you would have to give up your position in the Palace kitchen for that."

The girl leaned back, clearly overwhelmed. "I'm... I don't know what to say."

"Then don't say anything for now. Take your time and think about it."

Plia looked up. "I mean, I know that I want to do it, desperately! I would love to work with herbs, really!" She looked slightly panicky then. "Of course the work at the Palace kitchen is also fine - I don't mind the scrubbing and cutting and all it involves!"

Eryn smiled at her. The girl had not had very much in her life, so she was used to being extraordinarily grateful for everything she got or every favour that was bestowed on her. Being forced to choose between two options couldn't be easy for her, as it would mean considering one of them unfit and thereby seeming ungrateful.

"Then I will do everything to make this possible. You can of course continue to be friends with the cook. I would even recommend it. You might turn out to be a useful source of herbs for her, after all. And if she keeps on sharing her gossip with you, I'd be in favour of that, as well," Eryn chuckled and saw how the girl's eyes began to shine with excitement.

Two of their guards, Barul and Sebarn sauntered over to them.

"What is the plan for tomorrow?" Barul enquired. "Do you want to break camp after breakfast or is there some last-minute gathering to do before we return to the city?"

Eryn put aside the vials she had just filled and took out empty ones before answering, "There are a few more herbs I need. It should just be a short ride; we have almost reached the snowline. I propose riding up there early in the morning, gathering herbs there for about one hour and then returning here for a hearty meal before we break camp around noon."

Sebarn flinched, and they looked down at the cat hanging from his trouser leg, holding on to it with its claws. Eryn reached out and gently plucked it from the man's extremity, being careful not to rip the fabric.

"No climbing of legs," she scolded with a lifted index finger and rolled her eyes when the cat made to play with it. "I hope she soon ceases to be so cute, or I will have trouble punishing her."

"I dare say that will change alright. The longer the claws, the less of the cute," Sebarn commented and rubbed his leg where the cat had clung to it.

Eryn grinned. "I am glad she is still so small, or I would have owed you a pair of new trousers now. Of course we could have played for them. Or are you off the dice now?"

The man gave her a pained look and returned to his other two colleagues.

Barul crouched before Vern and said quietly, "I didn't want to say anything in front of the others, but I do have the strong suspicion that something is not quite right with these dice of yours."

Vern looked carefully blank. "Really? What do you mean?"

"I mean to say that your dice are loaded, young friend," the man said mildly. "I am willing to keep this a secret. But only if you return to me the four gold pieces you managed to obtain from me by unjust means."

The boy swallowed and then nodded, taking out his money pouch and removing the coins.

"No hard feelings?" he asked with a slightly uneasy expression.

Barul chuckled. "No. But it's interesting to see that you don't always seem to follow your father's strict principles."

Vern shrugged, then grinned and pointed a thumb towards Eryn. "That's her fault. She is a bad influence."

* * *

Eryn shaded her eyes and tried to make out if what she saw on the horizon were houses. She hoped so. They were supposed to reach a small town sometime soon, and she was eager to obtain some milk for the cat. It was in its cage, awake for a change, and only complained occasionally with a few impatient whines.

"Town ahead," Grend announced next to her. "We have made up some time, that's good. It's about one more hour until the light fades, and we should have reached the inn by then. How is your fierce little creature doing?"

"Plia is fine, thanks," she grinned and earned herself an indignant "Hey!" from behind her.

"The furry one seems also in good shape. Hardly any protests today."

"Yes, I have noticed. It seems to be getting used to travelling."

"She," Plia corrected him. "It's a girl, if you don't mind."

Grend sighed. "Alright, then. *She*. I assume the cat will sleep in your room tonight?"

"That was the plan, yes," Eryn nodded. "Unless you're in need of something warm and soft to cuddle for the night?" she grinned at him.

"Hardly," he said dryly. "I prefer my cuddling partners with fewer pointy teeth."

"So warriors don't seek challenges in all areas of their life, it seems."

"I would have thought that you would be aware of that. Your companion is a warrior."

Vern behind her giggled. "Yes, but he hasn't really chosen the easy road with *her*."

Grend smiled. "No, I imagine he hasn't."

Eryn shook her head at him. "You know what? Why don't you two ride ahead and make sure the inn has enough food and rooms prepared for us?"

Both boy and man nodded in assent, trying in vain to conceal their eagerness to let their horses run and enjoy themselves a little.

When they had ridden off, Sebarn took Grend's place next to her. "Where are they off to?"

"I've sent them ahead to get rid of them. They used their excess energy to tease me, and I thought this easier than striking them down. It makes carrying them along a nuisance, making sure they don't fall off their horses, don't stop breathing and so on."

"Ye-es," Sebarn said with a cautious glance at her, not sure if she was teasing *him* now or not.

She saw Garn now draw even with her horse, taking the place Vern had been only a minute ago.

"Only two more nights, then we are back again," the herb gatherer beamed. "I am very curious about young Vern's book. You did say that there will be a copy for every single one of us, didn't you?"

Eryn smiled at the careful question. "That is the plan, yes. But there are strings attached to that little gift: I expect every single one of you to memorise it and pass a test on the herbs and their proper handling."

Garn nodded. He had just remembered that bit, too.

"Well, that's only fair, I suppose."

She turned to him, looking earnest. "It's more than that, Garn. It ensures that you will find in us willing buyers for your herbs because they meet our quality standards. You wouldn't want to be sent away with full bags and an empty pouch after a gathering trip, would you?"

"True enough," he admitted.

* * *

The inn was not particularly luxurious nor was it cleaner than others of its kind, but the simple fact that it had a roof made it as attractive as a palace. Eryn had asked to be shown the room for herself and Plia first, so she could leave her feline travel companion there while she was eating.

Plia looked around the room and nodded approvingly. "Two beds. Excellent."

Eryn grinned knowingly and set the cub on the floor together with the bowl of milk she had obtained.

"Funny. I would have thought that sharing one bed with me can't be too bad after sleeping on the ground for several days. It seems I was wrong."

"Obviously."

"Come, let's get back downstairs before the men eat up everything." She lifted her heavy bag with the medicine vials and they went back to the public room.

Some of the herb gatherers squeezed together to make space for them on their bench. They had already been served generous portions of some meaty broth and dark bread.

Eryn was just about to order a bowl each for herself and Plia, when she heard her name called by a male voice from the bar. She looked up and saw a slightly familiar face belonging to a man about her own age grinning broadly at her.

"Look at that! Eryn! In the middle of nowhere! How crazy is that?" He came over to her and pressed to the surprise of all present at the table a hard kiss onto her lips and lifted her from the bench.

"Let me have a look at you! How long has it been? Three years, hasn't it?"

She smiled when she finally remembered where she knew him from. He had been a - well, a casual chum for a few nights when her bed was too big and cold.

"Yes, that sounds about right." She took his arm and steered him back towards the bar. Having him close to a table with two of the swordsmen who were also spying for city clients was not at all good.

"Say, what brings you here to this remote area?" she asked, desperately racking her memory for his name. In vain.

The man shrugged and pointed to a man at a small table at the back of the room. "I am here to deliver furniture to my uncle. He has ordered a chest for my cousin's marriage. And you? What are you up to here? Someone told me that you are a foreign spy! What nonsense is that?"

If her smile was rather strained, he didn't seem to catch it. "That was a little misunderstanding, nothing more. I have moved to the city and work as a healer there." Not bad, she mused. Not a single lie in there anywhere.

"And that group of men with you? Healer colleagues?"

"No, just a trip to gather a few herbs for medicines. We are on our way back to the city, actually."

"Really? So the herbs are all gathered?" He winked at her. "How about you let them travel ahead and stay here another day or two with me? We could pick up where we left off those years back."

She closed her eyes when she heard somebody behind her clear his throat audibly. Grend. Great, just fabulous.

"Eryn? Is everything alright?" he enquired with a muted smile. She could see from his expression that he must have overheard the last words spoken.

"Yes, I am fine. Thank you so much for taking the trouble of coming here and asking me that."

When he just kept standing there without showing any sign of returning to his meal, she sighed and smiled apologetically to her first conversation partner.

"I am sorry, it seems my boys want me back. Thank you for the offer, but no. This wouldn't be a good idea for either of us. Believe me." At least not if he was attached to his life or able to hide from Enric really well. She turned away and quickly returned to the table, where several pairs of eyes waited for an explanation.

"An old acquaintance of mine," she murmured and her tone warned them not to attempt any further enquiries.

CHAPTER 10

Returning Home

Eryn gulped when she caught her first glimpse of the city walls. About one more hour to go.

Her feelings were mixed. There was certainly the anticipatory pleasure of returning to what had in the last months turned into something very close to home. The thought of feeling Enric's arms wrap around her and pressing her close, his scent, his voice, made her feel a longing so strong that it was almost a physical ache. Yet, oh dear, there was the thought of facing him with the infant mountain cat. He would have learned about this at least two or three days ago already, so he would have had more than enough time to get used to the idea. Probably. Hopefully.

"You look nervous," Vern commented knowingly. "Dreading the reunion with your companion? Afraid he will not be too thrilled about the new toothed and clawed family member?" He nodded at the quietly snoring cub in its cage by her side.

She just gave him an annoyed look. He had been a nuisance ever since they had left the woods. He had, to the surprise of the four swordsmen who didn't know about the attack several days ago, insisted on sleeping in one room with Plia and her. He had gathered his blankets and slept on the floor of their room, no matter how often she had threatened, ordered and argued with him to leave.

To distract herself she made a list in her head of the things she needed to take care of when she got back. Checking the progress of the work on the healers' building, preparing the texts for the book for the herb gatherers and finalising it before ordering several copies, drawing up a schedule for the apothecary trainings, having a look at the applications for trainee healers and of course her regular everyday duties such as her studies, teaching Vern, and not forgetting the blasted combat training. She couldn't help a wry smile crossing her face at the thought of Rolan. He would not be too thrilled at having her back again. Junar would, on the other hand. And Orrin would undoubtedly be more than happy to have his son back unscathed and unmarred.

* * *

Enric stood at the top of the turrets at the city gates and watched the group drawing closer. After he had been informed that they were in sight he had climbed up, but then they were no more than a mass of indiscernible distant specks. Now he could distinguish between the horses already. He tried to find Eryn's, but couldn't. She obviously still hadn't changed her hair colour back and thus appeared only one of twenty-three blonde riders at this distance.

He wasn't wearing his robes today, had opted against them as he didn't want her to see him as any welcoming committee sent by the Order, but instead in his private capacity as her lover and companion.

Now they were close enough for him to distinguish between certain features. He spotted the only female figure at once and next to her a skinny, lanky one. Vern. The broad-shouldered swordsmen had split up - two of them at the rear of the group, two in front, just as they were supposed to be.

He felt the exact moment when she identified him and knew that her gaze had locked onto him even though she was still too far away for him to see her eyes.

When the group was about to reach the city gates, Enric returned to the Palace square and waited for the horses to pass through and enter the city.

He saw how Eryn looked nervous, and briefly wondered why. Afraid of how he would react to the cub, probably. Of course she was aware that he would have been informed about it already.

He smiled at her to let her know that his relief at having her back outweighed everything else and saw how she seemed to relax immediately. She stopped her horse not far away from him and was the first of the group to dismount.

Enric remained standing where he was, waiting for her to come to him. She did so more slowly than he would have wished, as if she was not sure if a passionate show of affection would be to his liking. Foolish, he thought, willing her to make haste, feeling how the anticipation of touching her made his fingers tingle. He would have loved to see her jump off the horse and right into his arms. But it seemed that they had not arrived at that stage in their relationship yet. He pushed aside the regret this thought triggered and concentrated on what he had been waiting for: finally having her back with him after what seemed like an eternity, but which had in fact been no more than ten days.

She stopped a few paces in front of him, looking at him.

"I am back," she just said and seemed slightly awkward.

"Yes, I noticed," he murmured and opened his arms. "Are you just going to stand there or will you finally come here so that I can hug you?"

Grinning broadly, she stepped into his embrace and felt that she had truly returned only when his arms wrapped around her.

She was about to press her face against his shoulder, but he buried one hand in her hair and made her lift her face up to his. He bent down until their lips were only a hair's breadth apart.

"Your hair. Would you mind?"

She smiled and quickly let the blonde masking disappear. Only then did he kiss her.

Her heart almost stopped. It had been a busy ten days, full of travelling, gathering herbs and making medicine. She had been exhausted enough to just fall asleep minutes after lying down, there had not been not much time or energy left to think about missing him.

How was it possible, that only now, that she was reunited with him, back in his arms, the full impact of it hit her like a landslide, mighty, unexpected and unstoppable?

He felt her hands at his collar, pulling him closer. She seemed to revel in his taste, her body tense, her breathing laboured.

"If you keep this up, my love," her murmured at her lips, "we'll need to find a more private place fairly quickly. Missed me, haven't you?"

She closed her eyes for a moment and exhaled before she nodded. "So it would seem."

He raised his eyebrow at the surprise in her voice but refrained from commenting on it. She obviously had been neither aware of having missed him nor expected that she would.

"I have heard that you brought a certain something back from your trip?" he enquired with a resigned expression.

"Yes, I suppose you could phrase it like that," she admitted slowly. She let go of him reluctantly and went back to the horse. Plia, too, had dismounted in the meantime and readied the cage in her hands for Eryn to take.

Enric stared at the small fluffy bundle, which seemed to be fast asleep despite the commotion around it, with interest.

"That is a very young cub. No more than four of five weeks old, I would estimate."

Eryn untied the cord that held the pointed top of the cage together and carefully lifted the small cat from its resting place. Slowly, it opened first one, then the other eye and stared at Enric, transfixed.

He shook his head slightly. Amazing. Its fur really had almost the same tint as Eryn's hair.

"I can't let you out of my sight for a minute," he sighed and took the furry bundle when she offered it. The cat immediately started licking his hand followed by his face when he held it closer. Eryn looked surprised.

"Oh dear," he said, turning away his mouth to keep it from being licked. "Let me guess, it's a female, right? I do seem to have a certain effect on those."

Eryn's relief made her start laughing; she watched the cub trying to climb on his shoulders to lick his ears with Enric trying to keep her from doing just that without making her fall off or causing her to use her claws to clasp hold of him.

"Can we put her back in the cage for now? I feel slightly besieged." Enric managed to pry the cat loose and set it back into the small container, where it immediately started mewling loudly in protest and clawing at the twigs.

"Now, would you look at that? What have we here?"

They turned and saw Orrin strolling towards them, one arm around Vern's shoulders, the other around Junar's waist. He looked smug, and his grin grew even wider when he saw Enric's narrowed eyes.

He gave Eryn a quick and hearty embrace and then nodded towards the cage. "So that's your little new friend from the woods. Couldn't live with the fact that Vern owns a cat and you don't, it would seem."

He stepped closer to take a good look at the animal. "Beautiful creature." He looked up at her. "You are aware that they get quite a lot bigger, aren't you?"

She sighed. "Orrin. Can you imagine how often I heard *that* statement over these last few days?"

Still grinning like a man possessed, he turned to Vern. "I suppose I should be grateful she only brought you a cat off the street. Remind me of this when I next complain about Ram'an."

Vern nodded with a lopsided grin. "I will, depend on it. Can we go home now? I really, *really* need a bath."

Eryn sighed happily. "Yes, that sounds fabulous. Little, ordinary things suddenly seem a lot more luxurious than before the trip, what did I tell you?" She turned to Enric. "Let's go. I want a bath, too."

She let loose a piercing whistle to get the attention of the members of the expedition and cleared her throat.

"I want to thank every single one of you for making this journey the pleasure it was. I enjoyed getting you know you and look forward to working with you in the future. The books with the information about the herbs I promised you will take some time yet, but my assistant will let you know as soon as they are ready. Now I don't want to keep you from your families any longer."

She saw heads bow to her and returned the gesture before turning to Plia. "I will send for you as soon as I have talked to Lord Tyront and Enric, little flower. I am so very glad you were with us on the expedition. I loved spending time with you." She kissed the girl on the forehead and then turned towards the Palace gates to return to their quarters. She frowned when Enric held on to her hand, but didn't move.

"No, my love. That's not the right direction."

"What?" She laughed and then suddenly turned serious. "You haven't really kicked me out because of the cub, have you?"

Enric stared at her and slowly shook his head. "No. And I am rather shocked at any assumption that I would."

"What is this about, then?" she asked and looked to Junar and Orrin, both of them smiling knowingly.

"Go on, Eryn. I am sure you will like it," Junar winked at her.

Enric nodded at them and tugged a still reluctant Eryn with him into Kingsway.

"Can you at least tell me where we are going?"

"Nope."

"Then tell me about what I will find there!"

"Nope."

"How much further is it? I have just returned from a really long journey, you know," she said pointedly.

"A few more minutes."

"We are headed towards the river." Her tone became panicky. "You are not about to drown the little cat, are you?"

Enric released a deep, heartfelt sigh and stopped to turn to her. He leaned his forehead against hers.

"Shut up," he said gently. "And just trust me, will you?"

He waited for her to nod hesitantly before he took her hand again and moved on.

A few minutes later he stopped in the centre of a street, facing towards two large buildings where some kind of construction work was going on.

"Here we are. You may ask your questions now."

"What is this?"

"Our new home."

Her eyes bulged. "Our *what*?"

"This is where we live now. At least the building to your left. The other one still needs some renovation to be taken care of. I am told it will be ready for use in about one month."

"You bought *two* buildings?" She stared at him, then at the structures on each side of the street. "Why? And how? I mean, how rich are you *really*?"

"The buildings are rather narrow, if you look at them." When she didn't look and instead kept staring at him, he grasped her by the shoulders and twisted her to face them. "You see? There is space for no more than three large or four smaller rooms per floor."

"But..." She calculated quickly. "That would make twelve large rooms in total! We were living in no more than four at the Palace!"

He chuckled. "That is true, but if you live outside the Palace, there is a certain infrastructure that is no longer available, such as servants' rooms, kitchen, storage and so on. The quarters we had were just for living in, not for any work in connection with them."

She blinked. Yes, that did sound halfway plausible. "And why two buildings instead of one? Isn't that a bit impractical?"

"No, not really. There will be one building for the servants, kitchen, storage space and so on, and the other one for us to live and work in."

"With a street in between."

"No. With what is shortly to become a garden surrounded by a wall as high as the buildings to keep a mountain cat inside."

Her eyes darted to the construction work. Only now did she realise what it was they were doing. They were removing the cobble stones from the ground and at the same time erecting what looked like a thick stone wall.

"You bought up part of the street as well?"

Enric nodded. "Yes, I suppose you could say that. But it is not an important one and can be bypassed easily. This is a quiet part of the city."

Eryn closed her eyes for a while and tried to collect her thoughts. All this seemed absurd, surreal.

"Why? I mean, you didn't just go and buy two buildings along with a street because I was bringing a mountain cat home, did you?"

He smiled. "It does sound rather crazy when you put it like that. And I am happy to assure you that the answer is No. Your choice of house mate," he nodded at the cage, "just influenced my plans and the timing of it."

"You wanted to move out of the Palace anyway? Why?"

"You didn't seem to enjoy living there very much from what I saw. And our quarters there were too small, anyway. I need a study, and so do you. Our quarters are not usually meant to provide additional working space. Usually the companions of magicians don't work. Well, not in the traditional sense of the word."

"The guest room could have been converted into a study for me," she pointed out.

"Yes, but then we wouldn't have had a guest room. A self-respecting magician does have a guest room, that's just the way it is."

She looked at the buildings again. "So we really live here? Already? Or are we just moving in?"

"Oh, we live here, alright. Our last possessions were removed from the Palace and brought here yesterday. Just in time for you not to face utter chaos upon your return. There is even a wash room ready for use, so you can take that bath you're wanting. Come."

He took her to the main entrance of the left building and opened the double doors for her to enter.

"Here to your right is a cubby-hole for your cloak, and then you are already in our new parlour."

She looked around and smiled at the familiar furniture. "You brought the inventory with you? Will the King approve of your leaving his rooms bare and empty?"

"Most of the furniture there belongs to us, my love. Magicians don't really like to borrow things."

"Alright, that makes things easier, I guess. At least we don't have to stay in an empty house for now."

He smiled. "Come on. Let me show you your study." Taking her hand, he led her to the right side of the building and opened a door. They stepped inside, and Enric saw the slow smile spreading across her face.

He'd had book shelves made that covered the walls from floor to ceiling, and her father's books had been sorted into the shelves already.

A large desk made of the same dark wood as the shelves stood in the centre of the room. She gingerly touched the smooth surface with her fingertips and walked around it to take a seat in the brown leather chair, just to try it out. She bent forward to slide open the three drawers of the desk and smiled when she found her new seal, the Order's official one, thick paper, sticks of wax, a box of matches to melt them, pens and two glasses of dark ink.

The third drawer contained the file with the collected paperwork on the planning of her trip.

"It's beautiful. Thank you."

"You are very welcome. I am glad you like it. You just order whatever else you need. Now come. There is still more to see."

She rose and took the hand he held out to her. He pointed to a door at the other side of the parlour.

"Over there is my study, but you can have a look at that later." He pulled her towards a broad staircase. "The bedrooms are upstairs."

He pushed open the first door to their right when they had climbed the stairs. The bedroom was slightly smaller than the one at the Palace had been. Smiling, she touched the same bed they had also slept in before.

"There are no curtains yet, and I don't see a carpet. Not enough time?" It seemed as if this was the only thing in the entire house that was missing.

"No. But you mentioned that you wanted to order both of them new when you finally agreed to sharing a bedroom with me. I didn't want to deprive you of that pleasure," he grinned when she laughed.

"So. The guest rooms are of minor interest right now, but I will now finally take you where you wanted to go even before you knew what awaited you: the wash room. Follow me."

Eryn stopped when she saw four more doors. "How many guest rooms do we have here?"

"Two."

"Alright, one wash room, two guest rooms. What is behind the fourth door?"

"Another wash room to be used by guests."

She blinked. "An additional one for guests only? That does seem a little opulent, don't you think?"

"What can I say? You asked me before how rich we really were." He kissed her forehead. "Filthy rich, my love. So I do enjoy a little opulence every now and then."

* * *

Enric sat on the floor next to the tub while his companion was delighting in her hot bath.

"I think I will go to bed afterwards and have a lovely nap," Eryn mused and released a small surge of magic into the water to warm it up a little more.

"To bed?" He raised his brows. "I know it has been a long trip, but it is only noon. I am afraid sleeping is not really on the cards for you yet. Tyront wants to see you sometime today."

"I need to meet Lord Tyront today?" she grimaced. "So much for a peaceful return."

"And there is another little something I want to show you."

She looked at him suspiciously. "I am not sure if I can bear another surprise today in addition to being relocated."

"I have great confidence in your ability to deal with new situations and am thus sure that it will not overwhelm you." He lifted the cub off a towel. "I think she has just peed on that. How does Vern deal with the cat's... excretory needs?"

"A box with wood shavings, if I remember correctly."

"Well, that should work for the moment. Later we will probably have to increase the size of the box. Or use a bathtub." He let the cub chew at his fingers. "Does she have a name yet?"

Eryn shook her head. "No. Any suggestions? What would be a good name for the first urban mountain cat?" she mused.

Enric looked up and grinned. "Urban mountain cat... Why not? Let's call her *Urban*."

"Really?" she asked doubtfully, but then shrugged. She had been more than lucky so far, so if he liked the name she wouldn't discuss that minor detail with him. "Urban it is, then."

She looked over to him and frowned. "How did the King react to knowing I had brought a wild cat into his city?"

"Cool and collected, as always. I suppose asking him for the permission to live outside the Palace precincts would have been much less promising without Urban."

"What? You need a Royal permission to move out of the Palace? Why? Not all magicians live there."

"The high command of the Order does - and has for as long as anyone can remember. We are the first ones to break with that tradition," he explained and then smiled and winked at her. "Not that it's the first one that falls victim to our waywardness, mind you. And probably not the last."

"So the King has generously granted us the permission to move out because he doesn't want to stay under the same roof as a fierce woodland carnivore?" she grinned. "So my bringing home the cat has actually helped you carry out a plan that might otherwise have been impossible?"

Enric waggled his head. "I wouldn't have said it was impossible, just considerably more difficult. I like to think that I would have managed to make him agree to it at one point. Whenever that would have been."

She laughed. "At least you are realistic. How have you managed to do all this within only the last few days?"

"Money," he just shrugged. "If you tell people you want something done quickly and are willing to pay enough people so a lot of things can happen at the same time, it is usually not really a problem."

"So you have really spent a lot in this last week, haven't you?"

"Yes, I have. But there is still enough left, so don't worry." He smiled and nodded at the bathtub. "How much longer are you going to stay in there?"

"Why?"

"Because we are due at Tyront's in about two and a half hours."

Furrowing her brows, she looked at him. "That would still give me plenty of time in here."

"No, my love." He rose from the floor and held out a fresh towel ready for her. "I very much want us to spend that time somewhere else. In fact, I insist," he added with a suggestive smile.

*   *   *

Tyront would have preferred to sit with them in the parlour, but it was better to take care of the Order business first, and for that his study was the more suitable setting.

"Lady Eryn," he said and handed her a warm drink. She looked tired but happy, and Enric seemed to be a lot more relaxed than he had been over this week and a half.

"Thank you," she smiled as she accepted the cup.

"That must have been quite an eventful trip for you. Why don't you tell us about it? I would guess you prefer this to writing a report."

"I do, yes. Though I imagine there is not a lot I can tell you that you have not already been informed of, unless I am very much mistaken," she added dryly.

Tyront grimaced. "With you I am not entirely sure. I was impressed that you worked out who my agent was. Enric and I compared our reports, and there was a considerable discrepancy one time. But I don't want to get ahead of your narrative." He nodded at her to start.

"Well, the first two and half days were no real challenge as such, unless you count the strain of getting used to spending all day long on the back of a horse." She saw Enric and Lord Tyront exchange a quick look. But when they remained silent, she continued. "We reached the woods according to plan, and I am glad to say that we found a great number of herbs in the area. The herb gatherers were all cooperative, without a single exception, and so were the guards. Fortunately, we were never really in need of their services. But it was good to have them there nevertheless," she added generously. "We had one night that was rather more eventful than the others. There was a huge storm, and we were not able to find shelter in time and were forced to make camp pretty much with nothing to shelter us from the gale. But Vern and I had a shield raised all the time to protect us from the weather, which worked quite well. I had been a bit worried about the strain of holding a large shield for such a long time, but it worked out brilliantly. Vern even managed to stave off a tree falling on us with his." She took a sip from her cup before she continued. "It was on the day after the storm when we found the cub. We heard a noise and found a dead, fully grown female, which had been crushed by another falling tree. The cub was alone and would have died, so we took it with us." She chuckled at the memory. "We were really worried about what to feed it without any milk anywhere close to hand, but fortunately the little thing took well to Plia's cooking. From a healer's point of view I can happily report that the expedition has been very successful. We were able to find the most important herbs for the cures I will need most frequently, and we even found a few less common ones that will also come in handy. Vern did very well with documenting the plants and methods with his drawings. I was very glad to have him there. And that is pretty much all there was to it."

Tyront studied her for a few moments and then pursed his lips. "I see. And this narrative of yours contains all information that would from your point of view be of interest to the Order?"

She nodded slowly. "I would say so, yes."

Enric cleared his throat and pulled a sheet of paper from his pocket.

"Eryn," he said with a warning undertone, "I am afraid you forgot to mention a minor detail. According to my information, there was an incident at the second night of your journey." He unfolded the paper and handed it to her.

She swallowed when she recognised the magistrate's name at the bottom. Oh dear. And she was so certain that she had managed to keep this from the swordsmen.

"Oh, that little fracas," she said weakly. "I had almost forgotten about it."

"Indeed?" Enric said quietly with an insincere smile. "How very fortunate that we have this report to help your memory along, isn't it?"

She barely managed to avoid wincing at the steely expression in his eyes.

"Talk," he just said and leaned back with folded arms. "And your story better fit my report, or I will use a truth block on you for all further questions we have."

She swallowed. Now that did seem a little extreme. She looked at Lord Tyront to see if he agreed with this and saw that she would not get any help from that side.

Sighing in defeat, she straightened. "Alright. It was during the second night. Plia and I were sharing a small room, and the bed was very narrow. I need a lot of space when I sleep, so she woke up when I almost pushed her off the bed. She then noticed that somebody was trying to get into our room because the door handle was being moved repeatedly. I had stuck a chair under it, you see, so the door would not open at the first attempt. There were no proper locks." She looked at Enric's grim expression and quickly returned her gaze to Tyront. "Plia then woke me, and I told her to hide under the bed. I had my herb gathering knife on the nightstand and quickly slipped it under the pillow. A moment later the intruder managed to dislodge the chair and entered the room. I had planned to raise a shield before he got to me, but he moved a lot faster than I anticipated. He was close enough to touch me when I wanted to shield, and thus it was too late for it by that time. So I used my..."

"Were did he touch you?" Enric interrupted her.

He wouldn't ask if he didn't know, she thought and cursed at not being able to omit that detail. "He was trying to strangle me."

"Was he *trying* to strangle you, or was he *strangling* you?" he enquired again.

Damn, damn, damn! "He was strangling me," she admitted reluctantly.

"I see," he commented, his voice cold. "Try to be a bit more precise, if you please."

She nodded and went on, "As I was saying, it was too late for shielding, so I had to resort to using the knife I had hidden under my pillow."

"One moment," Enric interrupted her again. "Did he give you to understand why he was breaking into your room?"

She swallowed. "I assumed he wanted to steal from us and had made the logical choice of robbing seemingly helpless women instead of the other rooms which contained two or three men each."

"So he didn't reveal any other motives? It does seem rather strange for a man to strangle his victim when grabbing your money and then running would have been so much easier." Enric watched her carefully.

"Well, he did mention something about having fun with me," she said slowly as if only recalling it now.

"I see. I would ask you to pay a little more attention to the details, if you will. Imagine I hadn't asked you. It would have slipped through our fingers." This tone had dropped from merely cold to icy sarcasm. She felt sweat start running down her back. Only an hour ago they had been in bed together, and now he was interrogating her like a criminal. How quickly things could change with him. One moment he was her lover, and without so much as a warning he slipped into the role of her superior.

"Go on," he prompted when she didn't resume speaking.

"I grabbed the knife from under my pillow and stabbed him in his side. I hit his lung so he was immediately helpless and I was able to shove him off me to the floor. I used a little magic to make sure he was unconscious and then sent Plia to fetch Vern. In the meantime I assessed the damage I had caused and kept him stable for Vern to do the healing."

"Why didn't you heal him yourself?" This time it was Tyront who asked.

She looked up at him a little sheepishly. "I thought this was a good opportunity for him to deal with a real medical emergency and heal something a little more complex than the usual injuries such as broken bones and cut skin."

Tyront hid a smile. So she had used her attacker as a training object for her healer trainee. That was surprisingly cold-blooded, but also amazingly efficient.

"Vern then appeared, along with the two herb gatherers who were sharing a room with him that night. The publican was also alerted, and they all watched us while we tended to the attacker. I didn't want to draw any attention to my person, so I had changed my hair to blonde and told the publican that Vern was the healer. I hid the fact that I was a magician as well, and Vern being seen to do the actual healing was very helpful." She thought for a moment and then went on, "I ordered Vern and the herb gatherers to keep the incident a secret. Vern was very angry at me because of the incident, and since then he has never let me spend a night without his being close. The next morning, the local magistrate, who had taken the attacker into custody, came to question Vern, Plia and me. And, well - you have a copy of his report."

"Where was your sword when you were attacked?" Enric asked calmly, watching her from under half-closed eyes.

Oh dear. This was not a good combination. Being questioned by her companion, combat trainer and superior in one person offered just too many possible attack surfaces for him to vent anger at her.

"In my bag," she replied weakly.

"Why was it in your bag?"

"Because I didn't think I would need it at the inn."

Enric nodded with pursed lips. She knew with absolute certainty what his next question would be and closed her eyes in dreadful anticipation.

"And where, if I may ask, was your sword while you were riding the horse?"

Her first impulse was lying, her second one self-preservation. An odd order of priorities, she mused. But of course he knew the answer and would not react well to any further attempts at concealment.

"In my saddlebag."

"So you were also counting on not needing it while you were on horseback, I assume. Tell me, when would you have been prepared to defend yourself? Clearly not in those situations when you were most vulnerable."

She didn't answer. It had not been a real question anyway, just a rhetorical means to scold her. She heard Enric take in a deep breath and then exhale slowly as if to calm himself.

"Is there anything else you would like to add to your report? Did you meet any interesting people? Anybody worth mentioning at all?" he added pointedly, and she had to bite her tongue to suppress the curse that had been about to escape her. So he had heard about that, too.

"On our way back to the city I met a man I knew from a few years ago in one of the inns we stayed at. He had been my lover for a few nights and asked me to spend one or two nights with him. I declined. That's it." She folded her arms, staring straight ahead at the empty wall above Tyront's head.

Tyront sighed. That had not been pleasant, especially not for two lovers following their reunion after ten days. But at least the worst part was now over.

"I am sorry I tried to hide this from you," Eryn finally said and looked at Enric. "But this is exactly the reaction I wanted to avoid. Everything turned out fine, and on the next expedition I will..."

"On the *next* expedition?" Enric interrupted her, mouthing each syllable with exaggerated precision. Tyront grimaced. Or maybe the worst part was yet to come.

"There will be no *next* expedition anytime soon. You will first have to prove to me that you are responsible and trustworthy enough to be let out of my sight again for more than a few hours at a time."

Eryn stared at him. "But I need to take them out there again for the summer and autumn herbs! This is important!"

"The *herbs* are important? Really? How about what is important to *me*? How about following a few simple, easily comprehensible rules such as not lying to me and taking more care about defending yourself?" Enric grabbed the armrests of his chair to keep himself from seizing her shoulders instead and shaking some sense into her.

They stared at each other, boiling anger in his eyes, defiance in hers.

After what seemed like an eternity of silence, she said quietly, "I am sorry. I know I didn't do very well. I also endangered Plia's life by being ill-prepared. It's not something I am proud of, something I hoped I wouldn't have to admit to. It was a cowardly thing to do."

Enric bent forward, braced his elbows on his knees and sighed. "No. A coward you are not," he said and the anger had vanished from his voice, replaced by resignation. "A fool, yes. But not a coward. I am glad you see that protecting yourself might help in protecting others, but I am not happy that protecting yourself for your own sake doesn't seem to be enough for you. As long as this doesn't change, you will not be making another journey alone. This is an order. We will talk again about this second expedition you wish to make in a few months. You might have to take Orrin with you if I still don't feel I can trust you with your own life. This is the limit of the concessions I am willing to make at this point." He turned to Tyront. "Do I have your support on this?"

"Yes, that you do," Tyront nodded and watched them. *Now* the worst part was over. "Lady Eryn," he went on, "there are a few matters as regards applications for healer trainees, but we can deal with them tomorrow if you have an hour for Lord Poron and me in the afternoon. We have eliminated the ones we both deemed unsuitable and which you would thus not be able to select on your own. The rest we can discuss later."

"How many are we talking about?" she frowned.

"After our pre-selection there are now nine candidates left," Tyront said and smiled when he watched her lean forward in surprise. "But let us not discuss this now. There will be time for that later."

Eryn nodded reluctantly. This would have been a topic she wouldn't have minded talking about for a little longer. But there was another matter to take care of, anyway.

"There is one more thing I wish to address," she ventured. "It is about non-magician medical staff."

"Ah yes," the older magician smiled. "I was wondering if you would want to talk about it today. Young Plia has turned out to be very talented with herbs, hasn't she?"

She nodded slowly. His spy, Sebarn, was obviously very thorough and hadn't failed to mention such minor details.

"Yes, and not only very talented, but also willing to put in the effort that is necessary to work with them properly, such as learning everything about them and then exercise and practise. I have found this to be a rare combination among people her age and would very much like to make use of it."

"So, what exactly is it you are asking me, Lady Eryn?"

"I am asking you to let me offer Plia an apprenticeship for a position as medical herbalist. Her place of work would be the healers' building, and she would be responsible for ensuring that the herbs delivered by the gatherers and the medicines produced by the apothecaries are up to the agreed standards."

Tyront studied her for a few moments, then looked at Enric questioningly. "What do you say to that, Enric?"

Eryn kept staring straight ahead, not daring to turn her head.

"I think this is a very good idea," he said, aware of her tense posture. "I would grant it." He saw her briefly close her eyes and exhale in relief.

"I agree. Make your offer, Lady Eryn. And now you may leave. I can see that you are exhausted and in need of a bed."

When he had closed the door behind them and they stood in the Palace corridors alone, she took Enric's hand and pressed her cheek into it.

"Thank you for your help with Plia," she murmured. "I value that very much."

"It was my pleasure," he replied and pulled her close. "I admit that I find it very hard to separate the different roles I play in your life. Reacting as your superior in a situation when your companion is involved as well is a challenge I have yet to master. It seems we both have some learning to do. I am not apologising, mind you. I meant every word I said. But the intensity was maybe not entirely appropriate for the time and place."

"You know," she said and leaned against him, "we should probably release you from one of your many roles then." She felt him stiffen.

"How am I to understand that?"

She shook her head and sighed. "What do you think? People keep telling me to use my brain, and yet they seem reluctant to do so themselves. There is a rather obvious answer to that question."

"There is nothing much you can do to release me of my role as your superior, and I assume you are not crazy enough to think that I will give up the one as your companion. That leaves the combat training. Are you telling me that you want to continue your training with somebody else? Orrin, most probably?"

Grinning up at him, she pinched his cheek. "Well done! You may yet amount to something. So, what do you say?"

"The difference in strength would be a problem. We try to make sure that the teacher is stronger than the student for obvious reasons. The teacher's strength determines more or less the limit of the skill level that can be reached by the student."

"I can wear shackles for the training," she shrugged. "You could enchant them in a way to reduce my strength to Orrin's level. Or even better, show *me* how to do it."

He looked down at her in surprise. "You would be willing to wear them again?"

"Only for a few hours a week, mind you," she emphasised. "So, what do you say? Will I be training with Orrin from now on?"

"Let's just say I am willing to let him do most of it. I will relinquish control of your training to him, but I will take the liberty of testing your progress from time to time." He smirked and shook his head. "I imagine his heart will miss a beat when you tell him that you have decided to train with him voluntarily. And there is always the chance that he will refuse."

Eryn laughed. "He won't. He likes me."

They started walking towards the Palace entrance.

"You know, I'm getting to like the idea of leaving the Palace when we go home. It doesn't make me feel like being somebody else's guest. And I have to say that I have a number of quite unpleasant associations with your old quarters."

"*Our* old quarters," he corrected her, almost unconsciously.

She ignored it. "It is nice to have a certain distance to all of this here."

He agreed, but was careful enough not to say so while they were still within the Palace precincts. The walls tended to have ears here.

"You know, the healers' building is not far away from our new home. We could make a small detour, and you can memorise the way home from there. Are you up to it?"

"Absolutely." The thought of going there even replenished some of her energy. "There should be some progress, it is due to be finished in about two weeks. I can't tell you how much I am looking forward to finally get things started there," she sighed.

Enric just smiled when they passed the Palace gate and turned into Kingsway.

The late afternoon sun was not yet strong enough for people to venture out without a cloak, but its rays did feel warm on her face. It was getting milder again. Low temperatures were not really that much of a problem for magicians - at least not as long as they didn't move around and just stood and warmed the air around them - but it was the quality of the light, the general mood of people around her, the sprouting of plants that made the real difference for her.

They reached the healers' building in a matter of minutes. Eryn frowned when they stood in front of it - she noticed how oddly quiet it seemed. "Where are the workers?"

"Why don't we go in and check?" he proposed and let her enter first.

She turned to him and narrowed her eyes. "This doesn't happen to be the surprise you were talking about earlier? Are you telling me that they finished ahead of time?"

"Yes, they did indeed." Probably to finally get the magicians off their backs. The workers had seemed rather agitated towards the end.

She slowly turned and looked over smoothly plastered walls, tidily finished floors and open doors around her.

"Then I can really use it? I can start furnishing and stocking it?" The thought sent waves of pleasure through her body.

"So it would seem, yes. Come. There is more." He took her hand and pulled her to the staircase that led to the first floor.

He passed several open doors, stopped in front of the only closed one and motioned for her to enter. She gripped the door handle and slowly pushed it down.

An irritated voice from inside complained, "Have you ever heard of knocking? It's considered polite before entering a room that's not yours. And this building is not yet open for..." Rolan's voice trailed off when he looked up from the paper he was bent over and he stared at Eryn, horrified.

"Good thing that I happen to own the building, then, and the room basically *is* mine," she said with wry amusement and cast her gaze around the room.

He had been busy, she thought to herself. This was a completely furnished office, and it looked as if it was in use already. Papers were stacked in neat piles around him, and he looked to be engaged in of some kind of calculation, or at least the sheet in front of him holding a long column of numbers would suggest that.

"Lady Eryn," he sputtered and hastily jumped to his feet. "And Lord Enric." He bowed quickly.

"Rolan," she said and nodded to him. "I see you have already chosen a place for yourself and have furnished it."

He looked at her uncertainly. "And this is not to your liking?"

"What? Why wouldn't it?" she shrugged. "I suppose then I'd better take care of getting a room ready for myself as well."

The young man walked across to a second door she only now noticed, and opened it wordlessly.

"I have taken the liberty of making arrangements as to that," he told her. "I thought it might be useful to have two rooms adjoining as we will probably need to be in constant contact for our work." His voice had taken on a noticeably resigned undertone, and she stifled a grin.

She quietly whistled through her teeth when she entered the room. It was large and spacious, quite a bit more so than she herself would have chosen for her study. Her main focus would not be up here, but downstairs with the patients. But it was bright and airy thanks to numerous windows. Here, too, an office had been prepared and was ready for use. Strange, she thought, she'd had to make do with an overstuffed guest room before she left, and now there were two real offices at her disposal, given to her on the same day.

"You did that?" she asked without turning.

"Yes, Lady Eryn. I hope it is to your liking."

"It is, thank you. I would like to meet with you tomorrow so that we can go through the things we need to prepare for the place to open." She marvelled at how calm her voice sounded when what she really wanted to do was dance and sing and jump around at the unexpected joy of finding herself in a fully finished and usable building instead of the construction site in its final stages she had expected. But expressing her elation like that would not impress Rolan in any way. She needed to work on earning his respect, not disconcert him even further with a lack of restraint.

"Of course. I will be here all day, so I am at your disposal," he said. "Would you like a tour of the place? I have your room plan here and a proposed list of items we will need to acquire. I have prepared a proposal for the Palace treasurer for funding; I only need the final list of items and the total amount."

"No, this can wait until tomorrow," Enric told the young man when she was about to accept the offer. "Lady Eryn needs to go home and rest now. This is an order," he added quickly when she turned to him to protest. "You look as if you are about to collapse any minute, and there is a small, wild mountain cat waiting for us at home that will probably have started to tear things apart by now. Come. You can avail yourself of your tour tomorrow." He nodded to Rolan and all but pushed her out of her new study.

CHAPTER 11

Orrin's Wrath

Eryn leaned back and yawned. It had been an exhausting few hours, and she was tired, but she wouldn't have wanted to miss a single minute. After all that time she was finally not only getting really close to being able to heal again on a daily basis, but also to making a real difference by offering services that exceeded the capabilities of only one person by far.

She had started the day by meeting Rolan and having him guide her through the finished premises. There were clearly some minor things that needed to be improved, but nothing that would put a brake on her plans.

To her surprise and great delight her assistant had furnished two teaching rooms with simple tables and chairs, so that, basically, they were ready for use. That in turn meant that she could start the apothecary training sessions as soon as the books were ready.

He had been granted the funding for the furniture by the Royal chief treasurer, as it had only been a minor amount. It seemed as if her assistant, Rolan was entitled to request money up to an amount of twenty-five gold pieces upon presenting a bill to be paid. For larger amounts Eryn's signature was required.

The morning passed quickly, and only when her stomach started to complain did she realise that half the day had already passed.

She had been really pleased with Rolan's efforts during her absence. It seemed that he had handled the apothecaries, who had turned out to be as demanding and difficult as she had anticipated, with grace and efficiency. They had contacted him almost every day - even though Rolan had reminded them repeatedly when she was expected back and that he was unable to decide anything without her.

There would have to be a meeting with them, but not today. First she wanted to talk to Vern about the time frame for producing the books. And there was the little matter of asking Orrin to resume training with her.

She decided to send a messenger to Orrin and see if he could be persuaded to meet her in his quarters, preferably with something to eat prepared. The reply came back shortly with the curt invitation so typical of him.

"Nice way of keeping your expenses low, inviting yourself for lunch at other people's homes. I suppose if you keep that up for the next few decades, you might save the money that your new residence has cost," he greeted her, beaming widely.

She sighed with theatrical remorse. "You have found me out, Orrin. I had hoped for some more time before you worked me out on this one, but it seems that I underestimated you. You are too smart for me."

"I am glad you finally saw that. Come, the food is getting cold." He led her to the dinner table. "Is there any particular reason to which I owe the pleasure of your unexpected company, or have you just been missing me?"

"I have, of course, missed you terribly. Vern is quite annoying at times, but still a poor substitute for you. And there is also something I want to talk to you about. Two things, in fact," she explained while she took a seat and smelled the aroma of food. "But let us eat first. I am starving."

"Yes, I can see that," Orrin remarked caustically as she took the first bite before he had even sat down with her. "You look tired. Didn't get much sleep last night, I bet." He grinned when her cheeks flushed red.

"Shut up, Orrin! After scolding me about unsuitable table conversations that one time, you should know better."

"Only for the boy - you are a grown woman. And there is not much that tends to make you uneasy, so I have to work with what I find," he replied, shrugging.

She continued eating, not willing to let herself be further teased by him before she had filled her stomach enough to deal with it properly. Smiling to herself, she wondered how he would react to her proposal of training together again.

"Why are you smiling?" he enquired, suspicious. "It makes me nervous, like you are about to hit me with something."

"Nervous? Big, unshakeable you? You destroy my illusions of your unflappability."

"Really? I wasn't aware you were harbouring such illusions."

She laughed. "How couldn't I? That's how people generally see you, solid as a rock, and unmovable as one."

He put down his cutlery and leaned back. "Do they now..." He waited for her to finish eating before he said, "So, out with it. What brings you here?"

"Don't you want to talk in your study?"

"Is it official Order business?"

She thought for a moment. "No, not as such."

"Then let's stay here." He rose and prepared two hot drinks, placing one in front of her. "I am listening."

"You arranged for Plia to be given that apprenticeship at the Palace kitchen back then. I wanted to let you know that I plan to offer her another one with me. She is very talented with herbs. I hope this does not paint you in a bad light or makes you feel that you wasted a favour for nothing."

He smiled. "Don't worry about that. I offered it to you back then to induce you to fight in Lord Enric's competition, so calling in that favour was useful in any case. This is quite a step up for her, and I have been told that she works hard and diligently. I am glad she can get this chance. Where will she live? You are aware that her lodgings at the Palace will no longer be available if she stops working there, aren't you?"

She shook her head and sighed. "No, I haven't thought of that. Though I should have - it's logical. I will have to think of something. Maybe Enric has an idea."

"But that's not what you came here to talk about, is it?"

"No, not primarily. I want to continue my combat training with you." She watched his brow first rise in surprise and then furrow into a frown.

"Why?" He recalled all those weary months of resistance, of her unwillingness, and his relief when that was finally over and the burden of making her fight had been taken off him by Enric.

"Because I need to stop Enric harassing me; he can't be my trainer, superior and companion. It weighs upon him, and subsequently on me when he loses patience with me."

"He has lost patience with you?" Orrin enquired mildly. That did not sound like Enric as he knew him, but then Eryn had already managed to cause quite a few rents in that seemingly solidly impenetrable exterior of his.

She thought back to the evening before, remembering their conversation in Lord Tyront's study. "Yes, I think he has. When he got up from that chair yesterday, his fingers had left marks from grabbing it so hard."

"Which chair?"

"In Lord Tyront's study. I was there to give my report on the expedition. I wouldn't say it went all that well." She shook her head at the troublesome memory as if trying to dislodge it. "Lord Tyront was just mildly disapproving in this way he has, but Enric was boiling under his stony façade. I was expecting him to explode any moment, but that wouldn't be like him, would it?" Her smile was thin.

"Good thing it isn't. I wouldn't want to be near once he does." He tried to think back to the reports he had received from Barul, if they had contained anything that would have justified such a reaction from Enric.

"What was he so upset about?" he enquired when nothing came to his mind.

"The attack at the inn. But that was hardly a justification for..."

"The *what*?" Orrin interrupted her sharply and leaned forward to stare at her in sudden anger.

Oh, bother! It seemed they hadn't told him about it. Damn them all, how was she to know that they hadn't even talked to Orrin about this? She was in no mood to face his wrath now as well. That was too much for two subsequent days, she had only just returned, after all.

Rising quickly, she smiled tensely. "You know what? I think I will come back some other time. It is not that urgent."

"Sit!" he barked and stared daggers at her when she didn't. "Now!"

She was about to point out that she wasn't obliged to take any orders from him, when she felt his hand close around her wrist and jerk her down onto the chair again.

"Orrin!" she exclaimed in annoyance. "You can't do that anymore! Things have changed, in case you hadn't noticed: I am no longer a prisoner!"

"Shut up," he growled and held on to her wrist. "The only thing I want to hear from you are answers to my questions."

She considered pushing him away with magic, but that would slice her chances of making him agree to train her again down to nothing. So she would have to endure this. Again.

"So you were attacked at an inn. When?"

"Second night," she murmured.

"Why haven't I heard about it?"

"Because none of the swordsmen was close when it happened, and I ordered Vern and the herb gatherers to keep their mouths shut."

"*Vern* was there as well?" His tone had become grave.

"Not during the attack, but afterwards," she quickly reassured him.

"Who was there during the attack?"

"Plia and myself."

"Where was the attack?"

"In our room."

"How many?"

"One. Now, is this interrogation really necessary? I feel like..."

"Shut up."

She did.

"What did he want?"

"A little fun with me," she said in a matter-of-fact tone.

"What did you do?"

"Stab him with my herb gathering knife."

"Why did he get close enough for you to do this?" His stare was intent, disapproving.

"Because he had moved close too quickly for me to shield."

"Close enough to touch you obviously, then. Did he hurt you?"

"No."

His grip on her wrist became stronger, and she groaned.

"Did he hurt you?"

"No! But you are starting to!"

"I can do this all day long if you keep lying to me. Did. He. Hurt. You."

How could he know that she was lying? She had been careful to avoid all the tell-tale signs. Damn! The answer would make him even angrier.

"A little."

"Where?"

"My throat."

"He was strangling you?" he asked with what she recognised as forced calm.

"Well, I would not exactly put it like..."

"Was he strangling you? Damn you, out with it or will use a truth block on you!" he all but shouted.

Swallowing, she nodded quickly. "Yes, he was strangling me."

"Then you stabbed him? With a knife?"

"Yes."

"Where was your sword?"

No, not that again! She'd had that discussion with Enric already, there was no need to be scolded for it all over again!

"I have been told off already, so please spare me your indignation!" She tried to pull her hand free, but he kept holding on to it. His eyes narrowed and she felt warmth seep from his palm into her wrist. He was obviously making good on his threat and using a truth block now. So his patience had started running out. Not good.

"Where was your sword?" he repeated his question. "And don't even think of fighting me, my girl," he hissed when she started drawing on her own magic to free herself. "I would make the incident public, and you would find it very hard to get another expedition approved any time soon. My expertise as combat trainer in assessing your self-defence skills would not shed a favourable light on your ability to lead others anywhere."

"Are you blackmailing me?" She stared at him in disbelief.

"I thought that was rather obvious. But if you need to hear me say it: yes, I am blackmailing you. And now answer me. I am tired of repeating my questions over and over again. Where was your sword?"

"In my bag."

"Where was the bag?"

"On a hook on the wall."

"Why was it not close by and handy for use?"

"I didn't think I would need it." There we go again, she thought.

"Really. You didn't think you would need it. And you also didn't think you would need the guards that were sent along for your protection, or they would at least have known about it. Why didn't you tell them?"

"I didn't want this to be reported. I didn't want to worry anybody here or be ordered back."

"And you think that finding out about it afterwards, and that you were trying to hide it is any less of a reason to worry for us? You idiot!" He let go of her hand and lifted his index finger. "You will not go on another expedition or leave the city for whatever purpose without either me or Lord Enric. Shut up!" he added when she was about to speak again. "And, in addition, ordering Vern to keep this from me is totally unacceptable. I am his father and I am responsible for him."

"He was not in any danger. The attacker was unconscious before I called for him," she said calmly, understanding that concern at least.

"I know that he wasn't. But you were, and unnecessarily so. And the girl was, too. It was your responsibility to keep the both of you safe. You failed," he added with finality.

Sucking in a sharp breath, she looked away. That remark had been well aimed.

"I won't have you fail again. I will train you." His voice was calm again.

She looked back at him and gulped at the smile on his lips. It was a rather alarming smile.

"If you thought that the months before were hard, you will soon learn that they were child's play compared to what you are going to face. I will see you tomorrow morning at the training grounds. Don't be late. You may leave me now."

When she stood in the corridor outside his door, she blinked and wondered how this ended up going so completely differently from what she had planned. It had been foolish and careless to assume that he had been told about the attack. But he had agreed to training her, hadn't he? That at least was something to be satisfied with, wasn't it?

This superior-subordinate relationship did not at all work with him, at least not the way it was meant to. Rather, it functioned in reverse. Using a truth block on her had been a risky move from his side. And making her endure it by blackmailing her all the more. But maybe that was something she would one day be able to use to make him do what *she* wanted.

She slowly descended the stairs, walking towards the exit of the warriors' quarters. She was due for her next meeting in about half an hour in Lord Tyront's study to discuss the applicants for the vacancies for healers with him and Lord Poron. She hoped that would turn out to be more pleasant than the encounter with Orrin. But then it could hardly turn out much worse, could it?

* * *

"You look like you've had a trying day," Enric commented when she arrived and hung her cloak on a hook in the cubby-hole.

She smiled tiredly and took a seat next to him on the settee, glancing at the book he had put aside when she had entered. Something on architecture. She thought about the many occasions when she had seen him sitting in the parlour with a book in his hands and only now realised that he really was a prolific reader. Why had she never consciously noticed that before? Especially with her own affinity for books? Was it because a literate fighter didn't fit in with her picture of the world?

"Good book?" she asked.

"It's alright. I am looking for some inspiration for the courtyard between the buildings."

"And have you been lucky so far?"

"There are a couple of things I am thinking about, yes. Such as a sheltered passageway from one building to the other."

She thought for a moment. "I suppose that would be handy for the servants, they could change between buildings without freezing or slipping in the winter; or getting wet when it rains. And they wouldn't have to brave Urban."

He smiled. "Yes, that was the idea."

Leaning against him, she took his hand. "That is very considerate of you, you know."

"I'm thinking it will be hard enough to get servants to work here once our little beast starts to grow. Some consideration for the workers might go a long way here." He lifted her chin. "Are you trying to avoid talking about your day for some reason?"

She smiled weakly. "Why is it so damn hard to keep something to myself these days?"

"Why don't you give up trying if you have already realised this? Who have you been trying to withhold information from this time?"

"Orrin. I visited him today to ask him if he would take over my training again."

"And? Did he agree?"

"Yes. But I am not sure I want him to do the training anymore."

Enric frowned. "What happened? Did you have a fight?"

"I am not sure if you could call it that. I think a fight would have been better than what he turned our meeting into." She shook her head. "I'd gone in assuming that he had been told about the attack and mentioned it. I soon found out that he had *not* been aware of it."

He grimaced. "My guess is he didn't appreciate the news."

"Yes, you could say that, if you wanted to grossly understate it." She found it wiser to keep to herself the nature of Orrin's means of persuasion for making her talk. There was no telling how Enric would react to the little matter of the truth block, even though he himself had threatened to use one on her only the evening before.

But then it might be a different case for him when he himself was resorting to such means compared with somebody else doing it. "He did agree training me, but I'm afraid that it is not going to be too pleasant for me."

"Are you regretting swapping me already?" Enric smirked.

"I think I am starting to, yes. Ask me again tomorrow after my first session with him." The thought of being at Orrin's mercy again was not a pleasant one right now.

"He is eager not to waste any time, it would seem."

"Eager somehow to punish me, I fear." She looked up at him. "And I don't see you taken aback sufficiently by that," she complained.

"You know what I think about the whole matter. And I have to say that it pleases me tremendously that Orrin seems to take a position similar to my own on this." He bent down to brush his lips against hers. "So you exchanged one demanding combat trainer for another. Pity you didn't choose one lacking any personal connection to you. I wonder if being trained by a father figure isn't worse than by your lover. He doesn't have to worry about your making him sleep in the guest room, after all."

She pressed him for more. "So you have accepted that I am not the object of his secret desires?"

"Yes, I am pleased to say that I have. Seeing him with Junar did make reaching this conclusion a lot easier." And seeing Eryn with a substitute father after having lost her own when she had been much too young to be forced to fend for herself was good for her, very much so. Even if she herself was not really aware that she was sometimes still in need of that figure.

"There is something else he said that has me thinking. It's about Plia and her apprenticeship in the Palace kitchen. If she renounces that job, she is no longer entitled to a room at the Palace. Does the Order have any non-magician apprentices?"

Enric shook his head. "No. The things taken care of by non-magicians are not administered by the Order. So we don't have any living arrangements for apprentices."

That was a troubling matter, she thought, and sighed. It needed to be solved before she could offer the girl a position. Maybe Plia could stay in the healers' building? There were still quite a few rooms that were not yet assigned to any particular function. But a girl of thirteen living alone in that building without domestic servants or even a kitchen? And she would be completely alone there at night, helpless if anybody decided to break in or worse. No, that was not on the table.

Enric watched her, obviously deep in thought, for a while before he said, "You know, there is a rather obvious solution to that problem, my love."

Eryn looked up in surprise. "There is? What is it?" How obvious could it be if it had not occurred to her, she wondered.

"We do have two unoccupied guest rooms upstairs. We could offer her one for the duration of her apprenticeship."

"What?" She searched his eyes to make sure he was being serious. But he wouldn't attempt a cruel joke like that. "You would be willing to let her move in with us? You are aware that it would be for at least two years and not just a few months, aren't you?"

"Yes. And yes, I am aware that it is a longer commitment." He put a loose strand of hair behind her ear and watched her swallow. "You are not going to cry, are you?" he asked softly.

Shaking her head, she blinked a few times and smiled. "Thank you. This is incredibly generous of you. I would never have dared asking for a thing like that."

Enric nodded. "I know. And I am rather sorry for that. I would very much like you to come to me when there is something you need or want. You know I have considerable means at my disposal."

Snuggling up close to him, she buried her head in the warm hollow of his neck and shoulder. "I will work on that. I promise. One day you will look back to this very moment and fervently wish you had never said this, when I start making one demand after the other. Jewellery, fancy clothes and all that."

Chuckling, he stroked her back. "I doubt that very much. Whenever I have a fancy gown made for you, it is a fight to get you into it. The day you start ordering them in great numbers is when I start worrying about your sanity." He breathed in the scent of her hair. It smelled faintly of the herbal soap she used for washing it. There was also some kind of fruit in there somewhere. He had come to prefer the scent to any created perfume he had ever smelled.

"How was your meeting with Tyront and Lord Poron? Have you agreed on the candidates?"

"Nothing final. I think I tried their patience a bit when I insisted on meeting the candidates before making a decision. There are things I need to ask that cannot answered by the sheets of paper they showed me. I need to get a feeling for the applicants, see if they are suitable, if I can imagine working with them."

"But they agreed to meeting them?" he enquired.

"Yes, they did. We have narrowed the list down to six, so we should be able to have a look at them within two days. Rolan has finished the teaching rooms, so basically I can start training them as soon as we have made the decisions."

"That sounds very good. Am I to assume that working with Rolan has turned out to be less of a trial than you expected?" She could detect a hint of amusement in his voice.

"For now, yes. He is surprisingly useful, I have to admit. But he doesn't like me. That makes working with him a bit of an effort," she sighed.

He kissed her forehead. "Give him time. He will fall for you, just like the rest of us."

She grinned up at him. "Like the rest? Who has fallen for me, apart from you?"

"Orrin. Vern. Junar. Plia. The King. Lord Poron. And to a certain degree even Tyront."

"Lord Tyront?" She grimaced. "That's not the impression I have."

"I think that is how he prefers it. It has taken him years to show me more than professional appreciation. He wanted to keep his distance, as affection makes leading more difficult. I have only now started to understand this," he added with a pointed look at her.

"The King hasn't exactly fallen for me, either. He enjoys me as a diversion, playing with me. He told me as much."

Enric raised both brows. "He did? When?"

"The day before my departure, when he amused himself with a little test in political strategy." She shifted uneasily at the memory. "He told me that he likes to touch me because it is meant to be reminder that he would have enjoyed taking me to bed that night after the ball if you hadn't made me agree to a commitment."

He pursed his lips. "He told you that, did he?"

She nodded. "Yes, he said that it would work even better now that I was fully aware of it. Devious man, isn't he?"

"Indeed. Very much so, considering his youth. But be assured that he will do nothing more than make you uneasy. He can't be seen to break a commitment he himself has forged. It wouldn't look good. Try not to let this bother you too much."

She shook her head. "I know, and I won't. There is something else he said, though. I only thought of it now. He knows that you lied to him about my shield."

Enric stiffened. "What?" His voice sounded alarmed. "Are you sure of this?"

"Yes. He said something about this being the point when he first thought of how to make me join the Order: when you lied to him about my protective field. I am not sure if he knows what the exact nature of your lie was, if he knows that you could have removed it or if he thinks that there was nothing there at all. Maybe that's why he was so confident that he would have been able to take me to bed."

"That is an unpleasant surprise, I'll admit," he said with a deep frown. "I will have to discuss this with Tyront tomorrow. Though there is one thing I don't understand." He shook his head. "When he summoned us to the throne room that day, we assumed that he wanted to inform us that he intended to use you to produce a magically gifted heir to the throne. If he was aware that I was lying, what has kept him from pursuing that plan?"

She thought for a moment. "Are you sure that this was his plan?"

"Tyront's informant seemed to think so."

"You know," she said with a grim smile, "I learned quite a bit about him last time. And I would not at all be surprised if he had planted that information for the agent to find and pass on. In

Tyront's place I would assume that this particular source of information is no longer anonymous. There might have been a plan behind it, but maybe not the one you thought."

Enric stared at her. "Look at you. Again you prove to be a very speedy learner."

"Are you very worried? He did not seem angry when he told me this."

He thought for a moment, then sighed. "Not exactly worried, more unpleasantly surprised. But he has not taken any action to expose or counteract my lie, so I assume that he either expected it, which probably should worry me as he might know me better than I was aware of, or that it has not made any real difference to him." He made to get up from the settee. "Come - it's late. Let's retire for tonight."

"Wait," she said and held on to his hand. "There is one more thing I wanted to ask you. How did you find out about the attack at the inn? I know that one of the two swordsmen, either Torvig or Grend, must have been your spy. I am pretty sure I managed to hide it from them. Orrin's informant had not known about it, so I think it was not common knowledge."

"I had two more agents following you. They are good at listening and buying drinks for the right people. They found out about the attack from the publican one day after you left and also obtained a copy of the magistrate's report for me."

"You had *three* spies set on me?" she asked incredulously. "And that does not seem rather excessive to you?"

"No, considering your hide-and-seek games, it seems to have been the required minimum, and I pride myself on my foresight. And I do like to keep an eye on what is mine. Several, in fact. You might want to consider that next time you are thinking about trying anything like that."

She smiled lopsidedly. "That you have me watched or that I am yours?"

"Both, my love. Both."

CHAPTER 12

Threatening Orrin

Orrin was waiting for her the next morning, leaning against the house wall with folded arms. Eryn noted that he was neither wearing armour nor carrying a sword. That was unusual for lessons involving fighting. What was he planning now?

"Good morning," he said in a mood that was much more relaxed than her own. It seemed his anger at her from the day before had melted away. Eryn just gave him a curt nod. She was still annoyed at him for his audacity with her yesterday.

"Take off your armour. We won't need it today. Bring it only every second time. Or better leave it here with me, and I will bring it when I plan on using swords. Come." He pushed himself off the wall and waited at the entrance to the training arena while she was unbuckling the leather protection.

"Sword fighting," he explained, "is the minimum requirement for every member of the Order. It is the one discipline we all have to train at, no matter how old or high up in status we are. But this doesn't mean that it is the only useful one there is. And with your reluctance to use weapons and your refusal to carry them in a way so they would actually be useful, I think we will have to try another approach: unarmed combat."

She laughed. "What? Fist fighting?" Her laugh slowly died away when he just raised his brows. "Oh, come on! You can't be serious! How can I ever prevail against a man in a purely physical fight without using so much magic that I would accidentally break a neck?"

"By learning how to do it properly. This is not about strength, but technique and reaction. If you have an opponent who uses a lot of strength against you, you can use this to your advantage."

"How?" she asked, intrigued. The idea of defending herself without the aid of potentially lethal weapons *did* hold a certain appeal.

"By using his momentum for a counterattack, for example."

At that moment a messenger arrived with a small wooden box. He bowed and presented it to Orrin with a note. Eryn frowned when she recognised Enric's seal on it. She watched the warrior open it and then a broad grin spread on his face. He turned the box so she could look inside, and she closed her eyes when she saw the golden bangles.

"How very considerate of him. He writes that you seem to have forgotten them when you left for the training session with me. Forgotten, eh? Lucky for us he found them, isn't it?" He took them out of the box and held them out for her to take.

She looked at them in annoyance. After talking to Orrin yesterday - or rather, after having been interrogated by him - she had decided to forego the manacles and benefit from her advantage in strength rather than putting herself at his mercy completely. But she hadn't told that to Enric as she didn't want to inform him of the truth block.

Orrin stepped closer to put them on her when she made no move to do so herself. She fought the impulse to step back and instead let him fasten the deceptively harmless looking jewellery on her wrists. She thought back to that evening, so many months ago, when he had put them on her the first time in his parlour. When she looked up into his face, she saw a faint smile playing around his lips.

"We have come a long way, haven't we?" he said quietly, obviously thinking of the same situation.

"That we have, yes. Though yesterday you made me question that impression."

"It was for your own good."

"Was it? That's pretty much what Ram'an said when *he* did this. Where is the difference, if I may ask?" She was proud of herself for keeping her tone calm and reasonable.

"Because my reasons were not selfish like his. I was considering only your safety."

He sealed the bracelets closed and she felt only a slight decrease in her powers. So that was how strong he was. He had considerable magical strength at his disposal, she mused. Not a lot weaker than herself, but then of course he wouldn't be. He was number five in the Order, after all, and had been number three before she and Enric had come along.

"In the future try not to treat me like a child," she said evenly. "I can't afford to indulge you like this if I want to save face."

"The way we are treated reflects the way we behave most of the time," he replied. "And saving face will not be an issue. I wouldn't have done a thing like that in front of witnesses."

"Are you telling me I behaved like a child? Because I decided not to share certain information with you? Would you accuse Enric of the same? I dare say there are quite a few things he doesn't tell you."

"We are not talking about confidential information here. We are talking of stupidity. If you hadn't been aware of how idiotic your actions were, you wouldn't have tried to avoid telling me. So stop being angry at me for being in the right."

"That is not why I am angry! Alright, you may have a point. I should have reacted differently, should have had my sword close at hand. But using a truth block on me was taking it too far, don't you think? I am your superior, after all!" Damn, she thought. This was not a good time to have her powers diminished.

"If you have to point that out so explicitly, this probably means that you don't fill out the role yet, don't you think?"

It was the smirk that made her say her next words.

"Really? Then I suppose a proper superior would report a violation of the rules such as that?" She regretted the words as soon as they were out of her mouth. But there was no taking them back.

He didn't react the way she would have expected. No anger, no apprehension, no sign of distress whatsoever. He just concentrated his gaze and asked mildly, almost amusedly, "You wouldn't be trying to threaten me, would you?"

"Why would that be so improbable? You blackmailed me yesterday. That was a threat." She folded her arms.

"You have a lot to learn, my girl." He gave her a smile loaded with heaviness. "And you are lucky, I am in the mood to teach you."

He then took her by the wrist and started walking towards Kingsway.

"Wait, what was that supposed to mean? Where are you taking me?" She tried to pull her hand free, but of course it was hopeless. She would have been able to free herself with her full powers at her disposal, but not when their magical force was balanced and he had the greater physical strength.

"We will pay Lord Enric a little visit. I assume he is working from his new residence?"

"What do you want from Enric?" Then she groaned. "You are dragging me there to tell him yourself? Just to show me that you can't be blackmailed? And you think you know him well enough to be certain that there will be no consequences for you? That is foolhardy, Orrin! I had no intention of telling him, so let's stop this little game right here."

He stopped and turned to her. "An empty threat, then?"

"Well, that would be one way of phrasing it, I suppose," she admitted sullenly. "I would rather call it *words spoken in anger that don't reflect my meaning clearly*."

Orrin shook his head. "Different words, but it still feels like an empty threat." He pulled her on.

Along the way she kept trying to dissuade him, but he ignored her. When they reached the building, Orrin pounded on the entrance door loudly, and it was opened by a servant almost immediately.

"I need to see Lord Enric," he barked and entered without invitation. The servant's eyes widened when he spotted Eryn being dragged in behind the magician.

"Then you had better come to my study." Enric spoke matter-of-factly, emerging on their left, doubtless perturbed by the assertive knock. He looked with some concern at Eryn as she tried to pry open Orrin's fingers around her wrist without success. It seemed the training was not exactly going well so far.

"What is it you need to see me about?" he continued, calmly closing the door behind them.

Orrin waited until Enric had taken a seat at the edge of the desk and was looking at them in anticipation before he released Eryn's wrist.

"Lady Eryn wishes to inform you of what she deems a violation of the rules," he said and turned to her. "Now go on."

"Orrin, you bloody fool!" she hissed. "Enric, I am sorry we have bothered you. It was a misunderstanding that has brought us here." When she made to turn and walk out again, she felt strong fingers close around her wrist again and relentlessly hold her back.

"Seriously, would you stop doing that? I am not a horse on a bridle, you know," she complained.

"Lord Enric," Orrin said and looked his superior straight in the eyes, "there is something I wish to make known to you. Yesterday when Eryn visited me to ask me to train her again, I made her tell me about the incident at the inn at the second night of the expedition."

Enric nodded slowly. "I am aware of that." What was going on here?

"Are you also aware of the fact that I used a truth block on her?"

Enric raised his brow. "No, this is new." Not good, Enric decided. That was the trouble with being told officially: now there was some kind of action required. He didn't mind Orrin's rather harsh course of action in this case, especially as he himself had been about to resort to the same means of interrogation only one day earlier. But now it had been officially reported to him, and there was the fact that Eryn was technically Orrin's superior so his action could be seen as insubordination. Eryn was obviously not very happy about this conversation, either.

"May I ask why you thought this necessary?"

"I was very worried about her personal safety and have taken it upon myself to better her ability to defend herself. For this I felt it necessary to judge the exact level of her incompetence without her trying to keep something from me."

"Incompetence?" she cried out, but both men ignored her as if she was an insignificant presence in the room.

"I see," Enric said slowly. "So she had asked you to take over her training *before* you used the truth block on her?"

"Yes," Orrin nodded.

"Eryn did not use her advantage in superior strength to stop you, so it seems. Why not?"

"Because I told her that her failure to cooperate would result in my recommendation as chief warrior trainer that sending her on another expedition anytime soon would not be advisable."

Enric pursed his lips and frowned to hide the smile that wanted to spread. "From where I stand you have acted in your capacity as her trainer to analyse the scope of what she needs to be taught," he said carefully. "May I ask why you have felt the sudden urge to come here and report your use of the truth block?" he asked mildly.

"Because Eryn felt that my behaviour was not in accordance with the rules."

Enric looked over to her. She was annoyed and kept scowling at Orrin. So it appeared she had tried to threaten or blackmail or otherwise set him boundaries, and he had taught her a little lesson of how hard it was to do this with a principled person.

"Do you still feel that, Eryn?" Enric enquired. "Is there any particular action you feel should be taken and that you want to request at this point?"

"No, of course not," she said stiffly and then added, "Unless you are willing to kick him properly for me for dragging me here."

"No, that would be inappropriate, I am afraid." He chuckled. "But as you have a training session scheduled right now, I would assume you can do it yourself. Or at least give it a try."

"Thank you for your time, Lord Enric." Orrin sounded very pleased with himself and politely lifted his hand to indicate for Eryn to leave the study first.

"Yes, great," she murmured with an evil look at him. "Suddenly we are concerned with politeness?"

Enric watched them leave and returned to his paperwork. He wondered how Orrin would have reacted if he had dealt him a punishment. Endured it, very likely. It would probably have made his demonstration even more effective.

"That was completely ridiculous! If you wanted to show off how luck runs with the brave, then you have succeeded," she grumbled.

"What I was demonstrating to you, you numbskull, was that you can't get away with threatening me with things like that. You already had your exam in political strategy, didn't you? My main one is to not do anything I can't justify to myself and that I am not willing to pay the price for. So for future reference: You can save yourself the trouble of trying to threaten me. The only thing you can effectively threaten me with is hurting the ones I love. And that wouldn't end well," he added grimly. Then he shot her an annoyed look. "As you happen to be among that select group, that also counts for you endangering yourself."

"Alright, message received." Then she grinned broadly and put her hand through his arm. "So you love me, hmm? That is so sweet." She pressed a quick kiss on his clean-shaven cheek, touched by the unexpected admission. There had not been many people in her life who ever told her that before. Only her father.

"Will that keep you from tormenting me too badly during our training sessions?" she asked, full of hope.

He stopped walking and turned to her to pinch her cheek and sneer. "Oh, Sunshine. Of course not."

* * *

Eryn looked up from the apothecaries' training schedule she was working on when a knock sounded at her study door in the healers' building.

"Come in," she called and Plia entered. She was wearing her kitchen uniform, looking neat and tidy with her hair pinned up.

"Hello Eryn," she smiled. "You sent for me?"

"Yes, I did. Why don't you sit."

The girl nodded and came closer to take a seat on the only other chair in the room in front of Eryn's desk.

"You surely remember our conversation out in the woods a few days ago. We talked about the chance of your working with herbs and leaving your apprenticeship at the Palace." Eryn smiled. "I am very happy to tell you that I am now in a position to offer you an apprenticeship here. The Order has agreed. You would train to become what we have decided to call a Medical Herbalist. You would be trained partly with the herb gatherers, partly with the apothecaries, and partly alone. As for your lodgings at the Palace, I was told that you would have to give them up, but Lord Enric has proposed another arrangement I hope will be to your liking. He has invited you to stay in one of the guest rooms in our residence for the duration of your apprenticeship."

Plia's hands rose to cover her mouth. "I really can work here? With you? And live in your new house with you?"

Eryn nodded. "Yes. Provided living with a growing mountain cat doesn't scare you enough to turn down that offer. So, what do you say? Do you need some time to think about it? Sleep on it?"

The girl quickly shook her head. "No, nothing of the kind. I accept. With all my heart!" She beamed and was obviously trying hard to continue sitting still on the chair when she would have preferred letting out the energy and excitement that was coursing through her. "When can I start? What do I need?"

"You can start as soon as you have terminated your apprenticeship at the Palace. How does this work exactly - can you just go there and say that you are leaving and be gone, or do you need to stay there for a while longer?"

"I don't know for sure. I need talk to Cook about that. As far as I know there is no major banquet, ball or something coming up, so it should be possible to leave soon." She darted up from her chair. "I will take care of this now and let you know." And without waiting to be sent away she all but ran out of the room.

The door connecting her own room with Rolan's opened slowly. "Is the orphan girl gone?" he enquired, sticking his head into her study.

Eryn looked at him tersely. "She has a name, you know. And I am pretty sure that you know it, it was on the list for the expedition. You better change that attitude towards her. She is about to become your colleague."

She saw the quick look of annoyance before he had his demeanour under control again. Privileged, arrogant young idiot, she thought and released a muted sigh. They would have to work on that. Fortunately, he was good enough at his job for this to be worth the effort.

"So the orph... Plia will start working here if I understand you correctly? In what capacity, if I may ask?"

This time her sigh was audible. She beckoned him to step into the room. "If you want to have a proper conversation with me, come in here and sit down. I find it distracting talking to you like this, perched in the doorway between two rooms."

Rolan seemed to consider that for a moment, then opened the door fully and walked to her desk to do as he had been bidden.

"Plia will start working here as soon as she has given notice of leaving her prior apprenticeship in the Palace kitchen."

"I don't see that we need kitchen staff here."

"She will not be kitchen staff here. I will train her as a medical herbalist, and she will be responsible for the herbs and medication we purchase and make here."

"Why was I not told about this?" he asked brusquely.

"Because the idea is still new and was granted by Lord Tyront only two days ago after my return. I am telling you *now*. We need to prepare a room she can work in here on the first floor. I will make a list of items she requires and give it to you. I am currently working on the teaching plan for the apothecaries and hope to finish it within the next three days. When they come back to pester you, you can tell them to mentally prepare for their training to start in about one month. The books should be finished and also copied by then."

"I had intended to refer them to you when they return, now that you are back," Rolan said, his expression slightly panicked.

She pretended to think about this for a moment, before she shook her head. "No, I like the idea of your dealing with them more."

"Figures," he murmured.

"Pardon?" she asked sharply and he rose hastily.

"Nothing. I need to get back to calculating the funding we need for the treatment rooms." He all but fled back to his office.

It was only noon. Too soon to try and get a hold of Vern, he would still be having lessons. Sighing, she pulled one of the books on herbs she had brought with her from her study at home towards her. There were still quite a few passages to prepare to accompany Vern's illustrations. Her father's books contained a lot of information about plant structure, but hardly anything about how to handle them and where to find them. She would have to add that. But that would not be that much of an effort as there were only about fifteen herbs they had worked with on their trip.

She prepared a note instructing Vern to come and see her as soon as he was free. She needed to see how far he had progressed in colouring his drawings. But he'd probably also had a lot to catch up on after missing his lessons for almost two weeks.

There was one thing that she could take care of without waiting for anything or anybody else: planning the healers' training periods. The rooms were ready, and there was not much more she needed - apart from her students of course. The only thing that needed taking care of was having a few books copied by the scribes. That was something she could arrange right now. She changed the note to tell Vern that he was to come and see her at her study at home instead of here and told Rolan where she was heading.

* * *

When she opened the door into the parlour, Urban came running out of Enric's office and started to attack a cushion on one of the sofas viciously. Eryn quickly snatched it away, but it was too late; the damage was done already.

"You are a little monster," she scolded the cub and picked her up. Small but sharp claws pierced her skin in a playful fight. "Oh my," she gasped. "I hope you'll stop that when you get older, or you're going to tear me to shreds with these paws of yours."

"Back already?" Enric strolled out of his study as she put the young cat down again. He eyed the latest casualty and poked his finger through one of four parallel slits. "Another cushion gone. I guess it doesn't really make sense to order new ones as long as she is growing."

"Hardly," Eryn agreed and wondered when they had reached the stage in their relationship where they discussed ordering lounge cushions.

"That was a very interesting visit in the morning," Enric mentioned casually and followed her into her study.

She turned to him, her arms akimbo. "Yes, I found that, too. Especially as you seem to turn unexpectedly lenient towards people who question me with the aid of magic. Where has that overly possessive urge to protect me gone?"

He shrugged. "Asleep for now. As Orrin's motivation was protecting you, I can hardly blame him. Would you have wanted me to punish him for this action?"

Looking helpless, she turned to her book shelves and started assembling the books of which she required copies for the healers.

"No, not as such," she admitted. "But scaring him a bit by telling him that next time he does a thing like that there will be dire consequences would have been nice."

"Doesn't work on Orrin, I am sorry to tell you. And I'd venture that this was what he wanted to teach you - that threatening him is rather futile, or am I mistaken?"

"No, you are not." She turned back to him, a stack of books carefully balanced in her arms. "How do you deal with a man like that? How do you direct him?"

"Certainly not by threatening him," Enric replied mildly. "He would see it as a challenge to show you that he can and will take whatever you decide to dish out to him. And more."

"Such as whatever punishment he might have got today?"

"Yes. He would have accepted it willingly. And he would have done the exact same thing again in a similar situation. That's principles for you. He is practically incorruptible, which has its downsides as well, I'll admit."

"That's alright, I can always bribe Vern," she grinned. "Fortunately, this seems not to be a family trait."

"How was your training session today?"

She groaned when she remembered. "I would never have thought that fighting without weapons could be so incredibly painful! Without my healing skills I would be black and blue all over and hardly able to walk by now."

"Unarmed combat?" Enric asked with sudden interest and looked thoughtful. "Good strategy. I imagine you will show less restraint when there is no danger of killing somebody in a fight."

"I was told that you can kill people with your bare hands if you know how," she pointed out.

"True, but usually not accidentally. How did your first lesson go, then?"

"He broke one of my ribs. Twice," she grumbled. "I don't mind telling you that I look forward to using the sword again next time."

"So he switches between armed and unarmed combat? Good, I was worried that he would neglect sword fighting. It is a compulsory discipline, after all."

She snorted. "Orrin neglecting anything? Hardly."

Enric watched her unload her book selection onto her desk and then took her hand. Her skin was marred by several bloody scratches from the cat.

"Would you allow me? I would like to keep in practice."

She smiled broadly. "By all means. Let's see if you do it properly."

He closed his eyes and a moment later she felt first the warmth of his exploratory magical impulse to determine the extent of the damage before he started working on it. He took his time and worked very accurately until every single scratch was cleaned and sealed shut again.

"Well done," she nodded and touched the repaired skin. "I am proud of you."

He brushed her cheek with his fingers. "I have been wanting to learn this since the day the apothecaries attacked you. I never want to see you hurt again without me being able to do something about it."

She looked up at the graveness in his voice. "It was only a harmless injury. Nothing life-threatening."

"It doesn't matter. I would have been content with healing the scratch you had on your cheek. Doing something, anything." He lifted her chin and kissed her. "I can't bear seeing you hurt. It tears me apart."

She swallowed and leaned against him, hugging him close. She wanted to say something in return, but there were no words she would have dared to utter.

He looked down at the books she had put aside and picked one up while he still held her close with his other arm. "A selection of literature for the new healer trainees?"

"Yes," she confirmed, relieved for the intense moment to be over. "I will have these copied for them."

"Why don't you have an extra copy made for me as well? I suppose as a high-ranking leader I should keep track of the changes in the Order," he said airily.

"That is very responsible of you," she nodded solemnly. "I wonder how you could have been such a bad student when you like reading so much. How is this possible?"

"Because they gave me the wrong things to read. And I was expected to do it, which was another demotivation to learning."

"So you were a rebel? Or just lazy?" She smiled at the image of young, careless Enric.

"Both, I suppose. My prime objective was disappointing my father, I guess."

His family, she realised with a jolt. She had never even asked him about it. "Where is your father now?"

"He lives a day's ride from here with my mother and my younger brother. I haven't seen him in a while," he murmured. "We avoid each other as best we can."

She took his hands and pulled him into the parlour with her and onto a sofa. "Tell me about it. I would like to hear this."

He smiled faintly without humour. "It's not a very entertaining story, I am afraid."

Shrugging, she made herself comfortable. "I don't mind. I have already had my share of entertainment today."

Enric studied her for a while. He was not particularly comfortable talking about his family, but he was touched that she showed an interest in his past, in him. His companion, he thought, and smiled. He could talk about this with her.

"My father is a merchant, a successful one. He took over the business from his own father and made it flourish. Hard work, discipline, long days and nights, countless trips through the country to purchase new goods - that has been his life ever since." There was a faraway look in his eyes.

"That sounds as if you didn't see him very much when you were a child," she ventured carefully.

"True. And I wouldn't have minded very much about that. But I was the oldest son, and so he was determined to groom me to succeed him in the business. The trouble was that I had absolutely no inclination to follow in his footsteps. He started training me and continued to do so for about three years. I got to know my father pretty well during that time, and I found out that I didn't like him very much. That is not a happy discovery for a young boy who is supposed to be spending the next few decades working with his father. I had to accompany him on some of his buying trips and saw him taking other women to bed when he thought I was asleep in my room at the inn." He shook his head in disgust. "My mother has spent her life raising his children and tending his house. She came from a wealthy family and fell in love with my father, who was lower in status, and at that time also income, than other potential suitors. She grew up here in the city and left the comfort and her friends to be with him." He shook his head in regret. "She turned into a sad, disappointed woman over the years. And who could blame her? In addition to my brother I have a sister; she, too, is younger than I. She lives as far away from our parents as she can manage. Only my brother has stayed behind to take over the business. He was much better suited for it than me anyway, and I think we were both relieved when my magical abilities were discovered when I was about thirteen years old."

She felt sorry for him, for the pain it obviously still caused him.

"I never talked about my family when I was sent here to the Order. But it turned out that Tyront had gathered information about my childhood, and quite thoroughly, too. When I was tested and turned out to be second strongest in the Order, he summoned me to have a little talk with him when I failed to meet his expectations." He shook his head at the memory. "That was quite a surprise. He told me to grow up and deal with these issues so I could finally get over not wanting to be like my father and turn into somebody who deserved respect."

"Which you managed, obviously," she smiled.

"Yes," he nodded. "I did. But the pressure I thought I had escaped by leaving my parents came back again, only worse than before. I started studying as I had never before in my life, made myself familiar with the players in the political game, was trained by Orrin. Obviously, a leader that high up in the Order has to be seen to be a formidable fighter, among other things. And I pretty much gave up the luxury of friendships. None of them survived my rise to power. Tyront told me that he'd had the same problem and somehow we became friends in the years that came."

"That does sound a little lonely," she said quietly.

"It was at first, but after a while you start getting used to it. Tyront encouraged me to take a companion so I would have at least one person to trust and be close to. But after seeing my parents as I was growing up I was not a great believer in finding happiness that way. And I had never met a woman I could have imagined having more than a casual affair with." He took her hand and kissed it. "Until you came along. You were so brave, so infuriating, so disrespectful, so captivating. Watching you from my window was at first no more than entertainment, seeing you exchange blows with Orrin and provoking him. But after a while it started to trouble me that you hated me so much." He toyed with her fingers. "After the Freedom Night I thought I had satisfied my curiosity, but it got a lot worse instead. I was, for the first time in my life, jealous." Smiling, he shook his head. "Because of a woman who hated me and who didn't even know that I had been her lover for one night." He laughed quietly. "I remember the amused and knowing looks Tyront gave me. He must have been very pleased. For his own plans it was perfect. The only magician in the Order strong enough to meet you head-on apart from himself falling in love with you."

"You changed the topic," she said in mild rebuke. "You are talking about me instead of your family."

"A more pleasant topic than the other, or any other," he said gallantly.

"So you have no contact whatsoever with anybody in your family?"

"I occasionally write to my mother and my sister. My mother keeps writing about how well the business is running and how my brother's children are her pride and joy. My sister ran off with a tree feller when she was eighteen. I sent them some money for a few years and they managed to acquire a saw mill and start their own, successful business."

"When did you last see her?" Eryn enquired. There was evident pride in his eyes as he talked about his sister.

"It must have been about four years ago. She's had two children since then."

"I would very much like to meet her," she said carefully.

Enric looked at her. "You would?"

She nodded. "Yes."

He nodded slowly and thoughtfully. "Maybe we should do it. Get away from here for a few days." Then he sighed. "But I imagine that will have to wait for a while until the healing business has started running."

"That would be useful, yes. I suppose I wouldn't be very good company when I kept worrying about all the catastrophes that could be happening every minute that I was gone," she laughed. She cocked her head. "There is one thing that surprised me a bit. You said they only found out about your magical abilities by the time you were thirteen years old. How is that possible? I remember that I was much younger than that when I started using mine."

"I was certainly aware that I could do unusual things, but it was nothing special to me. When I worked out that I was a little different from other children, I had decided that keeping this to myself was an advantage. I only could do little things, mind you. Nothing bold or shocking. I warmed myself when I was cold, ran faster than others and stuff like that. When I was angry at my brother and accidentally shot a weak bolt of magic at him, though, they figured out what I was. My father was really pleased. He had managed to make quite a bit of money, but there was always the matter of his social status. And a magician as a son would boost this, of course. He did not react well to my teachers' reports of my laziness and defiance."

"So there was no history of magic on your father's side of the family? You mentioned that your mother came from an influential family. That influence didn't happen to have anything to do with magical ancestors?"

He smirked. "It did, as a matter of fact. Great deduction, my love. My maternal grandfather was a magician. He was rather high up, too. Rank four."

"Did you ever meet him?"

"No, he was long dead when I came to the city. And I dare say that back then he wouldn't have been too pleased with me. My mother's family still lives in the city, but as she defied them to run off with a lowly merchant, her branch of the family was considered a dead-end. They tried to approach me when I was evaluated for second in command, but by then I had decided that I had no intention of letting them use me to enhance their power and glory." He looked up and saw her frowning. "I see that this must sound terrible to you. Your entire family consisted of only the one person you loved so much, and he is gone. You would probably give a lot for some kind of family."

She nodded. "Yes, I admit I am a little sad at the thought of someone having family but deciding not to have anything to do with them."

"Don't be on my account. I have learned that family has nothing to do with being related by blood. It is no more than a matter of chance which parents you are born to. And look at yourself. Orrin treats you like a daughter, Vern like an older sister. It looks to me as if you assembled your own family here." He pulled her into his arms. "And I have you. That is more than I have ever had before." He looked down at Urban, who had fallen asleep under the table. "And of course the wild creature you dragged home from the woods."

She shook her finger at him. "Don't talk like this about our love child!"

"Our love child?" He grinned. "I will remind you of this the next time she's destroyed something of yours."

Eryn perked up. "Maybe I could leave out one or two of Junar's dresses..."

"You do that and I will make you wear them nevertheless," he threatened. "And will have two more made for you as punishment."

"Very considerate. Junar will come over tonight to help me with the curtains and carpet upstairs. I will casually mention that you consider wearing her dresses an apt punishment for me. She will be so thrilled," she chuckled.

"Yes, and imagine how pleased she will be after I tell her that you intended to let the cat have your dresses to play with. Why don't we see who she is more annoyed with then?"

They both looked up at the knock.

"That is probably Vern. I sent for him to talk about his illustrations for the books." She rose from the settee. "That will be my first official meeting in my new study here. Can you see that we are brought some refreshments? I need to welcome my guest now," she said loftily and went to answer the door.

CHAPTER 13

Getting Started

Vern looked up from his dinner tray when the servant conducted Eryn into the parlour. "You are early. I am not yet done eating."

She shrugged and took a seat next to him. "The interviews with the healers didn't need as long as I had allowed for. Take your time; I don't mind a short break myself. Where is Orrin?"

"Out with Junar. They are visiting her sister and her companion; you know, the one you healed back then: Gara."

"What? Orrin makes social calls?" She laughed. "That image seems strange somehow. How did that happen?"

"Don't ask me. She mentioned that she intended to visit her sister, and he offered to accompany her - out of the blue. She was as surprised as you. More so, actually."

Eryn shook her head. "Well how about that. It seems as if he really likes her."

"Yes, he does. He keeps hinting that she should move in here, but she pretends not to hear it. It's quite funny to watch," he added, showing little compassion for his father's vain endeavours.

"Do you think she will eventually give in and move in here? Would you mind if she did?"

Vern shrugged. "No, I like her. And it wouldn't make much of a difference to me if she moved in with us. She already spends more nights here than elsewhere. And she doesn't try to take on a mother's role or anything awkward like that."

"You think he will ask her to become his companion?"

"Why don't you ask him yourself? You let yourself be beaten up by him every few days, so, there is ample opportunity for you to ask him about this."

"Very funny. When I asked him to train me I wasn't aware that I was going to fight him with my bare hands."

"No sympathy here. If you had kept your mouth shut about the attack, this wouldn't be the case." He laughed at the irony. "But I have to say I find it hilarious that you ordered *me* not to say anything, and then you inadvertently said something yourself."

"I thought he knew! How could I know that Enric only knew because he had sent two more spies after me? I thought it was known to all four of my diligent supervisors!"

"Yes, whatever you say." He dismissively waved off her excuses and shoved his tray aside. "How did the interviews with the healer candidates go? Are any of them suitable healer material?"

"Yes, we had a look at three of them today, and one seems pretty capable. Good impression, polite, respectful, good grades, eager, motivated..."

"But?"

"What makes you think there is a *but*?"

"There must be one; I can hear it from your voice."

She exhaled heavily. "I remember him from the assessment. He was the first one who attacked me when I had not yet learned how to shield myself."

He stared at her. "You are joking, right? He didn't attack you, he was ordered to test the strength of your shield. Well, if there had been one at all. That is the standard procedure when testing a magician's strength, not just a vicious way to put you through pain and mayhem. If you want to blame somebody, blame Lord Tyront! He gave the command."

"I know that in my head! But when I saw his face today, I saw myself standing in the throne room again with his shooting bolts at me from his outstretched palm."

"You've had Lord Enric shooting bolts at you more often than once, and now you live with him. Don't tell me this is an unsurmountable obstacle." Vern rolled his eyes. "How did he react when he saw you?"

"He looked slightly ill at ease. I suppose I was a little tense when I saw his face. And probably my surprise at seeing him was plainly visible," she admitted.

"So you made the poor man uneasy, and now you want to reject his application - even though he would be a good candidate - because he was made to participate in your assessment? Really now..." he scolded her.

"Alright, if you put it that way..."

"What did the other two say? Did Lord Tyront and Lord Poron approve of him?"

"Lord Tyront thinks he is promising, Lord Poron is a little sceptical. But I was told that he had a bit of a row with his father some time ago and so would not help the son some way if he could avoid it."

"So it's your decision. Your vote decides."

"Yes, it is. And I think I just made it. Felden will be the third healer trainee."

"We are talking about Felden? He wants to be a healer?" Vern's eyes bulged.

"Yes, why? You know him?"

"Not personally, but I have heard quite a few things about him. He had an affair with one of the Council members' companions a few years ago. Big scandal!"

"Well, even though we may question his judgement when it comes to choosing his bed partners, that does not exactly disqualify him as a healer, does it?" Eryn pointed out.

"No, of course not. I was just surprised he'd applied. But Lord Enric won't have much reason to be jealous because of him. Felden prefers older women..." he grinned.

"I had no idea you were such a gossip." She shook her head disapprovingly.

He shrugged unabashedly. "Little pleasures to brighten up my life. Who are the other two healer candidates that were chosen by your illustrious circle?"

"Onil and Lebern. Onil is Lord Woldarn's son, I am told. Whoever that is."

"You don't even know the names of the Council members? That is rather negligent of you! You should at least recognise their names when you hear them. I am not even talking about being able to identify them when you meet them. You move in the same social circles, after all. Even though lately you seem to have been letting that slip, too, from what I hear from father."

"I have work to do in the evenings, I can't dance from one dinner party to the next every time somebody high up is bored and feels it's time to invite whoever is important at that time. And I wasn't aware that your father gossips as well. Shame on the both of you!"

"Yes, sure. Says the one who has been fuelling most of the gossip in the city this last year."

"What? People have been gossiping about me?" she exclaimed, taken aback.

"Of course. Everything you did was broadly discussed, both at dinner invitations and balls - especially the bit at the Freedom Night. And as the entire city seemed to have been waiting for Lord Enric to finally take a companion, all eyes were on the two of you from that night on. Most of them had given up on any spicy titbits of news when you didn't find out about him for several months, though."

She closed her eyes and shook her head. "How do you know all this? You are too young to even be invited to these occasions!"

"Oh, please," he chuckled. "I have my connections and sources of information. Information is power. And power is a good thing in the game, you know."

She nodded slowly. "I do. I just wasn't aware that you were playing it already."

* * *

Rolan was just finishing stocking the supply cupboard in the final treatment room when Eryn walked in behind him and nodded approvingly.

"This does look very good, I must say." She let her fingers glide over the sturdy leather of the daybed, the backrest of the two chairs, the surface of the desk and the glass of the lamp.

"I have just finished stocking the treatment rooms with sheets, bandages, bowls, soap and whatever else was on your list, so basically they are ready for use."

"How about the changing room? Have the locks for the clothes cupboards been put in yet?" she enquired.

"Yes, everything's ready. The only thing that remains to be fixed is the plumbing in the upper wash room."

"The ones on the ground floor are functional, then?"

"Yes, they are now. It took the workers long enough, though," Rolan huffed. "And I am still waiting for the copies of the books for the healers. They were supposed to have been delivered yesterday."

"They just arrived," Eryn told him. "That was why I came down here, to tell you." She rubbed her hands. "That means I can finally inform our new trainees and tell them to be ready for their first lesson in three days."

"I will take care of this after lunch," he said.

"You don't have to take care of everything," she said, slightly annoyed. It wasn't as if she was completely helpless without him, after all.

He turned to her, looking expectant. "Then I assume that you have the addresses of the new healers somewhere handy and know where to send the messages?"

She sighed. Damn. "Alright, you do it. Send them a copy of the training plan for the next month as well. Did the scribes say anything about when the books for the herb gatherers will be ready?"

"No, nothing exact. They say the illustrations are taking a lot of time, especially as they have to colour them as well. They gave me a rough estimate of one month."

"One month!" Eryn exclaimed. "This is bad news." She paced the room restlessly. "I don't want to wait that long until I start training them. I need the herbs and medicines, after all." She stopped. "Well, then I will have to change the plan and start with the things I can teach them without books. They will have to take notes. The teaching schedules as such are finalised?"

"Yes, everything is ready."

"How about Plia's room? Has the equipment been delivered by now?"

"Almost. A few of the glass items were broken in transit and needed to be replaced. I expect this to happen tomorrow."

She nodded. Everything was looking fine so far. And Rolan had done exceptional work. She had come to rely on him more than she had planned to, more than she was really comfortable with. It was like somebody was constantly babysitting her by reminding her of things she would have forgotten, taking care of things she was too busy for and handling the things she actually *had* forgotten. It was unnerving. If he kept this up she would be as helpless as a toddler without him after a while.

But of course having him around was immensely useful, there was no denying that. There were so many things Eryn knew he would handle better than she ever could because she just had no patience for them. Such as communicating with the King's advisors, treasurers and whoever else needed a sheet of paper of whatever kind to grant this or that. Rolan seemed somehow to have worked out how to handle the torrent of paper and find his way through the jungle of bureaucracy. And what was even more amazing was that he seemed to be neither frustrated nor bored in the least by handling these matters.

She wondered if it wouldn't be sensible to have him explain all these things to her. It was certainly not too smart depending on him too much, especially in these monetary matters. Yet currently she was swamped enough with everything around her, and they had not even started offering healing services yet. So for now she would have to trust him to handle these things in her interest - whether she was particularly happy about that state or not. And it was not as if she was eager to gain an insight into these topics, anyway.

"Do you have a date in mind for the opening of this place to customers?" Rolan said into her thoughts.

She looked up at him. "Patients," she corrected him.

"What?"

"Patients. That's what we shall call people who come here with medical problems."

He shrugged. "Alright, patients, then. So? What about that date?"

"I have been thinking about that, but I don't really know," she admitted. "I need the healer trainees to be able to handle the basics before I unleash them onto the ill or injured. They need enough theoretical knowledge to handle the practical experience they are about to get."

"How about the boy, Vern? He surely is far enough along to do some healing on his own while you teach the trainees?"

She shook her head. "No, I can't use him as a healer yet, he still has a few years of magician training before him and needs to concentrate on that as well. He already has more lessons than any other boy of his age with the additional healer training. I am sure the Order would not even have considered him for a position as healer if he hadn't already started training in secret. He is too young for the double burden."

"So you have basically wasted one of the five positions for healers by training the boy," Rolan pointed out heartlessly.

"I can't really deny that there is a grain of truth in what you say, factually speaking. But I would appreciate if you refrained from calling Vern *a waste* of any kind. He is immensely talented and works very hard to meet the demands of the Order, his father and myself. What's more, he was brave enough to be the very first one to venture into this new field of using magic."

"Fine," Rolan sighed. "Do we have a date now or not?"

"No, we don't. I will let you know as soon as I have decided on one."

Both of them fell silent and turned towards the door onto the corridor when they heard a questioning voice calling "Hello?" repeatedly.

"Are we expecting anybody?" Eryn asked and frowned.

"No, not that I know of." Rolan went out to meet the newcomer.

She listened to him and was slightly taken aback at his less than friendly tone.

"What is it you want?"

An elderly male voice replied timidly, "I was hoping to see Lady Eryn. My companion here is in great pain."

"We have not yet opened the place. Come back when are ready to receive custo... patients."

"Will that be soon?" the elderly man enquired worriedly.

"We have not set a date yet. But we will announce it publicly as soon as we have."

"But my companion!"

Eryn heard violent coughing and shook her head impatiently. They would have to work on Rolan's social skills, seriously. That was no way to treat people who were looking for help!

"Rolan?" she called out. "Why don't you show them in? I will take care of this." It seemed she would now for the first time use the new treatment room.

The man who entered the room was not as old as she would have suspected from his voice; she estimated him to be in his late sixties. His arm was draped protectively around the shoulders of a frail looking woman about his age who looked ashen and was hardly managing to stay upright.

Eryn took her arm and lead her to a chair.

"Lady Eryn," the man said and made to bow, but she stopped him with a shake of her head.

"Good day to you." She sat down opposite the woman and smiled. "Why don't you tell me what is wrong?"

As if on cue the woman started coughing again. It sounded raspy and painful.

"I need to touch you to look inside you with magic to see what the problem is. Do I have your permission for that?" she asked and lifted her hand palm up.

A quick nod and a dry, hot, fragile looking hand was placed in hers. Closing her eyes, she found the problem almost immediately. An inflammation of the lungs, progressed far enough to be life-threatening.

"Why don't you lie down on the daybed? Lying down will be easier for you than sitting." And it would be less likely for her to fall to the floor.

The man all but carried his companion to the bed Eryn indicated and then stood there, unsure what to do.

Eryn turned to him. "This will take about half an hour. You can wait outside or go for a walk if you like."

"I would like to stay, if you don't mind, my Lady. I will not get in your way, I promise," the man pleaded.

She looked down at the woman who had extended a shaking hand towards her companion and nodded.

"Of course. Why don't you take a chair and sit at the head end?"

*   *   *

When she returned to her study more than half an hour later, Rolan knocked at her door almost immediately.

"Come," she called and dropped into her chair.

"I thought we were not yet open?" he asked pointedly. "Seriously, how am I to keep up with organising things around here if you keep changing plans? If you have any, that is."

"Sit," she commanded and folded her arms. "Your charming comments about my lack of plans aside, we need to talk about your less than respectful way of dealing with people who show up here."

"What of it? We are not yet open, and I let them know that," he shrugged with an uncomprehending frown.

"If people in severe pain come here, we don't send them away like that! This is the reason why I want to open this place, why I am training people to become healers: so we can provide help when it is needed."

"But we are not ready to provide help of any kind yet! We have no rates fixed, no proper way of keeping track of the earnings, no means of keeping the money safe until we can take it to the money lenders..."

"Really?" she interrupted him. "The reason why we can't help people yet, in your opinion, concerns organisational matters around money?"

"You make it sound like taking care of these matters is of no importance at all! You need money to keep this place going, whether you like it or not," he pointed out.

Eryn breathed in and out several times to calm down enough so as to stop herself from yelling, before answering, "I am very well aware of that, thank you so much. And yet I would prefer if you treated people who come here and seek help with more respect, even if you are not in a position to help them right then and there. If I ever again hear you talking to any patient the way you did today, there will be trouble." She gave him her best threatening glower.

He stiffened. "So I am to feign devastation when they come here even though we are not yet open?"

"Seriously?" She shook her head in disbelief. "Why would you even have to pretend to be sorry for them? If somebody came here in need of help, you'd have no bad feeling at all when you had to send them away again? What have you done to get assigned a position like this as punishment?" Ah, but she knew about that, didn't she? She had read his file.

"What have *you* done to get me assigned as your assistant?" he riposted. Then he smiled without joy. "Ah yes, there was the little matter of sending Lord Tyront to the ground. So it seems we are each other's punishment."

They stared at each other for several long seconds, before Eryn rose slowly and took three silver coins out of her pocket to put them before him on the desk.

"Here is the first money we have earned. I'm placing it in your custody, as you are so adamant about collecting it. I am absolutely sure you are more than capable of finding a place to keep it for now. You are dismissed."

Rolan rose and swept the money into his palm with a defiant glare. He didn't say anything when he returned to his own office and closed the door very, very carefully behind him.

Don't hurt him - it just wouldn't look good, it wouldn't be professional, she reminded herself.

*   *   *

Plia looked around the large, bright room at the healers' building. She smiled broadly, realising that from now on it would be her realm. It was about three times as large as the room she'd had at the Palace though still smaller than the guest room she'd moved into at Eryn's place no more than two days ago.

"So, what do you think?" Eryn asked and sat on one of the two chairs in front of a large table.

"I have no idea what most of the things here are for, but I love it!" the girl answered and curiously opened one of the doors of a large cupboard to inspect its contents. Glassware in different forms and sizes, a lot of it.

"You are going to be using every single item in here, don't worry. After a while they will be as familiar to you as ordinary cutlery."

"What is this for?" Plia asked and pointed to a small stone bowl and what looked like a round wedge. "We had those in the Palace kitchen, but what would you use them for here?"

"Pestle and mortar?" Eryn asked and then explained, "To grind herbs into powder. We should get a delivery of herbs tomorrow, then I can show you how to do it properly."

"So what am I going to do today?"

"Get familiar with the place, find space somewhere for your personal things. Go through the books again to remind yourself of the herbs we gathered during the expedition. We are going to use several of them tomorrow and I will ask you questions about them. In about one hour the apothecaries will arrive for their first training lesson, and you will join them."

Plia gulped in obvious dread and nodded.

"Don't worry, little flower, I will be there all the time. And if they try to give you a hard time, I will make my sentiments about that known to them." She sighed. "And I will have to stop using that pet name for you now that we work together. People would tease you because of it otherwise, I think."

"Don't worry, I wouldn't mind about that."

"But *I* would. And it would look as if I was giving you undue preferential treatment. That impression will be hard enough to avoid anyway now that you are living with me. Let's not make it harder than necessary for you." She looked at an empty shelf between two windows. "That would be a good location for your books, don't you think? It is always a good idea to have them close by when you work. There might be a little detail you want to look up and it's handy if you don't have to walk too far."

Plia nodded and watched Eryn rise from her chair. "So, don't forget - training in one hour. In the smaller of the two training rooms; there are only four apothecaries plus you. Do you know how to find it? It's the fourth door to your right as you walk out of here. We have yet to order plates for the rooms. And if you need anything, just ask Rolan. You know where his office is. I have to go and see Lord Tyront now. He wants a progress report." She looked at the ceiling. "And I have been avoiding that for the last three days, so he is getting impatient. He threatened me with having me dragged to his study if I don't show up there today. Can you believe that?"

The girl grimaced in sympathy. "He wouldn't really do that, would he?"

"You bet he would. Without batting an eyelid. So I'd better take care of it now. At least I can tell him then that I don't have much time as I need to get back for the training." She turned and left the room, calling "I'll see you in an hour, then," over her shoulder and made her way to the Palace to deliver her report.

* * *

"So, you have finally found your way here, Lady Eryn," Tyront commented cuttingly when she opened his study door after

154

knocking. He sat behind his desk, not bothering to rise when she entered.

"And a good day to you, too," she replied with a cheerfulness she by no means felt. "This is a very busy day for me today; but I told myself that I need to make time for a short visit nevertheless."

Tyront gave a smile that held no amusement. "So glad to be deemed worthy of your precious time, then. Come in and talk. If you are so busy I will try not to detain you for too long."

She approached and took a seat unbidden.

"So, how are things working out between you and Rolan?"

"So far everything is fine," she shrugged. "Very organised lad, listens when I tell him something, good with paperwork."

He waited for more to come and raised his brow when he realised that this was all he was about to get. "That's all?"

"Yes, pretty much." She frowned. "Do you need details? Such as what exactly he does? Furnishing the rooms, handling the teaching books, stocking the treatment rooms, taking care of the finances..."

"No, that's alright, thank you," he interrupted her. Pursing his lips, he thought of the letters of complaint he kept receiving from her assistant and decided that she could hardly be unaware of the tension between herself and Rolan. It seemed that in contrast to him, she had decided to deal with that on her own. Or she wanted to avoid giving her superior the satisfaction of seeing that his little revenge was working out well enough. But then she didn't seem annoyed or angry when she talked about Rolan. She was obviously determined to make it work somehow. Admirable, Tyront thought. And a pleasant surprise that she didn't complain.

"How is the training going?"

"The one I am receiving or the one I am holding?" she enquired.

"Both. Let's start with the first one, shall we? From what I hear your teachers have granted you some time to take care of the organisation for starting the healing services. I expect you to resume your studies as soon as the place is open and running." Then he smiled. "I heard that you have returned to Orrin for your combat training."

"Yes, you were informed correctly."

He sighed. She really didn't volunteer anything. "So, how is that going?"

"Painfully. He has decided that I am to be taught unarmed combat, which I am finding harder than expected."

"In addition to sword fighting, I assume? It is a compulsory discipline, after all."

She snorted. "Of course."

"How about your training for the apothecaries and herb gatherers, then? Have you started that yet?"

"No, I am about to in half an hour. The apothecaries will have their first lesson today."

"You need to start teaching in half an hour? This is all the time you take for me after avoiding me for so long?" Tyront pinched the bridge of his nose. "You are aware that I am accommodating you by having you deliver your reports orally instead of demanding anything in writing? And that I am also very forthcoming with regard to the interval of your reports, especially considering that you still try to avoid coming here unless I threaten you with consequences?"

He noted with satisfaction that she did look a little contrite.

"I apologise, Lord Tyront. It has been a busy time since my return from the expedition."

He looked at her intently and exhaled. "I don't hear you promising me any improvements for the future."

She thought for a moment, then nodded. "Alright, I promise to do my best to try and deliver my reports in a more timely fashion from now on."

"You'll do your best to try?" Tyront shook his head. "That's a vacuous promise if ever I heard it." He leaned forward. "Let me assist you slightly in motivating yourself: If you don't deliver the next report in whatever form you prefer within the next ten days, I will have you dragged here by liveried guards, no matter if you happen to be in the middle of a training session yourself, treatment of patients, or whatever else you currently occupy yourself with all day long. In addition, next time I will not bother with warning you. Have I made myself clear?"

Eryn scowled at him, but nodded. "Perfectly clear."

Tyront leaned back again, his smile considerably more predatory than happy. "Excellent. Then you may leave for now. Next time I expect you to bring a preliminary calculation of your expenses so far and details about the progress of your training sessions."

"Yes, Lord Tyront," she murmured and rose.

He watched her leave and shook his head in ironic amusement when she had closed the door behind her. She had adapted reasonably well to being part of the Order, particularly as she had not at all been eager to join them. Having her stall delivering her reports was a minor evil. And it was not as if he didn't have other, more thorough sources of information on her doings.

*   *   *

Eryn yawned and stretched. She noted with surprise how dark it had become outside already. Again. Somehow time did seem to pass too quickly these days. Enric usually awaited her at home in the parlour in the evenings, putting aside whatever book he was currently perusing to give her a look of mild disapproval.

Only one more test to correct, then she would call it a day, she promised herself. The apothecaries were doing reasonably well, considering that they were not exactly thrilled at having to do the training at all. Plia was the only one showing enthusiasm, and this was just one of numerous contrasts between her and the men. They had taken to ignoring her as well as they could, but Eryn saw the looks they gave the girl when she knew the answer to something they had forgotten or never even heard about. But Plia would be spending only one more week with the apothecaries, then she would transfer to the class of herb gatherers, which would undoubtedly be more pleasant for her. Those men had got to know and like her during the expedition.

She looked up in annoyance when a knock sounded at the door to Rolan's office.

"What?" she called out.

The door opened and Rolan entered, obviously none too happy about having to talk to her while she was in such fretful mood.

"Why are you still here? Go home!" she exclaimed. "It's getting dark already."

"I had to finish some paperwork for the Palace. They don't take well to waiting," he replied. "Lord Enric sent a messenger to tell you that you are expected to leave here immediately as you were invited to attend a dinner in about an hour's time."

She buried her face in her hands. "What? That was today? Oh no!" she wailed. "I just want to fall into my bed and sleep!"

"Would you like me to inform the messenger accordingly?" He couldn't quite hide the dark amusement in his voice and received a scorching glare.

"Are you mad? Enric would storm in here and drag me to whatever place we are invited to!" She rose. "Alright, I am leaving. And so will you." Grabbing her cloak and flinging it around her shoulders, she dashed down the stairs and out the main entrance, all the while muttering, "Damn, damn, damn."

In her head she went through what she had to do and in what order: getting home, having a quick wash, putting on whatever dress Junar had without a doubt already prepared, having her hair done. That should be possible in less than one hour, shouldn't it?

When she opened the door to her home, Enric was already waiting in the parlour, though not sitting and reading as usual, but in his evening attire already, standing there with a dark look, wordlessly pointing upstairs. She smiled apologetically and rushed up the stairs, where she almost ran into Junar, who threw her hands up.

"Finally! We had almost given up hope. Now go and get yourself cleaned up, and no dawdling! If I don't see you here again in five minutes, I am coming after you," she instructed without any greeting.

Eryn turned on her heel in wordless compliance to hurry into the washroom.

When she re-emerged soon after, Junar all but dragged her in front of the mirror and commanded, "Undress!"

She already had a pale-yellow gown draped over one arm.

Eryn groaned when she saw the colour. "Seriously? I will look washed out and pale in that!"

"I know!" the seamstress shot back. "I made it from leftovers and kept it for an occasion when I wanted to take revenge on you. Be grateful it is just a dinner invitation and not a ball, so only a limited number of people will see you in it."

"Revenge? Why? What have I done to you now?"

"You turn up here at the very last minute with no consideration whatsoever that I am supposed to make you look presentable! So I decided that next time you do this, I just won't bother trying to make you look better than you deserve." She shoved the dress over Eryn's head and pulled it down. Then she shook her head and exhaled. "I'll be damned - it doesn't look even half as bad as I had hoped. I really am too good at my job. Next time I will dress you in a sack."

Eryn smiled despite herself. "Maybe I am just too ravishing, and everything looks fabulous on me?"

"You wish! Give me fifteen minutes with a pair of scissors, needle and thread and I will prove to you that you are not. Now stop hauling that neckline up, it is supposed to be down there!" She pulled a chair close and pressed her unwilling customer onto it. "Just hold still, so I can try to tame that rat's nest on your head into something remotely elegant."

"Ow!" Eryn yowled when the brush hit a knot in her hair and was pulled through relentlessly.

"Shut up," Junar growled. "Come home earlier next time, then I'll have time for gentleness. Now hold that strand. No, the other one, the one I am trying to press into your hand."

Eryn stared into the mirror and watched capable and busy hands turn and twist her dark strands of hair into an elegant creation that made her neck look long and sleek.

"Now run," Junar commanded when she was done. "You should still be able to make it in time."

Eryn nodded to her and took two steps at a time as she hurried downstairs into the parlour. Enric raised his eyebrows in surprise.

"That was fast," he commented.

"What can I say? I aim to please," she replied loftily.

"I have no illusions whatsoever that the credit for this expeditious transformation does not belong to you, but to Junar," he retorted and took her hand to guide her out the door. Urban came running around a corner, aiming straight for the opening.

"No!" Enric said sternly, "You stay here." He quickly closed the door, careful not to squeeze a paw in the process.

"Where are we even going?" Eryn enquired with forced but feeble enthusiasm.

"Lord Remdel's. He lives down the street. We will still make it in time, even if we walk."

"Do I know Lord Remdel?"

"You have met him, yes. Member of the Magic Council, medium height, slightly grey moustache, bushy eyebrows. You will surely remember him when you see him, he has been at the banquets when the ambassador was here. Quiet type."

They reached an impressive looking building only a few minutes later and the double doors were opened before they even had a chance to knock. A servant bowed to them and took their cloaks, while another asked them to follow him into the dining room.

"Lord Enric!" a loud, painfully shrill female voice boomed through the room and a tall, middle-aged female in a dress that was slightly too tight and which hardly managed to keep her cleavage from exploding, approached him to clasp both his hands. "So thrilled you could make it! And Lady Eryn! What an honour to have you here, too!"

"The honour is ours, Inad," Enric replied with a polite smile and barely managed to free his hands again. "I see we are pretty much the last ones, aren't we? I hope we didn't make you wait unduly."

"Oh no, don't be silly!" their hostess laughed in her shrill tone. "We are thrilled to have you here, it was nigh on impossible to get you to come to our little gatherings before your commitment, so we are more than willing to indulge you. Come, have a glass of something before dinner."

"You have not exactly been the social type, eh?" Eryn whispered when they followed Lord Remdel's companion. "You shouldn't have changed that on my account. Really. I mean it. You should go back to being unavailable and avoid these occasions. This is a sacrifice I am willing to make to show you how much I respect your personal boundaries and preferences."

Enric grinned. "Very considerate of you, and so unselfish. I couldn't possibly ask you to spend your evenings quietly in the parlour or in bed when there is so much fun to be had beyond."

"Yes, I believe it," she grumbled and plastered a big, fake smile on her face when they encountered Lord Seagon.

The men nodded at each other politely, yet for Eryn he had no more than a pointed stare.

"Why does he hate *me*? *You* broke his nephew's nose, after all!" she hissed at Enric when they moved on.

He shrugged. "Because he isn't really happy about having you in the Order at all, I assume. He is not so young any more, adapting to revolutionary ideas such as a female magician is not easy for him. And my breaking that particular nose just confirms to him that you are trouble."

"Bloody nuisance that he is the Order's treasurer," she murmured. "Couldn't you have attacked somebody less inconvenient?"

"I'll be more considerate next time, I promise," he chuckled.

They finished greeting the other guests, in total about ten people, and then the whole party was lead to the lavishly laid table. Lord Tyront and Vyril were among them.

As was usual at such occasions, Eryn was not seated next to her companion but between two other gentlemen - luckily, neither of them being Lord Seagon.

Lord Woldarn, another member of the Magic Council, sat to her right, Marrin, the King's advisor to her left.

"How is that wild animal of yours doing in the big city, Lady Eryn?" Lord Woldarn enquired curiously.

"Fine enough, though our interior is suffering a little, as you might well imagine. We have given up replacing the cushions in the parlour for now."

"Keeping a wild mountain cat in a city is abominable," muttered a female voice opposite her. The companion of another Council member, Eryn remembered. But for the life of her, she couldn't say what the matching name was.

"Is it?" Eryn retorted calmly. "I decided that I found it more abominable to leave it in the woods to die."

"A noble sentiment," Marrin smiled. "And one that got you the permission to move out of the Palace."

She thought carefully about what to say to that. Admitting that she had all but appreciated being made to live at the Palace would not be a good move. The King would undoubtedly hear about it.

"An unforeseen side effect, but of course His Majesty's safety comes first," she replied with a sincere nod.

"Are you telling me that you regret moving out, Lady Eryn?" Marrin asked, clearly amused.

"Well, who would not? A convenient location, luxurious rooms, good infrastructure, disciplined servants..." she listed, using her fingers.

"Indeed?" he replied. "Then my perception of your reluctance of moving into Lord Enric's old quarters was a misconception on my side, I assume?"

"Well, it was certainly quite a change in my living circumstances," she improvised desperately.

"Compared to your cell at the warriors' quarters? That would be putting it mildly. It surely was a considerable improvement. So moving into the Palace certainly was quite a step up, unless I am very much mistaken?"

"Of course," she smiled. The glint in his eyes told her that he knew exactly what circumstances had led to her moving into the Palace. But this was neither the time nor place to talk about forced commitments and involuntary changes of residence.

"That healing place of yours," Inad asked casually, "how is it coming along? Have you set a date for the grand opening yet?"

"Yes," Eryn nodded. "In two weeks' time. The premises are ready, but there are still a few more things I need to teach the new healer trainees before we can start treating people."

"So people will have to come to your place instead of your coming to them? It was how the apothecaries used to work," Lord Seagon's sour-faced companion asked.

"Yes," Eryn replied with a saccharine smile, "but then my services are based on knowledge and expertise and aim to provide results, not convenience."

"What are your rates going to be?" Lord Woldarn enquired. His son was one of her healer trainees, she remembered.

"They will be based on the patient's income," she replied and waited for the storm of indignation that would very likely break loose.

"So we are to pay different prices for the same service?" the first unbelieving voice rose. "This is rather unfair, don't you think? If I went to the baker to buy a loaf of bread he would hardly try to charge me more than the stable boy."

That's as much you know, Eryn thought, but said instead, "My aim is to provide affordable services for everyone. You can surely afford to pay more for treatment and thus help keeping the system alive. And if you are not willing to pay my prices, nobody forces you to consult me."

A warning cough made her look at Lord Tyront who aimed a disapproving glance in her direction.

The first course was served, and when people around her resumed their conversations she hoped that they would leave her in peace for at least a few minutes. It was not to be.

"So - the apothecaries," Lord Seagon began, "they are no longer in business, are they? Forced out of it by you, am I to understand?"

"No, Lord Seagon," she replied evenly, "their efforts have been redirected to better fit their expertise. Instead of insufficient healing services they will now provide more effective medicines for the healers."

"So they are no longer permitted to consult on healing matters?"

"No, they are not. The quality of their services was deemed insufficient."

"By whom?" Lord Seagon sneered.

"By me," Eryn replied with a deadly stare. "Do you wish to question my expertise in these matters? In that case I challenge you to find somebody better suited in the Kingdom."

"You must let me tell you about my latest encounter with that impossible, self-appointed expert on interior arrangements," Inad's shrill voice burst out once more, silencing all other conversations at the table.

Eryn sighed with relief. She hoped the hostess broadcasting her disapproval would prevent any other attempts at returning to that topic for the evening. She kept her involvement in conversations as superficial as possible without appearing rude and limited herself to nodding and smiling for the rest of the meal. When they stood together with a glass of heavy sweet wine in the parlour after dinner and Enric had started hinting at their intention to leave, Inad took her aside.

"Lady Eryn," she said conspiratorially, "I must talk to you for a moment. Alone, if you please."

Thus she was pulled back into the now empty dining room.

"What can I do for you?" Eryn asked politely and hoped for her to get to the point quickly.

"It is about the orphan girl. The one whose face you healed."

"Plia? Yes, what about her?"

"Well," Inad went on, "this has certainly given rise to thoughts about the possibilities of your skills and the services you could provide."

"Really?" An unpleasant suspicion started to rise. Surely she was not hinting at misusing healing skills to correct minor imperfections for reasons of vanity, was she? "What would be the nature of such services you have been thinking about, if I may ask?"

If Inad had heard any warning in Eryn's tone, she had decided to ignore it.

"Little changes to external appearances that would make life so much more pleasant, for example."

"So what you are asking me is if I have considered offering cosmetic remedies?" She pretended to think for a moment. "Yes, I have." For about three seconds, just now. "And the answer is No. I am not going to use any of my energy and magic for enhancing beauty when it is so much better employed in healing people, alleviating pain and restoring their ability to work and provide for their families!"

With that she turned and stomped back into the parlour, leaving behind a gasping Inad who stared after her in disbelief. Eryn spotted Enric and went straight towards him.

"We need to leave here. Right this moment. Otherwise we will probably be seen to be thrown out," she murmured urgently.

Enric wordlessly put down his half-empty glass, nodded to Tyront and Vyril and had the servant waiting by the door fetch their cloaks. When they stood outside the grand house, he shook his head at her.

"So, talk to me. What was that just now? I assume you managed to insult the hostess after she pulled you aside?"

Eryn nodded. "I did, yes. But don't look at me like that. I was still polite, considering what I really wanted to tell her but kept inside. She wanted me to make cosmetic improvements! Can you imagine?"

They started walking.

"You did something like that with Plia," he pointed out calmly.

"I did, but that was completely different! You didn't see what Plia looked like before. Half of her face covered in burn scars, one corner of her mouth and eye distorted, others looking at her as if she was a monster and throwing stones at her! How would she ever have got into learning any trade whatsoever? But that spoilt, rich woman, who has nothing else to worry about than how to redecorate that huge house and keep herself from being bored to death during the day, has the audacity to propose a thing like that!"

"I hope you didn't use these exact words to make your sentiments known to her?" he enquired resignedly.

"No, of course not! Her companion is in the Magic Council, they would have made me pay for something like that, I'm sure," she grumbled.

They still might bring it up, Enric mused, but decided to leave it at that for now. If he was wrong, he would only worry her unnecessarily, and in case he was right, well - she would learn about it soon enough.

CHAPTER 14

Funding

Enric quietly knocked at her study door in the healers' building and carefully opened it when there was no reply. The room was dimly lit by a single lamp on her desk that bathed a motionless figure in a gentle glow. Eryn was lying there with her head bedded on her upper arm, the other one still limply holding a pen that threatened to slip from between her fingers any moment.

He sighed and came closer, taking the pen and laying it carefully beside her. She was the only one still in the building, everybody else had left, the healer trainees, Rolan, the patients.

"Eryn?" He gently touched her shoulder. "Wake up, my love. Time to go home."

She slowly opened her eyes, looking up at him in drowsy confusion. "Enric? What are you doing here?"

"Getting you home. It's midnight and I was starting to worry when you didn't come home." He took her hands to haul her up into a standing position and held on to them when she started protesting.

"Wait, I am not yet finished with my notes!"

"Falling asleep across them will not help you accomplish that, either. Come on. I am not going to argue with you." He extinguished the lamp and pulled her with him out the study and down the stairs. "Do you want to walk or would you like me to order a coach?"

She shook her head and stifled a yawn. "No, walking is fine."

"So, tell me about your big day. How did the opening go?"

He smiled when her face lit up.

"Incredible! At first it was utter chaos; the patients had no idea where to wait, the trainees were afraid to touch them and nervous about making mistakes, then we had too few chairs in the waiting area. Around noon we ran out of medicine for headaches, and Plia was almost in tears for not having prepared more. If it hadn't been for Vern and Rolan, I think I would have gone stark raving mad after a couple of hours."

"Rolan? What did he do?"

164

"He stood amidst all that mayhem, a calm, disapproving figure with a constant frown on his face. Then he suddenly let loose an ear-splitting whistle, and it was like the world had frozen. Every single pair of eyes was fixed on him, I swear. Patients, trainees, everyone. He started barking commands, pointing in different directions, making lists. I think they were all a bit afraid of him after that. Whenever somebody started to complain, one look at him made them shut up and sit down again." She laughed and rubbed her face. "I was so glad he was there. He was fierce, efficient, incredible. Don't tell Lord Tyront, he might feel that his punishment has not worked out properly and find another assistant to torment me."

"And the healing? You said Vern had been helpful as well?"

"Yes, without him I suppose none of the trainees would ever have dared touch a single patient. Vern and I split up, each of us took one treatment room and half of the trainees - two for him, two for me. We let them treat smaller injuries on their own and used more involved problems for demonstration purposes." She sighed. "You would be amazed at the flood of different things we had to treat today, from near-fatal infections to common colds, cut fingers to bone diseases."

"How did the trainees do? I expect they were a bit overwhelmed from what you are telling me now."

"All in all they did extremely well. Lord Poron had to be reminded constantly that increasing his knowledge is an important part of treating patients, but that making the problem go away instead of merely appreciating its complexity is also essential. I dare say he would have preferred sitting in a corner and writing everything down. Onil, Lord Woldarn's son, seems to have found his purpose in life. He more or less took over the treatment room. I had to push him aside to let Lord Poron try a thing or two. I suppose I will make them work together more often – one of them is eager to do all the healing, the other one wants to collect knowledge. A happy combination. Though I will need to check on them frequently or each will stick to his favourite task instead of taking turns."

"So Felden and Lebern worked with Vern? How did that go? I imagine taking instructions from a teenage boy might not have been so easy for them," Enric asked curiously.

"It was a bit of challenge at first, yes," she confirmed. "But when they saw him heal a spinal deformation before their eyes, they re-evaluated their attitudes towards him."

"This sounds as if it was a complete success."

She beamed, tired but happy. "It was, immensely so. I can't tell you how glad I am that it worked out like that. I was so afraid of no patients turning up or the trainees discovering that theory was one thing while actually treating patients was not to their liking. But the place was crawling with patients almost half an hour after we opened the doors. All the same, the collection of money ended up a bit haphazard. I am glad Rolan took over that. I wonder how he knew how much to collect, but it seemed to have been alright, people didn't complain."

Enric inclined his head. "You don't know how? He requested last year's tax lists from the Palace. They contain the names of all people in the city and how much they had to pay according to their incomes."

She whistled through her teeth. "He did? He never ceases to amaze me."

"How many patients did you treat today? It must have been quite a lot with you still sitting there at this time running through the paperwork."

"About fifty, according to Rolan's lists. I'll need to reconsider the opening hours, though. I thought about admitting people for about three hours instead of six. Otherwise we will have to work at least nine or ten hours every day we are open."

"Yes," Enric agreed, "that does sound sensible. Will you stick to your plan of opening every second day for patient treatment?"

"That is still the aim, yes. One day of training, one day of practice. I think I have a pretty clear idea what the most common ailments are in the city. I will focus on them in the course of the next few training lessons, so the trainees should be able to handle them without my assistance fairly soon. That would buy me quite some time," she sighed in blissful anticipation.

"So," Enric enquired, "your task for tomorrow is training the healers, then?"

"Yes, but first I am due at the training grounds for the regular excruciation with Orrin. Then two hours of healer training, and finally I need to finish up the notes I fell asleep on. I hope it will be an uneventful if busy day." She frowned when he cleared his throat. "Alright, what's the matter?"

"We have been summoned before the King tomorrow afternoon. Yourself, Tyront and me. It seems that Inad was not entirely satisfied with your little conversation at the dinner invitation that evening."

Eryn stopped and looked up at him in disbelief. "Don't tell me she has managed to make the King intervene over a thing like that?"

"Well, my love, her companion is an influential man, after all. He was a close friend of King Folrin's father, one of very few in that group. If he requests something, the King at least listens to him."

She groaned. "He is not going to make me do this, is he? I mean, he can't force me, can he? I thought my services and everything in connection with them was up to my own discretion!"

"Let's wait for tomorrow. Maybe your worries are unfounded."

"That's not really what you think! I can see it in your face!"

"I could be wrong," he conceded, without much conviction.

"But you don't think so."

"No," he admitted, "I don't."

*   *   *

They bowed as one when the King entered the throne room, both his advisors trailing a step behind him.

"Lady Eryn. My Lords," he nodded and stopped right in front of them. He first turned to Eryn.

"Before we get to the matter at hand, let me congratulate you on the opening of your building yesterday. I hear it was very successful and your services were well received. Well, I had expected nothing less. Your reputation in the city is very good, and after the apothecaries were relegated to producing medication without being allowed to sell it on their own, there is little alternative, after all, is there?"

"Are you implying that I pushed the apothecaries out of business to profit from the resulting need for medical services?" she asked brusquely.

The King raised his eyebrows. "No. This is not what I am implying. You are not devious enough for such a thing, my Lady. And even if you were, your services are far superior to whatever theirs were. But there is another little matter I have been asked to address with regard to your healing. As the Crown is funding your efforts, it is thought by some people that it should also be able to have influence over them to a certain degree."

"I see," she replied with narrowed eyes. "*Some* people think that? Among them Lord Remdel, I would assume. May I enquire as to the Crown's point of view on this?"

King Folrin sighed. "For myself, you see, I am more than happy to let you handle everything in connection with it. And of course I can hardly force you to act against your conscience, can I?"

She studied him closely. If this were all that was to be said about the matter, he would not have summoned them here. She wondered if he would try to blackmail her by threatening or hinting at the likelihood of his no longer funding her.

"Do not worry, Lady Eryn, I will not make that threat," he smiled, obviously guessing why she was watching him so intently. "To what avail, I ask you? The Order would very likely help you out, at least for a while. Or even Lord Enric, as he has considerable funds at his own disposal and is very eager to keep you happy."

Enric simply smiled at that.

"You know that Lord Remdel is an influential man, don't you, my dear? Then it might not come as any surprise to you that he has started looking for allies to increase the pressure on me to make you comply with his companion's request. You may of course stick to your decision and relish your victory over him, but I ask you to consider what this will mean for you, your healing services and, to a certain degree, to your companion's business interests. Running a business, whether it is trade or healing, Lady Eryn, does, as you will find out, depend on a great number of useful, reliable and benevolent contacts. You may in time find yourself in need of glass vials for your medicines, and it could turn out that the glass makers have been made to refuse selling to you. Or your load of deliveries might catch fire. There are numerous things that can go wrong, many of them mere nuisances that cause no more than minor delays. Others, though, have more unfavourable impacts."

Eryn stared at him and then took a step backwards, breathing heavily. "Is this your way of letting me deal with this?"

The King shook his head, impatient with her lack of understanding. "This was not a threat, Lady Eryn. It is a warning of what the consequences of your decision might be in the long run. I strongly believe in thinking of possible consequences before acting. I invite you to do the same." He then smiled thinly. "There is one more thing you might want to take into consideration. Vanity is a compelling flaw, especially among the more prosperous. Keep this in mind, would you?" He then nodded to all three of them. "You are dismissed."

Tyront took her arm and said quietly, "A word with you in my study, if you please. I trust you have no pressing appointments right now?"

She shook her head and turned to Enric who had fallen into step behind them. He gave her a reassuring smile.

"You are trying to make me do it, aren't you?" she said immediately after Enric had closed the door to Lord Tyront's study. She remained standing with folded arms, ignoring the chair she had been invited to sit on.

"I am not after trying to make you do anything you don't want to. Let's just say I would like to discuss our options here. I can see that you are agitated right now, but take a moment and consider the King's words and what exactly they mean for all of us," Tyront said placatingly as he took a seat behind his desk.

She whirled to Enric. "You own businesses? I didn't even know that! Are they in any real danger if Lord Remdel decides to tarnish you because of me?"

Enric considered the question for a few moments before answering, "There might be a temporary setback or two, but nothing that would harm us permanently. I have my own useful contacts to pay him back, in any case. Don't worry on my account."

"I should probably do what he wants and work on Inad a little. I am sure he would not appreciate it very much if her voice became even shriller or her skin turned yellow," she said through clenched teeth.

The two men exchanged a horrified look at the very notion of increasing the shrillness of that voice even further.

"Eryn, the King has given you two very powerful reasons to consider complying with Inad's wishes." Enric stepped closer and put both hands on her shoulders. "Please, calm down and start using that capable head of yours for something other than scary threats."

She blinked at him. "You mean protecting the healing services, or healing business, as he likes to think of it? But wouldn't that mean that I would in the long run have to do whatever others want me to in order to avoid being discredited in any way? I would make myself a slave to whatever demand a rich idiot might make!"

"Yes to the first, No to the rest. You only opened the building yesterday, and new ventures are especially vulnerable, even when they are not subject to threats like unhappy Council members' demands. You might one day be able to laugh off Lord Remdel, or rather his companion, but that time has not yet come. He goes a long way back in the Order, has close connections to the King and has very good contacts inside and outside the city. You are new in the Order, know hardly anybody here and depend on building up good reputations to be able to make your healing services a success."

She gulped. It didn't sound very promising when he put it like that. And that was only the first reason.

"What is the other reason the King gave me?" she asked with a defeated sound in her voice.

This time Lord Tyront answered with a broad smile. "A very significant one that should make pretending to give in almost a pleasure for you: independence from the Crown's purse."

"What?" She stared at him in confusion.

"He told you as much himself; the last thing he said. He told you that vanity is a great flaw among the rich. Don't you see?" He leaned forward eagerly. "It means you can charge premium prices for this by arguing that owing to the fact that you are not doing it out of medical necessity; and thus the procedures are not in accordance with the purpose of your business and take away much needed resources that must be compensated otherwise. Political strategy, my girl. This is one occasion to deploy it."

Both men saw her lean back with her head dropped, staring at the dark carpet, deep in thought.

After what had to be several minutes, she lifted her head again. The expression in her eyes had changed completely and was no longer angry, desperate or discontent, but instead calm and calculating. She straightened.

"I was giving the matter a lot of consideration and have reached a conclusion. I would not want to risk my own healing business or my companion's business interests. Furthermore, I do not wish to cause undue disharmony among the members of the Magic Council or inconvenience His Majesty. Thus I have decided to extend the healing services I offer in order to include, in addition to medical exigencies, procedures of a different nature." Then she bent forward and looked directly into Tyront's eyes. "This, however, would tie up resources - namely my own - and would make me unable to devote as much time and effort to the core purpose of the healing services as such. I would thus require an increase to the quota of magicians who are permitted to learn the profession of healing based on the demand for such new services. This will be an issue as soon as my current healers are far enough along to teach new trainees. I am sure that presenting this demand of mine to the Magic Council will not be a problem."

She watched a slow smile spread on Tyront's lips. He regarded her with what she strongly suspected to be pride and then nodded. "I will present your condition to the Magic Council to be voted on. Lord Remdel has a few allies in the Council, and then there are the votes of Enric, Orrin, Lord Poron and myself to support you. You should await the result of the vote with justifiable optimism."

"Then I suppose the only two things that remain to be done in this matter by me are calculating rip-off prices for cosmetic alterations and pretending to be reluctant because I was made to act against my own better judgement," she smirked.

"Two tasks," Tyront remarked, "and you will excel at both, I have no doubt whatsoever."

* * *

Enric looked up from his figures in surprise when he heard the entrance door being shut firmly. This was unusually early for Eryn to return from her work.

"Eryn, is that you?" he called out.

Only moments later she stood in his study door, the young mountain cat in her arms.

"This cat is growing like a garden weed. I mean, is it only my impression or has the little horror doubled in size since I brought her here?" She carefully freed her hand from Urban's claws and set her down on the floor.

"She has grown, that is right. But that is natural. She will continue to grow for another six months. Lifting her up like this will not be so easy after that," he smiled. "You are home unusually early today. Is everything alright?"

She shrugged. "I decided that I needed an afternoon off today. And after visiting Inad just now I feel I deserve it."

He grimaced. "So you went to see her about her cosmetic stuff? How did it go?"

"Better than I could have hoped, apart from her excruciating smugness. Restraining myself from punching her in the face every two minutes was a feat I am really proud of. Don't ever tell me again that I need to learn to control my temper. I not only controlled it, but wrestled it into submission and tied a gag on it before locking it away." Then she grinned. "I talked to Rolan about the price we should ask. The figure he gave me nearly made me fall down in a faint. But then I went there, listened to her congratulating me on finally coming to my senses and patting my arm and, well, what can I say? When I came to tell her the price I had agreed on with Rolan, somehow my brain came up with a different figure. Twice as much." Eryn shook her head and laughed. "And that proud fool of course could not show any sign of reluctance and so just nodded and told me to come by tomorrow to make her feet smaller! Can you believe that? She wants *smaller feet*! Have you seen her dresses? Nobody even sees her feet!"

Enric chuckled and rose from his chair to walk towards her and kiss her. "So, how much are we talking about here?"

"One hundred gold pieces," she called out and jumped up and down gleefully.

He stared at her. "What? That woman pays you one hundred gold pieces to have smaller feet? How could this be possible?"

"That's obviously what happens to women with too much money and too much time to fill their days when they don't work. You lucky, lucky man!" She pinched his cheek. "That is a problem you won't have to face. Ever. Your riches are safe from me because I have hardly any time to spend them."

"Well, that and the fact that you could do all your own cosmetic alterations without paying anybody else," he added and grinned when she scowled at him.

"So you think I am in need of some?"

"No. I am also pretty sure that Inad is not in need of smaller feet. Wishes are not always what we need, but just want for whatever reason. And you would be very welcome to spend *our* riches. I suppose I would just have to find a way of increasing them faster than you could diminish them," he smiled.

She regarded him thoughtfully. "*Our* riches. You still insist on this whole sharing thing between us?"

"I do, yes."

"Then you may start with sharing with me what exactly you are doing to make us so rich. What are these businesses of yours?"

He shrugged. "I try to spread them evenly. Trade, mining, farming for example. That sweet wine you like so much - I own the vineyards that produce it. And the source of flax to produce linen. Then I own a few mines extracting gold, iron and copper."

She nodded appreciatively. "That is a lot. How come you own all that? Family businesses?"

He shook his head. "No. I bought them one by one after I was promoted to Tyront's second in command. The allowance the Order pays me is generous enough, and I never really had any greater expenses. So I decided to invest the money in businesses, and to my own surprise I turned out to be rather good at managing them. It seems the training I received from my father was not completely lost," he ended wryly.

"No, obviously not," she agreed. "And they are all running well, are they?"

"Most of the time, yes. There are always minor setbacks in one enterprise or another, but that's why I spread the risk. The rule is always to have more businesses that run well than those that are experiencing difficulties. The wine business is very susceptible to bad weather, so if I depended on it alone to earn me money, there would be a real problem after every year when there was either too much or too little rain or sunshine."

"Look at that. You really are a smart one, aren't you? Considering that you are a warrior," she mused, and grinned when his eyes narrowed.

"What exactly is that supposed to mean?"

"Nothing, I am just teasing you a little. I had a day that was both a trial for my poor nerves and a triumph for that money box Rolan likes so much. I think I deserve a glass or two of that excellent wine we produce so expertly." Her eyes glinted. "Hey, maybe I can convince Inad that drinking robust quantities of it will help her feet stay small? We could make an even greater profit selling it to her!"

Enric laughed. "I am very glad you are a healer, my love. Your business ethics in trade truly scare me."

CHAPTER 15

Talking to the West

Rolan was waiting for her in front of the healers' building as the coach stopped. The coachman jumped off his seat to assist Eryn with the heavy wooden box that jingled suspiciously when moved. She yielded to his need to be courteous despite the fact that, with the help of a little magic, the weight would have been no problem for her.

She could see that her assistant was doing all he could to stop himself from drooling and stepped closer to take the small chest from the coachman and carry it inside. He had taken great care to have an extra room for their proceeds made as secure as possible. He had even added an extra wall, had the only window in the room bricked up to prevent anyone from entering that way, and there had to be at least four different locks in place which only herself and Rolan had the various keys to.

"Good to see that the lady has paid. I assume this is the full amount?" he asked when he put down the box in the vault.

"Yes, I made her pay in advance. She even paid for the coach ride here," Eryn grinned. "Our monthly expenses with the trainee allowances, materials and everything amount to about thirty gold pieces, am I right?"

Rolan nodded. "Roughly, yes. Not counting your own payment which you keep refusing to take."

She waved him off. "I don't need it, I have my allowance from the Order simply because I am a magician. And Enric takes care of all my expenses, so why would I need to take money that would be better employed at keeping this place running?"

"If you keep doing those cosmetic alterations we won't have to worry about this anytime soon," he commented. "Any chance that she wants her fingers shortened, neck lengthened or some such?"

"I don't know. She was immensely taken with her newly reduced feet, so I would assume that should keep her happy for a while. But she is the kind of woman to share her triumph over me with her fifty best rich friends, so there might be more requests of that kind in the near future." She grimaced. "I know you like to make money, but this was neither a pleasant nor a challenging task today."

"Be glad then that you managed to coax her to part with that much money," he remarked with scant sympathy. "And if you manage to take care of one such request a month, we should be well settled and can fund additional services."

She frowned. What was he planning now? "Additional services? Of what kind?"

"I have been thinking of preventative information campaigns or preventative examinations, for example. I can see in your notes some injuries happen more often than others, so why not instruct people how to avoid them? Or mothers-to-be. We could offer them regular check-ups to see if there are problems before they become obvious to a non-magician."

She stared at him open-jawed. He stopped and frowned. "We don't have to, I am just trying to make this work! It would in the long run enable us to make do with fewer healers. Don't look at me like that!"

"Shut up," she murmured, staring at the ground. "That's brilliant," she said, more to herself than to Rolan. "We could have non-magicians do a great deal of it."

Rolan straightened again, relieved that his ideas had met with a positive response.

"Oh," he exclaimed and slapped his forehead with his palm. "There was something I was supposed to tell you. I completely forgot."

"Been distracted by the heaps of gold, it seems," she smirked.

"I am not ashamed to say that I am excited about it. I don't see why you seem to regard it as something dirty or immoral," he replied with a tang of offence being taken. "Lord Tyront sent a messenger for you. You are to come to his study as soon as you are back from Lord Remdel's residence. Something about the Western Territories."

Eryn froze for a moment. Would that be good or bad news?

"Nothing more specific you can give me here?"

"No. Only that it would be of interest to you."

Well, that didn't sound too bad, did it?

"Then I suppose I'd better get going. The herb gatherers' lesson starts in about one hour. Send them a quick note that we will start an hour later owing to my being called away."

Rolan snatched a small notepad from his pocket and jotted something down. "Alright. Herb gatherers. One hour later," he murmured. "Anything else?"

She thought for a moment. "Yes, there is one more thing. Lord Tyront is due another report tomorrow. Can you prepare for me a pretty-looking calculation for the next three months, taking into account our hefty payment from today? I dare say that will give me some breathing space with him."

"Cost statement," he said and noted it down as well. "It will be on your desk when you return here later."

She nodded once in both appreciation and farewell and walked out the oppressive, windowless money chamber. She stopped in the door frame and turned back to him, grinning.

"By the way, there is a little something I forgot to mention. You remember the rate we agreed for Inad?"

He nodded. "Yes. What of it?"

"I took the liberty of changing it somewhat."

"Oh no! Why do I even bother calculating a rate for you if you just charge a different amount anyway? Judging from your attitude towards money you probably reduced it by half or something like that!"

"Wrong. Quite the opposite, I increased it slightly. We earned a hundred gold pieces instead of fifty."

Rolan's jaw was the one to drop this time and he stared at her, frozen in mid-movement. She laughed and turned, determined to remember this sight. It would warm her on cold nights - provided her new luxurious lifestyle did not put a permanent stop to something as common as freezing.

Her thoughts returned to mulling the matter at hand as she left the building. The Western Territories, she thought with slight unease. It had been about three months since Ram'an had left here. It was to be expected that there would sooner or later be attempts at making contact from one side or the other. He'd had two men with him to probe if there were any opportunities for trade, after all. She had never really enquired what the outcome of these talks was. That was negligent, she thought, and became angry at herself for not keeping up to date.

She reached the Palace and turned into the corridor to the stairwell that lead up to Lord Tyront's quarters, taking the steps two at a time.

Enric opened the door a few moments after she had knocked and kissed her demurely on the forehead before letting her in.

"Hello, my love. Come, we have been waiting for you."

He took her hand to lead her into their superior's study.

"Bad news?" she asked carefully.

"No, just news," he reassured her.

"Lady Eryn," Tyront smiled. "How did your appointment with Inad go?"

She shrugged. "Relatively satisfying on both sides, I think."

"Only relatively?" he enquired with concern in his eyes.

"Well, I had a very trying few hours, and she had to part with a considerable sum of money. So there was a downside for both of us."

"She has already paid in full?"

Eryn grinned. "Of course. In advance even."

"We may make a business woman of you yet," Tyront nodded.

"Enric tells me that my business ethics scare him, so you might want to rethink that ambition."

Enric chuckled. "Only when it comes to trade, my love."

"So, tell me about the news, will you? Rolan was rather cryptic, but so was your message from what I understand." She took a seat and took a sip from what looked to be Enric's cup.

"I am not sure how much you know about the King's efforts to establish and maintain communications with the Western Territories?" Tyront asked.

She swallowed. "I realised on my way here that I have been rather sloppy in keeping myself informed about that," she admitted.

"I see that there have been quite a few other matters on your mind," Tyront offered generously. "Certain steps have been taken to establish permanent communication. You may not have been the sole reason for them to seek contact with us, but you certainly were the trigger for it. Whatever happens in the future will surely involve you to some degree. The ambassador mentioned that you still have family in the Western Territories. I expect they will contact you. Be prepared for it and consider how to react if and when they do."

"You think? I would expect them to be rather disappointed in my staying here instead of hopping aboard Ram'an's ship to let him take me back there. They will probably decide finally to give me up as lost."

"After looking for you for more than two decades? I doubt that very much," Tyront said.

"But I don't really have close relatives as such. My parents are both dead, and I suppose whatever aunts, uncles and cousins who remain will hardly have any vested interest in me. From what Ram'an said I think they are trying to preserve the power in the families by making matches that produce offspring with strong magical abilities. I am no longer available for that, so I am basically useless to them."

"I am surprised you just discard a rather more obvious reason than that," Enric said. "The warm glow of having found the lost family member and curiosity about what and who you have turned into. Don't tell me you are not at all interested in them?"

She shifted uncomfortably on her seat. "I don't know. They might be angry at me for what my father did. Or be disapproving of me for some other reason. I might be too foreign for them, having lived here almost all my life."

"That is a possibility of course," Enric admitted. "Though the opposite is just as likely. They might be fascinated by you, surprised, intrigued."

"They might not be won over as easily as you," she said with some resignation in her voice.

Tyront chuckled and shook his head. "That is one thing I have never heard Enric described as before: won over easily."

"He is. I insulted, kicked, fought and tried to flee from him, and yet he couldn't get enough of me," she smiled.

"Still can't," Enric agreed good-naturedly and kissed her knuckles fondly.

"Stop it, the two of you," Tyront rolled his eyes. "This is supposed to be an Order meeting."

"So, how does the communication between the countries work, then?" she asked. "Using messengers, as they know how to cross the sea?"

"That was what has been done so far, yes. Yet the journey to Takhan, their capital city, takes some time, so it isn't the most efficient way to do this."

"How much is some time?" Eryn wanted to know.

"Four days from here, one way. So it takes about eight days for the travelling alone, and there is still what to write in the message to be considered," Tyront explained. "But there has been a new development. They sent us a new sort of messenger who can travel the distance in less than a day."

"What? Some kind of magical tool?" she asked, intrigued.

"No. More of a feathery tool," Enric smiled. "Messenger birds. They always return to their place of origin, no matter where they start from. They have sent us a few of them with instructions on how to make them breed. It seems they are quite demanding if you want them to raise young. Special kind of food with elevated, clean, sheltered perches and the like. The King has already arranged for an area on top of the Palace to be converted into a place they should find acceptable for nesting."

"So if we can make them breed here, they can be despatched to the Western Territories in case they want to communicate with us? But the birds would still have to be transported back by regular messenger, wouldn't they?" she frowned. "And you would need to breed a lot of them, if you can only use them for one-way communication."

"Yes, we can't completely forego the slower messenger service, but it would still save a lot of time. You would have to keep a larger number of birds, of course. Or have really short intervals for exchanging them again," Tyront elaborated.

"So, how fast are they supposed to breed? Are we talking about months here? And when are they mature enough to make that flight from here to Takhan?"

"We should be able to get them to lay eggs in little more than two weeks. We were told it is the right time for the year for them to mate now. And the chicks can fly long distances about two months after they hatch. They have been bred for their endurance."

"And you think that now that we are about to be able to communicate faster with the Western Territories somebody there will show interest in me?"

"Yes. That is just a matter of time now. The question is if you would like to declare your interest first by writing to your families there." Tyront observed her reaction carefully. She didn't seem very taken with the idea of taking a first step here. He was not at all disappointed in her lack of eagerness. The less interest she showed in the Western Territories for now, the better.

"I would rather not at this point," she said slowly. "Let's see how this whole relationship between the two countries develops, shall we? There might not even be any more contact with them a year from now."

Enric thought, that this was unlikely, and saw his assessment of the situation reflected in Tyront's expression.

"Alright, then I will let the King know that he need not wait for a message from you to add to his next missive," Tyront nodded. "Ah yes, and I am to convey to you Ambassador Ram'an's best wishes. He has also sent you a few bottles of something." He dragged an oblong wooden crate out from under his desk. It was filled with what looked like wood shavings and three bulgy glass bottles with gold paint on them. She smiled when she recognised what it was.

"That's what he got me drunk on that one evening in his quarters. Here." She took one bottle out of the box and handed it to Tyront. "Take one. It is excellent. I am told it is bad luck not to empty it once it has been opened, so make sure you don't drink alone. Unless you feel up to the task, that is."

Tyront raised his eyebrows in surprise at her generosity. "Thank you. I gladly accept it. If it is indeed as good as you say we might persuade the King to trade it for something."

She grimaced. "Then I suppose I am to give up another bottle to give him a first-hand taste?"

He grinned at her obvious reluctance. "Look at it like this: giving up one more bottle now might win you a steady supply in the long run."

"That will fail to comfort me when my now sole bottle is emptied," she said. "But take it and present him with it with my best regards. May he enjoy it."

"Me?" Tyront looked surprised. "Surely not. You will give it to him yourself."

She shook her head. "Absolutely not. He keeps teasing, scolding or lecturing me each time I meet him. I don't want to give him the impression that I appreciate that. Rather the opposite."

"Why not use the gesture to show him how little it bothers you, then?" Enric suggested.

"Because he would bloody well know that this was my reason for doing it. I swear to you, that man can read my thoughts."

"That's what he likes to make people think. He is just very good at drawing logical conclusions and reading people. And you are not as good at lying as you believe, so he doesn't even have to labour very hard at working you out," Tyront pointed out.

Enric shrugged. "So even if he divines why you are presenting him with the bottle, he will appreciate the motive. Or especially after that. He does so like games. And whatever puts him in a good mood might make him more susceptible to suggestions of trading."

"Alright," she sighed. "But how does one go about giving a present to a King? I can hardly give it to him when he next summons me to tell me off. Or at a ball, banquet or whatever. Or ask for an audience, give him the bottle and then leave again."

"True," the older man nodded. "But you wrongly assume that you will give it to him personally. You will leave it with one of his advisors, Marrin preferably, to have it passed on to him with your best wishes."

She considered that for a moment, then nodded. "Yes, I like that better anyway. It is almost the same as giving it to you to pass it on. I just exchange the middle man."

Tyront shook his head at her. "Middle man? You know, sometimes I have the impression that you do not fully appreciate my importance."

"Oh, but I do," she assured him. "Every time I make a decision, you are there to tell me why it's wrong. If Enric isn't faster off the mark, that is. So how could I not appreciate you accordingly?"

"It's a pity I haven't managed to teach you respect yet instead."

"Don't worry about that. Orrin has been trying that for almost as long as I have been here, so you are not the first one to fail with it, if that is any consolation," she grinned.

His smile was not exactly friendly, when he replied, "You seem to be under the misapprehension that I have given up on it. Rest assured that I haven't. But as you have presented me with a bottle of wine that you were obviously reluctant to share, I shall be lenient with you today. And now out with you. There are things I need to discuss with Enric that are none of your business."

"Gentlemen, then I shall leave you now. I know when I am not wanted any longer," she said in mock indignation and got to her feet.

"You should know it," Tyront grumbled. "I just told you plainly enough."

She just grabbed her bottles, one in each hand, and bent down to kiss Enric before leaving.

The men waited until the door closed behind her before they continued their conversation.

"So she is not willing to establish any contact with her family there. I admit I am relieved about that for now," Enric said.

"But they will sooner or later seek her out, no matter what she thinks right now. Ambassador Ram'an's visit has not yet been reciprocated. I strongly suspect that our new friends in the Western Territories have a clear idea of who they want us to send." Tyront pursed his lips. "The question is if the King would really send her. It is a risk, after all. Not dragging her off to their land is one thing, but keeping her there as soon as she has arrived would be much easier for them if they did indeed want her back."

"I don't think she would go there just like that at the moment," Enric chipped in.

"The King might order her to go."

"I don't think he would. Or would be able to, even. She is bound to the Kingdom by the magical oath. She just needs to convince herself that she will not return if she is made to go and would thus be stuck here."

Tyront frowned. "She would do that?"

"Depend on it. She is afraid of going there for now, I think. She didn't like what the ambassador told her about the magical bloodlines and how it affects the forging of companionships. And then there is meeting her family. She has not really got used to the fact that she is not alone in the world any longer. You heard what concerns she has about not being approved by them. And, finally, she has just opened her healing services to the public and is in the middle of learning how to run the place and training people."

"Alright, let's hope that you are right, then."

Enric thought for a moment. "How soon would we know if there was a message from the Western Territories that is requesting her to be sent to them for a visit? Are your agents that thorough?"

Tyront rolled his eyes. "Obtaining information from the King is more or less futile. He only lets my spies find what he wants me to know. He locks his desk, but only as a token gesture. I think he must burn the rest of the papers or hide them really well."

"You have no right to be unnerved by that. It's the same game you're playing with my spies," Enric chuckled.

"True. And doesn't it drive you mad?"

CHAPTER 16

Royal Plans

Marrin smiled without humour when the King, with an expression of discontent, let the letter from the triarchy - the ruling body in the Western Territories - sink and rest upon his desk.

"I assume the request for Lady Eryn to be sent to the Western Territories for a visit has finally arrived?" he asked.

"Indeed it has," the King replied. "Not unexpected, but still inconvenient. I was hoping for them to hold on a little longer with putting words to that particular need. She is still so very busy with getting her healing services to run smoothly and is hardly likely to be pleased at being sent away at such a time."

"Is it essential for her to be pleased about it, Your Majesty? She is hardly in a position to refuse a Royal order, is she?"

King Folrin rose from his chair and looked out the window. "You are mistaken. She is, and in more than one respect, too. The magical oath, you see, has its weaknesses. It is a matter of interpretation and what a magician can convince himself, or in this case, *her*self of. If she manages to talk herself into believing that I would send her there never to return, the oath would keep her from leaving the Kingdom. She is a smart woman. I am sure she is aware of this or would soon enough reach that conclusion if faced with such an order. And then there is the matter of angering Lord Enric immensely by despatching her to the Western Territories. I dare say he does not want to see her in proximity to the ambassador ever again."

"But you are willing to comply with the request to send her there, I assume?" Marrin asked.

"I must. There are several very good reasons to make those on the other side of the sea happy. Firstly, I hope they will show us how to overcome the obstacle that keeps us from going to sea. Secondly, they may in time show us how to free ourselves from whatever still precludes the birth of female magicians here, and thirdly, there is the transfer of goods and, even more importantly, of knowledge."

"So you have no concerns about their trying to force her to remain there? She still does have family over there, as I understand. Powerful *Houses*, as they call them."

"I am concerned about that, of course. With Ambassador Ram'an's obvious interest in her, not counting on this would be improvident of me. And this is exactly why she is not to go there alone under any circumstances, but to be accompanied by a person who will be very eager to see her return here again."

Marrin frowned. "You will send Lord Enric there as well?"

"Me?" The King raised both brows innocently. "*Send* him? I wouldn't dream of such a thing. I will merely grant his very urgent request to be allowed to go there." He fell silent for more than a minute before he continued, "I will need for Lady Eryn to be angry. No - not merely angry, but furious, enraged at her companion. Otherwise she will hardly be incautious enough for this to work."

"It has been a while since she was seen to be in such a state of fury," Marrin commented.

"I know. This is why we will assist her a little in getting there," King Folrin smiled darkly. "The essential part is to bring her to me immediately, before she has any chance to somehow vent her anger."

"And of what nature will that assistance be, if I may ask?"

"Lord Enric is not yet aware of his companion's very... open-minded handling of the changing room arrangements, I assume?"

"You assume correctly, Your Majesty. I suggest they would no longer be in place if he were aware of them," Marrin replied dryly. "So we will inform him of it?"

"We? No. He is so suspicious. We wouldn't want him to think that he is about to be manipulated, which would doubtlessly be his first thought if he received that bit of information from me. We will delegate this little task to somebody who has made it a habit of communicating small and unpleasant details to the Order's head. The matter being addressed in one of Rolan's letters of complaint should not arouse any premature suspicions."

"The young man has surely been aware of the changing room arrangement without ever making it a topic. What would induce him to do so now?"

"Ah, Marrin, the key is not the mere knowledge of it, but the more personal aspect of being directly affected by it. Until now he didn't care because it was of no relevance to him. Making *him* undress in front of her, however, will change that quickly. Judging from what I was told he is not the type to undergo something like that quietly. He still doesn't like her, and his attitude is not nearly as easy-going as the healers'. He will refuse to undress in front of her, I am sure of it. All that is required now is a little nudge. Prepare a note to Lady Eryn, will you? Inform her that I think it advisable to have every magician who works at the healers' building possess at least very basic healing skills. This should be enough for now. She needs to be observed very carefully then. When she has reached the state of exasperation I expect, she should be brought here immediately."

* * *

Eryn frowned at the note the Palace messenger had just delivered. It bore the Royal seal, something that was hardly ever good news. Sighing, she opened the folded paper and studied the words in evident surprise. Every magician who worked at the healers' building would need to have basic healing knowledge now? She wondered what had made him decide that. It seemed an oddly minor detail, considering that there was only one single magician concerned. She had no objection whatsoever to teaching Rolan healing skills; in her opinion every magician no matter where he worked should be able to do basic healing, just as Ram'an had told them was practice in the Western Territories.

Maybe that was a step in exactly that direction, she mused. But what would be the King's motives in enforcing that? And wouldn't it be sensible to coordinate whatever efforts he deemed advisable in this matter with her instead of phrasing it as an order?

She would ask him next time she saw him. Rolan would probably not be too thrilled about having to learn healing skills. Despite working in a place where healing was the daily business, he had never even once showed any inclination or curiosity to learn it himself. He seemed more than content with his office duties, which was fine by Eryn, as she preferred to concentrate her efforts on the healing part. And there was still enough paperwork left to be taken care of even with his help.

She got out of her chair and knocked at his door. He called her in and she handed him the note without comment. His eyes bulged, and he looked up at her from his sitting position, his expression slightly panicky.

"What? But why?"

"I have no idea. I just received the message and don't know any more than you. It was not my doing, in case you were wondering."

He handed her the note back. "I don't have to treat any patients, do I?" he pleaded.

She shook her head. "It doesn't say anything about that in here. But you will have to watch patients being treated and practice on them. As soon as you have mastered basic healing, you won't have to come near them anymore." Which was fine by Eryn, as his attitude towards patients was not the most compassionate.

He sighed in relief, which made her smile.

"I think one morning twice a week for the next month should be sufficient. You should be equipped to heal minor skin, bone and muscle injuries after that. The idea is not to make you treat illnesses and complex damage. We can start tomorrow, it's a patient treatment day."

Rolan studied her. "You are not very happy about this either, are you? Why?"

"I have no problem with teaching you. I am just confused about the order. It makes me nervous when he instructs me to do something and I don't understand why," she said thoughtfully and then shrugged. "But an order is an order. And I don't see any harm in your learning how to heal. I am sure you will find it a useful skill in your personal life."

He didn't contradict her, but his sceptical look bespoke his doubts.

* * *

She smiled when she came in and saw her trainees standing together in the corridor and talking animatedly, each of them holding a cup of steaming beverage. Rolan was there as well, but rather lost and off to one side. He was the new kid. That was comical in a certain way. It seemed as if behaviour patterns did not change that much when people grew up.

"Good morning, everyone," she waved and gratefully took the cup Onil pressed into her hand. Standing together and enjoying a hot drink before the mayhem of the day was about to start had become a habit among them on treatment days. Eryn appreciated that very much. It brought them closer together, gave them an opportunity to talk about whatever was on their minds - be it difficult or interesting patients, or private matters. Lebern and Lord Poron were currently discussing the best way to treat head injuries.

"Sending them to sleep is so much better. Head injuries especially need a lot of concentration, and extra activity up there," Lebern pointed to his forehead, "just makes it harder for the healer."

"I am afraid I have to disagree, my young friend," Lord Poron said with a shake of his head. "I fear that you would not be able to realise it if you were making any mistakes when the patient has no way of reacting to that. When this happens with a bone or muscle, you can repair whatever you did wrong easily enough, but the head is a completely different matter. You might damage somebody's ability to speak without noticing it and only realise it when the patient wakes up again and discovers that he is no longer capable of talking."

Both of them turned to Eryn expectantly. She thought for a moment before answering.

"My father would say that usually there is not only a single way of doing things correctly. I have to admit that I do not have great experience with head injuries, so I would keep the patient awake. A more seasoned healer might prefer the patient to be unconscious if he or she is experienced enough with the structures in the head."

She then took Rolan's arm and pulled him into the circle. "We will have company for the next month. You all know my assistant Rolan. He will be training basic healing skills two mornings each week with us. I expect you to be pleasant to him and help and explain things to him."

The trainees nodded to Rolan and then followed Eryn into the changing room.

Rolan swallowed hard when the men started to undress, not even bothering to interrupt their conversations. He then looked at Eryn and gulped again when she pulled her tunic over her head. When her eyes met his, he quickly averted his gaze and blushed. She sighed and put on her purple linen shirt and trousers.

"Grab a set and get changed. You must have been aware that there is one changing room for all of us; you furnished it, after all. No need to be inhibited. We are all professionals here."

She waited for him to move but he just stood there, rooted to the spot.

"Rolan? Hurry up. The first patients are due any minute."

He then swallowed. "I will change in my office."

When he heard her clearing her throat pointedly, he turned and saw her disapproving expression. She had folded her arms and stared at him with an impatient look. "No. You are going to change here. If you are not comfortable with your colleagues, how can you expect to be so with a person who needs your help? Looking inside a body is much more intimate than merely seeing the exterior."

"I can't change in front of you!" he blurted out in desperation. "You are a woman!"

Felden chuckled. "Come on, a strapping lad like yourself must have undressed in front of a woman before."

Rolan pointed at her. "Yes, but not... not... my superior!"

She rolled her eyes. "Gentlemen, leave us alone if you are ready. Start with a patient you can handle without me, I'll be with you in a few moments."

When they had all left the changing room and she was alone with him, she spoke slowly and in an exasperated tone. "Rolan, this is not about being a superior or subordinate, it is about being human. If I ever needed medical help from you, I would need you to be able to do something without bothering about who or what I am."

"But I would hardly have to undress in front of you, would I?" he said.

"No, hardly. But you were uncomfortable when I undressed in front of you as well, so it is clearly not only about you. Come on, Rolan! I have seen naked men before. There is nothing there that will shock me. And you can leave on your undergarments, even though you might find them a little uncomfortable after a while."

She folded her arms when he still didn't move and continued looking at her with a mournful expression.

"I am waiting."

"I can't," he said finally, in the voice of a small boy.

"Yes, you can. Turn around if it makes you feel any better," she suggested.

"It doesn't!" he exclaimed, then threw his hands up in the air. "And I don't see why I have to do this! This is demeaning!"

"How can it be demeaning when I just changed my clothes in front of you before?" she argued. "I am not asking more of you than I am willing to do myself! And have done, as you have seen."

"I am not going to go through this! And you can't make me! Damn you!" he shouted and turned on his heel to storm out the door. She heard him turn left, so at least he wasn't running out of the building but back into his office. That went really badly, she thought, and exhaled deeply. She wondered if she should have been more lenient with him. He was not a healer trainee, after all. What did it really matter if he was unable to get in contact with people on that level? It was just for one month, after all.

Yet then he was to be a part of the team for these few weeks, and this meant that he had to comply with the group's rules and not be treated any differently.

She wondered how to deal with this. Not doing the training with him was not on the table - there was the King's order, after all. And yet forcing him to undress in front of her seemed unlikely on past showing, as well. She could have flared off his clothes with a weak bolt of magic, she mused, and seen how he would have reacted to that. Maybe singeing a few chest hairs in the process. She chuckled and went out to join her trainees. She would ponder over how to handle that problem in the evening. Now there was work to do.

* * *

"There are another two requests for cosmetic alterations," Tyront shook his head. "It seems the ladies have the impression that sending them to me is more promising than contacting Eryn directly, as if I am the one to order her to do it."

"Considering how much money she asks for these particular services, I assume she will be willing enough to carry them out," Enric grinned. "One of them buys her at least a couple of months' financial independence from the King."

"It's a good deal for both of them. For the King, because he doesn't have to shell out for the expenses anymore and is safe in the knowledge that the Order doesn't increase its standing by funding it; and for Eryn herself, as she no longer has to be afraid of funding being cut off if something is not to the King's liking."

"I wonder that he is giving up that formidable advantage so easily," the younger magician mused. "It has been his most effective hold on her, after all."

"I am not so sure about that. He can still pass regulations, laws and orders that make her work harder or even impossible. You know, it is still in his power to strong-arm her effectively should he wish to do so. He just needs to be more creative now."

Enric smiled when they both heard contented snoring from under the table while Tyront looked a little edgy.

"Tell me again why you had to bring your fierce animal to this meeting in my study? I thought that wall you are having built would be finished by now."

"It is. But the yard is not yet finished. I had tree trunks and rocks brought in, but the earth is still fresh and when we let her out she gets too dirty to be let in again. And let me tell you one thing: bathing a half-grown mountain cat is not exactly a walk along Kingsway. At least I've had a few chances to use my newly acquired healing skills. Though one of the scratches was deep enough to damage a muscle and I had to let Eryn handle it." He shook his head at the memory. "So I decided to bring my feline housemate with me. She is bored at home alone and keeps ripping things apart and leaving scratch marks on the furniture. This is the second time I have brought her with me somewhere, and I have to say I am surprised at how well-behaved she is."

"I am surprised she doesn't run off," Tyront remarked.

Enric shrugged. "She likes me. She has taken to sleeping under my desk at home when I work. People are a lot more nervous when they come to see me now," he added with a knowing nod.

"Yes, as though your reputation wasn't enough to accomplish that already even without a mountain cat snoozing under your desk. Though I have to say that your reputation has certainly changed since your involvement with Eryn. People don't think you are heartless anymore."

"How nice," the younger man commented tartly.

"But more dangerous. Especially after the ball when you broke that man's nose."

"That's at least something. I can live with *more dangerous*."

A knock sounded at the door, and when Tyront called for his visitor to enter, a messenger came in, bowed and handed him a letter.

"Rolan to Lord Tyront," the older magician read out aloud.

Enric sighed. "Another letter of complaint? But then you do so enjoy them, don't you?"

"What can I say? They are entertaining," the older man chuckled and ripped it open. His smile slowly wilted while reading it.

"What?" Enric asked and frowned.

Tyront sighed. Oh dear. That was not good. And opening it in Enric's presence had not been a smart move. "Rolan has been made to learn basic healing skills and is not too happy about it," he explained vaguely.

Enric studied him for a few moments. "Why would she make him do that? She has been getting along with him reasonably well lately, so this surprises me rather."

"I have no idea."

"What else? There is more," he said slowly. "I can see it in your face. What are you not telling me?"

"This is something *I* might be better suited to handle," Tyront said carefully.

"Now you are really scaring me. You either hand me that letter right now or I will go and shake it out of Rolan myself. Which is it to be?"

Tyront pinched the bridge of his nose and handed him the letter with a sour expression. "As you wish."

Enric all but snatched the paper out of Tyront's hand, his eyes darting frantically from left to right. He had started breathing heavily and then, without warning, the paper in his hand went up in flames and disappeared completely within less than a second, leaving no more than wisps of smoke and a few flakes of ash that floated through the air.

"I am going to kill her." He got to his feet so quickly that his chair was pushed back and tipped over with the momentum. Then he cursed and rushed out into the parlour and then into the corridor.

"Hey!" Tyront called after him. "You forgot your cat!"

He looked under the table to the brown cat, awoken by the crash the chair had made when hitting the floor, and now staring in confusion at the man.

"Nice cat. Good cat. Don't try to eat me," he murmured. "I am old and stringy, you wouldn't like me. And I am a powerful magician. I would hurt you badly if you tried anything remotely predatory. Unless you are too fast for me, that is. Vyril," he then called out loudly. "Order some raw meat, will you? A lot of it."

*   *   *

Enric sent a strong gust of wind ahead to push the entrance doors to the healers' building open. Twenty-five pairs of astonished eyes were drawn to the tall, obviously angry, figure clad in dark blue. Nobody dared move as if each was afraid of somehow becoming the target of the wrath that seemed to make the air crackle.

His eyes wandered over to what seemed to be a line of seated patients awaiting treatment on wooden benches, when he spotted one figure in purple working clothes with a notepad.

"Where is she?" he snarled. Lebern, his eyes wide with panic, pointed wordlessly towards a closed door.

Eryn looked up in annoyance when the door burst open without warning. She was in the middle of showing Lord Poron and Onil how to seal off and remove an excrescence.

Her mouth, open to scold the intruder, remained open in dumbfoundment at the sight of Enric. His eyes burned blue with barely contained wrath. Without a word he pulled her up from her seat by her arm and dragged her out of the treatment room.

Only when she found herself in the corridor, did she come to her senses again and grabbed the door frame. "What do you think you are doing here?" she hissed.

"What do *I* think *I* am doing? Let's first talk about what you think *you* are doing!" he shouted.

Eryn glared up at him. The entire floor had fallen completely silent. Enric about to explode had that effect on his surroundings. She turned back to the treatment room.

"Onil, you know how to rebuild skin tissue to cover the hole. Make sure there is no scar afterwards."

After carefully closing the door, she took Enric's sleeve to pull him towards the staircase and into her office.

Then she whirled on him. "Have you gone completely mad? What do you think you are doing, storming in here, yelling at me in front of patients and my colleagues, and then interrupting the treatment of a patient?"

"No, just you listen to me," he said in a frightening, low voice and his index finger raised. "I just learned about your little custom of changing into your working clothes!"

She stared at him, waiting for more, then asked, "So, what?"

"*So, what?*" he shouted again.

She cursed and created a soundproof barrier around them. "Stop shouting at me! This is my place of work, don't behave like an idiot! I have a reputation to build here!"

He forced himself to breath in and out once. "Eryn. Your undressing in front of other men is not acceptable! Not at all! You will put a stop to that immediately - or I will!"

"What?" she snapped at him and came closer, arms akimbo. "Have you lost your mind? Do I come storming into your Council meetings to tell you how to do your work? This is the approach I have chosen, and you have to respect that!"

"I will not respect nor even endure your continuing to present yourself naked before the men who work here!" He wasn't shouting any more, but his voice was edgy, his expression set in grim determination.

"Very well. I will not ask you to respect it, then. But you will have to *accept* it, as I have no intention whatsoever of changing this practice. I have my reasons for it, which you haven't even bothered asking me about!"

"I don't care whatever reasons you think you may have to justify this. I will have this stopped, whether you cooperate or not. Don't make me come here every single treatment day to drag you out of that changing room. I am warning you!"

She ground her teeth and felt the boiling anger churning away in her stomach. "Oh, spare me your threats! I will not have this completely unwarranted jealousy of yours interfering with my work here! When have I ever given you any reason for it, I ask you? I am going to fight you on this, make no mistake about it! If you don't back off, I will have Lord Tyront deal with this, and even the King, if necessary!"

"You are really going to oppose me on something like this?" He grabbed her shoulders. "Stop this now! There is no way you could win any official dispute with me. I have been playing this game for more than ten years now, and you have only started to make out the edges of the playing field. I can have this put to a vote in the Magic Council, and they will not decide in your favour, I can promise you that with absolute certainty! They are all men; they will be with me on it, no matter what other differences there might be."

"We will see about that," she growled and freed herself from his grip. "Now get out of here! And don't you dare make a scene like that ever again here!"

The glare in his blue eyes had gone cold. "Have it your way, then." He turned and walked out the door, leaving it open.

Eryn balled her hands into fists and looked around for something to hit, punch or otherwise damage, then bawled in frustration when the only things she found were books and papers.

She braced her palms against the wall and forced her breathing to calm down. She had to return to the patients now. This was not possible in such a state of mind. She would somehow have to bury this until her work was done for today.

She looked up when she heard a knock at the door frame, the door still standing open. Half expecting Enric to have returned, she frowned at the liveried messenger who was clearly reluctant to get too close to her and was holding out a sealed letter for her to take.

She snatched it from his hand impatiently and turned it to have a look at the seal. Royal. She groaned and ripped it open. A summons to the throne room. Right this minute.

Staring at it in disbelief, she wondered how she was supposed to survive an encounter with the King at this moment without ending up in a dungeon cell.

The messenger cleared his throat. "I am to ensure you follow me to the Palace right away, Lady Eryn," he said with a grimace by way of apology.

"Do I at least have time to finish my one patient downstairs and change into different clothes?"

"No, I am afraid His Majesty's orders were very explicit. He wants you to come immediately upon receiving this message."

"Alright, then lead on," she sighed in defeat. She stopped when she passed Lebern downstairs in the patient waiting area. "Go on

190

without me for now, I have been summoned to the Palace. Seems to be rather urgent." Then she left the healers' building with the messenger, wondering if the day could turn any worse yet.

The guards at the high double doors to the throne room opened them for her in time so she didn't even have to slow down. She marched in, the anger lending her movements extra energy, and towards the throne, in front of which the King and Marrin stood, regarding her approach with obvious interest.

She bowed abruptly. "You sent for me? It has to be a matter of great urgency to summon me away from treating a patient, I would imagine," she said pointedly and was even more enraged when she saw the ghost of a smile on the King's lips. So he found her lack of respect amusing. What an excellent start. Well, there was more where that came from in case he didn't have a damn good reason for dragging her here like that.

"I apologise for my attire," she went on icily. "It seems there wasn't even enough time for me to change into something else. Is somebody about to die without my help?"

"Lady Eryn," King Folrin said mildly, "you do seem rather worked up at the moment. I will thus try your patience no longer and get to the point immediately. I have received a message from the Western Territories. They have offered to receive visitors from our side of the sea."

Eryn raised her brows. "How very fortunate for all of us. But I don't really see what this has to do with me. You surely don't need my assistance in choosing a delegation."

"They have specifically asked for *you* to be part of it, my dear."

"What?" she exclaimed in horror. "I can't go to the Western Territories any time soon! I have things to take care of here! What a ludicrous idea!" She exhaled and looked up at the ceiling. If this was why he had called for her, then it had been a total waste of time. Her time. "If there is nothing else you wish to discuss, I will now return to my duties."

She had already turned and was about to walk back to the doors when the King's sharp command made her halt immediately.

"Stop right there! Good. And now come back here. Excellent." His smile was cool. "You will leave here when I have dismissed you, not before. Have I made myself clear?"

She nodded stiffly.

"Pardon? I didn't quite catch that."

"Yes, Your Majesty," she said in terse obedience.

"I am so glad. There seems to have been a little misconception right now as to who is in charge here." He stepped down until he was only one step higher than her on the dais and looked at her thoughtfully. "You have been so restrained these last months, I had almost forgotten that temper that lies inside you. How refreshing to see that it has not yet been fully tamed. Please try to keep in mind who you are talking to, though," he admonished her gently.

Staring straight ahead she waited for him to go on.

"About the Western Territories," he continued. "I would, of course, not dream of ordering you to go there. There is a certain risk that they might decide to keep you there, after all. And we have all got used to you so very much, it would be a tragedy to lose you."

She felt blood pulse in her temples. Did he really think that teasing her right now was a sensible move?

"It is a pity, though, as I had the impression that your very... unconventional approach to diplomacy was well received by the ambassador. Apart from the little incident with the fork in his thigh, of course. I would advise you to refrain from expressing your sentiments quite so bluntly, even if with sharp tools, if you forgive my pun."

He smiled and walked around her, stopping right behind her left shoulder outside her field of vision, preparing to use an argument that he knew would not fail to make her react.

"I was not really confident that you would be willing to go, to be honest. But for the sake of what I hope are our soon-to-be friends in the Western Territories, I had to ask at least. And of course Lord Enric would hardly have approved, would he? You three weeks in another country..."

He watched her shoulders tense even further and walked on to stand in front of her again. He wanted to see her eyes. They were bright with anger. Excellent. She wouldn't fall for such an obvious trap if she was in her usual clear state of mind. But that she wasn't, he had made sure of that. Rage was such a helpful emotion when it came to steering people.

"Lord Enric," she said, pronouncing every word with extra clarity, "is not the reason for my decision not to go."

"Of course he isn't," King Folrin conciliated her at once. "A woman in your position can hardly base her actions on the approval of her companion. But fortunately this is not a dilemma you will have to face, as your decision not to go makes any confrontation with Lord Enric superfluous."

He saw a flash of renewed anger at his insinuation that she was just refusing because she wanted to keep her companion happy.

"I would go if it was possible, whether Enric approved or not."

He raised his brows. "Yes, you probably would. What a pity that there is now no opportunity for you to go, then. I mean, leaving the healers' place to young Vern for a time period of three weeks would clearly exceed his abilities."

She frowned. "No, it wouldn't. His abilities are beyond doubt. His schedule is what would make it impossible."

The King smiled. "Of course. So, who would you then recommend to be sent in your place? In your own interest it might make sense to pick somebody with healing skills so they might use the time there to pick up useful healing knowledge or have the right books copied for you."

He saw her swallow at the mention of healing knowledge and some of the fury in her eyes was replaced by restless longing.

"Are any of your trainees far enough along for that? Apart from young Vern, of course, who cannot be sent to a foreign country as a representative at the age of sixteen. Nobody there would take him seriously."

She covered her face with both hands. She needed to think this over in a quiet place, not in front of him and between audiences and treating patients. But there was nothing to think over, was there? There was no way she could go. The healers' place... could be run by Vern, as he had pointed out. The schedule would not be a real problem with some Royal intervention. Enric would be furious, immensely so.

"I will go," she said, her voice muffled behind her hands.

She felt warm hands grab her wrists and pull them away from her face.

"Could you repeat that, Lady Eryn?" the King asked quietly, his intent stare on her.

"I will go to the Western Territories," she said and swallowed.

"You understand that this is a binding promise?" he enquired firmly.

"I do, yes."

"Would you like to ask for permission first?"

The anger was back. "I doubt that the Order will stop me from going after you have commissioned me to. And I do not require my companion's permission for anything."

He smiled with obvious satisfaction. "Very well. I am glad we have reached an understanding. Then I will inform our new friends of your impending visit."

She watched him for several seconds, his fingers still around her wrists like the manacles she had been wearing for so many months. She wondered if it was meant as a symbolic gesture, as a reminder that her promise to go shackled her no less than the golden jewellery had.

He watched her breathing become more regular and felt the pulse under his fingers slowly returning to a resting rate.

She shook her head slowly.

"You have played me again, haven't you? And yet I can't see how you did it. I will very probably return home and be angry at myself for making such a foolish decision."

King Folrin loosened his grip on her wrists and let his fingers slide to close around her palms instead. "That I have, my dear. Why don't you give it a try? You were doing so well last time."

Her gaze wandered over the floor without taking in detail while she ran over the situation.

"What was the precondition for agreeing to, from your point of view, this seemingly unwise course of action?" he prompted.

"My anger." She frowned. "But how could you have known?"

"How could I, indeed?" he looked at her inquisitively.

"Agents?" she ventured. "But the chances of anything making me this angry were rather remote, weren't they?" She looked up into his eyes. "Unless you knew I would be. Or you made sure. But how? How could you have known that Enric would go there and shout at me?"

"Ah yes, I see there are still a few pieces of information missing. Why don't you talk to your companion or Lord Tyront? They will be able to fill in the blank spaces. Will you come to me again when you have pieced things together? But I have to warn you, this little game is not over quite yet. There are still moves to be made, one player in particular has to be considered."

"Enric?" she frowned. "Will he be able to stop me from going?"

"No, he will not," the King replied confidently. "On that you may safely rely."

"But he will exert some influence?"

"Oh, absolutely. I very much depend on him for it."

She shook her head in dismay. "So, when will it be clear that your plan has worked out to its full extent?"

"That, dear Lady, you will know immediately after a certain piece of information has reached you. Trust me." He released her hands again and took a step back. "Is there anything I can grant you in return for your cooperation in this matter, your willingness to embark on this journey into the unknown?"

She was about to decline politely, when her eyes widened and she drew in a quick breath.

"Yes, there is indeed a little matter I would ask you to decree in my favour."

"Go on."

"I don't know if you are aware of the changing room arrangements at the healers' building?" she asked carefully.

He smirked. "Your very open-minded approach to non-discrimination between the sexes? I am, yes. The number of applications for healer positions will very likely increase rapidly once it becomes public knowledge."

She ignored the heavy insinuation and went on, "Lord Enric disapproves of the arrangement."

"Indeed, does he now," the King replied with obvious amusement. "I can't think why."

"He plans to take the decision on how to deal with this out of my hands by having the Magic Council vote on it," she continued, determined not to let herself be distracted by his remarks. "As the healing services are officially still funded by the Crown, I ask of you to make it known that all decisions with regard to healing expertise, administration and organisation will continue to remain subject to my sole adjudication."

"That I will grant gladly. I will inform Lord Tyront of this tomorrow in a short note."

Eryn stood and waited. The King watched her a moment longer, then nodded approvingly. "It is good to see that you remembered my words about waiting to be dismissed. I will inform you of the exact time of your departure as soon as all arrangements have been made. It will be several weeks yet. You may leave now, Lady Eryn."

She bowed and left the throne room considerably less agitated than she had entered it.

Strolling back to the healers' building, she thought about the journey. She would be an ambassador. See Ram'an again. Meet members of her parents' families. As well as, she hoped, learn valuable new healing skills.

And she would teach Enric a good lesson. He had told her that she couldn't win against him. She hadn't merely won, but crushed him, even though he wasn't aware of it yet. She almost laughed out loud at what his reaction would probably be. He would learn about it tomorrow in Lord Tyront's study.

And in addition to this he would learn that she didn't need his permission for any of her decisions, not even when it came to leaving the country. She hoped that his being a few weeks without her would make him think twice the next time he planned to come dashing to her place of work to embarrass her.

* * *

Tyront read the note a second time. Enric was due any minute and compared to this, the bad news from yesterday had been little more than a minor nuisance. Two such blows in two days was not good. Even Enric's considerable command over his emotions might not be enough to let him keep his composure, especially as the note contained not only one, but two strikes.

Eryn had been summoned to the King immediately after Enric had left the healers' building. So he was carrying through another one of his little schemes. And this one didn't feel like it had run to the end yet.

Tyront sighed wearily. There was only one likely outcome of the gambit, though. He wondered if it would make sense to try and counteract it, but decided against it. The idea as such was not that bad, he had to admit.

Enric knocked once and didn't wait to be called in before he entered and took a seat. He looked harried.

"Good morning. Judging from the look of you I assume you didn't have a very pleasant evening yesterday after your tussle at the healers' building?" Tyront enquired.

"That would be putting it mildly. I tried to talk to her about it again, but she blocked all my attempts." He shook his head and a hardened expression showed in his eyes. "Then she will have to learn the tough way. I will call for a Council meeting and have some of her authority taken away from her. Several of the Council members think that she has too many privileges, in any event."

"I am afraid that is no longer something open to us, my friend," Tyront said calmly before handing him the letter.

Enric's face seemed to turn to stone as he read it.

"How is it possible that her undressing in front of other men suddenly seems trivial in comparison?" His voice was hardly more than a murmur, oddly free of any emotion. He covered his eyes with one hand for a moment and took a deep breath. "No wonder she didn't want to talk to me yesterday."

Tyront noted with a certain relief that anger had breached the icy surface. Good. It seemed a lot more natural than the eerie frostiness from before.

"The Western Territories," Enric hissed. "Of course they wouldn't just give up on her! And the King sends her there, just like that! How very convenient for them!" He rose abruptly. "Would you excuse me? I am going to try and talk some sense into the King. If he is deigning to see me after sending off my companion, that is."

He didn't wait for Tyront to dismiss him but left at once, forcing himself to maintain his pace merely brisk instead of the running he would have preferred.

When he reached the door to Marrin's study that preceded the King's own, he knocked and was admitted at once. Marrin nodded to him and then towards the next door.

"Go on in, Lord Enric. He is expecting you."

Enric walked on and entered the next study. King Folrin looked up from something he was writing and nodded to him.

The magician gave a rigid bow. "Your Majesty."

"Lord Enric. I assume you have come to talk about Lady Eryn's decision to go to the Western Territories."

"Indeed, I have," he replied, glad that they had got to the point right away. "I implore you to reconsider your plan of sending her there."

"Go on," the King said mildly and leaned back.

Enric noted that he was not offered a seat and thus remained standing.

"The risk of their managing to make her stay somehow is too great in my opinion. We have no idea what magical abilities they possess, only that they are superior to ours in many areas. She would probably not be able to defend herself against whatever magical means they might employ to convince or even compel her to stay there." He paused for a moment. "Eryn is too valuable for us to risk losing her. She has only started sharing part of her unique knowledge with us. She is important to the Kingdom."

"And of course to yourself. I am aware of all this, Lord Enric. You do not need to convince me of her uniqueness. The problem, you see, is that her visit has been requested explicitly, and we are not in a position to displease our neighbours after establishing peaceful, if wary contact only a short time ago." He smiled. "She agreed to it despite the rather unfortunate timing and the knowledge that you would disapprove, because she *wants* to go there. You must be aware of that. I admit that a little nudge was necessary, but in the end she needs to do it. There is family she has no memory of and knowledge she would otherwise have no chance of accessing."

"So she will go there as your ambassador, unprepared and vulnerable to everything they might do to her," Enric said coldly with a deadly stare. So much for appreciating Eryn's importance.

The King looked intensely at Enric. "As ambassador? No, surely not. You see, the status of her belonging might be considered… erm, disputable. We, of course, see her as one of ours, send her there as part of our delegation, have even bound her to the Kingdom by magic. But they might argue that she was born in their country, and not merely to two citizens but two powerful families, so it seems. In this case they would probably not acknowledge her title or function as ambassador." His gaze became more intent. "That is why she would need somebody to accompany her there. Somebody with considerable magical abilities to protect her from whatever she might otherwise fall victim to. Somebody who is used to interacting within high-born social circles and demanding the respect he deserves. Somebody with strategic prowess, a quick mind and restraint. And lastly and probably most important of all, somebody with both knowledge and experience when it comes to negotiating and finalising mutually beneficial trade agreements. You don't happen to be aware of anybody you can recommend for that position, do you, Lord Enric?"

Enric had closed his eyes somewhere after the *strategic prowess* bit. So that had been the plan all along. To facilitate his going there with her. He would otherwise never have agreed to take her to the Western Territories, even though he would probably have gone alone. But when the alternatives were either sending *her* alone or going with her, there was only one choice he could make.

He opened his eyes again and sighed in clear admission of defeat. The King had the good grace to refrain from smiling triumphantly.

"Your Majesty, I request to be sent to the Western Territories with Lady Eryn to represent our Kingdom."

"Granted, *Ambassador* Enric. I assume you would like to be the one to impart that piece of news to your companion?"

Enric nodded with a grim smile. "I would appreciate that very much, yes."

King Folrin nodded and took a sealed letter from his desk. "There is the official decree."

Prepared already, Enric thought without surprise. How very expeditious of him.

"I have already received a letter of confirmation from the Western Territories as to the acknowledgement of your status as ambassador, and they have graciously permitted you to bring your mountain cat with you to their capital city. Only provided it is no danger to the public, of course. Your departure from here is scheduled, you will leave in exactly three weeks. That should give you enough time to settle your affairs for the duration of your absence. Please do inform Lady Eryn of this as well. You are dismissed, Ambassador," he added with a smile.

* * *

Eryn was describing to her trainees the two major paths blood took through the body with the aid of one of Vern's drawings, when a knock sounded at the door of the training room.

Rolan poked his head in and scowled apologetically. "I am sorry to interrupt, but Lord Enric is waiting in your study. He says he would appreciate a few minutes of your time when you have your next break and not to hurry on his account."

She thought for a few moments. His coming here unannounced and interrupting her work was not something she wanted him to make a habit of. Though he had never even once admonished her when she had done exactly the same to him. She was still furious at him and considered letting him wait longer than necessary. But then he must by now be aware that he had been defeated quite thoroughly by her, and as a glorious victor she could afford to be generous.

"Tell him I will be with him in a moment, will you?" she instructed Rolan before turning to her trainees. "Gentlemen, the mighty leader calls, and I must answer. Take a ten-minute break. I hope I should be back by then. If not, try to work out the path of blood through the heart and present your findings to me afterwards. I'll leave the illustrations here on my desk. I'd also encourage you to look inside your body and observe the internals of your own heart. Be careful of the strength of the magical impulse you use for this, the heart is very sensitive and you want to avoid disturbing its rhythm."

She waited for any questions to arise and when none came, she left the room and walked the few steps towards her study. She was about to raise her hand to knock, but stopped and checked herself. It was *her* office, after all, even if she was being called into it.

Enric looked up from the book he had taken from her desk to leaf through. It was one of Vern's masterpieces. He had come to recognise the hand behind these skilled drawings at a glance.

She wasn't wearing her purple robes, he noted. She avoided that as well as she could, only used them instead of a cloak on her way here and then on the next hook they went and stayed there until she left the building again. He kept his expression neutral. She was very likely expecting him to be seething. There was a certain degree of anger in him, but he imagined that her own dismay would soon outweigh his.

"You are in my chair," she said brusquely instead of a greeting.

He leaned back flagrantly, remaining seated. "Let me tell you about my day so far," he began conversationally. "I had a very interesting meeting today, two of them, in fact. The first one was with Tyront. I learned about two things then. The first was that you have managed to obtain a Royal confirmation of your authority in all matters concerned with running the healing services. I was not happy about that, as you can imagine, but I was impressed at how fast you managed to finesse it. Our fight about that was only yesterday, after all. Then imagine my surprise when I heard about your decision to travel to the Western Territories."

He got to his feet now, putting the book back on the desk and walked the few steps until he stood directly in front of her. He saw her frown and look perturbed, and quickly grabbed her wrists when she made to step back.

"You stay right where you are," he said calmly, still showing no sign of agitation. "There is more to come. I had a nice little chat with the King and now I, too, have news for you, my dear." He smiled without humour. "I will be travelling to the Western Territories along with you."

"What?" she yelped and tried to retreat once more, forgetting that her mobility was somewhat hampered by his grip.

"You see before you none other than the new ambassador. For the duration of the journey my authority over you as your superior in the Order will be replaced by my new authority over you as ambassador. How considerate of His Majesty to keep the natural order of things intact, isn't it?"

"Why? I was to be the ambassador!" she exclaimed, making Enric sigh and shake his head at her.

"It seems that is not really possible with your status as citizen in the Kingdom being ambiguous. And from prior experience we both agreed that it was advisable to have somebody with you to keep an eye on everything and keep you out of trouble. Though I am not very confident that this is realistic. I may have to be content instead with getting you out of trouble," he added sardonically.

She gasped as it slipped into place: this was the final piece of information the King had said would reveal that his plan had worked. So he had wanted Enric to go there from the start, using her only as a means to induce him to go there when he might otherwise have been unwilling to.

"So he did it again," she murmured.

"Yes, thanks to all of us playing our parts so well," he confirmed. "Which brings me to your agreeing to a thing like that without talking to me first." The grip of his fingers became a little tighter. "I am well aware that the King has timed this very carefully and that your brain was awash with outrage and indignation and thus not working properly, but I think we can both agree that you did this to take revenge on me."

She stared up at him defiantly. "So what of it? You can hardly blame me for that after your behaviour yesterday!"

"Eryn," he said with forced patience, "making me sleep in the guest room is a suitable way of getting back at me, not trying to run off to a foreign country from where they might not let you return. And did you really think I would stand by idly while you wandered off alone to the place where Ambassador Ram'an lives?" He narrowed his eyes at her. "And I remember telling you repeatedly how I feel about your running off. It is a coward's choice and doesn't solve anything!"

"Don't you call me a coward!" she spat at him and once more tried to step away. He simply grabbed her wrists and turned her arms so she found herself pressed against him with her hands on her back, held there by one of his, the other grabbing her neck and making her look up at him.

"I didn't. I said you made a coward's choice; there is a difference. But that little matter is settled now, isn't it? Let's move on to another minor issue still disturbing me, especially as you so effectively thwarted my plans of involving the Magic Council. You may officially still be in charge of running this place the way you like, but let me assure you that I can make that a lot more difficult for you. I will accompany you here every second day to make sure that you are not changing into your working clothes together with your colleagues. Should you try it anyway, then your embarrassment at having me yelling at you in front of patients will be nothing compared to me dragging you out of that room."

She breathed in and out, forcing herself not to fall prey to her fury again. How was it possible that she had felt like a victor when she had come in only minutes ago, when suddenly *he* seemed to be on top of everything that had seemed to be going so well?

"So I am to tell the healers that I am not to change with them any longer because my companion's jealousy is more important than my own rules of learning to overcome physical inhibition?"

He smiled thinly. "Splendid. I am glad that you understood me."

A moment later she felt his lips hard on hers. The kiss was not gentle - it was a claim, very similar to the one after he had made her fight him in the streets. Just like back then, she was not required to reciprocate, but endure and accept her defeat.

The hatred and fear she had felt for him was gone, had been for several months. But she appreciated this way of kissing her into submission no more now than she had back then. She turned her head away angrily when he drew back again.

"Eryn," he murmured without releasing her, "don't make it so very hard for me to take care of you."

"You could try to let me take care of myself for a change," she said.

"I have. I was not pleased with the results. I surely don't have to remind you of the expedition." His tone became softer. "I expect you home on time today. There is a great deal of planning that remains for the trip. We will leave in no more than three weeks."

She frowned and he saw how the thoughts began racing behind her eyes, all the things she had to prepare, plan, take care of before then.

"Eryn?" he said into her thoughts. "Will you oblige me with this small matter and come home early today? No falling asleep at your desk again or taking care of everything yourself and making me worry when you are not home long after dark."

She sighed and nodded. There was not much else she could do while still in his vice-like hold.

"Thank you." He released her hands and put his arms around her instead. She was not one to take defeat well, he knew. So he wasn't surprised that she turned her head away when he made to kiss her again.

"Why do I have to kiss you when you deal me one blow after another?" she complained. "Just so you can prove that you can compel me?"

"To remind you why we put up with all the trouble that keeps coming our way. To show you that no matter how angry I am at you or you at me, that there is something stronger between us that makes it worth the effort of dealing with whatever troubles us. And because I really like kissing you. A lot. I also like that you can't really fight against enjoying it for long, even if you are angry at me."

She looked up at him in annoyance and saw him smile at her expression. He was right, that was the trouble. That he was aware of this made it even more of a nuisance. She did like kissing him very much, but she didn't have to like that she liked it so much that it overruled everything else sometimes.

He cupped her cheek quickly and lowered his lips to hers before she could answer, relieved when she didn't push him away.

"You know," he said with a lopsided grin, "if anybody had ever told me that I would have to fight my companion for a kiss three months after the commitment, I would never have believed it."

"If you had told me half a year ago that you are my anonymous lover and I would be joined with you a few months later, it would probably have unhinged me," she murmured.

"Tender words from my devoted lady," he chuckled and finally let go of her. "I will return home now. Remember to join me soon." He pecked her on the forehead and left.

Eryn leaned against the closed door and slid to the floor. So much for the lesson she had wanted to teach him. It was not as if the prospect of having him along for the journey was an entirely unpleasant one as such. Three weeks plus travelling time, four weeks in total, without him would have been very long indeed. She remembered her return from the expedition when his embrace had impressed on her how much she had missed him in those scant ten days.

Of course it had been stupid to agree to going there alone. But why did he always have to make a point of protecting her from herself?

CHAPTER 17

𝔓reparations

Vern leaned back and yawned vocally. They had been sitting together for more than three hours now, and it was getting dark already.

The dining table in Orrin's study resembled a battle field with numerous sheets of paper in various stages of being crumpled, stacked, ripped or loose.

Junar kept bringing them hot drinks and somehow managed to keep Orrin inside his study. His reaction to the news of Eryn agreeing to go to the Western Territories had not been a friendly one. He had asked her twice whether her senses had departed her completely in the light of what Ram'an had tried with his truth block, and had pointed out the chance of Eryn's finding herself bound and gagged in Ram'an's basement at some point.

When she had pointed out that Enric would be with her to avoid inconveniences such as that, Orrin had asked her very pointedly if her companion had even been made fully aware of the danger, or if he still hadn't heard about the truth block the ambassador had used on her.

By way of a reply, Eryn had just given Orrin a withering look and turned her back on him to wait for Vern. Maybe it had not been such a brilliant idea to arrange their meeting here in Orrin's parlour. But she had not wanted to have it in one of her studies - too official. And at her own home was not such a good idea, either. Vern had tended to be distracted lately whenever Plia was around.

"I need them to be able to take care of broken bones, damaged muscles and skin infections. Blood poisoning also seems to be rampant at the moment, so I would be grateful if you could include a lesson on that, too," Vern informed her. "I will take care of infectious diseases, organ damage and head injuries. How far along is Plia with her herbal knowledge? What medication can she make? And what about the apothecaries?"

Eryn pulled a sheet of paper out of her pocket. "I have a list here. These are the things we accept from the apothecaries at the moment. Plia can do the same things, but try not to anger the apothecaries by going to her instead of them. She will be busy enough checking the quality of whatever they are selling us. Only give to patients what she has approved."

Vern looked over the list and frowned. "Colds, sleeplessness, stomach upsets, tranquilizers... I don't see anything for increased blood flow here. Older patients especially will need something to thin their blood. I remember you once made something for that problem. You haven't taught them how to mix that together yet?"

Eryn shook her head and pulled her task list towards her. "Right. I will take care of that. Be careful though when you prescribe it to patients. And don't let the other trainees prescribe it for now. If they think it's necessary, you should be the one to make the final decision. Don't give the patients too much of it to take home; make them come back once a week to get more. If they take too much of it at once, it might otherwise be lethal as the blood is too thin if they suffer injuries and they might bleed to death. Unfortunately many of them suffer from the misconception that if a little is good, a lot must be even better. No matter how sensible they seem and how faithfully they promise you to adhere to the dosage, don't trust them. Ever."

The boy chuckled. "That is not exactly the philanthropic attitude towards patients you have been trying to impress on me in the past."

"Treating them with respect and showing sympathy shouldn't make you fall for their blithe assurances. I mean, examine some of their injuries and then listen to their stories of how they happened. Last week I had a man in his thirties who had a knife stuck in his arm, almost all the way to the handle. He told me he fell on it. I mean, really? Judging from the angle, it must have been *rammed* into his arm, probably during a drunken fight. But even in his half-drunken state he was ashamed to admit that he had done something stupid and fabricated a ludicrous lie that was easy enough to see through."

"So I am to distrust everything they tell me? That makes establishing a respectful relationship rather difficult," he remarked.

She sighed. "Well, you don't need to distrust everything. Just make sure the success of your treatment doesn't depend on their telling you the entirety of the matter. Be critical, but not impolite or unfriendly."

"But I can point it out when I discover that they are lying to me, can't I?" he asked.

"Not if you don't have to. There usually is a reason why a person lies. If somebody decides to hide the truth despite the fact that they have come to you for help, you can assume that there is a powerful motive behind it. So if you are aware that you are being lied to, do not expose the patient. The reaction would not be a happy one, trust me."

Vern rubbed his eyes. "Healing seems almost uncomplicated in comparison to this," he sighed.

She nodded. "I know. That's why you need a certain disposition for being a healer. An interest in the human body is a good start, but that's all it is. That's why I insisted on being included in the selection of the trainees. Lord Tyront would hardly have considered this, lacking any healing experience himself. But we are getting side-tracked again."

"That's because I can't concentrate any more. Can we leave it at that for today? I need a break and then I have to mug up for another hour or two. As I will be absent from my classes for an entire month, they are expecting me to do a few tests in advance."

She scowled. "Sorry to hear that, lad. But at least they are eager to make you finish your training on time despite the extra lessons and work in healing. It is more effort right now, but I am sure you will be glad not to have added another year afterwards."

"Yes, right," he snorted. "Remind me of that on the day of my testing, will you?"

She grinned. "I'll have Rolan scribble it down somewhere in this notepad of his. He will leave a note on my desk the day beforehand." She sighed. "Though right now it doesn't look as if we are going to be working together for that long. He fled even before his healing lessons were supposed to start because he didn't want to change in front of me."

"Don't be too hard on him. I was not exactly thrilled the first time, either. Though compared with him, at least I like you," he pointed out.

"So what am I supposed to do with him? Tomorrow is the next treatment day, and if he doesn't show up for his training session I'll have to think of something else. I can't bend the rules for him, it wouldn't look right."

"I thought Lord Enric was against your changing with the healers, anyway? So if you obeyed your superior for a change, that would solve both problems, wouldn't it?"

"Don't be ridiculous," she protested. "I can't be seen to give in to a demand like that in an area where I have the authority. Well, am *supposed* to have the authority."

"Didn't you say he threatened to drag you out of there if you change into your working clothes there again?" Vern enquired. "Don't get me wrong, I appreciate a good show, but it will not exactly strengthen your authority."

She smiled. "True. That's why I will oblige him in the mornings and wear my working clothes under my robes when I get there. But in the afternoons he will not be there to check on me."

He shook his head indulgently. "I bet that won't go well for very long."

"Let's see about that." She emptied her cup and selected several sheets of paper to take with her before she got up. "Now I'd better return home. Enric is waiting for me with more planning tonight. Won't that be so much fun," she sighed.

* * *

Tyront leaned back in his chair after calling in his visitor.

"Lord Tyront," Rolan said politely and bowed. He was clearly nervous, as was to be expected when granted a meeting with the Order's most powerful leader.

"Rolan," Tyront nodded. "Take a seat."

The young man did and waited for his superior to invite him to speak.

"What brings you to see me, young man?"

Rolan bit his lips before the words started bubbling out of him. "The matter with the changing room, Lord Enric... he was so angry at her, I shouted at her... she will surely kick me out now."

"I see," Tyront said slowly. So Rolan was plagued by a guilty conscience. How uncharacteristic. "Has Lady Eryn indicated anything of that sort?"

He shook his head. "No, but I suppose she would let *you* know first anyway."

Interesting, Tyront thought, he seemed worried. As if no longer working with her, or at least no longer working at the healers' place, was bothering him.

"Would that be a problem for you, young man?"

Rolan looked down, avoiding Tyront's questioning gaze. "Yes, My Lord. It would."

"That is not the impression I got from your letters, the last of which you sent to me only yesterday," Tyront pointed out. The one that had started the whole mess.

"It... it was wrong of me to send it. It was the reason Lord Enric made her angry enough to be willing to flee to the Western Territories," he said with a doleful expression.

Ah yes, there was a little detail he had wanted to ask the assistant anyway.

"Why did Lady Eryn decide that you have to learn healing? It is not part of your responsibilities in your current position, is it?"

He frowned. "She hasn't. His Majesty sent a note in which he ruled that all magicians who work at the healers' building have to possess basic healing skills."

Tyront's faint smile hinted at his wisp of pleasure. So that was how he had managed to start this little game. He had been aware of Rolan's habit of sending letters of complaint and had used him to make this particular detail of the unisex changing room known to Enric. The rest had only been waiting for Eryn to become really enraged and dragging her in front of the King. Then pushing the right buttons and so provoking her into accepting the assignment. Simple yet effective.

"I see. So what exactly do you wish me to do now, Rolan?"

"I wish to ask you if Lady Eryn has requested a replacement for me after I was rather... impolite yesterday." He forced himself to look up into those mildly amused eyes.

"No, she has not. And I doubt that she will do so in the near future," Tyront said.

Rolan looked at him in astonishment. "What? But she must have complained about me before!"

"What makes you think that? No, quite the opposite. Receiving your letters, I have asked her repeatedly how well your working arrangement works out. She has not even once expressed anything but appreciation for your work, your meticulous attention to detail, your organisational skills and how your performance has exceeded her expectations." He watched the young man's face grow pale and allowed himself a small smile. That had been a nasty shock, being commended by someone he had done his best to get into trouble.

"No complaints? Not even one?" he asked feebly.

Tyront shook his head. "No. She is not aware of your habit of sending letters of complaint to me so far, but I imagine that she will find out soon enough owing to the effect of your last one." He looked at his visitor pointedly. "I advise you to make sure that *you* are the one to inform her of this. Learning of this will of course not improve your standing with her, but it will surely be less of a blow to her if she learns of it from you instead of from somebody else. I wouldn't wait too long."

Rolan nodded slowly. "Thank you, My Lord. I will heed your advice."

Tyront was pleased to see that Eryn's assistant had become thoughtful, doubtlessly re-evaluating his impression of Eryn and considering his next step to minimise damage.

"If there is nothing else, you may leave now."

The young man stood and bowed. "Good night, Lord Tyront. Thank you for seeing me."

Pity, he thought. It seemed that the chances of receiving any more letters of complaint from him were slim to non-existent now. But for a man willing to pay in gold there were always useful sources of information.

* * *

Eryn closed the door behind her and saw that the one to Enric's study was open despite the two male voices she heard talking. So he had a visitor but did not object to being disturbed. Urban trotted towards her and rubbed her head against Eryn's legs.

"Hello, you," she said and bent down to scratch the cat's cheek. "Been a good kitty today, I hope? No furniture gnawed or people scared, hmm?"

"Eryn?" she heard Enric call from his study. "Come and join us, if you will. There is somebody I would like you to meet."

Urban followed her into the room and resumed her place under Enric's desk, daintily crossing her paws as she sat.

Enric was with a man about the same age as himself, well dressed, about Ram'an's height, thus only a little taller than herself. He had a pleasant face that somehow looked familiar. And eyes so light brown that they seemed almost golden.

Enric stepped closer to kiss her on the forehead in his usual greeting, then led her to the visitor.

"Eryn, I would like to introduce you to Kilan. He will be part of the delegation to the Western Territories." Then he turned to Kilan. "This is Eryn, my companion."

Kilan gave her a broad smile and bowed. "Of course. Lady Eryn hardly needs to be introduced, at least not to anyone who has lived in the city this last year. It is a pleasure to finally make your acquaintance."

"Nice to meet you, Kilan," she replied politely. "You are to come with us on that journey, then. May I ask in what function?"

"My two primary functions will be to keep His Majesty informed of what is going on in Takhan and then assist the two of you as well as I can. Organise things for you, find information and the like," he explained.

She studied his face for a few moments. "Where have I seen you before?"

"Probably at the last ball. I didn't have the pleasure of dancing with you myself, but considering Enric's reaction to men who get too close to you, that might have been good for my life expectancy," Kilan grinned.

Interesting, she thought. He didn't use the title *Lord* with Enric and made fun of him without showing any sign of fear. And he had been invited to the ball. That hinted at rank, some other kind of influence or a long-lasting acquaintance with Enric. Or a combination of those.

"He is getting better at restraining himself these days," she smiled. "Now he only roughs up one out of twenty men I dance with. So you have known each other for some time, haven't you?"

Enric raised his eyebrow. "What makes you think that?"

She chuckled. "Because, unlike most people, he does not cower in awe or fear before you."

"We trained together as boys," Kilan told her.

"It was quite a bit more than that," Enric corrected, in a mild tone. "We were close friends."

"Yes," the other man said with regret clearly discernible in his voice, "but then the testing, or rather the result thereof didn't leave you enough time for friendships anymore."

Eryn regarded him with renewed curiosity. "So you are a magician, then. And you knew Enric before he was all mighty and powerful. Is it true what people say? That he was a lazy student and a bane to his teachers?"

"Absolutely. It took my father two days to get over the shock of the test results," Kilan smirked, with a conspiratorial glance at Enric.

"Your father?"

"Marrin," Enric said. "This is the son of the King's advisor, so be careful what you say in his presence."

Kilan rolled his eyes. "Oh, sure, because the King has no other source of information than *me*. People are way too guarded with what they let me hear for it to be of any value to him. I don't even get to hear the gossip as it's fresh."

She frowned. "But Marrin is not a magician, is he?"

"No, but my maternal grandfather was," Kilan told her.

Eryn regarded him thoughtfully. "You know, that means that we should teach you basic healing before we leave here. Everybody in the Western Territories seems to be able to do it, and we wouldn't want to make the impression of being backward. Or let's rather say we should try to hide the fact that we are."

Kilan nodded. "Yes, that is something Enric and I were discussing before your arrival. I am glad you agree. I know you have a lot to plan and prepare, but I would appreciate it if you could squeeze me into your busy schedule somehow. I can adapt to whatever times would suit you."

She nodded. "I will contact you with regard to that. I am also supposed to be teaching my assistant basic healing, so maybe there is a chance to combine these. But I first need to work out how to coerce Rolan into giving it another try."

"Ah yes, the little matter with the changing room," he smiled and winked at her. "Then I will wait for your message about when and where to meet you. Enric and I have been thinking about products we need to bring to present to them as possible trading goods, such as wines, fabrics, samples of ores, spices, herbs and so on. If there is anything else you can think of, please add them to the list. Furthermore, you should order whatever you think you will need for the journey, such as formal clothes. But in your case, Lady Eryn, it might be advisable to have some clothes made up for you in the Western Territories as well. They will expect you to embrace your origins to a certain degree, and wearing the local fashion is quite an effective and simple way of demonstrating this."

"Wait, wait, wait," she stopped him with raised hands. "I don't know anything about that country, apart from the fact that it's warm and that they have excellent wine and berry juice there! How can I embrace anything from there? I will look like a fool trying to pass as one of them!"

Kilan shook his head. "No, you won't. The idea is not to pass as one of them, but to show an interest. And it would be advisable to have a nice mixture of both fashion styles at your disposal. They are very likely curious about how women in our country dress, so you need to provide some insight into that as well."

She gulped. "This sounds complicated, and we are still only talking about my clothes, aren't we? I suppose I shouldn't even open my mouth over there!"

"That would be an interesting change," Enric murmured and then grimaced when her elbow jabbed him in the ribs.

"Remember that I am the one they asked to be sent, you are just my accessory, *Ambassador*."

"That may be the case," he replied. "Though I would like to remind *you* that your diplomatic skills would most likely cause a war without me."

"Oh, dear," Kilan sighed. "I see I am going to have a lot of fun with the two of you there." He looked down at the brown cat under the desk. "I am told the cat will be coming with us. I suppose it has been trained not to eat anybody? It doesn't look fully grown yet, but we wouldn't want it preying on small children, would we?"

"I will not let her roam the city unsupervised, if that's what you mean," Enric said in a serious tone. "I will keep her inside our residence most of the time with the windows shuttered."

Kilan nodded. "Good. You are aware that you walking the streets with what is clearly recognisable as a fierce animal will definitely have an impact on how people regard you? But I suppose as you are meant to be negotiating trade agreements, that would probably not be an entirely unwelcome side-effect."

Enric chuckled. "What can I say, Kilan? You clearly have your father's analytical skills. That will be very useful, especially as Eryn tends to be rather... impulsive."

She rolled her eyes. "Says the man who stormed only yesterday into my work place and yelled at me in front of patients. Really now!"

Kilan looked at Enric thoughtfully for a few moments. "You know, it is kind of reassuring to see you like this again. Since you were promoted into the ranks of power, you were not seen joking around very much or showing any particular regard for anybody. Apart from Lord Tyront, and even that took several years. I am looking forward to this trip and to getting to know you again. A pity we didn't keep in contact. But I suppose you were too busy and I was too intimidated and insecure because I was categorised so much below your level. I should have risked rejection instead of staying back to avoid it."

Enric looked at him in surprise. "I thought you were resentful toward me for stumbling into fame and glory."

Kilan laughed. "Hardly. I remember your face when you came out of the exam hall. Completely pale, your movements awkward and your voice no more than a whisper. Believe me, I was very well aware that this wouldn't have been your choice. If there was anything I felt about you, it was sympathy."

Eryn grinned at both of them. "This is so endearing! A moment of true male bonding. Shall I leave you two alone now or are you done rediscovering your affection for each other?"

Two pairs of eyes turned to her in annoyance.

"We *have* to take her with us, don't we?" Kilan said sarcastically.

Enric nodded. "Yes, they specifically asked for her. But don't worry. They will see soon enough what they have let themselves in for."

*   *   *

Enric stopped Eryn in front of the healers' building when she was about to enter through the door and smiled down at her.

"Wait. Let me first see if you have your working clothes on under your robes," he instructed and nodded in approval when she lifted her eyes, but pulled down her neckline enough for him to recognise the purple linen beneath.

"Good. Can I rely on you to change back in your office or at home at the end of the day?"

"Why don't you come here and check on me?" she asked innocently, knowing fully well that this would be too time-consuming for him to undertake since nobody could predict the approximate time they would finish.

"As the end of your working shift depends on the number of patients, it might be necessary for me to wait hours until I can check on you. Unfortunately I don't have that luxury," he replied.

Yes, very unfortunate, she thought.

"Do you know that people have come to call the place *Lady Eryn's*?" he said.

She wrinkled her nose. "Really? That sounds like a tavern."

He chuckled. "Probably. But like a very noble one. Or a house of ill repute. Which is funny as there are some parallels, if you think of it." He held up his fingers to count them out. "People come in feeling bad, then they leave after a while feeling a lot better. You have beds in there. Your clothes unmistakably identify your profession. You ask immensely high prices for services that are outside the scope of your usual field."

Groaning, she gave him a reproachful look. "Thank you very much for that. I do so like being compared to a prostitute, especially by my own companion. You are not exactly a gentleman, you know!"

"That doesn't matter, my love," he smirked. "Most of the time you don't exactly qualify as a lady, either. I have heard some of your curses. Nothing for the faint-hearted."

He kissed her and then stepped back. "Have a good day and don't forget to contact Junar about clothes for the trip."

Yes, as if there was nothing more important to take care of right now than clothes, she thought, unnerved, but didn't say it out loud.

Instead she nodded obediently before she turned and entered the building. When she walked towards the small kitchen to heat some water for her morning beverage, she saw Rolan leaning against the wall, clad in purple healer's clothes, obviously waiting for her.

He pushed himself off the wall when he saw her and straightened, clearly nervous about something.

"Lady Eryn," he said and bowed.

"Rolan," she replied and looked expectant. So he was extra formal today. He was wearing the healer's shirt and trousers, so it seemed like he had decided to give the training another shot.

"I would like to start my training for basic healing skills today," he announced in case his intention was not clear.

"Yes, I guessed as much," she said carefully. "And I am very pleased about that. Will you give me a moment? I need to send a quick message to somebody I hope will be able to join us as well."

She rushed up to her study, wrote a short message to Kilan to ask him if he was available for starting his healing training right now and to apologise for this very short notice. When she had found a messenger to deliver the note, she returned to Rolan, who had not moved from his spot.

"I need to talk to you," he said and looked like he was not very happy about it.

Oh no, she thought. He would hardly tell her that he had decided to give up his position, would he? That would not make a lot of sense now that he had decided to learn healing to comply with the King's order.

"Yes?" she encouraged him warily.

He took a deep breath and then spoke slowly, "I have been sending letters to Lord Tyront to complain about you."

Her eyes narrowed and she pursed her lips. "I see. Since when?"

"Pretty much since our first meeting," he admitted with a grimace.

"And why have you decided to tell me about that now?" she enquired.

His mouth struggled to say the words. "Because of the trouble my last letter got you into." Watching her, he waited for her to reach the right conclusion and save him from saying it out loud.

She sucked in a breath when the truth dawned on her. "Are you telling me that this is how Enric learned of the unisex changing room? Because you sent a letter of complaint about it to Lord Tyront?"

He nodded, edging a little closer to the next doorway as if to make sure he had a chance to duck for cover in case she decided to send a bolt his way.

Closing her eyes, she exhaled. Now all the pieces fell into place. The King must have been aware of the letters and had issued the order for Rolan to be taught healing to make him reveal that little detail in his next letter. That had been the missing bit of information the King had mentioned.

But now there was nothing she could do against that any longer. The King's plan had worked, she and Enric were about to go to the Western Territories, whatever the outcome.

"I have to say that I don't appreciate your writing to Lord Tyront, Rolan. Not at all. If you are dissatisfied, talk to me. You might not always be happy with my reply, but I will at least listen to you. And if what you say is halfway sensible, I might even act on it." She narrowed her eyes at him. "If I hear about your sending him another letter ever again, I will get my hands on it and make you eat it. Don't think I couldn't do it. I would just stun you and force it down your throat. With a long wooden stick."

She had to suppress a grin when she saw the relief on his face when he nodded eagerly. "There will be no more letters, you may be sure of that."

"Good. Then go and prepare another set of working clothes for Kilan. He will join us soon, I hope."

"Of course," Rolan said immediately and then added quickly, "And thank you," before he hurried away.

Eryn rubbed her eyes. That meant she had to visit the King again as he had asked her to as soon as she had figured out his latest political strategy. Superb.

*   *   *

Vern turned when he heard his name spoken quietly and then looked on in surprise when he saw Lord Enric leaning against the wall next to his classroom door.

"Lord Enric," he said quickly and bowed. His classmates looked at him and the tall magician in blue curiously, and he heard them whispering as they retreated more slowly than they would have normally after their last lesson, maybe eager to catch a word or two to find out why this very important man was waiting for Vern in front of their classroom when he was in a position simply to interrupt the lesson instead.

Enric waited patiently for the boys to be out of earshot, before he spoke again.

"I need no more than a minute of your time." He pushed himself off the wall and looked down at the boy. Vern had grown a bit in these last months, and his cheeks no longer looked as smooth as they used to. He would soon have to start shaving regularly.

"What can I do for you?" Vern asked politely. He knew better than to take any liberties with this man just because he happened to be on very friendly terms with his companion.

"I was wondering if you could assist me with a little matter I have been pondering. You surely are aware of that one matter that has caused some... dissent between Eryn and me lately?"

Vern barely kept himself from bursting into giggles. *Dissent* was putting it very mildly.

"I am, yes," he admitted carefully.

"Good, that saves me some time. Eryn no longer changes into her working attire with the trainees, but I can't help but wonder if she uses the opportunity to change *out* of them again in the afternoons when the work is done. As this is a different time every day, I do not really have the chance to look in on her. She doesn't return home in her working clothes, so she must change out of them at the healers' building." He leaned forward slightly, forcing Vern to bend his head back a little further to look up at him, using his height to full advantage. "My question now, Vern, is if she does this in her office or in the changing room with her colleagues."

Vern swallowed as his mind raced. This was not good; he was stuck between giving Eryn away or lying to a man who would not take well to that. Enric's eyes narrowed when he hesitated.

"Vern?" he said in a low, warning tone.

The boy began to speak, his unhappy expression almost supplying the answer. "Are you *ordering* me to reply to your question, Lord Enric?"

Enric straightened slowly and regarded the boy for a few moments. "No, I am not. By asking that question you have made it redundant for me to order you. This is a more than sufficient answer." He pursed his lips. "It was a wise decision not to feed me an untruth. Give my regards to your father." Thus he turned and went away oddly noiselessly for such a tall man.

Vern closed his eyes and wondered if he should somehow let Eryn know that she had been found out. No, he decided, somewhat irked that she had indirectly put him in this situation just now. He had warned her only yesterday that this wouldn't go well for very long. She hadn't believed him. Well, she was about to find out who the smart one was now.

* * *

Felden froze in shock when he opened the door to the corridor to answer the knock and found himself facing Lord Enric, tall and imposing in his blue robes and clearly used to causing such a reaction.

"Felden," he spoke and gave the healer trainee a few moments time to recover.

"Lord Enric!" he exclaimed. "What can I do for you?"

"Letting me in would be a good gesture for a start," the tall magician answered laconically. "Not that this isn't a very clean and respectable corridor, but I find it rather unsuited to having a conversation in."

"Of course! Forgive me," Felden said quickly and stepped aside to invite his superior in. Why was it such a difference whether to deal with the number two or three in the Order? Working with Eryn every day somehow made people forget about her importance, as she was not one to flaunt her authority unless necessity demanded it of her. But not this one here. He sported his power like a shield - probably couldn't even turn it off if he wanted to.

"Why don't you sit, My Lord?"

Enric did and looked around the apartment unobtrusively. It reminded him very much of his own quarters before his promotion. Two rooms, suitable for a bachelor of medium importance. He would probably be assigned another one soon, Enric mused. The demand for healing services was high at the moment, and the importance of the healers providing it would almost certainly increase in the time to come as a result.

"I am here to talk to you about the changing room at the healers' building. I assume my attitude towards that is common knowledge by now."

"I admit it is," Felden nodded apologetically. "Though let me assure you that none of us would dare to look at Lady Eryn in any manner that would indicate an undue..."

"That is what I am assuming," Enric cut in sharply. "Otherwise this conversation would have begun in a lot less... friendly way."

Felden looked uneasy. This was *friendly*? Oh dear. He hoped fervently that it would not progress to being *un*friendly anytime soon. He waited for his superior to go on, too intimidated to ask the question that was on the tip of his tongue: What was *he* supposed to do now?

But fortunately Lord Enric seemed to want to talk about just that, anyway.

"Lady Eryn, as you know, is in charge of arranging all organisational matters around the services you all provide. This I have to respect, of course." He smiled thinly. "Though I know that she endeavours to provide a pleasant working environment for all of you and would hardly like to inconvenience anyone. A very commendable quality in a superior, I find." He looked at Felden pointedly.

The healer frowned and drew in a slow breath when an idea started to dawn on him.

"Inconvenience as in making us do something she thinks we do not want to do?" he ventured cautiously.

Enric smiled, but it didn't reach his eyes. "Indeed."

"So pointing out to her that a single changing room for all of us is not to your... ahem... *our* liking would induce her to provide different arrangements, if I understand you correctly?" Felden's face turned red at his little slip mid-sentence.

"Doubtlessly," the Lord agreed, pleased with the man's quick thinking, and nodded for him to go on.

Felden's eyes darted across the room in a desperate search for inspiration. "And we feel that the current arrangement is inconvenient on account of our modesty? And that our female friends and companions do not approve of it?" And that you are about to make me suffer direly if I don't comply, his thoughts added as completion.

"Very good," Enric nodded, obviously satisfied and rose. "I see we understand each other. I trust that you will not let too much time pass before you address the matter. Tomorrow morning would be a good time, don't you think?"

Felden nodded eagerly.

"A good night to you, Felden. Thank you for your time."

And gone he was. Felden let himself fall into the nearest chair and breathed out heavily. He couldn't help feeling that he had just narrowly escaped a rather unpleasant end.

*   *   *

Enric climbed the Palace stairs to the second floor. Lord Poron was the last one on his list. The conversations with Lebern and Onil had been as uncomplicated as the first one with Felden, but Lord Poron was not to be intimidated or manipulated easily, especially not by a man who he had more or less watched growing up.

Lord Poron was the first and only one to smile when he found Enric on his doorstep.

"Ah, Lord Enric! I was wondering when I would have the pleasure of welcoming you to my quarters, considering recent developments. Do come in, will you? Aurna has just brewed a nice pot of tea, and I hope you will take a cup with me."

Enric couldn't help but smile in return. So he had been expected. He shouldn't be surprised about this, he mused. Like Orrin, Lord Poron had never been an eager player of political gambits in the upper ranks, but he was nevertheless an experienced one.

"I would be happy to, thank you," he replied and took a seat after Lord Poron motioned towards a settee.

"So, I assume you have been making a few... social calls this evening?" the older man enquired with a quiet smile. "Though I imagine that is not what my young colleagues would call it."

"No," Enric agreed, "probably not. I admit they did seem rather tense for some reason."

"Did they now?" Lord Poron asked in mock puzzlement and handed his guest a brimming cup. "Well, you will not find me so disposed." A warning, though delivered in a friendly tone, Enric noted.

"And I am very pleased that I do not." Enric leaned forward. "Lord Poron, you know why I am here. Let's not offer any bluffing here between the two of us. In your case subtle threats won't work, and blunt ones will just amuse you even more. I am here for reasons of courtesy so you are not surprised when your colleagues approach Eryn tomorrow to request a separate changing room. But of course I would appreciate your support on this. Coming from you, the request would be even less likely to be refused. I would regard this as a great favour."

Lord Poron leaned back contentedly and studied his guest for a few moments. To talk openly like this was a luxury that people in their position didn't or couldn't afford often.

"I see your point. And as you have demonstrated how possessive you are of your lady, it doesn't surprise me. Though I admit I would have expected you to put it to a vote before the Magic Council instead. We are a rather conservative circle, to be honest. I imagine the outcome would have been in your favour."

Enric sighed. "That was the initial plan. But my lovely companion has managed to persuade the King to decree that her authority in all matters connected with healing and everything around it is not to be tampered with. As he officially still funds the services, even though they have started to become self-funding, this is within his rights."

The laugh began as a throaty chuckle and then Lord Poron's voice filled the room. "Has she? How very delightful! I am very glad she is starting to find her way around the traps and pitfalls of our political game here already."

"Yes, really delightful," Enric affirmed, though with considerably less enthusiasm.

"Oh, you can afford to be proud of her, Lord Enric," his host waved him off. "Your experience and skills are still far superior to her own, and will be for quite some time yet. It will take her years to defeat you. Otherwise you wouldn't be here to all but force her to give up arrangements that even the King himself has backed officially."

That made the younger man smile. "What can I say? Her unwillingness to take orders from me does make it necessary for me to resort to other measures. Can I count on you, Lord Poron?"

The older man nodded. "Yes, I will assist you in this matter. And as it happens, there is another little favour I would like to ask of you in return. You remember Grend, the man you sent with Lady Eryn on the expedition as one of her guards? His father is a close friend of mine. He has told me that Grend has just been deserted by his companion and could use a change of scenery. I presume you will be taking guards with you to the Western Territories?"

Enric nodded. He did remember Grend, of course. He had been not only a guard on that expedition, but also a useful informant. Taking him to the Western Territories would not be any sacrifice whatsoever - quite the opposite, in fact. Eryn had got along very well with the guards, so taking familiar people to a foreign country would be a comfort to her.

"I will ask him if he is willing to accompany us."

Lord Poron smiled. "Excellent. How nice of you to drop by, Lord Enric. I wish I had more such mutually satisfying visits."

* * *

Eryn turned the corner and saw her trainees standing together in front of the training room. She was about to wave them good morning, but felt the moment was wrong for it. Something was different today. The mood was somehow... strained. They whispered amongst themselves until Onil spotted her and cleared his throat. The others looked in her direction and stopped their conversation altogether.

"Alright," she sighed and stepped in front of them, arms folded. "What is going on here?"

She saw three pairs of eyes turning towards Lord Poron. So he had obviously been appointed as their speaker.

"We have been wondering, Lady Eryn, if you would be willing to reconsider the arrangements with regard to the changing room."

She stared at him. "Why? I wasn't under the impression that you had a problem with it once you got used to it."

"You see, there are other external factors to consider," Lord Poron said carefully.

"Such as?" she asked, suddenly remembering how late Enric had arrived home yesterday and how unusually smug he had seemed.

"Our companions and female... friends, for one thing. Not all of them are happy with us undressing in front of you."

She pictured Aurna and raised a brow. It was hard to imagine that woman being squeamish because her septuagenarian companion undressed in front of a woman who could be his granddaughter. This clearly pointed towards *another* companion who had very likely made his disapproval known to her trainees.

"I see," she said slowly and nodded. If Enric really had threatened them enough to make them request their own changing room, refusing it would mean damning them to a life in constant anxiety, which would be cruel. So as a considerate superior there was only one thing to do for her: admit defeat to ensure their comfort and wellbeing. And Enric knew her well enough to be sure she did just that. This was one of the rare moments when she really detested her job. That was the downside of being responsible for others.

"Alright then. I will have Rolan furnish another room for me to change in. Anything else?"

She saw relief evident on the faces around her when they shook their heads while she fought the urge to punch her fist against a convenient wall.

She couldn't even confront Enric openly with this as it would make it necessary for her to admit that she had been ignoring his threats before. At least this saved her from openly admitting her defeat to him. Again.

"Lord Poron, could I have a word with you?" she asked when the trainees started filing into the teaching room.

She directed him into her study and leaned against the door after she had closed it.

"It was him, wasn't it? Enric paid you all a little visit, didn't he?" she asked without introduction.

Lord Poron nodded. "Yes, I regret I have to admit that he did."

"I see how the others would respond to being threatened by him, but *you*?" she enquired pointedly and shook her head. "This somehow feels wrong."

"You are right; he didn't threaten me." He then smiled brightly. "We exchanged favours. But do not be displeased by this, Lady Eryn. You would have agreed to this whether I had backed it up or not. I just managed to get something out of it for myself."

She had to smile. "You let yourself be bribed? Wily men, all of you, no matter whether magician or not."

"True, all too true. But luckily we have managed to accept a wily woman into our circle. That has made things so much more entertaining."

"I am not wily. I am straightforward and direct."

The old man grinned. "That, my dear Lady, may currently be the case, but I am confident that you will soon employ more effective methods. You are a fast learner, after all."

CHAPTER 18

The Farewell Ball

Enric was bewildered by the sight before him when he returned from the briefing he and Kilan had just had with Marrin and the King. The parlour looked like a wardrobe had somehow exploded and spilled all its contents over all available surfaces.

"Ladies," he said and carefully walked towards Eryn, eager to avoid treading on any piece of fabric. She stood with arms stretched to her side while Junar marked off measurements by sticking pins into what looked like a white tunic in one of its many stages before completion.

"Lord Enric," Junar said, her voice muffled by several pins held between her lips, and nodded to him.

Eryn let him kiss her on the lips and looked down at the two envelopes he held in one hand.

"You have been with the King, haven't you? So whatever you are holding in your hand is very likely bad news," she said cautiously.

"Well, that would depend on your definition of bad news," he replied lightly. "But in your case we could probably say that, yes. The King has decided to mark our send-off with a ball."

Eryn groaned. "No, please - not another one! I detest balls! The last two were fiascos!"

Junar grinned and took the pins out of her mouth. "Looks like we are going to need another ball gown for you. Something bold that is worthy of whatever spectacle you will leave in your wake this time."

Enric looked at her and smiled as he handed her one of the two envelopes. "Make that two. You are invited as well."

"What?" She stared at the paper in his hand with dismay. "Where would the King ever get the idea of inviting me to a ball?"

"Yes," Eryn murmured with a pointed look at her companion, "where indeed?"

"I really have to go there?" Junar swallowed.

"Looks like it," Enric said nonchalantly. He then let his gaze wander over the heaps of clothes in the parlour. "You are aware that Eryn will be ordering some of her clothes in Takhan, aren't you? This looks like you are outfitting her for an entire year there."

"Hmm?" Junar slowly broke away from her distraction and looked up from the invitation. "Oh, these are just a few things for the first two weeks. The weather is much warmer there, so she'll need to wear thinner fabrics." She then started packing her things. "I am afraid I need to leave you now. It looks like I have to finish all this here *and* prepare two ball gowns."

When the door had closed behind her, Eryn turned towards him and folded her arms. "So he has personally invited her, hasn't he? I wonder what gave him *that* idea."

"Probably that I mentioned how much you would appreciate your closest friend being there to bid you farewell," he grinned. "Orrin owes me for that one. I have to make sure he finds out who he has to thank for it. Maybe you can hint at that when you dance with him. It would seem immodest if I mentioned it to him outright."

She shook her head at him. "I am trying to be angry at you for manipulating her like this, but as I am not particularly happy about having to go there myself, I don't really feel sympathetic for her right now. Misery does so much like company."

"Don't worry, my love. There is not a lot left that can go wrong anymore. I think we have already caused all the mishaps that could possibly occur at a ball."

"That's what I thought last time before you suddenly decided to break a nearby nose," she retorted caustically.

He chuckled. "A nearby nose?"

"Yes, a stand-in nose, so to say. You were not allowed to break Ram'an's, so you just found the nearest convenient one."

"You can utterly trust me not to break any bones at the next ball. I would only be expected to heal them again, anyway, as it is common knowledge that I can do so."

She rolled her eyes. "You can heal scratches and repair skin, but I would not like to see you unsupervised trying to put back together broken bones."

"I read one of your books about it. I think I know the basics. The greatest challenge seems to be the non-magical part, namely positioning the broken pieces correctly so they are not knitted together crookedly. The rest is just gluing back what was broken and making the patient eat the right food afterwards so the substances used for healing the bone are replaced."

One eyebrow raised, she regarded him. "I am surprised. That was a pretty neat summary. I would be interesting in seeing if you can also apply that knowledge in practice."

"Talking about practical application, how is Kilan doing so far? He has had one week of healing training now."

"Well enough. He will never be a professional healer, but that's not exactly his ambition anyway. I'll keep him there for another week, then he should be able to handle the basics. His schedule doesn't really allow for much more than that. The rest I will show him during our journey. I dare say there will be ample opportunity over those four days. And more than enough time to kill."

"How are your own preparations progressing?" he enquired. "Is everything under control so far?"

She sighed. "Yes, more or less. I have been working on a list of things the trainees should be able to handle in my absence and am now trying to cover as much of it as possible in the lessons. Unfortunately the patients are less cooperative. They simply refuse to provide the injuries I would need for demonstration purposes."

"How very inconsiderate," Enric shook his head in mock indignation.

"It's inconvenient. But there are still two more weeks. I suspect we will see another infected ear, severed sinew and damaged disc."

"A pity you can't place orders, what?" He laughed.

"Why do I even talk to you?" she growled at him.

"Because I am your superior and you want to keep me happy."

"I am your companion! Why not worry about keeping *me* happy for a change?"

He smiled and took her hand to pull her closer, but when she would have expected him to kiss her, he lifted her up and threw her over his shoulder. "You are right. Let me correct this injustice at once."

She felt slightly dizzy as he spun to walk up the curving staircase to the upper floor. Then she felt him halt abruptly.

"You are aware that Plia is at home, aren't you?" Eryn said urgently.

"I am now," he replied and gently put her back on her feet.

Eryn turned and saw Plia standing at the top of the stairs, peering down at them.

"Good evening, Lord Enric," she said awkwardly. "I can leave and visit friends..."

"No, that will not be necessary, but thank you," Enric replied earnestly.

Eryn looked from one to the other, both staring at each other in immense discomfort. And then she started laughing.

"You know, *that* does kind of make me happy," she sniggered and removed a tear from the corner of her eye. "Thank you so much!"

* * *

Eryn and Junar were standing in front of two large mirrors and regarding each other's reflections.

"Why does your dress look so much nicer than mine? It's simple and elegant," Eryn complained.

"Because I am but a humble seamstress and you are an important magician. We can't appear equally flamboyant," Junar stated matter-of-factly.

"Flamboyant? When have I ever been known for that quality? I usually run around in a tunic and trousers!"

"So you should at least display your status when going to a ball. I look elegant all the time, wearing dresses and the like. I don't need to convince people every now and then that I really *am* a woman."

"You make my tunics and trousers, so I look feminine enough. Don't think I haven't noticed how the necklines keep getting lower and lower on my everyday clothes," Eryn remarked. "Which is maybe not the smartest thing to do, considering how jealous Enric is."

Junar rolled her eyes. "Nonsense. He surely appreciates my efforts. And I am just slowly adapting your clothes to the current fashion without overstepping any boundaries whatsoever. Stop fiddling with that strand, I took me almost an hour to get your hair to stay in place like that!"

Eryn obediently let her hand sink. "Then let's descend to our escorts. I suppose they keep checking the time every minute."

"As they are entitled to. Just as we are entitled to be a little late in making an entrance," Junar explained.

"We are? Can you convince Enric of that little fact some time? He keeps insisting on punctuality instead of my making an entrance."

Both man stood in the parlour, talking quietly, each with a glass of wine in one hand, and then looked up when the women entered.

"You did fine work, Junar," Enric commented, "on both of you."

Orrin barely glanced at Eryn in his admiration of his lover. Of course he didn't have as many opportunities to see Junar dressed up for a ball.

The coach was waiting in front of the new entrance, which Enric had made as the original one now led into the courtyard for Urban and no longer opened on the street.

The ride took only a few minutes and they were soon standing in line behind Tyront and Vyril, waiting for the doors to be opened to parade along the path that led to the throne.

When once again they found themselves in front of the King and bowed, he smiled.

"Lady Eryn, have you managed to figure out how I set out my little game by now?"

She nodded and answered him with little enthusiasm. "I think I have, yes."

"Excellent. Then you must tell me about it later."

When they had taken their places to one side, Eryn sighed. "I find it rather mean of him to quiz me on the games he plays with me now."

Enric shrugged. "Not meaner than playing them in the first place, I would think. I'll admit that I find it a useful exercise for you to analyse them. And it's not only you he plays them with, if I may remind you."

"Great. Then why don't you have that little chat with him instead and explain to him how brilliantly he manipulated you yet again?" she said under her breath.

"Because he knows that *I* have no difficulties identifying his strategies. The trick is to do it before you fall victim to them," Enric remarked. "And I would imagine he finds conversing with you more pleasant than with me." He glanced down at her cleavage and sighed. "I wish Junar would be less frugal with the fabric when it comes to your necklines. I do enjoy the sight, but I am very reluctant to share it."

"That's what I told her. She says I need to remind people that I am a woman."

"I doubt that very much."

The last magicians were admitted to the ball room, and then the large double doors were closed.

The King waited for the murmuring to die down before he started addressing his guests about the happy occasion that had induced him to throw this little get-together in honour of the delegates who would so bravely venture into the unknown in service of their Kingdom and its citizens.

The audience applauded politely once he'd ended his short speech.

"How likely is it that I shall be made to open the ball with him again?" Eryn asked nervously.

"Not very," he assured her. "He is not supposed to favour one lady above all others, which would definitely be the impression if he bestows this honour upon you twice within such a short time."

"Yes, right, *honour*," she murmured.

"It is an honour, believe me. Do you see how all the ladies from rich and influential families are trying to catch his eye? Especially the available ones? The King is still a bachelor, after all."

Eryn looked up at the dais and regarded him thoughtfully, trying to see him as a man, not just an institution. He was not as classically attractive with the chiselled features of Enric, but he did have a certain *something*. Probably the power he radiated. Enric had that, too, but it was different with him. The more quiet authority that came with the confidence that his magical abilities and the rank that accompanied it wouldn't very likely encounter any insurmountable obstacle. The King communicated his own power mostly with his posture. And his eyes - piercing looks and cool stares. Though Enric was good at staring, too.

Power had always been instrumental in drawing admiring female glances, Eryn knew. Her father had told her more than once how power that came with rank and wealth was no real power, it could vanish any time. True power came with knowledge, personality, character – things that made a person who he or she really was, something nobody could ever take away. Strange, she thought looking up at Enric, how she had ended up with a man who very much represented everything her father had disdained.

He saw her thoughtful expression. "What are you thinking of, my love?"

"How my father would have reacted to my being joined to you."

Enric frowned. "Not very favourably, I would imagine from what you told me about him."

"Maybe not to your rank and all that, but I wonder how he would have liked you as a man, as a person."

He lifted her hand to kiss it and then smiled when the King chose Aurna, Lord Poron's companion for the opening dance.

"I like his sense of humour," he said. "I can't remember that he has ever opened a ball with a woman who was not joined to another man. He makes it a point of discouraging the eligible ladies."

"You yourself were an eligible bachelor for quite some time," Eryn said curiously. "I suppose you have received quite a few invitations, some of them undoubtedly worth considering?"

"True. But I like to be the one doing the choosing. I never liked it when women were flinging themselves in my path."

"This sounds as if my aversion to you must have been my most attractive feature."

He laughed quietly. "No, my love. Your revulsion was not what drew me to you. It was not exactly love at first sight, though I noticed your appealing looks from the start. I found you interesting, but more in the way of a riddle - more a puzzle to be solved than a woman to be conquered."

"You didn't really do any conquering, if I remember correctly," she said and watched Aurna beaming at the King while he talked to her during the dance.

"That would depend on your interpretation of *conquering*. If you refer to the expression as it is used in warfare, I think it would be fairly accurate," he pointed out. "As regards the other in connection with courtship involving presents, poetry and romance, I admit that we somehow skipped that stage. But I can't help thinking that presenting you with sweets would have ended with my picking them up from the floor after you had thrown them in my face."

She smiled. "That is a fairly accurate assumption, I admit. Though I would rather have let them burst into flames instead."

Lord Poron leaned over to them and nodded to his companion and the King on the dancefloor.

"She is a very good dancer, my Aurna," he said proudly. "She complains that I don't take her dancing often enough, but unfortunately I am not as young and nimble as I used to be."

Eryn made a pained face at him. "Lord Poron, you are a healer. That excuse is a poor one."

"Pardon?" the old man frowned.

"Whatever troubles you, be it your joints, tendons, bones or muscles, you can repair easily with a little healing magic. Don't tell me you have never thought of it?" she asked in surprise.

The old magician slowly shook his head. "It has always seemed rather frivolous to me to use my new abilities for my own comfort and vanity rather than healing people in need. And then you are known not to be in favour of using magic for this kind of purpose."

"Lord Poron," she sighed, "I spent an entire morning shortening a pair of feet for no reason more than the owner's sheer vanity. Believe me when I tell you that making yourself more comfortable and increasing your own well-being is a gift you may grant yourself without remorse."

"You know," Lord Poron said and nodded slowly, "I will consider this. Will you reserve a dance for me later, my dear?"

"It will be my pleasure," she smiled and stepped aside when the King returned Aurna to her companion.

It took her more than an hour to finally grab hold of Junar. She had been asked to dance so often that she had wondered how many men there could still be left to invite her.

"You are quite in demand," Junar marvelled. "They've hardly left you alone for a minute, have they?"

"What can I say? I am important, as you like to point out," Eryn snorted. "How are you doing?"

The seamstress grimaced. "My feet are killing me. The shoes have started chafing. I hope nobody else asks me to dance tonight. It would probably finish me."

"Give me your hand," Eryn instructed.

"Why?"

"To heal the pain, of course. Or did you think I was asking you for the next dance?" she smirked.

"Idiot," Junar growled but lifted her hand obediently.

Closing her eyes, Eryn sent a quick exploratory impulse into her friend's body and found the abraded areas of skin immediately. She dulled the pain and finally removed it completely, thickening the skin slightly to make it more durable.

She was about to retreat, when she stopped.

"There is a slight imbalance with one of your glands in your throat. It is a bit smaller than it is supposed to be, but I could counterbalance this by increasing its activity. Do you want me to take care of that while I am at it? It would only take a minute."

She felt the shrug. "Sure, knock yourself out. Nothing serious, I hope?"

"No, an imbalance, like I said. You will very likely feel a bit more energetic in the future," she murmured and then opened her eyes again when she was finished.

"Your feet should not give you any more trouble for the next few hours."

Junar moved them carefully and sighed in relief when the pain was indeed gone. "Thank you. You've saved the evening for me."

"Glad to be of service."

Both looked up when the King and Enric approached them from different directions.

Junar chuckled. "Want to bet who those two are aiming for?"

But to her surprise Enric, who arrived first, nodded to the seamstress and asked, "Junar, would you do me the honour and dance with me?"

Eryn grinned. "Pity, I should have taken that bet."

"Lady Eryn," she soon heard King Folrin's voice next to her and took the hand he held out to her in what was, as always, less an invitation than a demand.

"Your Majesty," she replied and put her hand in his to be led to the dance floor.

"Let me hear what you have figured out, if you please," he commanded without any detours when they had started dancing.

"You sent this order for my assistant to be taught healing. I remember that I was surprised at it, and a little apprehensive, as I didn't understand the reason for it. I didn't know at that time that Rolan was sending regular letters of complaint to Lord Tyront to share his grievances with him."

"Ah yes, the missing piece of information," he smiled. "Go on."

"You were also aware of something my companion had not known at that time, namely the shared changing room in the healers' building. Rolan of course mentioned it in his next letter to Lord Tyront, and thereafter Enric learned about it as well. As Enric has acquired quite a reputation of being jealous and possessive in the course of these last few months, it was not too difficult to gauge his reaction to that bit of news. And, alas, he complied beautifully by storming in to my place of work and yelling like a man possessed at me there. Due to this I was, in turn, just in the right mood to be manipulated into accepting an assignment to another country to take revenge on my companion."

"Well summarised, My Lady," the King nodded in approval. "But there is more, isn't there?"

She sighed. "Yes, indeed. When I thought I had successfully outmanoeuvred Enric, he came to see you, doubtlessly to ask you to change your mind about sending me. But as you had told me before, that was not in his power. So he did the next best thing, the one you had planned for him to do all along: he asked you for permission to accompany me on the journey. Though as he is now the ambassador, it looks more as if *I* am going to accompany *him*. You just used me to make *him* go there, he is the one you wanted there. Sending *me* is just a risk you have to accept, as they want to get to know me over there," she added bitterly.

"Do not be troubled by this, Lady Eryn. I would, indeed, have preferred to keep you here to avoid any risk of losing you, but the best I could do under the circumstances was give you an escort who would be quite sure to bring you back to us again. I am willing to send away two of the three strongest magicians of the Kingdom at the same time, mind you, so as to ensure you return safely. Fortunately, Lord Enric is a man of many talents, among them several very useful ones for this mission. Had it not been for their request to make you one of the party, I would have sent him there without you and instead invited members of your families to visit you here. But their wish to see you come to them arrived first, unfortunately."

She studied him for a few moments and he waited patiently for her question.

"Why didn't you just ask us to go there together? Why this scheme?"

"Because Lord Enric would never have agreed to taking you with him, and he would very likely have persuaded you to stay here. There is your healing business that you only started a short while ago and which is very important to you. So I had to make *you* agree to it first, and in a way that was binding for you. After that he had no choice other than to go with you."

"I see." And she did. Enric would indeed have tried everything in his power to compel her to stay here. "I know that you are very good at these things, and I understand in many cases why you do them. But I have to admit that every time I receive a message with your seal on it, I become really unsettled."

"Indeed? I am very sorry to hear that."

"Are you? I would have expected you to appreciate such an effect."

"Not in your case, My Lady. I do so much prefer making you nervous in person," he smiled and raised both her hands to his lips when the music slowly died down. "I haven't thanked you for the wine yet. It is excellent, and I am sure you will be glad to hear that I have asked Lord Enric to arrange for it to be among the goods we endeavour to obtain from the Western Territories."

She swallowed and was glad when he released her hands again. His little game still worked well, no matter how sternly she told herself to ignore that faint smile or tell-tale look in his eyes.

"I am glad to hear that, yes," she said and saw that he was rather delighted to sense the tension in her voice.

"I see your companion is about to remain with Lord Orrin's... escort for the next dance. Where would you like me to take you?" He smiled. "I see young Vern standing over there. He seems rather eager to dance with you, judging from those hopeful glances in your direction. You didn't have a chance to dance with him at the last two balls, did you?"

She smiled tensely. "No, not really. Maybe I should take the opportunity now before another cataclysm occurs and I am once again fleeing from the ballroom."

"So pessimistic, Lady Eryn?" he sighed. "I was hoping for you to stay longer this time, as there is nobody present whom Lord Enric feels is possibly in need of a warning. At least none I am aware of."

No, she thought - the one on the receiving end of his warnings lately had been herself.

"And I am confident that you will refrain from changing your hair colour to blonde tonight and stay true to your nature this time," he added.

She gave him another forced smile and just in time stopped herself from rolling her eyes at him. "I have decided to agree with your suggestion to dance with Vern. I would be grateful if you could take me to him."

Vern swallowed and bowed when the monarch stood before him. "Your Majesty."

"Young man," the King nodded and then lifted Eryn's hand to his lips once more before turning away.

"I thought I would never catch you between two partners," the boy sighed and took her arm possessively as another hopeful man approached them.

"Tell *me*," she murmured. "I haven't had a peaceful minute all evening. And the King has just told me that he wants me to stay longer, so no chance for a timely retreat."

Vern huffed and led her to the dance floor. "You had two very timely retreats twice before. I would think that one ball without any major incident is worth staying a little longer for. And there are quite a number of men who are still waiting to dance with you, judging from how their eyes follow you."

"Oh, I do thank you for pointing that out."

The music started and when she stepped closer to him, she grinned. "You have grown, haven't you? We used to be the same height, now you are a bit taller than me."

"A bit, yes," he said casually, not entirely able to hide that he was pleased about her noticing it. "Hey, have you heard that I am to get a full healer's allowance for the four weeks that you will be gone and I take over your work?" he asked brightly.

Oh dear, that was something she hadn't even thought of looking into. Of course he would need to be compensated for the extra effort he was about to put in. Luckily somebody else had seen to it.

"And so you should! Without you we would have been forced to close the place or just slim our services down to basic things such as healing broken bones and skin cuts. Who granted it?"

"His Majesty himself. I have an impressive letter with his seal and signature to present to the treasurer. I thought about buying a horse and putting the rest aside for when I move out of my father's quarters in a few years."

She looked at him, taken aback. "A horse? What for? You never leave the city!"

"How can I, without a horse? I think a man needs his own horse," he said, puffing out his chest and lifting his chin in what he clearly thought was a manly pose. "Your companion has a horse. He doesn't leave the city, either. Well, apart from the trip to Takhan, of course."

"Enric has a horse? I didn't know that."

Vern nodded. "Yes, quite a beast, I am told. But then he seems to enjoy surrounding himself with difficult characters," he grinned and then winced when she deliberately stepped on his toes.

"Oh dear, I am so sorry. How very clumsy of me," she sneered.

"Wasn't it," he growled. "You will be very popular in your home country, I can see that."

"Be careful how you address a lady."

"*Lady* may be your title, but it's certainly not an apt description of your character. Or your manners."

"You know, I hear that a lot," she remarked thoughtfully.

"Can't imagine why."

"Stop insulting me. Rather tell my why my companion owns a bloody horse. Has anybody ever seen him riding it?"

"Sure. He used to go hunting on it sometimes. Though not since you began gracing the city with your presence. I suppose his leaving here while you were busy plotting your escape was too chancy."

"Yes, probably. But he hasn't had to worry about that over these last three months. He could have gone then."

"You have been stumbling from one troublesome situation into the next, I suppose he simply had no time for hunting," Vern snorted.

"Idiot," she murmured and trod on his toes again for good measure.

"Ow! Can you stop doing that?"

"Why should I? You deserve it."

A nasty grin spread across Vern's face. "Lord Tyront has just given me to understand that he wants me to take you to him after this dance. It seems we know who your next dancing partner is going to be. Isn't that lovely? Good to see that you have turned into such great friends. But then this shouldn't be such a surprise for me, I haven't seen you shovelling horse manure for quite some time now." He deftly skipped a step when she made to stomp on his toes a third time and chuckled when she gave him a dark look.

The evening stretched on for Eryn - at least compared to the last two balls. Lord Tyront danced with her, then Kilan, after that one of the members of the Magic Council whose name she had no clue of, then Orrin, Kilan a second time, Enric and finally Lord Remdel, who was delighted to tell her how very happy his companion was with her work. Which was so very peachy.

* * *

Enric leaned back in the coach and grinned when Eryn exhaled in relief.

"Glad it's all over?" he enquired.

"Yes, very much so. And that nothing whatsoever happened. Apart from me being so exhausted that I considered taking a nap on one of the sofas once or twice. But I suppose that wouldn't have made such a good impression, my being one of the guests of honour."

He pretended to think for a moment before he wiggled his head. "No, probably not."

"You danced with Junar twice in a row. Isn't that rather unusual?"

"It is, yes," he admitted. "But we had a discussion I was reluctant to interrupt, so I stretched the rules of courtesy a little and held on to her."

"What discussion?"

"Business," he told her. "I make fabrics, she uses them for her profession. I offered her a special rate if she keeps buying mine and keeps mentioning where she gets them from. This should be of mutual benefit for our businesses. Mentioning my name will not harm hers - quite the opposite - and her buying my fabrics earns me more money."

Eryn yawned. "Why would she need your name? She happens to tailor for the city's sensation, namely me - in case you were wondering who that was."

"True. But it might be able to win her a few more male customers as well."

"I learned tonight that you own a horse," she said.

Enric furrowed his brow. "That's quite a conversational leap. From extending Junar's business to my owning a horse."

She ignored his remark. "I heard that you used to go hunting with it. Or on it, rather. Vern thinks you stopped that when I came here because you had to ensure I didn't decamp."

"Basically, yes. I was meaning to take it up again lately, but the last few months have been quite busy. But as we are living with a mountain cat now, I need to take her to the woods sometimes anyway. She needs regular opportunities for running and hunting."

"Isn't she a bit small for that?" she protested.

"No, not really," he shrugged. "If she had lived with her mother in the woods, she would have had her first hunting lessons by now. I will work something out when we get back from our journey."

The coach stopped and Enric didn't wait for the coachman but opened the door himself to exit first and then help his companion out.

"Do you think Plia is still awake?" he asked when he opened the door to their house.

"I don't think so. It's rather late and she needs to work tomorrow. Why?"

He grinned and pulled her close. "Because I can't take my eyes off your cleavage. And I don't want to keep my hands off you until we are upstairs."

"Behave yourself, Lordling," Eryn sighed. "Let's try to avoid scarring Plia for life before she is old enough to support herself after fleeing from what must seem like a den of iniquity to her."

"Den of iniquity?" Enric chuckled. "Hardly. There are laws that practically force me to bestow this kind of attention on you. I am merely trying to be a model citizen."

She shook her head at him. "I appreciate the sacrifice, I really do. You sure do know how to make a woman feel treasured."

CHAPTER 19

Departure for Jakhan

Dawn had only just started to break when she opened her eyes. It took her a moment to realise why she had woken at such an untimely hour. The bed beside her was empty. When had that begun bothering her?

She put her feet down onto the thick carpet and stretched. Too early, she thought drowsily and slipped into a fluffy robe before she carefully descended the stairs in the dark.

There was light in his study as she had expected. He looked up in surprise when she pushed the door open. He was sitting behind his desk, the cat sprawled on his lap, paws and head hanging down. Urban would soon be too large to fit on his lap, Eryn thought, amused. In fact she was already, but seemed not yet willing to give up the childhood privilege.

"I didn't wake you, did I?" Enric asked and put down what looked like another list. There seemed to be nothing else around these days, just lists in growing numbers.

She shook her head and came closer, sitting on his desk as Urban made no move to relinquish the cosy lap for Eryn to sit on.

"No, not really. Well, indirectly you have. It seems I've got used to you enough to miss you when you are not in the bed beside me."

He smiled with satisfaction and kissed her hand. "That was my wicked intention all along. I am pleased to see that it's worked."

"How long have you been up? This was to be our last night in our own bed for quite a while, so you must have been quite restless to give up the last hours in it just like that."

"A little, yes," he admitted. "I have been going through the packing lists to see if we have forgotten anything, the trade suggestions, the little information we have on the local customs. We don't really have a lot of documentation to prepare us for the trip, only what the ambassador has told us. This does make me rather nervous. I am not a great friend of the unknown. How about you? Don't tell me you are not nervous at all?"

"It's not so bad. I am trying to see it as a visit and not as a homecoming. I try not to think of what they might expect of me

233

over there. Alas, there are four days of travelling ahead of us - four days in which I'll have enough time to think about a lot of the things I would rather avoid right now."

He knew better than to tell her not to worry. If that could be turned off so easily, he would still be in bed, after all. His worries were of a different nature, however. Not succeeding in negotiating trade agreements would of course be unfortunate, but they had somehow managed without trading with the Western Territories in the past and would be able to do so in the future, if need be. What if the invitation for trade negotiations was no more than an excuse somehow to lure Eryn back there? Her family might just be powerful enough to arrange for a thing like that. How important was she to them? He hoped not the sole heir to rank or wealth or anything of that sort. If they really decided that they wanted her back at no matter what cost, there was not a lot he alone could do against it. He was a powerful magician, but there was a limit to how many others he could withstand.

"Then we will have to keep you busy," he smiled and then contorted his face as Urban dug in her claws to stop herself from slipping from his lap. "I should probably stop her from jumping onto my lap, she is getting too big for that."

"Probably," Eryn agreed. "Otherwise you will have to improve your healing skills to mend yourself afterwards. But she will soon be too big to fit on your lap anyway, if that is any consolation." She ruffled the soft fur on top of the feline head. "Has her crate for the journey been delivered yet?"

He nodded. "Yes, yesterday evening. It doesn't look too comfortable, I have to say, but then Urban will be sleeping all the time in there anyway." He shook his head when Eryn yawned again. "You should go back to bed and try to sleep another hour or two. You might fall off the horse otherwise."

"No, I don't think that would be wise. If I fall asleep now, I will be even more tired when I have to get up again so soon. And you are not exactly gentle when it comes to getting me out of bed," she added with a pointed look.

"That's because you tend to ignore all gentle attempts and bury yourself under all available bedding and pillows." He lifted the cat, who protested loudly, and put her down on the floor. "Well, it looks like we are neither in any state of mind to go back to sleep, and there isn't really anything to do as we had a minor army take care of all the planning. That means we have time for something else."

"Such as?" she smiled.

He rose and grinned widely. "A training session, my love."

She looked up at him in dismay. That was not the activity she had thought he had in mind. Or hoped.

"That's not funny."

He took her hand and pulled her out of the study with him. "It wasn't meant to be. You haven't trained with Orrin for more than a week. We don't want you to get out of practice, do we?"

"Oh dear me, no, we wouldn't want that at all..." she murmured, and pulled a wry face behind his back.

* * *

Eryn turned around in her saddle and looked back. The city of Anyueel sat stolidly in front of the grey sky as if sad to see them leave. She would have wished to see it gleaming in the sunlight to take the sight with her as a parting gift, but the weather was not obliging her at all.

They had left almost according to schedule, but saying their good-byes had taken a little longer than anticipated. Orrin, Vern and Junar had been there, of course. So had Plia. Rolan, too. Her healer trainees had assembled along with Garn, the herb gatherer. Marrin had come to see his son off and convey the King's best wishes for their journey.

She had been surprised and pleased to see Barul and Grend join them.

Grend rode in front of her and she wondered why he looked so strained. She led her mount next to his and smiled.

"I am still wondering whose spy you are," she said, which made him smile as she had hoped.

"What do you think? You successfully eliminated a few choice candidates already back then."

"Either the King's or Enric's, yes I know. But the King has basically sent his more or less official spy, Kilan, along, so I wonder if he needs you here in addition. What's more, Enric is here, so if you are his informant, he clearly hasn't brought you along to have your eyes on *me* this time."

"So you think there could be other interesting things than yourself in a foreign country?" he chuckled.

She looked at him with narrowed eyes. "Are you saying I am conceited?"

"I would never dare direct a thing like that at an important lady like yourself," he replied good-naturedly.

"Maybe not *say*, but *imply*," she pointed out.

"That, neither. I *am* ordered to have an eye on you, as is Barul."

"Who do you receive your orders from?" she asked.

"Lord Enric, of course. As does Barul. And in his absence, you."

"Who did you send information to during the expedition before?"

"I have no idea what you are talking about," he said with a faint smile and looked straight ahead.

"If you take my orders in Enric's absence, then I can make you tell me whose spy you were, can't I?"

He smirked. "Only in the case of the one who was allegedly receiving my reports being lower in rank than you. But as you think it must have been either the King or your companion..."

"Yes - no need to go on. They both happen to outrank me," she sighed. "Then I will assume that you worked for Enric. He surely had a say in what guards to take, and why would he decide to take the King's spy when he could have taken his own."

Grend nodded. "A valid conclusion."

"But not one you wish to confirm?"

He just smiled.

"Very well," she growled. "Then don't talk to me."

Enric joined them and noted her disgruntled look. "Is everything alright?"

"He doesn't want to tell me if he was yours or the King's spy during the expedition."

"Well, he isn't really expected to reveal that, is he?"

"You know what?" She pulled on her reigns to slow down her horse. "I think I am going to ride with Kilan for a while." She saw both men looking at each other and shrug as if to say *women*.

Kilan had the bridle of his horse tied to the back of the cart and was studying some papers. He looked up from them when Eryn appeared next to him.

"Lady Eryn. I am just going through the meagre information we have on the Western Territories. It's not much more than what Ambassador Ram'an told us during his visit. I didn't find anything useful in the library, either, so it seems we will have to do a lot of learning there. I will need to document and catalogue everything we learn there. I imagine you will be taking care of the notes on healing? I would hardly be much help there, I am afraid."

She nodded. "Yes, of course. Though I hope that I can mostly resort to buying books or have copies of them made there to take home. My efforts at writing in the past were more of the correctional kind. I don't think I am organised enough to write an actual book, to consider what order to put things in and all that's involved."

"I hope you won't have to put up with it, then. We will be there for only three weeks, and that will probably turn out to be rather short for you even without collecting and cataloguing information. You haven't had any contact with your family there yet, have you?" Kilan asked.

"I suspect you know very well that I haven't. Considering your connections to the Palace. I'm sure the King also reads the messages that are not addressed to him directly."

He shrugged. "I found this a more polite way to broach the subject than saying, *Hey, how come you haven't exchanged any letters with your family there? I know that for a fact because I would have heard about it.* I am supposed to be diplomatic, after all. Not that it seems to work very well on you, though."

236

"I came here to ride with you for a while because Enric and Grend were starting to annoy me. Now it seems you are not much of an improvement," she said with palpable crankiness.

"Does that mean you don't want to tell me about it? I would really be interested in that answer," he tried again. "Why haven't you written to your family? I can't believe that you are not interested."

Eryn sighed in defeat. "Of course I am interested. But I am also unsure of what to expect. I have no idea how close families in the Western Territories are. They haven't written to me, either. So it might be they are not that interested themselves."

"They were very likely the ones who insisted on making you one of the delegation," he pointed out.

"That's no more than an assumption. They might just be very possessive of their lost citizens."

"You are nervous about them, aren't you?" he asked, and leaned forward in what she thought was unwarranted delight.

"Why does that make you so happy?"

He grinned and shrugged. "I am not sure. Probably because you don't show a lot of weaknesses, so even a minor one can be savoured."

"What can I say? I am a beacon of strength," she said dryly. "If you would excuse me now, I think I will try Barul for a travel companion next. I wonder how interesting this journey is going to be when most of you have managed to irritate me within the first few hours."

She heard him laughing quietly as she steered her horse away from him to draw closer to Barul.

* * *

They reached the inn just after it had started raining heavily, and when Grend and Barul were about to lift the crate with the cat in it, Eryn shook her head at them and pointed a thumb at herself.

"Magician, remember? Strong bunch, also the girls."

Both men sighed.

"Still, it doesn't look good, letting a woman do the heavy lifting. No matter if you could lift a horse single-handedly," Barul said.

"Let me solve that dilemma for you then," Enric's amused voice said from behind them. "I expect you won't refuse a male magician carrying the box." Without waiting for an answer, be bent down and lifted the load from the cart without any apparent effort and carried it towards the inn's entrance door, which Kilan quickly opened for him.

"Now we have the problem of the highest ranking one of us doing the work. It doesn't get any better," Grend grumbled.

Eryn looked exasperated but simply grabbed their sleeves to pull them towards the inn and out of the rain.

"There is just no pleasing you, is there? We will make you sleep on the cold floor with the windows open to make up for your lack of effort in protecting the higher classes from doing any physical work, if that makes you feel any better."

The inn was not large and they had managed to book all three rooms it had available for guests. The guards shared one and so did Kilan and the driver of the horse cart. Enric carefully put the crate down on the floor of the room he would share with Eryn and motioned for her to close the door.

"Do you have the meat?" he asked.

She wordlessly held up the bowl of raw meat she had just obtained from the inn's kitchen and watched her companion open the top of the box. Urban lay spread among several blankets, breathing deeply and evenly.

"I am going to wake her now. Do you want to see how it's done? It might turn out to be a useful skill one day in case you need to wake me up again after knocking me out," she said with a reproachful look.

Enric smiled. "You know, that's not such a bad idea. I might even try it myself a bit later."

"Don't you dare," she warned and took his hand to lay it on Urban's torso. "Follow the stream of energy I am sending," she murmured with closed eyes. "There are several ways of sending somebody to sleep. I used a gentle one and stimulated the centre of her brain which produces sleep-inducing substances. I will now inhibit that production and at the same time stimulate the part which is responsible for the substances that increase the activity in the body."

She opened her eyes again and the cat stirred. "Normally a very weak impulse does the trick."

"What other ways are there to send somebody to sleep?" Enric asked, with obvious interest.

"There is your favourite one, of course: a strong impulse that overwhelms the nerves. And another more gentle, but also more dangerous one: slowing the breathing to reduce the intake of air. That shuts down the brain to a certain degree. The trick is not to stop the supply too much or there will be permanent damage. Those two options are more like knocking somebody unconscious and not so much like sleeping. Inducing sleep is less dangerous. Provided you don't just want to knock somebody out."

"But knocking somebody out is the quickest way, isn't it? I dare say you could easily counteract my efforts of just making you fall asleep?"

"I could, yes. Though I think that somebody with less advanced healing knowledge might not be able to fight it."

He grinned. "Then I will just stick to what has worked so nicely in the past."

She narrowed her eyes and warned him, "Just remember that you are just as defenceless when *you* are asleep. You might wake up with green hair or fingernails as long as a knife and as hard and impossible to cut. You would have to forge them off."

"Thank you for that image. I am sure falling asleep will be something of an effort tonight."

"Nonsense," she smiled, "I would be more than willing to assist you."

"Yes, that's what I was afraid of."

They both looked down at Urban, who had in the meantime opened her eyes and lifted her head to look around in bewilderment at the unfamiliar surroundings. After hopping out of the crate she completely ignored the bowl of meat and started sniffing around the room.

"She seems restless," Eryn commented.

"So would you after sleeping in a crate all day," he replied. "I wonder if we should try having her run along with us tomorrow. She is rather used to following me around by now."

"What if she runs off?"

"There are woods not far off. I'd say she would find a new home pretty quickly," he said and observed the feline scrutiny of the bedspread.

"You would let her run off just like that?" she asked in dismay, remembering that she had had pretty much the same discussion with Vern during the expedition, only with roles reversed. "She is still a bit too small to survive in the wilderness alone. She doesn't even know how to hunt properly. And there might be villages close by. She is used to humans and might get too close. They will be afraid and kill her!"

"That is the risk inherent in a life of freedom."

"Funny, you were not willing to grant *me* the privilege of a life of freedom several months ago, even though the risk would have been a lot smaller," she replied testily.

"Different situation, my love. By the time we had decided that you were not dangerous to us, we knew that we wanted you to stay because you were useful. And considering what Ambassador Ram'an told you, the search party from the Western Territories would have picked you up as soon as we had let you leave again."

Yes, she had to admit, that was very likely true. But she was not in any mood to acknowledge that openly.

"That's not something you were aware of at that time, so I don't really count this as a valid argument."

Urban returned to them and finally started sniffing at the meat before taking a tentative bite and judging it adequate.

"So you really want to let her stay awake and run with us tomorrow? I am not convinced this would be a wise move," she returned to the previous topic.

"Testing her willingness to follow us out in the open is surely less dangerous than doing it in a foreign city. I can always stun her in case she does something she is not supposed to. And she will be asleep for the two days we spend on the ship, so I'd say she'll need a little exercise before that," he pointed out.

"Whatever you say, Ambassador," she shrugged. "You are the one in command."

He knitted his brow. "That somehow failed to impress you sufficiently in the past. What's the difference now?"

She grinned. "You are an ambassador now. That is rather impressive."

"Maybe I can keep the title after we return if it makes you comply with what I tell you."

She shook her head. "Hardly. I think you have to stay in the country you were sent to and do some representing to be entitled to hold on to the title. And unless you have any relocation plans, that is rather unlikely, I think."

He nodded. "Yes, probably. Are there any other titles that you might find equally impressive? Maybe I can obtain one of those?"

"I like *King*."

He grimaced. "I need to usurp the throne to impress you? You are a demanding woman."

"You often complain that I don't ask you for anything. When I do for once, it doesn't please you, anyway."

"Because you never ask for the uncomplicated things a man would expect," he retorted.

"Like jewellery and dresses?"

"For example, yes."

She snorted. "I would more likely demand you to *stop* giving me dresses. But if I am lucky you will soon have an opportunity of giving me more than you ever wanted. Always depending on how expensive books are in Takhan, that is."

"Whatever the price is, it will surely be affordable. Fortunately their mineral resources seem to be less extensive than ours, so one of our gold pieces can buy almost twice as much as in Anyueel. I have brought along a considerable amount of our own gold. And the King has granted us quite a generous allowance as well - though he asked me tactfully to prevent you from spending all of it on healing books."

"Did he now?" she asked in annoyance.

"Yes. That's why I packed some of our own gold as well," he smiled and kissed her on the temple. "So you won't have to put any undue restraint on yourself when you go hunting for knowledge."

She took his hand and pressed it against her cheek. "Sometimes you are so sweet I don't know what to say. And usually that is right after you somehow mocked or insulted me so the contrast is even greater."

"I do that on purpose, of course. It's all a matter of presentation," he grinned. "Don't worry. It's not very often that I can buy something you really want, so I enjoy the opportunity, even if it costs a bit more. What's more, you don't have that chance very often, so I don't see any serious danger for our income being diminished significantly. And as I told you before, our gold is worth much more there."

"Yes, but you don't know how expensive books are over there. If they should be four times as expensive as in Anyueel we will still need twice as much gold to pay for them."

"That is rather pessimistic. According to your pendant you stem from a House of healing. They can surely assist you in obtaining affordable medical books. Do you have it with you, by the way?"

"My pendant? Yes. But I suppose I'd better keep it hidden for now. Somebody might take offence if I claim membership of two important Houses without first being invited to do so."

"That is probably a smart move, I'd say," Enric nodded. "But have it handy in case somebody wants you to make that connection. Maybe wear it under your tunic ready to be presented upon request." He got to his feet, pulling her up from the floor next to Urban's crate when he straightened again. "And now come. We need to eat and retire early. There is another full day of riding ahead of us tomorrow, and I am not sure how restful our first night on a ship will be for us."

Eryn waved him off. "I don't see how it could be so bad. I am a healer, after all."

* * *

Eryn, arms akimbo, grinned at the two guards who eyed the cat nervously.

"Shame on you! Two such strapping fellows as yourself afraid of a half-grown cat. Look at her, barely more than a kitten! She hasn't even reached knee-height yet."

"I remember when it was a kitten. I happened to be there," Grend said and watched the cat curiously sniffing the cart. The cart driver didn't look too relaxed, either, judging from the frequent glances he made behind him.

"I wouldn't worry about her, she is gentle. If I were Barul, however..." she trailed off.

"What?" Barul said and frowned.

"She might remember that you tried to kill her."

"Nonsense," he growled, but still took a small step back from Urban.

"Do you really think letting her run loose is a smart idea?" Grend asked. "People might get rather frightened, and so will the horses."

Eryn shrugged. "Don't ask me, it wasn't my idea. Enric wants to test if she is fit for unknown terrain and will keep close to us. I just hope she won't decide to take off for little hunting trips whenever she sees something moving somewhere. But she was behaving well enough in the city. We are about to see if she can be trusted out here in the wilder places."

Grend opened his mouth to reply, but shut it again as Enric came out the door. Interesting, Eryn thought. Questioning Enric's decision in his presence was obviously not something the guard was happy doing. She wondered if he would have continued if it had been *her* idea, if he would have been equally reluctant to criticise *her* to her face. Probably not, she mused and wondered about the reason. Was that due to Enric's being so much more intimidating than her or because Grend had got to know and like her during the expedition and so knew that she wouldn't bite his head off?

Kilan was right behind Enric and gulped when he saw the cat.

"I hope she doesn't find any of the horses particularly appetising. They do eat horses, don't they?"

Eryn nodded earnestly. "Absolutely, yes. Only if there is nothing easier to kill around, though."

Enric shook his head disapprovingly. "You should rather be endeavouring to make people around us more comfortable travelling with Urban instead of teasing them."

She shrugged. "You know, I probably would have done that if I had been made ambassador, but now that you are – again - the mighty leader, I will enjoy my position one step behind you and the lack of responsibility that comes with it."

Kilan interjected. "The King would never have made *you* the ambassador, Lady Eryn. Too dangerous."

"Yes, I know," she rolled her eyes. "Potentially unclear status of citizenship."

His grin had a hint of the wicked. "Actually, that was a minor consideration. The major problem is your approach to diplomacy. Such as forks that somehow mysteriously manage to get stuck into a certain ambassador's thigh?"

She frantically shook her head at him, but it was too late. The words were out. Enric, who was strapping the small pack with his personal belongings to the saddle of the horse, stopped and then turned slowly.

"Pardon? Would you please repeat that?"

Kilan looked abashed and gave Eryn a look that clearly stated that somebody should have told him to keep it a secret.

"It's nothing - forget it. I mixed something up. I didn't have a particularly restful night and am still a little slow," he said with an apologetic smile.

"Try again," Enric said coldly and folded his arms.

"It was just a little... discussion that got out of hand. Nothing serious, or you would of course have heard about it."

"I see," Enric said slowly. "Nothing serious. I think using a truth block on you right now might be regarded a rather... harsh course of action considering that you are with us to liaise with the King and are thus basically under his orders and thus more or less his protection."

Kilan nodded slowly. "That is a valid assumption, yes," he said carefully.

Enric turned to his companion. "But I am not under any such restriction when it comes to you, *my dear*. It is not much of a surprise to learn that here is another little matter you failed to communicate to me. Would you like to do so now? Voluntarily?"

She lifted her chin and folded her arms as well. "No, I am afraid I cannot comply with your request. I am under orders from the King and Lord Tyront to keep that information to myself."

"The King *and* Tyront told you to keep it a secret from me?" His voice was low, but his eyes had narrowed and the tension in the air became almost tangible. The horses started making uncomfortable little noises and tried to edge away to increase the distance to the magician.

"Yes," she said and was glad that it sounded more confident than she felt right now.

He pursed his lips and kept his eyes on her. "You *will* tell me about this in the end, make no mistake. But there is a time and a place for this, and it is not here and now. I don't care under whose orders you are, I consider my responsibilities and rights as your companion above them."

"That is an interesting statement on which I would like to hear the King's official judgement," she pointed out. "And I am sure that Lord Tyront would also like to think that his orders still carry more weight than yours."

Enric walked towards her, stopping when his nose was only a hair's breadth before hers. "Let that be *my* concern." Then he turned away abruptly and mounted his horse with a final angry look at her.

"What have you got me into?" she hissed to Kilan.

"I am so sorry," he whispered. "I wasn't aware that he didn't know about this! So he has also no idea about the tru…"

"Shut up!" She elbowed him none too gently. "Enric eavesdrops with his little air trick! If you go on, you might as well call him back and spill everything to him."

They both got on their horses and followed Enric and the horse cart. Urban had fallen into what seemed a comfortable trot next to her master's horse which, from the whites of its eyes, was clearly not too thrilled to have a predator that close.

"He said he will make you tell him. Can he do that?" Kilan asked quietly.

"You bet he can. All everybody sees are his cold stares and sharp words, but he uses more assertive methods on me if he sees fit. It's just a matter of time until he gets it out of me. I hope he decides to wait until we are back in Anyueel. That would make things easier."

"Yes, but how likely is that? He knows it has something to do with Ambassador Ram'an and will be eager to learn about it sooner rather than later. How long can you withstand Enric?"

She grimaced. "When he is determined and angry, he doesn't even hold off from using truth blocks and other *persuasions*, so probably not even an hour."

Kilan nodded slowly. "That will very likely make our stay a little more difficult than anticipated."

She smiled without humour. "True. But at least I can proclaim my innocence back home. I was not the one to bring it up, after all."

"Great," he sighed. "Thank you for your loyalty."

"You just made me the target for Enric's interrogation skills. Don't expect any loyalty from me right now. You will have to earn that back somehow. I could make you carry out a load of menial tasks for me in these next three weeks. You could serve me drinks, massage my feet, wash my clothes..."

He chuckled. "You know, I am beginning to think that I will somehow survive this trip even without your loyalty."

* * *

The second day of riding had gone by smoothly enough considering that they had a half-grown mountain cat running beside them. Urban had seen potential prey twice - first a rabbit and then some kind of bird, but Enric had been able to make her stay with the group both times. The first time he had needed a little warning shot of magic, the second time she had reacted to his verbal warning, though reluctantly.

Enric had been at the head of the party for the first few hours and the rest of them had been behind the cart; none had dared to ride up to him and start a conversation.

When they had stopped at an inn to have lunch, however, he had behaved as usual with no sign of anger or being offended. He had stepped towards Eryn's horse and held out his arms to help her dismount, smiling at her when he set her down and taking her hand as they went inside to eat.

The afternoon hours riding on the gravel road had been fairly pleasant. Enric had resumed talking to Kilan, discussing their living arrangements in Takhan.

Eryn knew better than to think that the matter was over and done with merely because for now he had decided to pretend nothing had happened. He would return to it, probably at the most inconvenient, unexpected time he could choose.

Enric rode next to her and looked up at the landscape to their left.

"This hill ahead of us should be the last one before we reach the village of Bonhet. It's small, mostly fishers," he explained.

"Will the ship already be there when we arrive?" Eryn asked.

"Yes, that is the plan. We will have a nice warm meal at a pub, then we will board the ship and leave the Kingdom tonight. At least if the weather is fit for sailing."

Eryn looked up at the clear sky with only puffy little clouds drifting lazily high above them.

"Looks fine to me," she shrugged.

"Sailors are generally a bit more exacting when it comes to the weather. It's not enough that it looks nice for the moment, it needs to last. They have their own little secret ways of divining that."

She recalled how the herb gatherers on the expedition had been able to predict the weather with surprising accuracy.

"Like a red sunrise being bad news, while a red sunset is good?" she smiled.

He nodded. "Yes, something like that. But from what I remember they have little devices that can do a lot of measuring as well. I imagine that your countrymen are a lot more advanced at this than we are. They are a few centuries ahead of us when it comes to seafaring."

"But there are fisher people here as well? So there must be some experience with the sea?"

Another nod. "But only for fishing. They don't venture out too far, as there is a phenomenon that has kept destroying ships for, well, three hundred years now. It can hardly be a natural event, as it coincides with the approximate time of the war. Probably a magical thing - maybe a barrier or something similar if that is even possible considering the size. Though a conventional barrier would only *stop* ships instead of destroying them. Learning more about that phenomenon is one of our priorities. But if they agree to trade with us, it's something which needs to be taken care of, anyway. We can hardly transport goods by ship if we can't cross the sea."

"They might insist on using only *their* ships to transport the goods," she pointed out.

"That is what we will have to make do with for quite some time, anyway. The only thing we have are fishing boats, more or less. They are hardly suitable for crossing the sea or transporting larger quantities of goods. But I will work on making them see that sharing with us the knowledge of how to cross the sea and help us build our own ships will benefit both sides."

She looked him up and down. "You will be quite busy there, won't you?"

He chuckled. "Why does this surprise you?"

"Ram'an didn't seem that busy to me back then."

"He had two attachés to put out their feelers. They were there to work while he was the one to take care of the social side of the visit. I am the one doing the work alone, which is why I very likely would have been the King's choice for this task anyway. I am used to negotiating trade agreements, and my high rank in the Order will ensure they respect me, as magical abilities in addition to social standing make me an acceptable delegate," he explained.

"So I am to all intents and purposes completely useless on this trip?" Eryn frowned.

"No, not at all. You are my opening for circles I would probably have difficulties being accepted into otherwise."

She shook her head. "I wonder if you aren't being a tiny bit optimistic here. I have no idea what social circles I might have been part of had I stayed there, and assuming that I could contrive to be part of them on this short visit is a rather bold assumption."

He smiled. "Don't worry. I think you may be surprised at how many doors will open for you. Ambassador Ram'an was sent to Anyueel to study you closely, and if his report had not been to the satisfaction of whoever ordered him there, they would not have insisted on your being sent along."

She was about to reply, but instead her mouth dropped open and she stared ahead, mesmerised at the sight the crest of the hill afforded her. The horizon was blue, but not merely from the sky above, but also a darker, sparkling, wide blue beneath. The sea.

The whole party had stopped their horses and looked at her with different expressions of amusement.

"You crossed the sea as a child to come here, so this can hardly be the first time you have laid eyes on it," Grend said.

"I don't remember that time," she murmured, still staring ahead at the calm, flat body of water that seemed to have force and mystery at the same time.

Kilan looked puzzled. "How can you not remember the sea? You were five years old at that time, weren't you? I remember things from when I was three years old, and my first impression of the sea I would surely not have forgotten."

"I just don't remember it," she replied testily, feeling as if she was again failing to meet expectations by not having memories at her disposal others expected to be there. Like Ram'an back then.

When she finally managed to direct her eyes away from the water, she saw the village Enric had told her about, close to the shore. It was indeed small, probably no more than thirty houses in total, all huddled together.

"The ship is already here," Barul said and pointed to a brown spot too large to be a fishing boat.

She narrowed her eyes and tried to make out details. "It doesn't look very big."

"Wait until you get closer," Enric smiled. "If we can identify it as a ship from such a distance, it is rather large, trust me."

Eryn didn't talk very much for the next two hours while they were riding downhill to the village. Seeing the ship, getting closer to the sea made it all oddly real. Riding off to travel to another country had seemed like a dream, but now there really was a ship, visible right there on the blue water ahead of her, sent here to take them away to a country she didn't remember anything about, to people who were curious about her.

* * *

She clung to what she had learned was called the *ship's rail* and got rid of the last remainders of her dinner. Her own words at the inn dismissing the possible inconvenience of travelling on a ship came to her mind, haunted her.

Kilan and Grend didn't seem to do much better than herself, but of course Enric, suave, superior and seemingly at home in whatever element he happened to encounter, didn't show even the slightest sign of unease but stood next to her with a sympathetic look.

To his credit he didn't repeat her words from last night at the inn back at her.

"Why can't I heal this away?" she wailed. "Every time I do, it is back a few seconds later as soon as the ship is tossed about by the next wave! Why don't you suffer from this... what do they call it?"

"Sea-sickness," he said. "I couldn't say. Iron stomach, I suppose. Barul doesn't seem to be affected, either."

"If that was supposed to comfort me, let me tell you that it didn't work," she scowled at him weakly and sank to the deck when no further reappearance of prior meals seemed imminent.

"I could always send you off to sleep," he offered.

"And have Grend and Kilan see me take the easy way out while they suffer through it? No, thanks," she huffed.

"Have it your way, then," he shrugged. "It's only two more days. You will survive that somehow, I am sure."

She wailed and buried her face in her hands, cursing her own pride, yet unable to act against it.

* * *

Enric leaned against the railing, staring up at the clear night sky with its countless stars. Eryn had finally fallen into a restless sleep and was tossing and turning on the narrow bunk bed. He had watched her for a few minutes and then decided to put an end to it. He put a hand on her forehead and deepened the sleep just as she had shown him earlier when she had sent Urban back to sleep for the journey on the ship.

Leaving the cat awake to prowl the ship would not have been a good idea. The crew would probably have thrown them overboard, cat included. So she rested peacefully in her crate until they reached Takhan.

Eryn stopped turning almost instantly at his touch and her features had softened. He had removed his hand again and decided that he needed fresh air.

Out on deck, Kilan stepped next to him, but didn't face the sea, choosing to keep his back turned to it.

"How is your stomach faring?" Enric wanted to know.

"Don't ask," he grumbled. "I am told that you get used to it after a few days, but I will hardly benefit from that, will I? We are meant to be arriving in little more than one day."

"Would you have preferred a longer voyage to have a chance to get used to it instead?"

"No, not really," Kilan shivered. "I greatly envy you right now. You seem to be completely unperturbed by this never-ending swaying and pitching."

"Luck, I suppose."

Suddenly both men felt a slight vibration going through the planks of the ship and each drew in a sharp breath. They looked down at their arms, at the goose bumps that had arisen.

"What was that?" Kilan whispered.

"I assume that was what destroyed our ships in the past. I hope we have crossed it."

They exchanged a look and then moved to where the helmsman stood, the wheel half his height in his hands, appearing calm but attentive.

"We just felt some powerful magic. Can you tell us that that was?" Enric enquired, careful to seem interested but not too eager.

The man smiled. "It was the barrier my ancestors erected to keep you inside and deflect any further attacks on us from your Kingdom."

So he had been right, Enric thought. It really was not a natural phenomenon.

"If it is a magical barrier, how was it possible for you to overcome it?" he asked.

The helmsman looked at him as if the answer should be obvious. "I use magic, of course. How else would I do it?"

"You are a magician?" Kilan exclaimed in surprise.

"Of course I have magic. Otherwise we would be a lot wetter and colder right now, as we would all be in the water," he explained indulgently, clearly finding this a less than stimulating conversation with the foreign men in their clothes that looked like dresses.

"Thank you very much," Enric said and bowed his head, grabbing Kilan's sleeve and pulling him along.

"A magical barrier that can only be crossed by sailors possessing magical abilities," Kilan shook his head when they were out of earshot. "No wonder we never found out how to cross it! Magicians would never in their wildest dreams have considered boarding a ship to do something as simple as steering it!" He snorted. "Makes you think about our elitist approach to working, doesn't it?"

Enric laughed quietly. "What a pity Eryn isn't here. She would very much have liked to hear you say that."

Kilan smiled. "Yes, I noticed that she has a more down-to-earth attitude towards work, doesn't she? Some of our fellow magicians are not too happy about one of us being willing to get her hands dirty." He raised his eyebrow. "I distinctly remember that you were not exactly one to consider hard work a desirable path for your life, either. Strange how things have changed. If you were still your old lazy self, your companion wouldn't even have spared you a second glance."

"No," Enric agreed with a sigh. "So it seems I have finally got my reward for my years of slaving for the Order."

"So it would seem. But judging from the tax listings you benefit a fraction from your work as well, don't you? You are among the five richest men in the Kingdom, my friend. Your father would be so proud. Of course you haven't told him to avoid just that, I bet."

Enric winced. "Nice to see that you remember the old stories. But yes, you are right. He thinks I live a life in comfort and revel in my high status without moving a finger all day long." Then he smiled in dark delight. "He even does some business with me occasionally without knowing it. I mostly avoid using my real name and send middlemen."

"So this time you will not only have to negotiate trade for somebody other than yourself, but also use your real name for a change."

"Yes," Enric spoke dryly, "a whole new experience."

"Eryn's family are probably hoping that you will favour their goods if they happen to produce any, considering your connections. So you might have to decide between either being seen to prefer them or to let them down gently and diplomatically. I don't envy you your task, to be completely honest. I will just sit next to you and hand you the information you need, watch you, marvel at how you do it and learn from you," Kilan smirked.

"So glad that you count on getting something out of it," Enric sighed.

"But so will you, won't you? Returning with signed trade agreements will have the King grant you whatever you like, I imagine. And I bet you already have an idea or two what to ask of him, don't you?"

Enric smiled. There was indeed one idea he had thought about bringing up. But that would very much depend on the outcome of the negotiations. If everything worked out the way it was supposed to, the favour he would ask the King to grant him would very likely catapult him to the top of the list of tax-payers in the Kingdom.

"Probably," he said noncommittally.

CHAPTER 20

Arrival in Takhan

Eryn shaded her eyes with a hand while she looked out over the wide, sun-flooded, sandy and rocky plains behind the river shore. Everything seemed so devoid of any plants. Fortunately there was some breeze so the heat didn't seem as oppressive as it had been a few hours ago at noon.

The man who had been introduced to her as the commander of the ship handed her a small brass telescope.

"If you look ahead, following the course of the river and the bend it makes to the right, you can already see the outlines of the city of Takhan."

Eryn lifted the telescope to her eye eagerly and after some moments found what looked like a collection of bright structures that were too evenly shaped to be natural but still too far away to be seen in detail.

"How much longer do you think we will need to get there?" she asked.

"If the wind keeps us heading at this speed, I would say not more than two hours. More than enough time to prepare for your arrival," he assured her.

She nodded to him and turned to look for her travel companions. She found Enric and Kilan sitting on the deck, leaning against the side of the mast that offered at least a modicum of shadow.

Grend and Barul each stood to one side of the deck, keeping an eye on their surroundings as good guards were expected to.

She crouched down in front of the two magicians. "It seems we are no more than two hours away from our destination. I suppose we need to change into our formal attires soon."

Kilan sighed. "Not a very pleasant prospect considering the temperatures here."

Enric nodded. "No, not really. I suppose one of the first things we need to take care of is finding a tailor and see if he can make us robes that are very similar in appearance, but a lot thinner. I don't want to spend the next three weeks here sweating."

"Is it really necessary to wear the robes? I mean, they will hardly recognise them as official Order attire, will they?" Eryn ventured.

Enric nodded again. "I am afraid we must. When they think back to this day, we want them to remember that we were dressed formally to show our respect and represented our Kingdom and the Order appropriately."

"Well, then maybe it would make sense for *me* to forego the robes, as there might still be different opinions about my belonging..." she tried again.

"Eryn," her companion said sternly, "you *will* wear your robes, no matter how hot you find it. And their seeing you representing the Order will be a good reminder of where *you* think you belong, so this is not a good argument at all."

She sighed and got up again. "Alright, whatever you say, *My Lord*. Let's just hope they don't have any lengthy welcoming ceremonies planned for us, or I am sure I will faint at some point. Deliberately, in case you were wondering."

Enric sighed. "You will do no such thing. You will be on your best behaviour. No intentional faints, no complaints about the heat. Politeness, respect, dignity. These are your guidelines."

Rolling her eyes in helplessness, she turned and walked away.

"Where are you going?" Enric called after her.

"To our cabin," she called over her shoulder. "I need to memorise my guidelines. We wouldn't want me to forget them, would we?"

Kilan chuckled. "She is a piece of work, isn't she? I bet you never get bored with her. Will she behave?"

Enric nodded. "Yes, I think she will. She does want to make a good impression, no matter what she says to us right now. Being obstinate just helps her to get rid of some of the tension."

"Well, then I suppose it's better for her to get rid of it now than later," Kilan shrugged.

"Exactly." Enric then whistled to the guards to come to him. "Gentlemen, we will reach Takhan in about two hours. Make sure you are clad in your uniforms by then."

Both men nodded once and returned to their lookout posts.

* * *

Eryn stood stiffly on deck in her purple healer's robes, letting her gaze wander across the large number of bright buildings in assorted sizes beside the piers the ship passed to reach what had to be their designated one. Ships in a variety of colours, styles and sizes were berthed peacefully at the piers. In contrast, people were running and climbing around purposefully on some of the ships, others seeming all but deserted. The wind had died down almost completely, but as the sun was dipping close to the horizon, the heat was at least bearable.

People she could see were dressed in simple clothing, but she recognised the general style as resembling what Ram'an had worn, though the working clothes of these men were less colourful and less extravagant by far. All of them, without an exception, sported various shades of dark hair.

Enric stepped behind her and laid his hand on hers on the railing without speaking. He, too, was busy scanning his surroundings. Despite the oppressive heat she welcomed the comforting touch and leaned back against him. Curiosity at all the new impressions battled the tension in the thoughts of what would expect her here. Everything she beheld seemed at the same time foreign and strangely familiar, as if a part of her that was too elusive or deep down to reach consciously, remembered it all.

They neared the end of the long procession of piers and the last one was empty, obviously reserved for their ship.

Kilan emerged from the below deck, dressed in his brown robes and stood next to them. Soon Barul and Grend also emerged. They had waited until the last possible moment to don their uniforms, and little wonder, as they mostly consisted of bulky leather armour that was not the most pleasant attire in this climate.

The ship finally coasted to a standstill, lines of thick rope were thrown to the shore, and a gangplank was lifted into place to allow the passengers to disembark first.

Eryn saw a group of four people waiting at the end of the pier. One of them looked familiar - even from a distance. Ram'an, she thought and smiled. It was good to have at least one familiar face there to welcome them, though Enric would doubtlessly have preferred an unfamiliar face to that particular one.

Enric was the first to leave the ship and waited for the other four to join him before he set forth to lead them to what seemed to be their welcoming committee. Three men, one woman, all dressed elegantly in flowing, thin and colourful fabrics, radiating wealth.

When they had reached the small group, Enric bowed to them and received their bows in return.

A man in his early sixties, tall and slim, with a sober expression and a piercing look, was the first to speak.

"My name is Golir, and I represent the Triarchy and the senate, an institution similar to your Council, as I understand. This here," he said and pointed to a woman in her late thirties, "is Malriel, a fellow senate member and Head of House Aren."

Enric barely managed to hide his surprise when he really looked at her for the first time. It was almost like he was looking at a slightly older version of Eryn, with the same dark brown hair held up by a complex-looking knot instead of being braided, the brown eyes, the curve of the forehead, the slightly fuller upper lip, the same slender build. There had to be a family connection of some sort, he was absolutely sure of it. Older sister? Aunt? Cousin?

He gave a surreptitious glance at Eryn, who either didn't seem to notice the astonishing similarity between herself and the stranger or had brought forth her acting skills to hide it. Kilan and the guards, however, had obviously been struck by the uncanny resemblance as well, judging from how their attention kept darting from one woman to the other and back again.

The woman's eyes didn't leave Eryn's when she slowly nodded to her.

"Ram'an you know, of course," Golir continued. "And this here is Valrad, Head of House Vel'kim and also a member of the senate."

The third man, in his mid-fifties with dark brown eyes and greying strands in almost black hair that reached to his collar, nodded to Eryn with a smile, his eyes shining warmly as if genuinely pleased to meet her.

"It is a pleasure to meet you all," Enric said. "I am Lord Enric and here," he took Eryn's hand, "is my companion Lady Eryn whom you have no doubt been very eager to meet."

Eryn smiled at each in turn and gave them a short nod. Something about the woman Malriel made her uneasy. Her gaze was too intent, the smile tense and expectant as if she were waiting for something.

Then Enric continued, "This is Kilan. He will be assisting me in all administrative matters. And our guards Barul and Grend. I noticed that you did not mention any titles. How ought we to address you?" Enric enquired.

Golir spoke again. "We do not use titles as they mostly refer to the positions we hold and are thus not relevant in social interactions. Addressing us with our names is sufficient and will cause no offence, Lord Enric."

Enric nodded. "Then for the duration of our stay here we would like to adopt your pleasantly uncomplicated way of address and also omit our titles."

Eryn hid an appreciative smile. That had been a slick move.

Ram'an smiled and took both of Eryn's hand to kiss them, ignoring Enric's cool gaze.

"Eryn, I cannot tell you how very happy I am to welcome you to your country of origin and finally to be able to show you your roots."

"Thank you. I admit I had not expected to return your visit to us quite so soon," she said and wondered if the tension between him and Enric would be there all the time until they departed for home.

Malriel stepped forward. "I admit I had hoped for some reaction from you at the mention of the names of our Houses," she said with an agreeably deep, throaty voice and looked at Eryn expectantly. "House Vel'kim is your father's House, and House Aren is on the maternal side of your family."

"Oh, I... see," Eryn stuttered, unsure how to react to that revelation. "Then I assume we are related, as you both are the Heads of the Houses?"

Malriel smiled and watched her like a hawk when she spoke again, "That is a valid conclusion, yes. The two of us are very closely related, even. I, my dear Maltheá, am your mother."

Enric's head snapped to his companion. How was this possible? Her mother was dead, wasn't she? Judging from Eryn's reaction - a frozen mask of disbelief - she had not been prepared for anything like that, either.

After standing there and just staring at the woman and her outrageous claim for several seconds, she then blinked rapidly for a few times and slowly breathed in and out.

Nonsense, she told herself. That was impossible on more than one level. The woman was obviously no more than ten years older than herself. Unless the usual age for having children was here a lot younger than back across the water, this had to be either a clumsy lie or a cultural misunderstanding.

She gulped and forced out a weak smile. "I am afraid I am a little confused right now, Malriel. It seems that my understanding of *mother* seems to differ by a long way from yours. Is the term in your country used as some kind of honorific for the Head of a House as the position includes great responsibility for the wellbeing of the family? Or anything of that kind?"

"No," Malriel said with a wry smile, "it is in our culture the general term to refer to a woman who has carried offspring in her womb for nine months before giving birth to them and who then raised them."

Eryn felt her patience wearing thin but forced herself to remain polite. It wouldn't do to insult the first people she met after disembarking from the ship. "I see. I have to admit that I find this statement rather hard to believe, considering two facts. First, I know my mother to be dead. And secondly, you look hardly ten years older than I."

"I see that your father might have felt it easier to make you believe in my demise than tell you the truth," Malriel of House Aren replied. "As for the second, I am a user of magic, dear child; I chose my appearance and the age it reflects at will. In reality, I am older than I look."

Only now did the panic start to rise and Eryn felt her breathing become shallower and faster. Her head swam. She felt Enric's arm wrapped around her middle, squeezing her reassuringly.

"I had hoped for a more positive and less distressed reaction, actually," Malriel commented with brows furrowed in displeasure.

Enric smiled at her as best he could. "I regret that this reunion is not going as happily as you would have wished for, Malriel, but please consider that Eryn has lived her entire life up until now with the assumption that her mother was deceased. Maybe somebody could show us to our accommodation now? I am sure she will better be able to handle all of this after resting herself after our journey." He needed to get Eryn somewhere private where she didn't need to control herself but could deal with that shock without worrying about the impression she made on others.

"Of course," Golir cut in. "Please follow me, it is not far from here. We will have your luggage brought to you."

Eryn looked up at Ram'an and addressed him sharply, her index finger pointing at his face. "You! You knew about this! You knew that I thought my mother was dead - and you didn't say anything! *I am not at liberty to tell, I am afraid*," she mimicked his words with a surprisingly accurate rendition of his accent.

"I am sorry, Eryn, I would have preferred to tell you, but I am sure you would not have believed me," he said and she saw the genuine sympathy and regret his eyes.

She then whirled to the fourth member of the welcome party. "Head of my father's House, aren't you?"

The man nodded cautiously. "That I am, yes."

"Any surprises from your side? If you somehow turn out to be my real father instead of the father I lost, I won't take this at all well," she warned, daring him to tell of any further shocking revelations.

"No," Valrad said mildly, "I am your father's older brother, your uncle. You seem under considerable stress right now. Let my help you calm down." Without waiting for her assent he took her hand, and a moment later she felt warmth on her skin and experienced an almost instantaneous sense of wellbeing. It rolled through her body in a powerful wave, engulfing with unstoppable force every negative feeling inside her. She wanted to tear her hand from his grip but simply couldn't come up with the angry energy to do it. Instead, she gently pulled it away.

"I must tell you that I do not appreciate being treated without my consent, if *treatment* is what you would call this infusion of really strange contentment, considering the circumstances," she explained with a smile that simply refused to be removed from her lips. She found the words did not come out nearly as sharply as she had intended. "How long will I continue to feel the effects of this?" Not too long, she hoped. She felt rather dazed and desperately wished for a clear head again to deal with this unexpected welcoming. Well, as desperately as that unbidden boost of positive energy would permit.

"One hour, two at the most," Valrad said. "It depends on the level of negative feelings inside you. If it is very high, the effect will not last as long."

"Good," she smiled beatifically, "then I should be back to normal in no time at all."

Enric strengthened his grip around her midriff. That strange contrast of her words and apparent helpless happiness troubled him. He had visualised how the first meeting with representatives from their host country might go, but this lay beyond his worst-case scenarios. Having her first traumatised and then, for lack of a better word, *drugged* into a scary half-submission, where underlying anger seemed to be fighting a trance of blissfulness, had exceeded the boundaries of his imagination by far.

Barul and Grend seemed uneasy as well, not sure whether Eryn had just been attacked or not and at a loss as to how they were to react in such a situation. Kilan was obviously fascinated by the whole unravelling of events.

Well, Enric thought, at least one of them could appreciate the entertainment value of the dramatic turn.

*   *   *

The residence that was put at their disposal for the duration of their stay was located close to the city centre, which was, in a city the size of Takhan, a considerable advantage as they did not require any transport to reach the hub of important buildings and social gathering places, as Golir had explained to them on their way there from the port.

Just like the other buildings in the city, the walls were bright in order to reflect the sunlight and thus minimise the heat within. Wealthier citizens had applied an additional layer with reflective stones ground into a rough powder to increase the effect.

The building's outline, Golir informed them, was typical for a residence in their country: the cooler storage rooms were on the ground floor while the central social room and the corridors that branched out from there and led to bedrooms and offices were on the first floor.

They ascended the stairs to the first floor and the main living area where Enric gently placed a still tensely relaxed Eryn on the large sitting area that consisted of large, colourful, soft cushions; in style resembling the space Ram'an had created in his quarters when he had visited Anyueel only months ago, but considerably larger.

Golir bade them goodbye and invited them to a formal dinner the next evening to give them time to work off the strain and exhaustion of their journey here. Not to mention the arrival.

Malriel, Valrad and Ram'an remained with their foreign visitors and now stood around the comfy seating island with Kilan and Enric, all looking down at Eryn, who stretched out comfortably and yawned.

A light wind billowed the gauzy curtains in front of the huge windows that afforded a view of an enclosed garden, and she watched them in fascination.

"I think it might be better to meet up again tomorrow," Enric murmured. "I am afraid she will not exactly be the kind of company you would wish for after the effects of that surge of happiness wear off."

"No, probably not," Valrad agreed. "Do you know how to send her to sleep? It might be that the news she has just received might otherwise keep her from having a peaceful night."

"No, none of that," Eryn smiled up at them. "Enric and I have a bit of a history with his sending me to sleep, don't we, darling? I don't take very well to it, and we tend to fight afterwards."

Enric raised his brows at the endearment. What a pity she needed to have her emotional balance tipped artificially to use it for him. Maybe he would have a little talk with her uncle to learn the skill, he thought with dark fascination.

"Would you like me to stay until she returns to her normal state?" Valrad asked.

Eryn laughed, her tongue slow, heavy and clumsy as if she was under the influence of alcohol. "Oh no, you would not like that, trust me. I think I wouldn't be too kind on you," she said thoughtfully and stared up at the ceiling. "Oh my, you paint your ceilings? How delightful!"

Enric cleared his throat. "I think it might be better for you to leave now. I hope you don't find me impolite, but for the sake of diplomacy I think it might be advisable to spare you whatever she will come up with when she is back to her old self again."

Ram'an flashed her a last worried look, then nodded. "I will drop by tomorrow morning after breakfast to see how you are doing."

Malriel stared down at her daughter, arms folded, and sighed, resigned to the fact that this was how the first encounter with her daughter after more than two decades would end. "I would like to invite you and Maltheá to have lunch at my place tomorrow. I will send a servant to guide you there. It is not very far from here; a pleasant walk that will give you an opportunity to take a first look at the city."

Valrad frowned, watching his niece with obvious worry. "Then I will see you at the dinner in the evening. I would like to invite you for lunch the day after tomorrow to introduce my family to you as well. I know she has a great interest in healing, so I hope she will find the connection to my side of her family useful."

When they were gone, Enric sent Kilan off and took a seat next to Eryn, pulling her close.

"I like it when you call me darling. Can we stick with this?" he asked and kissed her forehead.

She snuggled into his side and sighed contentedly. "Probably not. Ask me again when I am not all fuzzy and purple in the head."

"Purple?" he chuckled.

"Yes. It's my colour of peace and happiness, I think. Or fake peace and happiness. Funny, normally I don't see colours when I am happy. Must be a side effect. Nothing permanent, I hope. I don't even like the colour particularly."

"You don't? Then it was quite an unfortunate choice for the healers' robes, wasn't it?" He paused, then watched her when he said carefully, "We will have lunch with your mother tomorrow."

"My mother," she murmured. "This is like a really bizarre dream. I never had a mother. I mean, you know what I'm saying, don't you? No friendly older neighbour or elderly friend who felt the need to take over a mother-like role in my life, that's what I mean. I seem to have acquired a few father figures, though, especially in this last year. Orrin. Even Vern sometimes thinks he has to scold me and point me in the right direction. You."

He looked a little fazed. "You see me as a father figure? I don't think I am comfortable with that."

She laughed. "Really? And yet you keep disciplining and instructing me and using your authority on me all the time. I don't think we are on equal terms in our relationship, for what it's worth."

He looked down at her, considering her words. Even though she was not completely herself, they did make sense. He wondered if talking about this in her current state of mind was advisable, but then she would probably not be willing to go on with it later.

"Does this bother you very much?" he asked.

"Sometimes. Sometimes not at all. Sometimes I even like it."

His face turned to an expression of puzzlement. "Do you now? When?"

"In bed." She looked up at him with half-closed eyes. "Don't tell me you haven't noticed."

"I have. But it's still nice hearing you admit it. As for the other situations, it is less a fatherly role than one of superior authority I have to assume sometimes."

She shrugged and gave a smile. "Not much difference there, is it?"

"So Tyront and the King also assume father roles in your life?"

"Something like that, yes. The thing is, I have no female authority figure in my life, never had one. I wonder if Malriel plans on taking over that kind of role now." She lazily watched her fingers drawing circles in the air, marvelling at the lingering traces they left. "Wow. I need to ask... what was his name again? The healer?"

"Valrad?"

"Yes, Valrad. I need to ask him how he did this. I wonder if he will agree to teaching me. I could put you in such a state every time you are angry at me," she mused.

"What a charming prospect," Enric commented dryly.

"My mother. I hope I am not supposed to address her like that, am I? I am not even sure I like her."

"You haven't spent much time with her so far. Wait until tomorrow, then you will have the opportunity really to talk with her and make up your mind. Good-looking woman, though," he added with a smirk.

"You think?" Eryn frowned. "I don't see it."

"Love, she is almost your mirror image."

She laughed out loudly. "What? That is complete nonsense!"

He shook his head at her. "I can't believe you didn't see that. Everybody else did."

"You can't know that," she said with a lazy, dismissive wave of her hand.

"Judging from the shocked looks on the faces around me, I'd say I can," he countered.

Eryn yawned again. "I need to sleep now."

"Do that, my love." He kissed her on her temple and was about to ask her whether she wanted to sleep here or in their bed that had to be around somewhere on this floor, but her eyes were closed already and when he leaned away, she sunk back limply.

* * *

Enric looked up from the plate of unfamiliar fruits the servant had prepared for breakfast when Eryn came in from the adjoining room, her hair as well as her nightgown rumpled. At home she usually donned a morning robe after getting up, but it was too warm for this here. He appreciated the insights the gauzy material granted and watched her walking closer.

She looked resigned. When she had woken again yesterday evening, she had not been in a good mood - far from it. The effect of her uncle's little trick had worn off after her nap, and the anger that had been waiting for more than two hours had been eager to get out.

She had been at a loss who to be angry at; that had been a major drawback. Just ranting was not the same as giving it a purpose. She was aware that resenting her mother for being alive was somehow not right, and neither was cursing her dead father for giving that wrongful impression. Enric had suggested Ram'an as a target due to his withholding this information from her, but she saw through that manoeuvre at once and used the opportunity to take some of her frustration out on Enric instead.

It had taken almost another two hours before she had been exhausted enough just to sink back and bury her face in her hands. That had been even more disconcerting to watch than her outbursts. But she had found a way to deal with it for now. She would meet Malriel and talk to her. Find out what exactly she wanted, what both of them wanted.

The fruit on Enric's plate looked interesting. She picked a dark pink piece up and smelled it before taking a tentative bite. Sweet and juicy.

"Good morning. How are you feeling?" Enric asked and pulled her down on his lap.

She shrugged. "Better than yesterday. But I suppose that doesn't say much." She eyed the other pieces of fruit on the plate.

"Try the yellow one. It has a spicy aftertaste I think you will like."

She did and nodded approvingly before snatching another piece. "They are really good, much sweeter than our fruit varieties. I suppose that's because they have so much sun here. More sun develops a higher level of sugar in the fruits. We should see if they are willing to trade these." She saw Enric smile and sighed. "But you are far ahead of me again, aren't you?"

"I admit I have considered this option already, yes." He took a bulgy, gold rimmed glass and held it out to her. "Try this. It's something like a national drink here. Similar to our tea, but a lot stronger and more bitter. They sweeten it to make it palatable."

She took the glass and sniffed. "It smells horrible." She took a sip and kept it in her mouth for a few moments before swallowing it. "Doesn't taste much better than it smells. Is there an alternative?"

"Sure. It's not fit for children, so, there is a herbal brew they drink and many adults also prefer it, I am told."

"Where did you get all this information from?"

"From our servant. We talked a bit while she was serving me breakfast. By the way, she asked me about our preferences. It is customary here that servants are at your disposal no longer than until noon. They serve breakfast, clean the place and do the shopping according to your instructions. Then they leave and only return the next morning. I told her we were fine with adapting to their ways and do not require her longer than that. It seems that even in higher social circles cooking one's own meals is a skill everybody is supposed to possess. That will be quite interesting for us, I imagine. We are expected to cook our own lunch. People generally go out in the evening for dinner. So why don't we try skipping lunch for the next few weeks or make do with fruit?"

Eryn frowned. "Skip lunch? Why? I can cook."

Enric stared at her. "What? You?"

She laughed. "Spoiled rich boy! I grew up in the countryside as a country healer's daughter, so who do you think did the cooking? We had no servants in our cottage, we had to provide for ourselves - just like the majority of people, namely those born with neither magic nor inherited wealth."

Of course, he thought, feeling foolish for being surprised at this morsel of news. It was logical, wasn't it? But looking at her, he just couldn't imagine her in a kitchen, preparing a meal.

"So you will cook for us? I mean, that you can do it doesn't mean you have to."

She shook her head. "You think I am too important and noble for it now that I am joined to such a rich and powerful man as yourself? I don't think that preparing a meal is something that's beneath me. Quite the opposite, I am pleasantly surprised that they don't delegate the responsibility for their nourishment to their servants completely here."

"I was just surprised at there being a housekeeper somewhere underneath all your other talents," he said.

She frowned. "I wouldn't say housekeeper. I am glad enough we don't also have to clean the place, but cooking is a minor thing, and I think everybody should be able to provide for themselves. It is a basic survival skill I would have thought a warrior would appreciate, but which has obviously become obsolete with increasing wealth and no wars in aeons."

"What can I say, my love? Every word of yours is true. I stand before you, eclipsed by your wisdom and superior skill in keeping yourself well-fed."

She grinned. "Good. Don't you forget that anytime soon. I will have to familiarise myself with the local vegetables, fruits, spices and baked goods here before I try any cooking. But for the next two days our lunch is taken care of anyway as we are invited. You say the servant does the shopping for us? That is helpful. I wouldn't know where to get things."

They heard a loud knock at the downstairs entrance door and then Ram'an's voice when the servant permitted him.

"You'd better get dressed. I don't want him seeing you in your nightgown," Enric murmured and lifted her up from his lap just as Ram'an was led into the room.

"Too late for that," Eryn shrugged and waived her hand at their visitor, who clearly was surprised at the sight, but forced himself to keep his eyes on her face as he greeted her.

"Good morning, Eryn. Lord Enric."

Lord Enric, she thought and suppressed a groan. And that after Enric had asked them to address him without title. A deliberate sign that Ram'an wished to maintain his distance from him.

"Hello Ram'an. You have to excuse me for a moment, I have failed to get dressed in time as it would seem." She disappeared behind the door that separated the bedroom from the main room and quickly slipped into one of the thin tunics and trousers Junar had made for her. They did feel a lot more comfortable than the robes from yesterday.

When she returned, both men turned to her in what clearly was relief at not being alone with the other any longer.

"How are you doing today, my dear?" Ram'an said and took both her hands in his. "I imagine this was quite a shock for you yesterday. I know that you are not very happy with me for withholding this particular detail from you, but..."

"It's alright, I graciously forgive you," she interrupted him. "And I am generously granting you an opportunity to make up for it right now."

"Indeed?" he asked with some surprise and let himself be pulled towards the seating island at the centre of the room.

"I need information on social customs here. As you know, we have received three invitations for today and tomorrow that are centred around dining. We need to know what is expected of us."

He smiled and sat with her. "I am more than happy to help you here. Though you may expect a certain forbearance from your hosts considering that this is your first day here."

Enric took a seat next to his companion. "I would rather earn respect than be granted forbearance," he said coolly.

Ram'an nodded. "Of course. When you arrive at the Aren residence, you will be led to the hostess immediately. It depends on the personal preference of your host or hostess where you are received. Malriel tends to meet her guests on her terrace, as the garden attached to her residence is very grand and she likes to be complemented on it. That is the best time to present her with your gift."

"Our gift?" Eryn asked weakly.

"Yes. It is customary to bring a little something as a token of your appreciation. In your case a typical item from your country will do nicely as it is still unique as long as we are not engaged in any trade yet. A bottle of something to drink or some other speciality. Make sure the gift is not too extravagant or you might appear too flagrant, as if you wished to demonstrate your wealth. We do not look kindly upon this, even though we like to give subtle hints."

"Subtle hints?" Enric now enquired. "How subtle? And of what nature?"

"Let us say decking out your ears and neck with loads of gold is not looked upon kindly, but well-tailored attire made of high quality fabrics will never fail to convey the intended message in a more acceptable way. Eryn, did you bring the pendant I gave you?"

She nodded and pulled it out from under her tunic.

"Very good. Continue to wear it like that, invisible under your tunic, but be ready to use it when you see an advantage in doing so or if you need to verify your origins. That is why your mother gave me it to take with me on my visit."

Eryn swallowed her comment that handing her the gift her mother had given him for her would have been a fabulous occasion for mentioning that she was still alive. But after telling him that she had forgiven him for keeping it from her, it would not look good to reproach him for it now only a few minutes later.

"How do we greet her?" she asked.

"That is quite a difficult question in your case," Ram'an grimaced. "With your companion it is easier. He will take her left hand with his left and lift it to his lips for a moment before letting go of it. This is the formal greeting between men and women here. The formal greeting between two women is that they link the fingers of their left hands and nod at each other. The same goes for two men. But in your case the question is if you would not rather adopt a less formal greeting. In this case you would kiss each other on both cheeks."

"I think I will stick to the formal one for now," she replied.

"Are you sure about that?" Enric asked. "She might consider this an affront."

"If she wants to be affronted, she will find other opportunities soon enough. If she wants to provide the time I need for adapting to the state of not being an orphan any longer, she will accept it," she shrugged. "What rules do we have to follow during the meal? Do we have to wait until she starts eating or something like that?"

"No. Quite the opposite. A good host waits until all guests have started eating before doing so themselves so as to make sure every guest has found something to his or her liking. You are expected to wash your hands before you eat, though. For this purpose a bowl with water and a towel will be provided for your use. Wash and dry your hands." He then motioned to their own table at one side. "This table has been made for your comfort, but you will not find them in any of our houses. We like to sit on cushions on the floor, also for our meals. It makes leaning back comfortably easier after you are done with your meal. I remember that you prefer to change from the dinner table to more cosy seating arrangements later, but we like to move as little as possible after our meals for at least half an hour."

"So jumping up right after I have finished eating would not be received favourably?" Eryn asked.

"No, not at all. It would be an insult as it would imply that you did not enjoy your meal enough to stay any longer than necessary. Or that you do not appreciate your hostess or host sufficiently."

"Alright," she murmured and summarised what she had just heard. "Gift on the terrace, linking fingers of left hand and nod, wash hands before lunch, stay seated for another half hour afterwards. Anything else?"

Ram'an looked pained. "Do not concentrate so much on the rules, my dear. This is your first opportunity to really talk to your mother. This will not be about adhering to etiquette, but about the two of you getting to know each other."

"I haven't been in the role of a daughter in a very long time," she said quietly. "And I was not particularly good at it back then, either." She thought about her father's death and how she had precipitated it. "I was prepared to be somebody's cousin, niece, aunt, sister even, but long-lost daughter..." She shook her head. "I mean, she doesn't even look as if she were old enough to be my mother! I had no idea we could even do that! Do you do it, too? What do you really look like?"

Ram'an chuckled. "I assure you, this is my genuine appearance. For a man it is not advisable to look too young - or he might not be taken seriously. I will start changing my appearance in ten or fifteen years at the earliest."

Enric considered her thoughtfully. "Maybe they are willing to teach you this skill. Imagine when you offer it back home as one of your additional services. You would be able to make healing completely independent from the crown's funding."

She exhaled and scowled in dismay. "What an appealing thought indeed," she grumbled and shivered when she pictured herself spending her days removing wrinkles, tightening baggy skin and making varicose veins disappear.

"Teaching you the skill probably will not be much of a problem," Ram'an nodded. "Your uncle is a very influential and esteemed healer. Some would say even the most influential one there is. If he considers it a good idea to teach this to you, nobody will dare or even bother contradicting him. And you are part of his family, after all, even if it is only the paternal side."

"Only the paternal side?" she frowned. "That does sound rather derogatory."

"Not at all," he assured her. "A father's side of the family is always secondary to the mother's in our society, quite the reverse to what you are used to. When a child is born, it is considered a member of the mother's House. She makes all relevant decisions. Depending on the relationship between the parents, she might let her companion participate in them to the degree she sees fit."

"So I stem from a House that has brought forth generations of healers and another one with power-hungry politicians, yet the latter one is the one I am considered to be close to?" she exclaimed. "That is a cruel twist!"

Ram'an smiled at her sympathetically. "That is the case, I am afraid."

"Just fabulous," she murmured and lifted her eyes. "But Malriel doesn't have any real power over me, does she? I am not a citizen of your country."

"That is difficult question I cannot answer just like that. You are the first case of this kind we have known in recent centuries. The question whether your origins or the place where you spent most of your life determines where you belong is one that is being discussed among the lawyers right now, as it has been for several months now."

"So if your lawyers decide that I belong here, she could stop me from returning? Is that what you are telling me?" Eryn exclaimed and rose from her cushion.

"Factually speaking, yes. But do not be alarmed. She is a politician first and foremost, and forcing you to stay here might do her more harm than good, especially as your companion would not take kindly to such a course of action."

Enric smiled grimly. "No, hardly."

"So try to enjoy your lunch with your mother, Eryn. She is probably as unsure of what to make of this situation as you are,"

Ram'an soothed her. "Are there any other questions you have for now?"

She thought for a moment, then shook her head. "No, nothing for now, but I am sure that there will be a lot more later."

"Then do contact me. If you send a messenger to House Arbil, he will know where to find me. I will take my leave now. It was good to see that you have recovered from your shock of yesterday, and I look forward to seeing you again at the dinner tonight. I will be attending it in my father's stead." He nodded to her and bowed to Enric before walking out of the main room and down the stairs to the entrance door.

"That was helpful, wasn't it?" she said.

"Are you trying me make me like him?" Enric asked and folded his arms. "You are not likely to succeed with that anytime soon."

"Well, at least I can rely on your being diplomatic about it, Ambassador," she sighed.

"That you can, my love. May I in turn rely on your efforts to be diplomatic with your mother today?"

"Can we please not call her that for now?"

"Malriel, then. If you find that you can't be friendly, will you be polite at least?"

She sighed. "I will do my best, I promise. But somehow I have a feeling that she will not make that easy for me."

CHAPTER 21

Malriel

Eryn looked up at the imposing building and swallowed in trepidation. Clearly the residence of a very wealthy family, it stood two stories high with a façade that shimmered and gleamed in the sunlight. The servant that had collected them from the ambassadorial residence led them into a small ante-room and then offered them cool, wet towels to wipe their hands and face for refreshment.

"If you follow me now," the servant said, "Malriel is awaiting you on the terrace."

Eryn nodded. So far, just as Ram'an had predicted.

They walked along a cool corridor and up a flight of stairs. It seemed that having the main living quarters on the first floor was indeed common style in Takhan, just as Golir had told them after accompanying them to the ambassadorial residence.

They soon found themselves in a bright, airy room that could easily have contained the entire ground floor of their house at home. On the floor were two of these large sitting areas consisting of cushions. The walls were decorated with carpets with complicated tableaux of dancing and hunting scenes intricately woven into them. They followed the servant through an archway out to the terrace, where Malriel stood and turned to them with a smile.

"Welcome to my house," she said and approached them. Eryn quickly stretched out her left hand to avoid any misunderstandings as to what kind of greeting she preferred. But to her astonishment, the older woman looked down at it, chuckled and shook her head.

"No, Maltheá, surely not." And she pulled her daughter close and kissed both her cheeks before Eryn even knew what was happening. Eryn stumbled back, slightly taken aback and clenched her teeth to keep herself from commenting on this flagrant disregard for her own wishes.

Enric felt the tension and quickly stepped forward, taking Malriel's left hand with his own and pressing his lips to her warm knuckles for a short moment before releasing it again.

"Malriel, thank you for welcoming us into your home. Please accept this small gift." He handed her the bottle of dark wine and watched her smile in appreciation.

"Thank you very much, Enric. I admit that I am pleasantly surprised at you showing such consideration for our customs. Tell me about your gift."

"It is a special kind of wine, produced in our Kingdom. There are only three regions where it grows, and I happen to own one of them."

She smiled. "So it is a product of yours?"

He nodded. "It is, yes."

"My House also makes wine, though we do not specialise in it. Making wine is a matter of prestige - every House does it, but only three Houses produce on a scale large enough to sell. The rest of us just like to be able to offer it to guests. I'll freely admit that our own wine is not equal to anything House Partém or Arbil produces."

"House Arbil?" Eryn asked curiously. "Ram'an's House?"

"Indeed, child. It is nice to see that you have started to familiarise yourself with the Houses," Malriel smiled approvingly.

Child, Eryn thought. She was twenty-eight years old. A bit too old to be called a *child* by somebody who made herself look younger than forty.

"Your garden is a sight to behold," Enric said smoothly, shooting Eryn a warning glance when Malriel turned to the object of his admiration.

"Thank you so much. I must say I am very proud of it. The general outline was planned by my great-grandfather, and every generation aims to add a little something to make it even more distinctive. My mother's contribution was the patch of red bushes you see over there. She spent years experimenting and finally managed to combine two kinds of fruit into a completely new species."

Eryn looked over to the bushes with interest. "May I?" she asked and pointed towards them.

Malriel nodded. "Of course."

She went the few paces over to the three bushes and examined the leaves and the blossoms that had only started to grow. Closing her eyes, she sent a probing pulse of magic into the plant and examined it from within.

When she opened her eyes again, she saw Malriel's gaze resting on her.

"Very interesting. I can still make out what used to be the characteristics of the separate plants. It is impressive how they were merged."

"I am glad you like it," the older woman smiled. "We sold the seeds to House Partém, and they have managed to cultivate them on their plantations. They deliver a share of the profits to us. Come. Let me show you my own contribution." She took both Enric's and her daughter's arm and led them to a more remote corner of the large garden.

"This is it."

They stopped in front of a small tree not much wider than Enric's shoulders. "It does not look so impressive, but when it is the right time of the year, it bears two different kinds of fruit. It does not equal my mother's contribution from a scientific point of view, but that is not the ambition anyway. Every Head of House is meant to add something that represents her or his own strengths. Mine are of a more political, persuasive nature; and thus making two species share the same resources - namely the space and nourishment one tree can provide - corresponds with my abilities."

Enric nodded. "I like the concept very much. It unites the preservation of knowledge from your ancestors with the eagerness to develop and improve."

Malriel smiled up at him. "You are a smart one, Enric. I appreciate that in a man. But let us go inside now, I can see that the heat is not easy to bear for the two of you."

She led them to one of the two seating islands and pointed to two bowls of water. "I trust you are aware what to do with them?"

"Yes, we are, thank you," Eryn replied politely and sat down to wash her hands and dry them afterwards just as Ram'an had explained to them.

"I have prepared a mildly spiced meal for us today as Ram'an informed me that in your Kingdom you seem to use culinary herbs and spices a bit more sparingly than we do," she explained when she brought a large dark bowl filled with what appeared to be a colourful mix of various vegetables to their low table. Smiling, she placed the bowl at its centre. Then she brought three smaller bowls of the same colour and three pointed sticks.

They watched her filling all three bowls and place one pointed stick into each of them before handing them to her guests.

"Be pleased to relish," she said and nodded to them.

Enric carefully took his stick and skewered one of the pieces, which he then lifted to his mouth. He chewed it and then smiled. "Really tasty."

Eryn took a mouthful, then almost choked as she bit on something small and round that exploded into a painfully spicy sensation on her tongue. She smiled apologetically. "I think I just chewed something rather more potent than I am used to."

"I should have warned you. Avoid chewing the black seeds - or better, put them aside." Only then did she herself start to eat in the way a good host was expected to. "How familiar are you with the food which is eaten at a particular time of the day?"

"Not very much, I am afraid. Judging from our breakfast I dare say that fruits are customary in the morning," Enric replied.

"Yes, indeed. For the noon meal we prefer assorted cooked vegetables, but we usually let them cool a little before eating them due to the heat. The evening is the only time of the day where meat is served," she explained. "Normally, we do not eat alone in the evening, it is the most important meal of the day as it is the one we use to maintain and increase our social connections and contacts. We only cook at home if we have invited guests. Otherwise we either accept dinner invitations or go to public places where sooner or later somebody will come and sit down to eat with you."

So much for peaceful evenings with Enric at their residence, Eryn thought in dismay.

"You mentioned that it is the only time of the day where you serve and eat meat," Enric said.

"Exactly. Meat is a matter of pride in our society, you see. If you serve meat in your own home to your guests, then it is assumed that you were the one who went hunting and that it is your kill you are serving them. There is a black market in selling meat to those who are either not interested, disinclined or unsuccessful in hunting. However, that comes with the risk that if you are found out, your reputation is shattered and you will be mocked everywhere you go. It is better not to serve any meat at all than something you have not yourself killed on a hunt."

Enric leaned back and considered what he had just heard. "That is very different from our own customs. Where I come from, hunting is considered no more than a sport, at least for those of us who live in the city. We have farmers who breed animals that are then slaughtered and sold to whoever can afford the meat."

Malriel frowned. "That is indeed very different," she said, choosing her words carefully.

Enric smiled. "It must seem barbaric to you."

The older woman returned the smile. "Even if it did - I would hardly admit this to you, would I?"

"I have to say that I find your way of handling the consumption of meat intriguing," he said and pursed his lips. "I wonder if I could try it myself, or is it a privilege I am not supposed to usurp as a guest, a foreigner?"

"No, quite the opposite. It would show respect for our customs, something we appreciate a lot in our visitors. There are small hunting parties where a few people get together every now and then. You might want to join one of them for a start. They can show you good places to go hunting, where to find the different kind of game."

"I think I will, thank you," Enric nodded.

Eryn had finished her meal and placed the empty bowl back on the table. After avoiding the spicy seeds she'd found it undeniably delicious. And now there was the obligatory half hour to remain with the host, she remembered, leaning back.

"Are you sated, my dear? There is more if you wish," Malriel offered and indicated the still half full bowl on the table.

"I am, thank you very much," Eryn replied and smiled politely.

Malriel then put her empty bowl on the table as well and leaned back to study her daughter.

"You seem rather more collected than yesterday. I can see that you managed to deal with the shock. There must be a lot of questions you have for me, I imagine. And I have quite a few I would like to ask you in return."

Eryn steeled herself. "Alright. Why don't you start, then?"

"What did your father tell you about me, apart from the lie that I was dead?"

Eryn decided to condone the use of the word *lie*, however little she appreciated hearing it uttered in connection with her father. Especially not by that woman who was no more than a stranger and seemingly not at all well-disposed towards her father. "Not a lot, I have to say," she replied. "Except that he loved you very much, and that games of power were the reason he lost you."

"Did he tell you explicitly that I was dead? Or was this your assumption when he said that he had lost me?" Malriel asked and leaned forward.

Eryn tried to think back. "I assumed you were dead, and he didn't correct my impression. He probably thought it was easier for me than knowing that you were alive but beyond my reach."

"Yes. And also easier for himself, no doubt. Did he ever tell you why he left his home country?"

Eryn shook her head. "No, not exactly. But you know what? I am not sure I want to hear it right now." Not from you, she added silently.

"Oh, but you should." A flash of cold steel had entered Malriel's voice. "Everybody else in the city, and even the country, knows, and so should you. I imagine it will be mentioned in your presence sooner or later."

Eryn frowned at her. "I would rather not, if you don't mind." An undefined feeling told her that she would not be happy with the story Malriel was so eager to share with her.

"I do mind. And I do insist on you listening to it."

Enric quickly took Eryn's hand when she made to get to her feet. "Wait. I think you should stay and hear what she has to say," he said quietly.

She looked at him for several moments, into his blue eyes that urged her to lean back again and face whatever unpleasant truth was about to be revealed to her.

"Alright," she murmured and held on to his hand as she leaned back. She looked back at the older woman, who watched them patiently and seemed satisfied with the outcome of their exchange. Eryn looked at her and felt confirmation of what she had suspected before. She didn't like this woman, no matter what their family connection. She was inconsiderate, ego-driven and showed no regard for what other people wanted. This was the second time now she had ignored Eryn's express wishes to enforce her own.

"I will listen to you. But after that we will leave."

Malriel leaned back and folded her legs elegantly. "As you wish. I imagine you will not be very pleased with what I am about to tell you, that it will show you a man very different from the one you probably knew."

"Tell your story, then," Eryn said coldly.

"Not *my* story. *Our* story." Malriel took a deep breath and started. "Your father and I were intended for each other, as is customary in our society. I do not know if you are familiar with the arrangements yet - probably not. But let us leave this aside for now. You father courted me, and I accepted his proposal of companionship when I was eighteen years old. He came from a dynasty of healers, I from a long line of leaders, politicians. But we were in love and it did not seem to matter at that time. We decided to wait a little before having children, thinking that there would be enough time. We had you after three years, and we were all thrilled at having another girl for House Aren. Female descendants, you see, are what maintains a House's power."

"Ram'an mentioned something like that," Eryn said. "Go on."

Malriel nodded. "Alright. You were about two years old when a great discussion was started by a young woman who had become pregnant against her will because a man had forced himself upon her. We had very strict laws against healers ending pregnancies unless there were grave medical reasons for it. Your father was a great defender of this law, as his stance was that every life needed protection and nobody, not even a pregnant woman, had the right to end a life. This woman, however, tried to abort the foetus on her own and hurt herself so badly that she bled to death. The matter would probably have gone virtually unnoticed if the woman had not been a member of one of the twelve Houses. Her family fought for a law that permitted terminating pregnancies and eventually managed to convince the senate. Your father was furious. He was not willing to accept the decision and not only refused to carry out the procedure, but started assembling other healers who shared his sentiments. They started terrorising colleagues who adhered to the law and made them stop their work altogether to force the senate to rescind the law." She shook her head at the memory. "My House, you see, was one of the supporters of the new law, and this situation caused quite a rupture in our relationship, as you might imagine. We stopped talking to each other, and your father even moved back in with his family towards the end. It took the senate quite some time to take care of the situation, but your father was not willing to accept his defeat." Her voice had become bitter. "Not him. He tried to intimidate the few women who had dared seek the healers' services in that particular matter, threatened them and used his magic to force them to get in contact with the unborn life inside them. One of them was so traumatised, she broke down crying and it took the healers years to help her get over the shock and desperation. Your father was sentenced to a ten-year block on his magical powers."

Eryn was stunned. She realised he had not accepted that, either.

"You were five years old at that time. It was night when he came to talk to me about going away from here. He told me that he still loved me and that he wanted his family with him. I refused. He knocked me out with a single blow, and when I awoke, they had put me in my bed and I instantly knew that something had to be very wrong. My mother was the one to break the bad news to me. She told me that he had taken you and that the evidence suggested that he had stolen a boat and attempted to cross the sea to the Old Kingdom." Malriel's eyes had fire in them now. Anger at a man long dead for a deed long done, but neither forgiven nor forgotten.

"He took my only child away from me to a place so far out of my reach it took me months to persuade the senate to let me go after you with a search party. We had to understand how we could pass the barrier first, as it had not been attempted for three hundred years. But I prevailed. I found a weak spot and managed to get us through. Only when we reached the shore at the other side, did I finally learn that you had survived for sure and that my attempts had not been in vain. We roamed the country for two years looking for the two of you. Every single day in that place I hated him more. I thought of the things I would do to him when I finally managed to get my hands on him. Cruel, painful things to pay him back for every minute of fear for you he had made me endure. But he was very good at hiding his tracks. We sometimes found traces of his presence, but by the time we got there he was long gone, wiping memories and whatever other little tricks he knew."

Malriel rose and went to a small table with a carafe of water and poured herself a glass which she then drained in one go. She stood with her back to them while she continued.

"When I returned after these two years, the senate told me to give up my search, to give you up. But I couldn't. I paid one search party after the other to look for you. But to no avail. Nothing, no trace of you for more than twenty years. But one year ago, they found something. But too late. Your father had hidden your magical abilities well, but your accident in the woods had been only a few days too early. Only a few days."

They heard glass shatter and then a resigned sigh. Malriel turned and without showing any sign of pain started plucking splinters of golden glass out of her palm and threw them onto the small table. When she had all of them removed, she healed her hand and a moment later the few drops of blood on the glass was all that remained of her injury.

"You see, Maltheá, your father had his faults as well."

Eryn rose abruptly. The turmoil inside her made it impossible to stay seated any longer. She needed to get away from here, needed time to think. And she needed to talk to somebody else who could either verify or amend this story.

"Is this why you told me all of this? To show me how flawed he was? To show yourself in a better light? To make me return to House Aren, to return the power to you which the loss of a daughter had cost you?" She breathed heavily and felt Enric's hands on her arms pulling her back towards him.

"Don't," he whispered into her ear from behind. "Not now. Not as long as you don't have your emotions under control."

Malriel's narrowed eyes bore into Eryn's wide ones and she slowly came closer. She then lifted her hand to put it on the younger woman's shoulder.

Eryn gasped and the pain she felt made her knees buckle. Only Enric's grip on her arms made her remain upright. Desperation, fear, anger, hate, hope - all of that tied together in one tight, mighty ball inside her that almost took her breath away.

"Malriel!" she heard Enric's voice shouting. "Whatever you are doing, stop at once!"

The hand slipped from her shoulder and the painful emotions vanished instantly. The hand instead lifted her chin and Eryn saw cool brown eyes stare into her own.

"Power, Maltheá, was not the only thing this has cost me. This was a little taste of what life was like for me after you were taken away."

Eryn swatted the hand away and hissed, "Don't call me that! My name is Eryn."

Malriel smiled without humour. "No. This is just a name he has given you to keep you away from me. I will not use it. Ever. Your name, the one your grandmother gave to you, the one that carries half of my own name to signify where you belong and another part to make you unique, is *Maltheá*. And this is how I will continue to refer to you. Even if it is not to your liking."

Eryn nodded slowly. "As you wish, Malriel. Be not surprised, however, if I do not react to that name. Thank you for the meal," she continued coldly. "Please refrain from inviting me again. Ever." She turned to the staircase and stormed off without another look back.

Enric sighed and shook his head at their hostess. "That was insensitive of you. He was the only family she had known all her life. How could she accept a thing like that? You have made things very difficult for the two of you."

"You had better leave now, Enric," she said stiffly. "I will see you tonight at the dinner."

He nodded and turned to leave as well.

CHAPTER 22

The Dinner

Eryn stood in front of the mirror, staring at her reflection unseeingly. More than six hours later she still felt the imprint of the shock of emotions that had been forced onto her by Malriel.

She had wanted to discard the story, very much so. Going through it to find flaws, pieces that didn't fit, things that just couldn't be true, had not been helpful at all. She had considered contacting Ram'an, calling him to come over and tell her if this was true. But Malriel had mentioned talking to him more than once, so they were probably good friends and Ram'an might be willing to confirm whatever Malriel wanted him to. No. Valrad, her father's own brother, was the one she needed to talk to. If he confirmed the story, then it really had to be the truth. This was about his family, after all.

But it was too late for this now. They were due at the senate building in less than one hour, and even though he would be there as well, it was hardly a suitable setting for this particular conversation. She would have to wait until tomorrow to address this matter.

And of course *she* would be there. The thought of seeing Malriel again so soon made her hair literally stand on end and she rubbed her palms over her forearms to smooth them again.

She saw Enric's image appear in the mirror behind her, his expression worried.

"I wish I didn't have to drag you there right now," he murmured.

"I know. So do I. But it can't be helped, can it? Diplomatic duties," she sighed. "I just hope I don't have to talk to her, sit too close to her or have anything to do with her tonight. I think I would bite off her head."

He nodded. "It might be a good idea to avoid that for now. You will probably have a go at each other one day, but I hope that will be with a less public backdrop. It's time for you to get dressed now. Do you need help with your dress? I see it is one of those laced at the back."

"Yes, that would be nice."

She pulled the tunic over her head and threw it on the bed to slip into the dark blue dress instead. Enric stepped behind her and started pulling the strings taut and tied them into a knot the way Junar had demonstrated.

"All done. I am getting good at this. A pity, though, that it always takes longer to get you out of them than into," he sighed. "But maybe that's also a matter of practice. Do you need to do anything special with your hair? I am afraid we only have a few minutes until we have to leave, so whatever you do, it needs to be quick."

"I will just braid it in a more complicated looking style than usual, which should suffice for a formal dinner without a hairstylist available. How will we get there? Walk?"

He nodded. "Yes. I am told it won't take more than a few minutes to get there. Kilan has taken a walk through the city centre today, he knows the way."

He watched her nimble fingers parting her hair into four strands and then braid them by touch at the back of her head.

"I find this very interesting to watch. It looks completely straight, yet you can't see what you are doing," he marvelled.

She shrugged. "It is just a matter of feeling. I can sense if it is too tight or loose, if the pressure is a bit too much on the left or right side, so I more or less feel if it looks right. It's basically just practice."

He wondered how she had learned the technique but was afraid to ask. Her father might have been the one to show her, and that was a topic he thought wise not to touch upon right now.

"Lady Eryn? Enric?" they heard Kilan calling from their main room. "It's about time to leave. How much longer do you need?"

"We are as good as ready," Enric called back. He saw Eryn stare at the pendant with the two crests she still had around her neck.

"This is going to stay here," she said and opened the clasp. Enric nodded, understanding her perfectly. She would probably not be willing to wear it again anytime soon, he expected.

They walked into the main room where Kilan was standing, with a glass of water in one hand, in front of one of the large windows. He turned when they entered and nodded to them.

"Kilan," Eryn sighed, "you should stop calling me *Lady*. It seems a bit funny when Enric has asked people here not to bother with our titles yet we carry on using them between ourselves."

He nodded. "Very well. But as you are further up in the Order than I, I still had to wait for you expressly to grant me that. Protocol, you know."

"Oh, yes! Where would we be without our protocols in a foreign country?" she said with heavy sarcasm.

"We would be completely lost, my love," Enric said. "We like to hold on to familiar things, especially when everything around us is foreign. Human nature. Come, we need to get going."

Kilan nodded. "Yes, they are very keen on punctuality here when you are invited somewhere, I am told. While being early is never a problem, being late is a sign of disrespect."

"Not so very different from our own rules, is it?" she commented. "Somebody always pesters me to hurry when we are invited to something official."

Enric shrugged. "That's because you are not exactly a stickler for punctuality, are you?"

"I am punctual when it counts," she sniffed.

"Excellent. Then you will be the one to explain to the King why exactly you do not consider his invitations occasions that warrant punctuality," he smiled.

"Hardly. He would just look at me with that smile that really isn't one and make some kind of veiled threat I will probably only decode when I am back home again." She looked out at the dusky sky. "It is getting cooler; do you think I'll need to take something to keep me from freezing later? How cold are the nights here? I don't remember last night, the temperature was not a major concern of mine somehow."

"I would recommend taking something with you, yes," Kilan said. "There is quite a difference in temperature, it cools down a lot. A shawl or something should suffice."

She nodded and went back into their bedroom to return only a minute later with a pure white shawl around her shoulders.

"Gentlemen, I am ready if you are."

Enric took her arm and they descended the stairs to the door.

The twilight transformed the city completely. The buildings didn't seem as bright any more, but had taken on various shades of ochre and earthy brown. Lanterns and torches had been lit and bathed the streets in warm yellow. Unlike in Anyueel, the city was not about to retire, but genuinely seemed to be waking up now that the heat of the day was retreating. The local versions of pubs utilised a substantial part of the streets to put out piles of cushions for guests to sit comfortably upon, and they saw that blankets were provided to keep their customers warm.

Their group attracted attention in the form of curious glances due to both the men's hair colour and their foreign looking clothes.

Eryn smiled. "It's strange not to be the exotic one anymore," she commented. "Maybe I should change my hair to blonde again."

"Don't you dare try," Enric murmured. "Nothing good has ever happened when you did that, if I may remind you of the incident during the expedition and the other one at the ball."

She shrugged. "Minor setbacks."

"Promise me you'll keep your colour the way it is, however great the temptation to vex Malriel is. Just consider that she wouldn't be the only one who might react unfavourably to it," he insisted.

"Alright, I promise." Pity. Irking Malriel would have been sweet. She shook her head at herself. She had seen teenagers rebel against parents, but only from a distance. Was this her shot at making up for those lost opportunities in her young and wild years? Years she had spent learning how to make a living and taking care of herself instead of rebelling against her parents. The only rebellion she had indulged in so far was against her captors in the last year. But at least Malriel she would be rid of in no more than three weeks.

"I like the dresses," Enric said into her thoughts. "They are a lot more colourful than ours back home. Why don't you see a tailor tomorrow and have a few made up for yourself? I think the colours would suit you."

She grinned. "Trying to buy me clothes again?"

"What can I say? It's a never-ending quest. Let's do that tomorrow before we see your uncle for lunch."

"So you will accompany me to make sure I order something? Really?"

He nodded. "Absolutely. Here I don't have the luxury of just calling Junar and have her take care of everything like at home."

"I resent the implication that I am not fit to take care of my wardrobe," she huffed.

"That was not what I meant. I am not saying you are not fit, just that you are not willing to do it."

"I can't believe that we are having the clothes discussion again!" she exclaimed, causing several heads to turn in their direction out of curiosity. Smiling apologetically, she increased her pace.

"The clothes discussion?" Kilan asked with obvious amusement. "What's that? It doesn't seem to go the usual way of the woman saying she needs more and the man saying she can't have more."

"No," Enric sighed, "it's more the kind where I tell her that she needs them and she keeps complaining about my buying them for her."

"Indeed?" Kilan asked in surprise. "How does she react to offers of jewellery?"

"She snorts derisively and tells me she doesn't need anybody to provide for her as she was brought up to do that herself."

The other man whistled softly through his teeth. "Incredible. You don't happen to have any single sisters, do you?" he called to Eryn.

"Oh dear, I sincerely hope *not*!" she growled.

"Look at that," Enric marvelled when they had reached the senate hall. "Ram'an was right, there are traces of our architecture left here. You see the steep angle of the roof? The newer buildings here all have flat roofs or only slightly pitched ones. And the rounded façade?"

Kilan nodded. "Yes, now I see it. Reminds me a bit of the building the old warriors' quarters used to be in."

Eryn sighed and looked exasperated. "Are you done with your architectural studies? Can we get this evening behind us now?"

"That's maybe not quite the right attitude for facing this, you know," Kilan said. "Shouldn't you be a bit more eager to meet people from your home country?"

"I very recently had an extremely trying encounter with the person who calls herself my mother. And I am not exactly thrilled about seeing her again so soon."

"So the lunch didn't go very well, then. I am sorry to hear that. But we will be eighteen people at this dinner tonight. I am sure you will have ample opportunity to talk to other people. Your uncle will be there, after all."

Eryn snorted. "Yes, so he will be. The man who sent me into a dopey trance of happiness yesterday without my permission. If the lunch at his place tomorrow is equally distasteful, I will disown any connection to any of their families and return to the happy status of being an orphan that I was short-sighted enough to mourn before."

They climbed an impressive number of off-white stone steps and waited for the bulky, square double doors to be opened for them by two servants. They immediately found themselves in a high, brightly lit hall filled with what had to be the greater part of the guests already. They were standing together in small groups and turned curiously when the doors were opened, not hiding their delight at laying eyes on the foreign looking, fair-haired guests and the lost daughter from House Aren.

"We are not late, are we?" Eryn whispered.

"No," Kilan said. "But remember that being too early is here considered a virtue rather than a nuisance."

Enric took Eryn's hand and laid it on his arm when a richly dressed man, who seemed to be in his early sixties, approached them. It was the man who had welcomed them at the harbour, Golir.

He stretched out his left hand to Enric and smiled when he took it to link their fingers and exchange the nod.

"Welcome to our little gathering in your honour," he said and turned to Eryn to lift her left hand to his lips. He then took Kilan's hand and repeated the local greeting with him.

Golir waved to two figures not far away, a man and a woman about his age, who approached with a dignified pace.

"Let me introduce to you Torke'na and Abrak, my colleagues in the triarchy. These are Enric, Eryn and Kilan, our guests of honour."

Eryn had her hand kissed another time and finally carried out the greeting she had attempted to use with Malriel just a few hours before.

Torke'na's eyes searched her face and then she shook her head in bemusement. "The likeness between yourself and your mother is stunning. There is hardly a trace of your father visible in your features. An Aren woman through and through."

Eryn schooled her features into an expression of polite interest to hide her dismay at the similarity between her and Malriel being pointed out.

"Your mother is outside on the terrace, if you wish to greet her," Abrak pointed out with a smile.

"That is very friendly, thank you," she said with a nod and felt herself subtly edged towards the large opening by Enric.

To her relief, a familiar figure approached her after she had taken no more than a few steps.

"Eryn!" Ram'an beamed and took her hands. "Will you allow me to greet you like a friend?"

She nodded and murmured, "You can greet me however you want if you save me from having to go outside and greet Malriel."

He raised his brows questioningly, but first kissed both her cheeks before he asked, "That does not sound good. I assume your lunch was not particularly pleasant?"

"You may safely assume that, yes," she nodded. "I would like to keep out of her way as much as possible tonight."

"That is going to be difficult, my dear," he said with regret. "She needs to be seen to welcome you home and accept you into her House. Your staying away from her is exactly what she needs to avoid."

Eryn swallowed. "So I am supposed to play the grateful, loving daughter who has returned to take her rightful place in the family, or what?"

"That would be preferable for House Aren, yes," he said slowly. "But judging from your expression I am fairly convinced it will play out another way."

"Definitely," she growled.

"Eryn," she heard another male voice behind her and turned. Valrad.

"Valrad," she said with narrowed eyes. "I am in a bad mood and would prefer to continue to be so, if you don't mind. If you repeat your little *magical ecstasy* trick from yesterday, I swear I will find you and hurt you very badly as soon as I return back to normal."

The older man gave her a lopsided grin. "Threatening your poor, old uncle, my child? But do not worry, I have learned from my mistake and will let you be as disgruntled, miserable or angry as you choose."

"Good," she murmured and let him take her hand to kiss it. "Just to be sure that this is clear."

"Perfectly," he nodded and then turned to the other man. "Ram'an."

"Valrad," the younger man nodded back.

"How is your father doing?" the healer enquired.

"His situation keeps getting worse; he refuses to see a healer and keeps chewing the poisonous weed. I have taken over some of his responsibilities, as you can see. Some he still refuses to let me handle." He shrugged. "So basically everything is the same as ever it was."

Eryn squared her shoulders and lifted her chin when she heard the voice behind her.

"Valrad. Ram'an." Then Malriel came into view, a slight smile curving her lips. "And Maltheá."

She stepped closer to kiss Eryn on her cheeks.

"Don't touch me," the younger woman hissed almost inaudibly.

"Do not be stupid, Maltheá," Malriel replied without changing her expression at all. "Of course I will touch you."

She felt a slight magical tingle where her mother touched her arms, one that felt a lot like a warning, and then warm lips brushed first her left, then her right cheek.

Eryn was still wondering how strong the Head of House Aren probably was and if pushing her away with magic to find out here and now would be a smart move, but then the contact was over, leaving no more than a subtly sweet wisp of the doubtlessly expensive perfume she was wearing.

Malriel had turned to Enric, who had hurried to her side as soon as he saw Malriel.

"Enric," she purred and lifted her hands to his shoulders to pull him down enough to be able to kiss his cheeks as well.

He looked down at her, hiding his surprise at the warm greeting well and smiling. After the cool dismissal several hours ago this was unexpected. But she probably needed to be seen to get along just fine with the Ambassador and companion to her daughter.

"Come, there are quite a few important people the three of you should meet," she said and gently pulled his arm to lead him to a group of three men. Enric quickly grabbed Eryn's hand to pull her along.

"These here are Belkim of House Turbar, Kiral of House Partém and Tanif of House Landred. Gentlemen, may I introduce to you Enric, our ambassador from the other side of the sea. And this is my daughter Maltheá."

"Eryn," she cut in with a forced smile. "This is my name now, if you please."

She saw the youngest of them, Tanif, smirk at her interjection and give Malriel an amused glance. "Clearly your daughter, Malriel. In looks and temperament, so it seems."

"So it would seem, yes," Malriel agreed with a sideways glance and a casual smile. "The other exotic looking man here is Kilan, the third delegate and assistant to Enric."

They exchanged their formal greetings and before they had a chance to start a conversation, Malriel pulled Enric along to another pair, a man and a woman.

"Enric, these are Legara of House Finran and Uvel of House Tokmar. Legara, Uvel, Enric from the Old Kingdom and his assistant Kilan. And my daughter Maltheá."

Eryn ground her teeth. If she kept on using that name for introductions, she was more or less asking to be exposed.

"Eryn, if you don't mind," she corrected again.

The Heads of both Houses exchanged a glance and then smiled at her. Their eyes kept darting between the faces of both women in fascination.

"How very nice to see you again," Legara said. "It has been a while."

Malriel smiled at them and motioned to a man in his fifties to come and join them.

"Voreld. I would like to introduce to you the delegation from beyond the barrier."

The man nodded to the two male visitors and linked his fingers with theirs one after the other in the customary greeting before turning to Eryn.

"I am the Head of House Ordel," he said and lifted her hand to his lips. "I am very pleased you have found your way back to us. I wondered if you ever would."

She swallowed. "Only temporarily."

He smiled. "How unfortunate. But maybe you will change your mind and stay with us." His gaze wandered to Enric's cool expression. "Though I can see that the Ambassador would not be too happy about this. You are his companion, are you not?"

"I am, yes," she confirmed, skipping the rest. She had no intention of starting a discussion why relocating to a foreign country was not an attractive prospect at all.

"Where are Amgil and Anfer?" Malriel asked and looked around.

"Amgil had to be excused for today, his companion is in labour," Legara replied. "And Anfer will come a little later as she is on her way back from the plantations. They had an insect infestation problem, I believe."

"That leaves two more Heads of Houses that are present here to be introduced to you: Enkil and Koral," Malriel explained. "I think they are still on the terrace. But the meal should be served any moment, and there will be opportunity enough for further introductions later."

They heard a reverberating sound that started quietly and grew to fill the entire room before slowly decreasing after a few seconds.

"Ah yes, here we are, the signal for us to move to the next room and settle down." Legara smiled and took Kilan's arm, while Malriel held on to Enric's. Eryn stood around looking rather lost, when she felt a warm hand lift hers and turned to look at Valrad, who put her hand on his arm and smiled.

"Thank you," she murmured when they followed the others, "I was worried about being the only woman here who has to walk in there alone."

He chuckled. "You would not have been. I barely managed to beat Ram'an to offer you my arm. I had to more or less shove him aside and pretend to be sorry for it."

She smiled at the thought of the two men jostling for the privilege of accompanying her to the table. "Is there any particular sitting arrangement or can I just sit as far away from Malriel as possible?"

"I can lead you to wherever you prefer. If we slow down a little, she will be seated when we enter the room and I will make sure the distance to her is to your liking. I take it the meal you had together was not quite pleasant?" he enquired carefully.

She shook her head. "The meal itself was not the problem, the company was. There is something I need to ask you tomorrow. About my father. She told me a story, and I need to know how much of it is true."

He nodded, his expression serious. "I imagine you do. I will tell you what I know, but be prepared for it not to be too pleasant."

She sighed. So it seemed that at least part of it had to be true.

They went through another of the archways that seemed to be typical for the local architecture and she saw a very large seating arrangement on the floor. But unlike the smaller ones she had seen so far, this one was large enough to accommodate at least twenty people and was shaped like a half moon, as one large circle would have made talking to anybody else but the immediate neighbour rather difficult.

Malriel had managed to obtain a strategically advantageous seat virtually at the centre of the arrangement, so that at whichever end Eryn sat down, she would still be within reach for a conversation. That was unfortunate.

"Sorry, my dear. It seems she has anticipated your intentions," Valrad sighed and led her to one end of the half-moon arrangement.

She plumped down without much elegance and grimaced. "It seems I need to learn how to do this properly. I must look like somebody dropping a heavy sack when I sit down on these cushions."

A man next to her, one of the many faces she had been introduced to, smiled. "Do not worry about that, Eryn. You will have ample opportunity for practice, I think. But here is a little suggestion: try sitting down with legs crossed. It enables you to control the speed of your descent."

"Thank you, I will be sure to try that next time."

Valrad nodded at him. "Good evening, Belkim."

Belkim, Eryn repeated in her head and silently thanked her uncle for using the name and sparing her the humiliation of admitting that she had forgotten it.

"Valrad. How is that granddaughter of yours doing?"

Granddaughter? Eryn looked at her uncle. So he had at least one child.

"She is doing well, thank you for asking. Growing very quickly. Every time I see her she seems to have gained a little height," he replied good-naturedly.

"And now there is another addition to your family, though one I would not expect will grow any further," Belkim smiled and looked at Eryn.

"Not the natural way, no," she agreed.

"And you have no intentions of making yourself grow magically, I assume," the man grinned and looked up when Ram'an sat down opposite them. "Ram'an, how is your father doing? Still too stubborn to see a healer, is he not?"

"I am afraid so, yes," the newcomer replied politely.

Belkim turned back to Eryn. "You are a healer, are you not? But of course you would be, having been raised by Ved'al."

She stared at him. "What?"

"Your father's name," Ram'an said. "I never told you his true name. You would only know the one he adopted later in life."

She nodded slowly. Malriel had kept referring to him as *your father* instead of using his name even once.

"Ved'al," she repeated to herself.

"Yes," Valrad smiled sadly and took her hand in his. "We used to call him Ved. At least until his healer training was completed. He then insisted on being addressed with his full name, convinced that it would lend him more distinction."

Reining in her emotions, she tried to smile. Why did they have to keep mentioning him all the time? Why did it still hurt? But then she had never really taken the time or had any opportunity to talk about him to anyone who had known more about him. Nobody in the village had dared mention him in her presence in all these years.

Belkim seemed to notice her distress and returned to the topic he had started on. "You are the only healer they have over there, are you not?"

A safer topic. She nodded gratefully. "Yes, for now. But I have started training five healers, and their progress is highly promising. I was hoping to increase my own knowledge of the skill while I am here."

"That should not be a problem, owing to your connections to House Vel'kim."

She smiled and looked at her uncle. "Yes, I admit that this is the advantage I have been intending to make use of since I was asked to come here."

"I would be honoured to share some of my knowledge with you, Eryn," Valrad said earnestly. "We can discuss how to go about this tomorrow when you come to meet my family. Your family."

They fell silent when Golir, the first member of the ruling triarchy she had met, rose from his seat elegantly and waited for the voices around him to fade into silence.

"Friends, Heads of the Houses, you know why we have gathered here tonight. It is for you to meet our guests from a land we have not had any contact with for centuries. We will strive to establish a mutually beneficial way of exchanging goods and knowledge, and forge and nurture bonds of friendship over these next few weeks. But we are also here to welcome a woman who has been absent from her home country for more than two decades. For this, however, I would like to hand over to Malriel, for whom this visit means so much more than welcoming a delegation."

He sat down again and Malriel rose in his stead, smiling once all eyes were on her.

Eryn swallowed, hoping that she would not be forced to listen to another sad narrative of the hardships of a mother that had lost her daughter.

"Thank you, Golir," she smiled and then turned serious. "You are right, the delegation as such was only secondary in my mind after I finally managed to persuade you to send the letter to request my daughter be made one of the party. And graciously had it granted by King Folrin." Her gaze fell on Eryn. "Twenty-three years are a long time, my dear. A very long time. And even though I will have you here for only a short while to get to know you a little, I shall treasure this time and make the best of it. I want you to know, Maltheá, that you will always have a place at House Aren, should you need a safe haven for whatever reason."

Eryn forced herself to smile despite the use of the name she had asked not to be called and nodded in acknowledgement of the words. Rain would need to start falling upwards before she would ever consider *that* offer.

"But let me no longer stop you from the fabulous dinner that is about to be served. Maltheá, I drink to your return to me, to Takhan." She raised her glass and all others at the table joined her.

*   *   *

"Insincere, fallacious, perfidious, malicious bitch!" Eryn hissed when they had closed the door to their residence behind them. Holding the stream of profanities inside until they got back had been an effort that had bordered on mortal agony. It was an immense relief to finally let them out.

Kilan stared at her. "Who? Your mother?"

"Of course *her*! Did you glimpse any other insincere, fallacious, perfidious, malicious bitches there?" she snapped.

Kilan gulped and looked helplessly at Enric. "You know, it is getting rather late. I should retire to my own quarters and see you tomorrow afternoon when the first meeting with the senators is planned."

Enric nodded. "You do that. Sleep well."

And gone he was. Enric took her arm and led her up the stairs while she kept muttering curses under her breath.

"I am very proud of you, my love," he said while she all but ripped the scarf off her shoulders to throw on the cushions. "I admit I was rather worried that you would fly at her any moment, but you held back beautifully. I greatly admire your restraint."

"You should," she growled. "It was an ordeal, believe you me! I almost asked Valrad to drowse me with another dose of the creepy bliss to keep me under control!" She plopped down on the seating island. "Can you believe that woman? That devious, theatrical minx? I kept thinking of heavy objects to hit her with. That was probably the only thing that kept me from leaping up and throttling her right in front of her high-born friends."

"That would undoubtedly have made it an evening to remember for all of us," Enric said with a smile before he sank down next to her.

She stared at him for a few moments, distracted. "That looked really good. How do you make it look so elegant? I more or less drop down. I was told to cross my legs when I do it, but that's not how you did it."

Enric was taken off guard by the unexpected change of topic. "That's really what you would like to talk about now?"

She leaned back, closing her eyes in exhaustion. "No, not really. Tell me, Ambassador, what I can do to avoid her as much as possible without causing any diplomatic tensions?"

"By politely declining any invitations she makes in private and hoping that she doesn't resort to doing it more publicly," he mused. "And what's more, avoid being alone with her. You might go further and try to find out where she prefers to spend her time so you can refrain from going there."

Eryn looked at him thoughtfully. "You know, that is actually helpful."

"Thank you for your trust," he remarked laconically.

"No, I mean, I had expected you to lecture me on showing a bit more consideration for her feelings, but it seems as if you understood *my* point of view this time."

He looked weary. "How would siding with Malriel make sense? You would just be angry at *me* as well as at her. And I have to admit that she has not been particularly adroit in her attempts to subdue you."

"Why haven't you done something if you have noticed it? Where was that instinct to protect me against evil when I needed it?"

"How could I have intervened?" he asked calmly, looking straight into her eyes. "How would it have made the two of you look if I had? Neither of you would have thanked me for it. This is something between the two of you, something *you* need to settle with her. If I took care of it, it would make you seem weak and helpless. When have you ever appreciated those labels?"

She sighed, knowing fully well that he was right. Again. "Yes, I know."

"Come." He rose as elegantly as he had sat down previously, pulling her up as well. "Let's go to bed now. I told you I want to get up early tomorrow to see a tailor before we visit your uncle. Kilan has given me the name of one who was recommended to him."

Groaning, she flopped to let herself sink back to the cushions again, but felt herself being lifted over one of his shoulders instead and carried towards the bedroom.

"I'd thought the night couldn't become any worse, and then you compel me to buy clothes!"

CHAPTER 23

House Velkim

They stepped outside the tailor's workshop, with Enric shading his eyes against the glare of the sun.

"Now, that wasn't too bad, was it?" he said cheerfully.

"Speak for yourself," she sighed. "They kept marvelling at your stature and telling you what a fabulous and majestic posture you have. Of course *you* don't think it was so bad!"

"I let them measure me as well, didn't I? So you were not the only one to endure the endless torture with measuring tapes and polite chit chat."

She grinned. "Yes, you let them talk you into ordering something for yourself because you fell for their flattery."

"Hardly," Enric replied with dignity. "I just thought it would be a nice gesture to adapt a little to the local style and at the same time support some local businesses."

Laughing, she took his arm. "Sure, if believing that makes you happy, who am I to destroy your illusions?" She fished in her pocket for the piece of paper where yesterday evening she had written down Valrad's instructions on how to find his residence.

"According to my notes we need to retrace our steps to the large square where we started and then keep left until we reach a certain fountain."

"A fountain?" Enric sighed. "Are you serious? They more or less have a fountain on every corner here. That was the most distinctive landmark he could give you for orientation?"

"It's a particular fountain, one with a shiny gold or brass roof. Once we have reached it, we need to turn left again, follow the street to its end and then turn right."

"Or we could just go straight ahead here in this direction. Going back to the square would be a detour since we are headed southeast and are in the eastern part of the city already. The square is north from here."

Eryn thought for a few moments, trying to compose a map in her mind, but gave up as she didn't have enough information. "Whatever you say. If we get lost and end up being late, I will openly blame you for it."

"Which would only be right and proper," he agreed and took her hand.

They walked along the street, letting their gazes wander over the market stands with their colourful tarpaulins, taking in the busy haggling between sellers and buyers over goods on one side. Even though the object might be no more than a plain roll of fabric, the discussion seemed to require a number of exclamations and expansive gestures.

"Emotional topic, shopping," Enric murmured and nodded his head towards two men.

"I can relate to that. My primary emotion in connection with it is *hatred*," she said through clenched teeth.

"They don't seem to hate it, though."

"But they are fighting, aren't they?"

He shook his head. "No, that's no fight. They are just excited. Or pretending to be."

"If you find it so appealing, you should try it yourself. Maybe you can save some money when we pick up the clothes you ordered."

"You know, I think that is not the kind of shop where they would appreciate my trying to better the price," he chuckled. "That might be a sure and quick way of tainting our reputation. I am told that many rich and important people order their clothes there. This would spread like wildfire."

"Shouldn't we try not to be slaves to other people's opinions? You can't make everybody happy, so why not start with yourself?"

He looked at her with raised brows. "Wise words indeed. Unfortunately we are not in a position that affords us the luxury of heeding them. What people here think about us is ultimately what they will think about our country. So leaving a bad impression here, however happy that would apparently make *you*, is inadvisable as we would not be the only ones paying for it in the long run."

She sighed. "And even wiser words to counter mine. Alright, no leaving bad impressions for now."

"Good girl," he said approvingly.

"Stop that! I have heard you saying that to the cat!" she complained.

"True. Though Urban doesn't complain when I say it, but licks my hand instead."

"You would be stunned if I started doing that instead of complaining," she laughed.

"Yes, I dare say I would. My tastes don't really go in that direction." He looked ahead, narrowing his eyes when he saw a crest hewn in stone some distance away, to see if he recognised it. Then he smiled. "It seems we have almost reached our destination. There is the crest of House Vel'kim on that column to our left."

"Yes, looks like it, doesn't it? But where is the house?" She looked around in confusion.

"We need to turn left here, I think. Yes, there we are." He turned the corner and nodded appreciatively. "Look at that. Not a poor family, either. You do have wealthy roots, my love, on both sides of the family tree."

She nodded, impressed, and looked up at the hill on the top of which an elegant, airy residence with large windows stood surrounded by blooming gardens.

"So it would seem, yes. And now I have a wealthy companion as well. It seems I am meant to live with rich people." And Malriel would hardly have accepted being joined with a poor man, would she? She didn't seem the type to rank inner values above more material qualities.

"What a waste that you don't appreciate the luxury those riches can buy," he smiled.

They walked up the short paved road to the main building. Eryn stopped every now and then to have a look at the plants that grew along the way, wondering if they were medical herbs or just for decoration. They certainly didn't look like weeds.

Valrad himself opened the door when they had almost reached the house and smiled broadly.

"Welcome! Come inside quickly - this is the hottest time of the day." He ushered them in and turned to take a bowl with two cool and damp towels for them to refresh their face and hands, just like they had been greeted with the day before by Malriel's servant. Then he exchanged the formal greeting with both of them.

"The meal is in its final stage of preparation and should be finished in no more than a few minutes. Let us go upstairs and drink something while we wait," he said and preceded them up a flight of stairs into another large, airy room with the typical sitting arrangements on the floor.

"What may I serve you? Water or rather some variety of fruit juice? Or tea?"

"Water is fine for me, thank you," Enric replied politely.

"Fruit juice for me, please," Eryn said.

"Have a seat while I prepare your drinks," Valrad offered and went to a small cabinet from which he took five glasses, a carafe of water and two more carafes of juice, one a dark orange, the other bright red.

Five glasses, Eryn thought. So two more people would join them, it seemed.

"Father?" a male voice called from some unseen place behind a wall to their left. "I heard voices, have they arrived yet?"

"Yes, just a moment ago. Come here and introduce yourself."

"I will, if you come and help me carry the food. It is ready."

Valrad quickly placed the tray on the low table in front of them and poured them a glass each.

"Will you excuse me for a moment? I will be back in a moment with my son."

"So it seems your cousin is the one we will have to thank for preparing the meal," Enric murmured when Valrad had left the room.

"A man who can cook. I like him already," she smiled.

"That is a relief to hear, cousin Eryn," the voice - which had called out before - said, and she turned to look at a slim man in his early thirties, almost fragile in his beauty. Long lashes surrounded warm, dark grey eyes, his lips curved into a welcoming smile. His hair was longer than most other men around here wore it and reached down to his shoulders. His movements were elegant when he approached them with a large brass bowl in his hands, closely followed by his father, who carried a set of smaller bowls.

Both Eryn and Enric rose from their seats.

Valrad put down his load and then helped place the brass bowl with the food at the centre of the table.

"Vran'el, meet your cousin Eryn and her companion Enric."

Eryn lifted her left hand for him to kiss, but he laughed and pulled her closer instead.

"I am considered at bit of an oddity among my acquaintances, you know. I either greet people properly or do not touch them at all. Come here and let me kiss you, dear cousin."

She felt his warm lips firmly pressed to her cheeks before he held her at arm's length to let his gaze wander down and up again. Though he had disregarded the formal greeting just like Malriel, it felt completely different with him. This was not like having intimacy forced upon her, but being gifted with warmth where she had dared expect little more than politeness.

"You are a very beautiful woman, Eryn. What a delightful addition to the family. I know that external beauty is not all that counts, is not even important, but I do so appreciate looking at somebody beautiful instead of somebody plain. Call me superficial, but that is the way I am."

Eryn stared at him for a few moments, then laughed. "You know, you are the first uncomplicated person who makes it easy for me to like him instantly. Thank you so much for that!"

He waved her off. "Nonsense! You already met my father two days ago, and people usually are charmed by him after the first few minutes. Do not tell me you managed to resist that."

"Let's say he made it easy for me," she said with a sideways glance at Valrad.

"Ah yes, the little matter of his shock treatment. He mentioned that you did not take well to it." Vran'el then turned to Enric and kissed him on both cheeks as well before looking him up and down. "A very good-looking man you have found yourself, cousin. I like the exotic flair of the fair hair. Good build, too. They say you are a warrior, are you not? I wonder what you would look like in our local attire. I bet our cuts would suit you fabulously."

Enric swallowed, clearly a bit overwhelmed by the unusually intimate assessment by a complete stranger. A male stranger.

"Vran'el," he replied. "It is a pleasure to meet you."

"The pleasure is mine, Enric." Then his perfectly formed brows creased into a frown and he radiated impatience. "Where is Pe'tala? I told her to be punctual. If she does not turn up soon, we will start without her."

"Your daughter?" Eryn ventured, remembering that Valrad had a granddaughter.

"What? Oh no, my younger sister. I usually show a bit more patience with my daughter," he smiled.

"That is an immense relief to hear, brother. If you treated her the same way you treat me, she would soon refuse to visit us," a young female voice sounded from the top of the stairs.

"Pe'tala, my dear, come here. You have arrived just in time for the meal. Meet your cousin Eryn and her companion Enric," Valrad greeted her and then turned to his guests. "My daughter Pe'tala."

Pe'tala seemed to be in her mid-twenties, several years younger than her brother. Her build was slender and small, her dark hair was arranged into two long braids which were intertwined into a knot at the top of her head. She had her brother's long lashes and grey eyes, though hers were not warm, but appraising and calculating as she scrutinised Eryn.

"Oh dear. She really looks like her mother," Pe'tala said in a voice that made it very clear that this was not meant as a compliment. "The eyes, the mouth... there is a touch of Vel'kim in the nose, but hardly discernible." She came closer with a sneer. "So the great heiress of House Aren has returned and grants us the privilege of her visit. How charming."

Eryn stared at her, taken by surprise at the open hostility after her brother had been so welcoming only minutes before. Splendid. Now there was an unpleasant female relative on each side of the family.

"Pe'tala," her father warned her, "you are being very rude. This is not how I taught you to behave towards guests. You know that hospitality has always been very important in this house. Do not shame me in front of our guests."

"I apologise, father," she said earnestly and nodded to Enric before sitting down to take a bowl and fill it with food for herself.

"Heiress of House Aren," Eryn said thoughtfully. "That does sound very grand, but I am afraid it is hardly accurate."

Three dark pairs of eyes looked at her in puzzlement.

Vran'el swallowed what he was chewing before he spoke, "Why would it not be? You are the current Head's only child, which makes you next in line."

Now Enric leaned forward. "Are you telling us that no other arrangements for succession have been made in the more than twenty years Eryn was considered lost?"

Vran'el shrugged. "It is not really necessary. Malriel has one younger cousin who lives in the countryside and has two children. The older one would have taken over the House had it been required. But now that Eryn has been located, the original order of succession has been restored."

"I live in another country and have no intention whatsoever of coming here to take over a family," Eryn said carefully.

"It does not really matter where you live right now. As long as your status as Malriel's only child is intact, you are the heir to her position according to our laws."

"As long as the status is intact? Does that mean I could get rid of it somehow?" she asked with a certain urgency.

Vran'el chuckled. "Not easily. You would have to renounce your House, and that is something I would not recommend without very good reason."

"But people here can hardly assume that I will submit to your laws when I have spent most of my life in a completely different country and to which I will return in only a few weeks?" she ventured.

Her cousin nodded. "Shaky legal ground, yes. But of course we would like to assume that you will submit to our laws when the occasion arises one day."

Eryn exchanged a worried look with her companion, before she picked up her bowl and commenced eating.

Enric chewed while deep in thought. He would ask Kilan to have a good look into this particular matter. He did not want to have the threat of Eryn being called back to House Aren hanging above them like a menacing cloud, now that it was common knowledge where she could be found, when Malriel deemed it necessary.

"Is there a chance to study your laws? A library of some sorts that grants access to the public?" he asked finally.

Vran'el smiled. "You are very welcome to use my own personal library for that, Enric. I have studied law and thus collected quite a number of books on the subject."

Enric arched his eyebrows. "Indeed? That is very useful. And a generous offer I will take you up on."

"But if there are any legal questions you have, I would be more than willing to assist you with whatever you need."

Eryn saw a sceptical look in Pe'tala's eyes. What was wrong with that woman? Why was she not only refusing to be at least polite, but was also annoyed at her brother's friendliness? She watched Vran'el smile at Enric and felt that something was odd about him without being able to pinpoint it. It was not in the way he moved or spoke or smiled at Enric, all of which seemed perfectly normal if considered individually, but the combination of them.

"You said you had a daughter," Eryn smiled. "How old is she?"

Vran'el's smile took on an even softer quality. "Obal. She is four years old now and I swear to you, she becomes more gorgeous every day. She lives with her mother, but I see her as often as I can."

Eryn swallowed, not sure how to respond to that. He had obviously broken up with his daughter's mother not too long ago and would hardly be willing to broach the subject during a meal with strangers.

He seemed to sense her discomfort and grinned. "I can see how the thoughts behind your forehead race. Poor man, broken relationship. But let me assure you that this is not the case here. I have a special arrangement with Intrea, Obal's mother. One that is to the benefit of both of us and our families."

An arrangement that consisted in not being together?

Enric cleared his throat and took her hand. "My love, I think what Vran'el is trying to tell you is that conceiving a child was the main purpose of the arrangement, and that this has been accomplished." He looked into her eyes with a certain intensity, as if willing her to understand something else he didn't want to or couldn't put words to.

Both looked at Pe'tala when she chuckled. "She does not get it, does she?" She leaned forward with a certain gleeful pleasure. "Vran'el fancies men. He has a male lover, and after continuing the bloodline, he is free to do as he wishes and enjoy his freedom."

Eryn stared at her, wondering if this was supposed to be a joke, an attempt at making her fall for this absurd story and then laugh at her for believing it. But a look at Enric made her discard that possibility. He nodded to her almost imperceptibly.

"Oh," she said lamely. So that was that slight strangeness she had sensed about Vran'el.

"Is there a problem, cousin?" Pe'tala asked her pointedly. "We love Vran'el the way he is, and whatever he does in his bed chamber and with whom, we consider his personal business."

Eryn felt heat flush her cheeks. "Of course, I didn't mean to imply..."

"May I?" Enric said and looked straight at Vran'el. "I assure you that Eryn didn't mean to express anything but surprise. You must understand that our own society, our culture, does not handle these matters as tolerantly, as maturely. We do, of course, have men and women that feel drawn towards members of their own sex, but it is not talked about openly; they are forced to hide and are punished and ridiculed all their life if they dare to be open about their preferences. I greatly admire the openness with which personal choices such as this particular one are dealt with here. And that it is not the curse it doubtlessly is in my own country."

Valrad nodded appreciatively. "Well spoken, Enric. But do not make people here more considerate than they are. We, too, have people who decry a preference for same-sex intimacy as unnatural and an abomination. Some even say that it is an illness that needs to be treated by healers."

Eryn drew in a sharp breath. That last part had sounded worryingly familiar.

Valrad turned to her. "You recognised that one, did you not, my girl? It was a sentiment your father shared, unfortunately. If he had stayed here, I have no doubt that there would have been a great fight as soon as my son's affinity for other men was discovered. He was always so sure of his own picture of the world being the only true and trustworthy one, there never was much space for anything else." He looked at the others. "Have you finished your meal? Good. Then let us talk about what you are so eager to learn about, Eryn. The story of what really happened twenty-three years ago. You said that Malriel has told you about it already. A story, you see, is not always the same - it tends to alter with the people who tell it, and also with time. Had I told you about it fifteen years ago, it might have had more anger in it, less acceptance. Today I think there will be more gratitude, and also more sorrow, as I know that Ve'dal is no more."

He poured himself a glass of water and then leaned back onto the cushions.

"Our parents, Malriel's and my own, had arranged for the two of them to become companions one day. It is a custom, you see, to strengthen the bonds between the Houses at regular intervals. The one between Houses Aren and Vel'kim was in need of renewal, and two magically gifted children being born to both Houses in quick succession was a good thing to work with. House Aren has always been a powerful one: born leaders, people who see a problem and take care of it. Did you have a chance to look at their crest? It contains the sun as a symbol of leadership, so it is not mere chance that a member of that House tends to be part of the triarchy every now and then. But handling power takes a certain kind of person. Someone who learns to put their own aims aside in order to serve those around them. There are those who do not learn it and are merely out to feather their own nests, but their claim to power usually does not last very long. House Aren has been in a powerful position for a very long time now, so you may safely assume that they have learned well how to hold on to it. The dinner yesterday was a good demonstration of this. House Aren has suffered from losing you, and showing the other Houses that you are back reclaims some of the power. For this reason Malriel has dragged you from one Head of House to the next, addressed you by the name you wish to avoid and demonstrated to the people present a closeness between you which, behind the theatrics, is not there." Valrad took her hand in his for a moment. "Trust me, child, it was no pleasure for her, either. But she has a duty to keep her House strong, and she cannot shirk from it to save you from being uncomfortable." He took a sip of water before he continued.

"House Vel'kim is a completely different matter. We have never striven for leadership, but seen it as our duty to serve and make sure that those at the top performed their jobs well. But serving was for us never something that goes in only one direction. We also serve the public, thus our traditional inclination towards the healing profession." He looked at his son and chuckled. "There are runaways every now and then, such as Vran'el, who preferred the law to medicine, but compared to other Houses we do have a relatively high number of family members who have chosen the profession of healer. Healers and leaders, you see, have different sets of skills and values. Our values are the protection of life, the well-being of people including - and most especially - those who were not born into wealthy families. House Vel'kim has made a few very important contributions in the past towards making healing services available for even the poorest amongst us," he said with evident pride. "I think connecting two such different Houses, making them work together is a good idea. Every House can profit from the expertise and the different point of view their opposite number provides. But I doubt that Malriel and Ved'al were the right choice for each other. Both so headstrong, both so foolish and so convinced that theirs was the only way. For Malriel, that was normal since nothing less is expected of an Aren woman. But Ved'al... It always seemed to me that he had somehow been born into the wrong House. I was pleased when he decided to become a healer. I hoped that this would make him softer, more sympathetic. I was wrong, of course. He worked in a field where judgement has no place. And yet he could not help but judge. Helping others, you see, is not something you should do primarily for your own sake - to constantly prove your own value to yourself and those around you, or to take a position on the moral high ground to justify imposing your own convictions on others. It is supposed to be centred on the people that need help."

Eryn closed her eyes to control the moisture she felt welling up. Not in front of strangers, she told herself. She knew what was to come next. Valrad had told her this to lead her to where Malriel's story had more or less started, to prepare her for his confirming what she had heard yesterday at the Aren residence.

"The matter of unwanted pregnancies," she whispered.

"Yes. That caused quite a stir. And we are back to the values I told you about before. But values alone are not everything, it is also how you interpret them. Your father said that unborn life is life nevertheless and thus entitled to protection. A valid statement. And then there were people who said that a woman having a child forced upon her is also entitled to protection and cannot be made to pay the price for it all her life. Another very good argument. You see? There can never be a universal right or wrong in a seemingly simple question such as this. But there was only one answer for your father. And he was not willing to admit defeat. He carried on his quest even when it was obvious that it was a lost cause and all his former supporters had turned away from him."

"He wasn't one to forgive easily," Eryn murmured and then looked up at her uncle. "Malriel stood on the other side of the argument. He can't have taken this very well. Was taking me away from her an act of revenge? To her and House Aren?"

Valrad thought about the question for a few moments. "Not primarily, no. Do not think he had no love in him. He did. He loved Malriel very much, which was why it hurt him even more to stand against her. And you were his pride and joy. He took you with him to meet friends, having as much time with you as he could. He told me that he sometimes felt that Malriel was not spending enough time with you and he was worried that you might not feel as loved as you should. He might not have had the right attitude towards serving society as a healer, but he was an outstanding father. He did not take you away to hurt Malriel, or at least it was not his first reason. He took you because he would rather have cut off his arm than leave you behind. Do not ever forget that, no matter what you may hear about him. To this day his actions are still criticised severely, especially that he took you away. But your mother's standing is very strong, so you should not suffer any disadvantages from that."

"Unlike us," a hard female voice said and all eyes turned to Pe'tala. "We have been treated like criminals ourselves. Tainted by association. Let me tell you how agreeable it was as a child not being invited to some occasion due to being a child abductor's niece. And now we have you back among us, how very fine that is."

"Pe'tala!" Valrad hissed. "Stop this! You can hardly blame *her* for it, can you? And it were not only Ved'al's actions that were the problem, but also how your grandfather as Head of House handled matters back then. While House Aren did everything in their power to get them back, your grandfather was hiding in his study and hoping that they would never be found, hoping for them to have died and be buried beneath the waves of the sea to save him the shame of seeing his son brought back in chains. He let others fund the search for them, did not contribute a single chink of gold. That made House Vel'kim look as if we had condoned and even supported his fleeing with her. That was what ultimately harmed our reputation. So if you want to blame somebody, daughter, share it out equally among those who deserve it. *Your cousin* is the one you cannot blame, though. Do not let me hear you doing so again," he growled.

Pe'tala exhaled and gave Eryn a rare look of contrition. "I apologise. My outburst was uncalled for. Father is right. It was not your doing."

Valrad nodded to his daughter and then turned back to his niece. "Will you now tell me about your life in the Old Kingdom? I know very little of it, only what Malriel's search parties reported - and they never managed to find you, so I know hardly anything at all."

Eryn nodded. "My earliest memories are of moving around a lot. So many different faces and places. I don't know exactly how long we were moving around, but I think it must have been about four years before we settled down near a small village. He had changed the colour of our hair so we wouldn't stand out among all the blonde people there. He trained me to keep the shield for the colour intact unconsciously while I slept, so after a while I all but forgot that it wasn't my real colour. He trained me to talk and get rid of my dialect that would have marked us as outsiders. At the beginning he told people that I was suffering from a speech impediment, and everybody believed him as nobody knew that this was what people from the Western Territories sounded like. And when a healer makes a statement like this, people generally believe him."

Enric saw a faraway look enter her eyes as she continued.

"I remember that I was so relieved when we finally settled down. We were so careful all the time not to disclose ourselves as strangers, and suddenly we had this little house for ourselves, where we could afford to be a little less careful than out in the world. I had my own sleeping place for the first time in my life where I didn't have to worry about anybody else coming in or finding something incriminating after we had left again. I was about seven years old when my magical abilities started showing. My father had been waiting for them to surface and was of course prepared for it. He had started teaching me little things while we were moving around, but only started training me for real when we had our little house where we could cover the windows and practise together. He impressed on me that this house was our safe haven, that outside that door I was never to let my guard down, even if I thought that nobody could see me."

Enric put his arm around her shoulders, swallowing at the thought of the girl she had been, forced to hide what she was, living a life in hiding, keeping secrets from even her closest friends, if she had even had the luxury of friends at all. Vran'el hung on her every word, and even Pe'tala wasn't completely able to hide her interest in the story.

"He soon made a name for himself as a healer, and people started coming to him more and more often. I don't know if there was an official start of my healing training; looking back it seems to me as if I have always been in some stage of learning it. We were so very careful not to apply magic in any way that could be recognised. His favourite occasions were the ones when the patient was alone and could be sent to sleep. Then he would show me the things nobody else was supposed to see. We did a lot of work with herbs, as they were the most inconspicuous way of healing. He often gave them to people, even though he had already taken care of the problem to make it seem as if the herbs had done the work and not him. People came from quite some distance to him to seek his help." She frowned. "You know, this is a bit confusing. I learned only recently that search parties had been roaming the land, looking for us. How could they not have become suspicious of rumours of an unusually gifted healer? Wouldn't they have tried to find out about this? We can't have been that hard to find, ordinary people have managed it when they needed treatments, after all. Why not the search parties?"

"Your father was very skilled at manipulating memories, so I assume he used that skill to keep them from finding you. Or he might even have tracked them down and erased their own memories. That is the only thing I can think of," Valrad shrugged. "So Ved'al has lived a quiet country life among villagers, content with what he had?"

Eryn looked around the luxurious room. "Yes, and now that I see how he used to live, I am amazed at that. Our entire house would have fit four or five times inside this one room alone. He was good with everyday things such as repairs, cooking, gathering and chopping wood."

"Chopping wood?" Vran'el frowned. "What for?"

Eryn looked at him for a moment, then laughed. "For heating. And cooking. Don't you at least use wood for cooking? I can see that heating is not much of a consideration for you here."

He looked shocked. "Wood? For cooking! No, it is much too valuable for this! We use bundles of dried leftover plants from our plantations for that."

Enric listened to this with interest and made a mental note to mention wood as one of the tradable commodities. Funny how they seemed appalled by the idea of burning it here when in the Kingdom it was the cheapest way of heating.

"Tell me more about my brother, dear," Valrad requested. "You seemed surprised at what I told you of him, so I assume you got to know a different kind of man."

She nodded. "I did, yes. It seems he outgrew that fierce temper, or maybe he adjudged it too dangerous to hold on to if he wanted to avoid attention. I remember him as serene, composed, serious. And careful, always so very careful. He had his principles, strong ones I was not supposed to act against. He was strict about that. He impressed on me never to use magic against another person to cause harm instead of good, hurt instead of help. And I never saw him doing it himself. If he wanted to hurt somebody... let me rephrase that: if he saw no way other than causing somebody pain, he used his fists." She smiled faintly. "He did have a mean punch. People normally didn't make the mistake of provoking him a second time. That earned him respect. A man with a fist seemingly made of stone combined with a valuable skill such as healing, in a country where magical healing was unknown, was quite a piece of good fortune for a small village."

"So it is really true?" Pe'tala leaned forward, fascinated by the absurdity. "Magicians in the Old Kingdom have no idea how to heal themselves? They cannot even take care of a little scratch? A sore throat? A broken bone? That is so barbaric." She shook her head in disgust.

"They are learning it now, at least some of them," Eryn replied coldly. "And as it was your people who profited from the knowledge that was taken away to your country, I find it a bit of a cheek to call the victims barbarians because of it."

"Victims?" Pe'tala spat. "They were stupid enough to send away their healers and disregard the value of healing magic. If they fell victim to something, it was their own idiocy!"

"Stop this, girls," Valrad reproached them.

Vran'el looked from one woman to the other, his brow furrowed. "So that is what it would have been like to grow up with the two of you. Looks like I had a narrow escape there."

Three pairs of eyes stared at him in disbelief and astonishment at the crude attempt to make light of the deeds in the past. Only Enric grinned and then chuckled under his breath.

"That you had, my friend. It seems you and I are the only ones to have benefited from all this."

Vran'el smiled back at him. "I like you."

"I am good-looking, powerful, rich, appealingly quaint by local standards, and I will make sure you will be able to continue your life in peace by taking Eryn back home with me in a few weeks," Enric replied with a lopsided smirk. "Of course you'd like me, though worshipping me would probably be more appropriate."

"Not exactly the modest sort, are you?" Pe'tala remarked, with only a hint of sarcasm in her voice.

Enric smiled at her coolly. "No, that has never been one of my foibles. I have always considered modesty a failure in correctly assessing and appreciating one's own worth, though some people seem to think of it as a virtue."

Vran'el whistled through his teeth. "You know, keep putting Pe'tala in her place, and my worshipping you is something that we might actually witness. What a pity I have a hunting trip scheduled for this evening, I would have loved to take you and Eryn out for dancing. But I will do it tomorrow, I promise."

Enric leaned forward eagerly. "A hunting trip? At the risk of imposing my company on you, is there any chance for me to come with you?"

"I would be absolutely delighted!" Vran'el called out. "I have to warn you, though: using magic to kill your prey is not considered an accomplishment, but will get you laughed at. We all wear golden belts, so you need to be fit, agile and quick if you want to make a kill. We use spears, so you can neither increase the strength in your arm nor the accuracy of your eyesight," he warned.

"Good. I do like a challenge. Can I bring my cat? She needs to get out and I think this is a good opportunity."

"Your cat? Ah, yes, I remember something about a pet you were loath to be apart from and asked to be allowed to bring along." Vran'el frowned. "Will it not run away?"

"No, I hope not. But it would be useful to have somebody there who doesn't have his or her magical powers blocked, in case she does decide to misbehave." He looked at his companion and smiled.

Eryn frowned. "Have you just volunteered me to chaperone Urban on your hunting trip?"

Enric took her hand and kissed her fingertips. "I will let you put the golden belt on me to block my powers."

The first chance ever to have him before her without any magic at his disposal while she still had full command over hers?

"A chance I can't refuse!" she agreed immediately with a broad grin.

CHAPTER 24

Hunting

They walked up the path to the Vel'kim residence for the second time that day, but this time each was clad in a dark shirt and trousers that seemed to soak up the heat of the evening sun and bake them inside. Urban trotted next to them - her steps, too, with less bounce than normal due to the heat.

Three people were standing in front of the house and talking animatedly, Vran'el with another man and a woman. When they were within earshot, Vran'el turned towards them and froze for a moment, his eyes fixated to the dark brown cat.

"*That* is your cat?" he all but whispered. "I am about to crouch on the ground with my entire magic blocked while this creature is sitting behind me, very likely asking itself how I might taste?"

"Yes, cousin," Eryn smirked. "The only things between you and certain death are my keen eye and my fondness for you. Better be nice to me to make sure there is any of the latter remaining, eh?"

"That is not funny!" Vran'el exclaimed.

"It wasn't meant to be," she replied evilly.

"Intrea, this terrible woman who delights in threatening my life is my cousin Eryn," he introduced her to a rather tall and curvy woman whose eyes glinted humorously.

"I thought as much. Hello Eryn, it is a pleasure to meet you."

"Eryn, this is my companion Intrea."

Eryn looked at him, taken aback. "Your companion? But I thought..."

"Of course we are companions, a child hardly joins the Houses, it just preserves the bloodline," he said, amused.

"Be nice," Intrea scolded him. "Not everybody has studied the law and cares about such things. And she only arrived here two days ago, so how is she supposed to know about our customs?" She then turned to Enric. "You must be Eryn's companion, the tall blonde man everybody is talking about."

"Enric, yes," he introduced himself. "I am pleased to meet you, Intrea."

Another man, muscular and about Intrea's height, stepped forward. The lower half of his face was obscured by a short dark beard that made his glinting white teeth seem even brighter in contrast. "Allow me to introduce myself, as Vran'el seems to be too busy keeping his eyes on your animal. My name is Neval, I am Vran'el's lover."

Eryn was relieved to see even Enric, the epitome of stoic calm, show some surprise at that. His gaze wandered from Intrea to Neval.

"I would say any man who can take his companion *and* his lover hunting must be a very lucky man indeed," he said slowly. "Provided all three of you return unharmed."

Vran'el grinned broadly and slapped him on the shoulder. "Is he not amazing? I wonder if there is anything that throws him off balance."

Enric nodded at Eryn. "There is. Her."

"Really now? I would very much like to see that." He took in the measure of his cousin.

"You wouldn't," Eryn snorted. "It doesn't usually end very pleasantly."

"Well, maybe not for you, dear cousin. But I bet the audience would value the entertainment."

Yes, she thought, at least they had in the past, there was no denying that. Whether it was breaking a nose at a ball, on the training grounds when he threw her down after she had felled Lord Tyront, or at the healers' building when he had dragged her out of the treatment room. People always had something to talk about afterwards when Enric got angry at her.

"That is my sole purpose in life: enduring Enric's wrath to tickle other people's mirth," she murmured.

"That is the spirit!" Vran'el grinned and then turned towards the house where he had prepared an assortment of items that were leaning against the wall. "Eryn, you will not be participating in the hunt but providing magical services and watching over your cat, as I understand?"

"Magical services?" she frowned. "What exactly does that entail, apart from fastening your belts, obviously?"

"Well, that is one very important task. Another one would be unfastening them again afterwards."

"You don't say," she retorted dryly. "What else?"

"Healing, in case somebody gets hurt. Protection, in case we are attacked by either bandits or wild animals. This does not happen very often, but it is handy to be behind a shield in case something comes running with bared fangs and a hungry expression in its eyes." He shot a quick look at Urban. "That is pretty much it."

"Cat-sitting, healing and basic protection from criminal elements, pointy teeth and hungry eyes. Got it." She nodded.

"Good. Enric, I do not know which weapons you have used for hunting before, or how familiar you are with throwing spears." He bent down and picked up what looked to Eryn like a long and a short stick.

"This is a throwing spear with a spear thrower." Vran'el held up the shorter stick. "Here you have the handle on one end, the weight to balance the throw, and at the other end you see the spur that holds the spear in place when you throw it." Then he held up the longer stick. "The spear. The pointed bit is meant to land in your prey, the end where the feather is attached is where you stick it into the thrower. The thrower is meant to serve as an extension of your arm so you can throw the spear with more power. And this is the movement." He fixed the spear's rear end to the thrower, pulled back his arm and then flung the spear with an elegant movement forwards. After flying an impressive distance it landed in a bush.

"Hey!" an angry voice shouted from the roof terrace above them. Valrad stood there, hand on one hip, the other holding a glass. "This happens to be a very important medical herb, and I would thank you so much for not abusing it in hunting demonstrations! I hope it has not taken too much damage, or you will personally be tending it until it has recovered!"

"I am sorry, father," Vran'el called up with a pained expression.

Valrad murmured something about the indecent amount of money that plant had cost him and turned away with a final stern look at his son.

"Well, congratulations on your first prey tonight," Intrea grinned. "It is a bush! Remind me to tell your daughter about your hunting prowess. I do so enjoy it when she is proud of her father."

"Very funny. Let me get that spear back. And I'd better check that obviously so very precious bush for any damage," he sighed and went after his missile.

"That doesn't look too hard," Enric said and inspected another spear and thrower combination which was leaning against the wall. "I have thrown spears before, but in the usual way - which means in my case without a thrower. So if this gives me an advantage in speed and strength, I fancy I will manage somehow."

They saw Vran'el running towards them with the spear in one hand.

"No serious damage. I suppose I will live another day," he said with a careful glance up to the terrace.

"We have the spears plus throwers and carts for the horses," Vran'el went through the inventory. "Pouches with water, bread and of course the belts, which we will put on and have sealed by you, Eryn, when we get there. So if you are all ready, I say we should go down to the stables and leave, as long as there is still enough light for hunting."

They followed him around the residence and Eryn saw for the first time the garden that stretched out behind the house. It, too, was brimming with flowers, bushes and trees in different stages of growth and blossoming. She was mesmerised and didn't even notice that her pace kept decreasing.

"Eryn!" Vran'el called out impatiently. "Are you coming or not? You can look at the pretty flowers some other time. My father is crazy about the garden; he will give you a tour and tell you everything about his mystic greens, I promise."

She broke away from beholding the splendour before her and hurried after the party to catch up with them. The stables were painted in white just like the main building of the residence. Five horses, a lot smaller than the kind she knew from home, were ready bridled in front of it, each of them with a blanket and a narrow leather strap where the saddle would normally go. She curiously inspected the narrow carts that were attached by long rods to the leather strap around each horse's girth. Each cart consisted of what looked like a squat box on solid wheels.

"That is for transporting the quarry afterwards," Neval explained. "I suppose your cat can ride in one of them if she is too tired for running afterwards. What was her name again? It is a female, right?"

She nodded. "Yes, her name is Urban."

Vran'el looked down at the cat and shook his head. "Urban. Because she is going to become as large as an entire city when she is fully grown?"

"No, because she is the first urban mountain cat we know of," Eryn explained patiently. "You seem a tiny bit afraid of my kitten, cousin."

"Kitten? You have to be joking," he snorted. "How in the world does a couple which lives in a city come to share their space with a wild animal such as this?"

"Eryn brought her home from a herb gathering expedition," Enric explained. "Believe me, it was quite a surprise for me as well."

Intrea smiled. "Makes you question the wisdom of sending your companion on trips without you, does it not?"

"It does, yes. She had planned to come here without me as well, but I learned from last time and made sure I accompanied her."

"*You* accompanied *her*? But you are the Ambassador, are you not? It seems to me that this journey would not have happened without you," Neval enquired.

"According to my charming companion's initial plans, it would," he smiled thinly and put a hand on Eryn's shoulder to squeeze it none too gently.

Eryn grimaced and ducked away from under his grip. "Where are the saddles?"

"The what?" Vran'el chuckled. "Saddles? Not for this kind of outing, cousin. Just like our choice of weapons we also keep our mode of transportation more traditional when it comes to hunting and other short journeys on horseback."

He stepped to one side of the first horse and used a sling attached to the leather strap to mount up.

Eryn grabbed the mane of the next horse, placed her foot in the sling and pulled herself up as well to sit on the horse's back that felt oddly naked with only a thin blanket between her legs and the equine body.

When Enric was sure that she was perched on her mount safely, he mounted his own horse and turned to look at Urban, who was sniffing at the wheeled box behind him curiously.

"Vran'el? How long will this ride take?" Enric called out.

"About one hour," he replied.

"That shouldn't be a problem for her, even in the heat. And it keeps getting cooler," Enric mused and urged his horse into a trot.

"You are used to riding with saddles, then?" Intrea asked and led her horse next to Eryn's.

"I am, yes. In fact, I have never ridden without one. Is there anything I need to consider?"

Intrea thought for a moment. "It has been a while since I last had a saddle underneath me, but I think it is a matter of balance. The saddle holds you pretty much in the same position, and without one you need to concentrate a little more on staying upright, especially when you change direction. Riding with a saddle is easier, because it compensates for mistakes that will now probably make you fall off the horse."

"Good to know," Eryn murmured. "These horses are smaller than those we have at home. I suppose large bodies are not a good thing in a climate such as yours."

"No, not really. From what I know horses were never native to our country. We brought them here several hundred years ago and bred them for the characteristics that are important for us, such as withstanding swings in temperature from hot days to cold nights as well as surviving for some time without water. But this is not really what you would like to talk about, is it?" Intrea asked with an impish smile.

"What do you mean?" Eryn asked and shifted uncomfortably on her blanket.

"Vran'el told me about your reaction to our family situation."

"He did?" she grimaced.

"Do not worry, I am not offended that easily. I prefer if people show an interest and ask me about it instead of judging me behind my back. Not that I am saying that this is what you do, I just want to tell you that you should feel free to ask whatever you like and that I am willing to satisfy your curiosity."

"Alright. Did you know about Vran'el's... inclination before you joined him?" Eryn asked.

"Yes, I did. I welcomed it. My House had intended to join me with another man, but I was repulsed by him and refused. I had planned to remain unbound and enjoy the freedom and independence that would bring, but my family was not too thrilled about that. Daughters are valuable, as their children are the power base for the next generation. My children belong to my family's House, after all."

"So my cousin was a convenient way of providing your House with a child and you retaining your freedom at the same time," Eryn concluded.

"Indeed. And I must say that this is the best arrangement I could have wished for. I prefer it very much to being unbound. My daughter is a miracle I would not have wanted to miss out on. Vran'el is a caring and devoted father, as the men of House Vel'kim are known for being."

Yes, Eryn thought, it was virtually the only positive thing she had heard about her own father since she had come here.

"I find it very impressive that you manage to treat each other as friends and even include Neval."

"And why should we not? We have been each other's chance both for freedom and keeping our Houses happy. Had I met him under different circumstances, I would very likely have befriended him anyway. He is funny, intelligent and charming," Intrea smiled. "Just what I appreciate in my female friends as well."

"Are you saying that is what he is like for you - a female friend?"

"Sometimes, yes. He tells me what colours suit me and helps me pick gifts for various occasions. When Obal needs new clothes, I always send him to take her to the tailor. He just has the better eye for cuts, fabrics, colours and everything connected with apparel. And we talk about men. He tells me of the latest gossip and advises me which lovers would be a good choice and the ones best avoided."

"Really?" Eryn stared at her.

"Really. I bet your companion is a very able one, is he not?" Intrea enquired and made an appraising look ahead at the tall blonde figure who was riding between Neval and Vran'el.

"Pardon?"

Intrea took in her pained look and laughed out loud so that all three men turned towards her with questioning expressions.

"Not so comfortable talking about sexuality, are you? I am afraid avoiding this as long as you are in Takhan will be quite a challenge. We are very open and openly inquisitive about it. You can bet this will not be the last question about your companion's sexual prowess somebody asks you."

Eryn exhaled slowly. "Oh my. And I thought I was doing so well," she murmured.

"You are, my dear. I suppose people will show more restraint when they talk to your companion as he looks foreign. But despite your pale complexion from lack of sun you still look like one of us, though on the inside you are not, are you? Twenty-three years away from home is a very long time. Might I ask how you are getting along with Malriel?" she enquired with evident tact.

"Politely. I don't see our getting at all close anytime soon, I am afraid."

"I can see why. I am not especially fond of her myself, I have to admit. My House and House Aren have never really been allies, so I have no particularly close connection to her. I see her at official occasions and sometimes at the music evenings. She seems to me very cool, calculating and dangerous. Though she is also immensely intelligent, which is probably what makes her so dangerous. Being Head of a House like Aren cannot be easy. They are out in the open so much due to their involvement in politics."

Eryn gulped when she thought back to Vran'el's words about her being the next in line for that very position.

"Vran'el told me that your being the heiress of House Aren took you by surprise today. But do not worry about this too much - decades will pass before this discussion arises," Intrea smiled. "And you have very good connections to your personal lawyer, so I do not really see you caught in a position you do not want to take over."

They looked ahead at the three men in front of them. Vran'el and Neval were laughing at something Enric had told them.

"Vran'el is very taken with your companion from what he told me and also from what I can see. I hope you are aware that this is a purely friendly interest?"

Eryn smiled. "I am not worried about Enric breaking his heart, if that is what you mean. I have to admit that I am amazed at how well Enric has adapted to this place and the people here. He really was the right choice for being made ambassador."

Intrea chuckled. "That sounded very surprised. And just a little annoyed."

Eryn shrugged. "It's probably just envy. It is annoying that he is so good at everything he does. He is better at adapting to my own home country than I have been!"

"Now, I completely understand why you are vexed by that." Intrea narrowed her eyes at Enric's back. "How dare he!"

The three men turned back once more when they heard the two women behind them sniggering.

"You can call me suspicious, but I do get an uneasy feeling when there are two women behind me laughing and I have no idea why," Enric murmured.

"Not only you, brother," Vran'el sighed and grimaced, "not only you."

* * *

Eryn looked down at the dead animals that lay before her on the sandy ground and felt moved. Not long ago she had seen them sprinting and jumping elegantly between low bushes and high blades of grass, and now they lay there at her feet in a bloody pulp. Nothing was left of their grace and vitality. They were nothing more than dead bodies, mangled carcasses. She shivered and turned away.

"Is everything alright, my love?" Enric asked and pulled her close to kiss her on the temple.

"I don't know, it's just that seeing them lie there, lifeless and bloody..." she trailed off.

He raised his brows. "You have lived in the countryside almost all your life. Don't tell me you never had any contact with this sort of thing?"

She shrugged helplessly. "I know this sounds foolish, but what I got for cooking was not really recognisable as an animal anymore, just a red piece of meat chopped off, cleaned, skinned, plucked and generally made to look like a commodity. Seeing this is like... like seeing a person lying there. I mean, I have seen this creature jumping around and now that very same animal is dead! Imagine somebody had done this to Urban!"

Enric stared down at her. "I think I should probably not have asked you to come. I am sorry. I had no idea this would weigh so heavy on your mind."

"No," she took his hand, "don't say that. It is more like I had my eyes closed in the past. I really should know where the meat comes from, meat that I have obviously been eating for decades without thinking. I will get over this, don't worry. But I would prefer if I didn't have to look at the bodies right now."

"Alright, I can oblige you in that at least. We are done with hunting for today, so you can open my gold belt again now." He arched his eyebrows when she simply looked at him contemplatively, her lips pursed. "Eryn? The belt please."

"You know," she said and he saw a slow smile spread on her lips. "I think I am going to leave it in place for a little longer."

"Eryn," he warned her in a low voice.

She smiled and grabbed the back of his neck to pull him down. He tried to resist but she sent a little extra strength into her arms and pressed her lips onto his.

"Yes, the belt is definitely staying on for a while longer," she grinned broadly and met his annoyed stare. "I see now what you like about this. It is more fun being the stronger one, isn't it?"

"I am going to make you pay for this," he said softly.

She let one finger glide along the edges of his belt. "I know. But not tonight."

Her gaze fell on Urban and the mess of bloody smears on the ground before her. "She has been successful as well, hasn't she?"

Enric followed her gaze, still frowning. "Yes. Three small animals. Not bad for her first hunting outing, not at all. It seems that gutting our throw cushions served as sufficient preparation for the real world," he added dryly.

"Eryn?" she heard Neval call. "We are about to load the quarry into the boxes. A little extra strength for us magicians would be appreciated."

"I am coming," she called back and moved towards the three of them.

After unlocking their belts, she informed them, "I have decided to leave Enric's belt on for the moment. I would appreciate it if none of you opened it for now."

Intrea raised both brows. "No resistance from my side."

Enric rolled his eyes. "Boys? Can I count on you for a little solidarity?"

"That you can, my friend," Vran'el grinned lasciviously. "But my solidarity will consist in letting you go through this experience instead of robbing you of it."

"Neval?" Enric asked weakly.

"Same here. Enjoy the ride." He, too, grinned broadly.

He turned to Eryn and sighed. "You see? Now they all think this is some kind of sex game."

She raised her brow at him. "Who says it isn't?"

Enric opened his mouth to speak, but not a single tone came out. Eryn smiled at what had to be the first time of her seeing him speechless.

Intrea smiled appreciatively. "You see, Eryn? You are adapting beautifully."

* * *

Less than two hours later they sat together in the main room at the Vel'kim residence and Valrad opened a bottle of wine for his guests.

"Six gazelles – it was incredible!" Vran'el exclaimed to answer his father's question about their hunting success. "Enric used the spear as if he has been doing so every single day of his life so far! You really never used a spear with a thrower and without magic? Are you sure?"

Enric shook his head. "No, I'm sure I would remember it."

"And this cat! Urban, is it not? I thought I was going to die when she suddenly sprinted towards me and sprang!"

Valrad froze. "What?" He looked at the brown animal that lay peacefully under the table and was snoring quietly, and then to his son who didn't show any signs of having recently been mauled by a predator.

"She sprang - and I could only stare at her, frozen in shock. She landed right in front of me. Some kind of small animal had hidden there. She snapped her jaws, lifted her prey and trotted off as if she had not just given me the scare of my life!"

Eryn rolled her eyes. "Don't be such a baby! I had a shield raised in front of you. So even if she had planned to ambush you, she would have had a very rude awakening."

"I was scared, in total shock! And dawn had started to break, so how could I possibly have seen a slight shimmering in the air when my focus was the huge, fierce creature seemingly aiming for my throat?"

Several pairs of eyes wandered down to the dark brown paws of the sleeping cat that protruded from under the table and twitched occasionally.

"Yes - huge, fierce creature indeed," Neval chuckled and ruffled his lover's hair.

Valrad filled the glasses on the table and lifted his own when everybody had taken one. All eyes were on him when he started speaking.

"This is a very special time for me. I have seen the return of my niece, who I had not dared hope ever to see again, and who has turned out to be such a formidable woman that I only now start to grasp fully what a catastrophe it is to have lost these last two decades with her. Welcome home, my girl. You may return to Anyueel in only a few weeks, but I would like you to know that there will always be a place for you in my House. And my heart. This day has also bestowed upon my House a new friend, who through his connection with Eryn is also family now. Let us make sure not to lose this contact again when you are back at your home."

They raised their glasses and Eryn felt Vran'el's hand squeeze hers when he took a sip. She felt touched by these kind words, and for the first time in her life she could imagine what it was like to be loved by a family, to belong somewhere, to be one of many parts that formed a whole. It was both liberating and intimidating. Connections brought expectations and responsibilities with them, after all.

She looked at Enric, who winked at her and she felt awed and grateful that he, too, had been accepted into that circle.

Valrad made to refill the glass she had not been aware she had already emptied.

"Do not be too generous with the wine in her case, Valrad," Neval grinned suggestively. "She still has plans for tonight."

Valrad lifted a brow at his niece and then his gaze fell on the belt that was still around Enric's waist. "Ah yes, I see." He refilled her glass. "Then this shall be your last glass for today, niece. I would not want to sabotage your pleasure," he smiled good-naturedly.

"Oh dear," she sighed. "You people really are an indiscreet bunch."

"You will get used to this," Vran'el promised. "There is a lot more of it to come, cousin. By the way, you may consider the belt a gift. Keep it and have fun with it. I would not be able to look at it without getting distracted anyway," he grinned, then sniggered at Eryn's red cheeks.

CHAPTER 25

Getting Busy

Enric slowly opened his eyes a fraction. The bedroom was flooded with sunlight and the white, gauzy curtains at the windows were being moved around lazily by a mild morning breeze.

He lay prone across the bed, one arm under his chest, the other stretched away towards Eryn's pillow. Her *empty* pillow.

He felt the breeze that played along the curtains blow lightly over his naked skin. Only one leg was covered by the thin blanket, the rest of his body was exposed.

A noise that sounded like the clearing of a throat made him jerk his head up and turn it toward the archway leading to the main room. Two men were standing there, regarding him with very different expressions.

Vran'el was leaning against the wall, arms folded, grinning appreciatively at the sight. Kilan's discomfort showed all too clearly in his features and tense posture. Their difference in hair colour and style of clothing increased the visual contrast even further.

He felt his thoughts battle whether to jump up and cover himself or just avoid any sudden movements at all. He felt more disposed towards the latter. And what did it matter, anyway? Both of them must have been standing there for several seconds at least, so they had pretty much seen everything there was to see already.

"I am still wearing the bloody belt, aren't I?" Enric's voice carried a mix of slight annoyance and resignation and his hand moved down to his hips to touch the warm metal.

"Yes," Kilan said stiffly. "It is the only thing you are wearing, in fact."

"Look away if it makes you uncomfortable, then," Enric growled and rolled to one side, careful to pull along the thin sheet to cover his groin.

"I can't. Fascination of horror," Kilan shrugged.

"Do not listen to him, my friend. Your sight does not hold any horrors whatsoever. I like your accessory, it goes nicely with your golden hair," Vran'el grinned.

"Where is Eryn?" Enric looked around the large bedroom, half expecting to see her sitting somewhere and enjoying the situation she had put him in.

"With my father. She said she had woken early and could not stop thinking about his garden. He is giving her a tour right now. This will take a while, so I would not expect her back very soon. Healers and their playthings," he rolled his eyes. "It seems my cousin forgot to release you from the belt before she departed. How very inconsiderate of her." His broad grin belied the sympathy in his voice.

"Yes, that's it - *forgot*," Enric snorted. She would pay for that. Dearly. He sighed and rose, wrapping the sheet around his hips. "Well, it seems that one of you will have to free me from this thing."

Kilan took a hasty step back. "Would you mind dressing first? Then I will of course..."

Vran'el's laugh stopped him and he gave the man who had claimed to be Eryn's cousin upon his arrival an annoyed look.

"Come here, my friend. Be sure to always count on me when the need to touch a gorgeous naked man in distress arises."

Kilan's eyes bulged at the statement and grew even wider when Enric just rolled his eyes and indeed went the few steps toward Vran'el and let himself be touched lightly before the belt opened and could be removed.

"Thank you," Enric sighed and smiled faintly with closed eyes when he felt the previously blocked power surging through his body. "That's much better. I am going to get dressed, and then I need something to eat. I hope there is some breakfast left."

"Breakfast?" Vran'el said with raised brows. "Hardly. It is almost time for lunch. You slept a very long time. An exhausting night, was it not? You might want to use some of your regained magic to heal the bruises on your back and shoulders. Unless, of course, you wish to keep them as tokens."

Bruises? He wondered how that was possible. He didn't remember feeling any pain last night. But Eryn had been assertive, there was no denying that. He suppressed a smile at the memory of her obvious enjoyment at being in complete control of him for the first time since they had met, having him physically helpless and at her disposal to do what she liked with. And she had used that control to great effect, revelling in it. He did not generally appreciate being helpless and subject to another person's power, but the situation last night had still held quite some appeal. Being forced to submit to her was a completely new experience and made him think of the many times he had used his own strength on her and she had been the one made to be subservient. He decided that each way held its particular delight, but he preferred it if the one with her in control was rather an occasional occurrence than a regular one. He didn't want to give her any wrong ideas about who really *was* in charge.

"Reminiscing about the pleasures of last night?" Vran'el's amused voice brought him back to the here and now where he was still standing naked with two men in a sleeping chamber.

"No," he lied smoothly, "just wondering about where to get something to eat. This is the first time I have not been invited anywhere. Eryn promised to cook for me today, but it seems she has found a more appealing way to spend her day."

"Do not worry about this, I will prepare a little something for you and your men. That is actually why I am here: to feed you in your hour of want and teach you a bit about it while we are so engaged. The servants will surely have stocked the kitchen, so it should not take me long. Get dressed and join me. You are about to get your first lesson in cooking. A real man should know how to provide for himself, after all." He turned on his heel and left the two blonde magicians alone.

Kilan waited until Vran'el's steps had died away. He lowered his voice, "Say, is it possible that he is... you know..." He wriggled his eyebrows suggestively, at a loss or unwilling to find the right words.

"Attracted to men?" Enric supplied calmly. "Yes, that is indeed the case."

"And you just let him get that close to you? Aren't you worried?"

Enric chuckled and stepped over Urban, lying comfortably in front of the clothes chest in one corner of the room, to take out a fresh pair of trousers and a tunic. He pulled out his dark blue robes and eyed them with disdain. Wearing them to the meeting in the afternoon was necessary to represent the Order properly, wasn't it? But they were too heavy to be comfortable in the temperature here.

"No, I am not worried. He is in a relationship with another man, and I think he just likes to play around a bit to see if he can make me uncomfortable. You know, shying away would only increase the fun in it for him."

Kilan shook his head in wonder. "Incredible. Nobody will believe me when I talk about this at home. People at home bow to you or freeze in admiration when they see you, and this man just treats you like... like..."

"A friend?"

"I dare say none of your friends would treat you in *such* a friendly way," Kilan snorted.

No, Enric thought, the only friends he had left were more allies in the game than anything else and wouldn't overstep any boundaries. The most personal exchanges he had were with Tyront, and there was still the underlying understanding that Tyront was his superior and in command.

That was very probably why he liked Vran'el, he mused. No awe, reverence, veneration or fear masked as respect - just easy-going affection and acceptance of a complete stranger from another country. Eryn had not been as lucky when her own origins had been discovered. She had been dragged into a cell, locked up and then

314

delivered to the King as a potential spy - irrespective of her having dedicated so many years to taking care of others.

"So, did you have a good hunting trip yesterday?" Kilan asked, eager to change the topic.

"We did, yes. I learned about a new way of throwing spears. Quite effective. Eryn seemed a bit out of sorts, though. The sight of the dead animals drained the colour from her face. It seems she led a rather protected life in the countryside," Enric told him and slipped into the trousers. He closed his eyes for a moment to heal the bruises Vran'el had mentioned before slipping his shirt on.

"So, that belt. An equivalent of our golden manacles to block magic, it seems."

"Yes, they put them on for hunting to make sure none of the magicians cheats and has an unfair advantage. It is more practical for hunting, as manacles would probably get in the way or increase the danger of hurting yourself," Enric explained.

"And Eryn decided that not removing yours immediately would give her a nice opportunity to get back at you for keeping her shackled all those months?" Kilan asked carefully.

"Don't ask me what goes on inside that woman's head," he sighed. "I suppose I won't see her before we return from our appointment at the senate tonight if she really is talking about herbs with her uncle. I wonder if she will return here at all tonight. I'd better make sure she does and collect her when we are done later."

Kilan nodded. "And now you are going to let yourself be taught how to cook, did I understand that correctly?"

Enric shrugged. "Why not? It seems to be one of the skills a grown man is expected to possess here, like healing or hunting for your own meat. Come on! It won't hurt you to learn it as well. We are very probably expected to host a dinner here sooner or later, and I am surely not going to be the only one slaving away in the kitchen."

The assistant groaned. "You are not serious, are you?"

The ambassador grinned mischievously. "Oh, but I am. Very much so, in fact. Consider it an order. After you, old friend. Time to teach you some housekeeping skills."

*　*　*

Eryn leaned back comfortably in the shadow against a large tree and took a swig from the water pouch her uncle handed her.

"Your garden is a true miracle, Valrad. Never in my life would I have thought that there is one place where so many different healing herbs grow."

Her uncle sat down on the grass as well and smiled, pleased with the praise. "Gardens are a matter of pride for many of the Houses, though for different reasons. Did you see the garden at the Aren residence when you visited your mother?"

She nodded, not too happy about being reminded of that occasion.

"They delight in finding new ways of outsmarting nature. Our House likes to collect herbs and other plants for different purposes, though mainly for healing. There are a few other useful things as well. You see that dark yellow flower over there? The one with the five petals and the large pinnate leaves? If you dry the leaves and grind them into a powder and serve it mixed with water, it is a powerful aphrodisiac." He cocked his head. "You can take a few with you and try it with Enric."

She laughed and shook her head. "No, I assure you that there is absolutely no need for that."

"Something for the opposite effect then, to cool him down and lull him to sleep instead?"

Laughing, she inclined her head. "No, we haven't reached *that* stage in our relationship, either. We have been together for only a few months and haven't grown tired of each other yet."

"And from the look of it you will not anytime soon," he smiled. "I have written a few books on herbs that are not native here in this area. I was wondering if you would like to have a look at them?"

She leaned forward eagerly. "I would, yes!"

"Very good. I do so like to show them to people, but there is only a limited number who appreciate the topic, you see. Do not expect too much of my drawing skills, though. I have seen the book Ram'an has brought with him, the one with the amazing drawings. He said that the illustrations were done by a boy no more than sixteen years old? That can hardly be true, can it? I have seen people studying the arts for years without ever reaching that level of skill."

"Believe it, he really is as young as that. And I was the first person ever to appreciate his talent, as magicians are not really supposed to be artists back home." She shook her head. "Can you believe that? When I first showed him how to look inside his body, something like a drawing frenzy became unleashed and he spent the entire night in his room drawing pictures like a maniac of muscles, bones, skin and various organs. His father fetched me because he thought the boy had gone completely mad."

"I would very much like to meet this young man one day. His work shows a great deal of understanding of the human body. That is unusual in an artist."

"That's because he is not only that. He is also my most eager and talented healing student. He has taken over the healing services while I am gone."

Valrad shook his head in disbelief. "A mere boy has taken on this great responsibility? There was nobody else available to be entrusted with it?"

She shook her head. "No. He is the most advanced healer I have by far. The timing for this journey here was not a very good one."

"Yes, I can see that," he said slowly. "I am sorry for it. Malriel and I have worked together to convince the triarchy to ask for you to be sent."

Eryn nodded. "Enric suspected as much."

"But not you? You did not think your family would be eager to finally meet you again after all this time?"

"I don't know," she sighed. "I was afraid of hoping for anything like that, I think. Afraid of not meeting expectations, or worse, nobody expecting anything of me at all."

The older man took her hand and pressed it against his heart. "Not only have you not disappointed us, Eryn - you have brought us great joy."

"And you made me feel so welcome that I feel torn about leaving you all behind in a few weeks now after knowing you only for such a short time. I have disappointed Malriel, though, I suppose. But that fails to bother me at the moment."

Valrad smiled at her indulgently. "No, Eryn, to both. You have not disappointed her. You have turned out to be so much like her that the two of you getting along was an unlikely chance. I thought as much when you snapped at Ram'an for not telling you that your mother was still alive when he visited you. Aren temper, I remember thinking. And you are not as untouched by the tension between you and your mother as you would like me to believe, or as you would maybe even want yourself to think."

"I don't like her," she said sullenly. "That at least you may safely believe."

"Oh, I do. But the human spirit is a fickle thing, is it not? That we do not like somebody still does not always stop us from wanting to be liked or respected by that person, does it?" he asked mildly.

Damn him and his uncomfortably accurate insights, she thought.

"I think I just want to put her in her place, show her that she can't treat me as a figure in a game, place me where it pleases her to reach whatever goal she aims for."

"Respect it is, then, what you are after. Earning Malriel's respect is hard work, I feel I need to warn you."

Eryn sighed. "Yes, I can see that. But it would put her in her place and make her leave me alone, right?"

"No, my dear, I do not see any chance of that. Whatever you do, she will not leave you alone, trust me. She is your mother, after all. She may not have made a very warm or affectionate impression on you, but there is a bond between you, has been for the last twenty-eight years, at least on her side."

She grimaced. "Are you telling me I need to be more considerate of her feelings?"

He laughed. "Dear me, no! Show an Aren woman any weakness and she will crush you mercilessly. No, make sure to show her strength instead of consideration."

Eryn narrowed her eyes. "People look at me and keep calling me an Aren woman, so when you say a thing like that you are including me, aren't you?"

Valrad raised his hands palm up and shrugged. "We would have to ask Enric about that, would we not? I am hardly in a position to pronounce on you after only two days, am I? But you may ask yourself how much weakness you yourself allow other people to show you without your despising them for it."

"I avoid despising people as far as I'm able," she replied testily. "And a display of strength does not usually earn my approval. Enric showed a great deal of strength, and it made me detest and fear him for the first half year."

"Detest him? Indeed?" His expression had become worried. "So it is true what Ram'an told us? That you did not enter into your companionship voluntarily? He forced it upon you?"

She swallowed. This relaxed, cosy atmosphere had caused her to let down her guard and be careless with what she said. How to dispel his concerns without telling him too much, but to clear Enric of this sleight?

"I admit I was rather reluctant to join him at the time, but it was not him doing the forcing, you must believe me. He himself was manipulated into asking me." Oh dear, that didn't sound any better, did it?

Valrad stared at her in dismay. "You were both joined against your will? This is horrible!"

"No, it is not as bad as it sounds," she assured him hurriedly. "Enric told me he'd wanted to ask me anyway, but hoped to give me more time. We had been involved with each other back then already, though at that time I was under the impression that it was more a temporary physical thing than a long-term commitment. We were just pushed into making it official."

"To make sure you would not return here with Ram'an, I assume?" he asked thoughtfully.

She nodded.

"Would you have done so without the commitment to Enric? Would you have left Anyueel?"

She let out a long breath. "I don't know. Really, I couldn't say. I was angry when I heard that they had tricked me into this without telling me that a delegation was on its way. But then Ram'an told me that one of the search parties had been about to find me and would have more or less dragged me back to Takhan whether I had agreed or not. That had me wondering. And then there is the matter of what he said about preserving the bloodlines and producing magically gifted children..."

Valrad smiled sadly. "Your father was not a great supporter of arranged commitments, either. But for our system it is a helpful tool. Ram'an said your King is not a magician, yet he was the one to carry out the ceremony. This means there is no third level bond between you and your companion, unless you had somebody else put you under it."

"Third level bond?" Eryn frowned.

"A third level commitment bond, yes. There is none in place, is there?"

"I don't know. What exactly are you talking about?"

Valrad watched her for a while, then nodded slowly. "They would not know it any more over there, would they? It is used to permanently join two magicians, and they have not had that opportunity for a very long time with your being the first female magician in three hundred years. And it seems Ved'al never told you about it. But then he would avoid talking about his home, would he not?"

"A permanent bond between magicians? Like a magical oath?"

"Yes," he nodded, "exactly like a magical oath. Should you belong to a House, then your Head's permission is necessary for it. I am told you are under an oath that binds you to the Old Kingdom, are you not? They wanted to make sure you would not leave without the intention to return. We have three different kinds of magical oaths. The first level commitment bond is like a promise. We use it for business or private agreements to assure our partner of our honest intentions. The second level bond is pretty much the one you have entered into to bind yourself to the Old Kingdom. And the third one is what would bind you magically to your companion."

Eryn stared at him, her heart beating more quickly now. A magical bond between companions? That sounded extremely ominous.

"The second level bond I am under; it keeps me from leaving without the intention to return and would pull me back in case I decided to stay here. What exactly does the third level bond do?" she asked and dreaded the answer.

"It keeps pulling you back together. Long absences of one partner are a very hard trial for both. It makes lying to each other more difficult. And keeping secrets from your partner as well. You would feel an increased need to share your feelings and thoughts. It greatly reduces the risk of infidelity, as you might imagine."

"But it is no guarantee of a happy companionship, is it? I assume my parents were under a third level commitment bond?"

He nodded. "That they were, yes. Do not get me wrong, the bond is not meant to be a guarantee of eternal happiness or even fidelity. There is no such thing. It just helps two people who love each other take their relationship to the next level, make it easier for them, enable them to enter into a degree of intimacy that exceeds mere physical closeness or emotional attachment. But sometimes the differences between two persons are stronger than the bond."

Eryn stared at the grass for a few moments before asking, "So if the bond pulls people back together when they are separated for a longer time, how does it affect them when this isn't possible?"

"It starts draining their happiness after a while," he answered quietly. "Malriel had the bond removed after your father was gone. The senate granted it, as being bound to a man who had not only left her in such a manner, but also taken her child with him, was a burden they did not want to force upon her. It was a unanimous vote - even the Houses not allied with House Aren agreed to it at once. Ved'al, however, still had the bond to Malriel in place. I can only imagine what it must have been like for him. Maybe fighting its effects on him was what drained some of his temper over the years."

"That sounds horrible," she whispered.

"Not horrible, child. It is a fact that entering into a third level commitment bond is not to be taken lightly, it needs to be considered carefully. If there is a strong attachment in place between two people, then it is very likely a gain for both of them."

"But if something goes wrong, it becomes an enormous burden," she pointed out.

"Yes, I cannot deny that. But if the burden is too great, there is always the option of applying to the senate to have the bond removed again. If you manage to convince them, they will free you from it."

She shook her head in disbelief. "But when I can't convince them I am stuck with it?"

"Yes, I think that is a valid way of phrasing it." Valrad smiled without humour. "You are worried. Enric might want you to enter into it with him. But you would refuse, would you not?"

She flashed him a pleading look. "Don't tell him about it, please!"

He sighed. "As you wish. But this will not make a great difference. He will learn about it sooner or later, be sure of that."

She shook her head. "You don't know that. It is hardly an everyday conversation topic, is it? It must be possible to keep that little bit of information from him for a mere three weeks - two and a half now - mustn't it?"

"I would rather recommend dealing with the issues that stop you from considering such a commitment instead of trying to escape from it, dear niece," he sighed. "You can only run for so long, after all."

"It's the better alternative for now, believe me. I have yet to deal with the issues that have come up since I arrived here. I don't need Enric pressuring me about this right now."

* * *

Eryn looked up from the floor in her uncle's library when Enric came in and widened his eyes at the sight. It looked like mayhem. Books that had undoubtedly been stored in an orderly manner on the shelves around her were now occupying almost every available surface, some closed, many of them open. It seemed like she had started reading at the desk, but had at some point decided that it didn't provide enough space for everything she wanted to look at. She sat on the colourful carpet, surrounded by heaps of books that varied in size, thickness, colour and age. Currently she was carefully leafing through a grand book with fragile-looking, brown pages that crackled softly when she turned them.

"Did you do that or was there some local weather event that has caused this chaos? A whirlwind, maybe?" he asked and stepped closer, careful not to tread on any of the books.

She looked around as if only now taking in the chaos for the first time. She had created it step by step, always adding another book and had not really taken in the picture as a whole. Until now.

"Oh," she said in surprise. "It does look a bit messy, doesn't it?" She felt his fingers lift her chin and then his warm lips on hers when he greeted her.

"A bit? That is quite an understatement. You better make sure you get this back in order before you leave, or your uncle might never allow you in here again," he warned. "But it seems like you have found some things of interest. Have you asked Valrad if you can have some of them copied to take home?"

She smiled. "I have, yes. He doesn't mind. I have even started making stacks of what I want to have copied right now, what would be nice to have but is not necessary at the moment, and then there are a few books I already have, as my father brought copies with him when he left here. This does refute your theory about the whirlwind, you know. It's not random chaos, but organised, even if the untrained eye can't see it at first glance."

He chuckled. "Let me guess: The large heap over there that consists of five stacks so far is the one you need urgently?"

"How did you know that?" she grinned.

"I had a feeling. Then you'd better take care of that so that at least a few of them are finished before we leave for Anyueel again." He looked back over his shoulder to make sure they were alone, when he said, "You didn't remove the belt before you left. I found myself in a rather embarrassing situation with Kilan and Vran'el this morning."

A slow smile spread across her face. "Indeed? I must have forgotten. What embarrassing situation?"

"I woke up lying naked and undraped on the bed while both of them were standing in the doorway."

"Vran'el saw you naked?" She laughed. "I am sure he didn't mind. He doesn't seem to be the shy type."

Enric grunted. "No, shy he wasn't, quite the opposite. He told me I was gorgeous."

Eryn took his hand and kissed his palm, smirking. "He is right. You are."

"Don't try to stray from the topic at hand by flattering me. Kilan was not quite as comfortable with the situation as your cousin. And I need him to be able to look me in the eye; we are supposed to be working together, after all."

"Does that mean the meeting with the senators didn't go well because Kilan was distracted and uncomfortable, and you are blaming me for it?" she enquired with a pained expression.

"No, the meeting went well enough. I am just asking you not to leave me alone with my powers blocked next time. If there ever is to be a next time."

"Oh, I very much hope so. Vran'el has donated the belt to us for that exact purpose, hasn't he?"

"Yes, my love, but relinquishing control to somebody requires trust. And finding myself naked and vulnerable afterwards tends to make that slightly difficult for me," he replied softly.

She studied him for a few moments, then nodded. "Alright, I see what you mean. It won't happen again. Though I feel I should point out that *you* never seemed to care so much if I trusted you when you took control, at least at the beginning."

"Different situation. I had to take control to get you to trust me in the first place. I have become a lot more lenient with you in these last few months, haven't I?"

She raised a brow. "Hardly. If that were true, you wouldn't have stormed into the healers' building and shouted at me in front of everybody. That's not exactly my understanding of leniency."

"Quite honestly, it could have been worse. My first impulse was to throw you over my shoulder and lock you up in our house with shackles around your wrists. You see?" He smiled crookedly. "I was lenient with you by my standards."

Rolling her eyes, she got up and carefully closed the thick book before her, then lifted it to place it on a shelf. "That discussion will lead us nowhere. Let's agree that I have to work on not abusing my power and you have to work on your understanding of leniency. And now tell me about that meeting of yours. Have you signed any trade agreements yet?"

He shook his head. "No, my love. That's not quite how it works. We have only started carefully to approach each other, sizing up what each party is willing to talk about. We compared the goods each side has available for trade and considered which ones are attractive for exchange from each country's point of view. And then there are the Houses. They have hinted at wanting to discuss their own trade agreements with me."

"Can they do that?"

"It would seem so, yes. Though first the country itself in its capacity as a state needs to be supplied, before surplus goods may be distributed among the private parties. So the Houses may only attempt to obtain the goods after the public authorities have obtained their share in the name of the people. So only after the common good has been served, may the rich families buy goods from Anyueel for their own purposes."

She grimaced. "That does sound rather complicated, especially if you have to negotiate first with the country for the outline agreement followed by discussions with each single House for every single commodity."

He smiled. "It's not so bad. First we will agree on the general terms with the Western Territories, and only then will I deal with the Houses. I first need to see what is left to trade with them, anyway. And as soon as the prices and delivery conditions have been set with the Western Territories, only minor adjustments for the Houses will be necessary. Kilan can take care of most of that, I think. But there is still quite some work to be done until we get there."

"When will you be meeting them again?"

"Tomorrow afternoon. So it seems you will have to find a way to keep yourself busy again. But judging from the number of books that are still in the shelves, I'd say that won't be too much of a challenge," he remarked. "I am to pass on your mother's regards to you, by the way. As one of the senators she was there as well, of course. She has expressed an interest in trading the wine we gave her when we had lunch with her. It seems she liked it."

"Great," Eryn murmured. "I hope you charge her twice the price anybody else would have to pay."

"That's hard. There might be a thing or two we want from House Aren, and I wouldn't appreciate being overcharged for that in turn. Come on, get the place back in order now. Vran'el wants to take us out for dancing tonight, and we'll need to get changed for that. I sent Grend to pick up our new clothes from the tailor's so we won't embarrass your cousin tonight."

"Dancing? He said something like that yesterday, didn't he?" she sighed. "I suppose we must, then."

"See it like this: it is an informal social occasion that still enables you to meet the important people around here. I would have thought you prefer those to balls or banquets."

"I think I do, yes," she admitted. "At least I won't be the only one getting dancing lessons this time. You will be right beside me, making a fool of yourself as well. That comes as some consolation."

He chortled. "I won't make a fool of myself. I am a natural at everything that concerns coordination, style and elegance."

"And there is still no danger of you falling prey to the vice of modesty, is there?"

"None whatsoever, my love."

CHAPTER 26

Dancing

Enric was astounded when he saw her standing before him in her new dress. She looked different, very different. It was amazing how clothes could sometimes change a person to such a degree. Her skin looked a shade darker with the colourful material, as did her eyes. Suddenly, she seemed just as exotic to him as the other people in this country.

She really had come home, he thought, and his stomach clenched. The sudden stab of fear of losing her to this place came unexpectedly and he felt his hands balling into fists. He knew it was his own fault - he had insisted on getting her new clothes in the local style. He wished he hadn't. There was no denying that she looked brilliant, radiant. Yet he wanted to hide her away from the city out there, wanted to stop others from seeing her like that, from thinking that she really belonged here with them instead of with him and to the country he would take her back to when their stay was over.

Eryn kept plucking at the material, uncomfortable in the new dress. She frowned at him. "I hate it."

He smiled at her statement with genuine relief. He had half expected her to have adopted the local dialect to go with the new style, and these few simple words in her usual familiar way of talking, expressing her permanent disdain for new clothes, somehow restored his certainty that she indeed was his, belonged to him and no one else.

"Then take it off and put on something else," he said.

She looked at him in surprise. "Really? That is not exactly the statement I was expecting from you. I thought you wanted me to demonstrate to the locals that I embrace their culture? Use my origins to our diplomatic advantage?"

"Yes, I know. I have changed my mind. You shouldn't have to pretend to be something you feel you are not. If you don't like the dress, put it aside. Give it to Junar as a present when we are back."

She stared at him, disbelief on her face. "Sometimes you confuse me, really. Or are you trying to demonstrate that I underestimate your leniency? Whatever it is, I am determined to take full advantage of it if it saves me from wearing this dress. Do you see how long it is? How am I supposed to move in that? And it's too loose up here, too tight down there…" She paused to struggle out of the garment and flung it onto the bed, then continued, "and the sleeves are too long as well. Pity, though - I like the colours."

He looked at the dress thoughtfully. "Why don't you have it changed, then? Take one of your tunics to the tailor and ask him to use it as a model. He could make you a few tunics with the cut you are accustomed to and like and just use the local fabrics."

She considered that option while slipping into one of the thinner tunics Junar had made for her. "That doesn't sound halfway bad. I hope they won't object to my using their fabrics but not their cuts? It might be considered as only adapting to one part of the culture."

He shrugged noncommittally. He couldn't care less what people thought right now as long as she didn't go back to looking that foreign again.

"Make a bold statement, then. Demonstrate to the world that you embrace what you like best from each culture and combine them into something new. It's pretty much what you are anyway: a fabulous combination of two cultures, two countries. I don't see why your style can't reflect that, I even think it should."

A slow smile spread across her face. "I like that, I really do. You know what? I think I will pay that tailor a visit tomorrow. *Voluntarily*."

"Amazing," he marvelled. "Words I never thought I would hear from you."

He looked down at his own new set of clothes. He had done almost exactly what he had just recommended his companion to do, but the other way round. The local cut appealed to him, the tight fitting for masculine attire emphasised his broad shoulders and slim waist quite unlike the wide, loosely fitting tunics he owned. But the colours had made his skin seem even more pale than usual, especially in comparison with the local skin tones. So he had opted for the more advantageous cut, but chosen black. The tailor had warned him that he only stocked this colour for people in mourning, but Enric had insisted.

He slipped on the shirt and the rather baggy trousers and looked at himself in the mirror. The sight pleased him and he heard Eryn whistle behind him.

"You like it?" he asked, even though that was obvious.

She stepped behind him and looked at his mirror image. "I do, yes. Very much so. You look even taller, more imposing than usual, and that's saying something. And the contrast of the dark fabric with your blonde hair is really unusual after looking at dark-haired people with colourful clothes all day long. I think you will be the centre of attention tonight." She let her gaze wander down to his legs and up again. "And I see what you meant. Blending two styles

really works, at least in your case. I will definitely give it a try."
Then she grinned shamelessly. "The only thing that's missing now is
the golden belt. It almost matches your hair and would look very
good against the black shirt."

He snorted and remembered that Vran'el had said something
similar only this very morning. "No, thank you very much. I think I
will leave it like that. Are you ready?"

"Yes. Let's fetch the boys and then meet Vran'el in the large
square. He did say that we would get something to eat there, right?
I am starving. Valrad offered me fruit, but I didn't want to eat
anything as long as I was handling the books."

He nodded. "Yes, we will have dinner at the music house, as he
calls it."

Grend and Kilan were waiting for them in the main room, both
dressed elegantly.

"Where is Barul?" Enric asked.

"He will be here any minute," Grend explained. "When I left he
was still trying somehow to fit a large knife on his person without it
being visible."

"And I am pleased to report that I have finally managed it,"
Barul's voice came from the staircase. "I am ready if you are."

Eryn eyed him curiously. "Where have you hidden it, then?"

"Why don't *you* tell me?" he grinned.

"Can I touch you?"

"No," Enric growled and gave an annoyed look at Kilan, who
immediately stopped laughing.

"On your back. Inside your trousers," she guessed.

Barul shook his head. "No. The blade is too long, I wouldn't be
able to sit down all evening."

"Under your arm, then."

"No."

"Then you have it in your boot. There is no other place on you
for hiding a large knife. And there is a slight bulge in that right
trouser leg of yours, am I right?"

"Yes, you have found it. But as it took you three tries, I consider
it hidden well enough," he smiled and winked at her.

Enric took her hand and led them to the meeting point with
Vran'el. He was waiting there already and grinned broadly when he
spotted them.

"There you are! Very good!" He nodded at Enric. "I like your
clothes very much. Usually it is what people wear when they are in
mourning, but with your striking looks you can wear it. It
accentuates your impressive build. Very nice." Then he looked at his
cousin. "Eryn, what can I say? This colour makes you appear pale.
We will have to do something about that. Meet me at the tailor's
shop tomorrow after breakfast." He shook his head in dismay.
"Really, I cannot let you run around like this when people know that

we are related. It will make people think that I either do not care about you or that my taste has suffered badly."

She raised her brows. "Thank you so much for that. Being criticised after you praised my companion is a bit of a blow, you know. But you are lucky, I have plans to go and see the tailor tomorrow anyway. I graciously grant you the privilege of accompanying me."

"Good girl," he grinned and patted her cheek. "You will see that it is for your own good. And now come, let us get something to eat."

*   *   *

Enric studied the vegetables in his bowl with great interest. Funny, how learning to cook had changed his perception of food. It was no longer something that he took for granted as appearing on his table when it was time for a meal. He was more aware now that preparing it required time and skill - and that a task that was in his home considered fit for servants could even be a relaxing pastime. He was surprised at the satisfaction he had felt when sitting down to his first self-cooked meal, the sense of accomplishment when it had actually tasted good.

"I wonder how long it takes to prepare this dish," he mused.

Kilan wiggled his head. "I would say an hour. Chopping everything needs quite some time, but the frying doesn't take so long."

"I think not all of this is fried. The brown parts are steamed, I think. That takes some extra time," Enric remarked.

"Not necessarily," Vran'el cut in. "You can do the frying during the steaming, so it is basically only a matter of time management in what order you chop the ingredients. I could prepare this dish in no more than thirty minutes."

"Really?" Kilan exclaimed with delight. "That I'll have to see! Then I think we have found just the dish for our next lesson."

"You three are joking, aren't you?" Eryn said and shook her head in disbelief. "I can't believe I heard you having this conversation just now."

"If you think you can treat exchanges about cookery with such contempt, cousin, I would very much like to see how able you are in the kitchen. Tomorrow, after we are done at the tailor's, you should cook for me. And if the result is not to my liking, you'll join those two for the next lesson."

"Lesson?"

"I am teaching them cookery. We had our first lesson today, the next one will be in two days," Vran'el explained patiently. "And I will decide tomorrow whether it is taking place with or without you."

"My father taught me how to cook. And he stems from the same House as yourself, so you may safely assume that I know my way around a kitchen."

He clucked his tongue. "Sweetness, there is quite a difference between knowing your way around a kitchen and actual cooking. But let us discuss this no more, you will have the opportunity to convince me tomorrow."

"I don't need to convince you of anything. You just ingeniously invited yourself to lunch so you avoid cooking anything yourself."

"Please," he snorted. "For all I know I might be risking my life by eating what you serve me."

She grinned impishly. "You might - if I manage to sneak into your father's herb garden beforehand. He has an interesting assortment of plants that have a few very unpleasant effects unless they are handled with great care."

"You would not. Aren women do not poison people. That would be too subtle for them. They hit you over the head with a stick - preferably while standing in front of you, because they want you to know who has hurt you."

"Stop calling me an Aren woman!" she snarled and made several close by heads turn in their direction.

She heard somebody murmur, "Aren temper!" and her head spun around to make out the speaker. At once all eyes snapped away from her back to bowls and glasses in front of them.

Barul and Grend exchanged uneasy looks and resumed eating.

Enric smirked and put his empty bowl aside. "What about the Aren men? Do they suffer from that temper as well?"

"No, they do not. Aren men are generally more subdued, probably a survival technique to avoid being eaten alive," Vran'el grinned.

Eryn looked unfazed. "You know, the fact that you keep provoking me despite that allegedly fierce temper that is supposed to be slumbering inside me somewhere shows that you are either grossly exaggerating or not very attached to your limbs."

"What can I say, cousin? Vel'kim men are known for their stoic calm. It helps them when they have to face emergencies, which does tend to happen frequently when you work in the medical profession. I may not have chosen the profession, but I have inherited the calm and the contempt for death that goes with it."

"I always thought *I* was blessed with stoic calm," Enric said. "Then I met Eryn and now I keep erupting into anger at regular intervals."

"Do not worry about this, my friend," Vran'el sighed sympathetically. "A man who always remains calm in the face of Aren temper is very probably a dead man. They are known to tax even the greatest patience."

"Could you two idiots stop talking about me as if I weren't here?" Eryn hissed. "And if I hear the word *Aren* connected with me one more time tonight, there will be consequences. Painful ones."

Her cousin flashed Enric a look as if to say *You see?*

All five of them looked up when a figure halted at their table. Ram'an.

"Good evening," he smiled and nodded at them all. "What a nice coincidence to meet you here tonight. I am preparing a little dinner party for in a few days, and I would be delighted if you would accept my invitation."

"It is our pleasure to accept," Eryn smiled before Enric had a change to open his mouth.

"Excellent," Ram'an replied. "You will receive a formal invitation tomorrow. Eryn, I very much hope you might grant me the privilege of a dance tonight?"

She grimaced. "I am afraid that would not be a pleasant experience for you, Ram'an. I don't know any of your dances."

"It will be my pleasure to teach you at least one of them tonight. It would be a shame to have you just sitting here all evening."

"She will not," Vran'el smiled coolly at Ram'an. "I brought them here to show them a few dances myself."

"Of course," he said stiffly. "I did not mean to imply that you were neglecting your duties as a host, Vran'el. If you would excuse me now, my family awaits my return." He nodded to them once again and retreated to a table at the other end of the room, to a group of seven people.

"How nice to meet him here," Enric commented darkly. "What an unexpected pleasure."

"Yes, it is a small city, is it not?" Vran'el said without enthusiasm. "But it is not that unexpected to meet him here; there are only a few select places to go to in the evenings for certain circles. Though I understand very well why you are not pleased to meet him here, considering the liberties he took with your companion."

Enric's eyes snapped to him. "Liberties?" he asked seemingly calmly, but with narrowed eyes. "This doesn't happen to have anything to do with a fork that was mysteriously stuck into a certain ambassador's thigh a few months ago?"

Eryn swallowed. "Vran'el, I think it might be advisable..."

"Quiet," Enric barked without looking at her.

"This is neither the time nor the place..." she tried again and suddenly felt her wrist caught in an iron grip and his face close to hers, the expression in his blue eyes steely.

"You have two choices now, and I want you to listen carefully, as following any other course of action will leave you paralysed and unable to speak. Option number one is telling me about this yourself without omitting any details you might consider too burdensome for my frail constitution. Option number two is keeping your mouth shut while Vran'el tells me about it. Let me emphasise once more that the alternative - or option number three, if you like - is finding yourself immobile. Have I made myself clear?"

She bit her lip and nodded.

"Very good. Which one is it to be, then?"

"Vran'el," she said between clenched teeth.

"I see," he smiled without humour. "You hope that he is not in possession of all details, don't you? We will see about that. Should I feel that the story is incomplete, I will take the liberty of continuing this conversation with you; if necessary with the aid of a truth block." He then turned to Vran'el. "I would very much like to hear about the liberties that Ram'an seems to have taken with my companion, if you would be kind enough to share this information with me."

Vran'el looked at Eryn, a look of foreboding on his face. "I see that you are not comfortable with this, my dear, but I really think he should know about it. It was rather negligent of you not to inform him before you came here." He then turned to Enric. "I am not sure if I know everything, but I will tell you what I can. I would, however, ask you to keep calm here. We would not want to make a scene in public."

Enric nodded once.

"When Ram'an returned here, we were eager to learn about Eryn. He told us that she was a member of the Order of Magicians in your Kingdom, holding a position of power there due to her extraordinary magical strength. He also informed us that she was joined to a magician even higher up in rank and thus stronger than herself. He mentioned that he had heard rumours during his stay that led him to believe that her commitment to you might not exactly have been a voluntary one, at least on her side. He suspected that she had been made to join you in order to keep her from leaving the Kingdom as soon as she had the chance. And that chance would of course have arisen with the departure of the delegation. So he asked her about it. But Eryn was not quite cooperative in answering his questions, it seems. So he used what you call a *truth block* on her."

Enric drew a sharp breath. "Go on."

"He said that she had not realised what he was doing from the start, only became aware of it when she attempted to lie to him for the first time. She then managed to put together pieces of truth to tell him an obvious lie. When he wanted to continue his questioning of her, she managed to free herself and fled from his quarters."

Enric nodded slowly. "I see. Thank you Vran'el." Then he turned to his companion. "I see why you chose to withhold this information as long as Ram'an was in the city, but you should never have kept this from me when it was clear that we would be coming here." His voice was cold, and so was his stare. "And I don't care what Tyront or the King said, so don't you dare go using them as an excuse. I told you what I think of your withholding information from me, and I swear, if you don't start sharing things like that with me, I will put you under constant surveillance every single minute you are out of my sight. I mean it. I am sick of finding out that you keep matters of such gravity from me. Have I made myself clear?"

She nodded quickly and only then felt his grip around her wrist loosen.

"At least you showed him that you didn't approve of his actions," he said in a lighter tone. "I admit I like the simplicity of jabbing a fork into him. A pity you had no sword handy, really. But it doesn't really speak of good manners to bring one to a Royal banquet, does it?"

Eryn exhaled in relief. He seemed to have taken it reasonably well, considering that Ram'an was close enough to be available for retribution. And fortunately Vran'el did not seem to be aware that Ram'an had tried to confine her in his quarters with a shield she had only barely managed to break through.

She looked at Kilan and saw the same thought plain in his slightly troubled eyes.

"Let's not have this ruin our first evening out together," Vran'el said. "Put it aside for now, Enric, and instead let me share with you something that is important to us here: our love of music and dancing. You see the three men over there? They will be our musicians tonight. In these music houses, you see, we normally have different artists every evening. We have a number of very good ones in the city, and they chose different locations for their performances. They play an assortment of magical and non-magical songs. There will be a shield around the dance floor over there to protect those people who do not wish to dance from the effects of the magical music."

Eryn leaned forward with interest. "A shield can do this?"

"Of course. You can tune a shield to whatever you would like to pass through, be it magic, light or sounds. You can either stop them from passing through altogether or only filter out selected parts. In this case only the magic is filtered out, the melody itself can still be heard and enjoyed without any unwanted side-effects."

"Could you show me how to raise such a shield?" she asked eagerly.

"Sure, it is not very hard," he shrugged. "I will show you tomorrow. The musicians are preparing their instruments now, so they will be starting in only a few minutes as most of the guests seem to have finished eating. The first few dances are usually non-magical, so you will have to learn the steps instead of simply letting the music guide you. But even when the music contains magic, you can still see if somebody is a skilled dancer without the magic. Their movements are usually more elegant, more pleasing to the eye if a basic skill of moving is there already."

"So being able to dance in general will help?" Enric asked.

"Quite. Do you dance at home, Enric?" Vran'el enquired.

"Occasionally, yes."

"Then I very much look forward to seeing you dance tonight."

"I don't think I will," he shook his head. "At least not the non-magical ones. I don't know anybody to dance them with."

Vran'el frowned at him in puzzlement. "You do know me, do you not?"

"You?" Enric asked equally confused. "Wouldn't this appear rather strange?"

"Why would it? There are dances that are specifically meant to be danced by two men or two women."

"Really?" Kilan's brows rose in surprise. "That is very unusual by our standards, you should understand. We only have dances that are supposed to be danced by a man and woman together."

"Indeed?" Vran'el exclaimed. "How very odd! So if you happen to have more women than men at an occasion, they sit around and wait for one of the few poor, overworked men to ask them to dance? That sounds terrible!"

Eryn chuckled. "You know, when you put it like that it really does, doesn't it?"

"So, who generally requests a dance, then?" Kilan enquired. "At home it is the man, but if there are dances where either two men or none at all are involved, I wonder if there is a system of rank, age or social standing to consider."

Vran'el shrugged. "In general you may ask whoever you would like to dance with, but social standing is, of course, a consideration. Though in places like this you do not really need to be concerned about this. You will only find members of the Houses here, so you may basically ask whoever you like. In Eryn's case, however, she might want to consider the alliances and enmities between the Houses before asking or accepting somebody to dance with."

"I do?" she asked in surprise. "I don't even know about such political matters, not to mention who belongs to which House! How am I supposed to work it all out? Are you aware of all these things between all the Houses? Or just of House Vel'kim?"

He smiled reassuringly. "Relax, dear cousin. I have a pretty clear picture, and as long as you are with me, there is no danger of your dancing with the wrong partner. If you wish to venture out without me, however, I would advise you to take somebody with you who can help you with this. I could give you a list of acceptable people, but their names alone would not help you if you do not know the corresponding faces."

"You know, I have no particular wish to act like a member of House Aren, whatever Malriel or anybody else may be expecting of me. I am not here as a representative of her House, but of the Kingdom that sent me here. So if I happen to dance with or befriend somebody she doesn't approve of, I will not lose any sleep over it," she said sternly.

"As you wish, my dear. Just do not say I did not warn you in case your mother takes you aside to have a little talk because you get too friendly with her adversaries," Vran'el shrugged. "Look, the musicians are ready. The music is about to start. I will let you sit out the first one, but for the next one I claim your hand, Eryn."

"Alright," she sighed in defeat. "They're your feet, after all."

The music started and they listened in fascination to the unfamiliar tones the strange looking instruments produced. A skilled male voice climbed up to high pitches only to plunge to the other end of the scale in a mere moment.

They saw several people rise from various tables around them and step on the slightly subjacent dance floor. There were indeed a few couples that consisted of two men or two women among them.

"So this song is not aimed at any particular combination of dancers?" Kilan asked.

"No, it is not. A great many songs are not. So you do not have to worry about being considered a fancier of men if you are seen to be dancing with one," Vran'el smirked.

Kilan blushed and avoided his gaze, obviously uncomfortable at being seen through in this way.

"Speaking of fancying men," Eryn cut in to rescue Kilan, "where is your lover tonight? Why hasn't he joined us?"

"He has had to accompany his family to a dinner invitation and will join us a bit later. He is a very able dancer, so I am happy that I can show him off tonight," he grinned.

"They don't touch each other at all," Eryn noted after watching the dancers for a few moments. "That is interesting. We always have some physical contact with our dancing partners at home. Within specifically permitted areas, of course, but still."

"Some dances do not require any touching at all while others do. The seduction dances are in general a bit heavier on physical contact, as you might imagine," he leered rather suggestively. Then a frown dawned. "You are aware what a seduction dance is, are you not? You have them at home, I assume?"

Enric smiled faintly. "Oh yes, that we do. But as we didn't have any female magicians until recently, we never played them. I was the first in three hundred years to dance one of them again."

"Indeed?" Vran'el exclaimed in surprise, then slapped his forehead with his flat palm. "But of course, how stupid of me! It only works with two magicians, and couples of the same sex are not socially acceptable in your society. So of course you would not have known about them. So I dare say it was a very nice experience for the both of you. Dancing your first seduction dance with a person is like the first time of being intimate with someone. How wonderful for the two of you that you could experience this together. I am sure you will have other opportunities to dance them here as well."

Eryn cast her eyes downward and blushed a little, wishing Enric had not volunteered this information. Glancing up, she could see the uneasy looks on Grend's and Barul's faces.

"I suppose it would be good to dance another one, this time without masks," Enric smiled, relishing his memory of that first time with Eryn.

"Masks?" Vran'el asked and leaned forward, delighted at this information. "Are you telling me this was an anonymous dance? Really? How unexpectedly kinky! And there I thought that country of yours was completely prudish and stolid."

"Anonymous, yes," Eryn snorted. "For me. He knew who I was alright. Being the only person with dark hair in a country of blonde people rather makes you stand out."

Vran'el's eyes glinted with interest. "So he knew who you were but you had no idea who he was? When did you find out?"

"About three months later after he had beaten me mercilessly in front of an audience to punish me for a public insult," she told him with a sideways glance at Enric, who just smiled.

"He did? Beat you how?"

"In a sword fight he tricked me into with some kind of magical illusion that made me almost kill my combat trainer."

Vran'el whistled through his teeth. "That is not what I usually hear when I ask people how they found each other. Your story is a bit out of the ordinary, is it not?"

"Yes, you could say that," Enric nodded with an amused expression.

They looked up when the music stopped.

"Come, cousin. Let me show you how we dance here," Vran'el said and got to his feet before pulling her up and all but dragging her to the dance floor. She felt the slight prickling on her skin when they passed through the shield.

"Why is there a shield in place when they are not even playing any magical music at the moment?" she asked.

"Because it would be unnecessarily complicated to remove and raise the shield every time a non-magical song is played. So it is raised as soon as the music starts and at the end of the evening it is removed again. Plain and simple to avoid any mistakes, like the shield being raised too late or not at all. Imagine fifty magicians in one room that had no intention of joining the seduction dance, but suddenly feel the urge to just that - no matter if they have partners available or not. You would not want to be in that room, believe me."

She remembered her own reaction to the magical music. "No, I probably wouldn't."

The first notes of the song started and Vran'el listened attentively and smiled when he recognised it. "Ah yes, that is a nice and easy one. Take my hand. Move your left foot forwards like this and at the same time move your hips in a slow circle to follow the direction of your foot. No - more slowly. Like this."

Eryn watched him carry out the move elegantly and then repeated it.

"Better. Now do it again, only this time you move your left wrist in a circle as well. It is an outwards motion; use your little finger to guide the move. Yes, basically right, we will have to work on the smoothness. Practice will take care of that. Now everything at the same time: foot forward, hip and wrist circle. Not too bad. The hand a bit higher. Now I will lift our hands and you will turn to your right in a circle and pass through under my arm. Very good!"

When Eryn returned to her seat a few minutes later, she felt sapped, not so much from the physical exercise but from all the brain power involved.

"That looked pretty fine towards the end," Enric said and smiled at her.

She grinned. "Well, now is your chance to prove to me that amazing talent with everything that involves movement, coordination and style."

"Actually, it was coordination, style and elegance," he corrected and then looked at Vran'el. "Are you up to the challenge of making me look good on that dance floor? I gloated about my dancing skills and now she wants to see if I exaggerated."

"Enric, I doubt that whatever you do down there will make you look bad," he grinned.

Eryn huffed and watched them walk to the circle inside the shield.

"This is the first time ever I have to compete for flattery with Enric. Normally I am the one receiving it. I admit it is a bit disconcerting."

"Not jealous, are you?" Barul asked.

"No. Yes. I don't know. Oh dear, I hope he looks ridiculous when he tries to dance. Please, look ridiculous for once," she murmured and waited for the music to start.

He didn't, of course. As Vran'el had predicted, general dancing skills helped a lot when it came to learning new moves. Enric had to see the movement only once to be able to repeat it as if he had danced like this all his life.

"Damn him," she cursed. "Only once do I want to stumble across something he can't just pick up that easily and without any apparent effort. Bastard."

Kilan chuckled quietly. "Unfair, isn't it? I had that same feeling when we were in class together. He never cared a lot about his subjects or grades, but once in a while there was something he was interested in, and no matter how complicated it was, he mastered it in a matter of moments. I simply wanted to punch him. If he hadn't been so lazy most of the time, I wouldn't have dreamed of befriending him. It would have been too frustrating."

"I know what you mean," she sighed. "When we went hunting yesterday, he used this new type of spear with the throwing device they have here. And guess what? He excelled at it instantly. He had never used the bloody thing before and killed an animal on his first shot. Can you believe that? I even checked his belt afterwards to make sure I had closed it properly and he hadn't cheated."

"Makes you want to see him fail at something, anything, just to see that it is possible, doesn't it?"

"Tell me about it," she grimaced.

Kilan regarded her for a moment. "I think that is why people enjoy watching the two of you so much. For the first time after his transformation into this formidable Order lord, Enric seems vulnerable and human."

"Because of me?" She looked at him questioningly. "I hated him with all my heart, and now I am his companion. It seems to me like he has won there as well, wouldn't you say?"

"But it was not a smooth victory, not the kind we are used to from him. He actually had to fight this time, still has to. The first time people realised that not everything went according to his plans was the competition when you refused to fight him and even insulted him."

"He paid me back for that, if I may remind you. Successfully."

"That's as maybe, but that there even was a reason for him to pay you back showed that even great, powerful Lord Enric could be hampered sometimes, even if only for a short time." He grinned broadly. "When you moved out of his quarters as soon as the King had granted you the freedom to move around again, I thought that you were the answer to my childhood hopes of finally making him face defeat."

"Again, no permanent defeat. I was joined to him only days later," she pointed out.

"That doesn't matter, not at all. There is no way to permanently defeat him, Eryn. You need to be content with little, short-lived victories. Enjoy them; they are all we are ever going to get in his case," Kilan shrugged.

She looked at him in dismay. That was not a very promising prospect. She returned her gaze back to Enric on the dance floor, moving elegantly and in perfect harmony with Vran'el. No way to permanently defeat him. A challenge, she thought. But probably not one she was supposed to accept, was she?

CHAPTER 27

The Test

Eryn pulled the blanket up to her collarbone when she saw the three figures standing in the doorway to her bedroom. Enric, Vran'el and a girl of no more than four years were outlined in the light.

"What are you doing here?" she moaned. "Do you people here have no sense of decorum at all? This is a private room! Really now! Out of here, at once!"

Vran'el rolled his eyes and ignored her command by instead stepping closer.

"Good morning to you, too, sweetness. Obal," he turned to the girl at his side who stared at Eryn with big, almost black eyes, "this is your aunt Eryn. Do not mind her lack of manners - that is foreigners for you, darling."

"Lack of manners!" Eryn hissed. "Says the man who stands in my bed chamber while I lie naked in bed! Enric? Where is that cloying possessiveness of yours when I need it?"

Vran'el chuckled. "Obviously inactive when there is no cause for worries. Even if you were not family, you are still the wrong sex, sweetness. Now get out of bed and show me what other terrible clothes you have brought from your home. I need to see what I am dealing with here."

"Surely not while you are standing there! Out, out, out!" she cried.

Enric shook his head. "How is it possible that you have no problems whatsoever undressing in front of your healer colleagues at home, but make such a fuss here with your cousin?"

"At home it is in a professional context, this is private. I don't undress in front of other people at home, either! Not counting you, of course."

Vran'el turned to Enric. "The chest over there against the wall, is that where she keeps her clothes?"

Enric nodded and then looked down at the little girl beside him who still stared at Eryn wide-eyed. He crouched down next to her and his voice was soft when he asked her, "Obal, would you like something to eat while we wait for Eryn to get out of bed?"

The girl nodded silently and gingerly took the hand he held out to her to let herself be led back to the main room.

"Yes, there are a few things that do not look that bad. Here, put that on. I want to see what it looks like. The cut looks alright." He flung a blue tunic onto the bed and turned back to the chest.

Eryn hastily slipped into it and jumped out of the bed to grab a nearby pair of trousers and put them on.

Vran'el turned back to her and looked at her with one eyebrow raised critically.

"Good cut, suits you. Not as flowy and female as our fashion, but that seems not really your style anyway, does it? But it accentuates the right areas of your body. Despite looking like you are wearing a man's outfit you are still discernible as a woman. Enric is right, we will keep the cut and work with the fabrics here instead. Now try on that dress you refused to wear yesterday evening."

She sighed in defeat. It seemed the two men had been discussing her clothes issues before surprising her in what she had until now considered a private room. She went to the chair over which she had thrown the dress yesterday and slipped into it.

"Take off the tunic first, you idiot!" Vran'el growled, clearly reaching the end of his patience. "I will turn around to accommodate that unwarranted bashfulness of yours and count to ten. When I turn around you had better be wearing that dress properly."

He turned and commenced counting while Eryn quickly got out of both pieces of clothing and then slipped on the dress again and pulled it down over her thighs just as he turned back to her. He pursed his lips and came closer to take in the full view of her.

"Turn," he instructed and described a circle with his index finger.

She obeyed grudgingly.

"Yes, I see why this would not be to your liking. Not bold enough. The colours are a bit too vibrant for you. Yellow and bright red? I think not. Whatever made you think that these colours would suit you? You need rich, dark colours. Now get dressed in whatever you want to wear today. I will select a few items from that chest of yours to take to the tailor."

"Bully," she muttered but changed back into the tunic he had thrown to her before.

"Stop complaining and have breakfast so we can leave in a timely fashion. I find it incredible how long you stay in bed."

"I had a long night yesterday. I am not exactly used to staying up that late every evening. How do you manage with so little sleep?"

He turned to her and shook his head. "Well, we usually lie down after lunch for an hour or two until the hottest part of the day has passed."

She stared at him. "You do? I never saw anybody doing that! And I have spent three days with local people - I would have noticed if they had disappeared for a nap."

"That is because when there is a very good reason to stay awake, we can do without lying down for a day or two. But usually we avoid staying awake. As you are family now, you will see that we will not be letting your presence stop us from sleeping after lunch anymore. And there will of course always be a bed ready for yourself as well. Now go and eat something so that we can leave." He motioned for her to hurry and turned back to her chest of clothes.

She glared a last annoyed look at his back before walking out into the main room, where Enric and the little girl were sitting on cushions on the floor, a plate of fruit between them. The girl had just bitten off a corner of a yellow piece and held the rest in front of Enric's mouth, giggling when he snatched it out of her small hand with a growling sound.

Eryn stared at the pair of them, disconcerted by the scene. He seemed perfectly at ease with the child, bathing in the admiration he received and obviously enjoying the girl's company. He was aware that she had no intention of having children, wasn't he? She had been clear enough about that. Well, it had been implied, at least. Why then did the sight of the two of them make her that nervous? Maybe he was just enjoying playing the genial uncle for a short while and would be more than happy to get rid of her then.

"Is that my breakfast the two of you are gobbling up?" she asked lightly and joined them. She smiled at the girl. "Hello Obal. That is a pretty dress you are wearing. Did your father help you pick it?"

The girl looked up at her and nodded slowly before returning her attention to Enric and their little food sharing game.

Eryn shrugged. Engaging children had never been her forte, so being ignored by the girl was the lesser evil. As a healer she'd had to deal with some very unpleasant specimens in the past, some of them throwing things at her, spitting, howling, kicking and otherwise turning out to be true nuisances. Being merely ignored for a change was a relief. She snatched a piece of fruit for herself from the plate, earning a disbelieving look from Obal.

"Alright," Eryn murmured and rose. "I am getting myself another plate. Enjoy my breakfast, don't even think of sharing it with me. You are very welcome," she murmured and went to fetch more pieces of fruit from the kitchen.

When she returned with another plate a few minutes later, Vran'el had joined his daughter and Enric, a small heap of her clothes next to him on the cushions.

"Eryn! What have you been up to? Hurry, I want to leave soon," he frowned.

"If your daughter hadn't stolen my breakfast, I would be ready to go now," she shot back.

"Did she? Really?" he asked and rolled his eyes. "Let me guess: she overpowered you."

"Buffoon," Eryn murmured.

"Buffoon," Obal repeated with a broad grin.

"Eryn!" Enric scowled. "That is not an appropriate way of expressing yourself in the presence of a child. Watch your language."

"That is going to be quite a challenge. Her father is taking me to the tailor, after all," she sighed.

"Obal will stay with me while you take care of that. I can hardly risk her hearing the profanities you will surely let loose there," Enric remarked acerbically.

Eryn arched her eyebrows. Enric had volunteered to babysit the girl? Did he even know how to take care of an infant? She looked at Vran'el who did not at all seem to be burdened by such concerns and just smiled at his daughter who had got to her feet and carefully touched her fingers to Enric's blonde hair and then to her own to see if the strange colour felt any different.

"Let's go, then," she sighed, eager to escape that uncomfortably homely scene with Enric and the child. She stuck a few more pieces of fruit into her mouth and then rose.

"Very elegant, cousin," Vran'el commented when a thin trickle of juice ran down the corner of her mouth. "You are no good influence on my daughter, I must say."

She shrugged. "I have heard that before. Just tell her to do the exact opposite of whatever she sees me doing, and you should be on safe ground."

"It is a good thing she will spend some time with Enric, or I would have a hard time convincing her that there are not only barbarians over the other side of the sea."

"Are you saying I am a barbarian?" Eryn growled. "Say that again and I will show you how we barbarians deal with people who insult us. They trained me in sword fighting, you know."

He sniffed haughtily. "A lot of good that does you. They should have trained you in diplomacy and manners instead."

Enric shook his head when the bickering between them went on until the door had closed behind them and he was alone with Obal. He smiled down at her.

"How would you like to try on some of your aunt Eryn's clothes, little one?"

The girl beamed up at him and nodded enthusiastically.

*　*　*

"No." Vran'el was standing broad-legged with his arms folded determinedly. He shook his head. "No, and that one neither. Seriously? Have you looked at yourself in the mirror? You are too pale for these colours, that sunless place you call your home does

340

nothing for your complexion. These colours make you look like a walking corpse."

"Certainly not! I happen to like that colour!"

"Then you had better get used to liking it from a distance from now on. Here, these are what you *should* be looking at." He took a sample of fabric in dark green and gold and held it in front of her. "See? That makes your eyes look darker and the gold gives that skin of yours a warm glow."

She had to admit that it did. "Alright," she muttered in defeat. "What about that one? The dark blue with the white pattern?"

"No. White is not your friend, my dear girl. Neither is that light orange you are ogling presently. Stick to the dark colours, just as I told you. If I catch you ordering anything bright, I will personally soil it with the first indelible matter I manage to lay my hands on. Wine, probably. Though not the good stuff my father buys - it is too expensive to waste on your fashion blindness. Come over here. Dark red with a touch of black, purple with streaks of brown and that dark brown one. No, the other one. Yes, exactly! It is almost the precise colour of your eyes. These are your choices."

He motioned for the tailor who had been standing in one corner patiently, waiting for Vran'el to finish selecting his fabrics. It seemed people here were used to his taking command. A discussion ensued between them in the course of which Vran'el presented the tunics he had brought along and gave precise instructions as to the clothes he wanted made.

"Now, that went reasonably well, I would say," he said with obvious satisfaction when they left the shop about half an hour later.

"You selected, decided and ordered everything," she complained. "I wonder why you even brought me along. You discarded everything I said anyway!"

"Of course. Nothing you said made any sense, after all. But if I do not bring you along, how are you to learn anything? You are a big girl - you should really be able to pick out the right colours for yourself at your age," he said earnestly. "Come on, we deserve a nice cup of tea now. That was hard work. Have you seen those large tents on the squares and broader streets? These are teahouses. In the evenings the tents are removed as soon as the sun has set. I think you saw that yesterday evening, did you not?"

She nodded and followed him to one of the tents that shaded several cushioned sitting areas on the ground. Vran'el chose one and let himself sink down. He grimaced when she plopped down next to him.

"What now?"

"Your complete lack of grace never ceases to amaze me. Up you get again. We will have to get you practise that. You will be in contact with a lot of important people. That is not how you ought to sit down in their presence."

Vran'el rose with her. "The easiest way is to cross your feet before you let yourself sink down. Like this. Now you try it. No, you need to lean forward at little more. Watch me - I will show you again. You see? That looks a lot less like dropping a sack of stones and more like an actual person sitting down."

"Thank you so much," she muttered. "That was the easiest way. Which other ones are there?"

"Well, there is always the option of looking for a man to hold your hand while you sit down. Though I greatly suspect that this is not the impression of daintiness and petiteness you would wish to make on others."

"You suspect rightly. I will stick to the crossed feet. Belkim mentioned that little trick to me on our second evening here at the banquet."

"Yes, father told me that he sat next to you. How did you like him?"

"Well enough. Friendly man. He enquired about your daughter. Why? Am I not supposed to like him because he is from the wrong House?" she frowned.

"No, that is alright. Neither House Aren nor House Vel'kim are currently allied with House Turbar, but neither is there any enmity between them. You may thus safely admit to liking him," he replied.

"So glad to hear it. Nobody would want me liking the wrong people, would they?"

"Sarcasm is not an attractive quality, dear cousin," Vran'el scolded her.

"For your own sake I hope that is not true," she smirked.

"Well, just try to avoid getting friendly with members of House Roal, will you? Both our Houses have limited their contact with that House to the required minimum. There was a little incident with a case of fraud they tried to pin on us some time ago."

"House Roal," she murmured. "Alright, I'll try to remember that."

"Please do. It might please you to annoy Malriel by fraternising with them, but it would also reflect badly on my family, so please show some restraint here."

"I told you I will, don't worry. Displeasing others is not the main force that drives me, you know," she retorted. "I am a healer, after all. We are used to trying to make others feel better every now and then."

"You may be a healer by profession, my sweetness, but surely not by disposition."

"What is that supposed to mean? I am an able healer, even though I might not possess all the knowledge you teach your healers here. Yet."

"I did not say that you are a poor healer. I just said that your abilities and talents surely lie in a different area. There are certain character traits that usually are associated with healers, and you do not demonstrate many of those. But if you do not believe me, we can ask my father to arrange an aptitude measurement for you. It is normally done when people are rather younger than you are now, but I do not see why we cannot do it anyway," he said and gave her a challenging look.

"An aptitude measurement? How is that supposed to work?" she asked with a frown.

"It is a series of questions to answer and tasks to solve. Then the information is analysed by an expert, following which you receive an analysis of where your abilities and talents lie. It is helpful for young people who have difficulties deciding which direction to take, what purpose to give their life. The test results may give them an idea of what they are good at, what they might be interested in," he explained.

"And your father could arrange that for me? Not that I have any doubt whatsoever where my talents lie, mind you," she assured him. "But I would be interested in the procedure as such."

"Sure. Father can take the test with you, though he has to send the papers to House Arbil to have them analysed. They specialise in these matters. Great scholars, Arbil people."

"So somebody of Ram'an's family will do the analysis? I am not sure I am too comfortable with that. Why can't Valrad do it?" she frowned.

"Because it requires a bit more knowledge in this particular field than my father possesses. So, do you want to do it now or not? Not afraid of finding out that you are not really suited for the healing profession, are you?" he teased her.

"No, of course not! Alright, I'll do it."

"Good." Vran'el lifted a hand to summon a server, ordered a small pot of tea and asked for a piece of paper and a pen. He quickly scribbled a few lines and gave the message to the server with the instruction to have it delivered to House Vel'kim.

"I asked father to prepare the test for the afternoon. Enric will be at the senate anyway, so you have enough time for it today. It takes about two and a half hours."

"But I wanted to have a look at a few more books today," she complained.

"There is more than enough time for that tomorrow. The books will not run away. And judging from what I have seen after your last visit to my father's library, there cannot be that many left that you have not looked at yet," he discarded her objection.

They drank their tea and then Vran'el paid and stood up. "Come, let us return and see how Enric and Obal are getting along. And there is still the little matter of your having to cook lunch for me."

* * *

When Eryn returned to the main room with a steaming bowl, the two men and the girl were involved in what looked like a game of

343

balance. They stacked small wooden pieces onto each other to build a wobbly looking tower, careful not to let the structure collapse due to a careless movement or inexpertly placed piece. Obal giggled and clapped her hands when the tower they had erected finally did collapse.

"That is her favourite part," Vran'el smiled affectionately and pinched his daughter's cheek. "She is not yet fully aware of the game's real purpose, namely *not* to let it collapse. Or she has decided to ignore that for her own pleasure."

"Good timing - the food is ready," Eryn announced. "Enric, would you fetch the bowls and sticks from the kitchen?"

Her companion went obediently and returned with them a moment later.

"Well, cousin, let us see what you are about to bestow on us, shall we? It does not smell halfway bad, I have to admit," Vran'el commented.

"I used vegetables that looked and smelled similar to what I know from home, so I can't guarantee that they have been prepared the usual way. But if not, consider it artistic freedom," she shrugged.

She filled four bowls and then leaned back to observe how Vran'el judged her cooking skills. He took a bowl in his hand and took a careful bite, chewed it while savouring, then nodded slowly.

"You are herewith exempted from the cooking lessons, sweetness. I am pleasantly surprised at your cooking skills, though it pains me to say so."

"Sweetness," Obal crowed out and grinned widely while chewing a piece of vegetable.

"Obal, we do not like to see what is going on inside your mouth while you are eating. Close your lips while you are chewing, will you?" Vran'el reprimanded the girl in a mild tone.

Enric nodded at his own bowl. "I like it, very much. Maybe we should do some cooking at home every now and then; it's something I find a very relaxing pastime."

She smirked. "The servants will think we have gone completely loopy and will spread the news throughout the city: high and mighty Lord Enric has finally lost it."

He raised his eyebrows. "If binding myself to you hasn't made people think that already, a bit of cooking won't change a lot, I would say."

"Charming," she muttered.

"Vran'el has told me about your plans for the afternoon. Are you sure you want to take this test? You might not be too pleased with the outcome from what your cousin thinks," he warned her.

She waved him off. "Nonsense. I have been a healer all my adult life, I imagine the test won't reveal that I am actually a born warrior or a boat builder."

"Nonsense!" exclaimed the girl in obvious pleasure.

344

Eryn looked down at her. "That child surely does have at a talent for identifying the most significant word in a sentence, doesn't she?"

"Indeed. That is why I try to keep her away from profanities and curse words. They tend to stick. And if she repeats them back to Intrea, I will be in trouble. Again," Vran'el looked downbeat and then turned to Enric. "Will you come to my home after your meeting at the senate? I will prepare some of the meat from our hunting trip."

"I would like that very much, thank you," Enric nodded.

A thought occurred to Eryn. "Where is Urban? Did she behave with Obal? We have never tried to test how she reacts to small children. They are the ideal size of prey for her, after all."

"What a nice way of putting it," Vran'el growled at her. "But Enric took good care of this. When we arrived, he raised a shield around Obal. Your cat was friendly, though now she is hiding somewhere as my daughter's squeals of delight seem to have overwhelmed her sensitive feline ears."

"So I can bring Urban along with us to the Vel'kim residence today? Or do you think that is too risky?"

"No, bring her, by all means. I seem to be the only one uneasy around her," Vran'el sighed. "We will just not leave the two of them unsupervised."

"So, these tests. You said they are to be analysed at House Arbil?" Enric returned to the small detail that annoyed him slightly.

"Yes, that they are," Vran'el nodded in sympathy. "I can see why this is not to your liking, but they have devised the test and keep refining it, so it does make sense for them to analyse it as well. There will be a meeting between Eryn and whoever did the analysis, as there is some explaining to be done, especially as Eryn is not familiar with the test at all."

"Why do I get the feeling that this meeting will turn out to be with Ram'an?" Enric said testily.

"Considering his interest in her, that is a valid suspicion, I am afraid. But if it makes you feel better, we can ask him to come to our house instead of sending Eryn to his residence."

"Good," Enric nodded. "I don't want them being left alone."

"That is not really possible, actually," Vran'el shook his head. "It is a confidential conversation, as talking about one's personal abilities and character traits is not something you should have to do with witnesses around. But we can make sure there is no more than a door between them and us."

"Relax, you don't even know if Ram'an himself will come," Eryn sighed.

"I strongly suspect he will," Enric said grimly. "When I saw the two of you dancing last night, it was pretty obvious that he is more interested in you than ever. Be very careful around him. I don't have a good feeling about this. About him."

* * *

Eryn leaned back exhaustedly and gratefully accepted a cool glass of fruit juice from her uncle.

"Do you not want to come inside and sit there?" Valrad asked and looked down at her sitting in the grass, leaning against a tree.

"No, thank you. I like it here. I have been missing nature since I was taken to the city, so I enjoy spending some time around trees and flowers. Enric has a garden being constructed at home right now, but it will still take a few months to resemble a peaceful space. So I'm taking advantage of every bit of green I stumble across."

"As you wish," he smiled and let himself sink down next to her. "I have sent your test over to House Arbil. They will contact us when they are through with it. How did you find it?"

"I am not entirely sure. Some of the tasks seemed rather strange, to be honest. Building a house with bits of paper? I don't really see the sense in that. Or in which order I would save people from drowning if I came across a situation like that. And all these questions about how I think others perceive me... I mean, how am I to know that? It depends who you are asking, I would say. My assistant very probably sees me as a tyrant and the bane of his life, but my healers seem to like me."

"Your assistant?" Valrad frowned. "So you do not get along with this man you brought along, Kilan, was it?"

"What? No, not him. I have another person at home who works with me in the healers' building. We were assigned to each other as some sort of punishment."

"You got punished by being given an assistant? What an unusual way of disciplining somebody," he commented.

"No, the punishment was not giving me an assistant as such, just the choice of that particular person. We were never particularly fond of each other due to a few minor incidents when we were made to train sword fighting together. When I asked for an assistant, my superior chose him to take revenge for a little... thing I had done to him earlier. And after reading through my new assistant's file I had a pretty good idea what *he* was being punished for. He has a history of insolence and disobedience. So the idea behind it was to more or less let me taste my own medicine."

"A mean but effective way of teaching you leadership skills, I would think," Valrad smirked.

"Yes, I agree with *mean*. I don't know about effective," she rolled her eyes and took a sip from her juice.

"How have things worked out with your assistant so far, then?"

"Better now, I have to admit. Though it took a few minor altercations to get there. I am curious to hear how he is taking to accepting orders from a young man six years his junior. It might wound his pride even more than taking orders from me did," she grinned.

They both looked up when a streak of brown darted out the archway that led to the main room. Urban ducked behind a bush with an uneasy look behind. She then lay eyes on Eryn and ran over to her to rub against her shoulder.

"My, my, that little girl seems to get to you, eh?" she laughed and petted the cat's silky fur.

Only moments later, Vran'el and Obal appeared on the terrace and Urban flattened herself on the grass instantly.

"It seems my monster is scared of yours," Eryn called up to her cousin.

"Yes, I have to admit that Obal was none too gentle with your cat. But I am impressed that your animal runs away rather than hurts her. I doubt it would extend that same courtesy to me, though," he added with a sideways glance at the cat crouching next to Eryn's outstretched legs.

"Urban!" Obal exclaimed and made to run down the terrace steps, but Vran'el held her back.

"No, my girl, that is enough for today. Urban needs some time to recover from your attentions. And your mother should be here any moment to pick you up, so let us get you cleaned up before, shall we?"

The look of dismay on Obal's face communicated clearly what she thought about being cleaned up, but she complied reluctantly and let herself be led back inside by her father.

Eryn frowned. "There is one thing I wanted to ask you. I hope you don't find it too intrusive a question. Just tell me if you don't want to talk about it. Why are Vran'el and Pe'tala members of House Vel'kim? I thought children are usually considered members of the maternal House?"

Valrad sighed. "True, that usually is the case. But you have of course noticed that I do not live with a companion. I was joined with a young woman many years ago. Our mothers had arranged it. We were both not particularly in love with each other, but neither did we dislike each other so we agreed, as we were not involved with anybody else at that time. She ran away with a trader thirteen years later. The commitment was dissolved after that, and with her actions her House no longer had any legal claim to her offspring. They thus became members of my House."

Eryn swallowed. "I am sorry."

"Do not be," he shrugged. "We were never hugely attached to each other, and from a purely political point of view it was not a bad thing to happen for House Vel'kim. Your father and I had no sisters, you see. So our line of the family would have had to give up the leading role after I retire as Head of House. But now that I have both a son and a daughter in my House, one will take over the lead and the other will provide more offspring for the line to continue."

He smiled at her shocked expression. "That must all seem very cold and calculating to you, my dear. But I want to assure you that my companionship had none of the passion and affection your own all but radiates. It was more like a business arrangement. After Ved'al took you away, I was only glad that she left me our children. It saved me from going after her and taking them back. It was not easy for the children, though. Both of them would have needed their mother. Vran'el managed to deal with it more easily than Pe'tala, who grew angry and bitter for quite some time."

And still doesn't seem to have got over it completely, Eryn thought but decided not to put words to that.

"Talking about children," Valrad then said, "how about yourself? I know you have not been together with Enric for very long, but I assume you are going to have some soon?"

She shivered. "No, not anytime soon. There is so much I still want to do - a child would only be in the way. And I don't really see myself in the role of a mother."

"You are not afraid of being too much like your own mother, are you?" her uncle enquired mildly and smiled understandingly at her dark look. "You should not be. There might be certain traces of Aren temper in you, but that does not mean that you cannot be a loving and affectionate mother. No - do not look at me like that. Just because you did not get off to a good start with Malriel does not mean that you need to push everything in connection with House Aren away from you. Enric surely wants children, does he not? Considering his age, probably rather sooner than later."

She thought about the way he had been interacting with Vran'el's daughter and frowned. "I don't know. And I don't really care. He didn't bother to clarify his wish to be a parent with me before we were made to join, so he'll have to live with the consequences now, won't he?" she replied, with trademark stubbornness. "If he wanted children, he should have made sure to fall in love with a woman who is willing to accommodate him over children. And he has never mentioned having children, so I assume it is not as urgent as you seem to believe."

Valrad only sighed and shook his head slowly. "I see that this is not a topic you wish to discuss for the time being. Though I feel I need to warn you that Malriel will address it sooner or later, considering that you are the only heiress to her House and are thus expected to provide for another generation."

Eryn smiled thinly. "Imagine that. And yet I am so very indifferent to whatever her concerns may be in that."

* * *

Eryn looked up from the books in her uncle's library when she heard Valrad use her name. "Eryn? Ram'an is here. He has had a look at your test results and thought you might want to hear about them."

She lifted both eyebrows in surprise. "Has he now? How very considerate. That was very fast, wasn't it? You only sent the test to him a mere two hours ago, didn't you?"

"Indeed. It seems either he was particularly interested in them himself or is eager to accommodate you," Valrad frowned, clearly none too thrilled about either option. "Do you want to discuss things with him in here? It is private enough, and I am sure it will be interesting for you to hear."

"Fine, by all means," she nodded.

She had just started removing books from the chairs around the desk when Ram'an entered and smiled at the chaos she had caused.

"Eryn," he said warmly and took both her hands in his to pull her close enough to kiss her cheeks. "I see you are on the hunt for more knowledge. I dare say a healer's private library must equal a treasure chamber for you."

She laughed. "Yes, I suppose you could put it like that. I keep sending more and more books to be copied; I have probably spent a fortune already. But as long as Enric doesn't complain and keeps paying, I won't stop."

Ram'an's smile seemed a little more strained at the mention of Enric.

"You will be keeping the new books at the healers' place, I assume? There cannot be a lot of space left in those quarters of yours at the Palace."

"That's no longer a problem. Enric has bought two houses, and now I have a proper study with a lot of currently empty shelves that are all but screaming to be filled. But I will still keep a few of them close by at my place of work," she explained.

"Two houses?" Ram'an asked with a look of surprise.

"Yes, he wanted a garden for the cat and went on to buy two houses with a part of the street between them. A garden in the city is quite a novel concept in Anyueel, if you remember the houses there. We have several patches of green, but they are accessible for the public and not only for private use. I think the Palace is pretty much the only building in Anyueel that has a few small gardens. Here a garden is virtually standard, at least in the residences I have seen so far."

He nodded. "Yes, it is a blatant demonstration of wealth, to be honest. Maintaining a large garden in this climate requires quite some resources."

She smirked. "I imagined as much. Do you have an ostentatiously huge garden yourself or is your family above such petty attempts at impressing others?"

"I am afraid we are not. The gardens at the Arbil residence are quite extensive, I have to admit," he smiled.

She sighed in mock desperation. "It is amazing. Somehow I only manage to meet rich people here. Where are the hard-working citizens that have to earn their keep?"

"I resent the allegation that rich people do not in general work. There might be few who consider themselves above contributing their share, but these are more the exception than the rule. For my part, I have worked hard enough today already." He held up the sheets of paper she instantly recognised as her test. "Your handwriting, though charming to look at, is clearly not intended for lovers of uncomplicated reading material."

She shrugged. "I aim to express my uniqueness through any channel available."

"That would not have been necessary. Your results were unique enough."

"Were they? Then sit down with me and tell me about them." She motioned to one of the chairs she had just freed from a stack of books.

Valrad came in and looked for some space to put down the tray with drinks he held in his hands.

"Clear away some of the books on the desk for me, will you?" he instructed his niece and set down his tray once she had complied with this request. He accepted their thanks and gave Ram'an a thoughtful look before he retreated from the study again.

Eryn leaned forward, bracing her elbows on her knees. "Tell me that I was born to be a healer."

He furrowed his eyebrows before slowly shaking his head. "I am afraid I cannot go along with that, my dear. This is obviously not something you want to hear, but let me explain the principles of the test to you first."

Damn, she thought, and leaned back, setting her face in a scowl. Vran'el had been right, then. How unexpected. And unpleasant.

"This test aims to determine several dimensions of a person: abilities and talents, personality, and preferred methods of learning or otherwise acquiring knowledge and insights. The combination of these three indicates the areas where your greatest potentials lie. However, the test also allows for the chance of deliberate manipulation by the test subject. The first sheet shows that you tried to influence the test to show the result you wanted to see - namely, you attempted to present yourself as a healer as well as you could. The results of the other parts, however, contradict many of your earlier answers and thus indicate that you tried to concoct the results to fit the picture you have of yourself. Or at least, the one you wish to convey."

She folded her arms in dismay at having been unmasked.

"Well, what is the outcome, then?"

"That you have extraordinary abilities when it comes to the research and generation of new knowledge, do not shy away from taking risks, and that you value your independence very highly," he explained.

"I don't see how this contradicts a vocation as a healer, apart from perhaps the willingness to take risks," she replied in a slightly sulky voice.

"Then let me give you a short overview of the results we consider typical for what you would call a born healer." He consulted the sheets in his hands before he continued. "A high level of empathy and sensitivity, though you scored only average. Then we have patience, where you even scored below average. Interest in the field of medicine - the human body and science - however, is very high. Higher than work as a healer with a certain degree of routine will manage to satisfy in the long run."

"Are you telling me that I will soon become bored with healing?" she asked, incredulous.

"That is not very likely now that you have discovered a new, abundant source of knowledge by coming here," Ram'an shook his head. "But if you were forced to reduce your efforts to healing people without the chance of learning anything new, I predict that you would be frustrated soon enough."

She frowned. "Isn't that a characteristic for anybody who wants to be good at what they do? Realising where one's limits are and the willingness to push them?"

"There are two aspects to that, Eryn. There is the ability to learn and apply what you have learned, and then there is the drive to find out new things, constantly develop yourself and your field, avoid stagnation, discover what nobody before you has detected. While both are very valuable paths for a society and need to be promoted, none is more valuable or important than the other. The first ensures that the things that have worked in the past continue to be applied in the future to the benefit of all. There is no need to reinvent the things we know because we make use of them and pass them on to future generations and thus avoid forgetting them again. Yet this is not enough. Progress, improvement and development are what drives a society on, what brings it forward. Healing is one of the disciplines that requires both talents: one to learn, be patient and constantly apply what you have learned, the other to recognise new things when you see them, actively look for them in order to solve unanswered questions and then share that knowledge with others."

"But I am doing all of that, aren't I?" she asked. There was a slightly pleading undertone to her question. "I had to find out so many things on my own when my father died, and I had to learn how to apply them correctly. And now I am using them regularly and teaching others to do so."

"Yes, my dear, though not out of choice but out of necessity, as there is nobody else but yourself to take on all these tasks. This test does not describe your life the way it is, but indicates where your true strengths lie. Your strengths, Eryn, are clearly not in the mere everyday application of knowledge, but in experimenting and generating new insights." He took her hands in his, sighing at her obvious dissatisfaction. "These results are fabulous ones, so do not be dismayed by them just because they are not what you expected and hoped for. You have very high scores in intelligence, the ability to take in and understand things. What's more, you are very creative, not in the artistic sense, but when it comes to applying known methodologies in a new way. This ability is not only limited to the field of healing, even though you have probably not had that many opportunities to apply them in other disciplines yet. But think back - have there never been any surprises in the past when you have shown unexpected aptitude in areas other than healing? Or have you never managed to deploy knowledge acquired in a different context in the field of healing without anybody pointing it out to you?" he enquired.

She thought hard while fixing her gaze on the floor. Yes, there had been situations like that. Such as when she had discovered the new barrier that had shocked the magicians back home so much. And then she had more or less stumbled across a method of defeating her own barrier. She had started to use shielding, which had been taught to her as a defensive skill, in medical contexts to stem the flow of blood. Then there was the matter of finding out that mirrors reflected magical bolts to a certain degree.

"I have, yes," she nodded slowly and looked back up in his face. "Both. But my discoveries were more often a matter chance than not."

"This does not matter. That you cannot always see what made you act the way you did to accomplish your achievements does not mean that it had nothing to do with your abilities. Sometimes the way we act unconsciously reflects our personality and skills and thus provides outcomes others would never have managed to reach under the same circumstances," he smiled reassuringly.

"So what exactly does this mean for me? That I should give up healing and instead perform random experiments all day long?" she frowned.

Ram'an laughed. "No, hardly. It means no more than what you decide for it to mean, my dear. You can decide to continue your life and profession the way you have so far, to increase your medical knowledge and pass it on. Another choice would be to broaden your field, add new areas of interest whenever you happen across them instead of discarding them because they are not obviously related to the field of healing. Some of the greatest discoveries were made when somebody worked out that knowledge from one discipline can be applied to another one with outstanding results," he pointed out, which made her once again think of how she had used shielding techniques for medical purposes. Or how she had used healing skills as a means of harming another person; unbidden thoughts welled up and she saw Krion's face and broken arms before her.

"Such as shielding," she murmured.

"Yes, indeed. Having been trained in combat techniques, I assume you have learned a lot about how to use a shield to protect yourself. Here we mainly use them for medical purposes. But shielding clearly is a skill that is important in at least two very different areas." He smiled and his hair, brows, lashes and even the emerging stubble of a beard on his cheeks and chin turned blonde. "Or even for reasons of mere vanity."

Eryn laughed at the unexpected effect the changed colour had on his whole appearance. It looked wrong - ridiculous even. His eyes were too dark, and so was his skin.

"You know, I think that's not exactly your style," she chuckled. "It simply doesn't go with the rest of you."

"I imagined it would not," he smiled and transformed it back to the dark brown bordering on black. "Pity though, it seems to be what you prefer."

She stared at him for a moment, then tugged her hands from his grip and stood up to increase the distance between them. He had managed to turn a casual and relaxed situation into an awkward one with a single sentence.

"I don't like Enric merely because of his hair colour," she said stiffly. "And I am not comfortable with your saying things like that to me."

He got up as well. "I apologise, Eryn. It was a foolish thing to say and I regret that my words made you uneasy. You know that I like you very much, do you not? I would like to be your friend. Sometimes I seem to overstep your boundaries, though."

She considered him. Was she oversensitive? Had it been no more than a casual remark, a flirty joke on his side? Did Enric's jealousy influence her own perception enough to make her suspicious without reason?

Sighing she shook her head. "It's alright. I am probably a little touchy right now."

"Understandable enough," he said and took a sip from one of the glasses on the desk. "You have had quite a lot to deal with in these last few days. First discovering your mother to be alive when you thought her dead, and then the tension that arose between the two of you. But it is good to see that you seem to be getting along so well with your father's family. So, there is at least something here for you to remember fondly, now that I have managed to put my foot in it with you again."

She blinked. "You just said that last bit to make me reassure you that everything is alright and that you haven't offended me, didn't you?"

He grinned. "I admit I did. Does it work?"

She laughed and nodded. "Yes, I will accommodate you as you took the trouble of analysing my test in such a short time and coming here to talk to me about it. Ram'an, even if it wasn't for

House Vel'kim, I will still have you to remember fondly when I leave here again."

"Thank you," he nodded. "That does put my mind at ease. Will you prove to me that these are not just words to console me and have lunch with me tomorrow at the Arbil residence?"

She looked unhappy. "I don't think this is a good idea. Enric found out about our little disagreement before you left Anyueel and would not be very pleased at the thought of me visiting you at your place."

He nodded slowly. "I see. That is unfortunate. Will you instead agree to meeting me in the afternoon at a teahouse? He cannot object to that - it is a public place, after all. You may even bring along one or both of your guards, if you do not feel safe alone with me."

Groaning, she sat down again. "Don't be like that! It's not that I am afraid of being alone with you. I just have to take Enric's feelings into consideration as well. He is here in an official capacity, and I don't want to make his task any harder than necessary by diverting his attention like this. And there is the matter of the Houses wanting to negotiate possible trade agreements with him later, so his resentment towards you might have already reduced your chances of advantageous contracts."

"You are right, he is here in an official function. And thus he will also appreciate that our Houses are allied and that our meeting in public for a pot of tea is natural enough, especially as people here know that we know each other from my visit in Anyueel. Avoiding me would be considered suspicious and hardly a help to either House Aren or my own."

She released a long breath. "So no matter if I meet with you or not, there is a chance that I might cause harm?"

"Exactly. So why not just chose the path that is in accordance with your own preferences?" He crouched down in front of her chair. "Would you like to have a cup of tea with me, Eryn?"

She looked at him and then nodded slowly. "Yes, let's have a cup of tea, then." It was much the better alternative than taking lunch with him at his residence, she mused. "I will meet you tomorrow at the large square near the ambassadorial residence after the nap I learned I am supposed to take after lunch."

He smiled and got to his feet. "Excellent. Then I will see you tomorrow. Have a nice evening, my dear."

He kissed her cheeks again and then left.

She sighed, dreading the expression on Vran'el's face when she had to tell him that she was, indeed, not the born healer she had considered herself to be. Brilliant.

CHAPTER 28

Commitment Bond

Eryn saw the familiar slim figure of Ram'an leaning against a fountain when she arrived and waved to attract his attention. He smiled when he noticed her and pushed away from the basin to walk towards her. Just as the day before, he took both her hands to pull her close and kiss her cheeks.

"Eryn, I am glad you came. Did you have a restful noon?" he enquired.

She shook her head. "Not exactly. I am not used to lying down in the middle of the day. I was tossing and turning and couldn't sleep. That means that I will either be tired again in the evening or have a hard time getting up in the morning. Or both."

"You will probably get used to it after a while. It took me about two weeks to manage without sleeping after lunch in the Old Kingdom. Unfortunately there was then only one week left to enjoy the fruits of my ability to adapt before I came back here."

"Great prospect," she murmured and let him take her hand to lead her to a broad street and then a teahouse. "Vran'el took me to one of these yesterday after trying my patience at the tailor's. I like the concept. It is so much more comfortable, airy and open than the taverns at home. Of course you have the climate for them here, unlike us."

"I like them very much myself," Ram'an nodded and held on to her hand as she sank down on the cushions in a move that had hopefully looked as elegant as it had felt. It really was easier when somebody was holding her hand while she was sitting down, just like Vran'el had told her.

"It is nice to just stop on your way, take an extra few minutes and relax with a good cup. You need to know where to go, of course. Not all of them serve good quality beverages."

She grinned. "I assume this one meets your high expectations?"

"I would never have brought you here otherwise, my dear," he replied and sat down next to her. "Have you found some way to be content with your test results yet? I hope you have - being classified as an explorer is nothing you need to hide. Quite the opposite. We do not have many test candidates with such an explicit score for that."

"Explorer? That's what you call it?" It didn't sound bad, she had to admit; it had a ring of adventure.

"Yes. People with the ability, curiosity and wish to pursue the unknown - these are explorers, like yourself. And very much unlike most members of House Aren, you show hardly any desire for power. The only very distinctive score in that area is the wish to be in control of yourself, your need for independence."

She nodded. "I think I can live with that. The most unpleasant thing about it, I think, was admitting as much to Vran'el. He predicted that I wasn't really a healer by disposition and was very smug about being right."

"He grew up in *the* healing House in Takhan, so not believing him was a risk to begin with. He would know all about the typical character traits of a healer, having so many of them around him," Ram'an shrugged and ordered a pot of something with a complicated sounding name when a server approached them.

"How would you classify Vern? I know that is probably a bit hard to say without the test, but you have met him, maybe you have a basic idea."

He thought for a moment. "That is difficult - really difficult. In general I would say visual artist after looking at his pictures, but the combination with his intellect and interest in healing does not really fit the category. Usually artists have a fierce temper and are a slave to their impulses, and the more talented they are, the worse it is. But with a temper of this kind he would never be able to work as a healer or be patient enough to train for this challenging profession. I am a bit at a loss, I have to admit. I would love to run the test with him some time, it surely would bring some clarity."

"Have *you* ever been tested?" she then asked.

"Of course," he smiled. "As my House prides itself on being the originators, improvers and analysts, it would seem a bit strange not to take it as a member. Would you like to know what I turned out to be?"

"If it isn't too personal to ask, yes; I would be interested in hearing it."

"I am a scholar with a high score in that area, too. Not as spectacular as explorer, but not entirely unexpected in a boy with an unusually high interest in books. My brother is more the practical kind, good with plants and a problem solver. A good combination for our House, as we produce a lot of food and he is able to handle most of the things in connection with this."

"So, what is it you do? If I am to believe your claim that not all rich people here are idle, there must be something you dedicate your time to, unless you spend all your time reading books," she enquired.

356

"I have studied law, like your cousin Vran'el. I teach advanced students every now and then when they specialise in an area that has points of contact with my own. I am also considered an expert in ancient, but still valid, laws that have not been applied in a long time and are thus almost forgotten. In addition to law I have also studied history, so this is basically the background for my expertise," he explained.

"Enric is hoping to find a way to release me from my status as heiress of House Aren by gaining some insight into your local laws," she told him. "He isn't too comfortable with the prospect of Malriel ordering me back here one day to perform my duty, as it were."

"You may depend on Malriel's doing some research into the matter herself to prevent you from finding a way to avoid your obligation. The interesting thing about this situation is that if Lord Enric's efforts at negotiating were not so promising, this would probably not even be a problem. But as trade agreements tend to be a rather strong connection between two countries, this will also require a certain degree of respect for each other's laws. Your King would thus have to think it over very carefully if he wanted to stop you from coming here if summoned. He would even do well to insist on you leaving your home to come here if he wanted to avoid trouble," Ram'an explained.

"Are you telling me that Enric is just now laying the foundation for Malriel's being able to order me back here?" she groaned. "So he has basically the choice between his loyalty to me or the Kingdom?"

"Yes, it appears so," Ram'an nodded without any sign of regret or sympathy.

"How great are the chances of Malriel having another child? She is not much less than fifty, despite her efforts to appear younger. She could still conceive a child, couldn't she?" Eryn asked with little hope.

"Eryn," he said mildly and raised a brow, "do you not think she would have had another child years ago if she had intended to? Why would she do so now when you have turned out to be healthy, able and available?"

"Available? That is exactly what I am not!"

"From her point of view you are. But she will still be in command of her House for many years to come; she is a natural leader and will not give up her position for a long time yet. Who knows what will happen in the meantime? So do not worry over this for now," he advised and poured them both a cup when the server brought a steaming pot.

"Has your uncle taken you to the local healing place yet?" he asked, trying to change the topic from one that bothered her to something more pleasant.

"He hasn't, no. I have been busy with his books the last two times I visited him. But I will definitely ask him." Then she leaned forwards and picked up the cup on the low table to take a sip of something that tasted dark, complicated, silky and spicy. She looked inquisitively. "What is this? It is incredibly good."

He smiled with satisfaction. "It is a mix of plants my family grows and blends. I am glad you like it. It is considered a delicacy. The water needs to be the exact right temperature, and the mix needs to be allowed to infuse for precisely three minutes to achieve the optimum result. Otherwise the drink is either too bitter or too weak. How are you taking to the food here in general? It is rather spicier than what you are used to."

"I like the food, but I seem to have acquired a distinct dislike for meat since I accompanied Vran'el and Enric on their hunting trip. Every time I look at pieces of meat, I see dead carcasses lying on the ground before my feet. When Vran'el cooked for us yesterday evening, I simply couldn't eat it. The smell almost made me gag. Or rather the images it triggered." Her nose wrinkled in disgust at the memory. "I wonder how long it will take me to get over that."

Ram'an considered her thoughtfully for a while. "There are a number of people here in the city who have given up eating meat altogether. It is an accepted lifestyle here. In our society it is considered a more honest course of action to stop eating meat if you cannot or do not want to hunt it yourself. Most people who invite guests for dinner usually provide a meat-free alternative if they are not sure of their guests' preferences."

She stared at him. The thought of eating no more meat seemed altogether strange, outlandish, foreign. And intriguing.

"I don't even know how the human body reacts to a meat-free diet," she protested. "It could be harmful, couldn't it?"

"Then discussing this with other healers might be a sensible course of action if you are really interested in the topic. I should think that your closeness with House Vel'kim would put you right at the source for that. And I have a few acquaintances who have lived without meat for quite a while in case you want to talk to somebody who has experience with this lifestyle."

She stared into the dark, slightly greenish liquid in her cup for a while, then sighed. "I think I will have to think this over. I will talk to Valrad first and see what he says. I mean, I don't even know what to eat instead. There are only so many different vegetables, after all. It would hardly be a diet rich in variety, would it?"

Ram'an chuckled. "Yes, I remember the food in your country well enough. Calling it *diverse* would be rather flattering. But it is not just a matter of the ingredients, but how you prepare them. How you combine them and the spices you use. You can take the same ingredients and create a number of different dishes with them instead of just boiling or frying them to death then serving them next to a piece of meat. You just need to be more careful to eat more vegetables with nutrients similar to meat, from what I understand. But talk to your uncle about that, he will surely know a lot more about it than me."

"Yes, I will," she nodded and then chuckled. "Imagine if I return back home and refuse to eat meat. They will think that either I have gone completely crazy from the heat here, or that I have assumed a new foreign fashion to be different."

"Yes, imagine the consequences if you somehow unintentionally started a culinary revolution and the demand for vegetables rose immensely. This might overwhelm your whole system of supply and demand," he chuckled.

She snorted. "Hardly. There is quite a lot you can say about people at home, but that they adapt to changes easily is not one of them."

"You are a bit too harsh on them, I think," Ram'an objected. "From what I know they have accepted quite a few considerable changes only recently - like your turning out to be the first female magician after a long period without any, for example. Then they let you initiate healing services, a field entirely unknown to them."

"Yes, but turning out to be a female magician with brown hair earned me half a year of captivity, so..." She stopped abruptly and drew in a sharp breath when she realised what had just escaped her, and shut her mouth immediately.

Ram'an's gaze had become intent and his eyes had narrowed. "Indeed? Captivity. How very interesting. Do go on, will you? I would very much like to hear more about *that*."

She exhaled slowly, avoiding his eyes. "Thinking before speaking has turned out to be quite a challenge for me these days. Is there one of your scores that corresponds to it?"

He nodded. "Yes, impatience. But it is also a matter of letting your guard down. I feel honoured that you are less careful around me than you might consider prudent," he said gently, "even though I am not at all pleased about what I am hearing."

"Then I'll ask you to forget about it again," she pleaded. "Please! Spreading this about would only serve to make the situation between our countries more difficult."

Ram'an rubbed his face agitatedly. "Forget it? How can I? Knowing that you were first kept prisoner and then forcefully joined with Lord Enric is hardly something I can put aside just like that!"

She grabbed his hand and held it firmly between her palms, searching his gaze and holding it. The contact calmed him immediately and she felt his fingers close around one of her hands.

"Ram'an, I need you to listen to me very carefully: I am happy with Enric - whatever there was before. I was not happy about being kept in the city, but they didn't exactly lock me up in a dungeon cell." Though her sleeping quarters had been alarmingly close to that, she remembered. "I was free to roam the city, meet people, make friends and even heal. They had intended me to join them almost from the beginning and even taught me fighting skills, which is not exactly the usual way to treat a captive."

"But joining them was not in accordance with your wishes, or they would not have had to make you stay by force," he pointed out.

"No, it was not at first," she admitted. "My father had very distinctive views about the Order, and thus I resented the mere thought of joining them. But they didn't give up, and when my skills were advanced enough to meet with their regulations, they started negotiating with me. I wasn't forced into the Order; that would have contradicted their own rules."

"Would it now," he retorted dryly. "And yet your joining with Lord Enric was not voluntary." He lifted a finger when she opened her mouth. "I hope that you are not trying to lie to me again, Eryn. I know very well that you were made to agree somehow. Do not try to fool me, it would insult me."

She swallowed and stared at him for a few moments, then nodded. "Alright. I didn't join him voluntarily."

Even though he had claimed to have known it, his jaw muscles clenched and his grip around her fingers strengthened.

"So he made you do it. How?" Ram'an demanded, a dangerous glint in his eyes.

She shook her head. "It's not what you think. It wasn't Enric, but the King." She stopped. "I have said too much already. Please promise me that you will keep this to yourself."

He looked at her angrily. "You are really asking this of me? They kept you prisoner and then joined you with a man against your wishes! How can I keep this to myself instead of freeing you from such a situation?"

"Because I do not want to be freed, Ram'an! And I ask you to accept, no, even more, to *respect* that decision. They gave me the chance to make a difference by giving them what they didn't have before: magical healing. I feel like my life has a purpose there. What would I be doing here? I would just be one of many healers, less educated even with all these gaps in my knowledge. And then there is Enric."

"Do you love him?" Ram'an asked sharply.

"What?"

"I am asking you if you love him," he repeated slowly. "A simple question, I would have thought."

"That is... I mean... We never really... I don't see how this is any of your business!" she finally gasped and pushed his hand away.

"May I take this as a *No* or do you just have a very confusing way of expressing yourself?" he asked dryly.

"Whatever I feel for Enric, or he feels for me, is none of your concern!" She buried her fingers in her hair. "Will the two of us ever be able to spend more than an hour together without things getting awkward?"

She felt his hands on hers when he pulled them away from her head and touched them against his chest. "Eryn, I care about you. A lot. How can I be sure that you are treated well by him after all that has been done to you?"

Sighing, she noted the earnest concern in his eyes. "You may safely rely on that. He has always treated me very well, even when I punched him in the face in front of other magicians both above and below him in rank."

Ram'an lifted his brow in interest. "Indeed? Why do you not tell me more about that? Do not leave out the painful details."

She finally managed to laugh. "Surely not! I will hardly have you revelling in his humiliation! Shame on you!"

He smiled back faintly. "Why do we not call it a little consideration in exchange for my not putting about what you have told me unintentionally?"

"Alright then," she said. "I suppose telling you that story still means that I am getting off lightly." She leaned back again and told him about the apothecaries' attack, Vern's great revelation of his healing skills during the act of saving her from the King's punishment for disobedience, how Enric had taken control of her muscles and finally how she had punched him in the face and been sent to sleep in return.

Ram'an considered her for a while after she ended her story before he asked, "Where does this reluctance to punish your attackers come from? I am aware that you are a healer and that harming others is against your beliefs and your values; but we have healers here, too, and they do not normally object to justifiable death sentences." He leaned forward. "There is something else. Will you tell me about it?"

"No," she slowly shook her head. "I am sorry. I cannot."

"Alright, then I will not push you. Maybe one day."

"Yes, one day." Never, she thought. She couldn't even talk to Enric about it, had never shared it with anybody and would, she hoped, never have to.

He sighed, concerned. "That is not what your eyes are saying, my dear."

* * *

"Enric," he heard Malriel's voice at his side and turned to her with a polite smile.

"Malriel. Thank you for your support with the shipping matters today. I expect we will be continuing this discussion for quite some time yet, but I am glad to have it on the table. And you made sure that it won't be discarded lightly."

She smiled and took his arm. "It was my pleasure, Enric. I am in favour of showing you how to overcome the barrier, mind you, only if there are to be binding trading agreements. Otherwise there is little advantage and in fact more danger for us in making ourselves vulnerable to your Kingdom again."

He sighed. "You are very well aware that we are no real danger to you, I think. You know that we have no noteworthy harbours, no knowledge of either constructing or handling large cargo or battle ships."

"That I do know, of course. But you have no doubt also determined that while your Kingdom has continued training and improving combat skills, both magical and non-magical, this has not been the case here. As soon as you manage to cross the sea, you might again fancy an attempt at conquering us."

This time he laughed. "That's unlikely. It would be much more profitable for us to sell you our surplus raw materials and minerals, not to mention the manufactured goods, than to spend the gold on a war that might leave us isolated again for another few hundred years."

"Probably." She had started walking and pulled him along with her towards the exit. Enric let himself be led outside the senate building, curious to where she would take him.

"Have you been to one of our teahouses yet, Enric?" she enquired.

"No, I haven't. I have passed several of them, of course, if we are talking about the tents on the streets."

"Then let me treat you to your very first teahouse-experience."

He didn't reply to that, taking it as the demand it was intended as. She was obviously not concerned with waiting for his assent, anyway. A born leader, he thought with wry amusement. So Malriel was interested in talking to him alone, for whatever reason. He didn't mind - quite the opposite. And being seen in this woman's company would only increase his own standing. The fact that she looked so much like Eryn, almost as attractive as her, made him even more willing to accompany her than pure curiosity alone would have.

"I won't run away, even if you grip my arm less firmly," he said with a smile.

She looked up at him with brown eyes that were in shape and colour Eryn's, though not with the calculating and knowing expression lying behind them. "I know. Men do not run away from Aren women; instead they tend to run after us."

Enric laughed. "Yes, I can well believe that."

"From your own experience, I assume. I have known you for only a few days now, but I would expect that my daughter's not falling as easily for you as you might be used to was something which spiked your interest," she smiled, confident in her judgement.

"I must admit it did - there is no sense in denying it," he sighed.

"None whatsoever," she confirmed. "But let me assure you that being snapped up by a man is something we appreciate. It shows strength and determination, which is something you will need in abundance to stand your ground with an Aren woman."

362

"Yes, that, too, I have noticed," he remarked. They passed by three tents until Malriel steered him towards one she seemed to deem fit.

She caught a server's eye and pointed to three cushioned islands around the one she had chosen for herself and Enric to sit on. The server nodded once and disappeared into a building.

"Have a seat, Enric."

He did, and she gracefully sank down on the cushions next to him. He had noticed that people here did not sit opposite each other as he was used to from home, but preferred more physical closeness and frequently touching each other in non-threatening, casual ways.

The server returned with three dark red cards that he placed on each of the tables Malriel had indicated. So she had ordered some privacy, a thought which tickled him. The man then came towards them to take Malriel's order for a pot of her usual tea.

"Tell me about my daughter. How is she accommodating to life here?" Malriel asked without any detour. "And how much does she still hate me now?"

Enric pondered the second question. Telling this woman that her daughter indeed resented her was not a task to be undertaken lightly. But then she did at least not harbour any illusions in that regard.

"She is adapting well enough, I would say," he said slowly. "She very much appreciates the chance to learn new things since the availability of books for her areas of interest was limited to what she herself possessed. She is getting used to local customs quickly, especially little things such as washing her hands at the table before a meal or your ways of greeting. Other things are more difficult to adapt to, like lying down to rest after lunch or talking about sex openly."

She pursed her lips and waited for him to go on, but he didn't.

"Very diplomatic of you, Enric. Afraid of hurting my feelings, are you?"

"Why would you assume that?" he asked mildly, unperturbed at having been found out.

"Because otherwise you would have told me how well she is getting along with Ved'al's family - at least with the two men. Pe'tala is another matter, of course. You, too, are known to have got along with Vran'el very well. I am told he is teaching you cooking?"

Enric smiled, not really surprised at the wealth of information at her disposal and her decision to let him know that she had them well monitored.

"He does, yes. I lack talent in that area, I admit."

"Not Maltheá, though. She is an able cook, is she not? Or is she just refusing to learn it?"

"Vran'el has determined that her skills are sufficient so as not to require his tutoring," he answered.

"So her father taught her something useful in addition to healing. Good," she nodded. "Now tell me how likely it is that you will manage to persuade her to come to a dinner I will soon be hosting at my house."

Enric cleared his throat and looked at her pointedly. "What makes you think that I would wish to attempt such a thing after what happened last time we were invited to your residence, Malriel? I have no desire to make her suffer anything like that again. You may depend on me to fulfil my ambassadorial duties and attend whatever occasion you wish to invite me to, but I will not make her come against her wishes."

She smiled faintly and shook her head. "Ah, Enric. Between two Aren women has never been a safe place for any person, be they woman or man."

He held her gaze. "Are you threatening me, Malriel?" he asked softly.

"No, Enric. I am wondering about you, though. Stupidity or courage, I am not quite sure which one drives you. But then it has to be the latter, does it not? You do not seem stupid to me, and Maltheá would not have chosen a stupid man, no matter now persistent or physically appealing he might have been."

"Flattery now? I can hardly keep up with you," he replied with one arched eyebrow.

"And yet you are trying to be a step ahead of us, are you not? Your assistant has developed quite an interest in our local laws, it seems. Particularly in the area of legal succession?" Her smile didn't reach to her eyes.

"Has he now? Well, he is a very dedicated and thorough collector of knowledge. I am sure his interest is not limited to this one area," Enric lied, his expression imperturbable.

"Indeed? Then I must have misjudged his intentions," she said with a look that clearly stated that she was not taking it, however good his acting skills were. She observed him for a time, sipping at her tea and letting her eyes wander over him.

"I like your style of clothing. I remember what you were wearing when you arrived here and at the first meeting at the senate. You have adapted to our ways quickly, but only to the extent you are willing to. Your new attire communicates this quite clearly. A compromise between two worlds, but not one that was necessary, just one you happened to find appealing and decided to use to your own advantage. And advantageous it is. In a place of dark-haired people you have managed to become dark in your own way without denying your origins. The fact that our cuts enhance your impressive physical attributes even further is undoubtedly a convenient side benefit, is it not?" Her expression was earnest as she waited for his answer.

Enric cocked his head and smiled at the familiar, yet still so different face. "Are you flirting with me, Malriel? I have noticed your people's openness with sexuality, but I can't help the impression that you are toying with me. Maybe to see how I will react? To make me uneasy? Or even to test my loyalty to your daughter?"

She smiled lazily. "How unexpectedly modest of you to discard the most obvious reason of all: attraction."

He chuckled and shook his head. "The most obvious one it may be, but that doesn't make it the true reason. A woman concerned about her daughter's rejection would hardly try a thing like this with a mere carnal motivation. So it is less modesty than logic that causes me to discard it. Though I do believe that I might have been a target for your attentions of the physical kind had I not been Eryn's companion," he added with a smirk.

Malriel threw her head back and laughed. "I like your confidence. And I like even more that it is completely warranted. But I would not refer to your status as Eryn's companion too much, my friend. It is not as widely acknowledged here as you might wish to expect."

Enric stared at her in dismay. "Pardon me?"

"Ah, finally I have managed to catch you off balance. You did not make it easy for me, but it seems that I have found something now. Yes, Enric - your commitment was forged by a non-magician, thus it is in our eyes merely a legal one, a formality easily dissolved if need be. You may compare it with a simple, non-magical promise. Breaking it is not exactly considered polite, but will be forgiven. If a promise, a commitment, is not to be broken, we seal it with magic. The magical promise between two companions we call a third level commitment bond."

He stared at her. "My commitment to Eryn is not fully acknowledged here because there was no magical oath to bind us to each other?"

"Exactly. We would say it is more a plan, an intention to get committed at one time than a true bond. Or nothing other than a political connection. That makes it something which may be challenged quite easily."

Exhaling slowly, he narrowed his eyes. "Ram'an. So this is the reason why he did not seem discouraged by my claim to her, and apparently still doesn't. To him she is still available, and he thinks pursuing his interest in her is justified because there is no magical bond in place between us! And Eryn still thinks I am jealous for no reason, that he only wants to be her friend!"

Malriel raised her brows. "Does she now? Then let me encourage you to undertake a little journey to the historic archives in the cellars of the senate building tomorrow morning. Ask for Durgal and let him tell you a little about the Houses and show you around. I expect you will find a thing or two that will prove of great interest to you." She raised her hands to her neck and removed a silver pendant that equalled in style and appearance the one Eryn had in her possession, with two crests in different sizes, the larger one naturally of House Aren.

"Here," she said and handed it to him. "Show this to the guards at the entrance and to Durgal. It will ensure you are admitted into the archives. They are not meant for public access, too many valuable and delicate items are kept there. Just give it back to me in the afternoon when we meet at the senate."

He nodded slowly and put the chain around his own neck, wondering about what she wanted him to know but wouldn't tell him herself. "Thank you. I think."

She smiled as if understanding his deliberations. "Do not thank me yet."

"Alright, then, I won't," he smiled and leaned back comfortably. "I would be interested in learning a bit more about your commitment bonds. You said *third level* before. I assume there are a first and second level bond as well? How are they enacted? And how do your people feel about joining foreigners here?"

*　*　*

When he entered their bed chamber, he saw her sitting on the floor next to the bed, her elbows propped on the mattress, reading something. She had probably found another well of new healing knowledge and managed either to borrow the literature or obtain copies already.

She wore a white, slightly translucent gown that flowed around her, only leaving her arms and feet bare, her hair tumbling down her back in the kind of waves she always had when it had been braided all day long.

How was it possible that a gown that revealed hardly anything did so much for his imagination? It must have been a gift from Vran'el, he mused, and silently thanked her cousin for his considerate generosity.

He approached her and kissed her lightly on the head before he threw himself on the bed, careful not to crumple the papers she had spread on it in what seemed to him pure chaos, but was probably subject some underlying logic that revealed itself only to the trained healer eye. A quick look confirmed his suspicions. Drawings of plants and body parts with explanatory texts underneath covered about one third of the bed.

"You know, I learned something very interesting today," he said contemplatively, leaned back against the pillows and comfortably intertwined his fingers behind his neck.

"Hmm?" She didn't look up from her papers.

He observed her carefully while speaking the next words. "It seems people here have a fascinating way of sealing agreements. They call it *commitment bonds*."

He recognised subtle signs that he had her full attention now. The set of her shoulders had become slightly rigid, even if her posture as such had not changed. Her pupils that had before darted from one side of the paper to the other and back in rapid intervals were now fixed on one point. So she *had* known about that already and had kept it from him, he thought.

"Indeed?"

He marvelled at the hardly discernible tension in her voice. She was getting better at lying, he thought, tickled. But then he was getting to know her better, so she wouldn't really benefit from this when lying to *him*.

"Yes. The principle is similar to a magical oath as we know it, but it requires a commitment from both parties, the swearer of the oath and the one sworn to." He smiled when she gulped, still not looking at him.

"The strongest one of them - the third level commitment bond, as they call it - is meant to be exchanged between life companions. I find it touching that they consider this bond between lovers more important than the one between sovereign and subject, which is only level two."

"Yes, very interesting," she smiled faintly. He saw tiny beads of sweat forming on her forehead.

"A real magical commitment," he said reflectively as if to himself. "What an appealing concept."

She rose slowly and cleared her throat. "I need a glass of water. I will be back in a moment."

Yes, he thought, watching her all but run from the room and smiling grimly with narrowed eyes. You just run for now. This is not the last you will hear about this from me, be in no doubt about that.

He carefully collected the loose sheets of paper from the bed and neatly placed them on a nearby table. He didn't want to risk their being crumpled, as he was sure that after her return she would be eager to distract him from pursuing that topic any further. And he did so enjoy it when she was eager.

CHAPTER 29

An Unpleasant Revelation

Enric had decided not to reveal his little conversation with Malriel to Eryn for now. She would not have reacted favourably to it, and he needed to avoid her getting angry at him as well as he could for the next time if he wanted to convince her to take the third level commitment bond with him. He wondered how realistic the goal of getting her to agree to it was before they left here again. And then to have the ceremony carried out in the time they had left.

He descended the stairs down to the basement of the senate building according to Malriel's instructions and felt the temperature sinking with almost every step downwards. When he reached the last step, the air around him was pleasantly cool. Two guards sat on a bench in front of a large round, ancient-looking door and got to their feet when he approached them. Simply lifting Malriel's pendant permitted his entry immediately. He wondered if this wasn't a rather careless way of handling matters - he could have stolen the pendant, after all, and gained unauthorised access. But then stealing the pendant of House Aren's Head was probably considered an act either impossible or so risky that it bordered on foolishness, and thus the guards discounted that possibility immediately.

The air smelled old, Enric thought as he entered the hall, with odours of dry dust, sand and something else he couldn't quite place. Probably some material or chemical they used for the conservation of their treasures here. He looked up to the high, vaulted ceiling and wondered if he had really walked down that many stairs. He felt as if he had entered a realm deep within the bowels of the land.

Dark, massive, heavy looking shelves filled with books stood not against the sand-coloured walls but in the centre of the long hall, all in neat rows. Two men were standing in front of a table with an open book that stood about as high as Enric's outstretched arm and showed a faded image of intertwining trees and limbs that seemed oddly disturbing. The men didn't seem to notice him and continued their discussion about the right colours for the restoration of the picture, whether to use the original methods or benefit from the newer, more effective ways despite risking a less authentic result.

Nobody seemed to wonder if the blonde stranger had any right to be there or questioned his presence. It seemed as if being permitted by the guards was all the legitimation that was needed to be tolerated within this hallowed place.

He looked around for somebody who didn't seem absorbed in complicated repairs, absorbed in concentrated reading or otherwise preoccupied in a manner that would have made Enric feel guilty about interrupting them. After a few minutes of aimless wandering he saw a figure in motion and took the opportunity to stop a middle-aged man to ask him about Durgal. The man nodded once and beckoned for Enric to follow.

They stepped through a low doorway into another equally large room that was only partly filled with books; the rest seemed to be ancient weapons, different devices tarnished with age in varying sizes and for different purposes, pieces of broken pottery with crude, faded paintings on them, and oddly shaped stones with traces of craftsmanship visible that might have once been part of a building, sculpture or other man-made structure. His guide pointed at a man who was apparently in his late fifties. But who could really tell that in a country where people could shape their exterior according to their own wishes, Enric thought, and approached the man.

"Excuse me, are you Durgal?"

"Who wants to know that?" the man asked without looking up.

"Enric, Ambassador of the Old Kingdom to Takhan."

The man turned slowly and stared at Enric owlishly. "What? Who? And what is the matter with your hair?"

Both men stared at each other in confusion.

Enric cleared his throat. "You don't get out much, do you?"

"What for? Most of what happens out there will very likely have to stay happened for quite some time until it lands down here," the older man shrugged.

"Are you Durgal now or not?" Enric asked again.

"I am, yes."

Enric turned to thank his guide, but he had already disappeared.

"Malriel of House Aren sends me to you." He took out the pendant and dangled it in front of Durgal's eyes. "She asks you to tell me about the Houses and show me around."

"Malriel," he murmured.

"Yes, Malriel," Enric repeated carefully, wondering if the man was sane. "She is the Head of House Aren."

"What?" Durgal barked at him. "Do you take me for a fool? Of course she is the Head of House Aren! Has been for more than fifteen years. I should know, being her cousin."

"I apologise," Enric said stiffly. "I was under the impression that you had difficulties placing the name."

He snorted. "Show me one person in the city who has problems placing *that* name. People either admire, fear, loathe, envy or desire

369

her. She tends to polarise - and that is the way she likes it, always has done. Not a woman who takes lightly to not being noticed."

Yes, Enric thought, that he could imagine.

"Well, young man, come on then. The Houses, you say? How much time do you have? I can give you the long version, the very long one or the *really* detailed history."

Enric cleared his throat and frowned, slightly desperate at the thought of spending the next few hours being lectured on the history of Takhan nobility. Under different circumstances he might have welcomed the opportunity to educate himself on the topic, but not when he was looking for something specific - however little idea he had about what that was. "I was hoping for a rather more succinct insight, to be completely honest. Why don't we start with the very basics and then go as deep as we deem useful for my purposes?"

"Your purposes?" the man asked. "And what might those purposes be, if you do not mind telling me?"

"I should admit I am not too clear about that myself," Enric said slowly, feeling like a fool. "Malriel thought I might find interesting information here."

"Interesting information down here? We have loads of interesting information down here, though discovering all of it will take you decades. What were you talking about when she decided that you would find something here?" Durgal asked patiently.

"Third level commitment bonds, I think."

The man stared at him for a few moments, then a wide grin spread across his face. "You! Yes, they said you had yellow hair, I remember! You are little Maltheá's lover, are you not?"

"Her companion, but yes," Enric replied sternly.

Durgal shook his head. "Not really, I think. No third level bond in place, is there? But if it makes you happier, we shall call you her *companion*." He winked at the younger man. "But I think I have a pretty good idea what she wants you to find out. This is a matter of a few minutes, unless you are of sluggish mind." He eyed Enric doubtfully. "Half an hour, at the most. Surely no longer than one hour," he then amended after giving Enric another doubtful look.

Enric shot him a look of equanimity.

"But then maybe not," the older man shrugged apologetically.

The blonde magician followed who he now assumed was a historian through the long hall to a glass cabinet with twelve artfully designed golden crests, each about the size of his palm, displayed in two rows.

"These are the crests of the twelve Houses. I would venture there are at least two you are able to recognise," Durgal said, his tone now considerably more friendly.

"House Aren, second to the left in the first row." He continued scanning the intricately carved and carefully painted coats of arms.

"And House Vel'kim, the paternal side. Third from the left in the second row."

"Splendid," the man smiled approvingly. "The first one on the right side of the first row is the crest of House Arbil."

Ram'an's crest. Enric leaned forward and studied it. It wouldn't hurt to be able to recognise that one if he saw it somewhere.

"If you would care to look over here," Durgal said and pointed to a huge canvas almost as high as the room and half as wide, that was at first glance only a twirling mass of colours, but upon more careful inspection turned out to display some kind of family tree. Or several intertwining ones.

"At the top you see the crests of the twelve Houses. And if you follow the lines, you see which connections have been made by carefully planned companionships in these last ten generations. You can see here the alliances and how they have remained constant throughout these last two hundred years. We have older records that show quite a different picture, but the Houses seem to have found a balance that works for them."

Enric followed the lines starting from Eryn's maternal House, studying them carefully.

"It seems that House Aren has a steady cycle of companionships with four other Houses."

"Yes, Houses Vel'kim, Finran, Ordel and..." Durgal supplied happily before Enric swallowed and interrupted him.

"And House Arbil." He retraced the lines and then said slowly, "It seems there is quite a gap between the last connection between Houses Aren and Arbil." A very disconcerting suspicion had started forming in his mind.

The historian smiled. "Indeed. Any conclusions you have reached with regard to this?"

The man seemed to wait for him to reach a certain point, and with every moment Enric became surer what exactly it was.

"Considering the regularity of matches between the families I would assume that another one was or is now due. How many single persons of age are currently in House Aren?"

"Three," the historian answered.

"And in House Arbil?"

"Two."

"So there would be possibilities. But for some reason they have not been realised. What am I missing?"

"Consider what you know about our society, about what characteristics make a House powerful."

Enric narrowed his eyes when a notion dawned on him. "Let me rephrase my question, then. How many single persons of age *with magical abilities* are there currently in both Houses?"

The historian nodded with obvious satisfaction. "Ah, there were go. Two. One in each House."

"Eryn and Ram'an," Enric said darkly. "So their families had intended for them to enter into a companionship after reaching adulthood."

"Precisely," Durgal confirmed. "But due to her being taken away by her father, that never happened."

"Why has Ram'an never taken another companion?"

"Because both families have never really ceased their search for her and would have located her, moreover, had she not been taken away from the village only days before."

"They would have brought her back here and made her join him?" he frowned angrily at the thought. "She would hardly have agreed to that, believe me."

The historian shrugged. "From what I have heard about her, that does seem likely, yes. The families would in time have made a decision whether to wait for another generation to renew the bond or still make it happen in some way. And you never know, maybe Ram'an would finally have managed to win her, had you not been faster at that. He is what we would here consider quite a catch after all: good looking young fellow, charming, well-educated and, let us not forget, wealthy." The man chuckled at Enric's cold stare. "But I hear she has found a man with equally impressive attributes already. I can see this is not a topic that comforts you to converse about, so let us not hazard any more guesses as to what might have happened if fate had chosen a different path. As you have now learned what Malriel intended you to know, I assume you will be off again. Give my regards to my cousin when you next see her." And away he turned to saunter back to whatever he had been doing before Enric had interrupted him, clearly not in the least worried about leaving his visitor alone in this maze of towering shelves, ancient artefacts and priceless books.

* * *

Enric slowly stepped out into the sunlight and shaded his eyes with one hand. Interesting fact, indeed! he fumed. So Ram'an still considered himself to be the future companion of the heiress of House Aren, whether or not she herself believed that she was already in a binding relationship.

He slowly walked away from the senate building, feeling the anger bubbling inside him. He needed to do something about that before he was due at the meeting with the senate in the afternoon. This was not a mood to be in for conducting negotiations.

Thinking about the swords he had packed, he smiled grimly. It was time for Eryn to have another training session. They had arrived here one week ago, and her last lesson had been on the day of their departure in Anyueel more than ten days ago.

He took two steps at once when he arrived at the ambassadorial residence. It was still morning, he had needed not nearly as much time as he had allowed in the archives. Eryn looked up from her book in surprise when he strolled into the main room where she lay spread across several sitting cushions.

"That was fast. I thought you wanted to do some historic research? Not much history around?" she asked and frowned when she noticed his tense posture. "Is everything alright?"

"No, not really. But I need to do some thinking before I can tell you. Come on, I need some exercise."

She frowned. "Exercise as in...?"

"Exercise as in sword fighting."

"You brought the swords?" she groaned. "Why don't you ask one of the boys to play with you? I am sure they would be more than thrilled to accommodate you. You keep pointing out to me what an enviable privilege it is to train with you, so I feel I need to be social and share that burd... er... benefit with the others."

His smile didn't reach his eyes. "Not today. I am afraid they wouldn't be strong enough to get out of this unharmed."

Eryn swallowed and got up slowly, leaving the book on the cushions. Something had to be terribly wrong if Enric of all people didn't trust his own ability to maintain control over himself. And the prospect of facing him with a sword in his hand was not exactly so comforting right now.

"But you are not at all worried about hurting *me*? You do remember that I, too, am not your equal, neither in skill nor in power, don't you?" she ventured.

"Of course. It is my composure that is suffering, not my mind," he retorted and went into their bedroom to return little later with the golden belt. He closed his eyes for a moment and then handed it to her.

"Put it on me," he instructed. "The enchantment will reduce my power by one third."

She raised both eyebrows. "Really? You are that much stronger than me?" Funny, how she had never considered finding out how large the difference in power between them really was.

"No, not quite. But as you have pointed out, I am your superior in skill as well as power, and that should even the balance a bit more. And then there is my physical fitness, which is another advantage for me. Don't look annoyed at that. I am aware that you are fit as well, but your one year of training can hardly compete with more than twenty for me, can it?"

Eryn took the belt from his hands and sealed it shut around his waist. "I like this," she quipped, trying to lighten the mood. "It should be a part of your everyday attire."

He didn't comment and instead went back to their bedroom. She followed him and watched him kneel before the bed and pull out a long, broad box from underneath it. That was where they had been all the time without her knowing it?

"Where do you want to fight? On the terrace or in the garden?" she asked.

He shook his head and gripped both swords by their hilts to lift them out of the box. The smaller one he pressed into her hand.

"Neither. The sun would blind us. We will stay inside. The main room is large enough."

She turned around and eyed the interior warily. "Do you really think this is a good idea? Things might get broken."

"There are not many breakable things in here, and what we break I will replace later," he replied and pulled her along. The heavy hilt in his hand felt good. He itched to use the sword, to let out his frustration, fury and irritation, get it out of his system so he could return to the cool and sensible thinking that was so typical for him and that would allow him to find a way to handle this situation to his satisfaction.

She saw how he raised a shield in the archway that led to the bedroom, where the cat was dozing on their bed, to keep her safe in case she woke and decided to join the fun.

"Ready?" he asked and she nodded, expecting the first blow when it came and swiftly ducking away under it.

He attacked again and a third time when she sidestepped his strike. She ground her teeth and finally raised her own sword to block. This was not for training purposes, after all, it was for him to get rid of his tension. She wouldn't win this. Even though his magical powers were at the moment inferior to her own, she could see from the way he moved and the strength he put into his blows that he had used less magic in their former fights than she had thought. Another field where she had underestimated him, she sighed within. Sword fighting, of all things!

She decided to give up her defensive stance and instead attacked him, increasing her speed to see how far she could push him, how good he really was.

He didn't smile, but the glint in his eyes showed her that this was what he needed right now. He seemed more careful than normal, unusually concentrated and focused on her every move. Sure, she thought and aimed another stab at his side, it was not like he usually needed to be that cautious with his entire power at his disposal. Normally he could just compensate for any lapse with a subsequent quicker, magically aided move. But not now.

The thought cheered her up. Maybe this was the day for her to see *his* weapon lying on the floor while she was still holding on to hers.

She left a few openings, trying to tempt him into taking advantage of them, but he didn't fall for it and just shook his head slightly to indicate that he had seen through her manoeuvre.

No banter this time, she thought and wondered what could have happened to leave him that tense. He had said that he needed some time for thinking before he would tell her about it.

"Can I assist you with the thinking you said you needed to do?" she ventured and jumped back and into the circle of cushions on the floor, narrowly avoiding the table.

"No," he replied curtly and caught a pillow she threw at him to distract him from the sword that came swinging at him from the other side. He blocked it easily and joined her on the sitting area, the table between them.

"You insist on *my* telling you everything, but you are not exactly a good role model here, you know," she frowned and tried to gauge the position of the pillows behind her and whether they would hinder her if she tried to get out of the circle again.

He didn't answer, but his jaw muscles tensed visibly. No remark about this being his privilege as her superior, or joking about the right of the stronger one?

"You are worrying me," she said and slowly let her sword sink. "Tell me."

Shaking his head, he motioned for her to lift her weapon again. "Not now. I will, I promise you. Just not now. I need to talk to Valrad and Vran'el first."

"So it is about me, isn't it? It has nothing to do with your negotiations or the senate or anything like that." Her eyes narrowed. "I find that rather patronising. I don't want to be protected and kept in the dark for my own good! I want to know if I am about to get into trouble and be prepared for it!"

"I told you, not now," he growled and looked pointedly at her weapon, which was still pointing to the floor.

Sighing, she raised it and blocked his tentative attack. He struck again with more force when he saw that she was back in fighting mode.

They circled and crossed the large room several times, their swords meeting in regular intervals, ignoring Urban who was trying to get out of the bedroom but couldn't pass the shield and began complaining bitterly. The sound of steel against steel had obviously roused her interest.

Eryn watched his eyes, trying to make out some sign of an imminent attack, but he had been trained well and didn't give away anything that might have aided her. No blink of an eye or intake of breath betrayed his intentions.

She circled him slowly, pleased that she had persevered longer than in her prior fights with him.

"You know, if you had resorted to wearing gold during our training sessions before, I might have refrained from exchanging you for Orrin," she said lightly and jumped when she heard the loud clang of his sword hitting the floor. He grabbed her own sword and pulled it out of her grip to throw it onto the cushions before grabbing her collar.

She stared at the tense line his mouth had become. She had no idea why, but judging from his reaction, this had obviously been precisely the wrong thing to say. Instead of having released some of his tension it seemed to have increased further.

"Remove the belt," he said with forced calm.

She swallowed. "I am not sure this would be a wise course of action right now."

"Remove. The belt," he repeated, his eyes narrowed.

Her fingers touched the metal lightly and the seam opened and allowed him to remove the golden restraint. It landed on the cushions next to her sword. She felt herself drawn against him and a moment later he shoved his forearm under her knees to lift her up.

He removed the shield to let the cat out and carried his companion to the bed, dropping her on the soft mattress. When she tried to get up again, he pushed her back and caught her wrists to press them down.

"There is no exchanging me," he snarled.

"I didn't mean to..." she started but he interrupted her, paying no attention to her words.

"Ever. You are mine. And whoever doubts this will pay for it!"

Fabric ripped under his hands and she felt his mouth on her throat, her collarbone and finally her lips. The kiss tasted of wrath, of barely contained rage.

So apparently sword fighting had not quite seemed to be the right activity for him to deal with this wayward energy, she thought. She hoped this would be better suited.

"You are mine. Say it," he commanded.

"Yours," she obeyed, not daring to oppose him right now. "I am yours."

"Good," he growled and removed his own shirt. "And don't you *ever* forget it."

CHAPTER 30

The Memory Block

Eryn looked down at the colourful game board and frowned at the confusing constellation of the figures.

"So, when my pieces have surrounded one ship, they can sink it, can they? But only if the ship is still in the lower, dark blue portions where the water is deep. Your ship would be merely stranded if I sunk it now."

Vran'el shook his head. "No, because you need three magicians for that, and you only have two magicians and one smith."

"Why? The smith surely can cause some damage, considering that he is strong and able with a hammer. And why would you need three magicians to sink a ship, anyway? One is more than enough, *I* could do it by myself. It's just a matter of a few strong bolts damaging the hull - and down to the bottom of the sea it sinks."

"Eryn, this is a game, and you are supposed to follow the rules, not question them or discuss how to change them in your favour," her cousin sighed. "Even Obal knows that."

"That's because she is not yet encouraged or even permitted to think for herself. I am. And I resent these rules. They contradict reality."

Vran'el leaned back and rubbed his face. "Alright, no more playing board games with *you*. Are you just trying to drive me insane or are you always this averse to rules?"

"The latter," Enric's calm voice came from the opposite side of the cushion island. Both of them looked at him in surprise. He had been so quiet with the book on his lap this last half hour that they had almost forgotten that he was there.

"Hardly a surprise," Vran'el smirked and packed up the game pieces and board. "I wonder how you would have liked growing up here. We have quite a few rules, and maybe they would have shaped little Maltheá into an obedient soul."

"Keep on dreaming, cousin," she grinned back.

"Yes, you are probably right. There is a reason why no Aren woman has ever learned to play an instrument halfway decently. It would require too much patience and obedience."

"Instrument? A musical one, you mean? Why?" she enquired. "I am not a musician."

Her cousin rolled his eyes at her. "Because it is part of the general education. Playing a musical instrument makes you more sensitive to artistic influences and creativity, and it teaches you the beauty of creating something with your own hands. Am I to assume that this is not the case where you grew up?"

She shook her head. "No, not as far as I am aware. Being a musician is a trade like any other. Unless you wish to learn it, you don't just go off and start mastering an instrument. You wouldn't even find anybody to teach you just for fun."

Vran'el grimaced. "No musical education whatsoever for children? What a pity we did not manage to get you away from that barbaric place sooner!"

Enric cleared his throat without looking up from his book. "I happen to be very attached to that barbaric place, if you don't mind."

Vran'el waved him off generously. "No, I do not mind at all. We cannot help where we are born, can we?"

Enric frowned and closed the book. "Is it possible that there is a little misunderstanding? I wanted to point out that I find your calling my home a *barbaric place* rather insensitive. I didn't really ask for your forgiveness for having been born there."

The younger man sniggered. "I know. This is just my particular sense of humour. I am told it needs some getting used to."

"Yes, I can confirm that," Enric said and shook his head. "And if you had managed to find her and get her back here, she would never have met me. And neither would you. Are you telling that this is what you would have preferred the situation to be like? That my acquaintance is a burden to you?"

Vran'el grimaced. "I never wanted to imply anything like that! Please let me assure you that I value immensely the opportunity of getting to know a formidable man like yourself." He narrowed his eyes when Enric just grinned and returned to his reading. "Is it possible that I have just received a taste of your own brand of humour? A man after my own heart."

Eryn frowned. "I am still new to this kind of same-sex-attraction thing, but are you flirting with my companion?"

"Oh my, that *is* a rather blunt question, cousin! But yes, I am. Does this bother you, sweetness? You know he has only eyes for you, do you not? I admit I started it to make him uncomfortable at the beginning, his being so tall and powerful and from foreign parts and all. I wanted to rattle his composure a little. Many men find it disconcerting when they are considered attractive by a man of my inclination. They become insecure and wonder what it is about them that is unmanly. But Enric is too confident even for that. And now that he seems to take it as a compliment and does not treat me as an anomaly of any kind, I enjoy it even more." He nodded his head at her. "You, on the other hand, seem to be rather uncomfortable with the whole situation. I am really surprised at that, to be honest. You spent some time here before you were taken away, so I would have expected you to reconnect with your roots more easily. Your companion is much better at adapting to the local customs and practises than you."

"Why does everybody expect me to have jumped off that boat and be a slightly older version of the girl you used to know?" she exclaimed in frustration.

"Because we did not expect you to be so... foreign, I think," he shrugged. "I have memories from the time when I was younger than you were when Ved'al took you away, so you should remember at least *something*."

"I don't, really! Just snippets from dreams where I can't even tell whether they are figments of imagination or real events. So stop pressuring me!"

"I am not pressuring you. I am just saying that it is strange, nothing more. Is it possible that you are suppressing your memories for some reason?" he persisted.

"Shut up now, or I'll make your sister the oldest descendant of House Vel'kim," she growled.

Valrad entered from the terrace and shook his head in disapproval. "Children, you have known each other for barely more than a week and are exchanging death threats already..."

"He started it," Eryn murmured.

Vran'el rolled his eyes and then turned to his father. "Say, do not you find it rather strange that she does not remember anything from her childhood here in Takhan? What does an old healer like yourself say to that?"

"First of all, that I object to being called *old*. As for the other, that might be due to some trauma or shock. What are your earliest memories, child?" he enquired and sat down next to Eryn.

She sighed, resigned to the fact that the topic was not yet done with. "Pictures of people and villages, rooms, different smells. We used to move from one village to the next for the first few years before we settled down once father found it safe enough for us."

"So nothing concrete."

She nodded. "Yes, it would seem so."

She saw Valrad frown and then look at her thoughtfully for a while before murmuring, "It would have been punishable, severely so. But then he was a fugitive and would have been punished anyway if they had caught him. He probably thought that this single additional offence would make your discovery even less likely and was willing to risk it."

Eryn frowned. "What are you talking about?"

Vran'el drew in a breath. "You are thinking that he... but surely not his own daughter? I mean, everything about her mother..."

Eryn felt a lump grow in her throat and saw that Enric had put aside the book and leaned forward with a worried frown.

"Eryn, my dear, would you mind if I took a look inside your head? It will not be painful, I promise," her uncle asked in a calm voice that did not match the unease visible in his eyes.

"No." She folded her arms and leaned back. "First you tell me about what you suspect my father has done to me."

"I am reluctant to put an insinuation of such severity into words without first having proof, or at least fairly reliable hints, pointing in that direction."

"You think he did something criminal, then? You said he would have been severely punished for it. What is it? Come on, you can't refuse to disclose it after saying things like that! What has he done to me?" She stared into the older man's eyes. "Tell me!" she insisted.

Valrad shook his head sadly. "I should not, it would not be…"

"He thinks your father blocked or destroyed most of your early memories," Vran'el interrupted him and earned himself an admonishing glance from his father. "No, we must tell her if there is a chance that he really did that. She deserves to know. Especially now that you have unsettled her by already hinting at it."

"Blocked my memory?" she frowned. "You mean he might have removed them somehow? Like he presumably did with the search parties?"

"That is the question. Though in your case this would have been a manipulation to an extent far greater than with the search parties. He only had to remove snippets of their short-term memories to make them forget about their recent progress in tracking him. But with you he would have had to tamper with your long-term memory." Valrad looked worried. "There are two ways to do this, both expressly prohibited, though one is at least partly reversible. If he just blocked them, some of your memories might possibly be restorable. If he removed them altogether, then there is no chance of bringing those memories back. Removal runs the risk of permanent damage with the slightest mistake, and I doubt he would have taken that chance," her uncle explained unhappily.

"Why is it punishable?" Eryn enquired.

"Because taking away a person's long-term memory is like taking away a part of their personality. It essentially means interfering with a person's identity. Our experiences and the memories of them shape our personality to a large extent. Especially if it meant taking away a girl's only memory of her mother."

"But we don't know if he really did anything like that, do we?" Enric asked. "You asked to look inside her head. Could you find out that way? And if yes, could you restore these memories if he hadn't removed them completely but only blocked them off somehow?"

"I would very likely find traces of that, yes. But restoring it is a rather complicated matter that requires a great deal of knowledge about the brain and involves more expertise that I can offer in that field. But there is a man who I would trust to attempt it."

All three men looked at Eryn. She had closed her eyes and was suddenly feeling cold, despite the heat. Another crime her father might have committed. Wouldn't it be better not knowing at all? And how would this change the way his family remembered him? They didn't approve of his actions concerning this entire pregnancy issue and his subsequent escape with his daughter, but they seemed to understand them to a certain degree, even if they didn't dare admit it. But this would exceed even the leniency his brother was willing to show judging from Valrad's words just now.

"I don't think it makes such a great difference anymore whether we find out about this or not," she said nonchalantly. "I certainly can live without the memories. And there is a chance that I really just don't recall some things."

Enric noticed how she turned away from him and averted her eyes as if to avoid showing him something she didn't want him to see and that the other two men wouldn't notice. But he didn't need to see her eyes to know what was going on.

"We wouldn't have to make it public," he said calmly. "And your family here would doubtlessly rather have confirmation one way or the other than keep wondering."

"Enric, please," she whispered and gave him a pleading look.

"No, my love. There is no sense in trying to protect your father from whatever he might have done back then when there is even a slight chance of undoing it. And I very much doubt that the rest of his family has the same idealistic picture of him as you do."

Vran'el quickly took her hands as she attempted to get up from the cushions and pressed her fingers to his lips. "Eryn, I know this must pain you so much. He was everything you had for such a very long time, and you would not want to be forced to remember him any other way than you do now. But whatever he did was to keep you both safe, so resorting to measures that are not acceptable in our society does not necessarily have to make him a bad person in your opinion."

"He had his mistakes," Valrad said and leaned forward. "But loving somebody, my child, does not mean having a perfect picture in your mind. It means accepting a person entirely with both his good and bad sides. Imagine if love only depended on your seeing a person's positive sides. It could never survive for very long, because sooner or later our true self is somehow exposed. If he has put a block on your memories, it was his doing, was a decision he made. Does your love for him depend on his having been perfect? Then I promise you that you will not be able to hold on to that. There are probably more truths about him that you will uncover while you are here. Embracing them is the better choice, as closing your eyes can only work for so long."

Eryn pulled her hands back from her cousin's grip and covered her face. Wise words, she thought. But so painful. She was little more than a child when he had died, and questioning him afterwards had seemed like a violation of his memory. Even more so as she had been the one who caused his death. How was somebody like her even worthy of judging a man like him? A healer, a man who had helped others regardless of status, wealth, origins or character. And then there was herself - disobeying him, violating his most sacred rule and thus sentencing him to death.

She felt warm hands close around her wrists and pull them away from her face. Her uncle's kind face smiled at her sadly.

"I loved him, too, child. It broke my heart when he took you and fled from here. I knew that I would either never see him again or only in chains. I was torn which option would be worse and hated myself for even considering that it might be the second." He kissed her forehead. "Whatever I find in your head will not change my love or my anger at his deeds. But I would like to think that I could maybe change something for the better for you. Will you permit me to have a look?"

She looked into his dark brown eyes, same as her father's. Her own were not as dark, she had her mother's eyes, both in form and colour. The thought somehow made her even sadder. She nodded slowly and saw Valrad close his eyes before, a moment later, feeling warmth percolate into her body where he touched her. It seemed he didn't want to lose any time. Or risk her changing her mind. It was probably a combination of both.

The warmth spread from her wrists and moved up her arms and then shoulders and neck. She closed her eyes as well to see what he was doing inside her head. He probed with tiny, almost imperceptibly weak impulses that spoke of great skill in putting his magic to use, tested several areas of her brain where she assumed memories were located. She drew in a breath when he encountered a miniscule, nearly undetectable barrier and felt him do the same. Confirmation. So her father really had blocked her memories, walled away a part of her life.

Enric watched them both intently and saw Vran'el do the same from the other side. They exchanged a look when both of them suddenly drew in a breath at the same time. That had to mean that Valrad had found something to confirm his suspicion.

They both opened their eyes and stared at each other for some time, motionless.

"And now?" Eryn then asked and gently pulled her wrists from her uncle's hands. She seemed calm enough, but there was a tension in her jaw that bespoke control instead of relaxation.

"That depends on you, niece. There are two options."

"Leaving the block in place or having it removed," she said. "I assume we are talking about blocked memories and not the other option you mentioned? They were not removed completely?"

Valrad shook his head. "No. There would have been remainders of damaged nerves otherwise."

"What would you do in my place?" she asked.

"I do not know, I really do not," he replied and rubbed his face. "I can see how much tension there is between you and your mother. Maybe your memories would help you to overcome it. Or increase it even further. You would probably remember unpleasant things you would rather not confront. Like your first scolding, or discovering that fire burns your skin if you are not careful. But also pleasant situations, smells, voices. Like when you first saw your little cousin after she was born." He smiled faintly. "I remember the day well. I wonder if you would. You looked down at her when I held her in my arms and asked why she was so ugly."

Vran'el chuckled. "It seems to me the relationship between the two of you had already started pretty badly back then."

Eryn swallowed. Memories about her family. A family she had not had the chance to get to know and probably wouldn't spend too much time with once their visit here was over in only two weeks.

"I will do it," she said slowly. "Will it be painful?"

"Not physically, no. You will very likely be asleep as this works better in a relaxed state of mind. But there is no telling of the emotional consequences. You will need to be with somebody close to you right afterwards. It would be good if Enric were there as he is the one with whom you surely feel the safest. And somebody to guide you through the random pictures that will emerge and will very likely confuse you before they fall into place. I can do that if you like. Or there is your mother. I imagine she would be more than willing, as well."

Eryn shook her head quickly. "No, not her. She must not learn of the memory block." She wouldn't give that woman another weapon against her father. Or rather his memory. "Do I need to go somewhere or can we do it here? I would like to keep this as private as possible."

"I will talk to my colleague. I am sure we will find a way of doing this without drawing too much attention to it. He is very skilled in these matters. He occasionally puts memory blocks in place and accordingly he knows exactly how they can be removed," Valrad said.

"What? I thought they were forbidden? What about this severe punishment you mentioned?" Eryn exclaimed in confusion.

"There are situations that would damage the mind more than loss of certain memories. A trauma of some kind, for example. There are things people most sincerely wish they were able to forget. They can apply for a block. The severe punishment is for those healers who place one without having been given official permission for each and every case or doing it in the absence of the patient's express wishes. In your case, my dear child, it would have been punished, you may depend on it. Your mother would have made sure of that; she already had powerful connections back then."

She looked upset. "What would have happened to my father if they had managed to find and bring us back here?"

Valrad looked at his son. "You are the one versed in the law, son. What do you say? What is the worst punishment Malriel could have secured for the abduction of her only child and a memory block as well?"

Her cousin leaned back and blew out his breath. "There are a few possibilities. Banishment, but I think she would not have gone for that. She is the kind who likes to behold the punishment with her own eyes. Lifelong incarceration, probably. That would have enabled her to visit him and see him crumble. Or, his having been a devoted healer, golden shackles for the rest of his life."

Eryn had gone pale and Vran'el was smiling apologetically. "Sorry, sweetness. But you must by now know that in our society you do not become powerful by being kind. Or remain in power with that virtue, for that matter."

"Let us no longer talk about things that could have been. It is not a very pleasant topic," Valrad sighed. "I think you should show our guests a bit of the city nightlife, Vran. There is no official social event tonight which we need to attend, so why do you not take them dancing instead?"

Vran'el nodded eagerly. "Yes, let us go dancing. I would like to see if you remember any of the steps I taught you, Eryn. I have no doubt whatsoever that Enric does."

She flashed him a disgusted look. "Why do I even talk to you?"

"Because I am utterly adorable," he shrugged. "Is this not true, Enric?"

"Quite," Enric replied and nodded with a serious expression. "There can be no doubt about that."

Pe'tala entered from the terrace and rolled her eyes. "Does Neval know that you keep hitting on your cousin's lover?"

Your cousin, Eryn noted and watched the younger woman stroll in and lean against a wall instead of sitting with them.

"Are there any pastries left?" Valrad asked.

"There should be, yes," his daughter answered. "I will get them from the kitchen along with some tea, shall I?"

"That would be fabulous, my dear," her father nodded. He waited until she had left the room before he leaned towards Vran'el. "Take her with you when you go out tonight. She needs to get out more, meet people. I am worried because she works so much since... you know."

Vran'el nodded. "I will, yes."

Eryn frowned. Since what? Had something happened to her? But asking would seem indiscreet, wouldn't it? If they intended her to know, they would not just have hinted at it but put words to it.

Pe'tala returned with a large brass tray with five cups, a steaming pot and a plate of thin, rounded objects that seemed to be some kind of sweet pastry. She placed her load on the low table in their middle and started pouring tea into the small cups before handing them out.

Valrad accepted his with a smile and took one of the pastries before he leaned back contentedly. He laughed as he watched Enric taking a tentative bite.

"No, my friend, that is not how we eat them here. It would do permanent damage to our teeth. You are meant to dunk them into your tea first."

Eryn's head snapped up at his words and she stared at him when he dipped the round pastry into his tea and then took a bite.

"What?" he enquired, confused at the rapt attention this seemingly harmless action attracted.

Enric was the one to answer. "Dipping pastries into hot drinks is something Eryn has been doing all her life. It seems she has just realised where it comes from."

"Have you now?" Valrad asked, intrigued. "A little leftover from your early childhood, it seems."

She nodded slowly. "Father always tried to get me out of the habit, but he never really managed. I resorted to doing it whenever he couldn't see me. I always thought he didn't want me to do it because it was impolite or repulsive. But now I see that it was another indicator that we were strangers, and he wanted to avoid my giving out any sign of that." She frowned. "But wouldn't that have disappeared as well with a memory block?"

Her uncle shook his head. "No. There are actions that work automatically, that are not conscious but ingrained. Blocking conscious memories would not be enough to get rid of those."

She leaned forward and hesitantly took a piece of pastry in her hand, staring at it. "I haven't really dared to do this when others could see me in quite a while," she murmured.

Enric smiled at the memory of the first time he had seen her dunking biscuits in his quarters at the Palace several months ago. And that he had felt privileged that she had let her guard down enough to let him see it.

"It's cultural, my love," he said softly. "It would be undiplomatic not to adapt."

She laughed and dunked the disc into her tea, delighted at the simple pleasure of being allowed to do so more or less publicly.

CHAPTER 31

A Seduction Dance

Vran'el led them into a large two-storey building with wide-open double doors. The entire ground floor was one spacious room with columns to support the building's weight. The floor was interspersed with numerous circles of cushions with the usual low tables in their centres.

Eryn looked around curiously. This was not the same place they were at last time. It seemed less formal, more comfortable. Pe'tala was the first to sink down elegantly on an empty heap of cushions to one side of the room.

"Luckily this is still free - it seems to be rather full in here," Eryn remarked.

Pe'tala sneered. "That has nothing to do with luck. This is the regular reserved table for House Vel'kim. But today we are generously permitting you to sit with us." The words *as you are not one of us* seemed to hang in the air between them.

Eryn smiled at her coldly and tried to imitate her cousin's moves when she sat down as well. "How very generous of you."

"Well, I suppose it does not hurt to be seen to have Enric sitting at our table, does it?" she retorted with a sweet grin.

"And how about me?" Eryn asked, her tone acerbic.

Pe'tala shrugged. "Oh, why not? Our connection with House Aren is rather strained, after all."

"Yes, so is mine," Eryn murmured.

"Girls," Vran'el sighed. "Try to be civilised, will you? Let us not start what might appear to others as a public feud between our Houses."

"Don't call Aren *my* House!" Eryn protested.

"Do remind me to thank father for his suggestion of taking the two of you out tonight, will you?" he rolled his eyes.

"Maybe Eryn would like to sit at the Aren table instead?" Pe'tala jibed. "I see that Malriel is here tonight. I am sure she would be delighted to have her daughter with her. The long-lost heiress, the answer to all hopes..."

"Tala!" Vran'el hissed in such an uncharacteristically sharp manner that Eryn looked at him in surprise. He was either really annoyed by this hostility or had wanted to stop her from saying something that better remained unsaid. Maybe he had wanted to stop her from revealing something? Another secret to be kept from her? She stole a look at Enric, who still hadn't revealed what had put him in the scary mood in the morning. Secrets everywhere.

Vran'el ordered food for them and then made a wry face.

"I see that the table of House Arbil is occupied tonight as well. How lovely," he sighed and looked at Enric, who had turned to follow Vran'el's gaze. His eyes narrowed when he recognised Ram'an among the occupants.

Great, he thought. This day was getting better and better.

They looked up when Neval appeared at their table and bent down to kiss Vran'el on the mouth.

"Hello, everyone," he beamed and settled on a cushion next to his lover. "I am glad that I can join you earlier this time. No family obligations today. Have you ordered already?"

Vran'el nodded. "Yes, just a moment ago. But you can eat with me, I find their portions too generous, anyway."

Neval exhaled theatrically. "You know, without this last addition this would have been a very loving and tender gesture."

"I thought you were the loving and tender one?" Vran'el smiled and linked their fingers. "I am in charge of sarcasm and flamboyance. We really need to stick to our roles, Sunshine, or there will be chaos."

Neval rolled his eyes. "Dear me, how could I forget?"

"Nice allotment of roles. I like it," Eryn grinned.

"What are your roles, then?" Neval asked with a smile.

She thought for a moment. "He is superior and demanding, I am difficult and disobedient."

Enric considered this for a moment, then nodded. "Surprisingly accurate, I have to admit."

Pe'tala snorted. "How charming. At least you deserve each other."

"May I ask what I have ever done to you?" Eryn leaned forward and fixed her cousin with narrowed eyes. "The very first thing you said to me, or rather *about* me, was an insult and matters haven't really improved since then. What is your problem with me? I am sorry that you didn't get invited to celebrations as a child because I had the audacity to let myself be taken away from here, but it's time to forgive and forget, don't you think?"

"You know what?" Pe'tala rose stiffly and turned to her brother. "I am not hungry any more. Good night." Then she marched out.

Eryn stared after her and then looked at Vran'el. "What just happened exactly?"

Her cousin sighed sadly. "Do not take it personally. I will tell you about it one day. But not now."

She gave him an angry glare. That was the second time today she had been put off with this sentence. Why did nobody ever talk to her?

The food was served in dark green bowls, and Eryn was glad to see that it didn't contain any meat. But of course it wouldn't, would it? Meat was something that was served to guests after the host himself had killed it. This would not apply for a guest house, but only for gatherings at private homes.

She nodded appreciatively. "I like these dark red vegetables. The ones with the slightly sweet aftertaste."

"Good. You should eat more of them if you indeed want to give up eating meat. They are very nutritious," Neval pointed out.

She swallowed. "You know, I have not really reached a decision yet. I am still just thinking about it. I haven't even talked to a healer yet."

"How often have you eaten meat since we were hunting together?" he asked.

She thought for a moment, then said. "Not once."

"There you go," Neval smiled with satisfaction. "I would assume that you had made your decision already."

Staring at him, she wondered if she had indeed.

Several servers began collecting empty bowls, and Enric stacked them in a pile to hand them to one of them.

"The music is about to start," Vran'el said and looked at Neval. "How do you feel about treating my lovely cousin over there to the fabulous experience of dancing with you, light of my life?"

Neval grinned. "I would be delighted. Eryn?"

She nodded slowly and stood up. Somehow she couldn't help but feeling that she had just been sent off to play so that the adults could talk undisturbed.

Vran'el waited until they had reached the dance floor before he turned to Enric.

"Now talk to me, my friend. There is something that is disturbing you." His gaze was unusually intent and Enric saw the serious lawyer talking, not the flirty cousin.

"There is something, indeed. I found out about a certain prearranged commitment between Houses Aren and Arbil."

Vran'el nodded slowly. "I see. An unpleasant revelation, I imagine."

Enric agreed. "Yes, you could say that. One I would have appreciated being told about by you or your father instead of Malriel."

"*Malriel* told you?" he asked incredulously.

"Not directly, but she arranged for me to be informed about it."

The lawyer leaned back and quietly whistled through his teeth. "Look at that. You never know what to expect from that woman." His gaze darted towards the table of House Aren.

"How binding is it?" Enric asked tensely.

"Eryn cannot be forced to enter into a commitment with him, if that is what you mean. But officially the arrangement between the Houses remains intact," Vran'el explained.

"Which means what exactly?"

"Which means that nobody will object to Ram'an pursuing his interests and trying to win her for himself."

Enric rubbed his face. "What would need to happen to make people object?"

"Two things are possible, basically. Firstly, Malriel could dissolve the arrangement with House Arbil, but let me tell you that this is not very likely. It would be most imprudent of her to do this - it would equal distancing herself from an important ally. And secondly, there is the chance of Eryn's entering into the third level commitment bond with you."

"Right," Enric sighed. "A much more likely alternative."

* * *

"Enric," he heard a familiar throaty voice behind him on his way back to his table from the wash room and turned. Malriel was sitting on a pile of differently sized colourful cushions, smiling up at him. "Sit with me for a while, if you will."

She saw his gaze dart back to Eryn and Vran'el on the dance floor and chuckled quietly. "They are enjoying themselves. And as you surely know, he is no danger at all to her."

Enric hesitated still, wondering how Eryn would react if she saw him sitting with her mother.

"You know," she said, "you are connected to my House through your commitment to my daughter. It would seem strange to others if you declined an invitation to sit with me. I am, legally speaking, like a mother to you." She patted the cushions next to her. "Do not be concerned with what Maltheá will say for now. I am confident that you have your ways of making up with her."

It was the smirk at the end of her last sentence that finally made him sit down next to her. He found her confidence fascinating. Back home women were not as such without influence, but they were limited to wielding it in a more indirect manner by steering or manipulating men instead of holding public positions of power.

"I am surprised at your invoking our family status. I did not have the impression that you were satisfied with the situation as such. Or with Eryn's connection to me." He looked her straight in the eyes and was pleased that she didn't avert her gaze. These brown eyes, he thought, so similar to the ones he knew so well. But more calculating. A politician's eyes.

"I admit I was not. But then I had been told that Maltheá was made to join you against her will." She paused to give him the opportunity to comment on that, and went on when he didn't. "Will you tell me how much truth is in this? I see that Ram'an might have been eager to convey that impression due to his own interest in her."

Enric smiled thinly. "I am sure you appreciate that I could hardly tell you if this were true. What I can tell you is that Eryn and I were lovers already when we were joined. And I promise you that this was entirely voluntary."

Malriel leaned forward slightly. "Yes, I see that you are not a man who needs to compel a woman to be with you, are you? There is pride in you, a great deal of it. And affection for my daughter. Even if the commitment really was not voluntary as Ram'an told us, I doubt that you would have objected to it."

Dangerous paths, Enric thought and decided to change direction. "The mother's family is the one to make the important decisions in a child's life, isn't it? So you would have been the one to plan her commitment to Ram'an, unless I am massively mistaken."

She leaned back again. "No, you are not mistaken. It *was* I who planned it. Are you asking me, Enric, if I still intend to make this happen somehow?"

He nodded. "That question has crossed my mind, yes."

She studied him, let her gaze wander along his body and return to his eyes. "I was hoping to when you first arrived."

"Something has changed your mind, then?" he enquired impassively.

"You could say that, yes. When I look at Theá, I am astounded by how much of myself I see in her. Not only in our facial features, but on the inside." Her eyes wandered over to locate Eryn on the dance floor with her cousin. "She is strong - headstrong even - fierce and smart. I do not see how Ram'an would be able to handle her. He is too polite, too correct, too *nice*." She looked back at Enric. "But *you* know how to deal with her, do you not? When I look at the two of you, I can see that she accepts that you are the stronger, though reluctantly." She smiled. "But she would not be my daughter if she did not find a way around that occasionally, am I right? And I would bet you enjoy losing a good fight to her every now and then. Your pride goes further than your position and abilities. You are proud to have won a woman who will not bow to you so willingly all the time. And you are proud of her, because you are strong enough to know that real strength does not derive from never being surpassed, but from learning from it and re-emerging from your defeat as an even more formidable opponent to those who seek to challenge you in the future."

"So you are saying that Ram'an is not strong enough for her? This is why you have refrained from trying to join her with him any longer?" Enric asked, determined not to fall for her flattery but return to the topic that was on his mind and had been for many hours now.

"Let us just say it is one consideration." She lifted a finger for a servant to refill her glass. "Seeing that you so obviously love her makes it easier for me to accept your connection. And, I cannot help but think, you are somebody one had better avoid turning into an enemy. You would fight me until the bitter end if I were to go on with my initial plan. And then there is the political side to of all this. I might currently not be able to reaffirm our connection with House Arbil, but there is always another generation to come."

Enric lifted a brow. "And a close connection of your House to the top ranks of the governing magical institution of my home country is also nothing to cast aside carelessly, I would assume?"

She laughed. "Very true. And I am glad to see that you have not underestimated your own importance. But the final point in discarding my plans with Ram'an is a simple and uncomplicated one: I like you."

"Really?" He lifted a finger to have a glass of whatever Malriel was having and turned back to her, intrigued. "Do you now."

"Indeed. I admit that I find you fascinating. I have great respect for strength, be it physical, magical or in character. You, my dear, seem to combine all three - how very unusual. And how very lucky for my daughter that you were still available when she came along, considering your age. I would imagine you were never in want of willing women to choose from, were you?"

He raised both eyebrows at that statement. It was certainly rather irregular for something like this to be addressed by the mother of his companion, he mused. Or was that a standard conversation topic here? But the glint in her eyes told him that it was more likely that she was trying to see if she could make him uncomfortable.

"Are trying to make me brag, Malriel?" he asked with a faint smile.

"What if I told you that this is a cultural trait of our country? That recounting former conquests makes you rise in our esteem and earns you respect?"

"Then I would, with all due respect, take the liberty of not adapting to this one idiosyncrasy of yours and merely appreciate it from afar in accordance with my own culture's more modest ways of dealing with the topic," he replied smoothly.

"Well said. A diplomatic answer." She frowned when a faint bell was rung three times in a row. They both watched Ram'an cast a quick look around the room and then turn to walk in Eryn's direction.

"A quick warning," she whispered urgently, "and one I recommend you heed: do not let Ram'an dance this dance with your companion. It is of a rather... particular nature."

"A seduction song?" he asked sharply.

Malriel nodded. "Indeed. And unless you are very sure that there is no physical attraction whatsoever between them, I would intervene. But be aware that if you deny him the dance, you are expected to dance it yourself."

He rose immediately and all but ran towards Ram'an, who had already taken Eryn's hand in his and was smiling triumphantly.

"I am afraid I have to claim *that* dance for myself," Enric growled and stepped between them to break the contact. His eyes shot daggers at the dark-haired man.

Ram'an pressed his lips together in annoyance and balled his hands into fists, but stepped back and inclined his head towards Eryn before retreating with the words, "Another time, then."

"What are you doing?" she hissed. "That was uncalled for! You may not like him, but dancing is harm..." Her voice trailed off when the first notes of the song made her blood sing in response.

"Oh..." she murmured in surprise, understanding the nature of the song immediately. It was a sensation she had encountered only once before, but never really forgotten. This was stronger than what she had danced to many months ago, instantly recognisable for what it was, especially when standing close to a physically compatible and congenial partner.

"Yes, *oh*," he remarked grimly and took her hands when he felt the effect. Even though he fought to hold on to it, he gradually felt his anger at Ram'an subside in favour of the more pressing sensations the music around him awakened.

The first instrument filled the room with its low, suggestive rumble, and the tones seemed to vibrate in the air for a moment longer after they were released. Other instruments joined and created different layers of sound that appeared strangely independent from each other if listened to separately. When he gave in to the music and started moving, obeying its commands, the parts fused into a harmonic stream that lost its foreign quality almost completely, morphing into something he understood, recognised on a deeper, instinctive level. A high female voice began singing ancient words he had never heard before, but which made perfect sense. This was pure magic moulded into meaning, the words nothing more than a shell serving as a means to make expressing the essence behind them possible so that they were accessible to human senses.

Their content didn't seem to take the detour through his ears, but entered every fibre of his being at once, revealing its secrets, speaking of the power of surrender, the pleasure of defeat, the vigour of giving in.

He watched Eryn's chest lift and lower more quickly, and a slightly panicky expression entered her eyes. Smiling, he pulled her against him, stopping her a fraction before their bodies met, then turning her slowly until she stood with her back to him.

"Don't fight it, my love," he whispered into her ear. "You won't win this time, either. It's even more potent than the last one we danced."

She exhaled and closed her eyes for a moment. He was right, of course. This was not a conscious decision she had reached in her head - it was no more than a universal truth, like the stars in the sky or the warmth of the sun. The magic flowed through her veins and it felt as if all her blood had been exchanged for it. Concerns at being seen to relinquish control over herself, to react to him like this, to expose herself to knowing smiles, looks and possibly comments vanished, and her thoughts decelerated and finally came to a standstill.

He touched no more than her hands when he lifted both her arms to her sides and started steering her the way the music told him to. She complied, freeing one hand at the exact right moment to place it on his chest, leading him back and forward again, following the demanding rhythm.

She felt the increasing urge to touch more of him than the small areas the music permitted, but noncompliance was no option. Savouring every little contact she was allowed, she waited impatiently to see if the next movement would bring her closer to him. How was this possible? How could withholding contact with a man she had touched wherever and as often as she had wanted in these last months, at this moment cause almost physical pain?

He felt her hair standing on end when he gently let his fingers glide along her forearms and stepped back in time to catch her hands to guide them behind her back and make her bend backwards, making her lean back so that she presented her throat to him. Closing his eyes over the scent that emanated from her skin, images of himself closing the small gap between his lips and her throat caused his mouth to become dry from the strain of not being able to follow the urge.

Eryn almost groaned in frustration when she straightened again without feeling more than the touch of his hands and arms on hers. They intertwined their fingers, lifted them and after a quick turn that left her again with her back to him, she felt his arms settle around her, still joined at their hands, and so not able to touch her anywhere else.

He moistened his dry lips, caught between fervently wishing for the song to be over and release him from the forced restraint, and enjoying the immensely sweet pain it caused. Twirling her back to face him, he swallowed hard.

The intensity in her eyes when they roamed his body as if she, too, had clear images in her head of what she wanted to do with him right now, made his pounding heart increase its pace even further until he thought it must leap from his chest any moment.

He saw thin beads of sweat on her forehead, her throat, the top of her breasts from the strain of having the driving urge to touch him suppressed. Sheer desperation had entered her eyes and replaced the mere greed from moments before.

Commanding his legs, his feet to stop moving so he could finally submit to the tension that not feeling any more of her than the marginal touches had produced, he felt them move on to the music as if he was being held prisoner by his mind in his own body.

She wanted to fall to her knees in gratitude when she felt the song slowly subsiding, knowing that there were only moments left until she would again be mistress of herself.

When the last notes had faded, she grabbed his collar to pull him towards her violently while she felt his arms capturing her around her waist with equal rapaciousness. Their lips melted together in a tempestuous kiss that made him feel dizzy and had him fighting for equilibrium while a single tear of relief rolled down her cheek.

After what felt no more than a moment to them but had probably been a small eternity to the crowd around them, they slowly released their grips and stared at each other in utter disbelief for several seconds. The contact had taken the peak off the tension, the need for immediate action and merely left their bodies vibrating with suppressed sexual energy instead of the fierce, uncontrollable desire from before.

"I am stuck between desperately wanting to do this again and fearing for my life," she whispered, leaning her forehead against his shoulder. "Let's leave here. Now."

Enric swallowed hard and nodded. "Yes. There is just one more thing I need to do. Wait here."

The anger that had been dampened by the first notes of the song returned with a rush of fire now that he was back in control of himself.

He pressed a hard kiss into her palm and walked to where Ram'an was leaning against a column with folded arms, staring at him with an expression that was far beyond displeasure.

The man had intended to dance *this* dance with Eryn, something which shot through Enric's head like a hot spear. With *his* companion. He had been about to trick her into it, without her knowing what she would have been getting herself into. He wanted to choke, hurt, destroy Ram'an - make him regret the day he had laid eyes on her for the first time.

Before Ram'an even suspected what Enric's intention was, the fist connected with his jaw and launched him backwards across the entire span of a seating island. Only a column stopped his movement. Enric exhaled slowly. That had felt good, incredibly good. And he had been angry enough to punch that hard even without resorting to any magical assistance.

When Ram'an opened his eyes, it took the world around him several moments to swim back into focus. What appeared as a pale spot in front of his eyes slowly turned out to be a blonde head of hair close to his face.

"If you ever try anything like that again, I will make sure you pay for it. Dearly so," Enric's said in a deadly voice, so quietly only Ram'an heard.

"Are you threatening me, *Lord* Enric?" Ram'an choked out, throwing the title at him like an insult.

"No," Enric replied with a slight shake of his head, "No threats. Promises. And I pride myself on keeping them." And he simply got up and strolled back to Eryn, whose eyes were wide in bewilderment and shock.

She felt her hand enclosed in a warm grip and let herself be pulled out of the room into the cool night air. It was time to get back to their contemporary home. As quickly as possible.

* * *

Enric looked down at her satisfied smile. Her head lay on his shoulder and her hand on his bare chest, playing with the blonde hairs, twirling them around her index finger.

He had to tell her, he thought, and sighed. After what had almost happened tonight she needed to understand and be better prepared for similar attempts at seduction from Ram'an, especially if Enric was not around to protect her. But he was reluctant to tell her now and disrupt the cosy mood. And yet he had to.

"Eryn," he said and made her look up. "There is something you should know. It is the reason why I was so upset today, especially in the morning."

She lifted herself up on one elbow and regarded him warily. "That must be really bad news, then."

"It is nothing we can't handle," he assured her. "It is about Ram'an. There is an arrangement in place between Houses Aren and Arbil and has been for about twenty-five years."

He waited for her to make the connection. First she frowned, then her brow furrowed in disbelief.

"You are not telling me that I have been *promised* to him? As a companion?"

She sat up abruptly when he nodded. "Yes, so it would seem."

"But... that's ridiculous! It was such a long time ago! And I have no intention of complying with this arrangement!" She gripped his hand. "Can they make me? Please tell me they can't!"

"No, they can't," he assured her and with that she let out a long, relieved breath. "Though neither will anybody stop him from trying to take you away from me."

She slapped her palm against her forehead. "That's why you reacted so strangely when I said that I had exchanged you for Orrin, why you needed to hear me say that I was yours! The thought of being exchanged got to you, didn't it?" She lowered her hands and looked down at him. "You are not afraid that I am about to leave you for him, are you? I wouldn't, you know."

"Good. I wouldn't let you, anyway," he smiled. "Don't look so sad, my love. We will find a way through this."

She nodded. "I know. But despite everything, I still consider him a friend. Or have done so until now. He taught me how to change my hair colour and how to make magical medicine. We had tea together, and he told me about people who live without eating meat. He has enriched my life, and I am sorry that this will now have to stop. And I am sorry to see that his being pleasant to me was probably no more than calculated facade to make a politically advantageous connection for his House."

Enric sighed and pulled her close. If only, he thought. Crushing a man who wanted to steal his companion, his love, for mere political reasons would not have bothered him at all. But Ram'an had formed an attachment to her, and this was another matter entirely. Yet telling Eryn that Ram'an truly seemed to like her would make her breaking off contact with him even harder, so he didn't and just held her.

*   *   *

Vran'el strolled into the main room at the ambassadorial residence after the ambassador and his companion had finished breakfast and waved his hand.

"Good morning, cousin. Enric." He took a seat on the cushions next to Eryn and gave them a big smile. "That was quite a show you treated us to yesterday evening, I must say."

Enric snorted. "Then I assume Ram'an does not get punched in the face very regularly. I can't imagine why not."

"That was one thing, yes," Vran'el nodded and took a leftover piece of fruit from Eryn's plate. "But watching the three of you, that was really only a matter of time. With *the show* I was primarily referring to your dance. That was sight to behold."

Eryn frowned. "Why? There were two other couples dancing to it, so what of it?"

"Well, let me put it like this: the intensity we witnessed yesterday was... something above average, to put it mildly." He swallowed when Urban sauntered into the room and lifted her nose to sniff the newcomer in the air. Her amber eyes snapped to Vran'el and she stood for a moment as if considering her next step before she began pacing in a circle.

"What is that animal doing?" Vran'el sounded nervous.

"Playing with you," Enric smirked. "She can see, or rather smell, that you are anxious. Now she is going to circle you to make you really uncomfortable. At the end she will probably either jump on you from behind or sit in front of you to stare at you. It depends on her mood."

"What? Jump on me from behind? And then what?" Vran'el turned to keep his eyes on the slowly moving cat that did in turn focus on him.

"Don't you think we would have left her at home if she tended to rip out people's throats?" Eryn giggled. "Just try to relax. If she sees that her tactics aren't working, she may give up." Or try harder, she added silently. "Back to what you were saying. What do you mean with *above average intensity*? How can *you* know how intense it was?"

"You are joking, are you not? The people at their tables were hardly able to sit still after your little demonstration on the dance floor. We do not often witness two such strong users of magic dance together. It creates a certain kind of energy, especially as it was a powerful song. It cannot be contained by the usual shield that just filters audible signals."

"Yes," Enric nodded. "I have danced only one other, and the one yesterday was clearly more potent, very much so. Why does this affect people around us?"

"As I said, two strong magicians interacting creates a certain kind of energy, and a strong magical song can amplify it for people around them enough to become aware of it. And let me tell you one thing: People were *very* well aware of it yesterday. The entire room exhaled in relief when you finally kissed and part of that immense tension was dispersed. After you had left, all the windows were opened to let in cool night air to clear people's heads again."

Eryn exchanged an uncomfortable look with her companion. That had been much too personal a sensation to share with an audience, with strangers. But then sharing it with people she knew was not much better, either.

"You say you don't see this often. How often?" Eryn enquired.

"Well, the last time was when Golir, one of the members of the triarchy, took his companion. They are both very powerful. And before that," he looked at Eryn, "your parents."

She grimaced at the image of Malriel and her father experiencing what she and Enric had the night before. "Thank you very much for that delightful image," she groaned.

Enric watched Urban crouching in preparation for a jump, shoulders low, haunches slightly elevated, legs inching along the floor to prepare for launch. "Vran'el?"

"Yes, Enric?"

"Duck," he said mildly and moments later the cat sailed over the cushions and Vran'el's hastily drawn-in head and shoulders to land right in front of him.

"You are a monster," Eryn scolded her with a lifted index finger. "He is not your toy, he is a guest. This is not how we treat guests!"

Urban looked at her, ears and tail flicking nervously and then wandered off with a slightly sulky edge to her movements.

"What an incredible creature!" Eryn's cousin exhaled and shook his head.

"With an attitude like a queen," Eryn muttered.

He chuckled. "Yes, I wonder who she might have learned that from by watching."

Enric smiled, then became serious again. "What about Ram'an? How did people react to my punching him? Are there any official letters of reprimand from the senate likely to arrive anytime soon?"

"No, not very likely," Vran'el shrugged. "Your rivalry has become common knowledge now, and you did not resort to any magic to harm him."

"Well, no direct magic," Eryn said with her eyebrow raised in mild disapproval.

Enric smiled in quiet satisfaction and she was taken aback. "Oh, come on now! Don't tell me you punched him across an entire seating group without infusing your muscles? Not even a little?" She shook her head in disbelief. "Well, no matter how you managed to send him flying, it was a rather harsh reaction. I mean, he might not even have known what kind of dance it was that he requested of me."

Vran'el grinned. "Oh, he knew that alright, you can depend on it. There is a signal to announce them. A bell that chimes three times."

"And he looked around the room to see if I was anywhere nearby before he approached you," Enric added grimly.

"He did?" She frowned. "But how do you know that? How were you able to see him without his spotting you?"

Enric cleared his throat. He had hoped for this little detail to remain unmentioned. Vran'el smirked at him, clearly aware of his dilemma.

"He might have been a little sloppy in his survey of the premises."

"Go on," she said with narrowed eyes. There was clearly more to come.

"He had clearly not expected me at the table where I had taken a seat at and so had not bothered to check there."

"Oh no!" she groaned when realisation dawned. "Don't tell me you were sitting with *her*?"

"Yes, I did sit with Malriel. She invited me to do so, and I could hardly have declined, could I? I am the ambassador, she is an important politician," Enric stated reasonably.

"She is also a pain in my neck! Can't you keep away from her? And don't throw your political considerations at me!"

"She is your mother," he said reproachfully. "That was a personal consideration."

"That is an immensely ridiculous thing to say for a man who keeps his own family as far away from him as possible," she shot back.

He sighed. Well, he'd had that one coming.

"Why would you even *want* to sit with her? She promised me to Ram'an, after all!"

"That was a long time ago."

"Was it? Funny, I somehow have the impression that this decision is still very current. She hasn't publicly declared that she rescinds that decision, or am I mistaken? That must mean she still is in favour of it!"

Vran'el lifted his hand carefully. "Now, that is not as easy as it may sound."

Two pairs of eyes darted towards him.

"It would mean a public breach with House Arbil if she did. She does not really have another choice but to hope that Ram'an either succeeds, if she is still in favour of the union, or gives up in good time of his own accord."

Eryn shook her head. "But why doesn't he give up, can you tell me that? I am committed to another man! That should be a valid reason, shouldn't it?"

Her cousin lifted an elegant eyebrow at her. "You are serious, are you not? But I am too strict with you, how would you know about a thing like that." He leaned forward. "Committed you may be, but not in what we consider the final, authentic way. You have no more than a legal bond, forged by a non-magician, not a life-bond forged by magic."

She gulped hard. "He thinks I am still available because we have not entered into a third level commitment bond?"

"Indeed. Your bond is like… a promise, a plan. But you have been promised to him long before that, and as regards his point of view, you are still free to choose one promise over another."

Eryn jumped up and cursed. Then she looked up in sudden understanding.

"That day in his quarters!" she exclaimed. "That's why he was so damned pleased when I told him that our King is no magician! He had realised that there was no magical commitment in place! I need to talk to him. There must be an end to this idiocy. We can't go on like this."

"You surely won't want to talk to him," Enric said sharply.

"What? Why not?" She was about to add that she was stronger than him, after all, and had thus not much to fear from him magically speaking, but bit her lip in time. Enric would demand to know how she had found out about that, and saying that she had been able to break the barrier he had used to try and lock her in his quarters at the Palace would not be a wise thing to declare right now.

"Because he would very likely see your coming to him on your own as a sign of encouragement. *I* will talk to him."

"No. Why should he accept whatever you tell him? It is *my* decision to stay with you instead of him. So he needs to hear it from *me*. But I see your point how going there alone would not be so wise. Let's invite him here, then. I'll talk to him, you can be in the room with us. Visible, but not audible," she added in a warning tone.

He nodded slowly. Yes, he could agree to that. And who knew? Maybe another chance at punching him in the face would somehow present itself.

"What are your plans for today while I am at the senate?" he enquired.

"Valrad has offered to take me to their local healing place," she answered.

Enric nodded. "I was wondering when you would go there. You have been here for more than a week now, after all. I would have expected you to have visited it sooner. Vran'el, that means you will be at the senate meeting for House Vel'kim this afternoon when your father is taking Eryn sightseeing?"

Vran'el nodded and chuckled when Eryn flashed her companion an annoyed look. "I'll thank you very much not to call it *sightseeing*. I am not doing this for mere pleasure, but to learn something that will assist my efforts at making our Kingdom a better place."

"I apologise," Enric smiled. "In light of the fact that this is clearly more a matter of duty than joy. I see that insulting you by insinuating that you might actually be interested in seeing the place is outrageous, and I should be ashamed of myself."

"It is not going to be all fun. He will introduce me to the man who tomorrow will try to lift my memory block. He thought it might be a good idea for me to meet him beforehand, so he is not a complete stranger anymore and I am less nervous when he works on me."

"Tomorrow already?" Enric frowned. "When?"

"In the morning, after breakfast. Valrad thinks I should have an entire day to cope with the memories before I retire for the night. He recommended making no plans for the day after tomorrow, as the night will probably not be a very restful one. Memories might float up into my dreams and make them too realistic for me to sleep peacefully."

He turned to Vran'el. "Is there a chance that the senate will grant me a break from negotiating for tomorrow? I don't want to leave her alone after the procedure."

"I am confident that they will, yes. You just need to ask. Though I doubt very much that my father will leave her alone, whether you are there or not."

"Memory blocks are only granted under special circumstances, if I remember correctly?" Eryn asked. She continued when Vran'el nodded. "So, is the healer under any duty to report if he is asked to remove an unapproved block?"

"Are you afraid of Malriel learning about this?" her cousin asked.

She nodded. "That was a thought, yes."

"Then let me assure you that this is not the way she will learn about it." Eryn was about to relax, but then he went on, "Her information network at the clinic will have provided her with this little fact already."

"Damn it," she cursed.

"But why try to hide it from her, anyway? She could hardly object to your getting your memories back, especially as she may safely count on you to remember her as well, regain precious moments with her from your early childhood," Vran'el shrugged.

"Because she spoke of him like of a criminal, and I don't want her to know that there was even more to it," she sighed.

Enric took her hand in his, aware that his next words would not make her happy. "According to the local laws he *was* a criminal, Eryn. He would have been one at home as well; our own laws wouldn't have protected him from such a grave case of disobedience and child abduction, either. No, don't look at me like that. I am not judging him, whatever people might say about him. I was the one to profit from his actions profoundly, after all. But Malriel is entitled to a certain degree of anger."

"I don't like your taking her side," Eryn growled.

"I am not. I am on your side, always. But I am not entirely sure whether your side and her side are really two opposed ones."

Vran'el leaned forward. "There is no changing the situation, you need to find a different approach to working through it. Being angry at her only inflicts pain on yourself in the long run. So try to let go of it for your own sake."

"Philosophical words from both of you," she said coolly and stood up to go. "If you'll excuse me now, gentlemen, I need to brush my hair. Or braid it. Or whatever else a woman is supposed to pretend she has to do when she wants to avoid spending time with a man. Or two."

"Is not the purpose of pretence not to give away your true motives? We need to work on that, cousin," Vran'el called after her as she walked towards the bedroom.

"What can I say? I don't really bother with subtleties," she said without turning and walked on.

"No, of course not," she heard him murmur. "Otherwise you would almost certainly become the first Aren woman who did."

He sucked in a shocked breath when he saw a bolt of light fly towards him and lifted both arms before his face. A slightly blue shimmering barrier appeared before him, and the strike dispersed on it harmlessly with a faint crackle.

Eryn flickered an enraged look at Enric and turned on her heel to continue her way out of the room.

Vran'el swallowed and let his arms sink again. "Thank you, my friend. I was not prepared for that reaction. I probably should have been. I can see how combat training has prepared you well for a life with that one." He nodded towards the archway which she had just disappeared through.

Enric smiled. "Teasing her with the Aren temper for days and then not being prepared for it to bite you back is rather incautious, if you don't mind my saying so."

"Yes, I can see that now." He shook his head in disbelief. "And you fools taught an Aren woman combat skills? As if they were not dangerous enough already!"

"Only if you are slower and weaker. I happen to be neither," Enric remarked confidently.

CHAPTER 32

The Clinic

Eryn lifted her hand to shade her eyes while looking up at the building the locals called *the clinic*. It reminded her a little of the Vel'kim residence, which was probably no coincidence, considering that the family had very likely been involved in the planning of the place. Two storeys high, it gleamed white in the sunlight. She instantly recognised the large symbol which was painted in dark green over the massive double doors: a human palm emanating what appeared to be rays of light. The symbol of magical healing, just like on the Vel'kim crest.

Valrad waited patiently for her to take in the outside of the building and only walked inside when her gaze had returned to him.

She found herself in what looked like a waiting area with walls painted in different colours. It was currently empty.

"Is this just for decoration or am I looking at some sort of colour-based orientation system here?" she asked curiously.

"Very perceptive of you, my dear," her uncle smiled. "The colours do indeed have a purpose. They are meant to divide the patients according to their ailments."

"Really? Such as?"

"Such as broken bones and other injuries requiring immediate pain release in the red area, illnesses in the yellow one, and the green colour is pretty much for everything else except cosmetic corrections - for example, preventative measures. This is only part of what is offered here, though. We have an extra entrance for expectant mothers as they are not supposed to be in close proximity to people with infectious illnesses or have to look at injuries or other distressing accidents. It would cause them torment," he explained.

Eryn looked at the arrangement appreciatively. "I see. Very practical. My assistant Rolan mentioned a similar idea of preventative checks for pregnant women I intend to pursue when I am back home. But you offer them to other people as well?"

"Oh, absolutely," Valrad replied with emphasis. "We consider it one of a healer's main duties to make sure the patients stay healthy instead of just attending to ailments. They come here for an examination once a year. We tell them if we see something which might cause trouble at a future time and advise them what to do about it, be it a change in diet or more exercise, or less wine, less work, whatever we deem helpful in improving their life quality and long-term health status."

"So you basically treat them before they have even fallen ill?"

He chuckled. "Yes. A person is no less a patient just because they happen not to be ill at this moment. If a person attends his or her annual examinations regularly, we consider it the healer's failure if an illness cannot be prevented. For those who do not bother coming to us because they are too careless about their health, we limit our efforts to healing whatever keeps befalling them."

"This means you have fewer illnesses to cure but more preventive examinations to carry out, I assume?" she enquired thoughtfully.

"It does. We also table our prices according to the regularity of previous examinations. If they were few and far between, the treatment of an illness will be more costly. We aim to reward people for taking care of themselves. A healthy society is a strong society, after all."

Eryn's thoughts raced. Preventive measures instead of taking care of the damage afterwards, like maintenance work on a building. This would make everything so much easier to plan, to organise. Routine examinations could be scheduled - injuries and illnesses could not.

"Come," he said gently and took her arm to encourage her along with him. "We can talk about this in more detail once we are back home. I would like to show you the building and introduce you to a few of my colleagues. They are very eager to meet you."

She frowned in dismay. "They are? I hope not to assess my healing knowledge and have expert conversations with me? I will be sorely disappointing for them, I dare say."

"What? No!" He laughed. "They have each other for that. They want to meet this pioneer, who has taken it upon herself to push a seemingly backwards country into a new age of medical services. And there is the fact that House Aren is not exactly known for bringing forth dedicated healers, so they want to see the embodiment with their own eyes."

Great, she thought. It seemed that she was an oddity wherever she went. A sensation, once again.

They went along a long corridor with numerous doors leading off, some of them open, many closed.

"Are these treatment rooms?" she enquired and stopped in front of one open door to assess the complicated looking instruments laid out on tables.

"They are, yes," Valrad confirmed. "Go in, have a look around if you wish."

She entered curiously and cast her eyes over some intricate metal tools. She picked up what looked like a thin, very sharp knife.

"What would you need a thing like that for? Do you take your lunch in here as well?"

Valrad stared at her for a few moments, then his face contorted in what clearly was a heroic effort not to erupt in laughter. She waited patiently for him to regain his composure.

"No, this is a medical instrument. We use it to cut open tissue."

She stared at him in disbelief. "Why ever would you do a thing like that? Cutting people open?" She dropped the knife hastily and stared down at the other implements, imagining what horrible things there were used for.

"As not all of our healers are magicians, and we also try to get both magicians and non-magicians to learn and pass on healing skills without magic. We do not want to depend on magic alone for healing. Firstly, it would mean only a selected class of people had access to the profession, namely those born with magical powers, and secondly, there usually is a greater demand for healers than magicians alone could meet. Especially in small settlements and amongst desert tribes."

"Non-magical healers?" she whispered in awe and looked down at the metal items once more. Suddenly they didn't seem ghastly at all, but like slim, silver keys which would open hitherto closed doors. Non-magical healers in villages... she thought while staring at the array in front of her unseeingly.

What would she need to teach non-magicians as healers? What literature? Could she even do such a thing herself? She had no idea about healing without magic apart from by using herbs. How did they diagnose illnesses if not by sending an impulse into a body? Using mere external indications? But that was so prone to error, wasn't it? One symptom could have so many different causes, how could they ever discover the underlying cause?

Valrad's hand on her shoulder jolted her back from the muddle of different pictures and questions swirling around in her head.

"It seems this is another matter you will be eager to talk about tonight, unless I misinterpret your reaction," he smiled. "And we will, be sure of it. Come now, let us move on."

They stopped once more when Eryn discovered a room with shelves that went up to the ceiling, filled with what looked like files.

"What is this? Some kind of library?" she asked and was about to pull out one of the files when her uncle caught her hand and shook his head.

"No, you cannot just take them and have a look at them. They are confidential. These are patient records with the medical history of every patient who has come here and is still alive."

"Medical history? Such as which illnesses and treatments every single person in the city has had in the past? But that must be thousands of files!" she exclaimed.

"There are, yes," he confirmed. "This is just one of five rooms we have. But this probably sounds worse than it really is. We shelve them in a way that makes it easy for us to find the right file when we need it. They are generally divided by district and there is one section for members of the twelve houses."

She let her gaze sweep over the hundreds of files around her and nodded slowly. "So every healer can have a look at the file and see what a particular patient's previous ailments were without having to rely on their remembering or being willing to tell the truth. This is amazing! But it must take a lot of time to maintain these records, mustn't it?"

"Not really, no. Whenever you are finished with your treatment session with a patient, you take another few minutes to add your notes to the file and then put it aside and return it here before you leave for the evening."

Nodding slowly, she looked back at him. "You said this was confidential. Why was I able to walk in here just like that, then?"

He chuckled. "Because you are with *me*, dear niece. Had you been strolling along the corridors alone, somebody would already have stopped and escorted you to the exit."

"How important are you here, if I may ask? Is there any place you are not allowed to go?"

"No, there are no restricted areas for me here. I happened to be in charge of this place for several years, but have retired from that position. Heading a House and keeping the clinic running smoothly was quite a strain. I was working almost around the clock for some time, feeling the energy draining out of me little by little. And then there is so much administration; the time I wasn't spending bent over ledgers, reports and files I was on the go attending meetings. It did not really have anything to do with healing any more. I was more of a business man, a politician. This function I already have as a Head of House, I did not want here as well. This was supposed to give me some balance, the chance to live my vocation, but in the end it was no more than a burden, so I stepped down and resumed healing."

Eryn nodded thoughtfully. Was this what would sooner or later await her, too? Heading what she hoped would be a healing place growing steadily, would it eventually mean spending all her time in an office instead of treating patients?

"And now you are happier than before?"

"Oh yes, really." He smiled. "And the fact that people remember that I used to be in charge gives me quite a bit of influence here still. I also have taken over the area dedicated to illnesses, which is an interesting field as it requires quite a lot of searching around at times. You would be surprised at what people come down with. Only last month I had a patient who had been bitten by some kind of insect and kept falling asleep all the time. He had been far up north, where they seem to have quite a number of interesting animals, it would seem."

Eryn's brows rose. "An insect that induces sleep? Did you find out how exactly it worked? Did something stimulate the respective area of the brain? Or has the insect injected a substance to cause the effect directly?"

Valrad smiled. "The latter. I have written an article about it, if you are interested. A copy of it should be in my study somewhere."

"Is there any chance of sending an expedition there to catch some of these insects and examine them?"

He shook his head. "Not at the moment, no. Our political relationship with this country, Pirinkar, is currently rather strained. It is not a very good time for seeking permission to undertake research in their country. But I see that your test results were accurate. You truly have the mind of an explorer."

Her spirits sank. The test made her involuntarily think of Ram'an. And the revelation in connection with him.

She forced herself to push these thoughts away and followed her uncle to a group of three middle-aged people, two women and a man. One of the women seemed to tell the others a story about a patient and stopped in mid-sentence when she spotted Valrad and what clearly had to be his long-lost niece.

"Ah, there you are!" she called out. "We have been hanging about, waiting to lay eyes on her for a week now! What took you so long to bring her here, Valrad?" Then she turned towards Eryn. "Hello, my name is Alenéa. I am a colleague of your uncle's, though I do not work in his area. I work in the field of beauty corrections." She looked at the younger woman and shook her head in slight amazement. "You know, I have heard about you being easily identifiable as a member of the Aren family, but I admit I am still surprised at how striking the similarity to Malriel is. Welcome back here, Maltheá. Or do you prefer Eryn?"

"Good day to you. Eryn will be fine, yes." Finally - somebody who actually asked her what name to use.

Her uncle introduced the other woman. "This here is Dikea, another healer colleague. She has specialised in urgent treatments such as gaping wounds, broken bones and everything that looks vile and turns the stomachs of more squeamish types."

Dikea laughed and lifted her hand for the formal greeting. "Greetings to you, Eryn. Do not listen to him. Urgent does not necessarily mean bloody or involving any body parts hanging out that should not. Luckily, those are in the minority among our cases. And after a while you start getting used to even that. But I suppose you yourself have seen a few injuries that are less pleasant to behold, have you not? Being the only healer in your Kingdom does not leave people much of a choice who to fetch."

Eryn nodded and thought back to the last grisly injury she had treated: the table leg stuck in Vern's back while he had been lying in a puddle of his own blood.

"And this here is Rededar. He, too, works with illnesses, same as me," Valrad turned to the third person.

"I have been eager to meet you, Eryn," Rededar nodded while he took her hand to kiss it.

"Tell us about that healing place you have opened in Anyueel, will you? That must have been quite a task for somebody who grew up in a land without healers," Alenéa remarked.

"It has been, yes," Eryn nodded. "Walking around here shows me how much potential for improvement there still is. I imagine people at home will groan when I come back listing all the changes I want to make. You said your field was beauty corrections? I have started offering them as well, although rather reluctantly. As we comprise only six healers so far, I feel that it keeps me from treating the patients who need me for getting well again rather than for vanity purposes."

The older woman smiled. "Yes, but unfortunately the upper classes do not tend to get ill very often or injure themselves through doing hard manual labour, so if we want to get to their money, we need to cater to their whims in order to sustain the less lucrative but more important services." She shrugged. "And it is less stressful for the healer. You can table your appointments to your liking, as you do not have to deal with emergencies. Although I would not exactly say most of my patients are easy to handle. But when are overly vain and wealthy people ever easy to handle? A colleague of mine works in a different field of beauty corrections. He restores people's bodies after illnesses or injuries have left them disfigured. A much more rewarding field, but of course less well paid. Sometimes I ask him to change jobs for a day if I feel the need to do something sensible for a change."

"Now, Alenéa," Valrad smiled, "I know for a fact that you are just pretending to loathe your job, because I happen to know that you enjoy playing around with people's features. This artistic streak in you would simply shrivel away if you were made to heal bones or infections all day long."

"Ah, you know me too well, Valrad," she laughed. "But people do appreciate me so much more when I give them an impression of how much I suffer."

"So your artistic talent is not limited to visual moulding, but also includes acting. Good to know," Dikea grinned and turned to Eryn. "Your uncle told me that you have started training healers yourself. I imagine you will find quite a few books here which will be of interest to you, and which you will wish to take home with you. I have an extra set of books we give to our healer trainees in their first year and can give them to you, if you are interested. They contain the basics and are easy enough to understand. I imagine healing, teaching and running the clinic in Anyueel is quite time consuming, so your healers being able to learn a few things without you there might be beneficial."

Eryn nodded eagerly. "Thank you very much, I would be very interested! How do you train your healers here? I lecture mine for half a day every second day and oblige them to treat patients under supervision the rest of the time. It is pretty much what my father did with me."

Rededar nodded. "It is common practice here, too. But we only start confronting them with patients after their first year once they have passed all the exams and possess all the theoretical knowledge we deem necessary. In your case I see that this would be rather hard, as you would need them to be fit for service sooner and do not presently have the luxury of time we have here."

Eryn stood with them for almost an hour, asking them questions about procedures, administrative structures, working times, teaching methods and documentation.

Valrad finally cleared his throat. "Eryn, my dear, I am sure this is not the last time that you will come here during your stay in Takhan, so let us move on now. I would like to talk to Iklan before he leaves."

Dikea smirked. "Good, then you can tell him he still owes me a gold slip. I won a bet against him."

"I hope you two are not still betting on patients and illnesses? I thought we told you to stop that. It is tactless and reflects badly on us if somebody notices," Valrad scowled.

"No, not on a patient this time. Though on somebody who should be one. Iklan predicted Ahend would consult one of us within the next month. I disagreed." She shrugged. "I won. If he keeps up this stubborn attitude, House Arbil will soon need a new Head. What an old fool."

Eryn's head snapped up. This was about Ram'an's father?

Rededar sighed. "Do not be too hard on him, Dikea. He blames healers for his companion's death, so why should he trust them now?"

"But he trusts his sons, does he not?" Dikea shook her head angrily. "We showed Ram'an how to at least slow down the progress of the disease, but Ahend does not even let his son touch him. I wonder how much longer he will be able officially to lead the House before Ram'an has to take over, whether he wants to or not."

"Wait, what?" Eryn cut in, confused. "Ram'an is the heir of House Arbil? How is this possible, if his father is the Head of the House? I thought children are part of the mother's House?"

Valrad nodded. "They are. His mother was from House Arbil, his father is not. But after her death her companion took over the House as their sons were not of eligible age back then."

"So somebody who is not even a member of the House can be its Head?" she asked incredulously. "Your laws really confuse me."

She saw the other three exchange knowing glances.

Her uncle continued, "This was a special situation, you see. The initial plan was not for Ram'an to take over the House, even though he is the older son. He was meant to be joined with you, as you are now aware. As you are the heiress of House Aren, he would have given up his claim to leading his own House as we cannot have two companions leading different Houses."

"Then why didn't his younger brother take over?" she frowned.

"Because the situation with you and whether you would ever return was not clear. It still is not resolved from many people's point of view, if you forgive me for putting it like that. If Ram'an acknowledged your commitment to Enric and stepped back, he could take over his House without any problems. But he is still trying to win you, so this would mean that he cannot succeed his father. If he does not manage to get you away from Enric, however, he is next in line. So the succession at House Arbil is a rather delicate topic right now."

"Why would they even promise the oldest son to an heiress of another House? This seems like an immensely foolish course of action! Why didn't they promise me to his younger brother, then?"

"Because his younger brother had not yet been born at the time of the arrangement," Valrad explained. "And House Arbil was very eager to reaffirm its connection with House Aren. Had they waited any longer for another male child to be born to their House, you might very likely have been promised to another House in the meantime. There were several interested parties waiting in case there was no agreement with House Arbil, so they had to act fast."

"Then why doesn't his brother take over for now and step aside as soon as Ram'an realises that he is has no chance against Enric?" Eryn frowned.

"Because becoming Head of a House is not something you embark on for only a few months," Alenéa said and shook her head. "It involves oaths of loyalty from those members of the House who are related in a direct line and consequently would have a claim to leadership themselves, even though none are equal to the Head's. This is meant to prevent them from trying to assassinate him or her and assume power themselves. Then the Head takes over all the businesses that keep the family wealthy, in power and politically influential. They join the senate, taking their place there. It takes quite some time to grow into the position. To fill it with somebody just to keep the chair warm, so to say, is not advisable and might harm the House considerably."

"Which tells us that Ahend is still sane enough to realise this or he would probably have stepped aside already. He sends Ram'an to take over some of his duties already, though. So it seems he is not sure of the outcome of this triangle, but is not very confident that it will end in Ram'an's favour," Valrad remarked. "Ahend did not attend the welcoming banquet for the ambassador and Eryn himself, but sent his son. And he is absent from the negotiations at the senate with Enric more often than not, does not even send a replacement, which is very foolish. His resentment towards Enric for stealing his son's companion will very likely cost him profitable trading opportunities."

Eryn stared at her uncle in dismay. So Ram'an was endangering the stability of his own House with his obstinacy. What a mess.

Valrad took her arm. "But now we really need to get going, or Iklan will be gone for today and we have to visit him at his house, which is not polite without being invited or at least announced before. Come."

Eryn quickly bid her goodbyes and let herself be whisked along.

*   *   *

Though Iklan turned out to be much younger than Eryn was expecting due to his status as an expert, she had taken an instant liking to him. He seemed thoughtful, considerate, calm - exactly how the kind of person who would poke around inside one's head ought to be.

"Today the invitations for Ram'an's little dinner have arrived," Eryn sighed when she was back at the Vel'kim residence. Obal was there to spend the evening with her father and had ventured closer to Eryn to have a critical look at her knew, unusual clothes. Eryn had picked them up only this morning and was very pleased with the result. The girl didn't really seem convinced, though.

Eryn fixed her with a stare, and to her surprise Obal did not look away but held her gaze steadily. They continued staring into each other's eyes, each of them waiting or the other one to look away first.

"Will you go?" Vran'el asked and then frowned at them. "What are you doing? This looks scary."

"Staring each other out, I think," Eryn replied without looking at him but instead into his daughter's dark eyes. "I don't know whether I should go. I mean, I accepted the invitation when he asked us, didn't I? But this was before I learned that he thinks we are to be joined. And before he tried to seduce me publicly. He can hardly expect me to attend his little get-together after *that*."

"Yes, I agree," her cousin nodded. "You should refrain from encouraging him. You may be better staying out of his way as much as you can." He watched the girl and the woman for a few moments. "You know, Obal is really good at this. She has her mother's stare. Their House is famous for it. If they disapprove of you or something you have done, they do not say anything, they just stare you into submission."

Eryn frowned, holding eye contact with the girl. "Which House is Intrea from? Did you ever tell me that?"

Vran'el thought for a moment, then shook his head. "No, I do not think I did."

"House Feral," the girl supplied with what sounded like pride.

"Indeed, my heart. Not one of our usual Houses to connect with, but these were... extraordinary circumstances, were they not?"

The girl nodded, careful not to take her eyes off Eryn's. "Because you love men."

Eryn gasped and almost took her eyes off the girl to stare at her father instead, but caught herself at the last moment. She would not be a loser in a staring contest with a four-year old girl, no matter how legendary her family's ability to outstare others was.

"Don't you think that you are a tad too frank with her? Isn't she a bit young to be fully aware of the particulars of your relationship with her mother?" Eryn asked carefully.

Vran'el shrugged. "No, why would it? Children are cruel, and I want her to know what they are talking about in case they decide to be nasty, so she is able to defend herself properly. And I want her to grow up with this situation and see it as something natural that may not be what people usually have, but that still makes all involved parties happy. She sees me with her mother and feels that we are friends, that we love each other in a different, but hardly less devoted, way. We may not be lovers, but we have bestowed upon each other the gift of our daughter. Intrea is an amazing woman, and I am glad I can have a share in her life."

"He is mine, not yours," Obal growled at her.

"I wouldn't dream of taking him from you," Eryn replied solemnly. "But it would be nice of you to share him with me for a bit until I go home again."

"Where is your home?" the girl enquired.

"Across the big water."

"The sea or the river?" Obal frowned as if confused by this inaccurate description.

Eryn laughed, delighted at how smart the child was. "The sea."

"Why are your clothes so funny?"

"Because they are a mix of my home and yours. Do you like them?"

Obal shrugged. "No."

"Well, at least she is honest," Vran'el smirked.

"Yes, painfully so," Eryn remarked dryly. "But I will just take her with me across the sea to show her that all people there wear similar clothes."

The girl's eyes darted towards her father with a panicked expression. "She cannot take me!"

"Ha!" Eryn exclaimed gleefully, "I win!"

Vran'el sighed and shook his head. "Your aunt Eryn tricked you, my little darling. She is not going to take you with her, I promise." He looked at his cousin. "Are you proud of yourself now? Should a grown woman really have to resort to such methods to beat a little girl? Shame on you!"

"Shame on you!" Obal crowed happily, lifting her index finger to point it at Eryn.

"Oh, shut up, the two of you! Is being bad losers a trait of the Vel'kim family?" she grinned.

"No, cousin," Vran'el countered, "but being bad winners is clearly one of the Aren family."

"Careful, or I will treat you to another bolt, but this time Enric won't be around to protect you," she said with a lifted eyebrow and a cool smile.

"Yes," he huffed, "that bit is something we should discuss, should we not? Attacking family is considered in poor taste."

"It wasn't really an attack. It was only a weak strike, barely strong enough knock you out for more than a few minutes," she shrugged.

"Knock me out? And this is supposed to comfort me?" he protested.

"You would have deserved it! Or don't you think that I would have appreciated learning about the juicy fact that I am more or less still promised to Ram'an?"

"It was hardly my place to tell you, was it?"

She lifted her eyes in exasperation. "Yes, right! Like you are the kind who cares a lot about his place!"

Enric entered from the terrace, shaking his head at them. "I could hear you two bickering from out in the garden."

"He didn't tell me about the arrangement concerning me and Ram'an!"

"And she tricked a little girl because she would not have been able to outstare her otherwise!" her cousin shot back.

Obal jumped up from the cushions and ran towards Enric, arms outstretched. Enric bent down to pick her up. The movement seemed so natural that Eryn stared at them for a few moments before looking away.

"She does have good taste in men, I must say," Vran'el grinned. "A girl cannot start developing that too early."

"She just takes revenge on me because I asked her to share her father with me," Eryn muttered.

"Is there anybody in your family who you do not currently have an argument with?" Enric enquired and balanced the girl on his hip while she let her fingers glide through his blonde hair.

She thought for a moment, then nodded. "Yes. Valrad. *He* still likes me."

"Just a matter of time, you just wait," Vran'el murmured under his breath.

"I heard that," Eryn hissed at him.

"Good," he retorted. "Enric, what about that dinner invitation to Ram'an's? Are you going to attend? Eryn and I just discussed that it would not be wise of her to go, despite her premature acceptance. How about you? As the ambassador it is not so easy to attend dinners at one House and refuse the others, I would imagine."

He nodded. "True enough. I'll probably attend alone and convey Eryn's regards and apologies for not being able to come."

"Just do not tell them it is due to a headache. It would not sound very credible with her being a healer and all. But I suppose you are used to not believing that one anyway, eh?" Vran'el added with a teasing smile.

Eryn frowned. "Why would I use it with him?"

Both men stared at her and then looked at each other as if to question whether she was really serious.

"It is an excuse women sometimes are known to employ when they do not desire sexual intercourse and do not want to hurt their partner's feelings," her cousin explained to her.

She shook her head in confusion. "But if it is known to be a common excuse, why would any woman still use it? Wouldn't it be rather transparent, then? They could just as well say that they are simply not in the mood for it. Or am I missing something?"

Vran'el snorted. "No, nothing an Aren woman would understand. Why ever would *you* consider a man's feelings or that hurting them can be a bad thing? Even if it is a commonly known excuse, it still enables the man to save face when being refused by his woman."

"Firstly, stop bringing up the Aren name every time you are displeased with something about me. I suppose some of my less charming character traits can just as well stem from the Vel'kim side. And secondly, why would I want to be with a man who can't take a *No* without being devastated and who I would have to lie to?"

"Not much tolerance for weaknesses, eh?" Vran'el murmured.

She shrugged. "For weaknesses, yes. For weakness as such? No. At least not in my companion."

"Good to know. I will try to remember that," Enric remarked dryly.

"Oh, come on, Enric," Vran'el smiled, "this is hardly something which big strong you has to worry about, is it? And if there ever are moments where you need sympathetic words, just send me a note and I will gladly oblige so that you do not have to depend on that prickly companion of yours for comfort."

"Are you suggesting I am insensitive? You are aware that I am a healer, aren't you?" she frowned. "I am trained to be sensitive to other people's problems."

"Yes, sweetness, and a trained skill is all it is in your case. The sensitivity and empathy you have for your patients is only meant to go so deep or it would wear you out after a while. But people close to you do not want to be treated with a professional distance and merely the required amount of sympathy. They want the real thing. And from your words just now I take it that this is not one of your strong sides. Which is hardly surprising, considering..."

She interrupted him sharply. "If that sentence has the word *Aren* in it somewhere, I am going to stuff it back down your throat, I am warning you!"

Vran'el fell silent and shrugged.

Enric adjusted the girl on his hip and chuckled. "You are not a fast learner, are you, my friend? One of these days she will hurt you, and I won't be there to prevent her."

Obal looked at Eryn wide-eyed. "She wants to hurt my father?"

"Only if he deserves it," Eryn promised.

Vran'el scowled at his cousin when the girl let lose a pained cry and struggled to be set down to run to her father with outstretched arms, tears streaming down her pale cheeks.

"Very nice, dear cousin. You really do have a way with children," he reprimanded her. "And do not ever again dare discussing with me your natural inclination towards sympathy and sensitivity when I tell you that there is none."

CHAPTER 33

Lifting the Block

Eryn forced herself to sit on the cushions in her uncle's main room where Valrad, Vran'el and Enric waited with her for Iklan to arrive instead of pacing the room restlessly. Today she would have her memory block removed. They had just finished their breakfast and she wondered if her stomach would keep the fruit down.

"You are radiating tension," Enric noted and took her hand to pull her closer to him.

"Try to be calm - it works better that way," Valrad advised. "If you remain that nervous, we will have to tranquilise you as for this procedure the mind must be relaxed. It would be too hazardous otherwise. Depending how strong the block is, Iklan might even have to put you to sleep. But I do not want to get ahead of things. My colleague will guide you through this as he deems fit."

She bit her lip. Being asleep and at the mercy of a stranger was not something she had experienced, at least not in a medical context. How did the patients bear it? It probably helped a lot not being accustomed to doing their own healing on a daily basis, she thought.

But Enric would be there - he wouldn't leave her to face it on her own, would he?

"Will you stay with me while he is working on me?" she asked him quietly.

"Every minute of it. I promise," he replied and pressed her close to kiss her temple.

They glanced up when a servant preceded by two figures walked into the main room. The first one was Iklan, the second one a woman. A familiar one.

Eryn jumped up and beamed a furious look at her uncle. "What is *she* doing here? Did you tell her to come?"

But Valrad, too, looked puzzled about her presence, so Eryn discarded the idea again.

"No, Theá, he did not," Malriel replied calmly and gave Valrad a look of pure frostiness. "But he should have."

He rose slowly and approached her, hands raised in conciliation. "Malriel, I do not think this is a good time."

"Be still!" she commanded and was obeyed immediately. "You will not try to make me leave again, or you will be in serious trouble, old *friend*. You learned about a mind block having been placed upon a member of my House and failed to inform me of this as was your duty. If you attempt to have me removed from your residence, I will make sure you get into serious legal trouble. Vran'el? Why do you not inform your father that I am able to do this?"

Vran'el rose as well and stepped next to his father to reluctantly explain, "She can indeed. Your not telling her about it has obstructed her in the execution of her duties of protection towards members of her House. She can have you punished for it with at least three months of house arrest or golden restraints, or by one month of incarceration."

"So you are coercing him in order for you to remain?" Eryn fumed. "Pity then that it is not his decision who I want to have around for the procedure!"

Malriel smiled wanly. "Is it now, my daughter? Then I'd better concentrate my efforts on coercing you instead, should I not? Let me ask you a question, then. Is sending me away worth seeing your uncle being punished for trying to help you?"

"You would do that? You would punish him for something he has no influence over? For something I have decided upon?" Eryn asked, knowing the answer even before her mother raised both eyebrows in mild amusement.

"You do not really need me to answer that, do you?" Malriel replied and folded her arms, waiting for her daughter to speak.

Eryn lifted her chin. "Then there will be no lifting of the mind block." She turned towards Iklan. "I thank you very much for coming here. Unfortunately it seems that I have wasted your precious time for nothing."

"As you wish," Malriel shrugged. "Valrad, do prepare to be summoned by the triarchy within the next few days. Is there any preference regarding the punishment you prefer? I would have gone for house arrest as it would at least allow you time to work in your garden. Or would you prefer it to be over in one month but spent in a dungeon?"

Valrad gulped. "The house arrest will be fine, thank you," he said awkwardly. "I would, however, ask you to delay execution of the punishment until Eryn and Enric have left Takhan. I will need to attend the negotiations at the Senate, after all."

Malriel nodded once. "Granted."

Eryn stared at both of them. "Are you insane? I just told you that the block will not be removed! So, there is no reason to punish him! I am not excluding you from the procedure, it just won't take place!"

"Wrong. You made your decision - and Valrad is going to pay for it." Malriel's voice was cold. "There is only one decision I want to hear from you. Only one that will induce me to spare your uncle. It is not the one you just made. I want that block lifted. I want you to remember me." She nodded at the people present. "A good day to you." Then she turned and walked towards the stairs that led downstairs to the exit.

"Wait," Eryn pressed out between clenched teeth. Malriel just walked on.

"Do you want to stay now or not?" she called angrily after the woman who was the Head of House Aren.

Malriel slowed and finally turned and walked back towards the group. "So nice of you to offer, Maltheá."

Eryn just gave her a look of pure loathing and asked Iklan, "So, let's get this over with. What do I need to do?"

Iklan pursed his lips and looked around at the assembled people. "We need peace and quiet for the first part; for this we have too many people here. Is there another room we can go to where you can lie down?"

"There is a guest room if you turn and follow the corridor to your left," Vran'el said.

"Can I bring Enric with me?" she asked the healer.

Iklan nodded. "Yes, one person is acceptable and is even recommended as you will be better able to relax in his presence. I do not want to push you into a relaxed state of mind artificially if we can avoid that as it still causes underlying distress."

Eryn snorted and shot Valrad a dark look. "Yes, I remember that well enough."

Iklan turned to walk along the corridor Vran'el had indicated and Enric followed him, pulling her along gently.

"And now?" she enquired after they had closed the guest room door behind them, feeling more uneasy now that the procedure was about to start.

"Lie down on the bed, please. Your companion may lie with you if you prefer that. He can hold you or you put your head in his lap or on his shoulder, whatever is pleasant and makes you feel secure."

She nodded and Enric lay down, lifting his arm so that she could snuggle up against him with her back to him, feeling his warm body behind her, the movement of his chest against her back when he breathed, just as it was before she went to sleep at night.

Iklan sat on the bed in front of her. "Now I would like you to close your eyes and listen to your breath. It is a little too fast because you are nervous. There is no need to be afraid of this. I will not harm you or injure you in any way. If I find that I cannot lift the block, I will stop trying immediately. If you change your mind at any point, I will stop immediately. You are in control."

Eryn exhaled slowly. His last words helped indeed. The thought of control was a comforting one. It assured her that she was no one's victim, not her father's due to his enthusiasm to keep her from giving away their big secret, not her mother's for insisting on staying here despite not being welcome, and not Iklan's for invading her head. It was her decision and she could stop this any time she wanted to. That felt good.

"I will touch your head now. Do not try to concentrate on what I am doing inside your head. Do not see this as an opportunity to gain healing knowledge, but to learn something about yourself, about your past," his calm voice continued.

She opened her eyes for a moment and looked at him guiltily.

"I caught you there, did I not?" he smiled.

She smiled faintly and closed her eyes again. A moment later she felt his warm hand on her head, right above her left ear. Then there was more warmth.

"Yes, I see it," the healer murmured. "A block, very carefully set. Your father did not specialise in this kind of work, but he did well enough. It is not strong enough to risk any brain damage, but effective enough to hold back your memories. It is not entirely leak-proof, though. I expect you have dreams sometimes, impressions that seemed oddly real but nothing you could place?"

"Yes," she said softly.

"As I said, it was done very carefully. Your father was more willing for memories to slip out than to cause any damage to your mind. You will feel no physical effects of the block being removed. Removing it, however, will require the assistance of another, stronger magician."

Eryn opened her eyes again. "What? Why?"

"Because the block, you see, is nothing but an intricate shield placed at the exact right position. Your father was very strong, and as a weaker magician I cannot remove a shield placed by him. I am sorry, but it seems we cannot continue right now," Iklan sighed and she could hear the regret in his voice. "Your mother is not as strong as he was, and neither is your uncle."

"I am stronger," Enric said quietly. "Is there anything I can do?"

Iklan regarded him with surprise. "Are you? You sound sure of yourself. How would you know?"

"He placed a shield inside Eryn when she was a girl to protect her internal organs. I was able to manipulate it," he explained simply.

The healer nodded slowly, a smile spreading on his face. "That is excellent news. Yes, there is indeed something you can do. You will remove the block with my guidance."

Enric's eyes bulged. "I am expected to work inside her head with no more healing skills than repairing damaged skin requires? What if I damage something? I thought this is very intricate work?"

"It is, but you will not be the one doing the actual work. I will point you to the right spot and you will simply provide the energy that is needed. Do not worry, I will make sure you do not use more than is safe."

Eryn felt her heartbeat quicken. "How can you make sure of that? He is stronger than you, so you can't shield my mind from his energy if he uses too much!" she protested.

"True," the healer nodded. "That is why we will have your companion take over the shield and reshape it. He can feed it more energy and make it grow until it is no longer inside you but envelops your body. Then it can be removed safely."

She blinked a few times. That did sound simple enough. And plausible.

"It would avoid his using too much energy inside my head to remove the block," she murmured.

"Exactly," Iklan nodded. "But for this I need you to be asleep, Eryn. The nature of the shield is very dense, it is meant to block the impulses that transport your thoughts. So you would experience complete blankness for a few moments and this might cause you to panic. We cannot allow this. Are you ready?"

She drew in a deep breath and nodded. Iklan's hand returned to her head and a moment later she felt warmth, and then there was nothing.

Enric felt the tension drain out of her body and waited for instructions what to do.

"Put your hand on her head somewhere close to mine. Yes, this is a good spot. Now close your eyes and follow my impulses. I will lead you to where the block is. It is very hard to locate if you do not know where to look. Do you see it? It is a tiny spark of magic."

"I see it," Enric murmured. It looked oddly harmless and had yet such a remarkable effect. He hadn't even dared imagine that even memories could be blocked by shields.

"Make a connection to it - be very careful. Take the time you need. It does not matter if you use too little magic at first. Just increase it slightly for the next try. Yes, very good, you did it. Now very cautiously feed energy to the shield and make it grow at the same time. If you just feed energy without letting it grow, it will only become stronger, blocking off even more memories. Too much energy might also overwhelm her brain tissue and cause damage."

"Then I'd better make sure I let the shield grow, hadn't I?" Enric murmured. He sent a thin trickle of energy to the small, hardly discernible block and dared not use too much of it.

"Very good, take your time. There is no need to hurry. It is good to see that you have the patience for this work," Iklan said.

Patience, Enric thought. It was no more than sheer, pure panic at the mere thought that he could damage something that couldn't be repaired anymore.

The shield had now tripled in size and Enric felt that he started to get a feeling for the level of energy he needed to maintain relative to its size. Yet he dared not increase the speed of feeding it more magic.

After several minutes the shield was large enough to leave her head.

"And now? Do I increase it further until it envelops her entire body?" he asked, eyes still closed.

"No, that will not be necessary. Enlarge it a little more so that it stops at her throat. The tissue there is not sensitive enough to react to a sudden removal of the shield. Good, you can stop now. And now collapse it."

Both men opened their eyes after it was done and Enric let himself sink back, breathless.

"You did very well, Ambassador. There was no damage done whatsoever, and the impulses in the brain have already started accessing the area that was blocked off. She will probably first see unconnected pictures shortly after she wakes."

"I am glad it's over. Is this the usual way to do this?" he enquired.

Iklan shook his head. "No, Ved'al was an unusually strong magician, and removing anything he placed using my own powers, or that of most other healers, was impossible. This was the most uncomplicated way it could be done by somebody who was not trained as a healer, though often it is very risky. That you have such extraordinary command over the degree of energy you provide has made this very safe for Eryn. They say you are a warrior, are you not? I was not aware that fighting required such precision."

"It does if you are doing it right," Enric smiled. "The right amount of magical strength in a muscle can decide if you win or lose a fight. If it is too much, you might hit too hard or too fast, if it isn't enough - well, then you are too slow or too weak. Either may lead to defeat."

"I see. Not quite as barbaric as we here like to think of the discipline, then," Iklan nodded, apparently not even aware that he had casually insulted an ambassador and thus the country he represented. "Come, let us return to the main room. You can carry her and we will awaken her out there. She should not walk herself yet, it might cause dizziness otherwise."

Enric nodded and rose, lifting Eryn's slumbering body in his arms and following the healer out into the corridor and the room where her mother, uncle and cousin were waiting, each of them tense in their own way. Valrad was pacing the room nervously; Vran'el was sitting on the cushions, drumming his fingers on his knees; and Malriel was leaning against a column with folded arms and a worried expression on her face. Their heads turned as one when first Iklan and then Enric with his load entered.

"And? Did everything work out? Were you able to do it?" Valrad asked eagerly.

Iklan shook his head. "No, I was not able to." Three unsettled faces stared at him and then he smiled. "But Enric was."

"Enric?" Vran'el asked with a note of concern.

"Yes, it was a matter of strength. Ved'al had made the block very strong, so I could not disperse it. Enric is stronger than your uncle was, so I guided him through the procedure," the healer explained.

"You are stronger than *Ved'al* was?" Malriel said with a mix of calculation and fascination.

"Reconsidering the magical potential of your daughter's future offspring, Malriel? Then I am sure that Enric will meet your requirements even better than Ram'an would have," Valrad said somewhat reproachfully.

Very interesting, Enric thought, but remained silent. So it seemed that Ram'an was not his equal in magical strength. That was excellent news and very useful as it was probably only a matter of time until there would be a showdown between the two of them unless he gave up his pursuit of Eryn.

"She will now need to be guided through some of the images that will appear in her inner vision," Iklan explained. "As the three of you were part of her early childhood, you will very likely be able to supply information that will help her put the pictures in place. Enric, your role is equally important. Stay close to her so she stays as relaxed as possible. Make sure to maintain her in a positive mood; this will help her deal with the memories and connect their rediscovery with positive feelings, which will also influence how she remembers her childhood." He turned to the Head of House Aren. "Malriel, it is no secret that there is tension between you and your daughter. The fact that she did not want to have you here for this may also be a burden for her when she opens her eyes and glimpses you. She will be vulnerable and any argument you feel you cannot avoid may cause damage beyond repair right now."

"Are you telling me to be pleasant, *healer*?" She stared at him icily.

"I did not mean to be disrespectful. I was speaking from a medical point of view," Iklan replied stiffly, clearly worried that maybe she was not the right company to have around for Eryn right now.

Valrad nodded. "He is right. If you do not behave and are a risk to Eryn, I will have you removed from my house, whether you see fit to have me thrown into a dungeon for a month or not."

"Protecting my own daughter from me, Valrad?" she asked mildly. "How sad that you seem to deem such a thing necessary."

Iklan cleared his throat. "Then I will take my leave now. She may seem disoriented shortly after waking, but this does not need to worry you, it is completely normal."

Valrad grabbed both of the younger healer's forearms and squeezed them in a gesture of gratitude. "I am in your debt, Iklan. Thank you so very much."

"It was my honour to be of service to you, Valrad. Keep me informed, will you?"

"Of course."

Valrad accompanied the healer to the door and returned only a few moments later. They stood around Eryn's recumbent figure on the cushions and looked down at her.

Vran'el spoke first. "Shall we wake her, then?"

"Yes. I think we should," his father nodded. "Enric, you should probably sit somewhere close to her to give her a sense of safety when she wakes and is struggling to regain her sense of orientation."

Enric nodded and sat down next to her, pulling her into his arms.

Valrad crouched in front of her and lightly touched her hands. Only moments later she showed first signs of waking. First her head moved slightly, then her fingers twitched, and finally her eyelids opened slowly.

She stared into Valrad's face before her, taking in the brown eyes, the formerly dark hair now streaked with grey.

"Your hair is a lot shorter now," she said slowly. "I liked it better when it was longer."

He smiled. "It kept getting in my way. And Obal pulled at it a lot, painfully so. That is why I cut it short."

She turned her head and looked up into blue eyes that seemed oddly strange in this mix of dark-haired, dark-eyed people she had in her head. Golden hair, she thought dreamily and closed her eyes for a moment to breathe in the smell of him. He smelled delicious, familiar, exciting. Enric.

"You are not checking my body hygiene, are you?" she heard his voice vibrate in his chest. It had an amused undertone and it took her several moments to remember why. She saw herself in a dark bedroom. His bedroom. His arms had been slung around her from behind. It was what she had said to him when he had inhaled her scent.

"Shut up. You are destroying the moment," she repeated his own words from then back to him, smiled and opened her eyes again.

She stared ahead at a blank wall for a few moments, then she blinked several times in rapid succession.

"A bed, a child's bed. With green lace curtains," she murmured.

"Your bed when you were a child. You picked the curtains yourself. I wanted to order purple ones, but you protested and insisted on green. They reminded you of trees, you said," Malriel said softly and stepped forward and into Eryn's view.

Eryn's breathing quickened slightly. Her eyes wandered up and down the slim figure that looked so very familiar for more than one reason, and yet so changed.

"Mother," she said hesitantly and Enric saw Malriel swallow. It was the first time she had been addressed like this since their arrival here. No, he corrected his thoughts, the first time since Eryn, or Maltheá back then, was taken away so many years ago.

423

"Yes," she replied, obviously unsure if coming closer was too risky. She opted for keeping her distance after a quick look at Valrad.

"I screamed at you because you sent me to bed while Vran'el was allowed to stay up with the adults," Eryn said, looking at the floor, seemingly lost in her own world of pictures.

She looked up and to her left when she heard a low chuckle from that direction. "Yes, cousin, but then I was five years older than you, was I not? Almost a man - at least that was what *I* thought back then."

"You wanted to become a pirate," she frowned. "Whatever that is. But you said you weren't allowed to."

The grin grew even wider. "True. My father was very conservative about that. But I became the next best thing: a lawyer. It is a kind of pirate, but more respected."

She kept looking at Vran'el thoughtfully. "You helped me steal the jar with the sweet pastries from the top shelf in the kitchen. It was too high for me."

"That was you? I remember wondering how she kept managing to reach them!" Malriel exclaimed and shook her head at Vran'el.

"I once tried to eat a whole load of them and got sick," Eryn continued, seemingly unperturbed about her cousin having been found out as her childhood accomplice in theft. "They were not the hard ones that are dunked in tea, but softer ones. The hard ones... I remember a boy who showed me how to eat them properly. But not you." She looked at her cousin. "Another boy, only a little younger than you. Cute, dark, quiet. He took walks in the garden with me, because I liked the trees so much."

"That was Ram'an," Valrad supplied.

Enric swallowed hard. Childhood memories of Ram'an. His claim to Eryn had seemed absurd, something that might have been true or not, but hearing from her how he had been there, had been a part of a pleasant early childhood was disconcerting. He wished she didn't remember him that way, but as a nuisance, a bully who had pulled her hair instead of somebody who had shown her kindness that was there to be remembered by her now. He felt oddly outside it all, knowing that he was the only one in this room she would not find any memories of.

"Ram'an," she said thoughtfully. "Still pretty, still dark, still quiet. But he is not for me." She took Enric's hand and he felt his anger at Ram'an for being remembered by her almost completely evaporate. "Though he doesn't understand that yet." She shook her head. "I wonder how much more pain I will have to cause him until he does."

Enric closed his eyes for a moment, thinking back to when he had told her about the arrangement between the two Houses and how she regretted that she couldn't be friends with Ram'an anymore, that he had enriched her life. These memories would make Ram'an's obstinacy in trying to win her even more painful for her, as she realised how much Ram'an had been part of her life before. Being forced to hurt him would hurt her in turn.

She looked back at Malriel contemplatively. "I see a large round mirror with a golden frame. You must have been about my age, standing behind me and brushing my hair."

Malriel's normally cool and guarded eyes shimmered warmly. "I still have it, it is in my bedroom. You usually came to me to have me brush your hair after we finally managed to get you dressed in your night gown. You enjoyed playing around with my makeup and perfume - I had to spend some minutes every evening cleaning up the mess you made after you had fallen asleep," she said and swallowed once more.

Eryn lifted one hand to her forehead and closed her eyes for a moment.

"Is everything alright, my love?" Enric enquired worriedly.

"Yes, just a mess of pictures I can't quite place. There is one in a teahouse, I think. And one where I am dressing myself. But they are surely not connected. I see my father and other men I don't recognise drinking tea and looking so serious." Then she suddenly looked up at him. "He called me *little flower*."

Enric nodded slowly. "Little flower. Just what you called Plia." So many little things, he thought, buried so deeply but that had yet managed to surface unconsciously in these last years, as it seemed. He wondered what other remnants of her childhood here in Takhan had found their niche in her everyday life so far away from here.

"He had long hair like you," she said and looked at Valrad. "I played with it when he carried me on his shoulders, braiding it clumsily. It smelled of herbs."

"He used to make his own soaps from them," Malriel murmured. "He was good with herbs, always."

Eryn closed her eyes and leaned back against Enric's shoulder. "My head is hurting. But the pictures won't stop coming. I don't think healing the pain away will work here."

Valrad shook his head. "No, probably not. But I can give you some rest if you like," he offered and touched her hand when she nodded gratefully. A moment later her head lolled slowly to one side as she drifted off to sleep.

CHAPTER 34

Befriending the Enemy

Enric looked up and smiled when she entered the main room where he was sitting with Kilan after another long afternoon of negotiating with the senate.

"Hello, boys," Eryn yawned and went to sit next to her companion. "How was your day? Any progress in signing trade agreements?"

"Nothing ground-breaking," Kilan shrugged. "They are eager to get their hands on our timber and metals, but don't want to show it."

"What do we want to get our hands on?" she asked.

"Their knowledge, mostly. And their fabrics and wine. But the latter is only for luxury," he replied.

She nodded appreciatively. "Good. I like your priorities."

"We are about to make them agree to showing us how to cross the barrier," Enric told her.

"Cross it? Why don't they just remove it? It would be safer for them to remove it instead of showing us how to cross it. If we become dangerous again, they can simply re-establish it," she frowned.

"Hey, whose side are you on?" Kilan exclaimed and shook his head at her in mock disapproval.

"I was just wondering," she shrugged. "But if they prefer to show us how to get through it, I won't complain."

"I think they don't know how to remove it," Enric conjectured. "It is different from other barriers, has to be. It has long outlived the magicians who conjured it back then and is still strong enough to cause considerable harm. They have neglected their warrior skills here, and shielding is quite an important part of that."

"So you are saying that *we* probably have a better chance at lifting it than them?" she smirked. "That is hilarious! They should be begging *us* to do it, not we them to show us how to cross it."

"Fantastic idea. Why don't I suggest this tomorrow?" Kilan commented dryly.

"So what exactly is the status now?" Eryn asked. "Are we to trade goods with them anytime soon or will there be another delegation to continue negotiations after we have left?"

Enric's expression was smug when he replied, "No, another delegation is not very likely to be needed for this. I am confident that we will leave here with signed agreements. We have already agreed on quotas for certain spices, fabrics, herbs, wine, fruits and vegetables."

"Herbs?" she perked up. "Which herbs? Cooking or healing?"

"Both," he smiled and enjoyed the gleam his answer put in her eyes. "The Head of a certain House we know suggested it. He has also told us about an idea I find very appealing and which I imagine you will like as well: knowledge exchange for healers. He said that each side would benefit if one of the healers here were to go to Anyueel for a few months and help you set up an efficient organisation for your healing place and assist you in your training arrangements for the new healers."

"Really?" She leaned forward, excitement visible in her every feature and her posture. "Is this possible? Can we do that?"

"Probably. There would be quite a lot to consider, of course. All magicians in the Kingdom are members of the Order, and having a magician in the city who is not answerable to it will very likely be a problem. Having a citizen of another country join the Order would be equally difficult, as being bound to the King is a part of such a membership. But this is still far away for now; there will be enough time for the King and the Magic Council to work this out," Enric explained.

She leaned back, dazed at the chance of having a fully trained healer with the knowledge from this place at her disposal for a time. She didn't really worry about the organisational matters around this. She would certainly not let either the King or the Order mess up this exceptional opportunity.

Kilan stretched and yawned. "Can you believe that half of the time we have here is over already? Where has the time gone? There is still so much to be done."

Enric pursed his lips. Yes, the time was flying, wasn't it? And there was a thing or two he himself also wanted to accomplish before they left. There was still the matter with the third level commitment bond. He would soon have to face it again. If he waited too long, who knew when his next chance to take it would appear. It needed to be done here in Takhan as nobody back in Anyueel know how to apply such a thing.

He knew better than to surprise her with flowers, candles or whatever else a more romantically inclined woman might appreciate. She would need practical reasons for entering into the bond, he mused. Something that was worth the risk of binding herself to another person so inseparably.

"Kilan, I have been invited to House Arbil tomorrow evening. I do not think it advisable to take Eryn, yet can't decline the invitation without seeming petty or giving the impression that I feel threatened by him. I would ask you to accompany me there."

He grimaced. "Ah yes, the matter with the companionship arrangement. Sure, I will come with you. So, there is no way to take care of this mess properly?"

Enric shook his head. "At the moment it doesn't look like it, no." Not until he managed to convince her to take the commitment bond, he added silently. "But if he keeps his hands to himself until we leave Takhan again, I will be happy enough. Eryn, I suppose that means that you will have to either spend the evening at House Vel'kim or go out with Vran'el?"

She nodded. "Yes, probably. Though I would prefer a quiet evening in."

"Whatever keeps you out of trouble, my love," he nodded only half-joking.

*   *   *

Eryn waited in front of the clinic, leaning against the house wall. Valrad wanted her to see Iklan to make sure there were no unforeseen side-effects following the removal of her memory block two days ago. Yesterday she had spent the day indoors, sorting through pictures her brain kept throwing at her. Vran'el had visited her in the afternoon and helped her with finding the right context for many of them.

The first night had not been a particularly restful one, just as her uncle had warned her. The second night had been a lot better, and this morning she had even felt rested. Her brain occasionally came up with a new picture when an item or a place triggered a response, but otherwise it was pretty much back to its old form. She was able to concentrate on something else for a longer period again without being thrown off track all the time.

She saw her uncle's figure appear around a corner and waved at him.

"Eryn! Please forgive me for forcing you to wait. Obal did not want to let me leave; she spends the morning with Vran'el while her mother meets with a friend for tea." He raised his eyebrow at her. "Intrea asked me why Obal told her that you planned to hurt her father and then abduct her to take her across the sea with you."

Eryn scowled. "Oh dear, did she? Not very good with sarcasm yet, that child, is she?"

Her uncle sighed. "You need to work on your skills with children, really. It will be good practice for your own offspring one day."

"No problem there - I don't have any plans in that direction," she sniffed.

Valrad looked at her, clearly surprised. "You really do not? But you said as much before, did you not? That is a pity."

"Because it is a shame to waste the fabulous Aren and Vel'kim bloodlines?" she asked with an icy look at him.

"No, because Enric is very good with Obal and I would have thought that he wants children." He shrugged. "But that is a matter between the two of you. It is none of my business."

She sighed and felt immensely foolish. She was so poised to defend herself all the time, even against those who didn't mean any harm. Especially her uncle, who had proven to be a trusted friend during this very short time they had known each other.

"I am sorry, Valrad. I am probably a bit too sensitive when it comes to that topic. Everybody expects me to have children soon, and I feel under pressure."

"Do not worry on my account, my dear. I understand," he soothed her.

Eryn held on to his sleeve as he made to enter the clinic. "Wait a moment, will you? I wanted to thank you for what you have done for me. I wasn't aware that my request not to tell anybody about the mind block could result in serious problems for you. To think that you could have been punished like that..." She shook her head. "And that you were willing to accept the punishment without even challenging it... I don't know what to say."

"Come here, child," Valrad said softly and pulled her into his arms to give her a long, firm hug. "Family must stand together. And you are family. I will be there for you, always. Even if it means standing my ground against a certain member from the other side of your family."

Eryn nodded silently against his shoulder, squeezing him back. She fought back the tears that threatened to arrive at this demonstration of love and devotion. Suddenly she had to smile. She stepped back and looked at him.

"I remember the way you smell," she said. "Like a herb, but in combination with one of the spices that is used here a lot."

He chuckled. "That is because there are two bushes right next to my favourite spot in the garden where I like to sit every day in the morning for a few moments. They keep brushing against my clothes and the smell lingers. The smell is not unpleasant, I hope?"

She shook her head quickly. "No, not at all. It smells like... home."

Valrad looked at her, touched. Then he bent forward to kiss her forehead.

"Come now, Eryn. I want Iklan to have a look at you. And then there is somebody I would like to introduce you to. A certain healer I think you will be very interested in meeting." He took her arm and led her inside the building. "But first we will make sure that everything is alright inside your mind."

"You know," she mused, "under different circumstances that would have been a really cynical statement."

"I would not have phrased it like that under different circumstances. My daughter is in charge of cynicism in the family."

Eryn stopped herself from rolling her eyes. That she did believe.

He led her up a flight of stairs and along a wide corridor and into what appeared to be a study. A neat young woman sat in front of a tidy desk and smiled at Valrad when he entered.

"A good day to you, Valrad. Have you come to see Iklan?" she enquired politely.

"I have, yes. I would like him to have a quick look at my niece, Maltheá of House Aren. He has asked me to bring her by," he replied.

"Why do you not take a seat outside on the terrace as long as the heat is not at its peak? Iklan has a patient right now, but he will be with you as soon as he is done."

Valrad nodded and Eryn followed him out of the office again and to a wide, open terrace that afforded an impressive view over the city centre. She could also see the port and to the river glinting silver in the morning sunlight.

"Was introducing me as Maltheá of House Aren really necessary?" she asked and sat down next to him on a stone bench.

He smiled. "You may not like to be reminded of where you officially belong, Eryn, but being in a position to mention the name of a House after your name is a considerable advantage at times. This also requires using the name people here know you as. His assistant will slip you in before his next patient now that she understands you are Malriel's daughter. You might have been forced to wait longer otherwise."

She narrowed her eyes. "But surely not when I am in the company of the man who used to be in charge around here?"

"What can I say? It never hurts to be doubly distinguished, does it?" he chuckled at his own little joke and leaned back, letting his gaze wander over the view the terrace afforded them. He smiled when he looked at the harbour. "I just had to think back to the day of your arrival here. Your shock at finding out that Malriel was still alive. Was that really only twelve days ago?" He turned his head and regarded her. "Did the memories from your childhood alter your feelings about her in some way?"

Eryn rubbed her face. That was a question she had been asking herself already and not yet found a satisfying answer to.

"I am not sure. And I don't know if I would want them to. I remember that we had close moments, that there was love between us. And she has demonstrated very effectively what having me taken away from her has done to her. But still..."

"Demonstrated? How?" he frowned.

"A nasty cocktail of emotions she shared with me when we were invited for lunch the day after our arrival," she said and shivered at the memory.

"Did she now?" He sighed and shook his head. "Not a good start to your relationship. Aren temper. How interesting to see that there still are situations where she loses control of things. And how sad that you had to bear the effect of it."

"If she is usually so good at keeping herself under control, why is there all this talk of the Aren temper? I am sure other people get angry at times?"

Smiling, he wiggled his head. "Aren women are not known for losing control of their temper often, but it tends to stick when they do. Malriel's mother, Malhora of House Aren, once made a storeroom full of wine explode after her companion was discovered in bed with another woman. But fortunately the family can afford to pay for the damage they cause."

Eryn stared at him in dismay. Aren temper did not sound like a nuisance, it sounded positively dangerous. And she was supposed to have it, too?

"I have never done anything like that," she pointed out. "And trust me, in this last year I would have had quite a few reasons to cause harm." Careful, she warned herself. Don't make the same mistake as with Ram'an, speaking before thinking. No giving away information thoughtlessly again.

"You would? How so?" he enquired.

She shrugged. "Just this and that. Nuisances that kept turning up."

"Like being kept prisoner for several months? And being made to train fighting against your wishes? Nuisances like that?" he asked mildly.

She drew in a sharp breath and stared at him, taken aback. "How can you possibly know about that?"

"Enric told me," he answered calmly. "It was after I had sent you to sleep once the mind block was removed. He said he thought I should know about these things, being the closest family you have despite your more weighty legal connection to House Aren. It seems he has not told you about it."

She shook her head. "No, he failed to mention it."

"He cares very much about you. You are aware of this, are you not?" he asked quietly and went on when she nodded, "Then why do you not take the third level bond with him? It would put an end to the whole mess with Ram'an. He would have to accept that you have chosen another man."

"Surely not!" she protested and rose in agitation. She had expected to have a conversation of this sort with Enric sooner or later, but having it instead with her uncle right now was unsettling. Yet it was good practice for when she eventually had to face Enric about the bond, wasn't it?

"So you do not reciprocate Enric's feelings for you?" he asked with one raised eyebrow. "This is not the impression I got. You may not always be happy with his possessiveness, but that is only natural for a strong woman."

"I was made to join him once, that is enough. I was not ready for it then, I don't even know if I would be now. This is not about him, it is about me. I grew up in the knowledge that binding myself to people is dangerous, that it needs to be avoided. I know in my head that there is no reason for this any longer, but I can't just make that feeling vanish like that. Should I ever overcome this dread and decide to undertake this bond with him, it will surely not be to keep another man away from me. Not another time."

Valrad considered her and nodded slowly. "I see. I understand that argument. I really do. The easiest way is not always the best one, and if you join him willingly one day it will be for the reasons it is meant to be."

She nodded, glad that he understood her so well.

They looked up when the young woman who had received them stepped outside. "Iklan is now ready for you."

Valrad rose and motioned for Eryn to follow the young woman back to the study. Iklan was waiting for them and smiled when he saw them.

"Good day to the both of you. Come into my room, will you? Eryn, how are you doing today?"

"I am fine, thank you. No nightmares, disorientation, dizziness, headaches or other symptoms that would suggest any damage or unexpected side effects," she replied.

The healer chuckled and looked at Valrad. "Is it not always a pleasure to treat another healer? They are so eager to diagnose themselves. Will you still let me have a look at your head, or rather inside it? I would like to see if the level of activity has increased relative to the other parts of your brain."

Eryn nodded hesitantly and closed her eyes when he stepped closer and put one hand on her head.

"Very good," he murmured while he kept sending warm pulses of magic into her. "Your body has more or less reclaimed the blocked off area. There will probably be a few new pictures every now and then, but not what you must undoubtedly have been experiencing in these last two days."

"Good," she sighed and opened her eyes again when she felt him remove his hand. "It was rather diverting. I wouldn't want to suffer these concentration problems for the rest of my stay here. So there shouldn't be much more from my past to emerge from the depths of my memory?"

"Maybe the occasional recognition of a place when you walk through the city or situations that trigger a memory of a similar occurrence," Iklan replied and then hesitated for a few moments as if searching for the right words. "How did you experience waking up after the removal of the block? Was there anything unpleasant?"

She thought for a moment. "I felt confused and somehow caught between two worlds. I saw the room I was in with the eyes of a grown woman, but at the same time I remembered it through the eyes of a child. Then there were so many pictures, all mixed up, whirling around and wanting to be filed away."

"How about the circumstances you found yourself in?" His enquiry seemed oddly cautious.

Valrad smiled. "Eryn, he wants to know if Malriel behaved herself, but does not really dare ask you as bluntly as that. He warned her to be careful after waking you."

"Malriel?" She thought back. "She was guarded and careful, very careful considering my prior encounters with her. I would even say it was the first civilised conversation we had."

Iklan nodded satisfied. "That is good to hear. I am glad to say that you are perfectly healthy from a medical point of view. Be patient if there are memories you cannot place immediately. Put them aside until you have a chance to talk to somebody about them who can help you there. And now I am afraid I have to send you on your way as my next patient is due in only a few minutes and I have some preparation to do."

"Thank you for seeing us without an appointment," Valrad nodded at his colleague.

Iklan laughed. "How could I not? I was told that Valrad, Head of House Vel'kim has brought Maltheá of House Aren here. I did not dare for you to suffer waiting any longer."

"You see?" Valrad grinned at his niece. "It did the trick, did it not?"

She rolled her eyes and followed him out the study. "He would have seen us anyway. You just like to tease me." Once they were back in the corridor, she looked back and frowned. "He has his own treatment room? Why? From what I have seen your other colleagues share theirs."

"Because he is an important specialist in his field and it is an advantage if people know where to find him. And his expert status also affords him a certain importance, so he does not have to share his working space anymore," her uncle explained. "Now come. It is time to meet Sarol, one of the most famous healers in the city and probably even the country. And the interesting thing for you, my dear, is that he is not a magician."

Eryn stopped dead and stared at him. "What? How did he manage to become that famous without using magic for healing? What is he famous for?"

"For having an immensely sharp mind, being a brilliant healer and being extremely difficult to work with. What is more, he is no great friend of magicians, just to warn you."

"He isn't?"

Valrad shook his head. "No, and that is hardly surprising. He was not treated very kindly by them in the past. He is not the first non-magician to have learned healing skills, but certainly the most talented one that I and most others have ever seen. That did not sit well with his magically-gifted colleagues, and they were often patronising and disparaging him, making his life as hard as possible. He was almost not permitted to start training as a healer as he happens to stem from a House that has no history of healing expertise. It was Ved'al who made it possible for him to be accepted as a trainee."

Eryn felt pride well up inside her. Finally somebody had something positive to say about her father. "How so?"

"He saw Sarol help a man who had stumbled and fallen on the street. Sarol diagnosed the injury accurately without any magical help, and Ved'al verified it and decided to keep an eye on him. House Vel'kim, you see, has been on bad terms with House Roal, Sarol's family, for quite some time and his being accepted into a field that was dominated by our family was almost impossible. But your father looked past petty political considerations and saw the potential of the individual. It took him two months of almost non-stop pestering, threatening and begging to have Sarol accepted as a healer trainee." Valrad smiled at the memory.

"So he will probably go easy on me because I am Ved'al's daughter?" she ventured.

"I would not count on that. He has learned from his own experience that family connections are not a reliable way of judging a person's character or abilities. But be glad of it. House Roal is also not on friendly terms with House Aren, so being the product of those two particular Houses might otherwise stop him from talking to you at all."

They turned a corner and Valrad indicated a man sitting on a cushion on the floor, apparently asleep. "There he is."

"You are not suggesting I wake him, are you? If he is not fond of magicians, he will like me even less for waking him!" she protested in a whisper. "You do it."

"Afraid?" her uncle grinned.

"No, just reluctant to make a bad first impression with him," she denied.

"Then you should probably stop talking about me as if I were not even here," a raspy voice came from the floor and two eyes so dark brown that they seemed almost black looked up at her.

She looked down at a man about Valrad's age who was clearly enjoying her discomfort.

"I apologise," she said and came closer. The man didn't bother with getting up, just kept looking at her while he addressed her uncle.

"So this is that niece of yours people keep talking about. What an honour to have the privilege of her visit bestowed on a simple healer such as myself."

"Sarol, do try to be civil for a few moments, will you? She is here because she is interested in non-magical healing and is impressed by your accomplishments," Valrad sighed.

"Is she indeed?" the man on the floor said flatly. "We will see. Come and sit, then. I have another few minutes to spare, then I need to get back to my students and see if they have made a mess of the task I gave them."

Eryn sank down on a cushion opposite him and waited for her uncle to join them, but he just smiled at her and leaned against a wall instead. Probably to show Sarol that he was not the one who he was supposed to talk to.

"Valrad told me that you are doing incredible healing work without any magic. I would be interested in hearing about it."

"Why?" Sarol asked, somewhat bluntly.

"Because I think it would help me to better understand the field of medicine. And as magicians are only available in limited numbers, there would be better chances to provide healing services also outside the city," she replied.

"So this conversation is to satisfy your own curiosity and because you consider non-magicians a valid second choice to magically-endowed healers?" he huffed. "I should return to my students now."

"What? No! Wait," she cried urgently when he started to get to his feet. How could he have misunderstood her so completely? "Let me try this again. So far, I have learned of only two routes when it comes to healing: applying magic to make the problem go away or using herbs, where I have used magical impulses to locate the problem first. The idea of not becoming helpless with my magic being taken away is a very intriguing one for me. I don't want to depend on my magical abilities to be a good healer, but on what is up here." She pointed at her head. "And I don't want healing to be a field only accessible for those privileged with magic. Yet I don't know how to go about this and I wouldn't know even where to start teaching them. I have six people who work with me right now, and only one of them is without magic, as herbs are the only thing I know how to handle like this."

Sarol leaned back again. "Better. So at least you are aware of your shortcomings."

She furrowed her brow at him. "Nice way of putting it, but yes, I am aware of my limits. And I am not ashamed to admit to them. But if there is one thing that I do not appreciate, it is being ridiculed for them - especially when I want to improve myself," she added with a warning undertone. Being a legend in his field didn't give him the right to treat her like this.

"Did you take the test?" he asked and she blinked at the rapid change of direction.

"The ability test? I did, yes. Why?"

"Which category are you?" he continued without paying attention to her own question.

"That is a rather personal question, Sarol," Valrad threw in.

"She will answer it. She wants me to like her," he retorted unconcernedly.

Eryn stared at him in dismay, then nodded slowly. "I do, yes. But I am starting to ask myself how much I want it."

"While you are deciding that, tell me your category," he demanded smugly.

"Explorer," she told him after a few moments of consideration if rising and walking away from him would soothe her pride enough to make up for the lost chance of learning from him. It wouldn't, of course.

Sarol smiled for the first time. "Good. Just like myself. That is useful if you need to find out things for yourself because nobody in your area ever bothered with it before. But I suppose I do not need to tell that to somebody who used to be the only healer in an entire country."

"Not really, no." Her own smile was thin.

"Valrad? Take her to the library and give her my book on diagnosing organ failures." He turned back to her. "You will read it. I will meet you in two days at my usual teahouse and we will talk about it." Then he got up. "Now I need to get going." He nodded to them and off he went.

Eryn slowly turned to her uncle. "Did I just really have that conversation or was it a figment of my overactive imagination, a hangover from the memory block thing?"

He laughed. "You did, yes. He tends to have that effect on people when they first meet him. But you are to be congratulated - he seems to like you."

"That's what he is like when he likes somebody? I had the impression he barely tolerated me!" she exclaimed.

"That is the maximum extent to which he is known to show affection, so do not worry about it. And come now. There is the book I am to get for you."

Eryn shook her head. "He just ordered you to give it to me! Is that in accordance with your position?"

"Not at all," he smiled. "But he does not care about things like that. He used to talk to me exactly the same when I was still in charge of the clinic. It does not wound my pride; I choose to treat it as the request it really was."

She nodded and followed him along another corridor, considering his words. "He told me to meet him at his usual teahouse. He could have told me which one, even if his preferences are common knowledge here!"

"I will show it to you on our way back. I hope you do not have any plans for today and tomorrow. He expects you have read his book by the time you meet him and discuss it. And for the kind of books he writes that is a demanding deadline."

She would read that damn book, she promised herself, even if she had to stay up all night to finish it. That man would not find her wanting when they would meet in two days. Smug idiot. Well, genius. Both.

CHAPTER 35

Sarol

Eryn felt Urban sniffing around her legs, which were hanging over the bed. Next thing she knew, the cat had jumped nimbly onto the bed to examine the book that lay open.

"Careful," she warned the cat. "I would probably never hear the end of it if I returned his book to him in pieces. Or full of claw marks, drool or cat hair."

Urban retreated and then let herself fall on the bed, claiming one half of it by stretching across it. Enric would not be thrilled about this, he tried to keep the cat out of the bed; but well, he wasn't here right now and Eryn didn't mind. As long as the mountain cat didn't feel the urge to snuggle up to them at night, what did it matter?

She rolled onto her back and decided that her brain needed a short break from reading. She had spent several hours at it now, trying to memorise as much as possible. It was immensely interesting and had opened her eyes to the possibilities a healer had even without the aid of magic. So even without magic one could still be a very good healer with the right knowledge. At the same time magic without knowledge was more or less useless. But of course magic made everything easier, didn't it? Why learn all the symptoms when just sending a pulse of magical energy in was so much faster and required less insight into the theory of medicine?

Because knowledge was the key to progress, she thought. Without it one might stumble across a revolutionary new concept without even realising it. She wondered how her healers at home would take to being made to learn non-magical techniques out of the blue. If she decided that it was from now on part of their training, they could hardly do anything against it. But forcing an idea upon people was no more than a failure to convince them.

Would the King permit the training of non-magical healers? But why wouldn't he if he didn't incur any extra expenses in connection with it? Or any expenses at all, as for the moment the healing services were self-funding. The Order could not really object, either, as non-magicians were not part of their responsibilities. Her thoughts returned to what Enric had said the evening before about healers being answerable to the Order and how to handle this when it came to foreign magicians.

An independent institution that governed healing, she thought and sat up again. It would not only enable foreign magicians to work in Anyueel, but also allow non-magicians, who had no way of joining the Order, to enter the profession.

The King would probably not object to it, although the Order might do. It would take away some of its influence. She would have to test out the idea on Enric. If he was against it, there was not much chance for it to become reality as he would surely manage to convince Lord Tyront of his point of view.

Unfortunately Enric wouldn't return for several hours, she thought, impatient to talk to him about her idea. And when he did later, he would probably not be in a very good mood following dinner at Ram'an's place. Pity, she thought. She would have liked to see the Arbil residence, the extensive gardens, see if it still looked like the pictures in her memory, but not if it meant encouraging Ram'an. Pictures of him as a solemn boy who held her hand while telling her the names of the trees in the gardens of House Aren came to her mind unbidden.

And now she would have to avoid him as well as she could to make him understand that she did not intend to honour the agreement Malriel had made with House Arbil when Eryn had been no more than a toddler.

* * *

Enric balanced a steaming cup of tea in his hand and placed it on a small side table next to her side of the bed. Her posture had not really changed a lot since he had returned from the dinner at the Arbil residence last night. The book she had been reading these last two days almost without interruption was under her head, the cat was sleeping next to her; Eryn hadn't even woken from the feline protests when he had chased Urban away from the comfy sleeping spot. That had been a clear sign of how exhausted Eryn was.

"Eryn?" He shook her shoulder gently and sighed when she just turned away from him, clutching her pillow tightly and moaning something about liver diseases.

"Come on, time for you to get up if you don't want to be late for your appointment with the healer."

That worked. Slowly, she opened her eyes a fraction and turned back to him, regarding him thoughtfully.

"Is that tea I smell?" she asked hopefully and he smiled when he pointed to the cup. She stretched out her arm and grabbed the warm cup to take a careful sip. She sighed contentedly and smiled up at him. "You are my hero. I am going to keep you for now."

"Will you now? That is a great relief. Who else would I serve in the morning?" he retorted dryly.

"How was your evening?" she asked, hoping it hadn't been too tedious an occasion for him.

"Uneventful, fortunately. Ram'an enquired about you, naturally enough, and I told him that you were very busy and conveyed your apologies. I leave it to you to find an excuse should it be necessary. The Heads of Houses Turbar and Feral were there as well, they are allied with House Arbil. They took the opportunity to talk about trade with Kilan and I."

"Feral?" she asked and frowned when she tried to remember why that name sounded familiar. "Isn't that Intrea's House?"

"It is, yes. Her mother liked me instantly because it seems Obal talks about me a lot at home," he smirked. "It seems I have an admirer. But I have always had a lucky hand with females." He leaned back and laughed when she tried to swat his head.

"I noticed how quickly Obal and you became friends." She braced herself. This was as good a moment as any other, and it was probably time to clear that particular matter once and for all. "Do you want children?"

He noted her concerned expression. He would have to tread very lightly here. "Would you like me to want children?"

She scowled at him. "What kind of an answer is that?"

"What kind of a question was that? I thought you were decided on not having children?"

"People keep behaving as if I am violating some universal law of nature by not planning to have any," she sighed. "Not passing on the precious bloodlines seems to be an abomination. I just wanted to hear your thoughts on that. So, do you want children now or not?"

He watched her carefully. "At this particular moment I can do without children."

"So you don't want children?" she said with a frown.

"That's not what I said," he corrected her. "Just that this moment might not be the best choice. In the long run I wouldn't mind."

"So you want children?" Now there was slightly panicked edge to her voice.

He sighed. It seemed no answer was the right one here. "Do *you* want children, then? Have you changed your mind? Is that why we are having this conversation?"

"Stop pressuring me!"

"I am not. You are pressuring *me*, and I have absolutely no idea to what end. It seems to me that you are torn, but I am not sure about the nature of that internal conflict. You either want to have children but are not happy about wanting them, or you don't want children and feel that you should want them."

"Don't be an idiot! That sounds completely insane!"

"I think we should halt this discussion right here." He stood up briskly and took her hand to pull her with him, careful not to spill any of her tea. "Get dressed, eat your breakfast and then off you go to meet your illustrious new healer friend."

She looked at him uncertainly. "We haven't really clarified anything, have we?"

"No, we haven't. But if you really are dead set against children, I can hardly force you to have any, can I? Not that I would want to force your hand, mind you," he added quickly to avoid any misunderstandings here.

He rubbed his face as she was getting dressed. Oh dear. What a start for the day.

*   *   *

She spotted Ram'an as she left the street the ambassadorial residence was situated in and made herself smile politely. It was too late to turn away and pretend she hadn't seen him. He had made eye contact with her already and approached her.

"Eryn," he said with a bright smile and kissed her cheeks. "A good morning to you."

"And a good morning to you," she replied. "Have you been waiting for me here?" Please say No, she begged silently. Tell me that this is just a funny coincidence because you are meeting somebody here.

"I admit I have," he nodded. "I missed you yesterday evening and wanted to see if everything was alright. I wanted to show you the gardens we talked about."

She stared at him for a few moments, then thought of the book in her hand and lifted it. "I am sorry, I was more or less pushed into doing some extensive reading for an appointment today. That is actually where I am going right now."

"I know. You managed to obtain an audience with Sarol. I will accompany you on your way there. Only if you do not object, of course," he asked with a raised brow.

Sighing to herself she shook her head. "Of course not." At least she would only spend a few minutes with him as Sarol would probably not take very well to Ram'an's joining them at the teahouse.

He took her hand and put it on his arm. "So you are delving into the discipline of non-magical healing? Another new field that provides a chance to learn many new things - just what an explorer appreciates."

She shrugged. "I am not so sure this is about my personal inclinations but instead for more pragmatic reasons. The profession of healer is still something exotic for people in Anyueel, and currently I have a quota of no more than five healers I am allowed to train. The Order is still treating this as an experiment. Working with non-magicians might solve that problem for me and make me more independent."

441

"So, there is no fascination with the topic as such? Just considerations of how to increase the effectiveness of your services?" he asked, clearly not believing her.

She had to grin despite herself. "Well, maybe that is not exactly right. There might be a spark of interest as well, I admit."

"If it was only a spark, Sarol would not waste his time with you," Ram'an chuckled. "Not that a minute with you could ever be wasted, but that man is known to have quite an attitude. Try to keep the word *magic* out of the conversation if you can. It is general knowledge that he does not react too well to it," he advised her.

She nodded. "Thank you. Valrad warned me about that already. But I am hoping that he will be the one to do most of the talking, which should reduce the chances of my insulting or angering him inadvertently."

He looked down at the book she carried under her arm. "He gave you that book to read as preparation for your meeting today? That has surely kept you very busy, has it not?"

"That it has, yes. It is not exactly light reading and I hope he doesn't want to quiz me on the contents but instead is more inclined to answer my questions."

"Speaking of books," he said, "I showed your friend Vern's illustrations to a few people and they would be very interested in seeing more of his work. Is there a chance for him to send a few things here? A cousin of mine is a healer as well and currently is working on a book on foetal development during pregnancy. He says it is nigh on impossible to find a magician with both the required artistic talent and medical knowledge to do the illustrations for him. The trouble is that the good non-magician artists cannot look inside the body, and the magical ones have no idea what they are looking at when they do. He wondered if Vern would be interested in working with him by doing the illustrations. Say one picture for every week of the pregnancy to document the growth."

A broad smile grew on her face. "I bet he would be thrilled! It can't be too hard to find a woman who is willing to work with him there and let him take a look at the foetus once a week."

"Excellent. Then the two of us should have lunch together tomorrow and discuss the details."

She swallowed and saw with relief that the tent of Sarol's preferred teahouse came into view on the next turn the street took. "Tomorrow is not good, I am otherwise engaged. In fact, lunches are bit of a problem right now; I am spending a lot of time at the clinic currently. Why don't we talk about this when we meet somewhere in the evening next time? Or better yet, send me a detailed description of what exactly your cousin wants. I could pass it on to Vern directly." She saw Sarol sitting at an island of cushions with a book in his hands. "I am afraid I have to leave you now. Thank you for walking me here. I will see you soon."

She quickly kissed his cheeks and made to turn away, but he held on to her hands and his expression was troubled. "Eryn, is everything alright between the two of us? You seem agitated. And evasive."

"What?" she laughed too loudly. "Nonsense! Of course everything is alright. I need to go now. A good day to you." She turned quickly and felt his gaze in her neck as she approached Sarol.

* * *

Eryn walked next to Sarol. He had invited her to return with him and stay with him for the afternoon when he treated patients. She had agreed immediately, thrilled at the chance of seeing him in action.

Their conversation had been pleasant enough. He had not been particularly impressed by the feat of her having read his book in less than two days, almost as if he had expected nothing else. He explained to her some of the things she had not been able to connect in her head, such as certain symptoms that did not seem to have to do with anything which caused them. She had found out that she did have good anatomical knowledge due to her practice of accessing the human body directly through magic. However, her ideas about certain structures' place in the entire system and how they contributed to a smoothly running organism, how they influenced parts of the body that were located somewhere else could at best be called fragmentary.

"Is there any chance of my being allowed to copy some of your books? Or would you object to that for some reason?" she asked.

"Why would I?" he frowned and looked at her. "Carrying books home with you with my name on them would serve to spread my fame even further if I were a vain man. Using the things I have written to teach others would put my work to more good use if I were a devoted healer. Having the books aid you in discovering and creating new things would benefit the field of medicine if I were a passionate researcher."

She tried hard to hide her smile, but failed. "So which one is it, then?"

"They call me a genius, and they are right. It is all of them."

"My companion calls modesty a vice. I see that you have not fallen prey to it," she smirked.

Sarol raised his eyebrow at her. "And why would I? My work speaks for itself. Why would I pretend not to value it as highly as people around me do?"

"You undertake research, you teach and treat patients – that sounds like a lot of work. Why don't you just give up healing and concentrate on using that impressive intellect of yours for the other two areas?"

"Because that would let me forget the reason why I am doing all this. My test results showed a high score for explorer, which in many cases tends to correlate with a lower score in sympathy and compassion. So working with patients helps me to develop these areas, I am told. And many people want to be treated by me in particular as they are suspicious of magicians. They find it easier to be treated by one of them, so to say," he explained.

"So there are not many non-magical healers in Takhan if they need you to handle patients who are suspicious of magicians?"

"Not, not a lot. Most non-magicians who come here to be trained as healers leave the city again, as magicians are generally still regarded more highly in this and most other professions in the city. But if you are alone somewhere out in the desert or steppe, you do not discriminate if the choice is between suffering or being treated by a non-magician. Healing knowledge is respected out there, whether it be combined with magic or not. How will your people react to non-magical healers?"

She thought for a few moments before answering him. "I would say there will not be that much of a difference. They are not really used to healers anyway, so whether they are magicians or not is not really be the point there. In our case I am not even sure if magicians are allowed to live outside the city. The Order is an institution that has been established for purposes of defence, so having its members spread across the country would probably not be very helpful."

"And no healing whatsoever was done in the Old Kingdom before Ved'al came along? None at all?" he asked incredulously.

"Well, there were the apothecaries in the city. But what they did I would hardly term *healing*. And there is the odd so-called *wise woman* in a village here and there who has partial knowledge about herbs. That was pretty much it."

He shook his head in dismay. "Incredible. So all these magicians over there did was employing their magic for what, defence?"

"Yes, pretty much so," she nodded.

"Do they have that many wars, then?"

"No," she said slowly, feeling foolish because she could not really justify it, either. "Not really. The occasional skirmish or war with their own countrymen, but that was all it has amounted to in these last three hundred years following the war with your country."

He stopped and turned to her, regarding her thoughtfully. "You call this here *my* country. Which country is your country?"

"Well, the Old Kingdom, isn't it?" she frowned.

"Really? What would you say if somebody from there asked you where you came from?"

"I would probably say that I come from the Western Territories," she said slowly, surprised at her own answer.

"Very interesting. And here you talk of the Old Kingdom as *your* country. It seems to me like you are caught between your countries. Are you from both of them or from neither, I wonder? Why do you think that is, Eryn of House Aren?"

They had resumed their walk and she saw that the clinic had come into view.

"Probably because I am too obviously foreign to be considered one of them in the Old Kingdom. And even though my looks don't give me away here, I am a stranger and too unfamiliar with everything around to belong here, either," she mused.

"Interesting," he repeated, nodding.

"Why do I have the feeling that you are using me as a research item right now?" she said suspiciously.

Both his brows flicked up at her as if he didn't understand why there had been any doubts about that at all. "But of course I am."

"Right," she murmured. "Stupid question."

"Indeed," he agreed solemnly and entered the clinic in front of her.

She sighed. Sarcasm was clearly wasted on this man.

Suddenly she stopped dead and grabbed Sarol's sleeve. "What is *she* doing here?" she asked as calmly as she could manage.

Pe'tala turned and spotted her. And the all-but-pleased expression on her face.

"What do you mean, what she is doing here?" he frowned. "She works here." He lifted both brows. "Is it possible that you did not know that she is a healer?"

Her cousin came closer, wielding a triumphant grin. "No, Sarol, she did not. She never was interested enough to ask what I was doing."

"But your being from House Vel'kim would have allowed her to make an educated guess, I would have thought," Sarol remarked.

"Yes, *educated* is the key word here, is it not?" Pe'tala said in a chilly manner.

Eryn recovered from her surprise. "You really are a healer, then." The disbelief in her voice was all too audible, but she didn't care. Not with that one. "I would have thought that you needed human emotions for the profession."

"Obviously not," Pe'tala retorted, "or there would not be an Aren woman doing it."

"I thought we... *they* are known for their temper. I would have thought that constitutes a human emotion. Cynicism doesn't."

"Your behaviour is not very professional. I will leave you two to your bickering," Sarol offered and turned to leave. "I do not want to be associated with any of this. Eryn - find me in the East Wing when you are done with insulting your cousin. And colleague, for that matter. Somebody will point you in the right direction if you ask."

Eryn turned and called after him, "Wait! I am done now." She ran after him and aimed a final disgruntled look over her shoulder at her cousin.

* * *

"Maltheá," she heard a quiet voice behind her after she had left the clinic. Eryn turned to see Malriel lean against a house wall.

She froze for a moment, unsure how to react. This was their first encounter since the removal of the mind block.

"Malriel," she said, careful to maintain her neutral voice. "What can I do for you?" she asked politely.

"Walk with me for a bit, if you would," her mother replied and pushed herself away from the wall. It was late and the sun had already started setting. There would be no more than half an hour of daylight.

"Walk with you?" Eryn asked cautiously.

"Yes. There is a little matter I need to discuss with you, and I am under no illusion that you would come to the Aren residence to talk."

"What matter?"

"I would rather not address this right here. It is of a rather delicate nature. Come. I will accompany you back to the ambassadorial residence," Malriel insisted.

Eryn regarded her with a frown and couldn't help but wonder. She looked hardly older than Enric, a few years at most. Did he find her attractive? Especially as there was this uncanny resemblance between herself and the Head of House Aren? Malriel was more feminine, more refined, more subtle. Would this appeal to Enric?

She forced away the stab of fear and jealousy she felt at the mere idea of Enric feeling drawn to this woman.

"Alright, let's walk then," she replied more briskly then she had intended.

When they were out of earshot of whoever might have been behind a window or door at the clinic, Malriel turned to her.

"Theá, what I am about to tell you now will not be to your liking. But I want you to hear me out nevertheless without running off or snapping at me."

Eryn just raised an eyebrow and waited.

"It is about Sarol. I do not know if you are aware of the situation between his family and ours."

The younger woman nodded. "I was told that you are not exactly on friendly terms. What of it?" She chuckled. "I hope you are not telling me I can't play with him anymore?"

Malriel's eyes narrowed. "You may choose to treat this lightly, but your actions do have an impact on the people connected to you. House Roal and House Aren have been at loggerheads for some time now. House Vel'kim has been involved as well, but they had a reason to make an exception for Sarol that was generally accepted: his unusual talent when it comes to the healing profession. This does not apply for House Aren, you see, as we are not exactly known to be the healing kind."

2

"Then there are two choices for you now," Eryn cut in. "You either refrain from pointing out my connection to your House or you get used to a member of it being the healing kind with all consequences this may involve."

"Healer," Malriel murmured and shook her head. "Your test results do not point in that direction, and I very much doubt that you would have taken up the profession if it had not been the only one your father saw fit for you, if you had been given a choice. People have started joking about the *Aren healer*, the oddity they have to witness with their own eyes."

"How do you know about my test results?" Eryn asked in dismay.

"They are always sent to the Head of the family the test candidate belongs to. This is the standard procedure. Your results are not surprising. Your grandmother scored for explorer as well."

"This doesn't make any difference. My father was of House Vel'kim, and you must have been prepared for me to take after him and follow his profession."

"Ah, but you do not really take after him, do you?" Malriel smiled. "Neither in looks nor disposition. Now, do not look at me in that angry way. You may not like to hear it, but this does not change anything about the facts. You will feel better if you finally accept yourself the way you are, even if it means adapting your perception of yourself. But let us get back to the matter I wanted to talk to you about. Sarol."

"If you are asking me to stop talking to him, this conversation is over," Eryn warned.

She shook her head. "No. What I am asking you is to keep your interactions with him less public. Meeting at a teahouse for everyone to see you talking to him is not good. You are both healers, and nobody will have any objections to the two of you working together and associating on a professional level. But being seen to socialise outside the clinic has nothing to do with professionalism." She lifted her finger to silence her daughter when Eryn opened her mouth to speak. "And do not tell me that you were talking about healing matters. That does not make any difference to the impression you have made to a casual observer." Malriel exhaled. "Listen, some of your actions cause disadvantages for others."

"Such as?" Eryn enquired with folded arms.

"Such as the Houses allied with us right now putting our loyalty in question and wondering what we are up to. They might decide to terminate contracts we have or refrain from renewing them when the time comes. Furthermore, they may no longer support us at the senate, which would cause harm to the political influence of House Aren." She lifted her hands placatingly. "I am not asking you to stop seeing that man or profiting from his knowledge, but I would appreciate it if you did it in a less public manner. That is all that I am asking."

Eryn walked on in silence for a minute or two. It did not sound that unreasonable, she had to admit. It was Malriel's duty to protect her House from harm and keep it in power and wealth. And the unthinking actions of one person who was generally regarded as member of her House, however unhappy that person was about such status, had the potential to inflict damage. Her not forbidding any contact whatsoever but just asking this small favour showed an unexpected level of tolerance.

"Alright," Eryn finally said. "I understand your concerns and will from now on limit my interactions with Sarol to the clinic."

She heard Malriel next to her sigh with relief. "Thank you, Maltheá."

They had reached the ambassadorial residence. When Eryn nodded at her once and made to turn to open the door, Malriel took her hands and pulled her close to kiss her cheeks.

"Good night, my child. Give my regards to Enric." And off she went, back the way they had come.

CHAPTER 36

Ram'an's Unloading

She walked out of the tailor's shop and bumped right into a man who quickly raised his hands to steady her. She was about to apologise when, looking up, she realised that it was not a stranger who was all but holding her in his arms.

"Ram'an," she swallowed and took a hasty step back from him.

"Eryn," he smiled and held on to her elbow. "What a pleasant surprise."

Narrowing her eyes, she pointedly looked at his hand on her arm. "You are not pretending that this is a coincidence, are you? The city is too big for that."

He raised his brow and looked down at her. "What can I say, my dear? You are a smart woman."

"So you were either following me or lying in wait. I admit I find neither of those possibilities particularly reassuring." She tried to free her arm from his grip, but he only let go for a moment to take her hand instead.

"Eryn, I want to talk to you. I have the impression that you have been avoiding me. Do not deny it, I can see in your eyes that I am right. I will not let you go until you tell me why."

She looked around. People were passing them without paying much attention. But it was still public enough for her to be safe.

Trying to free her hand again, she scowled at him. "I don't like being coerced like this. I would have thought you remembered that."

He nodded slowly. "I do. And I also remember that you do not give away information willingly. I am serious, Eryn. Tell me why you are avoiding me. I will not let you leave here otherwise."

She breathed in and out. Twice. No panic, she told herself. That day in his quarters she had broken his shield. Not easily, but still. So she would just have to remind him that she was stronger and that he had no way of making her do anything.

Infusing her muscles with magic, she made to jerk her hand away from his grip and froze, when she felt his power flood her muscles, making them obey him instead of her commands.

449

What? How was this possible? She tried pushing against him, to make him release his control of her body, but it didn't work.

"You cannot free yourself. I am stronger." His voice was soft and low and he stepped closer to her until their faces almost touched and she could smell the scented soap on his skin.

"This is quite a surprise for you, is it not? And not a pleasant one," he murmured and smiled when he saw his words confirmed in her worried gaze and her heavy breathing against his chest. He closed his eyes and leaned to one side to let his nose softly glide along her hairline from her temple to her throat and inhaled.

He straightened again and let his thumb glide over her upper lip, then the lower. "I have wondered many, many times what it would be like to kiss you, Malthea," he whispered. "What you would taste like. If I could make you kiss me back."

He shook his head slightly when sheer panic had replaced the expression of worry in her eyes. "No, do not be afraid of me. There is no need for that. I will not impose myself on you. I do not want to take my first kiss from you by force, no matter how very tempting that might be right now. And trust me, I find it immensely hard to resist at this very moment." He closed his eyes for a moment and exhaled, as if to steady himself. "All I want from you is that you come with me. To a public place, a teahouse, and talk to me."

He released some of his grip on her and then strengthened it anew immediately when she began struggling.

"Not the answer I want, Theá." He leaned to her ear. "You either come with me to that teahouse or I will take you to my place. And I cannot vouch for my restraint there, no matter how strong my resolutions may be. I ask you only once again: Will you come to a public place with me where we can talk?"

She closed her eyes and waited for him to soften his magical vice on her muscles again. Then she nodded, not looking at him.

"Good," he sighed and held on to her hand to pull her with him when he started walking towards a large tent at the centre of a square on their left. The customary cushions were arranged in neat, cosy looking islands on the ground and he led her to one corner that was as far away from the other guests as possible.

Only when she had sat down did he release her hand and settled back comfortably onto a cushion next to her. She still avoided looking at him, her thoughts racing.

"Ask me, dear, I can see that you need to," he said softly.

Hesitating for several seconds, she considered a variety of options. Jumping up before he had another chance to grab her, for once. But his posture was not relaxed, as if he was already prepared to react to something like that. Hitting him hard. But touching him was the last thing she wanted. He would probably avert the attack and hold her defenceless once again. Not good. This time he would very likely not let go of her that easily.

He prompted her. "Have you decided on a course of action yet? Let me assist you, if I may. You will not be able to run; I will prevent you. Hitting me will not work, either. Though I would probably enjoy it if you tried," he added with a smile. "Screaming for help would be completely useless. I am too strong and too influential for anyone to challenge me here. Talk to me. It is the easiest way out for you."

She glared at him. "Alright then. Why are you suddenly stronger than me? Or did you mislead me on purpose that time in your quarters back in Anyueel?"

"I was stronger than you then as well, but I had used only part of my strength to erect the barrier that day. It was a coincidence, nothing intentional. Why have you been avoiding me these last few days?"

"I was busy," she replied stiffly.

Ram'an lifted a hand to summon a nearby server. He ordered a large vessel of tea for them and waited for the man to retreat before he took her hand and sent a warning pulse of magic through it.

"No lying, Theá."

"Don't call me that!" she hissed at him and pulled at her hand. He held on to it and she felt her muscles becoming heavier with every moment. He didn't paralyse her like before, but moving was a lot harder. It felt as if large stones were tied to her arms and legs and were pulling her down.

"Do not make me use the technique you call a truth block. This time there would be no escaping from it. You would have to endure it until I am done with you. This is not the way I want this conversation to proceed. You are making this very difficult."

"*I* am making it difficult? I am so very sorry for that," she snapped. She should have brought Barul with her, she thought and regretted leaving him behind.

"Yes, you are indeed. I do not think that asking you for an honest answer to a simple question should be such a trial for you."

She gave him an angry look. "Isn't it rather obvious why I am avoiding you after you tried to get me to dance with you to that particular song? I can't trust you! This is a foreign country for me, I need help to avoid the traps I don't know about, not be coaxed into them. And I learned about the little arrangement between our families when we were both children. It seems you have not quite outgrown it. You are dangerous."

"Dangerous," he repeated thoughtfully. "It pains me that this is how you see me. I would never endanger you; the opposite is the case. I wish to protect you. I would like to tell you a story, Theá."

"Stop calling me that! It was my name for only a short while a very long time ago."

"True," he admitted, but went on, "but that was a very important time. I still remember the day when they first showed you to me."

451

He smiled at the memory and his thumb glided over her knuckles in an absentminded caress. "I was five years old back then, you were two. You were a whirlwind - full of energy. I was told that I needed to take care of you, let nothing happen to you as you would one day be mine. I had not yet fully grasped the concept of companionship agreements and connecting the Houses for political purposes, but I accepted it as a universal truth. I watched you grow for only a few years longer, until I was eight years old. You were such a beautiful girl and I was proud they had chosen you for me." He looked up at her. "I was raised in the knowledge that you were *mine*, mine alone. Even after your father took you away. They were convinced that they would be able to find and bring you back."

Eryn closed her eyes in sympathy. What a cruel thing to do to a child, she thought. "I am so sorry, Ram'an..."

"No," he stopped her sharply. "I do not want your pity. This is not why I am telling you this. I want you to *understand*. Do not pity me," he repeated. "I could not bear it." He leaned back again. "Will you promise to stay if I release you?"

She nodded and felt the weight being lifted off her muscles almost immediately.

"I remember watching you in that small bed of yours with the green lace curtains while you were sleeping. I touched your hair, very carefully, afraid of waking you, but I could not resist. I needed to see if it felt as silky and soft as it looked." He smiled, the look in his eyes faraway as if he still saw himself standing in front of her sleeping form. "It did."

She remained silent.

"On the day of your fifteenth birthday," he went on, "I would have started showering you with presents, taking you dancing, stealing first kisses from you. I would have worked very hard at making you fall in love with me."

"What for?" she enquired testily. "I wouldn't have had much of a choice in becoming your companion, would I?"

Ram'an sighed and shook his head at her. "You think we are barbarians, that we force our young people into commitments and make them suffer all their life if they do not like the partner who was selected for them. This is not how it works. It is more like..." he thought for a moment, "the privilege of granting one particular candidate the first chance at winning you before you consider anybody else. A young man is expected to court his companion-to-be, not view her as a gift. If he does not manage to win her, he is not worthy of her hand and the families will very likely agree on a different arrangement."

Eryn sat up, intrigued. "So I could have rejected you? Or you might have decided not to try and win me because I wasn't to your liking?"

He laughed quietly. "The second option is not very likely. I was begging time to pass faster so I would finally be able to start courting you. And let me tell you one thing. Ten years is a long time for a young boy to wait." His face turned serious again. "Now it has been twenty-three years of waiting, and the struggle is of a very different nature from what I expected."

"There is no struggle. At least none you can win. Let it lie, for all our sakes."

"Days," he murmured, ignoring her words. "It was a matter of mere *days*. If they had found you only a little earlier, things would be very different now."

She looked at him coldly. "Why do you assume that I would have fallen into your arms like that?"

"I do not. But I am very confident that I would have turned your regard for me into something more, given time. I am persistent. And I have not given you up yet."

"I will not leave Enric for you," she said matter-of-factly and folded her arms. "Never."

"Then I should probably work on making him leave you, eh?" Ram'an said with a grim smile.

"And you think this would make me want to be with *you* instead?" She was about to jump up, but felt him close his fingers over hers again.

"Now, now, you made a promise to stay. Do sit back again, will you not?"

She exhaled and forced herself to lean back again. "You think the only reason I am not with you is because I am with Enric. You are wrong. If I weren't with him, I wouldn't be with anybody else." She took a sip from her cup. "I had no more than sporadic affairs in the past. This is probably the only thing you might have persuaded me to indulge in."

He lifted his eyebrows in wry amusement. "An affair would have been a very good start." He leaned closer. "Still would be. I am not afraid of proving my abilities in that area to you."

"Why can't you accept that I have chosen another man? You saw us dance the other night. I was told that all other guests could sense that there is something strong between us. Why not you?"

"Because you have not given yourself to him completely, have you? It is a matter of physical attraction to dance with somebody like that. Had he not intervened, *I* could have been the one you experienced this with."

"Hardly," she snorted. "Whatever you choose to think is between us can barely compare with..."

"Let us try it," he interrupted her with a hard look. "Dance with me. If there is nothing between us, then you should not feel any effect at all. The music only works with what is there already."

"Definitely not!"

"Afraid, Maltheá? I would not have pegged you as cowardly," he challenged with a sneer. "But let us make it even easier. Kiss me, and if there is nothing, I will not ask you again to dance with me."

He narrowed his eyes. "But if there is *something*, we will find out how much. Together. In a dance at my home, just the two of us."

"You must be delusional," she hissed. "How could you ever hope to top what you witnessed that evening?"

He waived a hand dismissively. "That was just a combination of physical attraction and your strong magical abilities."

"Then I don't see what would be different if *you* danced with me!" she exclaimed impatiently.

"I would prove to you that there *is* attraction between us, no matter how fervently you keep denying it."

"But this, too, would be no more than physical! Why would I want to exchange one relationship with strong physical attraction *and* emotional attachment for a purely physical one?"

"Because, my dear, your emotional attachment to him is not as strong as you would like to have me think, is it?"

"What?" She stared at him wide-eyed.

"You have not taken this last step. The final bond. And I have a pretty clear idea who of you is the one unwilling to enter into it."

She swallowed hard. "I am not going to do this just to stop your bothering me."

He smiled. "This is exactly what I am saying. Stopping *my* bothering you should not be the reason to consider it. Since you have obviously no desire to bind yourself to him that way, what you have now is no more than a legal bond, one that can easily be dissolved. A magical one, however, is a different matter altogether."

"Just because I am not ready to magically bind myself to anyone doesn't mean that am not sufficiently attached to Enric for you to respect my choice. I find it insulting that you need a third level commitment bond to accept my decision."

"As long as there is none in place, I will continue to fight for you."

"I see," she said stiffly. "Then I will make sure I avoid you for the rest of my stay."

"You can try that," he nodded. "But you will find that quite a challenge. This here is my city, after all. Whoever invites you to a social gathering will also invite me. I will find you when you are walking the streets or buying something, just like today. I will find casual ways to touch you or sit next to you at social events. You would need to lock yourself inside your residence for the rest of your stay, and that would not look good for yourself or the Ambassador, would it?"

She closed her eyes, imagining herself looking over her shoulder all the time and around every corner when she was outside, scanning each group of people around her to make sure he couldn't sneak up on her.

"Ram'an," she said in her most reasonable tone, "let's discuss this like adults, shall we?"

"By all means."

"If you continue your pursuit of me, we can no longer be friends."

"I do not want to be your *friend*, Theá, I want to be your lover," he said simply.

"Then there is nothing more I have to say to you." She shook her head in regret and rose. "Stay away from me." She all but ran from the tent, immensely relieved that he had not grabbed her hand to stop her this time.

CHAPTER 37

Enric's Revenge

Eryn stopped and braced her palms against a fountain when her lungs began burning like fire. In her mindless urgency to get away from the teahouse she had neither considered which way she was going, nor that enhancing her muscles would have been more effective than relying on her fitness alone. She took a few moments, let herself sink down on the paved street and leaned back against the fountain. Catching her breath was her first priority now.

She looked at the unfamiliar surroundings and wondered where her feet had carried her. Everything was clean and tidy, just like in the city centre, but the buildings here were less grand, less well restored in places where pieces had been chipped off.

She tried to remember the map of the city she had seen hanging in Valrad's study. She should have asked him for a copy to carry around with her, she thought. But then she had not really needed such a thing until now. People either described the way to her when she was expected to go somewhere, took her there, or Enric took over the navigation.

Where to go now, she wondered. Enric would be at the ambassadorial residence, but she didn't want to face him as long as she was this agitated. She needed some time and a quiet place to think. Like the Vel'kim residence.

Getting back on her feet, she decided to walk in the direction that had to be east judging from the position of the sun.

It was only a few minutes later that a servant opened the door for her and told her that both men and Pe'tala were out, enquiring whether she wanted to wait. She nodded and decided to sit outside in the garden. Although it was not yet noon, it was getting warmer almost by the minute, so she chose a large, bushy tree that provided plenty of shade.

She pondered what to tell Enric - if in fact it were wise to tell him anything. What would be the benefit? He was aware of Ram'an's intentions anyway, so why say something to enrage him? This would just cost him the energy he needed for his negotiations, wouldn't it? What if he did something that reflected badly on the Kingdom at a political level?

But what if Enric needed to do something here and now so Ram'an didn't continue under the impression that he could behave towards her like that without any consequence? Could she do something about him without involving Enric? But how? The unexpected discovery that he was magically stronger than her was a problem, there was no way for her to set him any boundaries this way. And he was clearly not open to talking about this matter in a reasonable manner that would not involve repeated invitations to become intimate with him.

Yes - she would have to tell Enric. The decision made her feel better immediately. At least he wouldn't find out by other means. That would only serve to make him angry at her again. Leaning back, she watched those horses they had taken hunting before, playing in the sunlight in an enclosure at the lower end of the estate and felt her entire body relaxing with the peaceful sight.

*   *   *

Enric found her lying on the grass, the sunlight bathing her recumbent form in a warm glow. She had probably chosen this place when the tree had still provided some shade. But he sun had moved across the sky and she was now fully in the rays. Her cheeks and nose were already slightly reddened from a slight sunburn.

He shook his head and sighed before he bent down to touch her hand lightly. Only moments later the reddened area of her skin reverted to the light tan she had acquired since their arrival here.

Her eyes opened slowly and she smiled when she recognised him.

"What was that? My cheeks are itching."

"I healed your sunburn," he said with only a hint of reproach in his voice. "Has nobody ever told you not to fall asleep in the sun, my love?"

She stretched and yawned. "When I fell asleep there was still some shade. What are you doing here, anyway?"

"Looking for you. I expected you back from the tailor more than two hours ago and this here seemed the most logical place to start looking. Come on, Vran'el has cooked lunch for us."

She held on to his hand when he made to rise again. "Wait. There is something I need to tell you."

He looked at her with a gaze that became intent.

"The reason why I didn't come back directly after the tailor was that I bumped into Ram'an, quite literally. He was waiting for me outside the tailor's shop and wanted to know why I was avoiding him. I wanted to stave him off with magic when he wouldn't let go of me, but it didn't work. He paralysed me and then made me go with him to a teahouse to talk."

457

She paused to hear if there was something he wanted to say or ask her at this point, but he just looked at her with an oddly calm expression. "Go on."

"He then told me about the time before my father took me away, how he had been told that I was his and that he has waited for me for such a long time and is not willing to give up. I told him to stay away from me for the rest of our stay here."

"That is all?" Enric asked with a raised brow.

She stared at him, appalled. "What is that supposed to mean? I just told you that I was waylaid by a man who then forced me to come with him! Yes, that is all! I am sorry I have wasted your precious time with a minor thing like that!" She felt his hand on her leg pull her back down when she tried to rise.

"This is not what I meant. No, stop struggling and sit still for a moment, will you?" He rolled his eyes when she infused her muscles with magic while he did the same to maintain the upper hand and pull her between his knees to hold her there. "Why are you always trying to fight me? There is no chance whatsoever for you to win. I am starting to think you enjoy being subdued by me."

She scowled at his amused expression. "And I am starting to think that you must have been dropped on your head as an infant. Repeatedly."

"There is no shame in admitting to it, my love, even for a strong woman. Or especially not for a strong woman. It is like a continuous challenge for her partner to prove being worthy of her as she wouldn't want to waste her time with a weak man."

"Is it comfortable in that dream world of yours? Can I visit?" she huffed.

"A discussion for another time, then. But we wanted to talk about something else anyway, didn't we?" he led her back to the initial topic.

"I wanted to, yes, but it seemed to be of minor importance to you!" she exclaimed indignantly.

"That is complete nonsense, and if you hadn't jumped up and tried to storm off, I would have been able to tell you what I meant by that already. I knew about what happened today with Ram'an before you told me. I have Grend or Barul follow you around when I am not with you," he explained.

"Pardon me? You are joking, aren't you?"

"I am not. After I had to learn from Vran'el that Ram'an used a truth block on you back home because you found it wiser not to inform me, I was not taking any more chances. And the occurrence today has proved me right. Walking around here alone is not safe for you."

"It is not as if being watched by a non-magician who can't intervene because he has no chance whatsoever to help makes it any safer for me!" she protested.

458

"No, but at least it considerably reduces the chances of your keeping important secrets from me."

She sighed and closed her eyes. "Which would not have made any difference at all as I have told you about it, haven't I?"

He nodded. "That you have indeed, and I am very pleased about that. It seems we are slowly getting somewhere with that communication problem of yours. What I wanted to ask you was why Grend was not entirely sure if Ram'an kissed you when he held you in the middle of the street. He told me that he couldn't make out any details, but from where he stood it looked as if Ram'an's face had touched yours. I would appreciate a few more details on that. That was what my question about this *being all* was aimed at."

Well, she had to admit, that did warrant an enquiry.

"No," she shook her head. "He didn't kiss me. He sniffed my hair or skin. He told me that he was tempted to kiss me, but wanted our first kiss to be voluntary."

"First kiss?" Enric asked grimly. "So he is confident that he will exchange more than one with you in the future!" He released Eryn and stood up sharply. "It is time to show him that his attentions are not welcome."

"Wait!" she called after him when he walked back to the house. "What are you planning?"

"I am going to have a little chat with our Ram'an. An intimate one," he smiled without humour. "Vran'el?" he called when they entered the main room through the terrace door.

Vran'el came in from the adjoining kitchen, carrying a large bowl of some vegetable dish that smelled spicy and rich.

"Ah, there you are. Just in time for lunch. Eryn, where have you been? We were told that you had come but we could not find you. I hope you have not been sitting in the garden all alone the whole time?"

"Vran'el," Enric said urgently, "I need your help. How do I find out where Ram'an is going to be tonight? I have to know where I should go if I want to meet him."

Vran'el carefully put down the bowl and shrugged. "That is easy. He has two favourite places he frequents when there is no private social occasion he is attending. Why?"

Enric scowled. "I feel the need to educate him with regard to a certain misconception he harbours."

* * *

Enric and Vran'el heard a slow tune coming from within as they approached the music house. After they'd had dinner at the first of Ram'an's preferred places and waited for him there for over an hour, they had decided that there remained little chance of his showing up there. So they had set out for the second location.

Enric spotted him almost immediately. He was sitting amidst a group of men and women, leaning back against the cushions and smiling while someone told a story. The quiet observer in the background, Enric thought. Not one eager to command all the attention for himself. Well, he was about to have numerous pairs of eyes on him soon enough.

"Would you like to sit, Enric?" Vran'el asked and started looking for an empty table. "This is not one of the preferred Vel'kim places, so there is no reserved table for us."

"No," the blonde magician replied. "I have no intention of staying here longer than necessary. I will take care of business and then leave." It was part of the impression he wanted to make on the witnesses around. He wanted it to be absolutely clear to everyone, Ram'an included, that the only reason he had come here was because of what he was about to do.

"What is your plan? You are not about to punch him in the face again, are you?" Vran'el enquired nervously. "Being seen to try and dance a seduction dance with your companion may warrant such action, but now without any obvious provocation it would not reflect well on you if you did so again."

"No, that is not the plan. Just wait here. This will only take a few minutes." He waited until the current song had faded away slowly and then started towards Ram'an's table. All of its occupants looked up at him in surprise, apart from the man he had come for. He frowned and gave the intruder a look of nonchalance.

"Lord Enric. To what do we owe the honour of your presence?" he asked.

"Dance with me," Enric said simply and stepped closer to Ram'an.

The other man stared at him. "Pardon me? Did you just ask me to dance with you?"

"I did, yes. I understand that unlike in my own culture, this is an accepted social ritual between men here. Oblige me, will you?" He placed his hand on Ram'an's shoulder and sent in a surge of magic to take command over his muscles. He made the man rise slowly, carefully keeping his facial muscles relaxed and led him to the dance floor. He felt the stares of the others at the table literally burning into his neck. Good. He needed an audience for this.

When they reached the dance floor and passed through the shield around it, he released Ram'an's facial muscles enough for him to speak.

"What do you think you are doing?" the dark-haired magician hissed.

Enric pulled him close, too close for two men who were not intimately inclined towards each other and started moving with him when the next song started.

"Why? I thought you liked this method of making others compliant. Or is it less pleasant when *you* are the one unable to move?" he replied, considering his dancing partner with his cold blue eyes.

"Is this what this is about? Paying me back for touching her? I was a perfect gentleman, though it would have been very easy and a lot more pleasant for me not to be," Ram'an managed to press out.

"A perfect gentleman?" Enric mused and pretended to think about this for a moment. "No, not from where I stand." He leaned down to the slightly shorter man's hairline and inhaled. "Or is this something you are experiencing as gentlemanly behaviour right now? Being touched like this by somebody who you have no wish to be that close to?" He smiled at the consternation on Ram'an's face. "No? I didn't think so." He increased the distance between them slightly, but not enough for it to be comfortable.

"You are a disgrace to your position as Ambassador," Ram'an growled while still helplessly moving with the music.

"Indeed? Well, you would know about that, wouldn't you? Having been an ambassador yourself. But you did not always act in accordance with your position either, did you? A truth block forced onto a citizen of your host country is not exactly considered good manners where I come from. And here neither, from what I have seen."

"Her citizenship status is not clear as I see it," the lawyer replied.

"No, it isn't, is it? And I am sure you are doing your best to convince people here that she still belongs with your country instead of mine. Being a lawyer must be so very useful right now," Enric said with a placid expression.

The other man didn't reply to that and just stared over his dancing partner's shoulder unseeingly.

Enric decided to increase the level of awkwardness a little further and leaned down to Ram'an's ear to whisper into it. "Your touching Eryn like this requires some sort of response from my side, you see? Both for political and personal reasons. I can't let you go on like this."

"There will be political consequences for your behaviour," Ram'an hissed back.

"No, I don't think there will. You are no longer an ambassador, so I am currently not subduing a country, only one single man. And should your country react to this by holding me accountable, they would - as I do happen to be an ambassador at the moment - offend and anger an entire nation. Why do you think a country sends a strong warrior as an ambassador?" Enric asked in the manner of a teacher with a child slow on the uptake.

"Because you would not permit Maltheá to come here alone," Ram'an snapped.

"No. I could just have been sent along as part of the delegation or as a guard instead of making me the head of the entourage. I was made Ambassador because the King wants to demonstrate strength. A strong ambassador to convey the impression of a strong nation. If I let you slight me by treating my companion like this without intervening, I would be perceived as weak and willing to turn a blind eye, which would reflect badly on my country. I can't allow that."

"So your revenge is making people think that we are sexually attracted to each other? This will not reflect favourably on you, either."

The blonde magician chuckled. "No, people here surely know you too well to think that of you, don't they? And even though I am known to get along very well with Vran'el, they will hardly believe that I would choose the man who is trying to take my companion away from me as the object of my desire." He shook his head. "Your face has conveyed to the observers that you are not happy about this dance, and that you are not dancing it voluntarily. I want people to see you defeated - under my control, subdued and defenceless. And each time you get too close to Eryn, we will repeat this little performance as a reminder to you. Having people watch this being done to you once is distasteful for you, of course. But believe me - their seeing you endure it repeatedly would do your reputation a lot more harm."

"So what is it you expect of me, Lord Enric? To avoid eye contact with her from now on, to leave when she enters a room and prevent myself from talking to her?" Ram'an asked through clenched teeth.

"No, nothing of that sort. That, you see, would only hurt Eryn. I don't wish to see her hurt. For some reason or other she has a soft spot for you, though nothing you should consider as encouragement. I want you to be polite to her, friendly even, within certain boundaries. I want you to avoid being alone with her, and also refrain from touching her, apart from greeting her, of course. Have I made myself clear?"

"Perfectly," Ram'an spat at him.

"Excellent," Enric nodded and stepped back as the last notes of the song died away. He held on to the dark-haired man's hand and finally made him bow as a gesture of reverence before releasing him. Then he turned and walked to where Vran'el was leaning against a column with folded arms and wide eyes.

"Come," Enric said quietly when he had reached him. "I am through here. Let's leave."

"Oh my," Vran'el whispered, his voice a mixture of incredulity and delight. "Call me a pervert, but that was really sultry. Can I be the one you do it with next time?"

Enric rolled his eyes when they left the building. "Go and cool yourself off in that fountain over there, will you? I don't think I can deal with any more intense male contact tonight."

CHAPTER 38

Talking to Malriel

"I don't like this," Eryn stated for what had to be at least the third time.

Enric held on to her hand and pulled her on towards the end of the road where the Aren residence was situated. "Come on, there is no harm in trying to talk to her."

"But you heard Vran'el! She will hardly dissolve the agreement as it would cost her the support of House Arbil," she protested.

"That may be so, but it might be possible that she knows another solution for the situation," he said calmly and knocked at the door without letting go of her hand.

"I thought you took care of Ram'an? At least judging from what I have heard."

"I have merely made him take a step back and be more cautious in the future. It will not stop him from trying again when he sees a chance. This will just make him consider his options more carefully and make sure that his next attempt is more successful. I don't want to take that risk."

Malriel opened the door and smiled at them. "Good evening. Do come in."

She handed them a cool, damp towel each and then kissed them, first Eryn, then Enric, on both cheeks. "Let us sit on the terrace, shall we? It is very pleasant outside tonight, a light breeze that carries the scents of the garden towards the terrace." She walked up the stairs ahead of them and crossed the main room. "What can I get you to drink?"

"Nothing," Eryn said stiffly.

"We will both have a glass of wine, thank you so much," Enric said and gave Eryn's hand a warning squeeze. Once Malriel had left the room to fetch a fresh bottle, he whispered to her, "This is not the way to behave towards somebody you are going to ask a favour of."

"A favour which, I'll bet you anything, she is not going to grant us," she whispered back.

Malriel returned and carried the bottle and three empty glasses with her as she went outside to a small table and cushions on the terrace. They followed and took a seat.

She handed them their glasses and then sat down herself. "Enric, your message said you wanted to talk about House Arbil. I can imagine what your concerns are, especially after what happened yesterday evening at the music house between Ram'an and yourself." She shook her head and smiled. "A man has to be very confident to do a thing like that." Her expression became serious again. "I regret very much that I cannot grant what you will surely ask of me: to annul the agreement and thus break with House Arbil."

He nodded slowly. "Yes, I admit I came here with the hope that there would be a way to achieve this somehow. I understand your position, of course. I saw the tapestry in the archives. Your alliance with House Arbil goes back more than one hundred and fifty years; you can't risk losing it for something like this."

"Very true," Malriel confirmed. "I wish I could do something for you, but it falls to you to resolve this matter. I cannot intervene."

"Is there maybe something House Arbil could be offered in exchange for foregoing the fulfilment of the agreement? I would be more than willing to bear the costs arising from whatever compensation they demand."

"What?" Eryn frowned and stiffened. "Did I hear you just offer to buy me off them? Like a horse?"

"No, Maltheá," her mother corrected her mildly. "He has just expressed his willingness to offer House Arbil some compromise that would allow them to step back without losing face and that would let the alliance between the Houses remain intact."

"That is an illusion," Eryn said coldly. "Ram'an will one day be the Head of House Arbil, and he will probably not be eager to remain on friendly terms with this House, especially considering that you are still suffering from the illusion that I am going to take over House Aren one day."

Malriel considered her for few moments with a raised eyebrow before turning to Enric. "She is not exactly in a conciliatory mood, is she? Although I suspect that she is not here entirely voluntarily. However, let us return to your question. I already tried to talk to them about this a few days ago. While Ahend, Ram'an's father, would be willing to negotiate simply to have the matter of succession finally settled, Ram'an would not. As he is the next in line for the position of Head, his word has quite some weight, no matter how paradoxical it is that his aim is to make himself ineligible for that position."

"So despite his efforts not to be the heir to his House, this status is what allows him to veto all amiable attempts to solve this?" Eryn asked incredulously. "This is ridiculous!"

"I admit it does seem a little unusual, yes," Malriel conceded. "But there is one thing I can do for you. While I cannot directly and openly welcome you as my daughter's companion into the family, Enric, I can show my approval in a more indirect way by letting myself be seen with the two of you. I could still argue that I am no more than socialising with the Ambassador who just happens to bring along his companion whenever he can. It is a mere coincidence that she happens to be my daughter," she smiled.

Eryn frowned. "I don't see how this would help us at all." She tipped back her head to empty the glass and got to her feet. "Thank you for your time, Malriel. We will not trouble you with this matter any longer." She flashed Enric a look that conveyed the words *What did I tell you?* as clearly as speaking would have.

"Not so hastily, Maltheá," Malriel said softly. "Showing my approval of Enric to the public will bring more social pressure to bear on Ram'an. We do not take lightly to losing face. Your companion understands this very well as his little demonstration yesterday evening showed. If Ram'an reaches the point where giving in is less painful than trying to win you back and facing the pitying glances people throw him, you have won. I can assist you there."

"Why would you want to assist us, anyway?" Eryn asked frostily. "You are the one who arranged for this, after all."

"Why would I not? Enric is a very good choice for you. And for House Aren, for that matter. I admit that seeing you leave here with him will not at all be a pleasure, neither will having my grandchildren grow up in Anyueel. But I am sure we will find a compromise solution for this in the fullness of time."

Enric sighed. That had not been a good thing to say.

"Grandchildren?" Eryn said calmly. "I am happy I can dispel your concerns about that matter at least: There will not be any grandchildren for you to miss. We are not planning on having children."

With delight she saw how Malriel seemed to lose control over her features for a moment before marshalling them into a mildly disapproving frown.

"No children?" she said slowly. "I see. That is rather unusual, I must say. It does seem to be a natural wish for a happy couple to procreate."

"Not this happy couple," Eryn retorted with an amused smile, pleased at how she caused some irritation for a change instead of being the brunt of it.

"Not much chance for me to do anything about that, is there?" Malriel sighed disappointedly.

"None whatsoever," Eryn emphasised and shook her head happily.

Her mother regarded her for a while, then she examined Enric. "The two of you really do not make it easy for me to be Head of this

House, let me tell you that. But what would life be without a challenge every now and then? Let me invite you to dinner here tomorrow. It will be a nice public display of approval."

Eryn frowned and hesitated for several moments before nodding slowly. "Alright. Just don't think this is going to become a habit." Then she turned and walked inside.

Enric suppressed the impulse to grin. Malriel had finally found a way to persuade her daughter to come to the dinner she had planned. The Head of House Aren winked at him before he, too, stood up.

*　*　*

Enric looked up from his notes, slightly annoyed, when he heard a knock at the door downstairs. He wasn't expecting anyone. Eryn was still at the clinic and he was currently skimming through the notes of today's meeting with the senators. He rose and went down to answer the door and expressed surprise to see Malriel smiling at him.

He stepped aside to let her enter. "Malriel. What an unexpected... pleasure."

"Enric. I dare say it is. Unexpected, I mean. And a pleasure I hope it will be." It always sounded a fraction more exotic when *she* said his name. He wondered if she did it on purpose. Probably. He imagined there was not a lot Malriel of House Aren left to coincidence.

"Wait, there should be bowl of water and towels somewhere..." He looked around and found the tray in a cubby hole. Malriel smiled and refreshed herself quickly before following him up the stairs into the main room.

"What may I offer you to drink, Malriel?" Enric asked when she had taken a seat.

"I would very much like a glass of that fabulous wine you make. If you have some to spare, that is. I would not want to deplete your stock unduly."

He smiled. "Of course. I enjoy sharing it with somebody who appreciates it."

"I promise you will not find me lacking in that respect," she laughed.

He took two glasses to the sitting arrangement and sat down next to her, as was custom in the Western Territories.

"What is it I can do for you, Malriel?" he asked after they had clinked their glasses and both taken a sip of wine.

"Right to the point, I see. You are not afraid of Maltheá coming home any moment and finding me here, are you? She is still at the clinic and will be there for at least another hour or two. They are letting her work with patients now."

He raised both eyebrows in surprise. "Are they?"

"Yes," she confirmed. "Though I am not exactly happy about the circumstances which made this possible, as you surely know. Befriending somebody from a House we are on bad terms with is not the most helpful course of action." She put her glass on the low table. "The reason why I am here to see you despite having spent almost the entire afternoon with you at the senate is a little issue I would like to talk about. It concerns the matter of offspring."

Enric stiffened. "Pardon me?"

"Maltheá is against having children with you."

"Not with *me* in particular," he remarked dryly. "I would say it is more the idea of having children in general. Should she ever choose to have any, I would like to think it would be with me."

"So you are not averse to having children yourself?" Malriel asked, not entirely able to conceal the hopeful undertone in her voice.

"What is the purpose of this conversation, Malriel? Even if I wanted to, she does not. And this is something I respect." He chuckled. "Moreover, it is not as if there was any other choice, is there? She is a healer, after all, and can influence her body in a way that will make sure she doesn't conceive a child unless she plans to."

Malriel smiled quietly and pulled out a small, thin glass vial from her shirt sleeve. She held it up for him to look at. It had a narrow, elongated neck that broadened into a slightly bulgy, rounded bottom. It contained what looked like an opaque dark red liquid. There was a strange, pulsating glow as if whatever was in there was eager to get out and make things happen.

"There is always another choice, Enric. You just need to make it."

He swallowed, fighting a feeling of unease, hoping against hope that this was not what he suspected. "What exactly am I looking at here?"

"This little vial here is your choice, your key to having a child, even if Maltheá continues to control her fertility cycle. It is an enormously powerful mixture. Not only does it take away her control, it also conceals the loss of it. That is why she has no way of counteracting the effect in time," she said calmly and held it out for Enric to take. "Do make sure not to let anybody find out about it, though. It is not exactly legal. At least not if the recipient does not agree to having it administered."

He stared at the potion for several moments before closing his eyes and slowly shaking his head. "No."

She pursed her lips. "Are you sure, Enric? Absolutely sure? It might be your chance of a little daughter with Maltheá's eyes and temperament. Or a son with your facial features and strong willpower. It is easy to apply. Just mix it with a sweet drink to conceal the bitter taste and make sure she drinks it all up."

He shook his head and got to his feet. He needed some distance. From her. From that little vessel that he had been so very tempted to accept and yet knew that he couldn't ever use.

"No, Malriel." His voice was hard. "I appreciate the offer, but accepting it would be far too dangerous. I might lose her if I did a thing like that to her. And rightly so. She would never again be able to trust me after that."

She stood as well and held the vial against the daylight, catching his eye with the darkly shimmering swirls that caught the light from behind her. "I understand your concerns, of course. But she is not the only one entitled to making decisions in your companionship, is she? What about your wishes, Enric?"

"Do not try to manipulate me so bluntly," he warned her. "And do not pretend that your worries about my unfulfilled wishes are what brought you here with that illicit and thus very likely immensely expensive little gift. Your only daughter refuses to have children. This is not good for House Aren. But your House will prevail, whether your direct bloodline is in charge or not. And even if we had a child, it would not grow up here but in Anyueel far away from House Aren. There is nothing you can win here."

She smiled at that and shook her head slightly. "So indignant. Noble Enric. So understanding of your companion's needs and wishes, denying your own. And yet I saw a spark in your eyes when I told you what I was holding in my hand. That was more than mere interest, was it not? Greed. Only for a very short moment, but it was unmistakeably there."

He held her gaze steadily. Denying wouldn't make any sense. She was right and they both knew it. A woman like her would have ample experience in recognising greed in a man's eyes, very probably having been the cause of it more often than not.

"You are right," he admitted calmly.

She smiled triumphantly. "Ah, I do so enjoy my conversations with you, Enric. You do not insult my intelligence by denying what we both know to be true. You are a man who acknowledges his weaknesses and thus makes it impossible for others to exploit them." She stepped close to him, lifted his hand and pressed the small, warm vessel firmly into it. Then she closed his fingers around it. "Take it. Do not use it if you do not wish to. Consider it a... souvenir, will you?"

He shook his head. "No. I cannot take it. I might use it in a weak moment and that would cost me dearly. A prudent man never risks more than he is willing to lose. Your little game, Malriel, would make me risk far more than that." He gave the vial back to her and she took it with a deep sigh.

"As you wish. Men with principles are hard to find nowadays." She smiled. "And I am very glad about that. It is so immensely hard to make them comply with my wishes. I admire your resolve, even though we would both have benefited if it were not quite so strong."

She stood on her tiptoes and lifted her hand to his neck to pull his head down so she could kiss his cheeks. "Good night, Enric. I will see you later for dinner at my residence. I would appreciate it if you did not mention our little conversation to Maltheá. But you were not planning to anyway, were you? You want us to get along for her sake." She smiled and left, leaving him standing there, looking after her with a worried expression.

CHAPTER 39

Dinner at Malriel's

Eryn lay on the bed with her head comfortably resting on her forearms, observing Enric in front of the full-length mirror as he pulled another shirt in the local cut over his shoulders, a dark blue one this time. It nearly matched the colour of his robe of office.

"Are you done yet?" he asked when he caught her glance in the mirror.

She shrugged. "Sure. I am not planning on putting on any makeup or fancy clothes, if that's what you mean. It is just a dinner, after all."

"A dinner with a number of important people, no doubt. You could at least change out of the clothes you have been wearing all day at the clinic," he sighed.

She affected astonishment and reluctantly climbed off the bed to look through the clothes in her chest. She pulled out a bright red tunic.

He shook his head. "No. You are doing this on purpose."

"I have no idea what you are talking about," she huffed, knowing exactly what he meant.

"You chose something from home to demonstrate to your mother and her guests that you do not consider yourself connected to her House or her country. You are not taking any of it seriously." He stepped next to her and pulled out one of her new garments, a long tunic in a symphony of dark colours. "Here."

She took it and slipped into it, mumbling something about surely being old enough to dress herself without male interference.

"That is a brave claim to make considering that your male cousin picked your clothes when you ordered them," he said. "What about your hair?"

"What about it?" she asked innocently.

"You are not planning on just letting it hang down like that, are you? Do something to make it more elegant."

She laughed loudly. "Is it possible that you have forgotten who you are talking to?"

"Hello?" They looked up when they heard a male voice from the main room calling.

"In here, Vran'el," Enric replied and only moments later Eryn's cousin strolled into their bedroom.

"Enric, you look fabulous, as always." He eyed his cousin critically. "You look passable enough, if we do not progress further than your shoulders. Is this rats' nest a deliberate style to annoy your mother or were you planning on doing something civilised with it?"

Enric smirked at her. "Funny, we've just had a similar discussion."

"Alright then, I'll braid it. Satisfied?"

"Yes, if we were on our way to a hunt," Vran'el snorted. "But not to a dinner at House Aren. Sit on the bed. Where are your hair accessories?"

"On that table, the dark box," she said, defeated, and pointed at it.

He picked it up, opened the lid and grimaced. "There are only ribbons in here! How am I supposed to pin up your hair with ribbons? Where is all the rest?"

"What rest?" she frowned. "That's all there is."

Vran'el turned to Enric with an incredulous look. "That is it? Are you sure your companion is a woman? I know horses with more hair accessories than this!"

"She was a woman the last time I looked," Enric remarked dryly.

"Oh dear," Vran'el groaned. "I will be back in a moment." And out he walked.

"What is he up to now?" Eryn frowned and looked after him.

"Sounds like he is going to the kitchen. Probably in search of tools for the hair style he has in mind for you."

"I swear to you, if he tries to keep my hair up with spoons and sticks, I am going to kick him out of a window," she growled.

"From any other person I would have considered it an empty threat," Vran'el remarked, returning to the room with several small objects in his hands. "But I have no intention of making you look like a cooking utensil drawer has been emptied over you. Sit now."

She did so hesitantly, eyeing the little items he was holding. They did not look particularly kitchen-like, she had to admit.

He sat on the bed behind her, motioned for Enric to toss the hair brush to him and, after catching it expertly, stared brushing her brown mane.

"Is that a grey hair?" she heard Vran'el ask behind her.

"So what?" she shrugged. "I suppose it is going to get some company soon enough. Ow!" she exclaimed when she felt him rip it out. "Stop that!"

"I could not resist. A single one just stands out."

"How is there ever going to be more than one if you rip them out? I prefer going grey to being bald!" she protested.

"Stop whining. You are worse than Obal."

"Really? How many of her grey hairs have you had to remove to be able to compare us?"

He didn't reply but she felt him tug at strands of her hair, anchor them to her scalp and then move on to other strands, twisting and arranging them as he saw fit. It took him no more than a few minutes until he got up and nodded towards the mirror.

"Go and look at yourself."

She climbed off the bed to step in front of the mirror.

"Look at that." She turned her head from one side to the other, trying to see as much as possible from each angle. "You are really good at this." She turned to him. "How is this possible? You don't even have long hair to practise on yourself. How did you get that good at it?"

He grinned. "I have a younger sister, who was very eager to look pretty at a certain age. And Intrea is more than happy to let me style her. So is Obal. Plenty of subjects to practise on, you see." Then he clapped his hands. "And now hurry. We need to leave or we will be late. That is not something a host looks kindly upon. And we do not want to walk into a room where everybody is already seated and stares at us latecomers."

"Where I come from a woman is entitled to being late so she can make a proper entrance," Eryn told him.

Vran'el laughed and then stared at her. "You are serious, are you not? Really? Being late is something women do intentionally over there? Oh dear. I mean, you would of course get attention here, too, for being late. But not the pleasant kind."

They walked down the stairs and out the building. Dawn had already broken and the teahouses were removing the tents as they were no longer necessary to provide shade.

"Malriel is a very accomplished cook," Vran'el told them. "I think you will enjoy the food at least."

"Oh yes, just like that is my main concern when I have to spend an entire evening with her. The food," Eryn murmured.

"Try to be nice," Enric said soothingly. "See it as a business arrangement: You demonstrate to the world that you accept your status as her daughter, she in turn shows them that she approves of me as your companion. This is a setup we should all benefit from."

"Why does this sound too good to be true? And why does the thought of accepting my status as her daughter make my hair stand on end?"

"You got off to a difficult start," Enric replied. "That was unlucky. It does not mean that she is a bad person. She likes you very much, but is not really used to dealing with a fully-grown daughter after all these years. She has a strong character, and so do you. It would probably take a lot more time than we have here for the two of you find your way into a harmonic relationship."

472

Vran'el sniggered. "More time than any single one of us has left on this world, I would think." He shrugged when they both gave him a disapproving look. "What? Aren women from different generations are not generally known to get along well. There is a reason why Malriel's mother does not live in the city any longer."

"Another stereotype about how all Aren women fit one pattern? Really?" she rolled her eyes. "Why did she even invite you? I thought there is still some tension between the Houses?"

"There is," he nodded. "But now that you, the link between the Houses, are here, this changes things. Especially as you have shown very clearly that you feel more connected to us than to her. She knows that treating us well means that you will be more inclined to tolerate her. At least for short periods of time." He pursed his lips. "It is that time of the year again, I wonder..."

"What?" Eryn demanded.

"Be prepared to be invited on a two-day hunting trip," he replied. "She generally invites a number of close friends and strategic allies to join her. It is quite the occasion and people hanker for an invitation to go every year. She does not always take along the same people, though there are a number who are invited without fail, of course. But some are granted the privilege only occasionally, and it is evidence of your importance if you are considered worthy."

"A hunting trip?" Enric interjected, his interest awakened. "Where?"

"On one of the Aren estates. At this time of the year a lot of animals raid the plantations at night as the fruit is ripening. The Aren family has managed to turn this nuisance into a social event. They have a convivial gathering in the evening with very fine wine and food - everything done in style."

"This would hardly be possible," Eryn cut in. "Our departure is scheduled for no more than three days' time. I don't see how a hunting trip is supposed to fit in with that." And neither the thought of hunting down animals nor spending time with Malriel was particularly appealing.

"Well, I wouldn't say it like that," Enric mused. "The negotiations have virtually reached the end, we are more or less waiting for them to make a few decisions that will enable us to sign the agreements."

She groaned. "Really? You might want to go? But there is not really any need for me to accompany you, is there? I mean, would they really expect somebody who is revolted by dead animals and has stopped eating them to join their hunting party?"

Vran'el nodded. "The hunt itself is not the most important part of such a trip. It is merely a pretext. Many people who go there do not hunt at all. That was a *Yes* to your question, in case you were wondering."

"Will she invite you as well?" she asked.

473

"This time that is very likely. But I do not flatter myself on having risen to a hitherto unknown level of importance. She will just invite me to make sure you do not decline the invitation," he explained unabashedly.

"Wouldn't that be a perfect occasion to demonstrate to her that she can't just use people that way? Let's show her! We will decline the invitation in the event that there is one. What do you say?"

Both men looked at her pityingly and shook their heads as one.

"No, my sweetness, it would not look good for House Vel'kim if I declined. And then there is the little matter that I really *want* to go. I have been invited four times so far, and every single one was an adventure. I dare say with you there it will hardly be less of one," he grinned.

"But *we* don't have to accept, do we?" she took Enric's arm and looked at him pleadingly.

"Well, my love, it would kind of defeat the purpose of going there tonight if we declined an invitation such as that. Inviting me will prove her acceptance of our relationship even more publicly."

She sighed and glared at the residence that had come into view. Maybe there wouldn't be an invitation. Maybe there wouldn't be a hunting trip this year. Maybe it would be later, when they were already gone.

Who was she trying to fool? Of course there would be an invitation. And Enric would accept it for both of them. Before this she thought that she couldn't dread this evening any more. How splendid that there was always room for improvement.

Malriel herself opened the door only moments after Enric knocked and stepped aside with a broad, welcoming smile. "Good evening. Do come in."

She took a large silver plate from a small table and held it out for them to take a cool towel each. The light was almost gone, but the heat of the day still lingered.

The main room held what had to be the larger part of the guests already and the murmuring among them didn't subside completely at their entrance, but decreased in volume for a few moments before swelling back to its former intensity. Eryn recognised many of the faces, among them a few Heads of Houses. Valrad waved to her and smiled before continuing his conversation with a young woman. Then she saw another figure and stopped in her tracks. Her gaze locked with Ram'an's and he slowly put his glass aside to approach her.

"Eryn," he said without the usual smile on his lips when he greeted her. He stood awkwardly for a few moments as if not sure how to greet her, if kisses on the cheek would earn him another punishment. He gave Enric a hard look and raised one eyebrow in question.

When Enric nodded once, he leaned forward but stopped when she was about to take a step back. Enric put a steadying hand on her back and said in a low voice, "No, let him greet you the way he used to do. We don't want to create any impression that there are tensions between the three of us."

Yes, she thought angrily, because that would be a wrong impression indeed. Pretence. How she hated that. Politics and diplomacy, they were supposed to keep people from fighting - but would a decent, honest scrap not be better to settle matters? Get it out in the open? Deal with it instead of pretending nothing was amiss?

She felt Ram'an's warm hands take hers and then his lips upon her left cheek for a moment, then on her right before he stepped back again, letting her fingers glide out of his gentle grip.

"Lord Enric, Vran'el," he then said and nodded to each of them. Then he returned to his conversation partner.

"Why is *he* here?" Eryn asked Malriel as calmly as she could manage.

"Why would he not be here? He represents his father, and House Arbil is allied with us. What is more," she added pointedly, "I would have thought demonstrating my approval of Enric to *him* of all people is in your own interest. Even though you are obviously not particularly relaxed in his presence."

She had a point there, Eryn had to admit. When she didn't reply, Malriel stepped towards a small table to collect three empty glasses and press them into their hands before filling them from a bellied bottle.

"Come," Vran'el said and pulled Eryn along. "Let us not stand here like outsiders, this is a socialising event. Mingle."

Two more guests arrived after them, and the whole party was led outside to the terrace where quite a number of cushions had been added to the few that had been there only yesterday when they visited Malriel to talk about the agreement with House Arbil.

Candles burning inside artfully-wrought gilded lanterns lent the location a soft, welcoming glow with just the right intensity to set a private and welcoming, yet not too intimate, mood.

Eryn sighed when Enric was among the first guests to take a seat. She would have preferred to see where Ram'an was sitting and keep her distance. Sinking down next to him she observed Ram'an from the corner of her eye, as he walked to the other side of the circle to sit as far away from her as possible, though exactly opposite her, so each time she looked straight ahead she would see him. How delightful.

She looked up when Malriel stepped behind her and bent down to her. "It is customary for one guest to help the host in serving the food at larger gatherings. Being chosen for this is considered an honour. Will you assist me tonight, Maltheá?"

Eryn stared up at her for a few moments, then nodded when she felt Enric's soft nudge at her side.

"Alright. Yes. Sure. Very well," she replied without much enthusiasm and accepted Malriel's hand, which pulled her to her feet.

Enric watched the two women disappear back into the house through the terrace door and then turned when a man in his fifties he recognised as the Head of House Ordel, one of the Houses allied with the Aren family, spoke.

"Seeing them beside each other like this is still a minor shock to me. Incredible, this similarity." The man smiled. "And to see them reunited after all this time... Yet I admit I cannot help but half-expect an eruption of some kind. They seem friendly enough with each other, but I can sense the tension between them. I have known Malriel for a long time. She is not so relaxed when her daughter is close by, even though she manages to convey quite a different impression, does she not?"

Enric nodded. "She does indeed. But then she is used to not showing any weaknesses, I'd imagine."

Voreld of House Ordel nodded. "Yes, that is true. The last time I saw her show any sign of vulnerability in public was when she collapsed at the senate some days after Maltheá had been taken by Ved'al."

Enric remembered how he had heard about that. It was probably quite a feat keeping all the desperation, frustration and frustrated hopes within, hidden from the people around her, who might have considered showing it a weakness. And seeing her only daughter again after all these years did not really turn out the way she must have been hoping it would.

He looked up again when Eryn and Malriel returned to the terrace, both carrying a large steaming bowl of something.

"My daughter will be happy to serve those of you who prefer a meat-free meal if you raise a hand," the hostess announced.

Three hands went up, among them Ram'an's. Eryn forced herself to smile and kneel down next to a young man who lifted his bowl for her to fill. The second one looked familiar, though she couldn't remember where she had seen the woman before. Probably at the clinic. It was Valrad's conversation partner from before. And finally she approached Ram'an who smiled faintly at her when he lifted his bowl.

"How are you adapting to your new diet? Do you miss the meat?" he asked casually.

She looked at him for a moment before answering. Was he really pretending nothing had happened between them?

"Well enough, thank you." She made herself smile politely and stood again to return to her seat and fill her own bowl. She saw Enric raise an eyebrow at Ram'an who ignored him completely and commenced a lively conversation with the person on his left.

They waited until Malriel had served the other guests and taken her seat next to Enric before everybody began eating. The hostess was the last one to pick up her bowl, just as was considered polite here.

The dinner conversation bubbled along, interrupted by occasional laughter. Eryn didn't join in but was content watching people around her. Only a few more days in this strange country before she returned home. Her gaze fell on Vran'el and Valrad who were discussing something with a third man and she felt her heart grow a little heavier. She would miss them a lot, achingly so. Then she looked at Malriel, who was in an animated conversation with Enric and another guest. Regret and relief formed an odd mix inside her. Regret that she had not managed to make herself esteem her own mother the way a daughter was expected to. Combined with relief at soon being free from that woman's unsettling presence.

She looked straight ahead when she felt someone looking at her. Ram'an. He was observing her, smiling knowingly as if he had guessed her thoughts. She lowered her gaze, avoiding his eyes, wishing he would leave her a moment of private pondering instead of beaming his attention onto her from across the table.

When all guests had emptied their bowls after the first or second helping, Malriel cleared her throat.

"Friends, there are two things I would like to say. One of them concerns the negotiations with the Old Kingdom." She turned towards Enric and smiled. "I am very pleased to tell you, Enric, that the senate and the triarchy have agreed to sign the most recent version of the agreements." A round of polite clapping erupted. When it had died down, she continued, "In addition we have decided to share with you not only the knowledge of how to cross the barrier, but also how to go about building large cargo vessels."

Enric smiled broadly. "That is excellent news, Malriel."

She nodded. "It is indeed. It is now up to the Houses to agree with you on their separate trading agreements, but I think your assistant Kilan has been toiling away on that for at least half the time of your stay here already. I expect most of these contracts are ready to be signed." She turned back to the rest of her guests. "The second matter I want to address tonight is the annual hunting trip House Aren organises. This is the last opportunity to do it if I want to have our guests join us on it. I would thus like to invite all of you on this year's little hunting party. We will leave here tomorrow noon, so there is still time to take care of finalising agreements in the morning."

She looked at each and every guest until he or she had nodded in acceptance of the honour. Though most of the guests seemed to have been expecting the invitation, there was still a variation in eagerness, relief, satisfaction and joy on the faces. Finally Malriel turned to Eryn and Enric.

"I would be very happy and honoured if the two of you would be part of this."

Enric nodded. "The honour is all ours. It will be our pleasure to accompany you."

Eryn gave her mother a guarded look, but her reply was not required in any case as her companion had already spoken for both of them. Ram'an would be there on the trip. How could that woman dare to place them together in such a situation? Making them go on a two-day hunting trip together, forcing them to spend time together showed some nerve, especially as Eryn had made it all too clear upon their arrival that she was not keen on spending even a single evening with Ram'an.

Only three more days, Eryn reminded herself. Then she would be free of Malriel's scheming, attempts at manipulation, demands and political manoeuvring. She would get these last few days behind her somehow. Additionally, Vran'el and her uncle were invited, so this trip would at least not rob her of any precious time with them.

"Get rid of that dark expression on your face," Enric murmured only for her ears. "We have just been extended what is considered a great honour. Don't concern yourself over Ram'an. He will not be a problem."

She plastered a smile on her face. "I wish I had your confidence."

CHAPTER 40

The Aren Estate

Eryn shifted uncomfortably on her horse. Riding bareback was definitely not her favourite mode of travelling. Urban trotted next to them in what was a relaxed pace for her, careful to remain in the shade the horses cast. The horses had to be calmed with a little magic every now and then to stop them from bolting for their lives.

"How much longer until we get there?" she enquired for the third time in one hour.

"About one more hour," Vran'el sighed. "And now stop that. You are worse than my daughter."

"Have you noticed that you keep comparing me to a four-year-old child and I always lose? Why did I have to come?" she complained. "I don't even hunt! And I am not going to consume anything you kill."

"I told you before, the hunting itself is not the main thing. It is the socialising in the evening and being seen to be part of the illustrious circle of names who were invited," he explained patiently.

"I can easily forego that honour. I would much rather spend the time with Sarol and learn something or read another book. Or just have dinner at your place."

Her cousin chastised her, "Stop whining and enjoy it instead. You may not be too thrilled about spending time with Malriel and Ram'an, but they are not the only ones there, after all. Be grateful father and I have come along as well."

"I am. Though I would have preferred spending my last evenings in a rather more subdued and private setting with you."

Vran'el leaned over to squeeze her hand. "I know. But we have to make the best with what we are given. And it is a nice chance for you to meet your grandmother. She is quite a piece of work."

"That would be the one who blew up a wine store once?" Eryn wanted to know.

"The very one, yes. I am very curious to see how the two of you will get along. Malriel has her problems with her, so there might be a chance for the two of you to get to like each other. Or you will finally be able to bond with Malriel owing to both of you having a difficult mother. Which would be rather strange, as her being a difficult mother is pretty much the reason why you do not have a good relationship. Or they both disapprove of you so much it unites them against you. That would be interesting to watch as well," he reflected.

"You are quite a piece of work yourself, you know," she growled. "No matter how bad this is for me, you see the entertainment value for yourself in every scenario! Where is your compassion, I am asking you?"

He shrugged. "Must have left it at home. It would only have got in the way of enjoying myself."

Valrad and Enric led their horses next to theirs. Her uncle smiled at her downcast expression.

"Do not let him tease you, my dear. He has had so much practice with his sister, so he is good at it," her uncle told her.

Vran'el shrugged. "I like to think I have a talent for it. One of many."

Eryn scoffed at him and then turned towards Valrad. "You know, there is one thing I have completely forgotten to ask you about. I can't believe I have thought of it only now." She looked around to make sure no others were within earshot. "Ram'an told us about there being a magical barrier that was originally intended to stop people in the Old Kingdom from having any more magically gifted offspring. In their heads, I mean. But they did it wrong somehow and it only managed to eliminate magic in the women. Can you tell me more about that? How does it work? Is there a way to undo this? Would you be allowed to tell me if there was?"

Enric cut in before Valrad could answer. "I asked Kilan to do some research on the topic, but he has not found anything useful in the books in the library. I didn't want to ask the senate about it before the trade agreements are signed."

Naturally, she thought - he would not have forgotten about it like she had. But then he was the Ambassador, after all, wasn't he? He was supposed to keep matters like that in mind.

"You would not find a lot about this in the books," Valrad explained. "Shielding has in these last few hundred years not been used or improved for anything but medical and agricultural purposes. Blocking magical skills does not really fall into either category, just like the barrier in the sea that stopped your ships from crossing."

"Are you telling me that you don't know how it works? Or how to remove it?" she asked in dismay. That was not good news.

"That is the case, I am afraid. Though the matter has been discussed every now and then - on a purely intellectual and theoretical level. There was never any experimentation or research done. Which is a pity, considering your very understandable interest in the matter."

Eryn nodded slowly. "Can you tell me what theories there are?"

"Well, first there is the matter of how magic can be blocked in the human body. Whether or not a child is born with magical abilities can already be seen while it is still inside the mother's womb. There is an area in the brain that is only active if you are a magician. Even though a child is not able to access the magic before a certain age, the activity is there already."

"And deactivating this area would block the magic in a person completely?" she asked, appalled at the idea.

"It has to be done before the person has access to it, so while he or she is still a small child. Once magic is being used consciously, you can no longer block it off. And neither can you restore magical abilities that have been blocked after a certain age."

"So whatever shield there is would have to do what? Block off any magical ability in children? But how? Where is this shield located? And a shield is no more than a barrier stopping objects, elements or magic from passing, so you would basically have to place one inside every child's head for it to work. And why does it only work with girls while boys are not affected at all?" she frowned.

"Ah yes," her uncle smiled. "The explorer has awoken, I see."

"It never really sleeps," Enric added. "But I would be interested in the theories, too."

"Alright, there is one I have been toying around with. But a theory is all it is, mind you. It might be valid or it might be conjecture. Let us start with the reason why it does not work with boys as well, as was probably intended by our ancestors. Male and female brains differ in quite a number of areas, such as mathematical understanding, language, social behaviour and abilities, sexuality and so on. As they do when it comes to magic. This was very probably not known back then when they placed the shield. They may have had enough healing skills to locate the relevant area in the female brain, but had not considered that there might be a difference between the sexes."

Eryn nodded. "Very well. That answers one question. But what about how the shield was put in place?"

"Patience, my dear girl," her uncle said calmly. "I was about to get to that. Some of our old books contain information about methods of punishment that were used in the old days. One of them was blocking off an entire family's ability to produce magically-gifted offspring. The interesting thing is that they did not have to renew the punishment every generation; it was carried out once and then remained in place. As if it were being passed on from one generation to the next."

Eryn stared ahead, thoughts racing through her head. Enric leaned forward, intrigued.

"So your theory is that there is a shield inside us that is passed on from one generation to the next, blocking the brain areas that would allow magically-gifted daughters? I would have to have such a shield inside me as well, then, wouldn't I?" he enquired.

Valrad nodded. "Yes, that you would indeed."

"The fact that I have never detected a shield inside me works against your theory."

"Oh, but then you would not know where to look for it, would you? We are talking about miniscule barriers so weak that detecting them by chance would be nigh impossible. The reason why the activity in the brain is so effective is that it does not need large amounts of energy. So blocking a small part of this activity would not require a strong barrier, either."

Eryn turned to him. "But how can passing on a shield through your parents be possible? This sounds completely..." She stopped herself in time.

"Insane?" her uncle asked with an indulgent smile. "Maybe. But then a few things which seemed equally insane turned out to be true in the past, did they not? We know that if you go down really deep, you can influence what is being passed on and what not."

"But wouldn't this have required very detailed healing knowledge? Missing the little detail that the barrier does not work on males does not seem very advanced to me," Eryn pointed out.

"True, but then we cannot really be sure of what their true intention was, can we? It is generally assumed that they wanted to block all the magic, but maybe this is not what they were aiming for. Maybe they thought it was too cruel and instead merely limited their efforts to blocking magic in females on purpose to generally weaken the magic within the country. We will never know now," Valrad shrugged.

"So, why have you never asked me to let you verify your theory by letting you search for a shield inside my head? It would have to be there, or I wouldn't be able to pass it on," Enric asked. "This is the first time you have had somebody from the Kingdom here, so that would have been a good chance to investigate it."

The older man nodded. "Yes, you are right, of course. I would have loved to do so, but I was asked to hold back. Before your arrival there was no way of telling how we would get along and whether alerting you as to how this barrier could be removed would be a wise idea. I think that after signing the trade agreements today this will no longer be an issue." He looked at Enric thoughtfully. "If you are willing, I would like to ask the triarchy for permission to look into the matter after we have returned to the city tomorrow afternoon. That would leave us one evening, which very likely will be more than enough."

Enric nodded. "I am more than willing. If there is a way of working out how to undo this, I am eager to assist in finding it."

Valrad's eyes sparkled, when he smiled. "Excellent. I will contact the triarchy immediately once we are back. It would indeed be a shame to let this opportunity pass."

Eryn thought about the tumultuous welcome they would receive if they indeed managed to bring home knowledge that could lead to lifting that mysterious barrier. Female magicians, she pondered. That would bring quite a few changes not only to the Order, but also to society as such. She cautioned herself not to expect too much from her uncle's theories and that they could be confirmed that easily and turned into reality like that. Yet it was a start - every change had to start somewhere.

* * *

Eryn had emptied her second water bladder when the Aren estate came into view as they passed two large rocks. It looked magnificent, she had to admit. Glowing in a soft reddish brown, the luxurious residence amidst extensive areas of green filled with various bushes, trees and vines seemed to have been built from the same stone that formed the broad valley.

It looked quiet, harmonious, imposing and welcoming. A collective sigh of relief seemed to emanate from the party as they beheld their destination, promising something cool to drink and relaxation over the last few remaining sunny hours of the day.

Malriel had left earlier than her guests, going ahead to make sure that everything was prepared for their arrival. As most of the guests had been on one of her hunting trips already, they knew the way well enough without her, so there was no danger of getting lost in the forbidding terrain.

The horses, too, seemed eager to reach the place quickly, and they arrived at the house not much later. After the riders had dismounted, the main door of the building opened and Malriel stepped out, smiling broadly. She greeted every single guest, kissing most of them on both cheeks, apparently not minding the dust that clung to their damp skins.

Servants appeared from one side of the house to lead the horses into the shadow and take care of them.

"My dear friends," the hostess announced, "let me show you to your rooms. As you have spent the time of your usual rest on horseback, this is now a good opportunity to refresh yourselves and lie down for another hour or two so that you are fit for the evening."

Smiling gratefully, the guests picked up their bags and followed her into the cool building and up the first flight of stairs. They tried to stay clear of the mountain cat at Enric's side as far as they could.

The main room on the first floor was almost as large as the one at the Aren city residence and just as elegantly furnished and decorated. Not exactly what Eryn would have imagined of a house in the countryside which here was little more than rocky outskirts of the desert they had just ridden through.

Several corridors branched out from the room, and Malriel led a small group down each corridor to their respective rooms while others waited.

Enric noted with relief that Ram'an was part of the first group, so his room would be far enough away from theirs and they would not bump into him accidentally on their way to their room later.

The guest rooms were cool, airy and furnished with simple elegance that spoke of studied quality instead of parsimony. Eryn dropped her bag immediately after Enric had closed the door behind him and all but sprung out of her clothes to make use of one of the two large bowls of water and the towels.

Urban just plumped herself down on the cool stone floor and fell asleep almost immediately.

When Eryn was dressed in fresh clothes and the dirt from her skin was floating in the bowl which had been completely white and clean previously, she sighed in contentment.

"I feel like a different person. Isn't it remarkable what difference a little water and soap can make?"

Enric took out a fresh shirt from his own bag to put aside for later and smiled. "Yes - the little things in life. I will lie down for a bit. You look quite awake and restless, so I assume you are not going to join me?"

She shook her head. "I don't think I can sleep now. All of a sudden I have the feeling as if our time here is running out and I shouldn't spend any of it sleeping when I don't absolutely have to. I will take a walk around the gardens, see what they are growing here."

"Alright, but don't think that this is an excuse for you to retire early tonight," he warned her.

She made a sullen face, resigned at having her plans unveiled so easily. "Would I ever?"

Enric rolled his eyes and didn't even bother commenting on that.

*   *   *

Eryn had spent more than an hour strolling through a garden that was not quite as large here as the one in the city; but then maintaining a large garden in this place would not make too much sense, especially as the plantations provided more than enough greenery that was not only pleasant to look at, but also more useful than vegetation for purely decorative purposes.

She was walking along one side of the imposing residence and was about to return to the main entrance, when a sharp voice to her right made her stop and turn slowly.

"Come over here and let me look at you, you fool." A woman seemingly in her late fifties or early sixties sat on a heap of cushions and stared at her in a none-too-friendly manner.

Eryn turned to see if there was anybody else around who the hardly very flattering term *fool* could have been applied to, but she was alone.

"Me?" she asked hesitantly.

484

"Of course you! Or do you see anybody else here?" the woman replied impatiently.

Eryn considered ignoring the blunt command, but decided against it. Her curiosity was awakened. She had at times been treated in an unfriendly way, but hardly ever by people she had not even met before - at least if one didn't count Pe'tala. She studied the woman while edging closer. There was an unmistakeable resemblance to another face she had come to know better than she cared to. Malriel's. This was an Aren face, there was no doubt about that. And there was obviously also a generous portion of the charm Aren women were infamous for.

"You look absolutely ridiculous, Malriel. There is nothing to say against a bit of vanity in a woman, but you have overdone it. People are undoubtedly laughing about you behind your back. You have gone back an entire generation now! I remember telling you more than once that maintaining your physical appearance is something to be handled with care. Nobody will take you seriously in the senate anymore with a face like that. Add a few wrinkles, at least!"

Eryn slowly raised her eyebrows. So it seemed that she had her grandmother sitting before her. And that woman thought she was talking to Malriel! Ridiculous, she thought angrily. The similarity between them was not great enough to confuse a family member who had known her own daughter for several decades, was it? Or maybe Malriel's mother was suffering from an eye-condition or similar. But then this was a country of magicians and advanced knowledge in healing. A member of such an influential family would have had that healed away in no time.

"Do not just stand there, say something!" the woman demanded.

Eryn considered the woman through narrowed eyes. This person clearly deserved some sort of lesson. Why not have a little fun at her expense? She seemed unlikeable enough. If she limited her own contributions to the conversation to short remarks, imitated the local dialect as best she could and pitched her voice a little lower, she might pass for Malriel for a short while at least.

"Rather not," she said and folded her arms, careful to let the Rs roll over the tip of her tongue and prolong the vocals.

"What is the matter with your voice? Did you play around with your vocal cords as well?" The old woman shook her head in exasperation.

"So what? My choice," Eryn shrugged.

"Yes, your choice, daughter. You would of course not listen to the voice of reason if it is not your own, would you?"

"True," Eryn smiled faintly, enjoying herself immensely. She hoped Malriel would somehow have to pay for this cheek later.

"You probably did it for that new lover of yours people are talking about. The one from House Partém. You are known for always taking younger men. Does this one have any issues with bedding older women? Is that why you transformed yourself? To keep him interested?"

Eryn stared at her. What a despicable thing to say to one's own daughter. At least now she had a pretty good idea from where Malriel had derived her own twisted notions about motherly warmth and affection.

"None of your business," she said calmly.

"None of my business?" the woman spat. "Whatever you do reflects on House Aren, you idiot! Of course it is my business if you ridicule yourself and with it our House! I still happen to be a member of it, though I have started to question the wisdom of allowing *you* to head it."

"Too late for that now, is it not?" Eryn smiled coolly and turned away to return the way she had come. She had to leave immediately or she would burst out laughing.

"You come back here right now! This is no way to talk to your mother!" she heard the woman's voice shout after her.

Eryn kept on walking and turned a corner before she clasped a hand over her mouth to stifle the guffaws that couldn't be held inside any more. So that was her grandmother. What a displeasure to meet her.

* * *

She watched Enric putting on the clothes for the hunt that was due to start in little more than one hour.

"Aren't you getting ready a bit early? We could have used that time otherwise," she smiled with a suggestively cocked eyebrow. "Maybe even put that golden belt to good use again."

He smiled down at her. He was very tempted to accept that offer, but there was something more important he wanted to do before meeting the other hunters.

"Why don't we take a little walk through the garden? You said it was nice to look at."

Eryn didn't hide her surprise. "You are declining my offer in order so as to take a *walk* instead? Really?" She shook her head in puzzlement. "We have come a long way in a short time, my friend. But let's walk if that is what you want."

He just nodded and took her hand to lead her outside. The cat followed them, stopping occasionally to sniff items she had been too tired to pay proper attention to when they had arrived, and then running to catch up with them again. The main room was empty apart from a servant who was arranging final details for the gathering in a few hours. Enric pulled her towards the terrace door and out into the gardens. Dusk was falling already and the servants out there had just finished lighting the lanterns hanging in the trees and placed on the ground. The lamplight lent the place a charming, unreal quality.

"This is delightful," she commented. "It reminds me a bit of the Freedom Night, when all these lanterns were fixed to tree branches."

He smiled. He'd had to think of the very same picture. He walked on towards the lower end of the garden behind which crops grew, separated from them by a chest-height barrier of bushes.

Eryn bent over one blossom and exclaimed in surprise, "When I was here before, this bud was closed! Look at that, you can watch the blossoms opening in the dark! Isn't this incredible? They have several species here that can do that!"

As she was about to dart across to another bush, he caught her hand. He had not brought her here so she could indulge her fondness for botanical studies.

"Eryn, stay with me for a moment, will you please?"

She looked up at him and he could feel the tension in her arm at his serious tone.

"Yes?" she asked carefully. Was she in trouble? She tried, but couldn't think of anything she had done or withheld from him that he might disapprove of.

"I want to tell you how much richer my life has been since you became a part of it," he started and took her other hand in his as well when the first signs of unease began to show in her eyes. "I told you once that I would work hard at not making you regret binding yourself to me and I hope that despite minor... differences you never had reason to wish that things had turned out differently."

She felt the weight of the moment on her. He was obviously waiting for her to say something. Very likely that she didn't regret joining him. Was that really true? She thought about the fights they'd had in the past, how they had been resolved, what it had been like afterwards.

"Eryn?" he interrupted her thoughts, worried when she didn't answer.

"Enric, where exactly is this going?" she asked with a dreadful sense of foreboding.

He sighed. So there wouldn't be any exchanges of intimate confessions of love and affection.

"I am asking you to enter into a third level commitment bond with me, Eryn," he said calmly and clenched his teeth at the sudden panic she began to emanate.

"But... but..." she stammered and thought frantically, "that would not make a lot of sense, would it? I mean, we are about to leave here, and thus Ram'an's failure to acknowledge our companionship will no longer be a problem. And at home nobody would know what to make of it, anyway. We are joined already, so there would not be any difference."

"I wouldn't be doing it for Ram'an or the people at home," he said calmly, "but for the two of us. However, I can see that you are not in favour of it."

She gulped. Of course he was hurt now, and she felt crushed for being the cause. But was there any way to refuse an offer like that without doing harm? Very probably not. She should have been prepared for it, she thought. He had expressed his interest in the custom before and now that their time here was nearing its end, there was not much time left for him to pursue this. What could she say now to make her rejection sting less?

"I am sorry," she said and lifted their joined hands to her lips to kiss his fingers. "I can't. It scares me. The thought alone of being bound by magic - to a person, a place, anything - makes me shiver." She shook her head. "I have to think of Malriel and my father, or of Valrad and his companion. Things break apart all the time, and there is nothing we can do about it. We would be chained to each other. Imagine - there might be a time one day when we don't even want to look at each other any longer but would still be compelled to undertake the journey here together to have the bond removed."

He sighed and pulled her closer, regretting that he had asked her. He had known about her issues with committing herself to anybody and had failed to take into consideration that she had been made to do so against her will once already only months ago. Entering into an even tighter bond had to be intimidating for her. It was his own fault that trying to put his own wishes before her needs had not worked out the way he had hoped.

"Don't worry, my love," he said soothingly and kissed her temple. "You are clearly not ready for it. I will not speak of it again."

Now he was being cheery about it. Great. As if she didn't feel bad enough already.

"Don't do that," she groaned. "I feel like a heartless monster, crushing your feelings under my heels, and then you tell me not to worry about it."

"I mean it. I did not ask you to make you feel bad. The third level commitment bond needs to be something both parties desire, and my being the only one is not enough. And I respect that you do not feel ready for it now. This will, however, not stop me from hoping that you will be one day. I can wait for that day." He lifted her chin and kissed her mouth tenderly.

She nodded and then stepped back, breaking the physical contact with him. She needed to be alone for a few moments, collect herself.

"Go," he said softly when he saw her gaze flash across to the terrace door. "I'll see you after the hunt. Try to enjoy yourself while you are waiting impatiently for me to return," he added with a reassuring smile.

She smiled back at him gratefully and then walked back towards the house.

When she had disappeared inside, Enric exhaled loudly and covered his face with both hands. That could not have gone any worse, could it?

He looked up when he heard a noise to his left and stopped himself from cursing with an effort when he saw the last person he wanted to face right now lean against a tree, considering him with a satisfied half smile and folded arms: Ram'an.

"That was interesting," the lawyer said slowly. "I admit I was not feeling particularly joyous when I came out here. Seeing her with you generally does that to me. But right now I have to say that my mood has improved considerably."

Enric walked towards him until no more than a few paces separated them.

"You had better be careful what you say to me right now, or I will use you to unload my frustration onto," he growled.

"Really?" the other man retorted. "What will it be this time? A straightforward punch on the jaw or another dance to publicly humiliate me? I just wonder why a man who pretends to be so sure of himself and the woman he unjustly keeps referring to as his companion needs to threaten the competition."

"You are no competition. This does not change anything for *you*. She may not be willing to bind herself magically to me, but that does not mean that your chances have become any better because of it," Enric shot back.

"Then I wonder why you seem so tense, Lord Enric, if you have nothing to fear?" Ram'an smiled calmly, obviously enjoying himself.

"Because I don't want you to make her feel bad again. She feels guilty because you had to suffer due to the arrangement. This is the only feeling you trigger in her: pity."

Now anger flashed in Ram'an's eyes. "If this is what you need to make yourself think so as to feel safer, I will not try and topple your illusions."

Both men looked towards the house, when the dark clad figure of Vran'el appeared on the terrace. He looked around and seemed to freeze for a moment when he saw the two men standing together. Drawing in a deep breath, he made himself walk towards the two obviously displeased men who were each magically stronger than himself.

"Enric," he said with only a hint of warning detectable, "I was looking for you. Your cat has just eaten, or at least thoroughly chewed on, an expensive-looking cushion. Any attempts at taking it out from beneath her paws result in hissing and low growls. We have so far been too considerate to stun her, but that might change any moment."

Enric nodded and turned abruptly to walk back inside the house to get his cat under control. And his anger.

*   *   *

Vran'el was the first of the hunters to join the party on the terrace after his return. Considering that he was very much in touch with his female side, it was rather surprising to see him being the first who had managed to make himself presentable. He strolled outside and smiled when he saw his cousin standing in one corner, trying to attract as little attention as possible.

"Tell me I do not look like Malriel," Eryn murmured and took a glass from a nearby table.

Vran'el looked uncertain. "You know that it would be a lie, even if I did say it, do you not?"

"Doesn't matter right now. I just need to hear it. Go on," she pressed.

"Alright, then," he sighed. "Here we go: Eryn, you do not at all look like Malriel. Not one bit. No similarity there at all."

Eryn smiled. "Thank you."

"Why did I just lie to you?"

"It would seem I met my grandmother earlier. She thought I was Malriel and demonstrated what I think people refer to as the *Aren charm*." She shivered despite the warm evening air. "Ghastly woman. But at least there is one similarity between Malriel and myself which I can't deny: we both have appalling mothers."

"I told you so, did I not? Did you introduce yourself to Malhora?"

"No. She mistook me for her daughter, so I led her along in believing I was Malriel and gave her back some of the impertinence she dealt."

"So Malhora is now angry at Malriel for your flippancy?" he chuckled. "That is really mean. I like it." He pointed his glass towards the terrace arch through which Malriel was stepping just now. "She does not appear too happy. If I had to guess the reason, I would say she has probably just had an unpleasant conversation with her mother."

Malriel searched the crowd and narrowed her eyes when her gaze came to rest on her daughter. Eryn grinned impishly and raised her glass in a salute to her before draining it in one go.

"You!" she heard her grandmother's voice from behind her and whirled. "What do you think you were doing, pretending to be Malriel? That is no way to show respect to your elders!"

Eryn watched Malriel come closer and gave a silent groan. Now she would have to deal with both of them at once. Not good.

"I didn't notice anything or anybody that gave me the impression showing respect was necessary," she shot back, deciding that a defensive stance was surely not a good strategy.

The guests around them had stopped their conversations and every pair of eyes was turned towards them, some expressing fascination, others seeming slightly aghast at the spectacle.

"Maltheá," Malriel's icy voice said, "do not embarrass me."

"Embarrass you, *mother*?" she sneered. "That would be something of a challenge, as people obviously delight in talking about your habit of bedding younger men. Whatever I say to your mother is still minor in comparison to that."

"That girl has no manners at all!" Malhora hissed. "You think being dragged to that barbaric place across the sea by that worthless father of yours justifies such behaviour upon your return?"

"You be very careful what you say about my father, old woman!" Eryn warned her with a raised finger.

"Do not talk to her like that, mother," Malriel cut in. "Being abducted as a child was hardly her fault, was it? And it was you who arranged for Ved'al to be her father, if I am not very much mistaken."

"I shall talk to her as I see fit," Malhora snapped back at her daughter. "She is obviously in need of someone to teach her manners!"

"That hardly falls to you, does it?" Malriel shot back.

"I do not see *you* taking care of it," the old woman said with narrowed eyes.

Enric walked out the terrace and his eyes bulged at the scene in front of him. Three women, two of whom he recognised instantly and a third one - who was too similar in appearance not to be of Aren blood - were facing each other in what seemed like a verbal battle which shortly would develop into something more physical. It seemed like each one was fighting against the other two.

"What's going on here?" he whispered after quietly stepping next to Vran'el, who was following the exchange with rapt attention.

"An Aren clash," he whispered back without taking his eyes off the three women. "They normally do not happen publicly. Do not interfere, do not get too close, do not draw their attention to yourself. You might get hurt badly."

"A clash?" Enric asked in confusion. "You mean a fight?"

"No, my friend. A clash is a bit more. It is a powerful fight between generations. They happen, as is natural. But among magical families, they tend to be a little more... energetic," he explained and kept watching the three women. "Aren clashes, you see, are particularly dangerous owing to their renowned temper. Did you ever wonder why the Aren residence does seem so much newer than the more traditional residences of the other Houses? They have to rebuild it occasionally because their clashes tend to get out of hand, at least when they are real ones. The last one that required major reconstruction work was between Malhora's mother and her mother. And this one is between *three* generations even!"

"What?" Enric hissed. "If they are so dangerous, why are people standing around them like idiots? Shouldn't they be running for cover instead?"

Vran'el shrugged without taking his eyes off them. "Morbid fascination, that is all I can say. Those of us who survive will have something to tell our children and grandchildren about."

Enric stared at him in dismay.

"I don't need either one of *you* to parent me," Eryn exclaimed and folded her arms, her stance broad. "But I can certainly see why Malriel is so cold and heartless. She can't be blamed for it, it seems she hasn't really had a very good role model herself."

Both of the other women turned on her.

"How dare you!" Malhora screeched.

"Cold and heartless?" Malriel hissed.

"How strong are they?" Enric asked urgently.

"Malriel is a little weaker than Eryn; about Malhora I am not sure. But Aren women tend to be rather strong, the House usually gets the best companions to breed with. I mean, look at yourself. You fit the bill really well."

"Alright," Enric murmured, ignoring Vran'el's comments about his suitability for breeding, "I need another strong magician, then. Two shields should be enough to separate them. Look around and tell me who of the present magicians you know to be stronger than Eryn."

Vran'el finally managed to tear away his eyes from the scene in front of him to stare at Enric in horror. "You want to interfere in an *Aren clash*? Have you gone completely insane or do you have an urgent death wish? If it is the first one, we can have you treated for it. If it is the latter, let me suggest a number of less cruel ways to die."

"If they make buildings collapse, I am going to stop this fight before it turns really dangerous," Enric insisted.

"Oh, come on! Nobody has died in an Aren clash. Well, not for quite a while now."

"People have died?" He forced himself to remain calm. "Vran'el, you either show me a strong magician here right now who can raise a shield strong enough to contain Malriel, or I will shake this information out of you!"

"Ram'an, for example," Vran'el obliged. "Over there, next to the exit. Smart position, by the way."

Just perfect, Enric thought. The very one person he did *not* want to work with here. "Anybody else?"

"Not really, no. But the chance of your finding anybody who is tired enough of life to get between three Aren women is not that great, anyway."

"Alright. Then I will knock one of them out and separate the two remaining ones with a shield", Enric murmured more to himself and nodded. "Yes, I can do that. Knocking the old woman out will not earn me any points with the local dignitaries, and Malriel would have my skin for it." He sighed. "That leaves Eryn. And she does so hate it when I do that."

"You know the reason why I don't want children?" they heard Eryn exclaim. "Because I am afraid I would turn out as atrocious a mother as each of you! Aren women are clearly not fit for motherhood! I would be too afraid of being too much like either of you to burden a child with that!"

"You talk of burdens, you ungrateful brat!" Malriel had both her hands balled into fists. "If you want to see a burden, try taking a look into a mirror!"

"What for? People keep telling me I am your mirror image, so everything I would see in a mirror is you! Which fits your statement just fine – because seeing you when I look into a mirror truly is a burden!" the younger woman spat back.

"She is a catastrophe!" Malhora threw at her daughter. "This impudent horror is expected to take over the House one day?"

"I have no intention whatsoever of taking over your precious House," Eryn laughed derogatively. "Remember? I was trained as a healer, so there is a trace of humanity left in me. Clearly no Aren material, me."

"Oh, inhumane, are we?" Malriel growled with bared teeth. "I am so glad you have returned from what you now consider your home to show off the true virtues of yours! Such as loyalty, duty and providence for a family that depends on you!"

Enric braced himself, reminded himself that showing weakness was not an option and stepped forward.

"Ladies," he barked, "this needs to stop before somebody gets hurt." Like myself, he added silently when three pairs of furious brown eyes stared at him. He could very probably withstand every single one of them, but not if they managed to combine their fury into one well-timed shot each. If three powerful bolts hit his shield at the same time, that would not end well for him. But for the moment, coordination of any sort did not seem to be an imminent danger.

"Stay out of this, Enric," Eryn hissed.

"This is the man you call your companion instead of honouring the agreement your House made for you?" Malhora said in what was clearly less of a question than a statement.

"Shut up, you," she spat at her grandmother, "What do you know, anyway?"

Enric braced himself, then stepped next to Eryn, putting an arm around her centre and sending her off to sleep. He caught her without any effort, holding her pressed against him and immediately raised a shield between the two remaining Aren women who just stared at him. He knew that if they were both about as strong as Eryn, they would be able to break his shield sooner or later if they battered it from different sides. He bent down to lift Eryn over his shoulder and then stepped next to Malriel, who reacted too late and was about to step away from him hastily, when he touched her hand and took control of her muscles. Two of them were out of the game, and the third one wouldn't be able to penetrate the shield. Moreover, there was no reason for her to try anymore with both her sparring partners incapacitated. Unless *he* was now a more interesting target due to his audacity to interfere.

"I want the two of you to stop this," Enric said calmly. "Or I will send you off to sleep as well, one after the other."

"Threatening me, boy?" Malhora growled with narrowed eyes. "An Aren woman does not react well to threats. We tend to see them as challenges."

"I know." He smiled without humour. "But that is not the way I meant it. I am but a simple man from a barbaric country which breeds nothing but mindless warriors. We threaten, then we strike. We don't have female magicians, so we never had to bother with wondering if they should be spared."

"Savage," the old woman threw at him.

He kept on smiling. "Was that a No?"

Malhora sent him a last devastating glare before she turned on her heel and stalked off towards the terrace door with her chin lifted proudly.

When she had disappeared inside, they all heard something shatter against a wall, followed by silence.

Enric turned towards Malriel and said quietly enough for only her to hear, "I know that you are very likely in a mood to do something very unpleasant to me, thus let me warn you that I am prepared for it and you will either end up on the floor or over my other shoulder."

He released her and stepped behind the shield he had raised between her and her mother. She blinked a few times and then gave him a cool smile that did not match the fire in her eyes.

"Enric," she said calmly with only a light timbre that bespoke the effort that appearing collected cost her. "What an impressive demonstration of courage. But I suppose living with an Aren woman and a wild cat would have prepared you for a thing like that."

The guests' relief was almost tangible as they let out their collectively held breaths and laughed uneasily. Enric nodded at her in appreciation of her ability to control herself so marvellously.

"I think it probably would, yes. Though I admit that I only did it because I judged my chances at survival to be higher if the legendary Aren temper did not have the chance to run its course."

That made more laughter ripple around them, again aimed at Enric, and Malriel's smile became slightly less frigid. Acknowledging the power of the Aren family after stepping in their way was at least some consolation to her injured pride.

He kept his gaze firmly linked with hers as he removed the barrier between them. "I will take Eryn to our room now and wake her up. She should probably not be around polite company when she makes me pay for this."

More laughter at his expense that unloaded some of the humiliation from Malriel.

"Do that. Do not take too much time over it though, dinner will be served in a short while." With this she turned away, took a fresh glass of wine and smiled as she walked towards her guests.

* * *

Eryn kept her smile polite, dutifully making conversation with the other guests during breakfast. She glared frostily at those who were taken in by her apparent friendliness and thought that humorous remarks about the evening before would be acceptable to her.

She had decided not to talk to Enric for now, and he accepted that. Resigned to his fate, he was packing their belongings while she gazed out the window. It had a prospect over the garden, the same spot where he had asked her to enter into a third level bond with him. And to think she had felt bad about refusing him! Right now she would be feeling a lot worse had she accepted it.

She didn't turn when she heard a knock at their door and left it to Enric to deal with. She closed her eyes when she recognised Malriel's voice asking to talk to her for a moment.

She turned and fixed her mother with detached composure. "What do you want?" Only one more day, she thought, then she wouldn't have to deal with this woman any longer.

"I would like to ask you for an hour or two of your time before you leave here," Malriel replied calmly.

"You had plenty of time with me yesterday. I believe we have had as much contact with each other as we would wish for."

"Time *alone* with you," her mother replied. "There are things I would like to know. Things about your father. After you have gone there will be no further chance for me to hear about them."

Eryn stared at her for a few moments. She could allow her an hour. Refusing would only cause feelings of guilt to haunt her for a long time, that she knew. "Very well. One hour. When and where?"

"Come over to me this afternoon. I would prefer the Aren residence as the matter is private and I do not want to worry about being overheard or observed."

Eryn nodded and turned back to the window, listening to the sounds of Malriel's footsteps receding and Enric closing the door behind her.

"I am glad you agreed to what she asked of you," he then said.

She whirled to him angrily. "I am not talking to you right now!"

He sighed and finished his packing. "Of course. How could I forget that for even a moment?"

CHAPTER 41

Sharing the Secret

Eryn braced herself and lifted her hand to knock at the door of the Aren residence. She was exhausted and would have preferred spending the afternoon lying down with a book - maybe falling asleep over it.

The ride back from the Aren estate had been tense. People had just about avoided riding too close to her horse, which had been more than acceptable to her. Vran'el had tried to lift her spirits with conversation, but gave up after about half an hour. Enric had ridden next to her for the first few minutes, but after receiving very pointed and very brooding stares from her repeatedly, he had chosen to let himself fall back with the others. Valrad had remained with her, riding next to her without saying a word. Having somebody next to her who accepted her need for silence unconditionally but still kept her company had been comforting, she was surprised to admit to herself.

Enric had let her wallow in her dark thoughts for several hours, but had then felt the need to put an end to it as soon as they had arrived at the ambassadorial residence. When had made to all but flee into their bedroom, he grabbed her arm and pulled her back.

"Alright - enough of this now. You had plenty of opportunity to be angry at me. The only thing I could think of while listening to Vran'el's stories about buildings collapsing and people dying when Aren women fight, was how to prevent it. You were the only one I could send to sleep without political consequences."

She had tried to pull her hand out of his grip. "Well, Ambassador, then you certainly made the right choice. But while you may have avoided political consequences, you still have to deal with the personal ones."

"I have been dealing with them for many hours now. You either get it out of your system now by sword fighting, sex or any other means you see as suitable, or this last day here in Takhan will become an unpleasant memory for both of us, which would be a shame as we don't know when we can return here again."

She stared at him for a few moments, and then infused her arm and shoulders with enough magic to punch him right in the face. Unfortunately he had been prepared for it and had ducked in time.

"Good."

That had gone on for almost half an hour, until she had slumped to her knees, panting heavily. She had not managed to land even one hit.

"Better?" he asked and crouched down next to her.

She just nodded.

"Good. You can put the golden belt on me now if you like - and still have enough energy left."

She looked up at him in astonishment and then started laughing at his incredible boldness.

"Maltheá," Malriel said into her thoughts after opening the door. "Do come in."

Eryn was offered the customary cool towel and then followed her mother up the stairs into the main room. They would sit inside this time as there were several hours of daylight and thus heavy heat left.

"What can I offer you to drink? Water? Juice? It is still a little early for wine, I am afraid. It is not a good idea with this heat."

The younger woman took a seat. "Water is fine for me."

Malriel joined her a few moments later with a round tray containing two ornate glasses and a carafe in a similar design.

"Alright," Eryn said after she had taken the first sip. "I am here. Ask away."

"I would like to know how you grew up. What moving from one place to the next was like for you. About living in that village where you were still staying until you were taken to the city of Anyueel. About your healing training."

Eryn nodded and started talking. She was determined to answer the questions as briefly as possible, but Malriel kept asking for details until she began supplying them unprompted. After a while she even added personal impressions, memories, feelings that she thought she wouldn't have been able to share with this woman.

"Would you show me what you looked like with blonde hair? What everybody there saw when they looked at you?" Malriel asked.

Eryn nodded and changed her hair colour.

Her mother first looked at her with a frown, then chuckled. "Forgive me, but it really is atrocious! Your skin, your eyes... how could they not have seen that there must be something wrong?"

"It's easy for you to talk," Eryn replied, smiling. "You only know me with dark hair. They never saw me as anything else than a blonde. And I was paler back then; it does not look so bad without the tan I have obtained here."

Malriel waved a hand. "Nonsense, blonde goes very well with a tan. Look at Enric - he looks fabulous."

Eryn swallowed and remarked pointedly, "How very astutely you have observed him."

"Ah, Maltheá, you need not worry about my showing any undue interest in your companion, even though I am known for delighting in the company of men younger than myself. He is yours, and I respect that. And now tell me about how Ved'al taught you healing without any patients to practise on."

Eryn then talked about practising on injured animals they had found in the woods or the rare opportunities when they had been alone with an unconscious patient and could thus perform some magical healing.

When she had finished, Malriel got to her feet and motioned for her to follow. "Come with me. There is something I would like to show you."

The younger woman got up from her seat hesitantly. "What?"

"Your old room. Do you think you can find it on your own?" she asked.

Eryn nodded slowly. "Yes. The first corridor to the left." She walked in that direction and then accidentally entered the wrong room when she took the second door to her left instead of the third.

Eryn looked around the large room, emotion surging. It looked almost exactly as in her memory. The bed with the green lace curtains, the large window with the view of the garden, the colourful toys and pictures on the walls.

"You left everything the way it was. Why?" she asked, astonished at having walked into what seemed like a memory come alive.

Malriel smiled sadly. "It was everything I had left from you. The room you shaped according to your wishes. You even picked the pictures. This room reflects the character of the child you were when you left here. I could never have allowed for it to be turned into anything else. Many have tried to persuade me to do just that, to spare myself the pain, but I could not. If the pain was my only connection to you, I needed to keep it alive."

Eryn stared at her, feeling her chest tighten. She reminded herself that this was probably no more than a good performance by a master politician, and yet this failed to persuade her body to stop reacting to it. Her heat beat a little quicker, her hands started sweating. Malriel's words about keeping the pain alive... it was exactly what she herself had done after her father had died. She had kept looking at his possessions, reading his books to keep him close, however harrowing that had been. And Malriel had obviously done the exact same thing with her lost daughter.

"But let us not talk of this. It is not a pleasant topic. I do not want to spend this last bit of time I have with you whining about my suffering." Malriel chuckled. "Aren women do not like to admit to weaknesses. That makes us fearsome opponents. Yet after meeting Enric I wonder if we should work on this."

Eryn frowned. "Why?"

"Because one of his most formidable strengths is embracing his weaknesses, admitting them proudly so that they cannot be used against him so readily. And once you embrace a weakness, you can begin working on it. How can you work on something you refuse to acknowledge even to yourself?" She smiled. "Come, let us return to the main room. It is less... haunted by the past."

Malriel then asked her to describe the house they had lived in, the people in the village, the surrounding areas where they had gone to gather their herbs and many other small details of their everyday life.

After more than one and half hours, Malriel sighed and leaned back. "There is one more thing we have both avoided mentioning so far. An important bit for me, Maltheá, because I need to close this chapter of my life somehow. I know that talking about this must be trying for you, but I would not ask it of you if it was not very important for me. Will you tell me about it?"

Eryn stared at her and gulped. Talking about it. She didn't have to ask what she meant. Her father's death. They had talked about everything else. Could she? Would she find the words? Where there even any right words for this? She had never before talked of it to anybody - at least not of the entire truth. There was always the one fragment that she had left out, the piece that had actually led to his death. Her own contribution. But telling Malriel? She had not even told Enric about it, didn't plan to. But she didn't have to tell every last bit. It would not make a difference to Malriel if she knew about this or not, would it? She could still bring her issues to a close.

"Alright." She took another sip of water and commenced the narrative with a good-looking baker's son called Krion who paid a particular young girl more attention than the others and made her feel special. Malriel's eyes flashed when she came to the point where he had tried to force himself on her, and Ved'al, or Treban, as she had learned to known him as, had broken the boy's arm when he had rushed to her defence. Then she continued with the baker coming to their little house, threatening the healer and earning himself a painful reminder that being in the profession of helping others did not necessarily equal physical weakness or the inability to defend oneself.

She told about Krion breaking his other arm somehow in the course of his work and how the baker had been convinced that it must have been the healer's doing, stabbing him in the back - murdering her father to make him pay for it.

Malriel nodded slowly. "Thank you very much. I appreciate that you went through all of this again for me. I can see that it is still painful for you to talk about it. But there is more, is there not?" she asked calmly, looking at her daughter, her gaze piercing.

Eryn stared at her, her heart beating much too rapidly. "What makes you think that?"

"There was something in your eyes when you talked about the boy, about how he broke his other arm," the older woman said slowly. "What happened really, Theá? We may not have been able to connect the way we should have, but let us be honest with each other at least. No half-truths between us."

Eryn's hands had gone cold despite the warmth and she clenched them together to warm them. Malriel reached over and took Eryn's hands in her own, sending a little magic to warm them. The caring gesture touched Eryn, and she looked away, unsure how to react to it.

"I will not judge you, whatever happened back then. But I would like to know," the older woman said calmly.

"I don't know if I can speak of it. I have never told anybody," she murmured.

"Then just close your eyes. Pretend I am not here, pretend you are alone. Let the words come to you."

Could she really tell this woman about something that personal? They had not had a harmonious relationship with each other so far, had been separated by a magical shield only the evening before when who knew what might have happened. But then this also reduced the risk, didn't it? Even if Malriel was not true to her word not intending to judge her, that would not be such a great problem as she wouldn't lose the high regard from somebody who was so very important to her. Talking about this to Valrad or Vran'el would have proved impossible.

She nodded slowly and closed her eyes exactly as Malriel had suggested.

"I remember sitting in front of the fire that evening after Krion had tried to... you know. Father made me sit in his special chair in front of the fire and offered me something strong to drink. I had expected him to scold me for being so careless, being out after sunset even though he had warned me about this so often. But he blamed himself instead. Blamed himself for not warning me about this particular boy, who was known to have done the same thing to another girl already. He then said he would make him pay for it. And I implored him not to. *I* wanted to be the one who made the boy pay. I kept thinking of how to exact revenge. Of painful, barbaric things I could do to him. But then after several weeks it kind of happened. We ran into each other on the street and he was with a group of boys and started teasing me. I provoked him, hoping I could make him touch me so I could use magic to inflict something on him that would teach him a lesson. It took a few insults, but finally he did touch me, and I used my healing knowledge and my magic to weaken the bone in his arm enough to make it snap at the next above average strain. Being the baker's son, that was only a matter of time." She let go a long breath and opened her eyes. Malriel looked at her with concern.

"When father heard that the other arm had broken, he knew immediately what I had done. He was so angry, he shouted at me and for the first time I wondered if he would strike me. He didn't. He stormed out again and I waited for him to return. But he didn't return. Once it had begun to get dark outside, I started worrying. I kept waiting, but he didn't return." She stared at a blank wall, the pictures coming back unbidden, a little paler than they had been a few years ago, as if time had made them lose their tint. "I remember the torches as the villagers arrived at the house to convey the bad news. That the baker was convinced that my father had caused Krion's arm to break and had killed him in revenge. In revenge for something I had done. They killed the baker after that."

She saw from the corner of one eye Malriel stirring, but didn't turn to look at her. She froze in surprise when she felt arms surrounding her and pressing her close to a warm body.

"My poor girl," Malriel whispered. "I am so sorry. To carry this enormous burden alone at this tender age, taking care of yourself when you were little more than a child!"

Eryn let her head sink onto her mother's shoulder. How could it feel so good to be held by somebody she had spent three weeks cursing?

Malriel pulled back and held Eryn's face in her hands. "You are aware that you are not to blame for any of this, I hope?"

Her daughter stared at her. "How can the blame not fall on me? Didn't you hear what I just told you?"

"I shall tell you what I heard. I heard how a young girl who had not learned how to protect herself had sought use of the only weapon she had, the only chance she had of countering an opponent's superior strength. You did not make that baker go berserk. He was not right in his head and might have done something like that sooner or later anyway. What man murders another man because he suspects him of breaking his son's arm? This is not normal - you could not have foreseen this! If the man's son had cut himself with a bread knife, his father would probably have blamed Ved'al for it as well and acted on it the same way," Malriel implored her.

Eryn blinked. The words felt good; believing them would make her troubled memories so much easier to bear. Yet it wasn't quite that easy, was it? But she didn't want to discuss this here. She needed open air. Space. Solitude.

"I must go," she said and rose abruptly. "Sorry, but I need to get out of here." She all but ran down to the entrance door and felt Malriel's hand on her arm before she could open the door.

"Maltheá. I am sorry this causes you so much pain. You must deal with this or it will never let you go," she insisted. "Talk about it. Tell Enric."

Eryn sighed. Enric? What an idea! Surely not. But she didn't want to discuss this, either.

"Will I see you again before we leave?" she asked instead.

Malriel gave her a slow smile. "Depend on it, my child."

Eryn turned and walked away, breathing more easily under the open sky.

CHAPTER 42

A Revelation

Eryn's feet carried her towards the Vel'kim residence almost without any conscious input from her brain. She tried to understand how she felt after putting words to every single detail of what had happened all these years ago for the first time in her life. Relief? Not exactly. For so many years she pushed the memories away each time they had returned unbidden. For a while they had haunted her dreams, but after a while that had stopped as well. But the memories had been there, as if they were waiting for her to allow them to break into the open again. They had been slightly faded at the beginning but had become clearer and painfully colourful after only a short while, as if a layer of dust had been swept from them.

She thought about Malriel and how she of all people had been the one who heard this story. But then people said that sometimes talking to a stranger was more helpful than opening up to somebody close. Malriel was not much more than a stranger to her, an acquaintance at best. And not even one she was very fond of. Malriel had told her to talk about this with Enric. A shiver ran down her spine at the mere thought. Facing one's weaknesses was one thing, but making somebody else face the abyss was a different matter entirely. Her personal abyss - a vortex of guilt, regret, loss and desperation.

She walked up the street to the Vel'kim residence where Vran'el was the one to answer her knock. He looked her up and down.

"You look pale. I take it your little meeting with Malriel did not particularly well?" he asked with a sympathetic grimace.

She shook her head. "No, it was not so bad. Surprisingly." The towel he handed her felt clammy and too cool, although she rubbed her face with it to get some colour into her cheeks and avoid more enquiries as to why she was so pale.

When she entered the main room after her cousin, she immediately felt the excited, cheerful mood.

Valrad jumped up when he saw her, laughing and rubbing his hands. "Come! Look at this! I have found it! It really is there, just as I thought!"

Eryn stared at him for a moment, before realisation dawned on her. "What? Oh, the shield! Really? Where?" Good news was a very welcome diversion.

Her uncle took her hand to lead her across to where Enric was sitting on cushions on the floor, then placed it to Enric's forehead. "Follow me, I will show you."

She closed her eyes and followed the quickly fading path of magic her uncle left to a remote area of the brain.

"Do you see it?" he murmured.

Frowning, she shook her head. "No. Where?"

"Go deeper. The shield does not envelop the entire area of the brain, but only that essential part which enables passing the ability on. A magician with his powers blocked like that during childhood cannot pass on the ability. Magic does not follow the usual rules of inheritance like the colour of your eyes or hair."

"I can't see it," she said, impatient with herself.

Valrad opened his eyes and really looked at her for the first time since she had arrived. "No wonder, you are clearly not in any shape to do precise work." She felt him put his hand on hers and felt warm magic pass through her skin.

"Increased heartbeat, temperature too low, digestion turned off. That was quite a stressful meeting with Malriel, I suggest."

Eryn jerked her hand away from him and glowered at him. "I don't like uninvited intrusions! I would appreciate it if you stopped that!"

Enric took her hand and pulled her closer towards him. "Don't be angry at him, he is just excited and eager to show you his momentous discovery."

She sighed and nodded. "I know. And I would love to see it, I really would." She held her hand out to Valrad. "Can you do your relaxation thing? Just a little less highly dosed than last time, if you don't mind."

He nodded and she felt herself sink into a state of peace and contentment almost as soon as his hand touched hers again.

She then turned to Enric once more, putting her hand on his cheek. She returned to the area in his brain her uncle had indicated before and scanned it again, more slowly and thoroughly this time. It took her almost a full minute, but then she finally saw it. A small source of energy, almost impossible to detect if one didn't know where to look and still difficult enough if one did. She whistled through her teeth.

"This tiny block has such a remarkable effect? Incredible!" She opened her eyes again and stared at Valrad. "Can we remove it?"

"I am not sure. It is a very weak barrier, so I would say it is possible. But I do not want to do this without a brain expert. You never know the unknown side effects it could have if you just remove something that has always been there. I would not want him to go into shock or something," her uncle explained.

"Can't you send for somebody? Iklan, for example?" she asked impatiently.

"I already have, we are expecting him any minute. But the question is whether I am even permitted to remove the barrier."

She frowned. "But they gave you permission to look for it since the trade agreements have been signed. Doesn't this include removing the block in case you manage to confirm your theory?"

"Unfortunately it is not that easy. Removing the barrier and sending you home with the knowledge of how to do this will have quite an impact on both our societies and must therefore be considered carefully. The triarchy will have to decide on that."

"But we are leaving tomorrow!" she exclaimed in frustration. The effects of the calming infusion seemed to be wearing off quickly. "There is no more time for any of your bureaucracy!"

"I understand your impatience, my child," Valrad said softly, "but I cannot act on my own initiative here. I have a House that would pay the price for doing so. Do not despair, my dear. If Iklan finds that removing this shield need not cause any negative effects on his brain, we can always send word to Anyueel about how it may be performed, or even send a healer to show you."

She nodded hesitantly. That was better than nothing, even though it would not be easy leaving here with the knowledge that they had, after three hundred years, finally determined how to have female magicians again but had no access to how it might be done.

They heard a second knock and Vran'el went once more to admit a visitor. This time it was Iklan.

He was out of breath as he entered the main room.

"You wrote that you were able to confirm your theory?" he panted without bothering with a greeting of any sort. "Show me. And I am warning you, if you have made me run here for nothing, I am going to…"

"Do come and take a look for yourself instead of threatening me unnecessarily," Valrad said with a smug smile.

Iklan stepped closer and crouched in front of Enric, who looked resigned to having people poking around inside his head. Iklan then touched Enric's forehead and closed his eyes. Even without Valrad's guidance it took him only a little over two minutes to locate the block. They saw him draw in a sharp breath and then exhale slowly.

"Amazing," he murmured. "It is limited to a very small area, but highly effective. A shield connected to his life force. I did not know they were already able to do this back then."

"Can it be removed without causing harm?" Eryn wanted to know, working hard at keeping her excitement in check.

Iklan remained silent and motionless for another few minutes before finally removing his hand and opening his eyes again.

"I do not see why not," he said slowly and turned towards her. "But I hope that you see why I cannot show you at this particular time how to go about it."

She nodded impatiently. "Yes, Valrad already told me that you need to ask the triarchy first. But this will take too long! We will be gone by then!"

Her uncle chuckled. "You have managed without female magicians for a few hundred years. I do not think that a few weeks longer will make such a great difference."

It was easy for him to talk, she thought, but remained silent.

They turned when Pe'tala entered and grimaced when she saw Eryn.

"How charming. A last chance to spend some quality time with my dear, dear cousin. What a pity to see you leave tomorrow. I hope you will forgive me if I do not find the time to come to the jetty and wave you off," she griped.

Eryn rose from her seat and narrowed her eyes. A target for her frustration. And one she would not at all mind insulting or hurting. Good.

"Oh my, how will I ever get over not having seen *you* on my last day here?" she smiled sweetly. "It will be like a day without sunshine, a meal missing spices, a..."

"Do you really have to fight on our last evening together, girls?" Valrad sighed.

"Please, father, do not interrupt the high-born Lady. She might strike us with her wrath if she has the feeling that she is not getting the attention and admiration she is owed," Pe'tala sneered.

"Careful, or you will get what *you* are due. Like the smacking you have been begging for these last three weeks," Eryn shot back.

"Threatening me, *Cousin*?" Pe'tala hissed and balled her fists. "But you may try if you feel up to it. Do not cry afterwards if you find yourself once more in the role of the helpless little damsel in distress you have turned out to be so good at."

"Helpless little damsel in distress?" Eryn repeated through clenched teeth. "Well, what can I say? We can't all be frustrated, sour-faced, impolite, aggressive botherations like yourself."

Pe'tala's raised palm was about to connect with Eryn's cheek, when a firm hand grabbed her wrist and pulled her aside instead. Enric glared down at Pe'tala and held on to her hand when she tried to free it.

"This is enough," he growled and pulled her back towards him when she made to retreat. "What exactly is your problem with Eryn? Since the very first time you saw her you have shown her nothing but hostility and contempt and have kept insulting her. What is the matter with you?"

Pe'tala stared up at him for several moments. Then she slowly lifted her free hand to his shoulder, stood on tiptoes and without warning pressed her lips onto his. Enric froze for a second and then took a deliberate step back, breaking contact of both their faces and their hands.

"Pe'tala!" Vran'el exclaimed. "What do you think you are doing, you idiot?"

Eryn just stared at her cousin in ultimate bewilderment, unable to believe what she had just seen. Had that woman really just done that or was she going insane? Were hallucinations a side-effect of the magic her uncle had sent into her? Or a reaction to the stress at Malriel's place beforehand? Or had she really and truly seen that arrogant creature kiss her companion?

"I want her to see what it feels like when another woman has her claws in her man," Pe'tala wailed and covered her face with both hands.

Enric blinked, then turned to Vran'el, whose face was a battleground of conflicting emotions. Sympathy, pity and pain fought anger and impatience.

"Isn't it time to share with us what you have kept a secret?" Enric asked quietly, putting his arm around Eryn, who was still staring at her cousin in utter astonishment, but would awake from her shock soon enough to try and rip out Pe'tala's hair, limbs or other body parts she was doubtlessly attached to.

Iklan swallowed audibly. "You know, I have the feeling that this is a family moment. I will take my leave now."

Valrad nodded gratefully and waited until his guest had left before he turned back to the others.

"Very well. I see that the time has come to tell you. I was hoping we could forego that revelation, but it seems that we cannot. Sit down." He went to his daughter and put an arm around her shoulders. She didn't resist when he pulled her onto the cushions next to him, holding her against him.

"It was about a year and a half ago when Ram'an's father and I entered into an agreement," he began. "Ahend was tired of waiting for some sign of Eryn to be found and decided that it was time for his older son to be joined with a woman and then finally take over the position of Head of House Arbil."

Eryn's eyes became wide in surprise. "You promised them to each other? Just like that?"

"Not just like that, my dear. Both Pe'tala and Ram'an agreed to it, though when I look back it is clear that Ram'an did so out of little more than duty while my daughter had formed an attachment to him."

Pe'tala turned her head away in embarrassment at having the story of her unreciprocated feelings told openly.

"But then people here heard about Eryn being still alive and in Anyueel," Enric concluded.

Valrad nodded. "We did indeed. Ram'an urged the senate to contact your King and establish a tentative diplomatic relationship. He offered to go there as ambassador, and Malriel supported him, of course."

"And you?" Eryn asked calmly.

"I did, too. Though I admit that I was not pleased at Ram'an's eagerness to go there after he was about to be joined with my daughter. But you are Ved'al's daughter - how could I not want to know what had become of you?" he sighed. "After Ram'an's return, he immediately terminated the arrangement with our House. He told us that you had been made to join a powerful magician there against your will, but that it was no more than a legal bond as you were either not familiar with the principle of a third level commitment bond or had managed to resist being forced into that as well. We were appalled and did our best to convince the triarchy to request your being one of the party when sending out their invitation for a diplomatic delegation. I was surprised to see you with Enric. He did not match the picture of the barbaric savage who had made you his trophy to compel you to bind yourself to the Old Kingdom and thereby stop you from fleeing the country. And Ram'an is still determined to win you for himself, even though by now it must be clear to him that you are not with Enric because you have no other choice."

Eryn stared at her cousin, unsure how to react. Pe'tala had been ditched by Ram'an on a whim yet didn't have it in herself to hate him for it. But of course she could instead hate the person who had somehow been the cause for all this: her long-lost cousin. How very convenient.

She shook her head. "Why do you despise me so much? Why are you blaming *me* for what Ram'an did to you?"

Pe'tala gave her a hateful glare and spat, "Because everything revolves around you, whether it is justified or not. What have you ever done to be considered so special, I ask you? Being born to two influential families seems to be the sole accomplishment in your life so far. Oh yes, and being rare enough with your hair colour in that country across the sea to have caught the eye of an important man. You just dance through life, snatching the best of everything as it passes, do you not? Even the things you do not want or need, such as other women's men!"

Breathing in and out slowly, Eryn folded her arms to keep herself from punching Pe'tala. "You insensitive imbecile, how dare you say things like that to me? You think my life has been some kind of lazy dance which makes the time pass somehow, like your own? You listen to me very carefully: all my life I've had to work hard to make a living. I lost the only family I knew when I was still a girl and had to learn to survive alone somehow, never letting anybody come close enough to learn of my secret, labouring only for my food and other simple things I required, teaching myself what I needed to heal others from books." She shook her head at her cousin. "You imagine that was such a pleasant experience? Then I invite you to try it yourself, because I say it would do you good to stand on your own two feet for once and take responsibility for your life instead of lamenting what other people keep doing to you."

"Really? I can see how hard your life with Enric is," her cousin sneered. "So it seems that a few years of living alone paid off well enough for you."

"Oh yes, because being dragged from the only home I had into a city where they kept me prisoner for many months and forced me to fight every day is a superb way to meet your companion and be forced..." She stopped herself.

Her cousin's brow rose. "Come on, do not be shy," she prompted. "Ram'an told us that your commitment was not voluntary from his point of view. So why not say it out loud? I wondered if it was true, and it seems I have my answer now. That makes me hate you even more. Two good men for one woman who is too ignorant to consider what she has. But that is not such a great problem for you, is it? Luckily you have people around you to force you into happiness," she hissed.

"Just shut up, you idiot!" Eryn shot back. "I was never forced into happiness, only used to create a favourable political situation, however romantically you choose to view the whole matter. I might have done it willingly one day, but never got the chance to decide for myself. But a spoilt brat like yourself who has never bothered tackling anything on her own would hardly see the point in that. Making your own decisions would require using that brain of yours instead of waiting what others make happen to you and then complaining about it."

"Thank you so much for sharing your wisdom with stupid, little me, oh powerful and mighty lady!"

"I never said you were stupid, just that you are an idiot. What self-respecting woman cries after a man who left her in such a manner? Why would you even want him back? What is the matter with you? I would punch him in the face so hard he wouldn't even be able to remember his own name for a while!" She shook her head in disbelief. "You are rich, pretty and are pining after a man who initially accepted you as second choice and then discarded you like an old shoe? Is that what you think would make you happy, what you deserve?" Breathing out, she sent her cousin a last disgusted look. "Why do I even talk to you? You make me sick." Having said that, she turned and left, glad to get away from that unthinking, self-pitying creature.

Enric rose and waved a quick goodbye before following her down the stairs and out into the street.

"I am sorry that your last evening with your family turned out like that," he signed and took her hand.

She exhaled. "Me, too. But at least I know now why she has been treating me like that and that I am not the one to blame for anything. I am glad I don't have to see her again before we leave. Valrad and Vran'el will come to the harbour tomorrow, so I can bid them goodbye there. Let's get back to our place. I really feel like spending my last evening here in peace and quiet."

CHAPTER 43

Departure

She checked throughout the spacious bedroom to see if they had forgotten anything. To her surprise she felt a little wistful at the thought of leaving here, but her eager anticipation when she thought about returning home to her friends, her work and her own house outweighed that easily.

Enric walked in, the cat at his heels. "Are you ready? Valrad and Vran'el have just arrived to pick us up and accompany us to the port."

She nodded. "Yes, I think I am. What about Urban? When do you want to put her to sleep?"

"Before we go aboard. I want to do it at the last possible minute so she has a last chance to move around a bit before she rests for two entire days," he replied and put an arm around her shoulders. "Are you very sorry to be leaving here?"

"Yes and no. Yes, because I am leaving my uncle and cousin behind, the only family I have left after such a long time. Also there are so many things I could learn here - books to read, people to teach me. And no, because I am not sorry to get away from Malriel and Pe'tala."

"Don't worry, my love. I am certain that this is not to be our last visit here," he smiled and they went into the main room where Barul and Grend were standing with Valrad and Vran'el.

"Where is Kilan?" Eryn asked and glanced around.

"Fitting our precious trade agreements into waterproof containers," Enric told her. "From what I have seen his efforts will probably ensure they remain dry and undamaged should we even end up at the bottom of the sea."

"Sure, because that will definitely be my priority if the ship sinks," Grend murmured, "Saving the bloody paperwork."

"Right you are," Eryn grinned. "Better save the bloody magicians first."

"As if you needed any saving," Barul threw in. "I suppose you could just create a shield that keeps the water away from you."

She pursed her lips and looked at Enric. "I have to admit that I have no idea. Can we do that? Under water, I mean. I know that keeping water away works in general." And she had proven that already during the expedition with the shield that had made it possible to sleep out in the open during a thunderstorm.

Valrad answered instead. "For a short while, maybe. But it would take a very strong shield as you would have to combat the pressure of immense amounts of water."

"So saving the magicians it is," Grend sighed with a wink at her.

"You should not have sounded so reluctant," Kilan said when he entered, carrying a wooden chest in his arms. "It makes me doubt whether I will make it back home."

"As long as you have that chest in your custody, you are the most important person on the ship. So your chances of survival are quite high, I would say," Enric remarked wryly. "If all of us are ready, I suggest we leave now. The ship is due to leave in less than one hour and there will probably be a few people there to say goodbye to. Our belongings are on the ship by now, I assume?" The question was aimed at Kilan, who simply nodded.

They stepped outside and Vran'el took Eryn's hand as they started their walk towards the harbour. "It will be very quiet without you around, sweetness. I will almost certainly be bored no end. Make sure you write to me often. And do come back to visit us."

"I would love to. But I think we will have to see how things turn out politically and if private visits without being part of an official diplomatic delegation are on the table anytime soon," she sighed. "But as soon as trade has started, writing will be no problem."

Valrad smiled. "We will not depend on trade for this. I have taken the liberty of sending along a few of our birds to be packed with your belongings. They will return to our residence when you release them as they were hatched there. If you manage to make them breed on your own roof, be sure to send some of your birds to us by messenger."

Eryn smiled broadly. That was excellent news. They would be able to write to each other regularly without depending on a human to deliver their messages. And it would be much faster as a bird didn't need longer than one day flying from Anyueel to Takhan.

"Very good, that was thoughtful of you," Enric said with a delighted smile.

"Listen," Valrad said, his expression pained. "I am very sorry about yesterday evening. And the way my daughter treated you before. I hope you have it in you to forgive her. For both her behaviour in general and what she did yesterday evening. It was not appropriate." He glanced at Enric.

Eryn shook her head. "Don't worry, Valrad. I see why she is unhappy and why it was easier to be angry at me than Ram'an. And I will leave here today, so we will have a lot of distance between us soon enough."

"I would wish for you to remember your stay here fondly. It would be terrible for me to know that she ruined this for you, especially as you did not get along so well with your mother."

Eryn stopped and took her uncle's hand to squeeze it. She looked into his eyes and smiled reassuringly. "Nothing whatsoever could cast a shadow on the time I have spent with the two of you here. Your House may not officially be the one people prefer to think that I belong to, but in my heart I am Vel'kim. When I think of my family, it will be the two of you who will come to my mind."

Valrad smiled and nodded without saying a word, turning his head slightly to hide a giveaway damp glint in the corner of his eyes.

They turned into the street that would lead them down to the jetties.

"This was where you infused me with happiness when I arrived here to soothe the shock of finding my mother alive," she grinned.

Vran'el chuckled. "I wish I had been there. That would surely have been a sight to behold."

Her uncle shook his head. "It was scary, that is what it was. She was smiling like a maniac, but I could still sense the anger and helplessness underneath. Not something I would like to watch again. I was glad when Enric told us to leave them alone for the evening so I did not have to be present when the effects wore off."

They rounded the last corner and saw a group of people waiting in front of the jetty they had arrived at three weeks ago. From the looks of it, it was the same ship that would take them back.

Some of the healers from the clinic where there, among them Iklan and the three she had met when she had visited the healing place for the first time. Intrea, Vran'el's companion, waved to them, keeping her hand firmly around Obal's wrist to keep her from stepping too close to the water.

Eryn tensed slightly when she discovered Ram'an. But he had lost. It was probably a gesture of acknowledging this fact that he had come here to say goodbye.

She frowned when she let her gaze wander over the farewell-wishers and didn't find Malriel among them. Saying good-bye to her would still have been pleasant, especially after their conversation yesterday. Could she have forgotten? Hardly. She tried to shrug it off, but found that it did annoy her. But who needed Malriel, anyway?

Making herself smile, she stepped towards Intrea, causing Obal to hide behind her mother's legs.

"I will not come with you! You cannot take me!" the little girl exclaimed with a worried look.

Eryn shrugged. "Well, I will just have to accept that, won't I?"

That was obviously a great relief and the girl moved forward again and lifted her arms to Enric to be lifted up. He obliged her and placed her on his hip. She immediately started playing with his hair.

"It looks like she fancies yellow-haired men," Intrea sighed with a humorous twinkle in her eyes. "Where am I to get one for her, I ask you? I am meant to be arranging a companionship for her, after all."

"You could change the colour of a boy's hair for her," Eryn suggested.

Intrea laughed. "No, trust me - it would just not be the same. You would not manage to make Enric look like one of us by making him darker."

They turned when they heard a number of heavy food-steps behind them. A group of what suspiciously looked like guards in identical uniforms and with curved swords hanging from their belts turned the corner and walked towards them, looking official and serious.

"A formal fare-well ceremony?" Eryn asked and lifted a brow. "That is rather surprising, considering that our welcoming back then was so low-key."

Enric narrowed his eyes and slowly shook his head. "No, this is nothing of that kind. I don't have a good feeling about this."

They waited until the ten men had come closer and stopped a few paces away from them. The man in front of them had different insignias on his uniform and was obviously in charge. He cleared his throat and unrolled a piece of paper.

"Maltheá of House Aren, you are summoned before the senate to vindicate yourself in view of the allegations that have been brought forward against you."

Those who were not staring at the guards in surprise started whispering.

Vran'el was the first to find his speech. His voice was bare of emotion and cool when he spoke.

"Allegations of what nature exactly?"

"Allegations of having used her healing skills to wilfully harm a defenceless non-magician and thus causing the death of Ved'al of House Vel'kim," the head guard stated.

Enric blinked, then looked at his companion to see what effect that ridiculous claim had on her. She had frozen and gone completely pale under her tan.

"Eryn?" he murmured urgently. "What is he talking about?"

"Malriel," she choked out and all of a sudden started breathing too quickly as if she couldn't get in air quickly enough. "That's why she is not here. She knew I wouldn't be leaving here now! I am going to kill her!"

"Steady," Valrad warned. "You will start hyperventilating. Easy breathing."

Eryn's vision swam before her and she grabbed Enric's shoulder to keep herself from falling forward. Her secret. Her shame. Her great fault. It would be laid out openly in front of everybody. In front of Enric. He of all people would know what she had done to

514

her own father. How she had violated the most sacred law of healing - never to use the skill to cause harm. How would he ever again believe her when she spoke of principles, how could he again feel safe when she touched him after this? How could anybody?

Enric quickly put his arm around her shoulders when she covered her face with her hands. His gaze shot to Ram'an, but he was looking just as surprised as the rest. Vran'el had taken the document from the guard to read it through. He looked up with a worried frown.

"It is official. We must go to the senate. There is no other choice," he told them matter-of-factly.

The guard chief spoke again. "All members of the senate are summoned to attend this assembly as well," he announced and then stepped towards Eryn.

"Maltheá," he said, unsure of how to proceed with the obviously very distressed woman in front of him. The blonde magician with his arm around her had a menacing look about him.

"We will follow the summons, of course," Vran'el said stiffly.

"I can't," she whispered and shook her head, her face still covered. She couldn't face all these people, couldn't face anyone right now. She just wanted to crawl away into a dark, solitary place and curl up into a ball, neither seeing nor hearing anything.

She almost stumbled when her cousin took one of her hands from her face to gently pull her along. "Come. We need to go. Let us not give them the impression that you are not cooperating," he said softly.

Enric saw Ram'an leave his place among the audience to walk with them. Of course, he remembered - Ram'an had a seat in the senate and had also been summoned. Valrad exchanged a worried glance with Enric.

Eryn looked up in surprise when they stopped in front of the large, majestic building that housed the senate. She didn't recall a single detail of the way here, just a warm hand that had made her go on and a reassuring arm around her shoulders.

The guard who had read the summons out stepped forward to enter the great round hall before them to announce their arrival. The other guards stayed with them as if to make sure they were not about to bolt. Valrad and Ram'an each gave her a worried look before they, too, entered to take their seats.

"Is it true?" Kilan asked quietly. "Do they have a reason to keep us from leaving here?"

Enric looked back at his companion. It did not take a truth block to see that she felt guilty about what they were claiming she had done.

"I think they will keep us here until this matter is resolved."

"I thought they were still debating whether she is subject to their jurisdiction or not?" Kilan frowned.

"It seems they have already reached a decision on that," Enric replied dryly.

The doors were opened again for them to enter. Barul, Grend and Kilan were requested to sit in the last row of chairs while Enric, Eryn and Vran'el were led to the centre of the room, where they faced the elevated seats of the triarchy and had the other senators on their other three sides.

Eryn sucked in a breath when she saw Malriel sitting in the front row to her left. She stared at the woman with an expression that clearly conveyed the hurt, humiliation, embarrassment and disappointment she felt. But there was no energy in her left to mask her feelings; it was all required for preventing herself from running and hiding somewhere. The urge returned and had to be forced into submission anew every few seconds.

Enric looked up at the three members of the triarchy in front of them. Golir at the centre, Abrak to his left and Torke'na to his right.

Abrak turned to Eryn and raised his voice. "Malthéa of House Aren, you have been accused of having used healing magic to cause harm to a non-magician who had no knowledge of your magical abilities and no way of defending himself against you. As you are part of a diplomatic delegation we need to proceed with this very carefully, as I am sure you can imagine. For this reason, rather than the local magistrate, the senate will take it upon itself to reach a decision on the matter. We herewith deny you the permission to leave the city of Takhan for the duration of these proceedings." He turned to Enric. "You, Ambassador, and your assistant and guards are of course free to leave our country."

Enric nodded. "I acknowledge your permission and will confirm to whoever desires to know that you have made no attempt whatsoever to hinder me from leaving here. But I instead wish to request your permission to remain here in Takhan as well for now."

All three members of the triarchy nodded. His request was obviously no great surprise to them.

"It is granted. You may stay here," Abrak announced. "We will start with a first hearing tomorrow morning in the course of which Malriel of House Aren will stand before us as a witness."

Eryn forced herself to look straight ahead. She had expected nothing less, yet each of the words felt like a whiplash. Her own mother had done this to her. She had informed the triarchy of what Eryn had told her confidentially following her own request. Come tomorrow she would stand there and continue to condemn her own flesh and blood.

Now Torke'na spoke up. "Ambassador, we hope you will understand that we will have to separate you and Malthéa for the duration of the proceedings, as you are both known to be unusually strong users of magic, even though we are not aware of the exact extent of your strengths. Yet in combination we are convinced that the two of you may turn out to be a serious risk if you should decide to leave here without permission."

Enric swallowed but didn't speak and waited for her to go on.

"We have decided against asking you to let us bind yours and Maltheá's powers with gold," she went on, "but instead put each of you in the custody of a magician superior in strength." She turned to the assembled senators. "Who of those of above average strength would be willing to take over the guardianship for Maltheá of House Aren for the duration of these proceedings? This will require accepting her into your home and not leaving her unsupervised at any time."

All eyes turned when Ram'an rose. "I am. My powers exceed hers and I am willing and able to guard her."

Enric felt hot wrath rise inside him and forced it down with iron willpower. Of course. This was just too convenient a situation not to take advantage of it.

"How can you be sure that your powers exceed hers, Ram'an of House Arbil?" Torke'na asked.

"I have tested them against hers and prevailed," he replied.

"How have you tested them?" Abrak enquired with a concerned expression.

"I took control over her muscles and she struggled to free herself in vain," Ram'an explained.

"I hope," Torke'na threw in with narrowed eyes, "that you did not behave in an untoward manner and force your attentions upon Maltheá? This would not be looked upon benignly."

He shook his head. "No, I can assure you I did no such thing. It was done in public, so there should be sufficient witnesses who will confirm that there was no inappropriate behaviour whatsoever from my side."

"Could you tell how much stronger than her you are?" Abrak then asked.

"Noticeably, but not considerably," Ram'an told them.

Torke'na pursed her lips. "I see. This means that Maltheá is very strong indeed. This reduces the number of possible candidates for this task significantly." She looked at her two male colleagues for confirmation and then continued, "Ram'an of House Arbil, we confirm your role as guardian for Maltheá of House Aren. She will stay at your residence..."

"No." Enric's voice had not been loud, but it was not the volume that had stopped the triarch in mid-sentence and caused all present to stare at him. There had been a low rumble, a vibration that had shaken the building slightly. Motes of dust that had been loosened from the ceiling floated in the air around them and many eyes darted upwards nervously to see if they were about to be buried by several tons of masonry from the domed roof.

Only one pair of eyes seemed almost amused when it rested on the blonde magician. It certainly showed interest. Golir's.

"Your disapproval of this arrangement is duly noted, Ambassador, but we do not have many magicians to choose from as Maltheá is obviously very powerful," Abrak explained.

Valrad's voice came from their right. "House Vel'kim offers its hospitality to Maltheá of House Aren."

"You are a strong magician, Valrad, but no equal to the powers of your niece, I am sorry to say," Torke'na said with regret. "And even if you were, there is the matter of your personal connection with Maltheá that might induce you to act unwisely."

"What if the invitation was extended to Ram'an as well?" Vran'el added.

"Would this be an acceptable compromise for you, Ambassador?" Abrak asked Enric, who nodded hesitantly. The triarch then turned towards Ram'an. "Would you be willing to move to the Vel'kim residence in order to carry out the duty of guarding Maltheá?"

Ram'an looked at Eryn and back to the triarchy. "I would, yes."

"This leaves the matter of Enric," Torke'na mused. "Ambassador, you have proven to be exceptionally strong. Not only just now, but the story of how you danced with Ram'an of House Arbil has gone around."

Golir rose, descended the few stairs at the back of the podium and came closer until he stood right in front of Enric. Then he spoke for the first time since they had arrived.

"Raise a strong shield, if you will. Make it as strong as you can."

Enric raised a barrier and waited. Golir lifted his hand and reached right through it to touch Enric's shoulder. He retracted it again and shook his head.

"Enric, this is not the strongest shield you can create. We will attempt this again, only now I would ask you to refrain from attempting to appear weaker than you are. Trying to mislead us would not cast a favourable light on your willingness to cooperate." The warning in his voice did not fail to impress his opposite.

Enric nodded curtly and increased the level of power as much as he was capable. Golir reached out again, but this time he was more careful when he touched the shield, frowning in concentration when he made his hand go through it again.

"Yes, this is more like it," he nodded with satisfaction and turned to the other two members of the triarchy. "The ambassador will reside with me for the duration of the proceedings. I doubt there is anybody else in this city or even the country who would be able to contain him if the occasion called for it."

"What about my cat?" Enric asked.

Golir looked down at the brown, knee-high predator next to the magician.

"Your creature may move in with me as well. Just make sure it behaves itself," Golir warned him.

"Who will act as Maltheá's legal advisor?" Torke'na asked and looked questioningly at Vran'el, who nodded.

"I will," he confirmed.

"We shall forward copies of all protocols and documents for your perusal," she nodded and then rose. "This gathering is herewith adjourned to tomorrow after sunrise. Each House is to send one representative to the senate for each and every hearing that will take place in the case. You may leave now."

Enric looked at Eryn, who just stood staring straight ahead as if wandering through another world altogether. He put one hand on her shoulder and slowly turned her towards him.

"Eryn?" he asked tenderly and lifted her chin up. He wasn't even sure how much of what had just happened she had consciously taken in. "You will have to return to the Vel'kim residence. Did you understand that?"

She shook her head slightly as if to clear it. "Not to House Arbil?" she asked faintly, looking confused.

"No. Ram'an will stay at the Vel'kim residence with you." He pulled her close and into an embrace. Being forced to let her leave like this without being there for her was almost unbearably painful. He looked over to Ram'an, who was waiting at what he gauged a safe distance, observing them both with a carefully neutral expression.

Enric glared at him with narrowed eyes, vowing without words to inflict unspeakable agony if Ram'an didn't behave. Ram'an seemed nonchalant and pointedly looked towards Valrad and Vran'el as if to imply that Eryn was not the only one being guarded.

"When will I see you?" Eryn murmured into his shoulder. Enric looked at Golir, who looked down at the clearly very distraught woman.

"Tonight after dinner," Golir said and Enric nodded gratefully.

Valrad stepped towards them, putting a hand on Eryn's shoulder. "Come," he said quietly.

Enric carefully opened the fingers she had closed over the fabric of his shirt and kissed them before releasing her hands reluctantly.

Golir then turned to leave and Enric had no choice but to follow him.

Ram'an stepped closer as soon as Enric had left the hall, ignoring Vran'el's cautioning look. Eryn looked up when she felt warm hands take hers and was about to take a step back when her gaze fell over Ram'an's shoulder on Malriel.

"You," she whispered and then repeated the word loudly enough to make all heads turn towards her. "You!"

Before anybody had a chance to react, she hurled a gleaming blue bolt in Malriel's direction. People threw themselves down on the floor and dived for cover. The strike hit a stone wall and left nothing more than a slight dent and a black spot.

Ram'an quickly grabbed one of her hands again and she felt all tension drain from her muscles when he once again took command of them. She felt him put one arm around her and press her firmly against his side. Only then did Malriel slowly rise from behind a leather chair. Her face was stony and for a moment she looked as if she was about to come closer, but she decided against it and instead turned to leave quickly.

"Will you behave if I release you?" Ram'an murmured close to her ear and released her head so she could answer.

She nodded and when she felt she was able to move again, slowly stepped away from him and then turned and ran after Malriel. After no more than a few steps she felt a strong arm around her waist lifting her up. Ram'an set her down again a moment later then turned her with her back to a wall, facing him. He shook his head indulgently.

"Why do I even bother asking?" he sighed and took her hand. When she tried to pull it away, he squeezed it with his eyes narrowed. "You have three choices now. One, you come with me to the Vel'kim residence without trying anything like that again, holding my hand so I can react if you do not behave. Two, I will take your hand *and* assume control of your muscles to make you walk there with me. Or three, I send you to sleep and carry you there over my shoulder. Which one will it be, Theá?"

"Eryn," she murmured and then added, "One."

"Good. Should you change your mind on our way there, you will not have that option a second time. Do you understand me?" he asked slowly and insistently.

She nodded without looking at him and let him guide her out the building, her cousin and uncle walking right behind them.

* * *

Enric turned his head and watched his companion being marched out by Ram'an, who was clasping her hand tightly and did not seem at all relaxed but in a hurry to get her away from the building. It probably had something to do with why Malriel had left so quickly no more than a minute ago.

He watched the four of them until they had turned a corner before he turned back to Kilan. Golir had granted him a few minutes with his assistant. He raised a soundproof barrier.

"I need the three of you to leave here today. Don't lose any time. Return and inform the King of what is going on here right now. Give him a few of the birds Valrad has sent along so he can contact Eryn and me directly at the Vel'kim residence without his message passing through any other hands."

"I am not going to leave you here!" Kilan protested, wide-eyed.

"Listen," Enric insisted, "I need you out of here. If things go wrong here for some reason, I don't want to have to worry about you. It seems I am stronger than just about everyone else here but Golir; Eryn is very strong, too. We can battle our way out of here if there is absolutely no other way. But you would be a liability. And the King needs to hear of this. Perhaps he will be able to intervene somehow."

Kilan did not at all look happy, but nodded reluctantly. "As you wish. Do you want me to return here with Lord Tyront?"

"No, categorically not." Enric shook his head emphatically. "That would make things appear as though she is guilty and we require him to free us from here. We first need to wait and see which conclusion they reach."

"And should they find her guilty?"

"Then I will have to make a decision. But until then Tyront must not interfere. Leave now and do not concern yourself too much. I will send word as soon as I have an opportunity. Farewell, my friend." Enric clasped the other magician's hand tightly, nodded to Barul and Grend, then collapsed the barrier to walk over to where Golir was waiting for him.

*   *   *

Eryn fought the urge to tug her hand from Ram'an's grip. It was not that she was reluctant to return to the Vel'kim residence as such; it had been the most delightful location for her in the entire city. But being dragged there by this particular man felt wrong. Additionally, once they had arrived there, there would be no way to avoid facing Valrad. She wondered why he had offered to let her and her guardian stay at his house. To make sure nothing would keep her from facing the trial and get what she deserved for indirectly causing his brother's demise? Or to diffuse the tense situation and demonstrate that he was still supporting her? The thought that she would find out soon enough made her stomach clench.

"I will send a message to Intrea," she heard Vran'el say to his father behind her. "I will ask her to let Pe'tala stay with her until this whole tangled mess is over. I do not think having the three of them together under one roof is a wise idea."

Eryn shuddered at the thought of her cousin seeing her and the man she was in love with together in her home. But it was not as if her relationship with Pe'tala could get any worse. Not that this was top of her list presently. There was still the minor matter of having her secret exhibited to everyone here, and soon enough to people at home as well. Every single one of her few friends would know about it. Then she would see soon enough if they still were her friends. Unless they were about to throw her into some kind of dungeon here for the rest of her life, that is. A shiver ran through her body at the very thought.

Ram'an slowed and turned to her, cupping her face in both his hands, leaning his forehead against hers.

"Do not fear, Theá, everything will be alright. Whatever Malriel's aim is, having you come to harm is certainly not a part of it."

She tried to turn away when a tear ran down her cheek, but he held her face in place.

"You can't know that," she whispered, touched that after all that had happened between them, he was not showing any sign of condemning her. But then he didn't yet know that the allegations were true, did he?

"Of course I can," he smiled and lifted his head to press a kiss to her forehead. "Come. You should get some rest. This has not exactly been a peaceful morning for you."

Rest? How was she supposed to sleep now? But a few hours of solitude sounded good, so she nodded.

When they arrived at the Vel'kim residence, Ram'an turned to Valrad. "Do you have a guest room with two beds? Guarding her requires constant supervision."

Eryn took a step back, appalled at the idea of sharing a bedroom with him.

Vran'el smiled thinly. "No, I do not think your duties as her guard require quite that much selfless effort on your side. Sharing a room with her will not be necessary. We will give you two adjacent rooms. You can shield her windows and door as long as she remains in there alone. The guardianship rules do not stipulate that you are to spend every second with your charge, only to ensure she is well guarded by whatever means appropriate to the situation."

Ram'an pursed his lips, clearly not too thrilled at having another lawyer inform him of rules he had decided to interpret in a way that catered to his own preferences. He gave a single nod and followed Vran'el along a corridor that led away from the main room, holding on to Eryn's hand.

Her cousin opened a door into a room with a pleasant view over the gardens and motioned for her to enter. She pulled her hand free and walked to the bed immediately, laying down on it so she was facing away from the two men. She saw a faint shimmer in the air as Ram'an created a shield in front of the window. How very conscientious of him, she thought wryly, wondering if he enjoyed this chance at being commissioned to make her remain close to him at all times.

"Come," she heard Vran'el say to Ram'an, "let us give her some privacy for now."

She exhaled in relief when the door closed behind them and she was alone. Now she had ample opportunity to stare at the walls and wonder how she could possibly have been naïve enough to assume that she would never be held accountable for what she had done. Perhaps punishment would finally deliver some peace of mind.

* * *

She looked up and turned when she heard a hiss in front of the closed door to her room. Steps approached and then a muffled discussion between Vran'el and Ram'an ensued.

"You put a bloody barrier in front of her *door* as well? What if she wanted to come out to join us or go to the bathroom? Really now, she is not a caged animal!" Vran'el complained.

"How about giving her some privacy for now? What are you doing, trying to sneak into her room?" Ram'an demanded without responding to his questions.

"She has been left to herself for two hours now. I think she might just need some friendly company," she heard her cousin say in a hostile tone which was very probably accompanied by a pointed stare.

"You do not even know if she wants to see you," Ram'an countered.

"I bet she prefers seeing me to being in the presence of a certain other person in this house," Vran'el growled back.

"She might not want to see anybody at all. Or she might be asleep."

Eryn sighed and got up to open the door and glower at the two men from behind the shield.

"Even if I had been asleep, I would surely have been aroused from it by your bickering," she said calmly.

Vran'el grimaced. "I am sorry, sweetness. Your eager guard here has barred my way through to you. I wanted to keep you company. Father is cooking lunch and we were hoping that you will join us when it is ready."

She shook her head. "I don't feel like eating - but thank you."

Ram'an looked at her. "You need to eat, Theá, to preserve your strength, especially now."

"I would appreciate it if you stopped calling me by that name," she replied stiffly.

"I do not use it to upset you, dear, but because you have been Malthéa to me all your life. It means that you are one of us, that you belong here."

She made to step forward to give him a good shove, but hastily pulled back when she encountered the barrier she neglected to remember was there.

Ram'an removed the shield. "But I am not an unreasonable man. If you resent being called by that name so much, I would be willing to accept a little deal. I will stop calling you Malthéa, if you sleep in one bed with me tonight."

"You conceited, insensitive idiot, are you completely out of touch with reality? What in the world makes you think I would agree to thing like that?" she spat at him, balling her hands into fists, ready to punch him.

"I did not think you would. But seeing you angry is not as painful as seeing you desperate, my dear," he replied quietly.

She exhaled slowly, her anger draining away. So he had provoked her to get her out of her depressive mood.

Vran'el elbowed his way into the room and stood between them. "Do you want me to kick him out for you, sweetness?" he asked her.

Ram'an snorted derisively. "You can try it if you feel like receiving a good beating."

"That is no way to treat your host. Or is that how House Arbil shows gratitude for hospitality?" Vran'el jibed.

"The host is your father, strictly speaking. And do not pretend that your hospitality was aimed at me. You wanted to make sure Theá did not stay at my place. That is the only reason I am here."

"That is your own fault. Had you not treated my sister like this, you would still be a welcome guest at our home," Vran'el hissed.

"Just because *you* are content in a companionship that is no more than a political convenience does not mean that this is what everybody else prefers," Ram'an replied and folded his arms.

"Political convenience? You cold bastard! It was a lot more for Pe'tala!" He stopped himself when he realised that he had said too much.

Ram'an frowned. "Wait, what? But we were never..."

"Forget what I said. It does not matter anymore. The fact remains that you cast her aside for another woman who has no intention of being yours, however unable you have proved for accepting this."

"Are you telling she was in love with me?" Ram'an enquired with disbelief, ignoring the other man's attempts to change the course of the conversation.

"Right - as if the great heart breaker could be too surprised about this," Vran'el murmured and shook his head. "Just because she is probably one of the handful of women in this city whom you have not yet taken to bed does not mean that..."

"That is a gross exaggeration!" Ram'an interrupted him, appalled at being made to appear as a shallow womaniser in front of the woman he wanted to win for himself.

Eryn closed her eyes for a moment. "You really have come in here to fight? Is it less fun without an audience or why do I have to listen to this?"

Both of them fell silent, looking at her sheepishly as if her words had made them realise how inappropriate their behaviour was in light of her own troubles.

"Forgive us, sweetness," Vran'el then said. "I came to keep you company. I am worried about your being holed up in here all alone. I want you to know that your family will be at your side, we will get through this together."

She gulped, fighting the teardrops she felt building in her eyes. "That is very sweet of you, thank you." She exhaled. "But before you offer comfort, I feel I should tell you..."

With a wave of his hand he shushed her, then wrapped his arms around her. "Whatever happened back then, dear cousin, whatever mistake you may have made, you surely did not do so intending your own father to be killed, did you?"

She shook her head, unable to speak.

"And that is all I need to know for now, sweetness." Vran'el pulled her across to the bed with him and lay down, motioning for her to snuggle up to him. She hesitated for a moment, then lowered herself onto the bed as well and put her head on his shoulder. After a few moments she felt another weight on the bed when Ram'an sat behind her without touching her.

"I remember when you were four years old and I was beginning to realise that my interests were not the same as those of most other boys. I once tried to do your hair, but you resisted, shoving my hands aside and telling me that a boy cannot make a girl pretty as he has no idea." Vran'el snorted. "That shows how much you knew. But I am glad to see that you changed your mind about that misconception. Now it seems that of the two of us I am not the one who has no idea how to deal with a woman's hair."

"I hope that makes you proud, my friend," she murmured, grateful for his efforts at distracting her.

"I admit it has its merits," he replied good-naturedly. "My daughter and Intrea are a lot more eager to have me style them when they go out than you were back then."

"What can I say? I clearly failed to recognise greatness when it was before me," she smiled tiredly.

"Well spoken, sweetness. Consider yourself forgiven," he announced solemnly then went on, "I remember that you were fond of spending your time out in the gardens - not only at the Aren residence, but wherever you went. They hardly ever managed to keep you inside for long when there was a terrace door in view." He paused for a few moments before he continued, "Ram'an used to take walks with you outside. His mother told us that he sat down at home to learn the names of plants and trees so he could tell you about them when you asked. Malriel was very pleased about that. She said that she had never seen a boy make such an effort at so young an age. It was to her a confirmation that she had chosen well for you."

Eryn turned slightly to look at Ram'an, who was leaning against a bed post with a faint smile on his face. She remembered his having taken walks with her, but not that he had actually studied to please her with his knowledge of plants.

"You had a favourite flower," Ram'an said quietly. "It was the one you were named after. Your uncle had somehow managed to make a few of them grow in his garden, which was quite a feat as they normally require high altitude and a cooler climate."

"How sweet of you to remember," she murmured.

"We can take a walk in the garden later, if you want," he offered. "I think I still remember where they grow."

She swallowed and shook her head slightly. "I don't think we should."

"Give it up," Vran'el smirked. "She will not fall for you, however sweet you were as a boy. Enric is a lot more attractive than you."

Ram'an smiled. "No, he is not. It seems you were misinformed on that account."

"I do not have to rely on anybody else's assessment of male attractiveness. My own judgement is quite reliable in that area."

"Indeed?" Ram'an lifted both brows. "Then you are telling me you do not find me attractive? I am devastated."

"That is not what I said. I said you cannot compete with Enric. Hardy anybody can. He is marvellous," Vran'el sighed.

Eryn raised her head to give her cousin a worried look. "Are you falling in love with my companion? Do I need to warn you that this will end up in having your heart broken?"

Her cousin laughed. "No, do not trouble yourself on my account, sweetness. I know that he is well outside my ambit due to his inclinations in general and his attachment to you in particular. And I am extremely fond of Neval. But I admit that watching him dance with Ram'an that evening made me a bit envious."

"Did it now," Ram'an commented dryly. "You are very welcome to take my place next time."

"You had better be cautious. There might very well be a next time unless you are very careful how you behave towards my cousin. I imagine Enric would not appreciate seeing you on the same bed with her right now, or even near it."

"I doubt that his wreath would be as great as you imagine as long as you are sharing that bed with the two of us," her guardian smiled thinly. "But you can go and help your father in the kitchen anytime you like."

"Shut up, the two of you, or I will be the one leaving you to share this bed with each other," she growled.

Vran'el smiled lazily, raising a suggestive brow at Ram'an. "What do you say? Would that not be a happy experiment for you? I promise I would be extra gentle with you."

Ram'an shook his head and chuckled. "You can stop trying to play your games with me. I am very well aware of what you are doing and it will not work on me."

"Me? Doing something?" he asked in mock innocence. "What would that be, pray?"

"You delight in making other men uneasy by pretending to be attracted to them."

Vran'el raised an eyebrow. "So the idea of my being attracted to you would not bother you at all?"

"What can I say? I am very confident in both my sexuality and my appeal. So even if you were genuinely attracted to me, it would be completely understandable."

Eryn watched how her cousin stared at Ram'an for a moment before he burst into laughter and said, "One point for you. What a pity you are an insensitive dolt! If it were not for my sister and my cousin here, I might actually like you."

*   *   *

Enric paced the room he had been given. Golir had turned out to be a member of House Partém, which was not a very pleasant discovery. He remembered from the tapestry that it was one of the Houses Ram'an's family regularly connected with through arranged companionships.

He turned when he heard a knock at his door and went to answer it. Golir stood in the door frame.

"Dinner is ready, Enric. Join me." At this he turned and walked along the corridor to the main room.

That had clearly not been a request, rather an order. So it seemed the powerful man either wanted to make sure that his guest was well-fed or intended to talk to him. Probably the latter, considering the circumstances.

Enric sat down on the cushions and nodded gratefully after he had accepted a bowl containing chunks of cheerily coloured vegetables, spices and dark meat.

"If I remember correctly, you do not share Maltheá's dietary preferences, especially as you have turned out to be quite a skilful hunter if I am to believe the rumour," his host said and waited for his guest to start eating.

"You are right - I do not share them," Enric smiled and took the first bite. It was very good, though not quite as richly spiced as what Vran'el generally served; but then, hardly anything was.

"From what I have seen you have adapted remarkably well to our country within a very short time," Golir commented.

Of course, Enric thought, he would not come directly to what was on his mind while they were eating. It was very likely not considered polite to interrogate or warn guests while they were trying to enjoy a meal.

"I like to think so," he replied. "Though I have to say that people here made it very easy for me to adapt. Considering that my country is considered a somewhat barbaric place I was shown great tolerance and acceptance."

Golir smiled. "You have managed to change our perception quite a lot. We had not exactly expected somebody as... cultured and able, to be completely honest."

Enric chuckled. "Instead, a barefoot figure clad in furs?"

"Not quite that crude, but you get my meaning," his host replied.

"So the reports you received from the search parties and Ram'an about their stays in the Kingdom were not that favourable, I suspect."

"Let us just say they might have been a little superficial," Golir said diplomatically and set aside his empty bowl.

Enric finished as well, bracing himself for whatever was to come now.

"Would you like some more? There is more than enough left. I have asked my family to have dinner elsewhere to allow us some privacy."

He shook his head. "No, I've had sufficient, thank you."

"Good." Golir leaned back into the cushions and gave his guest a calculating look. "There is one matter in our reports about your country I dare not dismiss: your expertise in everything connected with fighting and warfare. It is essentially what kept us from making contact with you before. We did not want history to repeat itself by making us once more the target of a belligerent country we failed to assess adequately. And you are the second highest ranking magician in an institution that has dedicated its energies to defending the country. Thus I assume that you have in addition to your considerable powers also vast knowledge of the discipline of fighting at your disposal."

"You assume correctly," Enric replied calmly. It would make little sense to deny it.

"This knowledge, I imagine, may also turn out to be useful when it comes to fighting a stronger, if less skilled opponent?" Golir enquired and watched his guest carefully.

Deciding upon honesty, Enric nodded. "Yes, that is the case. Though I have not really had an opportunity to test my abilities against a stronger magician and prevail so far."

"So Lord Tyront, the leader of the Order, is either your equal in skill or his powers are superior enough for this not to matter. Or a combination thereof," his host nodded. "I will not ask you which one is the case, as it would in this current situation put you in an awkward position. You would either have to lie to me or tell me plainly that you will not share this little detail with me, neither of which would exactly make our arrangement here more convivial."

"Then I thank you for your consideration."

Golir smiled. "Do not as yet. The fact that you might be in a position to overpower me makes me feel the need to warn you in case this advantage would induce you to do something foolish. Should you decide to take matters into your own hands and try to flee from here with Maltheá, consider that you may prevail against me alone, but probably not against a greater number of magicians that would finally take you down. Have I made myself understood?"

If Enric felt any unrest at this announcement, his face did not show it. "Perfectly," he just replied.

"No honest promises that you would never even consider anything of that kind?" Golir smiled with his eyebrows raised in question.

"No. However honest they might be, you are hardly likely to believe them, are you?"

"I am not, no." His host then rose. "Come. I am sure you are eager to meet Maltheá. Ram'an will be at her side the whole time, so if you feel any surges of jealousy I would ask you to deal with those without me having to intervene because you feel you have to make another point. Violence will at this point not cast a favourable light on yourself or on her."

"I will do my best to maintain my jealousy to a socially acceptable level," Enric replied coolly.

"Make sure you do. If you attack her guardian in any way, you will be held accountable for it. As will I if I fail to restrain you. So however he might try to provoke you, remember that he is the only one who would benefit from your anger, either by seeing me restraining you or him accusing you publicly."

Enric just nodded, dreading whatever Ram'an might be considering doing to take advantage of that situation.

CHAPTER 44

Confessing

Eryn looked up sharply when she heard a knock at the door downstairs. Finally!

Ram'an was sitting beside her and put aside the book he had been reading and quickly seized her arm as she was about to jump up. Vran'el rose and walked downstairs to admit the visitors.

"No." He shook his head when she looked at him in annoyance. "You will stay close to me where I can touch you."

Touch her? She frowned and pulled at her arm. Having Enric see him touching her throughout the evening would hardly be very pleasant for either of them.

"Theá," he warned her, "do not make this more difficult for yourself than it has to be. Making it permissible for the two of you to be in the same room is a courtesy bestowed upon you by both Golir and myself. I can withdraw that privilege at any time if you do not follow my rules."

She looked at him with a wavering expression. Was that true? Could he?

"Your rules? What exactly are they, if I may be permitted to ask?"

"What I explained before: Stay close to me, so I can touch you at all times. You may choose the nature of the way I touch you, such as my arm around your shoulders or holding my hand, for example. Whatever you feel most comfortable with."

Whatever she felt most comfortable with? While Enric was watching them?

"There is no way you could touch me that I feel comfortable with!" she complained.

He nodded. "Very well. My choice then. That suits me fine."

When Enric and Golir entered, Eryn was on the verge of jumping up and running across to him, but felt Ram'an's arms close around her from behind, pulling her back and against him.

"Let go of me! Is that supposed to mean I can't even greet him?" she cried.

"I told you. I expect you to stay within my reach at all times. This is well within my rights as your guardian, and as he is stronger than myself I adjudge close contact between the two of you too risky. You can greet him *without* touching him," he explained calmly and met Enric's warning gaze with equanimity without removing his arms from around her waist.

"Ram'an, you are a brute," Vran'el said disapprovingly and shook his head. "Stop provoking him. It is not professional."

Ram'an merely smiled as if notions of professionalism were beyond his concerns for the moment.

Valrad entered the main room from the terrace and nodded to the newcomers. "Golir. Enric." He stepped towards Enric to squeeze his arm in a gesture of understanding and sympathy. "Have a seat. Tell me what I can get you to drink."

Golir motioned for Enric to take a seat opposite Eryn and so be as far away from her as possible before he sat next to him. Valrad returned with a tray full of drinks and sat between Golir and Ram'an while Vran'el took a seat next to Eryn.

"How are you doing, my love?" Enric asked, trying to ignore her unhappy expression at being locked in Ram'an's embrace.

"Confused. Angry about being a prisoner yet again," she grimaced. Scared at having to talk about what I did back then and what the reaction to it will be, she thought.

"We will get through this," he said with more confidence than he felt. "Have you talked to Vran'el about the case against you yet?"

Her cousin shook his head. "No. I thought you would want to be here when she talks about it. I assumed that you needed to hear this as well."

Enric nodded. "Yes, I do." He looked at Golir. "Is there a chance of a little privacy? This is a confidential matter, after all. She would probably compromise herself by talking about this in the presence of a member of the triarchy."

Golir thought for a moment, then nodded. "I will stay in the room where I can see you, but you may raise a barrier for privacy."

"Thank you," Enric said and bowed his head. Then he looked at Ram'an. "I would ask you to leave us now as well for the duration of this conversation."

"No," he said sharply.

Eryn turned her head to him and looked at him pleadingly. "Please?"

"No," he repeated more gently and shook his head. She wondered if he really thought it too dangerous to leave her in such close proximity with Enric without keeping them apart of if he just wanted to hear the story. But then maybe this was what would finally convince him to give up his claim on her. He might just be disgusted or appalled enough to retreat.

"Can you release me from your grip at least?" She wriggled, demonstrating that she couldn't even move her arms. "I feel quite restricted."

"Will you let me take your hand instead?" he asked and released her when she nodded hesitantly after a moment. Seeing Ram'an holding her hand would surely be easier for Enric to watch than her being pressed tightly against him. She felt his warm fingers link with hers and wished they were Enric's. She looked at her companion, who apart from his implacable gaze gave nothing away of his displeasure at first glance. But she had come to know the tiny, less obvious signs of annoyance he tended to display, as she had provoked them often enough in these last few months. His jaw muscles were slightly more tense than usual, and so were his shoulders.

"Will you raise the barrier?" Enric asked Ram'an icily. "I suppose you will not appreciate my doing it. I might try to suffocate you, after all."

Ram'an wordlessly raised a soundproof shield and put one arm behind Eryn while pulling her hand onto his lap, all the while keeping eye contact with Enric to make sure that he understood this as the punishment it was.

"This will be over one day," Enric warned him slowly, "and then I shall be free to pay you back for all of this. Just keep that in mind, can you?"

"You are not threatening me again, *Ambassador*?" Ram'an replied with a raised eyebrow. "Such a thing would not be wise, would it? If I am under the impression that I am to be made to pay anyway, I might decide that I should at least make the cause for the punishment worth my while." He let his arm, resting on cushions behind Eryn, slip forward so it came to lie around her shoulders.

"Stop that!" she hissed and sent him a glare that neither impressed him nor made him retract his arm.

"She is right," Valrad said tiredly. "This is hardly the time for your little power plays. We have more important things to consider now." He turned to his niece. "My dear girl, it is time for you to tell us what really happened back then, however reluctant you may be to talk about it. You will have to sooner rather than later anyway, and we as your family should not have to hear of it along with everybody else. Have you ever told anybody about this before?"

She hesitated briefly. "I told Malriel yesterday afternoon." Her voice was all but a whisper, hardly able to believe her own lack of good sense in having done so.

He nodded. "Then she acted very quickly. Getting the triarchy to detain you here in only one evening was quite a feat. But then House Aren has always had good connections to the upper ranks. It does not pay to underestimate the woman. This is why you must tell us everything, even - or especially - if there was something you withheld from her. In contrast to Malriel, we will not use anything you say against you."

That remained to be seen when he had heard what she had done, she thought, but instead turned her head to look at Ram'an.

"You might."

He pulled her head towards him to kiss her forehead. "I would never assist others in harming you, and having you think that I would do so pains me a lot, Theá," he said and sighed with regret.

Enric closed his eyes for a moment, trying to ignore the affectionate gesture her guard was using with her, so naturally as if he had every right to do so. He had no right whatsoever to exchange tender little touches with her and keep her away from her companion.

Eryn took a deep breath. "You all know how my father died, don't you?"

Vran'el nodded. "We do, but you should tell us the complete story. It will help you sort your thoughts. Consider it a preparation for when you have to speak in front of the senate." His tone had become lawyer-like.

How had she managed to get herself into a situation that required telling that particular story not only once but repeatedly, she wondered. By putting trust in the wrong person, that was how. But the damage was done already, wasn't it? It was not as if there could be vastly more harm done by repeating it now. Yet there would be more harm of course, another part of her brain chimed in. The people underneath that barrier would know about everything, would see what kind of thoughtless, carefree creature unworthy of the healing profession she had been, and maybe still was. But that could not be helped now. This would be the first part of the price she finally had to pay.

She told the story again, but unlike the evening before, she did not try to omit the incriminating details. She looked straight ahead and down over the low table while she was talking, avoiding eye contact with any of the four men around her. They listened attentively, not one of them interrupting at any time. She felt Ram'an's fingers squeeze hers as she talked about the incident with Krion when her father had intervened and again a second time when she recounted how she had been informed of her father's death.

Enric watched her helplessly from across the table, feeling the waves of anxiety radiating off her and wishing that he could be in physical contact with her for just a moment, to hold her and tell her that everything would be alright, however bold that promise was right now.

When she was finished with her story and fell silent again, none of them spoke for a while.

"Say something!" she demanded desperately.

Valrad stirred and stepped over his son's legs to squeeze between him and Eryn and pull her into a wordless embrace. She felt the tension in her muscles loosening and her knees becoming weak. He did not despise her for what she had done to his only brother.

Enric watched the relief on her face and thought about all the years she had been keeping this secret to herself with no one to talk to about it. What was more, she had kept blaming herself for everything that had happened.

Her uncle loosened his grip on her so he could look at her face. "Eryn, this was not your fault."

She shook her head, stifling a sob. "I really do value your saying that, but your kindness can't alter the facts."

Valrad sighed and took her head in both hands to stop her from turning away to avoid his gaze. "Now you listen to me for a moment. I want to tell you about the natural development of magically gifted children. You would not know about it, as you grew up without other magicians around you."

"Whatever you want to say, you can't make things..." she started, but when she felt warmth from his palms seeping into her throat, her voice trailed off.

"I told you to listen to me, my girl," he said sternly. "And listen you should, because this picture of yourself and your deeds you hold is a twisted one that causes you needless suffering. I am not saying that you should not be mournful about the tragic end your father met, but blaming yourself for it is nonsense." When she touched her throat, he added, "I have just hindered your vocal cords for the moment. I will restore them as soon as I am done. Do not try to heal them yourself - better to pay attention to me now." He waited until she was looking at him again before he continued. "It is in the nature of the very young to test things that are forbidden to them. It is a way of exploring the limits of their surroundings, seeing how far they can push. For healthy development it is necessary to question the rules others make instead of obeying them blindly. Otherwise nobody would ever uncover anything new; we would be stuck in our society without progress or improvement of any sort. Using healing or any other magic against people who cannot protect themselves against it is a grave offence indeed, I am not going to lie to you about this. But then you yourself were put into a similar situation by that baker's son before: he had been about to use his superior physical strength on you and would have succeeded. Your retribution was therefore not unprovoked since you made use of the only means by which you were able to prevail against him. In a society where it were publicly known that you are a magician, this situation would very likely not have arisen as we are generally treated with more wariness by non-magicians. So your circumstances back then were a lot more involved and cannot be compared to our own here. Yet what I can tell you is that you did not cause your father's death by breaking the young man's arm. Yes, there is the principle of cause and effect.

However, applying that principle here would be completely ridiculous."

Enric nodded. "True. And yet Malriel aims to accomplish just that very thing. She wants the blame to be placed on Eryn. Why? What punishment can she wish to be inflicted on her?"

Vran'el thought for a moment before he spoke, "I would say that under normal circumstances the triarchy would not even bother with a case such as this, especially as all the events occurred such a long time ago. Additionally, there is some dispute whether the accused is even subject to our local laws as she has lived most of her life in the Old Kingdom, which is also where the alleged crime took place, even though Ved'al technically remained one of our citizens. The only reason why this has been put before the triarchy and the senate is Malriel's considerable influence. The question is if that influence is great enough to make the senate decide in her favour and risk diplomatic tensions with the Old Kingdom."

"That was not really an answer to my question," Enric said in mild rebuke. "What kind of punishment could Malriel have in mind? I assume having her own daughter incarcerated in a dungeon is not what she intends."

Valrad shook his head. "I would not imagine so, no. Neither is having her barred from the country. The only thing that would seem logical to me would be to compel Eryn to stay in the city instead of allowing her to return to Anyueel. Legally speaking she still is the heir to House Aren, and Malriel is doubtlessly eager to have her own direct bloodline in charge of the family."

"So she might try to keep Eryn from leaving here ever again?" Enric frowned. "Is that possible? How great are her chances for success if that is indeed her plan?"

Vran'el shrugged. "That is hard to determine. With the right number of votes in her favour and the triarchy not objecting, it would theoretically be possible to push it through. But I doubt that matters will come to that. Many of the Houses would risk losing the advantages that trade agreements will bring them if Eryn is held here against her will, not to mention the political relationship with your King that would no doubt suffer direly. Ram'an?"

The other lawyer nodded. "I agree with your evaluation. The Houses which have signed trade agreements will be eager to have them put into effect. And then there are the ones that are opposed to House Aren and will vote to set Maltheá free again just to have the Aren family weakened by the loss of their only daughter and heir."

"What about me?" Enric asked tensely. "I am her companion, after all. Putting me in the custody of a stronger magician shows that they are uncertain what to expect of me. They will surely not assume that I will accept my companion being kept here just like that?"

Vran'el nodded. "You are right about the first assumption. They are very cautious about you. But your status as her companion will not make much of a difference since you are only bound legally, not magically. Sending you home while she stays here is theoretically a valid option as there is no third level commitment bond between you."

Enric nodded slowly and then looked at Eryn. "Then we will take that bond as soon as possible."

Eryn stared at him, trying to put words to her thoughts, but nothing came out of her mouth. She waved her hands in front of her uncle's face to get his attention.

Valrad took her hands in his to squeeze them reassuringly and turned to Enric. "I am afraid this is not so easy, my friend. Eryn is a member of House Aren and thus depends on the approval of the Head of the House to be permitted to enter into such a bond. You may trust to Malriel's not being overly eager to agree to it," he added dryly.

Eryn rolled her eyes impatiently and turned to Ram'an, pointing helplessly at her throat. Whatever her uncle had done there, she was not sure how to repair it.

"Valrad?" Ram'an said with an amused smile, "I think your niece would appreciate it very much if you restored her command over her voice."

"What?" Her uncle turned and looked at her for a moment, before remembering. "Oh, yes, of course. Forgive me, my dear, I had completely forgotten about that." He placed a hand on the side of her throat and a few moments later she was able to speak again.

"What did you do to my vocal chords? I had no idea how to heal that!" Then she turned towards Enric. "A third level commitment bond? Have you gone completely insane?" she exclaimed and tried to stand up, when she felt Ram'an's arm pulling her down again. She turned to him angrily and growled, "And you don't have to look so damned pleased about my not wanting to enter into the bond just to avoid being kept here! It does not mean that I am not attached to Enric, nor does it increase *your* chances in any way."

"Whatever you say, my dear," Ram'an replied and pulled her back towards him. "Try to remember my rule about maintaining physical contact with me, even when you are agitated," he reminded her.

She leaned back reluctantly, letting him put his arm around her shoulders again and restraining herself from pulling back when she felt her hand being taken into his. She looked to Enric.

"Did you really think I would do this just to escape here? The first commitment to you was an escape. I will not do anything like it again for such a reason!" She saw the torment in his eyes only briefly before he had himself under full control again.

"So for you there would be no other reason to do this?" he asked dangerously calmly.

"Don't give me that," she growled, "you know exactly how I meant that! If you want me to do it for any other reason, don't suggest it as an easy way out of my troubles here."

He nodded, ignoring Ram'an's smug smile while he played with her fingers. "Alright. Then let's talk about it no more, especially as it is not really a choice anyway without Malriel's permission."

"It would also not be a choice *with* Malriel's permission," she clarified. "If you want this commitment, you will have to wait until I am ready for it. Then you may at least be sure I agreed to it for the right reasons."

Enric nodded without words. This had been the second time she had refused him, and even though he could hardly blame her for it, it still pained him. And to have Ram'an witnessing it a second time did not make it any easier to bear, either.

"So what am I going to do now?" she asked and turned to her cousin.

"There is nothing much we can do for now, as we will have to wait for Malriel's testimony tomorrow," Vran'el explained. "Maybe we can challenge some of the information she presents as unprovable and thereby invalid for the proceedings. It might be that she is not in possession of all the facts. After that we will have to see what punishment she demands. If it is too outrageous and bears no relation to the alleged offence, she will have undermined her own credibility. Nonetheless, I would not count on that. She has not risen to where she is today by making stupid mistakes like that."

Valrad then turned to Ram'an. "Could you lift the barrier for a moment? The air is getting a little stale in here."

He nodded and complied.

"I think we are done anyway, so we can all enjoy the benefit of fresh air," Vran'el said and got up to stretch and inhale deeply.

Golir noted the removal of the shield from his position next to the terrace door and returned to the cushions to sit next to Enric again.

"How long do proceedings like that normally take here?" Enric enquired.

"Not much longer than ten days," Golir replied. "But that depends on how cooperative the witnesses and the accused are, how controversial the matters of the case are and whether there is political relevance to the proceedings."

"Would political relevance slow proceedings down because you need to consider the outcome more carefully or would it speed them up?" Eryn asked suspiciously.

"We try to handle matters of high importance as swiftly as possible without being unduly hasty," Golir told her.

"*Swiftly without undue haste* gives me no useable information at all!" she complained.

"Eryn," her uncle said with a warning undertone.

She looked at Golir with a pained expression. "I apologise. I suppose insulting you is not a very smart move right now."

The triarch nodded. "You are right. It is not," he said pointedly. "But I understand your impatience and that your situation is not exactly a pleasant one and will thus allow you some lenience. For now."

Alright, she thought, and made a mental note, warning received.

Enric leaned forward. "That little thing of touching her all the time, I hope this is only a matter of caution as long as I am present and not something you shall insist on at all times?"

"Such as at night, you mean?" Ram'an said, making no attempt to hide his amused smile.

"Yes."

"We are still discussing that."

"No, we are not!" Eryn protested, elbowing Ram'an in his belly hard enough to make him groan.

"He will shield her window and door for the night," Valrad threw in. "Plus we will ensure he takes no advantage of his position as her guardian that would cause him to be released from that task and harm his reputation."

Enric nodded. The warning to Ram'an had been clear enough judging from his less than thrilled expression.

"I would like to give my companion a hug to comfort her and show her that her unfavourable view of the past events is not repugnant to me. Will you grant me that favour?" He turned first to Golir, who nodded briefly, and then to Ram'an.

"Tell me one thing," Ram'an said slowly with narrowed eyes, "Why did your companion, as you never tire of referring to her, omit to share this particular, very burdensome detail of her life with you? From where I stand this seems to indicate a certain lack of trust."

Enric did not reply at once. Muscles around his mouth tightened, although he showed no other sign of distress. It was not a question he wanted to hear from this particular man. Or anyone else, for that matter.

"I don't know. But I would assume that sharing something that you have never managed to forgive yourself, with others, is not easy. I trust that she would have told me one day," he replied stiffly and waited.

"What would one embrace be worth to you, Lord Enric?" Ram'an then asked speculatively.

"What do you want?"

He seemed to consider that question for a moment. "How about a shipload full of goods that you produce? Wines, fabrics, a splendid mix of everything."

"That is outrageous! You really have the nerve..." Vran'el spat out, but was interrupted by Enric.

"Agreed," he just said and got up.

All of them stared at him in utter surprise, Eryn included.

"You must be either rich beyond imagination or very desperate," Ram'an said and shook his head slightly.

Enric made no comment on that but stretched out his arms to help Eryn get up from the cushions and away from Ram'an's possessive touches. As soon as her hands touched his he pulled her up and right into his arms in one swift move. Her arms wrapped themselves around his chest almost of their own accord and held on to him tightly. She felt him exhale a long breath of relief and felt his lips trail kisses along the top of her head, her temple, finally finding her mouth after lifting her chin.

"We will take care of this. Do not worry yourself about it. I hope you can find it in yourself to appear strong tomorrow. Strong and in control," he murmured. "No loose Aren temper. It would only make you appear more like Malriel."

He waited for her to nod before he went on quietly, "Do not provoke Ram'an into taking any liberties by challenging him unless he seriously exceeds tolerable limits. In this case inform your uncle or Vran'el."

She sighed and nodded again. She didn't want to talk or hear about that right now, just enjoy his warmth and smell without having to think of what awaited her in these next few days, perhaps even weeks.

He released her again, pressing a last tender kiss into her palm and stepped back again before Ram'an saw fit to separate them.

"You will have to send a ship to pick up the produce, we do not yet have any that are fit for the purpose of transporting a greater load of goods," Enric said to Ram'an.

"This does not matter," the other one smiled thinly. "I have no intention of collecting that debt. I was just curious about how you would react to a demand like that."

"Then I hope I did not fail to entertain you," Enric replied coolly.

Ram'an smiled and took Eryn's hand into his own again. "Oh, no, you did not. But then grand gestures never fail to entertain, do they?"

Eryn watched Golir rise and indicate to his house guest that it was now time to leave. When both men had left the main room, she turned to Ram'an and scowled at him.

"You know, sometimes you make it almost impossible for me to remember what it was about you that made me like you in the first place."

"Strong words from a woman who lives with a warrior while despising the profession so much," he retorted mildly.

"If it weren't for my cousin, I would very probably start despising the profession of lawyer even more," she said pointedly and stood up. "If you will excuse me now, I am going to have an early night."

She frowned when Ram'an stood as well. "What now?"

He lifted a brow. "Your windows and door, Theá. I need to secure them."

She thought back to Vran'el's words several hours earlier. "What if I have to go to the bathroom or somewhere?"

"Then you will have to knock on the wall to my room."

"Like a small child?" she grimaced.

"Or like somebody accused and under suspicion of having broken the laws," he pointed out. "Whichever take on your case you find more appealing."

She sighed and thought of Enric's warning not to provoke him unduly before nodding and walking ahead.

CHAPTER 45

The Proceedings

Eryn pulled her blanket over her head when she felt somebody softly shaking her shoulder to awaken her.

"Go away," she growled without opening her eyes.

"As much as I would like to let you sleep, I am afraid that I cannot. We are due at the senate in little more than one hour."

She opened her eyes in her fabric cavern immediately. Wrong voice. Too exotic. Too serious. Ram'an.

Pulling the blanket back from her head, looking up at him and sighing in resignation. "You know, I was really hoping that all this had just been a bad dream."

"Well, it is reality I am afraid," he said with what was in her opinion unwarranted serenity.

Frowning, she sat up. "Why do I have the feeling that you are delighted at my being kept here?"

"Because, my dear Theá, I do not have it in me to condemn circumstances that make you the first person I lay eyes on in the morning," he smiled and stood so she could get out of bed.

"Terrific," she murmured. "I am glad Vran'el is the one providing legal advice to me and not you. You would probably make me incriminate myself enough to be kept here over the next decade." She narrowed her eyes at him when he didn't reply. "I see you don't deny it."

He shrugged. "Why would I? It is true enough."

"What about not aiding others in harming me? Was that just yesterday?"

"I would consider locking you in a dungeon harming you, not keeping you here in general. You could stay here quite comfortably, for instance, under my continued guardianship for a few years," he said mildly.

She narrowed her eyes to determine whether he was jesting with her or really meant that seriously, yet she was not entirely sure. "For your own sake I hope that this was a misguided attempt at making fun of me."

"If that makes you any happier, please do."

She got up and folded her arms. "Are you one of the representatives of the Houses who will cast their vote on what is going to happen to me?"

"I am, yes," he replied with a complacent smile she did not at all find reassuring.

"Is there a way for me to get you kicked out of the senate for the duration of the proceedings? For being biased against me?"

He chuckled. "If there were it would be foolish of me to tell you, would it not? But let me assure you that my bias is never against you, but in your favour."

"In my favour as in respecting my wishes or as in doing what you think is best for me?" she enquired testily.

He shook his head in amusement. "I am afraid you would not like to hear my answer to that on an empty stomach, my dear Theá."

She swallowed and looked at him incredulously. "So you really intend to vote for keeping me here? Away from my friends, my work, my home? No matter how unhappy that would make me?"

He stepped forward, placing his hands on her shoulders when she attempted to step back. "You have family here. And you have made friends here already. As for your work, you could learn and accomplish so much more here than back in Anyueel, benefiting from knowledge and progress here. And I would give you a home, Theá. A very nice one, even if I say so myself."

She pushed away his hands and pointed to the door. "I would like to get dressed now if you don't mind. Or is that so risky an endeavour that you feel you need to insist on supervising me?"

He nodded slowly. "Very well. But just one little thing before I step outside: ask yourself why Enric was not on your list of things you would leave behind among friends, work and home."

She stared at him when he closed the door behind him to give her privacy. He was right, she had not mentioned Enric. Because the thought of losing him due to being made to remain here was unbearable. Because she knew that he would not leave her behind like that, didn't she?

He was leaning against the wall opposite her door when she stepped out fully dressed.

"So? Have you found an answer to that, my dear?"

She smiled thinly. "None *you* would wish to hear on an empty stomach."

Vran'el stepped out from another corridor, yawning expressively. He smiled when he saw her.

"Good morning, sweetness. I was on my way to wake you, but I see your eager guardian was faster than I."

He preceded them to the cushions where one large bowl of fruit and four smaller bowls had been prepared by a servant.

Eryn sat and looked at the food doubtfully. Her tense stomach was not in any shape to react well to being made to work.

Valrad stepped in from the terrace door.

"Good morning to everyone," he said cheerfully. "Eryn, the food is not meant to be stared into submission, but eaten. I understand that you are very probably not too thrilled at the notion of eating, but you will need your strength today. And the fruit contains sugar, which is what the brain needs to work properly."

"Excellent," she murmured and took a bowl to fill it. "Patronising homilies and a lecture on health in one compact morning package." She flashed Ram'an, who had sat down next to her, an annoyed glance. "But I should probably be more careful of what I say to you, or I might create another senator around who votes against me. Or conceivably, being as great a nuisance as I can will better coax you into making sure I am sent home again."

Valrad looked at the two of them alternately. "It seems you did not have a very good start to the day, my dear girl. But considering Ram'an's efforts at urging you away from Enric, it cannot come as such a great surprise that he would take this opportunity to keep you here, can it?" he asked in his usual calm manner.

Eryn looked at him with a raised eyebrow. "Sometimes your equanimity is really trying, uncle. You could at least *try* to be indignant on my behalf. Would that tax you?"

He shrugged and took a bowl. "It might do in the long run, yes. Increased heart rate and production of stress-inducing substances..."

"Right, that's what you get for talking to a healer," she sighed.

Vran'el smiled. "Tell *me*. I live with two of them. Whenever I eat something containing too much sugar or fat for their liking, I am treated to a litany of illnesses that might soon befall me unless I mend my ways. When there is a day I am not feeling so good, they instantly agree that I am the only one to blame for it, as my lifestyle cannot result in anything other than pain and illness."

Valrad rolled his eyes. "My poor, long-suffering son. Then you should probably thank your cousin for bringing another lawyer to our house as they are known to be such pleasant company."

Eryn stared at him in mock astonishment. "Dear me, was that actual sarcasm from *you*?"

"What can I say? You seem to have been a bad influence on me," he smiled.

"After living with Vran'el and Pe'tala for such a long time, I seriously doubt that a few weeks with me could have done that to you," she grinned.

Her uncle winked at her. "Ah, but is it not the dose that does the trick?"

"That would make *me* the overdose, then, would it? How delightful," she sniffed and put her now empty bowl aside. "Do you know how many Houses have signed trade agreements with Enric and Kilan?" she asked.

Valrad nodded. "Eight out of twelve. Two others refused to accept the terms and conditions and the remaining two have decided not to do any business with the foreign barbarians."

She turned to Ram'an. "Where does House Arbil stand?"

He grimaced. "I am afraid my father is one of the two Houses refusing to consider trade with the Old Kingdom. But at least this will not put me in the dilemma of choosing between causing a disadvantage to my House or voting to keep you here."

"So you see that your father's course of action is not good for your House? But from what I was told you could take over his position as Head anytime! Why don't you do so?" she urged.

He looked at her in surprise as if this was obvious. "Because of you, of course. I would give up my claim on you if I succeeded my father as you are the only heiress to House Aren and cannot be joined with another Head of a House."

She had known this, of course, but hearing him confirm it in such a matter-of-fact way was unnerving. Taking his hands into hers, she leaned forward, looking into his dark eyes.

"Ram'an, I want you to listen very carefully to what I am telling you now," she insisted.

"Of course, my dear - I always hang on your every word," he smiled, squeezing her hands.

"I am not worth a sacrifice of that magnitude. Give up any childish claims on what you consider your rights due to some agreement our parents made and find yourself a pleasant woman who melts into your arms," she implored.

His smile became indulgent. "I thank you for your advice, my dear. Only I am afraid it is not as straightforward as that."

She stared at him. "It's not?"

"No. The problem here, you see, is that I am in love with you. Very much in love."

She took a deep breath and forced herself to remain in control. "No, you are not," she explained patiently as if talking to an infant. "You have had a lot of time to make yourself believe that, but it is no more than an illusion, it is wishful thinking. I am very sure that I would never manage to match that picture of me you have created over these last two decades and that you would be very disappointed at being stuck with me."

He shook his head and lifted one of her hands to his lips. "No, Theá, I am afraid you are the one who suffers from a misconception here. My being in love with you is not a matter of creating a perfect image of you in my mind, but a result of meeting you in person back in Anyueel. Believe me, I had not been prepared for it, either. And if I had had any choice in the matter, I would have preferred not to have had any feelings of that kind for you - a woman in a relationship with another man - but to have returned here and entered into a commitment with your cousin. Yet what cruel fate would it be for a woman to be bound to a man who is deeply attached to another?"

Valrad nodded slowly. "Indeed," he murmured. "Though being discarded for somebody else is not a pleasant circumstance, either."

Ram'an sighed. "I know. And I am sorry for it. But as her father I think that you would wish your daughter to be committed to somebody who appreciates her the way she deserves instead of a companion who longs for another woman. I am convinced this was the lesser evil for her." He paused for a moment as if looking for the right words. "I know it cannot be easy for you to have me here under your roof while your own daughter has fled somewhere else because of my position. I thank you for the courtesy that you have shown me so far. I would not have blamed you for being less civil."

"You have never been an unkind man, Ram'an," Valrad sighed, "but circumstances have not been in favour of joining our Houses. I do not wish you anything bad and seeing that you are as unlucky in your attachment as my daughter in hers does not make me feel any better."

Vran'el smiled without humour. "So you are saying you do not deserve my sister. But you are convinced that you deserve my cousin?"

Ram'an looked back at Eryn. "If I am not the man to deserve you right now, Theá, I would dedicate my life to becoming that man."

She felt her chest tighten and pulled her trembling hands from his grip, shaking her head at him with an unhappy expression. Why did people think that declarations of love were generally a good thing, she wondered. Whenever Enric expressed his feelings, she felt fear rising inside her and she needed to stop him, terrified that he would say that one thing to her that she would choke on if she had to reciprocate in words, even though he was the one man she wanted to feel like this for her. In Ram'an's case it was at the same time less frightening as he knew that she did not reciprocate his feelings, but on the other hand so very frustrating as he kept forcing her to push him back and hurt him for feeling something he couldn't help.

"Let us not talk about this any longer, Theá," Ram'an said gently. "I am sorry that my admiring you the way I do upsets you. It should not. Try to consider it as a gift, even though you might not feel at the moment that you can return my feelings for you."

Valrad nodded in agreement. "Considering that you need to face Malriel in less than one hour, I will second that. It was not a very good choice to bring it up at this particular time anyway, but that cannot be helped now." He stood. "Come. We cannot be late for the hearing. It would cast a bad light on Eryn and aid Malriel."

* * *

Eryn entered the great senate hall behind Ram'an. He had held her hand all the way here and she started to wonder whether her being shackled in gold would not have been easier on both of them. But it would send the wrong message as the King back home would certainly hear of it.

Ram'an led her to the first row of seats and motioned for her to sit between him and Vran'el. She let her gaze wander over the other seats, which were arranged in semi-circles, to see if she could spot Enric somewhere. She wondered if Golir would insist on keeping him as close as Ram'an kept her. Probably not. Her own guard very likely delighted in carrying out his duties so diligently because it served his own ends as well.

She caught a glimpse of a fair head of hair between the senators standing around talking to each other. She saw Enric stop in front of a seat in the last row where Golir said a few words to him, although she was too far away to catch their content. Then the triarch left his charge to approach his own seat of office on the podium.

Enric did not have to scan the room for her, his look was drawn to her immediately. He smiled at her reassuringly and took his seat, knowing better than to approach her without having Golir at his side. She looked somewhat shaken, he noted, and wondered if she had been able to rest at least a little last night. He hoped that her uncle's words had managed to keep the guilt brewing inside her at bay, or maybe even diminish it a little. He wondered who had woken her in the morning and how she had experienced waking up without him beside her for the first time since her expedition a few months ago.

He looked to the door when Malriel entered. She looked different - a little older. He studied her features for a few moments. She had added a few wrinkles here and there, so the effect was not unintentional. While she had until now appeared not much older than himself, she had chosen to alter her facial features in a way to reflect an age closer to her real one and appeared about ten years older than Enric now. He calculated quickly. According to what she had told them at their first dinner together, she had conceived Eryn when she had been twenty-one years of age, so she had to be forty-nine now.

Remarkably, she had not lost any of her feminine appeal by adding a few years, but looked more sincere and credible - which was doubtlessly the impression she intended to create. She smiled faintly when she passed him, seemingly unperturbed by the resentful look he gave her.

Eryn stared at her mother open-mouthed and only reigned in her facial features when Vran'el's foot trod heavily on her toes. She muffled a curse and healed the pain away before leaning closer to him.

"What has she done?"

"For a change, she has made herself look like she could actually be your mother instead your older sister. She hopes to appear more trustworthy, I would think," he whispered back.

"Will it work?" she asked, unable to take her eyes off Malriel. The change was not extreme as such, she had perhaps added seven years, but from one day to the next the transformation was still astounding enough.

Vran'el thought for a moment, then sighed. "I really cannot tell. With some of the senators maybe; with those who know her well and have fought at her side or against her probably not."

Another thought occurred to her. "Can I get rid of Ram'an somehow?"

Her cousin frowned. "Of course you cannot. He has been appointed your guardian. You cannot just have him exchanged because he is not to your liking. It would in effect defeat the purpose of guarding you in the first place."

"I meant that I want to have his right to vote in this matter taken away from him," she rolled her eyes.

"You are aware that I can hear you, are you not?" Ram'an said dryly from her right side.

"Also you are aware that this is a conversation between myself and my legal advisor, so I would kindly ask you not to interfere if you can't manage not to eavesdrop," she growled at him. She then turned back to Vran'el. "He is clearly biased as his priority is not justice, but pursuing his own interests. You and Valrad have witnessed him admit it. This should count for something, shouldn't it?"

Vran'el grimaced and shook his head. "Hardly. My word as your counsellor would not count for much, and neither would your uncle's. One could argue that we are biased as well, though in your favour."

Ram'an's smile was relaxed. "This is *exactly* what one, namely me, would argue."

"So I depend on not enough Houses supporting Malriel? Just marvellous," she grumbled testily.

"It is not only the Houses that will be voting, but also the triarchs," Vran'el explained. "Their votes each count for two senator's votes, so they will very likely tip the scale. We may safely count on Abrak voting in Malriel's favour, but with the other two it is hard to tell."

She watched the other senators walking to their seats and soon after the noise level died down to no more than an occasional whisper every now and then. When Torke'na on the podium cleared her throat, even that subsided.

"Let us commence, senators. I herewith call upon Malriel, Head of House Aren and senator for House Aren, to present her case against Malthea of House Aren. We will first listen to her and then you are invited to present your questions," she stated and nodded to Malriel, who stepped before the assembled senators and triarchs to speak.

"Colleagues," she started and interlaced her fingers before her. "All of you know my own and my daughter's tale, how my companion Ved'al took her away from me so many years ago and that I laid eyes on her after so many years only a few weeks ago." She sighed and closed her eyes, causing Eryn to narrow her eyes at the obvious display of well-dosed emotions. Obvious to her, at least. She hoped that the others around her remembered who they were currently listening to and would thus not fall for this performance, not matter how convincingly it was carried out.

"Believe me when I tell you that standing before you today to have Maltheá justify her actions from several years ago pains me in extremity." She looked over at her daughter, who stared at her coldly, arms folded. "Maltheá," she continued, "told me herself of the true circumstances surrounding Ved'al's death and her part in them only two days ago, and her narrative closed one or two gaps in the reports I received from the search parties." She motioned to a thick file on the table to her side before she continued. "Let me impart to you what really happened when Ved'al lost his life so you may decide if Maltheá is to be held accountable for her part in it."

It was completely hushed in the room as she commenced her tale about how Ved'al had moved through the Old Kingdom for a few years with their daughter, successfully eluding discovery through the locals and the search parties that must have got quite close to him time and again. She continued with how he had taken on the name of Treban and settled in the village where Eryn would spend the next seventeen years of her life, talking of how he had made himself a name as a healer, and trained his daughter in the craft in the years which followed.

Then she came to talk about the evening when Eryn had returned from collecting the roots her father had sent her to get and how the village baker's son had almost succeeded in overpowering her but for the intervention of Ved'al, who had broken the boy's arm in the process.

Eryn closed her eyes, unnerved by the eerie situation of hearing her own story, the secret that she had kept for what seemed now like eternity, retold by another person. By Malriel. She felt a warm hand closing over her own on her right thigh and squeezed it back gratefully. For the moment she would simply pretend it was Enric's instead of Ram'an's.

Malriel proceeded with recounting how Eryn had provoked Krion into touching her so she could use her healing skills to deplete the bone in his arm enough for it to break a short time after that. Her voice was calm, her features collected as she spoke of how the baker had assumed that Ved'al must have had something to do with his son's injury as nobody had really been sure of the extent of the healer's skills. She paused for effect before continuing with how the healer had ended up with a knife thrust in his back and how the baker had in turn been lynched by the villagers as punishment for his deed.

When it was clear that she was finished with her story, Torke'na straightened and addressed the senators.

"You may now pose your questions."

Nobody said anything for a while, then a male voice asked, "Why would you accuse your own daughter, Malriel? What do you hope to accomplish, I wonder? It does seem rather heartless, even for you."

Eryn turned curiously. That did sound like a potential ally.

"Who is that?" she whispered to Vran'el. "He looks familiar."

"Uvel, Head of House Tokmar. You met him on your second evening here at the dinner."

"Not a great friend of Malriel's?"

Her cousin shook his head. "Not exactly."

They returned their attention to the figure in front of them. Malriel cast a cool look in Uvel's direction.

"The law is the law, Uvel. If the Heads of the Houses do not abide by it, how can we expect others to?" she replied.

"Pretty words. But even though I suppose that all of us here would wish to appear law-abiding, most would not go as far as incriminating our own children," Uvel returned mildly.

"As you are surely aware, Maltheá is the heiress to my House. I do not want this to catch up with her one day when she is about to take my place; it is better to take care of it now. I do not believe that House Aren has the reputation of shirking or stalling conflicts."

"No," the man smiled thinly, "that is true enough."

"I would like to hear Maltheá's confirmation as to the truth of this tale," another voice said.

"Legara of House Finran," Vran'el whispered unbidden. "*She* does happen to be a friend of Malriel's, unfortunately."

"Maltheá, is there anything about your mother's story you would wish to challenge?" Abrak asked from the podium.

Eryn nervously looked at her counsellor who slowly shook his head.

"No, not at this point," she replied quietly.

"Are there any other questions?" Torke'na asked.

All eyes turned when Enric got to his feet. "I am aware that I am not a member of your senate and thus not as such entitled to address questions to Malriel on this occasion, but as I have a vested interest in the outcome of these proceedings I nevertheless kindly ask you to grant me that privilege," he said formally.

Torke'na nodded. "Unless there are any objections from the senators, I will grant it."

Enric glanced around to see if anybody wanted to protest and when nobody did, he looked at Malriel.

"What punishment would you presume appropriate for your daughter's actions?"

"I will ask the senate to keep Malthéa under observation here in Takhan in a private house for a period of two years," she replied.

"This does rather look like you are trying to prevent your daughter from leaving you again so soon after the reunion between you," another senator commented.

"Amgil of House Roal," Vran'el supplied.

"Roal?" Eryn asked quietly. "The one Sarol belongs to, the one which does not get along with House Aren? So I suppose I may expect to have his vote, too?"

"That is very likely, yes," her cousin confirmed. "And it is a good thing that this particular statement did not come from Enric, but somebody else."

"How old exactly was Malthéa when she used her healing skills in the manner described?" Uvel of House Tokmar enquired.

"Fifteen years old," Malriel replied and added, "mature enough to be held accountable to a certain degree, but not fully."

"Then old enough to keep her here for you to see her whenever you want to, but still too young for a block of powers or being put in a dungeon," Uvel smirked. "This seems very convenient. It makes me wonder if we would be here today if she had been older - say twenty years old - and thus subject to a markedly more severe punishment."

"Try to limit your efforts at analysing to the case under consideration instead of speculations about what might have been," Torke'na warned him. "Malriel's motives are at the moment not what is of interest, only whether her claims are justified." She then waited for a few moments before she went on, "If there are no more questions for now, this hearing is adjourned. We will convene here again in three days. Any questions that arise in the meantime will be dealt with at the beginning of our next hearing, in the course of which you will also hear what Malthéa of House Aren has to answer in the matter."

The senators waited until the triarchs had risen and stepped down from their seats at the podium before stirring.

"Two years!" Eryn groaned when the noise level in the senate hall had risen. "She wants to detain me here for that long? What for?"

"To reconnect with you, I would assume," Ram'an supplied.

Eryn shivered and pulled her hand away from under his. When he left his own lying on her thigh, she looked pointedly at him.

"That is overly friendly, if you don't mind," she said and then roughly pushed his hand off when he merely smiled. "You are going to stumble into Enric's fist again one of these days if you go on like that," she murmured.

"Not as long as Golir is there to keep him reigned in. It would not look good for him to be seen as being too lenient on his charge," Ram'an remarked soberly.

"Something you clearly enjoy taking advantage of," Vran'el commented acerbically. "Twofold, in fact. I do not see *you* hesitate when it comes to reining in your own charge, whether it seems necessary or not."

"What can I say?" Ram'an smiled unabashedly, "I am very diligent in the execution of my duties."

Eryn didn't reply but watched Golir and Enric leaving the senate building through one of the three doors. Only when they were out of sight, did Ram'an take her hand and pull her up as well.

She drew in a sharp breath when Malriel stepped in her way, hands lifted placatingly in front of her.

"Theá, I want you to know that I am not doing this because I am convinced your father's death was your fault," she said in a low voice, yet still with urgency.

"And I want you to know, *mother*," she menaced the final word, "that, looking at you now, I feel the urge for another Aren clash rise inside me. Unless you want my next bolt of magic or my fist to meet its target this time, you had better get out of my way."

"Behave, my dear," Ram'an warned her mildly. "I will not be seen to be letting you get away with that a second time. It would not look good for me."

"And it would not help your own case either, sweetness," Vran'el threw in and added dryly, "Although I suggest that this would obviously be no major hindrance for your ardent admirer here."

Eryn looked serious and then turned towards the door. "Well, then let's leave if I can't hit her. Would a nervous breakdown with lots of tears do me any good?"

Vran'el grimaced. "Not really, no. It would look like an admission of guilt. Be superior, confident and unperturbed. Pretend you are Enric."

"Thank you for that last bit," she growled and all but pulled Ram'an along with her as she approached the closest exit.

* * *

Eryn frowned when Ram'an took a seat on the cushions right beside her.

"I think your remaining that close to me when we are in this house without any visitors present is a bit overzealous," she pointed out when he put his arm around her shoulders.

He shrugged. "Just to get you used to it, my dear."

"How very unselfish of you," she jibed and rose to take a seat opposite him. She stopped abruptly when she saw the faint shimmering of a barrier in front of her and turned to look down at him incredulously. "Really? That's how desperate you are?"

He took her hand and pulled her down next to him again, pretending to consider her question for a few moments.

"So it would seem, yes."

Valrad and his son entered the main room, carrying lunch and bowls to the low table.

"Ram'an, you know better than to beleaguer a woman like that," her uncle sighed.

He smiled. "Do I? From what I gather this is how Enric managed to get her to give in to him. It might also work for me now that I have the chance of spending some quality time with her."

She swatted his fingers away when he began playing with a strand of her hair.

"Stop that now or you will find yourself picking bits of hot food from your lap," she growled.

"You would not do that," he retorted casually, "it would show great disregard for the meal your uncle prepared for us."

She considered the dish her cousin pressed into her hand for a moment and then nodded reluctantly. Yes, some way to express contempt for no one but Ram'an would surely be the better course of action, she mused. And she had to do something soon, because his touches and advances were becoming more and more frequent and intimate. He was superior in both physical and magical strength, but there was a slight chance she could outwit him if she was quick. She would have to think of something.

"The hearing did not go too badly, did it?" she asked her cousin. "I had the impression that a few of the senators were a little sceptical of Malriel's motives."

Vran'el swallowed a mouthful of food, then sighed. "That may be true, but I am afraid I have to open your eyes to the cruel reality: It will not really matter whether or not the senators think that you are to blame. This is about politics and nothing more. What we need to accomplish is collecting the required number of votes to win this. Malriel has Houses Arbil, Finran and Ordel on her side, and Houses Turbar, Partém and Ulverd will vote for whoever Ram'an asks them to. Then there is Triarch Abrak whose vote will be in her favour as well. That makes eight out of seventeen votes in her favour already. We do not know where the other two triarchs stand. She needs only one more vote to win the case and keep you here."

Eryn stared at him. "Then what I am going to say at the next hearing will not make any difference? None at all? I could go there naked and gyrate in front of them all, the outcome would be the same?"

"Well, that might be a little counterproductive, as those who are generally against Malriel might reconsider detaining you here for mere reasons of entertainment," Vran'el remarked dryly with a raised brow. "For the senators it will not make much of a difference, you are right. But there are still two triarchs left. Golir belongs to House Partém, but he is not especially thrilled about the affair between his nephew and Malriel. And he is spending a lot of time with Enric right now, something which might induce him to vote in your favour. With Torke'na it is hard to tell. Her House is neither allied to nor at odds with House Aren, so anything is possible."

"But didn't you say that the Houses which signed trade agreements are likely to vote for me to be sent back home again as the arrangements might not otherwise become effective?" she asked.

"That is not something we can safely depend on. While the trade agreements with the Old Kingdom are a positive thing for most of the Houses, losing the favour of a powerful local House like Aren would be a high price to pay for such an opportunity. It might be possible in cases where the Houses are allied with the Arbil family, though," Vran'el added as an afterthought.

"I take offence at that," Ram'an frowned.

"You should not," her cousin smiled without humour. "Your House's status and influence have declined ever since your father took over position as Head. If you had been less determined to ignore the needs of your family in favour of running after a woman you cannot win, that might have been different now. You have no one else to blame for it but yourself, and certainly not those people who dare telling it to your face."

Eryn was surprised to see that this seemed to have silenced Ram'an. So this was clearly a sore spot. She saw a mix of guilt and torment from his features - by his frown and lips pressed tightly together.

"Why wasn't I born into House Vel'kim?" Eryn sighed, deliberately steering the topic away from Ram'an's family and what her cousin considered the negligence of his duties. "This would surely have made things a lot easier. My association with House Aren has turned out to be quite a burden."

Ram'an slowly turned to her, regarding her for a while until she shifted uneasily.

"What? Do I have something between my teeth or on my nose? Why are you looking at me like that?"

"You could always renounce House Aren," he said deliberately.

She gaped at him in surprise, as if rocked by a revelation. "I could?" Then she looked at her cousin. "You said something like that a while ago, didn't you? You advised me against it, but it was more of a jibe back then." She held her half-full bowl in one hand and stared into the distance while pondering Ram'an's words.

"Eryn," Vran'el said urgently, "that would not be a very smart move right now."

She looked at him, displeased about his trying to dissuade her of what sounded like a quite ideal course of action.

"Why not?"

"Because the Houses standing against House Aren may not be as keen on voting in your favour any more if they cannot hurt Malriel with it. And if you renounced her House right now, that would be what happened, as she would be losing you anyway. Moreover, if she manages to win this case and keep you here, you will need the protection of a House if you are to stay here as a stranger for two entire years," he pointed out emphatically.

She groaned and put the bowl down on the table. "So the only way of my being able to sever the connection to her and her House is to first win this farce?"

"Yes. If you are permitted to leave here again soon, it does not make a great difference whether you are a member of a House here or not. And maybe that is not such a bad idea, after all. If you no longer belong to her House, she has no more claim to call upon you as the heiress of her House," Vran'el mused.

Eryn's eyes had begun to gleam and she leaned forward. "Alright. How do we win this thing? I want her out of my life. Is there anybody I can bribe, blackmail or otherwise convince to vote for me?"

"There is me, for example," Ram'an chimed in and smiled when she stared at him in confusion.

"What do you mean, there is you? You left no doubt whatsoever that you will vote against me! Why would you suddenly change your mind?"

Vran'el narrowed his eyes. "Because if you renounce House Aren, he can have both. He could have you *and* become Head of House Arbil. And in addition to that, any children you would have would belong to his House instead of Aren and thereby secure the succession at House Arbil."

She shook her head and turned to Ram'an. "But you can't have me, no matter if I belong to House Aren or not! How can an otherwise smart person be that stupid when it comes to comprehending such a simple fact as that?"

"Yes, that is what makes me wonder as well," her cousin agreed, considering the other man thoughtfully. "Why ever would you be that confident that you can make Eryn stay here with you when being cleared of the charges would allow her to return to Anyueel?"

Ram'an shrugged. "I have every hope that after spending some more time with me she will finally realise that she is with the wrong man and correct her error."

Eryn lifted her eyebrow at his comment. "That is quite some audacity you display here. But if it makes you vote against Malriel, I am more than willing to let you lie to yourself."

He smiled indulgently. "I did not say that I would vote in your favour, just that I might be open to your attempts at bribing me. Make me an offer, my dear. Do not bother with anything Lord Enric could buy." His gaze wandered from her eyes to her mouth and stayed there. "Make it personal."

"I am not going to kiss you," she explained calmly.

He sneered. "I am talking about offering you your freedom and you think I would be content with no more than a kiss? It seems I am not the only one with a claim to audacity here. Kissing, my dearest Theá, would only be an opener."

Why even get worked up over a statement like that anymore? She simply gave him an angry look and leaned back.

"Bold words from a man who demanded a shipload full of goods for granting two people in distress an embrace," Vran'el threw in. "Too bad he accepted and thus made you look like a greedy opportunist. Remind me why you think you are the better choice for her."

"Which other senators can I try to convince to vote for me?" Eryn insisted.

"None. I am your best chance. One night with me, Theá. Think about it. It would not only be my vote, but those of three more Houses you would obtain into the bargain," Ram'an proposed.

She breathed in and out once before replying calmly, "What makes you think that I will ever agree to a thing like that when I could not even bear to let you kiss me?"

"I admit that is something you have on that point," he nodded. "Make me another offer, then."

"I will have Enric agree to another round of negotiations for House Arbil after you have taken over the House to make up for the chance your father missed."

He thought for a moment, then shook his head. "That is very generous of you, but I asked you to make it personal."

"I am not going to do anything with or for you that will encourage you in your misapprehension that you and I are, or will ever be, destined to be together," she explained patiently.

He nodded. "That is very considerate of you, my dear Theá, but let me assure you that my misapprehension, as you like to term it, does not depend on your encouragement."

She narrowed her eyes. "Yes, I did get the impression that reality does not have much of an influence on your perception."

"My sweet Theá, your wit is exceeded only by your beauty," he said.

Vran'el rolled his eyes while Eryn grimaced. "You are either making fun of me, which is something I do not appreciate, or you are being completely serious, which disturbs me greatly. I honestly can't say which of the two I prefer."

"You will get to know me well enough to distinguish my meaning in time," Ram'an smiled with unwarranted confidence.

She sighed and leaned back. "You really are a persistent person, I have to grant you that."

"I am, yes. You know, I am still waiting for you to make me an offer that will induce me to aid you in your current legal problem."

Valrad looked at him reflectively and pursed his lips. "I really wonder why you are *that* confident that you will not lose her by helping her. It worries me. I cannot help but believe there is something you know that we are not aware of." He shook his head. "Eryn, I would advise you to be very careful here."

"So I should not try to persuade him to vote for me?" she frowned. "Look, I have no intention of being stuck here for two years!"

Her uncle rubbed his face. "I know. I am not saying you should not take the chance, just be careful not to agree to anything that would lead to your somehow unintentionally assisting him in reaching his goal of holding you here. If you agreed to spending the night with him, you would very likely drive Enric away or at least cause severe damage to your relationship."

She snorted. "That is putting it mildly. He would kill Ram'an and leave me here without another word."

"Apart from the detail where I lose my life I rather like that scenario," Ram'an nodded.

"It is only available as the combined package," she retorted with a glare at him.

"Alright, then we will try something else. As you keep avoiding making me an offer, let me propose something. I offer you my vote and those of my allies in exchange for a certain kind of dance with you."

"Surely not!" she exclaimed. "This would just end up with Enric badly beating you up which would lose us another few votes!"

Ram'an considered for a while and then looked at her. "Then how about dinner? An intimate one, just you and I. At my home."

She pondered that suggestion. It was the most innocuous one he had brought up so far.

"Exactly how intimate would that dinner be?" she enquired, her words deliberated.

"Nothing that might be framed as your being unfaithful to your current lover. Unless you wished to, of course," he added suggestively.

"You refer to my *companion*, I think," she pointed out.

"Not from where I am standing, my dear," he retorted, unruffled.

"No touching?"

"That, Theá, would not be *intimate* at all. Of course I would touch you. I intend to do so a lot, in fact. And you would refrain from resisting, just for a change. Though I promise that I would keep my hands to the socially acceptable regions of your body," he stated.

"No kissing, then," she insisted. "About that I am absolutely adamant."

"Not even on your cheek?" he asked, looking expectant. "I used to greet you by kissing you on the cheek, so that limitation does seem rather irregular."

"Take it or leave it," she replied and folded her arms as standoffishly as she could.

He nodded. "Then I will take it. Dinner it is, then. I expect you to dress nicely, just as you would for a dinner with Lord Enric. Something stylish and clinging."

She looked at him in displeasure. "Enric would never ask me to dress up for a dinner with him. He knows how much I hate doing so."

"Then I should consider your doing it for me as a special privilege. Make sure to pin up your hair. I enjoy looking at your neck."

She clenched her teeth and nodded. "Is that all?"

He thought for a moment. "Yes, it is. Be ready at sunset."

"Today? So soon?" she asked, startled. "I need to talk to Enric first."

"You will do no such thing, my dear Theá," he said and shook his head. "This is between the two of us; he has no part in it. He would only try to prevent you."

"I certainly will not do this behind his back!" she protested.

"You have no other choice. As I have no intention of letting you meet him, you will have to inform him of our little tryst afterwards."

"I am not happy about that," Valrad scowled. "I did not think that I would ever see you resorting to such measures as this, Ram'an. Eryn has agreed to your terms, so you might at least grant her a meeting with Enric."

"No. His reaction would not be a favourable one and I have no wish to let him punch me again." Ram'an shook his head determinedly.

Eryn folded her arms and bit her tongue to hold back the profanities she wanted to hurl at him. Hitting him would be such sweet delight right now. But without taking away his powers this was no more than wishful thinking. Why were there never any golden shackles handy when she needed some?

She caught her own thoughts. Or a golden belt! Just like the one Vran'el had given them a few weeks ago, the one she had packed among her belongings. It had to be in one of the chests in her room here. She measured her exhalation, careful not to give away any sign of excitement. She *would* see Enric, whether Ram'an approved or not. It was time to show him what it was like to be pushed around, locked up and treated as a child.

CHAPTER 46

Dinner with Ram'an

Eryn rose wordlessly from the cushions to walk back into her room, trying to recall which one of the four chests the belt had to be in.

"Where are you going?" Ram'an called after her.

"To my room to select a damn dress for some compulsory romantic evening with a man who is too stubborn to recognise a lost cause when it is right before his face," she cast over her shoulder without stopping.

"Let me help you. I am the one who has to approve of it, after all."

She gulped when she heard his steps behind her. This was not going to make it easy. She needed the belt hidden and ready in one hand. That would hardly be possible if he were present while she was looking for it. She stopped abruptly and felt him bump into her from behind.

"I can see that you are eager enough to return to my bedroom, but I would very much like to have a few minutes to myself, unless you can't handle not supervising me for even that long. I will call you in to pick a dress when I have narrowed down the choice." She didn't turn and waited for him to either insist on accompanying her or leave her alone.

"So be it," she heard his amused voice behind her. "Though you have to understand that I shall insist on placing a shield on your door and windows as long as you remain in there alone."

"Do what you must," she murmured and opened the door to the room to let him place a barrier in front of the windows. Then she stepped inside and waited for him to add another one that blocked the door frame before she closed the door in his face.

She listened until the sound of his steps had receded and then opened the first chest for a quick search. She found a dress that would probably qualify and threw it onto the bed and another one at the bottom, but no belt. She had progressed, elbow-deep with her hands in the second chest, when she felt the familiar outline of the belt with her fingers. Her lips twisted into a lopsided smile and she pulled it out to look at it. It gleamed in the sunlight when she held it up. Too bright, she thought, and looked around for some piece of fabric to disguise it so Ram'an would not spot it prematurely. She would have to be very quick about it; a golden glint one moment too early would probably be the only warning he needed to fox her plan.

The trick would be to distract him for a short while, and the dresses were a good way to divert his attention away from her for a few precious moments. She just needed to be careful that he did not replace the shield at the door immediately after entering or she would be stuck in here with him. That would not be a lucky outcome.

Two dresses would make the decision too straightforward for him, so she pulled out another three to make sure he required more time for choosing one.

Where to place the belt until she was ready to use it? It would look suspicious if she stood close to him holding a long, thin item wrapped in fabric in her hand. She looked down at herself and decided to put it on herself and pull her tunic over it so it would remain out of sight until she could safely employ it.

She felt her heart beating in her throat and leaned against the wall to draw a few calming breaths. If this did not work, he would never be that careless or let her out of his sight again while the trial was in progress. On the other hand, he would keep her under his watchful eye all the more even if it *did* work.

She stepped towards the door and opened it, calling out for Ram'an, being careful not to touch the shield.

He appeared only moments later and she stepped aside for him to enter. He had removed the shield, she noted with satisfaction instead of simply stepping through it.

"I hope your educated taste will not find my small selection of elegant gowns wanting," she said in a haughty manner.

He smiled and stepped closer to the bed over which she had draped the garments. Her heartbeat quickened as she moved behind him. No hesitation - she urged herself on and fumbled to remove the belt from around her waist without any noises to alert him. When she held the belt in her hands in front of her she saw that he made to turn to her and hastily wrapped her arms with the belt around his waist.

He looked slightly surprised, then looked down at her hands with an amused expression which lasted only a moment, before she managed to connect the ends of the belt and make the seam disappear.

"What have you done?" he gasped when he realised what she had just accomplished. The look on his face was menacing and he grabbed her wrists roughly. "You remove that belt at once or there will be trouble!"

She shook her head and used a little magic to free her hands, then pushed him easily onto the bed, before she walked over to the unsecured doorway and stepped outside the room. When he jumped up again and attempted to follow her, she quickly raised a barrier that kept him confined inside the room.

"Maltheá!" he shouted when she started running down the corridor towards the main room and from there down the stairs to the exit.

Vran'el watched her with a frown and got to his feet to see where she was off to, but turned when he heard his name called.

"Vran'el!" Ram'an shouted a second time, his voice urgent. "Come here quickly!"

He ran to Eryn's room and goggled at the sight of Ram'an held behind a barrier, wearing a golden belt and looking furious.

"Get me out of here! Now! I need to stop her!"

Vran'el didn't take the time to laugh, jibe or argue. This was too serious. He shot a strong bolt at the shield, but it held.

"Father! Come here! And fast!"

They soon heard Valrad's steps and he, too, looked at the scene before him incredulously.

"Can you help me remove this shield?" Vran'el asked urgently. "Together we should be able to break it."

Valrad motioned for Ram'an to step aside and together with his son he aimed a strong strike at the magical barrier. It wavered slightly at the impact, though it needed a second bolt from each of them to make it falter and collapse.

"The belt," Ram'an ordered and Vran'el touched it briefly and made it fall off.

As soon as he regained his powers, he started running, infusing his muscles with magic to increase his speed.

* * *

Eryn scouted around. Her first step would be to get off the broad street; it was too exposed by far. It would probably not take Ram'an very long somehow to free himself from her little trap. When he came storming out of the house in pursuit, she had to be out of sight.

She ducked into the first smaller road that branched off and ran. It was noon, so not many people were around - something which was both a blessing and a problem. Disappearing into a crowd was easier than hiding in what appeared to be a mostly empty city at the moment, but not having to dodge passers-by meant that she could move faster.

Direction was no priority now, only gaining distance from the Vel'kim residence. She would have to ask for directions to the residence of House Partém later when she could be sure that she had shaken Ram'an off. Although he would probably guess where she was heading. This promised to become problematic.

"Eryn!" she heard a voice call from the street behind her and turned to look at Vran'el, who did not look particularly thrilled at having to follow her in this heat.

Damn, she thought. They had obviously found Ram'an very quickly. Too quickly. He had very probably shouted loudly enough for Ram'an to hear him if he was close enough. She increased her pace, glad that her cousin was no match for her, magically speaking. He would not be able to draw level with her.

"Stop! This is stupid and dangerous!" she heard him shout after her.

She cursed when she saw a large square appearing in front of her. It was too open here, with precious little cover. But turning around was not something she wanted, either. She quickly raised a strong shield for protection and started sprinting across the square, careful to hug the outline of the buildings to her left to have at least one side where no one could surprise her.

She heard a pair of feet with a rhythm different from Vran'el's approaching her from behind and to her right, also faster than Vran'el's. Not daring to look and hoping against hope that it was her uncle instead of Ram'an, she infused her muscles with as much magic as she could manage without weakening her protection.

When the steps behind her did not become any more distant, she knew that this was not her uncle but somebody at least her equal when it came to magical strength. Ram'an. She concentrated for a moment and increased the density of her barrier before splitting it in half to create a space empty of air inside the two layers. She felt her energy draining more quickly now, and her muscles started protesting when the magic that had driven them was redirected into the shield.

She heard a bolt of magic being swallowed by the outside of her shield. It did not reach the inside.

The steps behind her seemed to decrease in speed and she imagined Ram'an's incredulous face at his strike being held off by what he knew to be a weaker magician. But he seemed to recover fast because she soon heard his footsteps again and from the sound of it he was catching up with her quickly enough.

She felt the breath in her throat burn and looked for some path she could slip through and then block quickly to gain ground, but there was nothing in sight. Another bolt penetrated the outer shield and she turned a corner into a narrow side alley. The barrier in front of her appeared so suddenly that due to her momentum she had no chance avoiding it and hit it at full speed.

The blow to her forehead and nose made her stumble back several paces, dizzy and disoriented. She was about to collapse to the ground, when she felt arms wrap around her from behind, keeping her from falling.

Only now the pain in her face penetrated the shock and she gasped in agony when the hot, burning sensation in her nose almost made her double over. Something warm ran down her lip. She squeezed her eyes shut to brave the wave of anguish, too distracted by it to be able to put an end to it. There was no way to concentrate on healing as long as the ache was that powerful.

She felt herself being turned around and a moment later there was a wall in her back. A warm hand grabbed her neck firmly and she felt the pain inside her subside almost immediately. Stifling a sob of relief, she leaned against the warm stones behind her and slowly opened her eyes to find herself looking up into Ram'an's face, his features livid.

He removed his hand from her neck and pulled a piece of fabric out from the inside of his shirt, lifting it to her face. She turned her head away, irritated at his move to wipe her nose as if she were a small child.

Her muscles suddenly grew heavy, just like on that one day when he had made her come with him to the teahouse. She felt him clean away the blood and inspect her nose for any residual damage before putting the now blood-stained handkerchief back once he seemed satisfied with his healing efforts. Only then did he allow his fury to erupt.

"What do you think you are doing here?" he hissed. He grabbed her hair and pulled her head back to face him when she had managed to fight the heaviness in her muscles enough to slowly start turning her face away from him. "This would have looked very bad for both of us, you foolish, unthinking..." His voice trailed off when his eyes locked on her lips, which were half open owing to the downward pressure on her hair.

Panic rose inside her when he just stared at her mouth as if transfixed by the sight. They stood like this for several long seconds before he exhaled slowly. He was close enough for her to feel his breath on her lips.

"No," he murmured as if talking to himself, "not like this. The first kiss will be voluntary."

Her knees almost buckled with the relief she felt, but his arm around her kept her upright. His eyes narrowed and focus returned into them.

"Consider your rule about my not kissing you tonight suspended," he said. "Should you feel the need to object to this, let me warn you that my concession to touching you only in socially accepted areas will be the next to fall."

Her eyes widened and she did not dare make a move for fear he might interpret it as protest.

"A very interesting barrier you had there, by the way," he said, his tone clearly conveying that he was anything but happy about it. "I want you never to use it against me in the future."

She felt warmth seeping into her body through his palms, then her heavy muscles gave in completely as she sank into oblivion.

*   *   *

Enric glanced up from his book when somebody knocked at the door of the guest room he had been assigned.

"Come in," he called and Vran'el stepped in. He was about to greet the lawyer with a smile but instead looked concerned when he saw his visitor's serious expression. "What has happened?"

Vran'el closed the door before he said without a greeting, "One or two things you are not going to appreciate, I am afraid."

"Ram'an?" Enric asked simply, his eyes narrowed.

"Yes. He has agreed to vote for Eryn and make three allied senators do the same."

The blonde magician blinked in surprise. "That is unexpected. Why?"

"She plans to renounce House Aren in case she wins the trial, and that would enable him to have both her *and* the lead of House Arbil. He says he wants to use the time without your being around to make her see that she is with the wrong man and choose himself instead so that she will decide against returning with you," Vran'el explained.

Enric raised his eyebrow. "That shows a great deal of confidence considering that so far she hasn't left him in any doubt she is not interested in him. There must be more."

"That is what my father thinks, and I agree. Though I wonder what he could have in mind for compelling her to stay here. Blackmailing her? Yet with what? Harming you? Or me, or my father? Whatever else he may promise her would not impress her enough to abandon you." He shook his head, clearly at a loss.

"Are there any mind control techniques he might use on her?" Enric enquired.

"Mind control?" Vran'el looked at him, puzzled by the question. "You do have a very interesting concept of what we can do here."

"So it seems we have to wait for his next move to see what he is planning. Has he asked for something in return for the votes?"

Vran'el nodded. "Yes. I will spare you the first few *rewards* he proposed; I am sure you can imagine them well enough. What they finally agreed on was that Eryn is to have dinner with him tonight. Alone. At his residence. Dressed up. With his being allowed to touch, but not kiss her. Though I am not sure how strictly he will adhere to that last one after the stunt she pulled just now."

Enric closed his eyes. "Wait for one short moment, will you? You are telling me that he is very probably planning something devious by helping her win the trial and nobody is sure what exactly that could be. Then she is to be with him tonight for some kind of romantic dinner where he intends to have his hands all over her and that *there is more*?"

"There is, yes. She tried to come here to talk to you about whether to accept his condition for his votes or not, but he denied it. She did not want to do it behind your back, so she somehow managed to bind him with the golden belt I gave you, then lock him inside her room while she tried to run over here," Vran'el told him with a sympathetic expression. "Father and I freed him and then we went after her. I was too slow, but Ram'an caught up with her. When I reached them, he had already sent her to sleep and carried her back to the house. She had traces of blood on her cheek - he told me that he had raised a barrier to stop her and she had bumped into it and hurt her nose."

"She is hurt?" Enric jumped up and then controlled his fear when he reminded himself that she would already be well again with her uncle being a healer and two other men around her who also had basic skills in that area.

"No, not any more. Her nose was bleeding, but Ram'an healed that on the spot. It was only a minor thing, really. My father checked her over when we brought her back, and everything is alright with her. I promise."

"I told her not to provoke him," Enric growled and rubbed his palms over his face. "Why is there mayhem whenever she is out of my sight for more than a few hours? How is this possible? It is as if trouble is following her around, just waiting for me to look the other way!"

"Ram'an has written a note to Golir," Vran'el said carefully.

"To inform him of Eryn's attempt at running over to me? Why? It will look good neither for him in letting himself be tricked like that, nor for her."

"I think it was due to Eryn's using a barrier of some sort. One that is effective against stronger magicians. Ram'an has imparted that little detail to your guardian to warn him in case you intend to use it. He said that he did not write under what circumstances he learned of it."

Enric looked up at the ceiling. So she had not only given Ram'an a reason to cling to her even more closely, but also given away their secret of the special barrier. So much for that strategic advantage. But at least she had done it while trying to get to him for advice on how to deal with Ram'an.

"Is there a chance that Ram'an will permit me to see her if I can convince Golir to accompany me?"

Vran'el indicated negatively. "No, I am sure he will not today. He does not want to risk your spoiling his plans for the evening."

Enric nodded slowly. "I see. How is she doing in general, apart from being unconscious because she tried to run?"

"Well enough. I think that talking about the situation of her father's death was maybe not such a bad thing for her; she has been carrying that burden for a long time now without allowing anybody the chance to put things in perspective. And Ram'an at least maintains her anger, which distracts her from whatever else she might feel or think of." He crouched in front of Enric and put a hand on his shoulder. "You are not worried that she might be yielding to him, are you? From what I see she is not thrilled about his attentions. Not at all."

"That is hard to answer," the blonde magician sighed and tipped his head back, staring at the ceiling. "In this last year it has turned out that not only am I a slave to jealously, but am also surprisingly poor at dealing with it. I had to fight for her, and achieving the feat of bedding her turned out in hindsight to have been the easiest part. She is still not *completely* mine. I asked her to enter into a third level bond that evening at the Aren estate. She refused me." Enric paused, then added with a downcast look, "Now there is another man fighting for her, refusing to relent and using every advantage he can seize. The mere thought of his touching her makes me want to hurl him off a high building. Or a clifftop."

"But she does love you, does she not?" Vran'el enquired, with both eyebrows raised in question.

"I am fairly sure she does, yes. But she isn't aware of that yet. I am not even able to tell her that *I* love her, or it would scare her, which I can't afford right now with another man pursuing her so relentlessly. She needs to feel safe with me." He looked at his visitor. "Can I give you a message for her or will that get you into trouble?"

Vran'el winked at him. "I would not care, even if it did."

Enric smiled and squeezed his arm. "Thank you. I am glad you are there to keep an eye on Ram'an. I think I would be going spare here otherwise."

They both looked at the door when another knock came.

"Enter," Enric called once more and Golir opened the door, holding a piece of paper in one hand, which was no doubt Ram'an's message.

"So it is true," the triarch said and strolled in, considering Enric pensively. "I suspected that you might have had a trick or two up your sleeve. He took a seat on the bed and looked at the letter again, scanning it in search of a selected passage. "*A barrier that manages to withstand a stronger opponent's magical attack,*" he read out and returned his gaze to his house guest. "Show me."

Enric didn't waste any thoughts on pondering whether demonstrating the double barrier was wise or not. It was somewhat late for that and refusing would only give an impression of unwillingness to cooperate. He concentrated on creating a double-layer shield and nodded to Golir when it was ready. The triarch then slowly lifted his hand and shot a bolt from his palm at the barrier. He watched in fascination as his strike was swallowed up in no time and just disappeared without any apparent effect.

"Amazing. There will, of course, be dire consequences if you decide to use this barrier against me as long as I am your guardian. I hope I have made myself clear."

"Perfectly," Enric nodded. "I will only use it if I find myself in desperate straits already."

"I can only say I will have to trust your judgement on that," Golir replied. "I wonder how Ram'an found out about this. He did not give any particulars about the circumstances that induced Maltheá to demonstrate this ability. Her being of the Aren family, I would assume that they were probably not particularly amiable ones." He raised a questioning eyebrow at Vran'el. "Would you care to elaborate? I assume you are in the know."

Enric caught Vran'el's uncertain gaze and thought quickly. Refusing to tell the triarch might offend him and make him more likely to vote in Malriel's favour, but informing him of what had really happened would cast a bad light on Eryn for acting against the senate's orders. That, too, might induce Golir to vote against her.

He decided to take the chance that would make staying here not unnecessarily unpleasant and opted for honesty. He gave his visitor a curt nod to go on.

"You are right - a friendly situation it was not. She tried to outwit Ram'an so as to run here and discuss a proposal with Enric she was not sure whether to accept or not. When Ram'an refused permission for her to come here, she decided to try it anyway."

The triarch nodded. "I see. Of what nature is that proposal, if I may ask?"

"He wanted her to spend an evening with him at his residence, alone," Vran'el supplied.

"Has she agreed to that?"

"She has, yes."

Golir pursed his lips for a moment. "Then I assume, Enric, that you would appreciate spending the evening at the Vel'kim residence to await their return and be sure everything is in order."

Enric straightened in surprise. "I would appreciate that very much, yes."

Vran'el grinned broadly. "Then allow me to invite the two of you to dinner."

The older magician rose from his seat and nodded. "We shall be there at sunset."

Golir then nodded to both men and turned to leave the room. When the door had closed behind him, Enric got up to take a pen and paper from a small, exquisite-looking table to write to Eryn.

*   *   *

Eryn stirred, then groaned when she opened her eyes. She had pins and needles in her arm due to the angle it had been trapped at under her body for who knew how long. Pictures of herself hitting a magical barrier and being pressed against a wall by the furious Ram'an arose before her eyes and she lifted a hand to her nose. It did not feel any different, so he had obviously done a good job of healing it.

A long piece of fabric was draped on the bed next to her, and upon inspection it turned out to be one of the dresses she had laid out for him to choose from. He had chosen a dark red and black one with short sleeves. It would leave more of her skin exposed to his touch.

Judging from the quality of the light, there was not much time left before sunset, maybe one hour. This meant it was time to get up and dress. He had requested that she pin up her hair, she remembered, and wondered whether Vran'el would be assisting her there once again. Or would he consider it an act of betrayal towards Enric to help her prepare herself for another man?

She got out of bed and took the dress under one arm to take it with her to the bathroom. She would need to wash herself before getting into anything remotely clean after her chase through the city. A quick look into the mirror revealed tousled hair, smudges of dried blood on her chin and one cheek, and a patina of dust mixed with sweat that clung to her skin.

She opened the door and almost bumped into Ram'an's barrier.

"Ram'an?" she called out and leaned against the door frame. When she heard nothing for several seconds, she added, "Ram'an! Move on or I will be late for your dinner! Don't you dare go blaming me for that if you won't let me out of here!"

Only then did she hear steps approaching from the main room. Ram'an came into view, looking elegant in dark grey. He was obviously already done with dressing. She noted with relief that he did not show any residue of the anger from several hours before. He had either got over it, was hiding it really well or had decided to put it aside for the duration of the evening.

"You are awake. Good - I was about to wake you." He removed the barrier and followed her to the bathroom. She stepped aside to let him place a shield in front of the window and then closed the door behind her.

Somebody had prepared clean towels and a tub of water for her. She smiled and heated the water to the right temperature with a light touch of her fingers before stripping off her clothes and letting the warm water envelop her.

Her thoughts circled around Enric and what a huge shame it was that she had not at least managed to talk to him before Ram'an seized her. Would he have advised her against agreeing to this dinner? Would he have had another idea how to extricate her from this mess?

She wondered what staying here for two entire years without him would be like. Two years. That would be twice as long as she had known him so far. Would he want to wait that long for her? Did she expect him to? Would Ram'an continue his attempts at winning her with such determination during her detention here?

Then suddenly pictures of her father emerged unbidden and she clenched her teeth and closed her eyes. That was the trouble about not being pestered, chased, challenged or otherwise preoccupied: the mind had time to wander. She briefly considered pushing the images away, but decided against distracting herself. She let them come and accepted the wistfulness they brought.

She realised with surprise that something had changed about how she saw the incident that had led to Ved'al's death after telling it to the four men. Each of them had without hesitation acquitted her of any guilt in the matter - even Ram'an, who had at that time still been determined to vote against her. Even manipulative, devious, untrustworthy Malriel told her that it had not been her fault.

And Vran'el had explained to her that the trial was not to determine whether she was guilty or not, but a trial of political strength where the Houses would either demonstrate their solidarity with Malriel or another House allied with her, or take the opportunity to teach her a lesson.

Something deep within that had been drawn tight and rigid for a long time uncoiled a little. Was this a sign that her soul was finally starting to heal? Was dealing with this matter, sharing it, making herself vulnerable to the judgement of others instead of locking it away deep inside her the way finally to leave it behind her? Would it hurt any less?

She pushed aside the memory of Malriel urging her to talk about it to Enric as they parted on the evening before their intended departure. Her mother had definitely not done this to provide some kind of cure for her, but had used confidential information that Eryn had shared in a moment of weakness to drag a painful matter out into the open for her own purposes. No, she decided, she did not owe Malriel any gratitude, none at all.

The water had gone cool and she decided against reheating it. She would have preferred soaking a little longer, but there was no time for that right now. Rising with rivulets of water cascading down her now clean skin, she grabbed the topmost towel from a stack to her left, causing a piece of paper folded between the material to fall out and land on the stone floor. She towelled herself off quickly, dried her hair with the aid of a little magic and then, without bothering to dress, bent down to retrieve what looked like a letter. Unfolding it, she sucked in a surprised breath when she recognised Enric's energetic strokes on the paper.

Her eyes darted along the lines, absorbing the words his flourishing handwriting spelled like a dry sponge dropped into water, and soon a relieved smile spread on her lips. He wrote of missing her, thinking of her day and night and pondering how to end Ram'an's life in a both creative and elegant way that could never be traced to him - even though everybody would of course know. She smiled about that. She had missed his wry sense of humour that often left her wondering how much truth it contained.

His opinion of her attempt to get to him today was however not a favourable one, but he wrote that he understood her and approved of her desire to see him and that he himself had considered sneaking out at night, but had discarded the idea repeatedly as it would only have complicated their situation if they were caught. He repeated his warning not to provoke Ram'an unnecessarily and to be aware when being more or less at his mercy in the evening. He expressed understanding why she had accepted the deal and promised her that he would make Ram'an pay if he hurt or otherwise harmed her in any way.

He ended by promising that they would somehow get through this together, that he would not leave the country without her - whatever the outcome of the trial was.

She felt concerned at the last bit. What did he mean by that? Was he telling her in some elliptical way to prepare for escape or was he hinting at staying here himself should they decide to detain her for the two years Malriel was aiming for?

She squared her shoulders. She hoped that this would not be an issue if Ram'an kept his promise to help her with the votes after she spent the evening with him. She could endure his touches if it meant that she would be able to return home with Enric. Home to the house he had bought for her and the feral cat he had adopted on a whim after she brought it back from the expedition.

Something inside her tightened when she thought of all the things he had done for her since she had been made to join him. Both grand gestures and small, which he had never expected any thanks for. Nor had he practically ever received any. What he had expected, she had time and again refused him: openness and honesty instead of keeping secrets, not bolting when there was trouble but facing it, and finally, reciprocating his feelings for her.

That evening at the Aren estate outside the city came to her mind again, when he had tried to tell her how important she was to him. She had panicked and blocked him off, refusing his proposal for a third level bond.

But surely he knew that the bond itself was the problem, not himself? That he, of all people, was the only one she could remotely imagine one day taking it with?

Her joy at finding the letter had somehow transformed into its exact opposite, and she checked herself from indulging in anger at herself and the world in general. Ram'an wanted a pleasant evening in exchange for his help, and achieving that and at the same time keeping him at bay would be hard enough even without pondering the state her relationship with Enric was in. And her relationship was the reason why she was doing this, after all.

She slipped on the dress and opened the door again. Ram'an pushed himself away from the wall he had been leaning against and indicated for her to return to her room.

"Your cousin is waiting for you to take care of your hair. Do not let him pin up all of it, I like it when a few strands frame your face," he remarked and gently brushed one unruly strand from her face.

A corner of her mouth curved upwards in lopsided half-smile. "As you seem to have very clear ideas what I should look like, perhaps you would like to take care of my hairstyle yourself? And apply some makeup as well? Pick the colour for my lip-gloss and so on?"

He pretended to consider that suggestion for a moment, then shook his head. "No - unlike your cousin, I have neither the patience nor experience of handling a woman's hair that artfully. I am afraid I lack the dexterity for such tasks." He smiled back at her. "In other areas, though, my fingers leave nothing to be desired, I have been told. As regards making-up your face, please do refrain from putting anything on your lips. It would only get smeared."

He then turned with a smug grin at her irked expression and walked towards the main room. She reminded herself, through rising indignation, of how she needed to stop making it so easy for him to provoke her. Ram'an was a lawyer, he was used to countering verbal attacks of any kind swiftly and eloquently, so she shouldn't fret about his managing to unnerve her with his words.

Vran'el sat on her bed with an assortment of equipment draped on one side and looked up when she entered.

"Good, it is about time. He is expecting you to leave here with him at sunset, and that is in less than half an hour's time." He got to his feet and inspected her hair. "Did you dry it completely? There cannot be any dampness left or it will soon start slipping out from whatever implements I use to pin it up." She felt his fingers combing through her waves and then warmth when he dried residual patches of moisture. "Now, sit here."

"I could wear it in a simple braid, just to antagonise him," she suggested.

Her cousin shook his head. "Do not forget why you are doing this, sweetness. Avoid opposing him in such minor matters - you will very likely need to swat away his hands tonight. Give him the impression that you are cooperating a little, at least."

"Very well, then. He said to leave a few strands hanging down to frame my face," she murmured.

"A man who knows what he wants. How delightful," Vran'el commented and started twisting and forming her hair in different directions, pinning it up with some of the numerous pinning devices he had prepared, then finally loosening a few strands to hang about her face.

He delicately took her chin between his fingers and turned her head this way and that, eyeing his work critically.

"That should do the trick," he judged and nodded. "We do not want to make you any prettier than necessary. Though that will not make much of a difference to him; unfortunately he is crazy for you, no matter what." He paused and then added in a lower voice. "Did you find Enric's letter?"

She nodded. "I did, yes." Then she asked impatiently, "So you saw him while I was knocked out? What did he say? How is he doing?"

"Obviously, missing you a lot. He appears to be indulging in rather violent fantasies about injuring Ram'an."

"Yes, I gathered that much from his message. But if I have to restrain myself, so does he." She rose. "Am I ready?"

He shook his head. "Certainly not without adding a pair of shoes to the ensemble. I do not have to tell you that they need to be either black or dark red, do I? That is unless you have another accessory in a different colour - such as a shawl - then the shoes could match that colour as well."

She didn't deign to respond to that but instead stepped towards one of her chests and pulled out a simple pair of black shoes.

He rolled his eyes. "I failed to mention that the colour is not the only characteristic that counts. The style needs to match as well. This pair you can wear with one of your pairs of trousers, but not with a dress such as this." He pushed her aside and rummaged through the meagre collection of footwear. "Seriously, how can you survive like this? I know horses that possess more shoes than you!"

"No wonder, they have twice as many feet! I notice how you keep comparing me to horses. It seems they are very well equipped in these parts; they seem to possess both more shoes and more hair accessories than I," she retorted and waited with folded arms for him to pull something out that he approved of.

"There we go! I was about to give up." He pulled out a pair of delicate and slim black shoes and handed them to her. "Put those on. They are not as shiny as I would have hoped for, but you are not the glimmering sort anyway."

"Are you telling me that I am plain and boring?" she asked with a lifted eyebrow while slipping on the shoes.

"No, but you do not need *me* to tell you that with two gorgeous men competing for your heart, sweetness."

"I like to think they are attracted to my inner qualities," she replied with mock haughtiness.

"Yes, of course. That must be why Ram'an keeps looking at your backside whenever you leave the room," he chuckled.

She grimaced. "He does? So much for the sophisticated scholar."

"There are things that no degree of education can overcome. Such as being born a man, for example. Enric does it as well, by the way."

"Am I ready to go now or do I have to keep on listening to this?"

"Ready? You must be joking. Sit down again. We need to take care of your eyes. The rest of you can remain as it is. As you are to be having dinner together, lipstick would just be gone after the first few bites or end up clinging to your teeth," he explained.

She nodded slowly. He had a point there; and it was not as if she was eager to make herself up more than was considered absolutely necessary.

"You know, normally I am only being prepared like that when there is a ball or official dinner. I find it really strange to do it for this man who doesn't leave me in any doubt that he would prefer me naked anyway," she pointed out.

"Ah, the games we play," Vran'el sighed and started applying powders in different shades of grey and bronze to her eyelids with a small brush.

* * *

Ram'an looked up when she entered the main room, a delighted smile spreading across his face as he beheld the full sight of her. He stepped towards her to take both her hands in his and kiss them. Vran'el leaned against a wall close to them with folded arms.

"I hope you will behave yourself, Ram'an," he warned.

The other man winked at Eryn. "I will. Mostly. First I want us to lay down mutually agreed rules for this evening. I would like us to spend a pleasant time together. I have no intention of chasing you around while you are desperately trying to get as much distance as possible between us. I told you that I intend to touch you frequently without your shying away. If I touch you in a way that is definitely not acceptable to you, you must let me know, then I will respect it. As a consequence of your attempt at seeing Lord Enric without my permission today, I will take the liberty also to kiss you, despite your rule against it. Though I do not want you to consider this a punishment, but rather a little reminder that I am being very lenient with you still."

She shook her head. "No, that is not acceptable."

"I know. That is why I am making a few concessions as to that part. I will only kiss your hands and face, exactly as I have done before without your objecting to it. The difference will be that this time I want to kiss your lips as well. Your closed lips," he added when she opened her mouth to protest again. "Like this."

He cupped her cheek before she could turn away and pressed his warm lips onto hers, kept them there for only a few seconds and then pulled back again. "You see? Harmless enough. Almost brotherly," he smiled.

"Hardly," Vran'el commented dryly. "That is certainly not how I kiss *my* sister."

Ram'an ignored him and lifted a questioning brow at her. "Do you think you can stand this for the duration of one evening, Theá?"

She gave him a pained look. "This is not about my standing it, Ram'an. I do not feel repulsed or anything when you touch me, but this feels as if you expect me to assist you in torturing yourself." The only thing she had felt was a pleasant soft warmth and a slight tingle - nothing that made her heart beat faster or sent shivers down her spine. None of the things Enric managed to elicit when he touched her.

"I am a grown man, my dear. Let that be my concern, will you?"

She looked over at Vran'el who just shrugged. "Your decision, sweetness. Just consider the intention behind it and be aware of it at all times. He is trying to get you used to more and more intimate physical contact, and if he keeps up this pace you will sooner or later find yourself in his bed, wondering how it happened."

Eryn rolled her eyes at him. "I am not *such* easy prey, just so you know!"

"Just be careful around him. He had a lot of practice."

Ram'an took her hand and led her downstairs towards the exit. "Come, my dear. Let me show you my home and regale you without any unwanted remarks."

She waved goodbye to her cousin and looked at Ram'an enquiringly. "They are not true, then?"

He thought for a moment, then smiled apologetically. "I did not say that. Just that they are unwanted. But let us not talk about this, it is a topic highly unsuitable when trying to woo a woman." They stepped outside and started walking.

"Don't worry on my account, I will remain un-wooed in any case. It just does not seem to match your status as a scholar. Usually the bookish kind don't get the girls, or so I thought. Such is the general perception where I come from. Vern is very worried because of it as he has quite an affinity for books himself."

Ram'an gave her a pained look. "I really do not want to talk to you about my conquests, Theá. None of them counted for much. But your young friend may rest assured that books have never been an obstacle when it comes to women. He just needs to make sure to mind *what* he reads."

"You mean the *right* books?" she enquired.

He smiled. "Yes. Plus quite a number of the *wrong* books."

She looked at him for a moment, then had to smile. "A scholar's approach to taking a woman to bed. I can't help picturing you as an adolescent boy hiding under his blankets while leafing through forbidden books."

"That is a pretty accurate portrait of me, I have to admit," he laughed and kissed her hand before linking their fingers.

"How far do we have to walk?"

"Not very far. It is a bit further than House Aren, but not much. We will be there before the sun has set completely."

Eryn watched the routine of tents being removed from the streets to afford the guests of teahouses and music places a clear view of the night sky.

"You know," she pondered, "I have been here for more than three weeks, and there was not a single drop of rain all that time. How do people here keep their gardens from turning to dust?"

"By drilling deep boreholes in the ground where the water is and transporting it to the surface. We have constructed devices that pump the water up. They can be powered either manually, or in case of the Houses, with magic. Very effective," he explained. "I will give you a tour through our gardens after dinner and show you. I am curious if you still remember them when you see them."

"I would not count on that if I were you," she replied doubtfully. "It was more than two decades ago when I was there last time, after all."

"True, but memories behind a block tend to be more complete as they are less prone to the usual process of fading after a time," he explained. "You should have experienced the newly recovered memories as more vivid and clear in comparison to things you remember from, let us say, fifteen years ago."

She pondered this for a moment and then nodded slowly. "I have not really thought about that, but now that you mention it... Yes, they are unusually lucid."

"Am I right in assuming that you have rediscovered a few memories of me as a boy?" he asked with a smile.

"You are, yes. There are indeed images of a handsome, dark-haired boy, serious and unusually gentle. I remember taking walks with you in the garden."

He chuckled. "Unusually gentle. Not an attribute that makes growing up easier for a boy. But I admit that it has its merits now as an adult."

She raised both eyebrows. "At least with the ladies, I'd bet. But I do not have the impression that this description of you is still as valid as it seemed back then."

He nodded. "It may not be as unconditionally applicable as it used to be, but then it would be a mistake to equate gentleness with weakness. Dealing with you, my dear, requires quite a lot of both - gentleness and strength."

"Does it now. I don't think that strength is what you need to get along with me. A certain amount of respect will do well enough," she replied coolly.

Ram'an squeezed her hand. "No. Strength is exactly what a man needs in your case - both in magic and character. You would not respect anything less."

"That is complete nonsense! There are a number of people who I respect even though they are either magically less capable than me or have no use of magic at all," she protested and started listing. "Vern, Junar, Orrin, Plia, Vran'el, Sarol, Valrad, Kilan, Barul..."

"Ah," he interrupted her, "but I did not say people, but *man*."

"I had non-magicians as lovers. So that is a misconception on your part."

He sighed. "Taking a man to bed and respecting him as a partner in a relationship are two very different things, Theá. A man with less magical strength than you would have a very hard life with you as he would have no chance whatsoever to set you boundaries."

"Set me boundaries?" she frowned in dismay. "I am not a stubborn child, but a grown woman! I do not appreciate it if people think they have to set me boundaries. And especially when it comes to my men." Why did she seem to attract only men who seemed to think that subduing her was a fabulous idea of late?

"And yet you would not respect a man who could not do it as you would not allow him to get close enough to you otherwise."

"So you think a man needs to be able to force himself on me so I am able to respect him? This is a truly disturbing image of me you seem to have, and I reject it outright!"

"I think you are misunderstanding me deliberately," he replied with control. "Forcing himself on you is not what would make you respect a man, but there is so much pain inside you that sometimes it seems that you need a more persuasive approach when it comes to accepting gentleness. It is what Lord Enric appears to have accomplished to a certain degree already, but not yet completely. And it is what I have been working on since your arrival in Takhan."

"So you think *forcing me gently* is the way into my bed, heart or whatever your current priority is?" she snorted with a derisive laugh. Yet his words did make her feel slightly uncomfortable. He was so very confident about his assessment of her that she couldn't help but wonder if there was some truth in it. Her history with Enric certainly did convey that impression, didn't it? And whatever Ram'an had done so far to displease her had ultimately ended up in him taking her out on what he termed an intimate dinner where she had agreed to be touched and kissed by him within agreed boundaries.

"I will not answer that question. I can see that you are thinking about what I said, and that is confirmation enough for me." He then lifted his hand and pointed ahead. "Look, we are almost there. It is the house at the end of the road."

"That large residence with extensive greenery around it, I assume," she remarked dryly. It was not as if there was any other building around that could have been mistaken for the residence of the leading family of a local House.

"The very same," he confirmed and a little later opened one of the wing doors of a heavy metal gate to let her enter the premises first. He then again took her hand into his and walked with her to the ornate entrance door.

"Will I be meeting your family?" she asked, feeling ambivalent at the prospect. They would hardly be very thrilled about meeting the person they had to see as the cause for Ram'an's refusal to take over leadership of the House. But then their presence would mean that she would not be dining alone with Ram'an, who would then have to be more careful about how close he got to her.

"No, Theá, not today. This is just you and me. You can meet them at some other time. A family evening is not what I consider an intimate dinner," he clarified, opening the door for her to enter first.

He turned to a dark green bowl with two rolled up dampened towels on a small table and took one out. When Eryn reached out to take it from his hand, he shook his head.

"No, please, allow me."

Without waiting for her reply, he unrolled the towel and delicately wiped her forehead, temples, cheeks, the sides of her nose before progressing to her throat. He took his time, traced the sinews of her throat with his cloth-covered fingers. She stood rigidly, waiting until he was finished and had put the cloth away.

Then he took the second towel and cleaned his own face and hands before bending down and pressing a quick kiss onto her lips, smiling at her look of surprise and dismay.

He linked their fingers and urged her up the broad stairway and into a main room that was as large as she was used to from other residences she had seen, but not as scarcely furnished. Side-tables, bookcases, high bulging vases in bold colours and naturally the cushions that formed sitting arrangements on the floor. Artful tapestries decorated those walls not taken up by bookcases and lent the room an ambience that was probably exotic even by local standards.

Ram'an's eyes remained on her while she was letting her own wander over the many items in the room.

"How do you like it? I am sure it is quite different from what you have seen here so far. My family favours a somewhat less light and airy style of furnishing."

Eryn stepped towards one of many bookshelves, considering the collection of old and valuable looking books.

"I find it impressive. But then a room with books in it hardly ever fails to impress me," she smiled and tilted her head when she tried to decipher one of the titles. "I can't read this."

"This is our ancient language, the one that was spoken here more than five hundred years ago. Hardly anybody can fathom it nowadays," he explained and pulled out a book to show her the arcane-looking symbols that made up the text inside.

"Can you?"

"Yes, I am one of the few who still bothered to learn it. But then I am a historian, so who would learn it if not I?"

She eyed the book curiously. "But this book is not five hundred years old, is it? It looks old, but not that old."

"No, it is a copy. We have a few old originals, but we do not keep them here out in the open. They are too valuable and delicate. Of course we also treat the copies with a lot of care – it is hard enough to find scribes still who are able to copy them without making too many mistakes because they do not know the language and so do not realise when something does not make sense."

"What are these books here about?"

"Old laws. Many of them are outdated, some are still in effect, even though hardly anybody is aware of them these days."

"But you are. So I suppose that winning a legal argument against you must be quite a challenge?" she asked, only half-jokingly.

He smiled and put the book back. "There is no way for me to answer that question without casting myself in an unfavourable light. If I agree, it will seem immodest and you would think that I am bragging. If I deny it, it will look like I am not a very proficient lawyer. I shall leave it to you to make enquiries and satisfy your curiosity as to that with the help of sources other than myself."

She raised her eyebrows. "An option you are hardly likely to point out unless you are sure enough of the favourable answers I am very likely to receive. Which means that you are very probably a proficient lawyer."

He laughed. "Although is it not far better for me if you learn this from somebody else? It certainly makes it more credible."

"And you do not have to sink so low as to praise yourself."

"Yes, there is that." He took her hand again and pointed to an adjoining room. "There is the kitchen. Join me."

"You want me to watch you cook?"

"If you like. Though I would prefer it if you helped me."

She looked surprised. "I have to work? Really? What's next? Cleaning the floor?"

He frowned for a moment, then said slowly, "I sometimes forget that you are not familiar with our customs here. If your host offers to let you participate in the process of preparing a meal, this is a great compliment. Guests do not normally consider it a burden."

"So, being asked to help serving food is an honour already, but being invited to prepare it with you is an even greater show of appreciation?" she enquired.

"Indeed. Though preparing food together is a little more than a demonstration of appreciation. It is an invitation into an area that is normally reserved for family and close friends only."

She sighed and cocked her head. "I suppose refusing this honour means insulting the host? No matter if you would rather not be considered somebody that close?"

"Very true. I know that you are a very direct person who does not always value diplomacy or the rules a society sets too highly, be it your own society or mine. But you would surely not wish to make me doubt that you are upholding your side of our deal here tonight."

She stared at him in surprise. That had been an unusually direct warning. Nodding slowly, she gulped. So no more displays of reluctance for tonight. He wanted an evening of illusions? That he could have as long as he behaved himself. She smiled, trying hard to make it look authentic. "Of course not. I gladly accept the privilege. I thought it wise to learn about what to avoid here in your country in order to avoid causing inadvertent offence."

He regarded her for a moment. "Do not try to be diplomatic with me, Theá. It does not wash with me. I prefer honest disagreement to cool and polite detachment."

She was about to tell him that honest disagreement was clearly not what he wanted from her, that he had more or less excluded that very thing with his conditions and his warning just now, but thought better of it. Alienating him was surely not a good idea. There was still the little matter of those four votes which would undoubtedly come in handy.

"Though we agreed on a thing or two that will, I hope, keep the need for that to a minimum," he added, as if deducing her thoughts. "Come now. Let me show you the kitchen here. Though the rest of the house is furnished in a more traditional style, you will see that we have a very modern and effective approach to cooking."

He led her into a spacious, brightly lit room with large windows which overlooked the garden, now lit only by the light of dusk. Broad, new-looking shelves displayed a number of different pans, bowls, knives, graters and jars in assorted sizes and colours.

The cooking place and work surfaces gleamed and looked sparkling clean and new as well. A long, narrow bench at one end of the room held about ten different flowerpots with herbs growing in them.

She nodded appreciatively. "I admit I am impressed."

Smiling, he took two aprons from a hook on the wall and turned her towards him to fix one of them around her neck and waist before protecting his own clothes the same way.

"I have had the ingredients for tonight brought up and cleaned for us already, so we can start peeling and chopping right away." He indicated a large bowl filled with various kinds of vegetables and took a menacing looking knife and chopping board from one of the shelves.

He took several items of vegetable, explained to her how he wanted them cut, then took a smaller knife to remove the peel from others. He watched her for a few moments, then sighed and shook his head.

"Wait, I cannot watch you working like that. You may be a healer, but I would still like to avoid gaping wounds and loss of blood in general. This is a well-honed knife - if you cut yourself with it, that will be rather messy." He put aside his own blade and stepped behind her, putting his hands on hers. "You need to hold your fingers curved inwards like this so you cannot slice off your fingertips, but at worst only graze your knuckles slightly. Now the knife. Do not use your index finger to press down on the blade but let the tip touch the board at all times. Just lift the part that is close to you like this."

She watched his fingers over hers guiding the movements he expected her to copy and felt his cheek against her ear. He smelled of soap and some kind of subtle spicy fragrance. She had not used any perfume herself and wondered if this was good or not. Someone's natural scent was to the right person a powerful aphrodisiac, and masking it with something else might have been advisable. But then he might have seen it as an encouragement as he would surely have thought that she had put it on to please him.

"You are not with me right now," he commented. "That is not a wise thing considering that we are working with very sharp tools here. Even though I like to think that I have managed to distract you from your task," he smiled and stepped back. "Now show me how to do it properly so that I can return to peeling without worrying about your losing parts of your fingers. The dish would not be free of meat after that."

She stared at him, shocked for a moment, then chuckled. "That was a very insensitive thing to say!"

"And yet it just earned me your first honest laugh for tonight. He stepped towards a high cupboard filled with bottles of wine and took one out to open it. He poured them a glass each and handed her one.

"To a pleasant evening we will each remember fondly," Ram'an said solemnly, raising his glass.

She took a sip and then put it aside. "You just told me to be careful with that murderous weapon you handed me for cutting the vegetables, yet you give me alcohol. Is that wise?"

"It is a very mild wine, I am confident that you will manage to stay free of intoxication until the dangerous part of cooking is over. And only then I will switch to the more potent beverages that will make you compliant." He rolled his eyes at her bewildered expression. "That was said in jest, Theá. If I were planning a thing like that, I would hardly warn you in advance about it, would I?"

Eryn exhaled and nodded. "I am sorry. I admit I am a little tense."

"We will work on that, my dear. You have nothing to fear from me." He smiled before he added, "Well, not tonight."

* * *

She leaned back contentedly after completely emptying her bowl. "That was tasty, very tasty. Though I am aware that my contributions were not exactly of a nature that had any impact on the taste."

Ram'an shook his head. "That is not true. The way you cut the vegetables, the size of the chunks, all have influence over the taste of the final result. So you may rest assured that you have contributed sufficiently to our culinary satisfaction." He got up slowly and picked up both their empty bowls to take them back to the kitchen. "I do not have to shackle you, shield you or otherwise keep you in place if I leave the room for a short moment, I hope?"

She waved him off. "Go on. I promise I will behave."

He returned only a moment later and reached out for her. "Come, my dear. Let us take a walk in the garden."

When she took his hand, she felt herself being pulled to her feet with more energy then was required and ended up in his arms.

He smirked. "Dear me, how very clumsy of me."

"Yes, how very clumsy," she said and rolled her eyes before stepping away from him.

Holding on to her hand, he walked towards the terrace door. It was completely dark outside by now, but a large number of small lanterns hung from branches or were attached to sticks in the ground for illumination. The light they cast created a delightful ambiance. A gentle breeze brushed her skin and caused the lanterns to swing slightly without extinguishing the flames.

Eryn let her gaze wander over the extensive green, the large number of bushes and trees that were only occasionally interspersed with flowers. It was quite the contrast to Valrad's garden which consisted mainly of herbs.

"It is not as flowery as most gardens in Takhan. There have been no healers in the family for quite some time, thus the interest for herbs and flowers has decreased considerably over this last century. What you see here is more or less what has managed to survive without any particular care," he told her while they were strolling along a row of high bushes. "Nonetheless we have managed to create a few very nice quiet spots that serve as safe havens, as it were. Scholars tend to appreciate solitude every now and then. Though if there was a healer in the family again," he added casually, "I would be more than happy to dedicate parts of the garden to growing medical herbs."

She kept her eyes straight ahead and decided not to comment on that remark. What would be the point in her repeatedly rejecting the idea of living here with him if he just kept refusing to acknowledge that she was serious?

They passed a large tree with low hanging branches and dark orange blossom. She stopped, looking up. Images of a similar, but much smaller specimen came to her mind.

"I think I remember this one here," she said slowly.

Ram'an touched the bark with his flat hand. "It was planted by my grandmother on the day I was born. She told me that she had intended to plant a different kind with sweet fruit, but bought the wrong seeds."

"It is still pretty, though," she said and sniffed one of the pretty blooms.

"I like it, too," he agreed and plucked one of the blossoms to stick in her hair. "I appreciate the idea of things working out to mutual satisfaction even if they do not seem to progress the way they were initially planned."

Her smile had taken on a slightly waxen quality when she moved on, determined not to react to this remark, either. This evening would be quite a test to her patience if he continued like that.

"Wait," he said softly and held on to her hand when she made to move on. "Sit with me for a moment."

Looking around in confusion, she frowned. "Where?"

He stepped aside and revealed a low stone bench behind him. She sat down when he patted the spot next to him, waiting.

"How are you doing, my dear?"

"Pardon me?" She looked at him, frowning. "What kind of a question is that? You have been with me almost every minute since I was placed under your care. I would assume that you know pretty well how I am doing."

He sighed. "I mean on the inside. You have not had much time to recover from everything that has happened. You look tense, but I am not sure if it is because of my proximity to you or because the circumstances of your father's death were revealed."

Gulping back her emotion, she shook her head. She didn't want to talk about this, neither to him nor to anybody else. Was it too much to ask to be left alone?

She gave him a forced smile. "Let us not spoil the evening." He held on to her arm when she began to get up.

"This is important, Theá. You need to deal with this. Otherwise it will haunt you for the rest of your life, just as it has been torturing you for the last twelve years. Talk to me," he insisted. "It wounds me to see you suffering so."

"What makes you think that you are the one I would want to talk to about this?" she replied coldly.

"I am not saying that I am. But I have the impression you have no intention of talking of it at all. Lord Enric learned about this matter at the same time as your family and me. So you obviously do not have *anybody* you wish to talk to about it," he countered reasonably.

She hardened her voice. "Don't push me. This is none of your business."

He smiled faintly. "You agreed to an intimate evening, my dear Theá. There is more than one kind of intimacy."

Eryn looked at him in dismay. "Excuse me for asking, but I am not very good with such subtleties. You are surely *not* telling me that I am violating our deal by refusing to talk to you about this? I do not remember agreeing to anything of that sort!"

"But neither did you explicitly *exclude* anything like it. So it is a matter of interpretation which we would have to base on common practice and custom - namely, the general understanding of the term *intimacy*."

"Don't use your lawyer talk on me, Ram'an," she warned him. "I am in no mood to play semantic games with you right now."

"Good. Comply with what I am asking of you, then I will no longer bother you with them."

"I don't like being blackmailed!"

He nodded unabashedly. "That I understand. Hardly anybody does."

Staring at him, she pulled her arm out of his grip. "I am not a child you can press into confessing."

He stood and took her hand, pulling her to her feet as well. His voice was cool. "You are right. I cannot make you. We are both adults and there is no shame in admitting when something does not work out. Let us return to the Vel'kim residence."

She froze. "What? That is it? You are ending this? Just like that?"

"Yes. I am sure you will find another way to make certain that the senate will permit you to return to your country."

Her heartbeat had quickened and she felt a light throbbing in her temples. That was not going well, not at all. Whatever she had expected of this evening, his drawing the line under it like this had definitely not been one of the outcomes she had imagined. In fact she'd envisaged quite the opposite scenario, rather expecting him to detain her here as long as he was able.

She held on to a tree when he took her arm to lead her back inside.

"Wait! Is that your way of reacting to the honest disagreement you pretended to prefer over forced politeness? If it was, then I will avoid being honest with you from now on - you are not handling it very well. Let's sit down and talk, shall we? I will tell you how much the whole thing pains me and what a great relief talking to you is, and how from now on my life will never be the same because you managed to heal me by finally convincing me to share this entire wretched mess with you!" Her voice had become loud towards the end and she exhaled slowly.

He watched her with an unreadable expression and then folded his arms, both his gaze and posture calm and unrelenting. "My votes, my terms, Theá. Make your choice."

She narrowed her eyes at him and nodded slowly. "You want to talk? Alright, let's talk. But keep in mind that this is nothing more than a business deal. I am not doing this because I trust you or feel the need to share anything with you."

Ram'an nodded, unfolded his arms and motioned for her to sit on the bench again. "Duly noted." He took a seat close to her. "Please keep in mind that I am making you do this because I care for you. A lot. I do not enjoy watching how you keep torturing yourself. If making you face this makes you angry at me, I am willing to live with it as long as it helps you in the end."

She swivelled her head away as he bent forward to kiss her lips. "Spare me your pretences of selflessness. They are wasted on me. You are doing this because you hope it will make me break down crying and turn to you as the only one close who will hold and comfort me."

He chuckled. "Hardly. I very much doubt that you are the type for it, though your letting me comfort you would indeed be a side benefit, however unlikely that is. This is not the type of woman House Aren breeds." She felt his hand turn her chin back to him. "And turning away from me just now was another violation of our agreement. I will exercise leniency if you correct that little matter."

She braced herself for another kiss, but he kept looking at her, obviously waiting for something.

Then it dawned on her. "*I* am to kiss you?"

"Yes. I think that will be a happy change," he nodded and raised his brow when she didn't move. "I am waiting."

She gulped and looked at his lips. Maybe it was not so bad if she was the one who did it - then she would at least be in control of how long it took. His eyes stayed on hers as she slowly leaned ever closer until their faces were almost touching. She paused for a short moment, took another breath and then pressed her mouth onto his lightly for no more than a second before leaning back again, feeling him lean forward a little to follow her move and prolong the contact.

"That was not so hard, was it?" he enquired with a faint smile.

She decided not to comment on that and folded her arms in front of her chest. "What do you want to hear now? Please be very specific about that - I wouldn't want to endanger the fulfilment of my side of the bargain again, would I?"

"Firstly, I want you to get rid of the sarcasm; and secondly I would like to hear about what your life was like after Ved'al's death."

"What do you think it was like?" she growled, anything but happy that he was forcing her to recall and describe this painful time. Taking another breath, she went on more calmly, "I was told that my father was dead, which meant that I was alone in the world with no one to teach me how to take full responsibility for my life, earn my keep or increase my healing skills. There would be no one to share my secret any longer, either. The villagers took care of me for a while, but that was no long-term solution of course." Her eyes avoided Ram'an's face and stayed trained on a nearby tree. "My father had not been an advocate of dependence on others and had impressed on me the importance of never letting anybody else do for me what I could do myself. I was crying for three days, kept to my bed and refused the food they coaxed me to eat. But on the fourth day, when no more tears were there to be cried, I got up. I washed, dressed and took control of my life again, taking over my father's work as well as I could. And that is what I was doing until I was taken to Anyueel."

"How do you feel now when you think about your father?"

She shrugged. "Sad. Remorseful. Forsaken."

"Guilty? Angry at yourself?" he supplied.

"No," she replied with control. "These feelings are long gone."

His hands covered hers and she felt warmth from his palms permeating her skin as he applied magic.

"Do you still feel guilty when you think of your father?" he repeated his question.

She was not pleased when she felt the effect of the truth block stopping her from denying it again, but it was not much of a surprise. Not really. Suddenly she felt tired of fighting. It seemed she had done little else recently. Nodding, she looked up at him. He wanted to hear it? Alright, then.

"Yes, I feel guilty. He impressed on me that this one law was most sacred to him, warning me of the consequences. I broke it and he died. Without my disobedience he would still be alive. There is no denying that fact. I have learned to live with the guilt, but admitting it to others is... hard. I never had to deal with what anybody else might think about it."

"You never shared this with anybody? Nobody at all? No close friend or lover you trusted enough?" he asked with a worried frown.

"No. Never. Malriel was the first one ever to hear of it," she replied.

The ensuing silence stretched on until Eryn's sigh broke it. "What now? Aren't you going to tell me how it *really* wasn't my fault? How I couldn't have foreseen the consequences? How the whole world around me - circumstances, the baker, the stars - were to blame, but not myself?"

"Back to sarcasm, I see," he remarked factually. "No, I am not going to tell you that it was not your fault. You would not believe me, would you? But let me tell you a little about growing up as a magician in Takhan. I was about twelve years old when I was first summoned to the Council for juvenile offences." At her questioning look he explained, "It is an institution that was established to deal with children and adolescents who used their magic in ways which are not approved of. It is meant to impress on the young that, should they disobey the rules, it will not go unpunished, and to show them more leniency as they are still in a process of socialisation and need to learn to control their magic. Their impulses as well, of course. It is also meant to intimidate them to a certain degree, appearing big and frightening with stern looking older people scowling down at them from their elevated seats; a hall that is much too large and so makes them feel small and vulnerable."

"And you were summoned there because...?" she enquired, interested despite herself.

"Because I bestowed a rather nasty rash on my music tutor when he kept striking me on my fingers with a stick each time I produced a wrong chord. He was a non-magician, you see, something that makes it even less acceptable as he had no defences against it - neither when it came to warding off the attack, nor to healing it afterwards. They made me do several hours of charitable work such as cleaning fountains and helping out in the clinic."

"You said it was the *first* time you were summoned there. So there was a second time?"

He nodded and then smiled. "A third time, even. Though I generally was considered a very smart boy, that was an area where I proved to be a rather slow learner. I was never the brawling kind, but rather uncommonly gentle, as you have put it. Using magic just seemed easier and less messy. And there was the hope, of course, of not being found out."

She stared at him, taken along by the story. "How did a troublemaker like that end up studying the laws?"

"Probably a desire to learn how to better break the rules without getting caught," he grinned and then rolled his eyes at her look of dismay. "Do not tell me I have destroyed your illusions about my always having been a respected pillar of society? I had my rebellious phases, just like most young people do. But let us return to the Council. Vran'el was summoned only once, if I remember correctly. Pe'tala, too, though her offence was a rather spectacular one. Would you like to hear about it?"

Of course she wanted to! What a question. But it would not do to appear too eager. It would only give him the impression that she appreciated having been made to talk about this despite her initial objections.

"I wouldn't mind hearing about it," she replied casually, trying and failing to appear ambivalent.

"She was about fifteen years old when she refused the boy her family had chosen as a prospective companion for her. He was not particularly happy about that, as you can imagine. Being refused by somebody you were promised to indicates certain deficiencies in the suitor. So he tried to change her mind by inviting her time and again to go out with him - only to be refused. The gifts he kept sending her were returned to him unopened, she turned away whenever she saw him and towards the end even refused to talk to him. But he was determined to sway her. He waited for her after a private gathering at one of her friends' houses and stopped her to make her talk to him. I do not know the particulars, but it seems to have turned into a battle of magic that ended with his lying stunned on the ground. This alone would not have got her into trouble, but instead of walking away, she then caused all his hair to fall out and gave him illusions of giant birds of prey chasing him. She had already started her healing training by then, so her revenge was quite effective, carried out with the considerable skill Vel'kim healers are known for."

"But a skill she was not supposed to use for purposes such as that," Eryn murmured and looked down at her own hands. Fifteen.

That was how old she herself had been when she had decided to teach a lesson to another boy who couldn't accept the answer *no*. Strange that Pe'tala and herself should have that very thing in common. "What did the Council decide?"

"That she was to make his hair grow back and apologise. The manipulation of his brain was a bit too delicate to be taken care of by herself, so Valrad was asked to remedy it instead. He was at that time still in charge of the clinic, so it was not good for his reputation to have his own daughter, who was being trained as a healer herself, do something like that. It did also not show the Vel'kim family in a good light. Nonetheless this incident put a stop to the attentions of her over-eager admirer. The Council warned him that they might look the other way next time if he did not stop pestering her. This was a rather lenient decision, very much in Pe'tala's favour. Some of the Houses - especially those associated with the boy's family - were not happy about it, claiming that she was being shown unwarranted preference because of Valrad's standing. Pe'tala was watched over carefully for a while to see if she could still be trusted to continue her training and help people instead of harming them. If there had been another incident, however innocuous, she would very likely have been barred from the healing profession entirely."

So Pe'tala's life had not exactly been easy, either. And then she had fallen in love with a man who not only did not reciprocate her feelings, but had dropped her as soon as he had seen a chance to be with her cousin. Well, *dropped* was maybe a little hard as he had not actually been involved with her at that point. That would have made it even worse.

"So what you are telling me is that every single magician you know was caught out using magic in pretty much the same way I did and put before that Council for juvenile delinquents?" she asked sceptically.

"Not every single one, no. Not all of them were caught. My brother, for example. He is what you would call the mischievous type. I very much suspect that as a boy he used his powers to harm somebody at least one time. But he has always been very good when it comes to hiding things. But what I am trying to tell you is that disobeying one's elders is an essential part of healthy development. In the case of magicians this means using our powers not only in the way we are supposed to. Consequences like the ones you had to suffer are not normally what happens when you break somebody's arm. Or do you also blame yourself for being made to grow up in a place where a thing like that was even possible?"

She didn't respond to that. The way he said it - it sounded so logical, so harmless. But causing her father's death was not something that could just be talked away like that.

"I appreciate your efforts at easing my mind," she said slowly and deliberately, tired of dealing with the topic yet again, "though whatever you say, I am very well aware that this was a matter of cause and effect. The same action may not have caused the same consequences here, but that is not the question, is it?"

He furrowed his brow. "I am not trying to tell you that your actions did not lead to his death. That would hardly be true, would it?"

She tightened her mouth and stared at him. "You are not?"

"No. You triggered his death at that time, but that does not mean that you caused it."

"That is complete nonsense! I do not see any difference," she objected.

"You do not? Let me give you another example, then. Your friend Vern. He is a very talented artist, and even though you may have provided the chance for him finally to do something with his talent which earns him praise and acknowledgement, you are hardly the cause of it. The cause is the ability, the skill he was born with."

"And I was not the cause for the baker's actions, it was just a convenient reason to do something extreme?" she asked, doubting him.

He leaned forward. "How many people do you know who would react like this to a suspicion of having their child's arm broken? Beating somebody up? Standard reaction. Destroying somebody's reputation? Sure, why not. But waylaying a person in order to kill them? That is not the reaction of a man in his right mind. This man would surely have done something terrible one day; you just provided the setting for it to happen then and there."

She turned his words this way and that, but couldn't find any weak spot in his arguments. The trigger, but not the cause, she mused. Would that make living with the past easier? Probably, she decided. She would never stop wishing that she had acted differently that very day, but the nagging feeling of guilt might in the future find less fertile ground in her mind.

He smiled at her thoughtful expression. "You look like I gave you food for thought. Good." He stood up, as always tugging her upright with him. "Come. I will not ask you to admit that talking to me helped you, you would probably choke on the words."

"I bet you could somehow manage to argue that my doing just that was part of our deal as well," she said quietly, annoyed that he was right with both assumptions. Talking to him had helped her. And admitting it was not something she was willing to do in front of him.

"Probably," he nodded and started walking back towards the terrace. "But I do not need to hear it from you. I am very confident in my assessment."

That made her smile. "Yes, I have noticed that you are not exactly the self-depreciating type." She stopped dead when she beheld two musicians in the main room. His words about figuring out the level of physical attraction between them by dancing that special kind of dance at his place came back to her.

"No," she exclaimed and freed her hand from his, taking a step back while vehemently shaking her head. "*This* was never part of our agreement, whatever smart reasons you may have to support it!"

Ram'an looked about in confusion, then understanding dawned on him. "Theá, I have no intention of tricking you into bed with me. It would hardly aid my long-term objectives with you. They will not play *that* kind of song tonight. If you wish, we can keep the music completely non-magical. I wish to spend a pleasant evening with you, and I am determined to make sure that our conversation just now was the last disagreeable aspect for tonight. I will take advantage of the opportunity to hold you a bit more tightly than may be considered polite, but I promise that there is no need to fear me." He held out his hand. "Will you do me the honour and dance with me, my dear Theá?"

She exhaled slowly, relieved that she was not on the brink of prematurely ending the evening and potentially losing her four votes for the second time. She nodded and put her hand in his, letting him pull her inside to where the musicians were waiting patiently.

CHAPTER 47

New Expertise

Enric kept listening for the sounds he was waiting for - namely, the arrival of two people. It had been more than four and a half hours since they had left here according to Vran'el. He participated in the light conversation around him enough not to appear disinterested or impolite, but he could see that the other three men were aware that his thoughts were not with them entirely. He wondered what exactly Ram'an was doing at this very moment. They would have finished dinner more than two hours ago. Would he be walking with her through his garden, just like he had done as a boy? Probably. Touch her whenever possible? Undoubtedly. His hands balled into fists at the mere thought of Ram'an's hand around hers or wherever else he felt like touching her.

Images of hurting Ram'an badly returned to him, as they had so often in these last few days, like welcome friends which managed to lift his spirits for a short time. Maybe one day, he thought wistfully, when he was no longer an ambassador and bound to the necessities of diplomacy but a mere visitor here...

His head jerked upright when he heard the downstairs door opening and low voices reached his ears. A moment later he was on his feet and moving over to the stairs, Golir not far behind him. He stopped at the top of the staircase, looking down at the two of them - Eryn with her back to him, Ram'an looking up and into his eyes for only a brief moment before turning back to her.

Enric could hear his low murmur as Ram'an spoke to her.

"Theá, my dear, this is where our evening ends. I demand one last kiss, then I will consider this agreement of ours fulfilled." Without waiting for her consent, he cradled her cheeks between his palms and lowered his lips to hers, obviously enjoying the contact.

Enric felt a torrent of heat rising inside him, begging to find release with only one well-aimed bolt. It would take nothing more, just one hit. He saw her stiff posture and how her hands that hung down her sides balled into fists. Oddly enough, this sight helped. The relief at seeing that she did not enjoy Ram'an's touch was soothing for his strained nerves, yet it also caused new anger to flare at seeing her being made to endure such intimate contact with another man. He folded his arms to keep himself from acting on the impulse.

He saw a faint shimmer in the air before him and half-turned to Golir with a raised brow. It seemed his guard did not have great confidence in Enric's self-control.

When he turned back to the pair at the foot of the stairs, he saw Ram'an finally release her lips after what seemed like an eternity and then kiss her forehead. Enough was enough, Enric decided and cleared his throat loudly.

Eryn whirled at the sound and her face lit up when she spotted him. Before her guardian could react and hold her back to make her obey his prerequisite of not approaching her strong companion, she had already climbed two thirds of the stairs and opened her arms, when she suddenly hit Golir's barrier and stumbled backwards, slipping and almost toppling back down the steps.

Enric watched in horror, unable to penetrate the stronger shield and come to her aid. Then suddenly her descent stopped and she seemed to lean in mid-air. Golir had removed the shield in front of her and raised another one at her back to check her fall. Enric quickly moved forward, grabbed her hand and pulled her towards him and into his arms, pressing her close to him, inhaling the scent of her hair, her skin.

When he released her to kiss her mouth, he frowned in dismay when he saw a thin trickle of blood run down one nostril. He directed a small amount of healing magic to where the damage was and made sure the injury was healed before claiming her mouth, pushing aside the thought that only moments ago Ram'an's lips had been on that exact spot. He would not let this man diminish the pleasure of touching and kissing her.

"I would kindly ask you to remove the shield you have raised between my charge and me. It constitutes a violation of the rules," Ram'an said coldly to the triarch.

"Forgive me, nephew," Golir replied calmly. "You are right, of course. Though you surely acknowledge that I did it to keep her from getting hurt."

Enric and Eryn both stared at Golir, then at Ram'an.

"Nephew?" she ventured. "Really?"

Golir smiled at their surprised expressions. "Indeed. Ram'an's father is a member of House Partém; he is my brother."

Eryn bent to her companion's ear to whisper, "Is this good news or bad?"

"I don't have the slightest idea," Enric admitted equally quietly.

"Theá, do step away from Lord Enric," Ram'an instructed. "I am sure you remember my conditions when it comes to permitting you to remain in the same room as him."

She sighed and gave Enric a look of exasperation before removing her arms from around his neck and reluctantly returning to stand beside her guardian, whose arm possessively encircled her waist a moment later.

"Shall we return to our hosts or do you prefer staying on the stairs?" Golir asked dryly when the two younger men just stared at each other in muted hostility.

Enric stepped aside to let them enter the main room before him, then followed them to the seating cushions, from where Valrad and Vran'el watched them approach with concerned frowns.

"Sweetness," Vran'el smiled with forced cheerfulness, "how was your evening? I hope he did not try anything that would warrant challenging his status as your guardian?" His tone made clear that he was hoping for an opportunity for exactly that.

She shook her head wearily. "No, he adhered to what he thought were the rules. Though it seems that they contained unexpected aspects as he interpreted them."

"Did they indeed?" Enric's smile was dangerous. "Such as?"

"Personal conversations," she replied and immediately regretted mentioning it. She was in no mood to elaborate on their exact nature and hoped that nobody would ask. She sent Enric a pleading look and he seemed to understand immediately, nodding almost imperceptibly and letting himself sink down onto the cushions.

Ram'an led her to the spot furthest from Enric and motioned for her to sit as well before he took a seat next to her, close enough so he could put his arm around her shoulders. When Eryn motioned to lean away surreptitiously, he murmured, "There is always the option of your sitting in my lap instead, if my arm around your shoulders is not to your taste."

She stilled immediately, imagining Enric's reaction to that little scenario. She knew that his control over his impulses was far superior to her own, but judging from the looks he kept shooting Ram'an, he would probably not react favourably to any additional provocation after watching them kissing downstairs just now. Golir would have to rein him in if he attempted to inflict injury on his nephew, and that was something she wanted to avoid. For now.

"How was your day?" she asked conversationally.

"Tense," Enric replied. "I kept worrying about you after what Vran'el told me. I remember asking you not to do anything that might be seen as a provocation. Let me reassert that request." He looked at her pointedly.

She nodded and then gave her cousin an annoyed look. "If it wasn't for my dear cousin who freed my guardian, I might at least have managed to talk to you so that my little attempt would not have been completely in vain."

Vran'el sighed. "Sometimes you really make me want to give you a good spanking. Do you have any idea what the legal consequences of not freeing him would have been? He was assigned as your guard and you violated the rules. Had I assisted you in doing so by keeping Ram'an locked inside your room and unable to bring you back, the senate would very likely have decided that staying at our residence made it harder for him to carry out his duties. They would have ordered you to stay at House Arbil without any further consideration of Enric's disapproval. So next time you had better think twice before trying a stunt like that. And I am not even going to mention the consequences for me personally if I, a man of the law, have to account for breaking the rules so blatantly."

Eryn swallowed and blinked a few times. "I am sorry. I had not really considered it like that."

"I know," he retorted acidly. "Aren temper is not exactly known as the character trait that facilitates proper thinking before taking action. But looking at Malriel, it is something even an Aren woman may learn in time." He shook his head. "You are a smart woman, sweetness, but from what I have seen this intelligence seems to be limited to acquiring knowledge, not to deploying common sense. I really wonder how you managed to live alone for such a long time before you were taken to Anyueel."

She clenched her teeth and decided not to comment on that statement. The trouble was that there was nothing much she could say. Enric smiled faintly at Vran'el as if he was glad that somebody in the room shared his sentiments.

She flashed her companion a cool look. A little support would have been nice instead of silent assent to these less than flattering statements.

"Children," Valrad said placatingly, "this is not a good time to be fighting each other. Concentrate your efforts on the matter at hand and how to deal with it. Vran'el - consider what she has been through in these last two days. We need to grant her that at this moment not all of her actions might be being guided by reason. Eryn - Vran'el is right, there was no other way for us to act than to assist Ram'an. This might at first sight look like an act of disloyalty, but let me assure you that it was your interests we had in mind. I hope this settles that matter. And now I think it is time to end this evening, I need to be at the clinic early tomorrow. Eryn, if your guardian is willing to accompany you, you are very welcome to join me there. I assume using your time here instead of sitting around and waiting for the next hearing is more what you would like."

"We will be ready," Ram'an nodded before she had even turned her head to ask him.

She exchanged a relieved look with Enric. At least she would not be alone with Ram'an most of the following day. That was *something* to be glad about at least. Her guard got to his feet, pulling her up with him as usual.

"Come. Let us get you tucked in bed for the night. I will wake you in time. From what I have seen today you are not much of a morning person."

Enric's eyes narrowed. So it seemed he was about to make entering her room while she was still asleep a habit. Ram'an caught his gaze and smiled thinly as if guessing the other man's thoughts.

"Good night, everyone," he called out and waved them goodbye casually while he ushered his charge towards the corridor where their rooms where.

* * *

Eryn awoke with a start and yelped when she felt something cool at her toes.

Ram'an sat fully dressed at the foot end of her bed and laughed. "Still as ticklish as back then when you were a girl."

She groaned and let herself fall back into the cushions. "Go away! This is no way to wake somebody! One of these days I will strike you down and you have nobody but yourself to blame for that!"

She held on to the blanket when she felt it being pulled off her. "You stop that right now or there will be trouble!" she hissed and gave him a glare of anger. "I am, as you yourself pointed out only yesterday evening, not exactly what people would call a *morning person*. So do not make the mistake of thinking of anything I say as an empty threat," she warned him.

He nodded earnestly. "I have noticed, yes. And no, I would not dream of *not* taking you seriously. But this only results in me protecting myself better; it will certainly not make me cease my attempts of getting you out of bed. Make haste - Valrad is already up and you surely do not want to keep him waiting. Unless you have changed your mind about accompanying him to the clinic," he added casually, "and would rather spend the day here with me."

"Alright, alright," she grumbled and swung herself feet first out of bed, pulling down the rucked-up nightgown when Ram'an's eyes began wandering along her uncovered legs. "And stop staring! That's not for you to look at."

Shrugging good-naturedly, he rose and took her hands to pull her up into a standing position. "Whatever you say, my dear Theá. Now get dressed and join us for breakfast at the terrace. I will be waiting in front of your door."

Murmuring something unintelligible, she waited until he had closed the door behind him and then pulled out a dark brown and gold tunic and a pair of trousers from one of her chests. When she stepped outside, he was leaning against a wall in the corridor and smiling at her.

"I like it when you wear your hair down." He brushed a wayward strand behind her ear.

She gulped back an acid remark about too intimate touches. It would only tickle him.

Vran'el stepped out into the corridor behind them and yawned loudly. "Oh my, I hate mornings. Why can days not start at noon?" he complained.

Eryn grinned at him. Finally a kindred spirit. "I suppose they could for you, rich boy. You don't really have to work to make a living, do you?"

Her cousin grimaced. "Not exactly, no. But being rich and idle is generally looked down upon, so I should do *something* to protect my standing in society. And being a lawyer is not the worst kind of work there is. It is mostly pushing around contracts nowadays. As well as advising the odd family member when she stumbles into trouble."

Her face fell. "Thank you for that little reminder. What better way to start the day."

Vran'el chuckled. "As if having your very own guardian following you around wherever you go would not remind you of that, anyway."

Rubbing her face, she started walking towards the main room. "Don't pester me in the morning. Better feed me instead."

Both men followed her onto the terrace, where Valrad already sat with a plate of fruit on his lap and a bundle of papers in one hand. He looked up when the three of them joined him.

"A good morning to you. So you finally got up," he commented with a look at Eryn's sour expression. "I hope your mood brightens after you have eaten something, or unleashing you on unsuspecting patients will be quite an adventure."

She rolled her eyes and filled her plate with fruit, making sure to get as many of the sweet, yellow pieces as possible.

"Hey!" Vran'el protested, "Those are my favourites, too! Do not be so greedy!" He quickly snatched a piece of fruit from her plate before she batted away his hand.

"Then you had better get up before me," she said and thought of how much this scene reminded her of herself with Vern. She wondered how the two of them would get along. Probably like a house on fire, one of them too grown up for his age by far, the other one still stuck in some kind of adolescence despite his dry profession. Maybe it was his way of compensating.

Somehow Ram'an seemed so much more suited to this line of work: distinguished, calm, collected, scholarly and yet with the ability to switch on iron-hard determination if need be. This was a great difference between him and Enric, she mused. Her companion did not need to switch it on, it more or less radiated off him all the time. That was probably why people, namely herself, were surprised to find it so unexpectedly in Ram'an while with Enric nobody harboured any doubts that it had been there all along.

"What is the plan for today?" she enquired of her uncle. "You mentioned *unleashing* me on patients. Good. I am itching to do something useful."

"Yes," Valrad confirmed, "we will do some healing today. Though I cannot allow you to work unsupervised, as you will surely understand. Our rules here require an official certificate obtained through training at the clinic for this."

She nodded. "Of course. I am in the process of establishing something similar in Anyueel." Then she looked at him thoughtfully. "You mentioned the chance of sending a healer from here to my city. This would mean that we need to find a way somehow to compare abilities, or neither my healers nor yours here will be able to work in the other city. I have had a look at the books your healer trainees have to go through, so I dare say I have a basic idea what obtaining this certificate entails. Is there a chance I can take these exams here?"

Her uncle pondered her question. "I would need to talk to the head of the clinic about this. From where I stand, it should be possible, but then you have never trained here and we would also have to test your practical abilities apart from your theoretical knowledge. What he will probably offer you will of course depend on the outcome of the trial. If the senate lets you return, we need a quick way for you to accomplish this. If the judgement is not in your favour, there would be more than enough time for you to do some training here."

She scowled at him. "Thank you for remembering that last option. Though I don't really see how I can work at the clinic if Malriel manages to get me marooned here, under house arrest, for two years."

"But you have managed to secure Ram'an's votes for yourself, have you not?" he asked with a raised brow. "This should make it rather unlikely for you to be forced to remain here, I would venture. I just mentioned it for completeness' sake." He picked up the pile of papers he had put down next to him and stood up. "Are the two of you done eating? It is time for us to leave now. My shift starts in half an hour and we have to find something for you to wear yet."

Eryn nodded and pushed her plate aside. "What about you, Ram'an? You don't have to come, you know. I'd imagine that waiting in front of the treatment room for several hours is hardly going to be very pleasant for you. Why don't you return to your residence and pick me up in the afternoon? I am not likely to run away and make my uncle look bad, am I?"

Ram'an smiled. "That is very considerate of you, Theá, but do not worry on my account. I have sent a messenger to bring some of my paperwork to the clinic. I will find a table within sight of your door and catch up on a few things. I have no doubt that you will make no further attempts to flee, but I cannot be seen to be delegating my responsibilities of guarding you to anybody else. It would raise doubts about my commitment to the task at hand."

Of course, she thought, everything else would have been too good to be true. So no message to Enric to ask him to visit her at the clinic while Ram'an was gone. Pity.

She sighed and took his hand when he offered it to help her up. "That is very conscientious of you. I admire your thoroughness."

"No, you do not. You are irked because you will not be able to meet with Lord Enric while I am away. But you cannot really complain about that after what you tried yesterday morning, can you?"

She decided not to pass comment on that. He had said that with such conviction that denying her intentions was probably not much use. Shooting him a sideways glance, she went towards the bathroom to wash herself before leaving for the clinic.

* * *

Eryn leaned back in her uncle's chair when the patient had left the treatment room.

"That was the third one presenting with a slipped disc today. Is that such a common affliction here or is it a coincidence?" she enquired.

"Neither," Valrad replied, "it is due to the harvest season. A lot of heavy lifting, not enough people to do the work, and the ones doing it needing to lift more than they should. This will go on for another three or four weeks, then it will be no more than an occasional occurrence." He smiled at her. "I am very pleased with your work, my girl. Considering that you had no more than a few years of training as a child with an actual healer, your abilities are more advanced than I had dared hope for. I will leave you here for a short while and see if the head of the clinic has time for me to enquire about your request to obtain the certificate." He went to his desk at one end of the room and put the flat of his palm on a stack of papers. "I will leave you here for now. Do not hesitate to peruse my notes if there is something you would like to look up."

She looked puzzled at the intense stare he gave her, then looked down on the papers on which he had placed his hand. His faint smile was strained and he nodded once almost imperceptibly, then went towards the door. "I should be back in no more than half an hour."

Then gone he was. Eryn looked at the door and shook her head in confusion. Her gaze wandered back to the papers on the desk and she leaned across to see what he had been so eager to draw her attention to. Her eyes widened after reading the first few sentences and she drew in a sharp breath. It was an essay or report on the nature and the removal of the barrier inside the heads of the Kingdom dwellers! She quickly flicked through it to see how voluminous the report was. About ten pages. An amount she should easily be able to work through and memorise in about half an hour.

She thought seriously when the implication of what her uncle was doing dawned on her. He had provided her with this knowledge without the triarchy's permission and very likely risked an enormous amount by doing so. If they ever found out about this, he might lose his position at the clinic.

Her head jerked upright in sudden panic and she dropped the sheets to the floor when the door unexpectedly opened without knocking. Ram'an looked at her expression that suspiciously resembled frozen panic and furrowed his brow.

"What are you up to *now*, Theá?"

"Me? Up to? Nonsense!" she exclaimed and laughed. "Why do you always think the worst of me?" She bent down to pick up the report.

"Let me help you with that," he said and started to retrieve the two sheets that had landed closest to his feet.

"No!" she called hastily and quickly snatched them away from under his hands, causing him to narrow his eyes at her.

"Alright," he said slowly and deliberately, "you either tell me what is going on here or I will find out without your cooperation."

She took two steps backwards and away from him, letting her hand with the papers hang down her side to make them seem less conspicuous. He turned to close the door behind him and she saw a moment later a faint shimmer in the air in front of it that meant that there was no escaping from this room. Telling him that there was nothing whatsoever going on would be pointless. She had tried to trick him once too often for that to work.

"Your silence means that I will have to resort to the latter, I assume." He stepped closer and reached out to take the sheets from her hand. She quickly took another step away from him and hid them behind her back.

"Please, Ram'an!" she exclaimed pleadingly when he followed her and reached behind her to relieve her of the report. "This is just something Valrad has written about a medical phenomenon, nothing to cause harm or require your interference! I promise!"

"Why, then, are you so adamant about not letting me see it, if I may ask?" he replied calmly and plucked the sheets deftly from her hand with magically aided speed.

She tried to get them back, but he held them out of her reach and raised his brow at her.

"You either stop that, Theá, or I will immobilise you," he warned and waited for her to consider her next course of action.

Exhaling, she raked the fingers of both hands through her hair and leaned against a wall. There she allowed herself to slide down to the floor with a miserable, resigned expression.

Ram'an leafed through the papers until he found the first page and started reading. After a few moments she heard him whistle through his teeth.

"Look at that. So they have been able to finally confirm one of the theories of why there are no female magicians in your Kingdom. And it seems Valrad was the one who was right." He looked down at her. "Judging from your reaction he is not authorised to pass on that knowledge as yet. I dare say the triarchy will not permit it before the outcome of your trial is clear. So he was willing to risk quite a lot in sharing this with you." He looked at her with a fixed gaze. "Imagine that. So, there is also a rebellious side to good, old Valrad. Who would have thought?"

Eryn swallowed audibly, cursing herself for not being more careful about this and landing her uncle in difficulties. Of all the people who could have learned about this, it had to be a man of the law who knew exactly how illicit the unauthorised conveyance of information was.

"It is not his fault," she said quietly. "As soon as he left to talk to his superior about my being allowed to take the examinations here I was the one who went through his papers. He didn't surrender them to me himself."

Ram'an crouched in front of her, placing his free hand on her knee. "Indeed? So it was pure coincidence that these particular papers were arranged in such a way that you would find them only seconds after he left the room?" he asked in an even tone.

She gave him a pleading look. "What are you going to do now?"

Ram'an sighed heavily and considered the report in his hand. "Nothing, my dear." He let the papers sink into her lap. "Nothing at all. What could I do? Give Valrad away? Causing difficulties for your family would not earn me any points with you, would it? I am still determined to win you for myself, Theá. I would only be sabotaging my own aims. For all I care, people in the Old Kingdom might as well have their ability to have female magicians returned to them. It was never our place to take it away. What is more, it would make you stand out less among them; they may be less insistent on your returning to them in exchange for that knowledge."

Eryn stared at him and then at her uncle's report before nodding slowly. "So you will not expose Valrad?" It could still be dangerous for her uncle later in the event Ram'an decided to take revenge after she left from here with Enric and he would have to face his defeat, however. "For now?"

He smiled thinly. "Not now, not ever. You are worried about what I will do in case you do not stay here with me, are you not? Do not be concerned about that, I promise you that I would not make your family pay for it. Will you trust me on that, my dear Theá? I am willing to repeat this promise under a first level commitment bond."

Her thoughts raced. First level commitment bond? Ah, yes - that was the one that sealed earnest promises. She shook her head hesitantly. It would hardly look good if she doubted his words and demanded a gesture like that.

"That will not be necessary, but thank you."

He took her hand into his so that their palms were pressed against each other. "But I would like to. It will ease your mind and keep you from worrying about your uncle. I can see that you find it hard to rely on my words. I do not blame you for it - it must seem to you that we are on different sides at the moment. So let me do this for your peace of mind. I insist."

She felt warmth seep from his hand through her skin when he started speaking. It was like back in Enric's quarters when she had promised him not to use her special barrier on him before he had removed her manacles for a short while.

"I promise not to expose Valrad with regard to the information he has made available to you despite the fact that he is not authorised to do so. Neither will I expose you and make it known that you are in possession of it." The magic stopped flowing and he kissed her hand before releasing it.

She smiled at him in relief. "Thank you. That was considerate of you. It really means a lot to me; I would have found the idea of getting him into trouble for doing me this great favour unbearable."

He nodded and pulled her back to her feet. "I know. Then I propose that you better get through learning the details of it before he returns. I will stand guard outside and make sure nobody disturbs you while you are at it."

She held on to his hand and lifted it to her cheek for a moment before breaking the contact. The prospect of soon having to distress Ram'an by finally smashing all hopes of her ever being with him was a lot harder to bear when he did things like this for her.

* * *

She stood in front of the window in the treatment room and looked out over the street and the people passing by when Valrad returned. He shot a quick glance at the papers on his desk and smiled at finding them in a different spot than where he had left them.

"I have spoken with my superior and he is open to the option of letting you take the exams. Though he first wants to find out how great the gap in your knowledge is in comparison to our own healers in their last year of training. This will influence his decision."

Eryn nodded. "Thank you very much, Valrad." She stepped close to him and took both his hands in hers. "I appreciate what you are doing for me. Everything." Her gaze darted towards his desk and back to him.

He nodded and smiled. "My dear girl, that is what family is for - being there for you when you need them. And occasionally being a real nuisance."

"You have never once been a nuisance, Valrad," she replied, laughing.

"That is because I delegate less amiable tasks to others," he smirked. "I think my children are better suited to that particular one. It is time for lunch now. Sarol has learned that you are here and asked me to convey his wish to eat with you today."

She lifted her brow. "That does not sound like Sarol."

He smiled. "You have it. He more or less commanded me to inform you that he expects you to have lunch with him today. As you suspected, there was not much *asking* involved."

"Well, then let's oblige him, shall we?"

"I am afraid I will not be able to join you for your meal. I have been called to one of my colleagues to advise him. There is a patient he wants a second opinion on. You go there, the eating hall is not hard to find. Just keep to the right and follow the stream of hungry-looking healers." He unclipped a small silver symbol from his collar and handed it to her. "Wear this and they will feed you."

She looked at the small silver hand that was the symbol for magical healing. "Did you get that when you started working here?"

He shook his head. "No, it is what we get when we pass the exams and are officially considered fully trained healers. Who knows - you might soon be granted one yourself. It makes you recognisable as a healer and entitles you to certain privileges, such as dining for free at healing places in addition to being granted access to patient files and medical libraries everywhere throughout our country."

She followed the outline of the delicate symbol with her finger. "And people here will not mind if you let me wear it for now?"

"Not for one hour in order to get you fed, no. If I let you run around with it outside the clinic, I would definitely get into trouble for it. So do not let me forget to claim it back from you later. And now you had better leave. Sarol is not known for his patience, as you are surely aware."

She stepped outside the treatment room and looked around for Ram'an. He was sitting in one corner at a round table with books and papers spread about him. He lifted his head as soon as Eryn closed the door behind her and smiled when he beheld her.

"Theá, my dear. According to my stomach and the steady stream of people in the same direction it should be time for lunch now."

She nodded and watched him push his chair back. "It is, yes. I have been invited - or rather instructed - to eat with Sarol."

He lifted a brow. "Instructed by who? Valrad?"

"No, Sarol. He is very assured in his importance and assumes that if he wants to have lunch with somebody that person will not refuse."

Ram'an chuckled. "It seems that his confidence is not entirely unwarranted, is it? You are complying, after all."

"I am, yes. I admit I feel rather honoured he wants to spend time with me. He is known to be wary of magicians, so I think I must be privileged at being considered worthy."

"Well, he is known to be more accepting of magicians stemming from House Vel'kim, considering all your father did to get him accepted into being trained here. As well as that, your uncle has always treated him well."

She snorted. "Thank you very much for reducing my unique character traits and abilities to my connection to House Vel'kim. When I first met him, he did not really give me the impression that this little detail got me an advance in his esteem."

"I did not mean to diminish your uniqueness, my dear Theá," he said. They walked on and his gaze fell on the silver symbol at her collar. "Your uncle has lent you his insignia, I see. Well, well, I suppose it will only be a matter of time until you will be wearing one of your very own."

She smiled at the thought. "May your words turn out to be prophetic. I was wondering about having something similar designed for my own healers. Something to distinguish them as healers, something subtle that nevertheless makes them easily recognisable. Though borrowing the symbol of another country for use in Anyueel is hardly appropriate."

Ram'an raised both brows. "Why would it not be? It is where their knowledge comes from, after all. And as they do not really have their own symbol of healing over there, you would not be showing any disrespect for local traditions, would you?"

A valid argument, she admitted to herself. And yet it did seem wrong to take another culture's symbol for it instead of creating something for themselves. What is more, she had a very talented artist at her disposal to work something out here, didn't she? The thought of Vern made her smile. She wondered again how he was doing in his temporary position, whether several weeks in charge of the place had made him either desperate or reluctant to give up his position of power ever again. She tried to imagine how he had reacted to learning that he was supposed to continue filling in for her for yet longer without knowing exactly when he would be released from his duties. Worried, most likely. Even if he welcomed the chance to be in charge a little longer, learning about her troubles would surely have upset him.

"I like this faraway smile of yours, Theá. What is it you are thinking of?" Ram'an asked gently.

"Vern," she told him. "I am missing him. A lot. He is pretty much the first real friend I have ever had. With him I can be myself, which is quite a relief as I am now responsible for so many things back home. At work we are professionals, colleagues, and when we spend our free time together, we fight, insult each other and laugh together. From what I have seen this is a rare thing to have."

He nodded. "It is indeed. And I am glad to see that you treasure it."

She stopped and turned to him. "And yet you are determined to keep me here and take all this away from me."

His expression became strained and he lifted both hands to put them on her shoulders. "I would never take away more than I am willing to give back to you, my sweet Theá. You will have knowledge here, family, colleagues..."

"Let's not discuss this now. I am sorry I started it. I know that you do not intend to make me unhappy, but I want you to know that I am terrified of being stuck here."

He just nodded sadly and took her hand to lead her into the eating hall. A great number of tables were spread unevenly throughout the room. She scanned the occupants and saw a hand lifted in greeting to her left and the familiar slightly bored voice of Sarol called out to her.

"Eryn. Come over here. You may bring your guardian. You probably have no other choice, anyway."

She froze when she saw who was sitting with him. Pe'tala had stopped midway in chewing a bite of food and stared at Eryn with obvious displeasure.

"Sarol," she hissed, "you could have told me that you planned to dine with *them* before letting me sit down with you!"

Eryn saw several pairs of interested eyes turn towards them and felt Ram'an's hand on her elbow.

"Come on, let us not provide material for entertainment and gossip for now. Sit down and try to get this behind you in dignity."

"Seriously?" she whispered incredulously. "You are making me sit down at the same table with the two of you? Shouldn't you be more reluctant to eat with the woman you discarded *and* the one you are trying to shackle here?"

He just smiled tensely and pushed her on towards the table and then down on a cushion next to Sarol.

Pe'tala's icy stare fell on the silver insignia immediately. "So father lent you his pin. Do not become attached to it too much; it is something only *real* healers are supposed to wear."

Eryn swallowed the retort that she hoped she would be wearing her own one soon enough. It would be so much sweeter to just show it to Pe'tala once Eryn had passed the exam and to observe how her expression, without doubt, would collapse.

"And it is a pleasure to meet you again, too," she replied instead with a false smile.

Once Ram'an had taken a seat between the two women, a female server approached them with two bowls of food and nodded when she saw Eryn's silver symbol. She waited until Ram'an had handed her two pieces of the local coinage and then left the group.

"I hope you will manage to spend a few civilised minutes in each other's company, or I myself will leave," Sarol commented and kept on eating.

"That is a risk you were obviously willing to take, considering your very interesting choice of luncheon companions," Ram'an said tartly.

He shrugged. "You are all grown people. Professionals, too. More or less. Whatever the results of your little love triangle here may turn out as, I do not see why I have to let this ruin my chance of spending some time with two good healers."

Pe'tala stared at her colleague for a moment, then shook her head and laughed. "I am never sure with you. You either have just a very cruel sense of humour or you really are as unconcerned with the feelings of other people."

"As your situation fails to amuse me, I would assume it is the latter one," Sarol admitted unabashedly. "Now tell me, Eryn, what you have been working on today. As you will probably leave here soon in case the senate votes in your favour, you might want to use the remaining time here to your best advantage."

Eryn blinked in surprise. "Slipped discs from the harvesting, mostly. I appreciate your concern, but I am not really in a position to pick my assignments here. I am glad enough that Valrad allows me to work here at all."

He shook his head with a dismissive wave of his hand. "Nonsense. I dare say you have worked with enough injuries to be able to repair every possible kind of tissue. How able are you with infectious diseases?"

She thought for a moment, then snorted. "That depends if you consider handling an outbreak of a lung disease in a village without giving away your magical abilities a sufficient challenge for a healer."

He seemed to think for a moment, then nodded. "Adequate enough, I would think. Cosmetic corrections?"

She grimaced and shook her head. "Spare me. My expertise in that area is about as advanced as I care for."

Sarol raised a brow at her. "I sense great disdain here. I would not disregard this area if I were you. Pe'tala, elaborate, will you."

Pe'tala looked at him in annoyance. "You are making me lecture her here? I do not believe this is happening!"

She sighed and rolled her eyes when he just stared at her, seemingly at a loss as to why his request met any resistance from her at all.

"So be it. It is a clear signal of an advanced and tolerant society to value the individual's wish for self-improvement due to his or her own requirements. This improvement is to be carried out in a way that ensures the individual's wellbeing and continued health without causing undue inconvenience or pain." It sounded like she was quoting that from a book.

Eryn chuckled. "You have made catering to vanity a principle of your healing services? How lovely."

"Yes, dear cousin," Pe'tala sneered, "because in comparison to your oh-so-very-advanced country across the sea, we have no priorities other than beautifying people instead of pursuing knowledge and development. How many healers did you say there were again before Ved'al and yourself?" she added, in a sweetly sour voice.

"It is also a convenient way of keeping the money flowing in to support the services that are not self-funding but necessary as opposed to cosmetic corrections," Sarol cut in.

Eryn nodded and sighed. That was no different here than back in Anyueel.

"In order to be in a position to ask high prices for these services, we need to provide high quality standards, of course," he continued. "As you are in a position of heading healing services back in the Old Kingdom, I would have assumed that this connection was self-evident."

Pe'tala smirked at his last statement. "Yes, one would think that."

"I see the connection well enough, but unlike yourselves here, I am forced to work with limited resources back in Anyueel. I have a staff allocation of currently no more than five healers, and keeping them busy with cosmetic alterations means that I cannot provide as much necessary healing. I am reluctant to neglect legitimate medical patients in order to cater to the whims of vain, rich people," she explained with a stern expression and folded arms, daring either of them to contradict her.

Sarol nodded. "I see. That is an understandable sentiment, of course. Why do you have no more than five healers?"

"Because the Order is concerned about my undermining their primary function of defence. So they make sure there are a lot more warriors than healers around," she replied darkly.

He frowned. "But that limitation would then only apply to magicians, would it not? What keeps you from taking on non-magicians as healers? Is there no place for them in your elitist approach to this noble profession?" The last sentence had been a lot less sober than his usual statements. His history of not being taken seriously due to his lack of magical powers clearly swung in there somewhere. She decided to reply to it the way he deserved.

"No, you bloody fool, that is not why I am not training them! It is because I do not have a lot of practise in training in general and no idea how to train non-magician healers in particular. So it is my own shortcomings that stop me from acquiring the people I need in order improve my organisation, if you need to know."

She noted with satisfaction that she had finally managed to unsettle him. Pe'tala, too, regarded him with interest. So this displaying some sign of unease was clearly not a common sight.

"I can provide you with a training plan for this purpose," he murmured, his eyes on the food in his bowl.

Eryn hid a smile. "Good. You do just that." Then she decided to push her luck a little further. "And you should make some time to come to Anyueel in order to see if your plan works out the way it was supposed to. It is the least you can do after calling me a magician supremacist."

He looked at her with an alarmed expression. "I never called you that!"

She shrugged. "But it was implied. Don't deny it. So, do you agree to vising Anyueel or not?"

Sarol stared at her for another few seconds, then nodded slowly. "I do." Then he straightened, returning to his usual confident self a moment later. "You will keep me informed of your efforts and I will decide what time would be convenient for me. Not to mention interesting enough, considering your progress."

Eryn hardly managed to keep her face calm. Yes! He would be the key to no longer being forced to limit her efforts to the staff quota the Order granted her! She wanted to leap up and perform a victory dance, clap her hands or otherwise express her joy, but remained seated with a placid expression. She saw Ram'an hide a smile and wondered if he was aware of her excitement. Pe'tala just threw a reluctantly impressed glance in her direction before rising.

"You will excuse me for now. I need to get back to my work."

Ram'an stood up with her. "Pe'tala, it was unexpected to meet you here, but a pleasure nevertheless," he said gallantly with a warm smile at her.

She lifted her brow at him and regarded him coolly. "Really. Was it now." Then she turned away and left the eating hall.

"You are not trying to get her back, are you?" Sarol asked. "She would not take you, no matter how rich and pretty you are. Very proud, that one. Yet people say you are still besotted with the other one," he nodded at Eryn. "Or have you finally given up on her and decided to take over your House?"

Eryn gulped at that very blunt statement and looked up at Ram'an, who probably did not have to deal with this kind of remark very often due to his position in society. It was rather what people said behind his back instead of to his face.

"I think it is time for us to return as well," he said stiffly and took Eryn's hand to lift her from her cushion. "Sarol, I wish you a productive afternoon."

He took her hand and walked back towards Valrad's treatment room with her. When they were out of earshot, he smiled in amusement. "That was very well done, Theá. Even Pe'tala was impressed, though she is probably rather reluctant to show you any appreciation whatever."

"You mean when I asked Sarol to come to Anyueel?"

"Yes. He showed you one weakness, and you exploited it mercilessly by making him look like a fool for insinuating ulterior motives and then even admitting to your own limits. That set him thinking. In the end there was not much more he could do than to agree when you insisted on his travelling to the Old Kingdom, at the same time demonstrating great appreciation for his skill and thus exploiting another of his weaknesses: his vanity." He shook his head in wonder. "Remarkable. I bow to your quick thinking and determination. And you knew exactly how to handle him. Apologising for causing him distress would have been the exact wrong thing to do. Instead you talked him into submission by giving to him what he likes to deal out to others: a proper reprimand."

Eryn smiled widely, more than satisfied with his assessment of her deeds, dimly aware that he was very probably catering to her own vanity right now. But a girl needed to indulge herself every now and then.

CHAPTER 48

Defending Herself

Eryn stood in the main room at the Vel'kim residence, patiently waiting until Vran'el was done scrutinising her appearance. He had insisted that she needed to look strong, confident and serious. She had proposed wearing her healer's robes for this purpose, but he had immediately dismissed that idea. Emphasising her otherness was not a good strategy here. He had already sent her back to her room to change twice and she was waiting for his judgement on her current attire, some bright red tunic and black trousers. He had not discarded it right away, which held promise.

"I think we can work with this, yes," he nodded finally, making her exhale in relief. Good. Otherwise she would run out of options soon.

"I don't really see why we are bothering with this," she complained. "This is little more than a farce as it is not about judging me fairly but seeing which side is stronger - the one supporting Malriel or the one against her. So what difference does it really make how I am dressed? As I said before, I could probably turn up naked and sing a bawdy song instead of answering the questions, and the result would be virtually the same!"

"An intriguing plan," Ram'an said from the cushions on which he sat and observed them. "Would you like to demonstrate here, so we can decide together if it is a valid course of action?"

"Very funny," she returned.

Vran'el unclipped the ponytail that hung down her back. "Braid that. It looks more dignified and no-nonsense."

She obeyed and lifted her hands to quickly intertwine the strands of hair into the style he wanted.

"Yes, that is fine. You are basically right; what you say will probably not make much of a difference. But your adhering to our protocols will nevertheless make a good impression. In addition, it will very probably influence your dealings with our country in the future, whatever the outcome of this trial is."

"Right now I don't really feel like I want to deal with this accursed place any more after I am gone," she growled.

"Nonsense," Vran'el said in a harsh voice that made her look at him in surprise. "If I were to assume that letting you leave here would mean never hearing anything from you again I might be less inclined to assist you in making this turn out in your favour."

She was chastened. "Forgive me. I didn't mean to imply that I would willingly give up my family connection to you. I just felt the urge to air my frustration over this whole mess."

He exhaled and nodded slowly. "Good. As long as you do not make any mistake about that."

She stepped close to him and wrapped her arms around him, pressing her cheek against his. "You are a nuisance and a pain in my neck. But I love you. I will continue to let you annoy me with the messages these fabulous birds you breed will bring me."

She smiled at his low chuckle and felt him squeeze her for a moment before releasing her.

"It is time for us to leave now. The hearing will start in less than half an hour and we cannot be late."

Eryn breathed in deeply, then nodded. There was basically not much to be afraid of, she told herself. The senators determined to support Malriel would not be swayed by whatever she said today, and neither would those against her. And yet answering their questions and talking about that matter once again was not a happy prospect. At least she would see Enric there, however small the chance of her being allowed to get close to him was.

She shaded her eyes against the morning sun as they stepped outside and felt Ram'an take her hand in his and squeeze it reassuringly.

"There is no need to be nervous, Theá," he said in a soft voice. "As you pointed out so eloquently, you cannot really mess anything up today since this is no more than a political game in which you happen to be the prize."

"I know. But I am not sure if that doesn't make it even more scary. It means that I have practically next to no influence on anything that happens. Others are in control of what is going to happen to me."

"That is not entirely true, is it?" he said mildly. "You are playing your own part in this game. You have managed to secure four votes in your favour already, have you not?"

She looked at him. "How certain are these votes really? Have you received any confirmation that these three Houses allied with you will comply with your request? What if Malriel has managed to bribe them to make them vote in her favour instead?"

Ram'an shook his head. "Do not worry about that, they have all promised me to vote the way I asked them to. I assume Malriel will not really count on losing those votes, as she very probably still counts on my voting in her favour in order to keep you here."

Which brought them back to the reason why he really was doing this for her. He had to be aware that she was nowhere close to giving in to him and leaving Enric. Why was he still so absurdly confident about her staying with him after the trial was over? She decided to worry about that later. One thing after the other. First the trial, then she would deal with Ram'an and whatever devious plans he might have hatched.

But he was right. She had done something that might very likely tip the scales in her favour, so she was not entirely a victim of circumstances. How marvellous it would be, winning this farce against Malriel, she mused. She would of course not gloat. Well, at least not openly. Not in Malriel's presence, that is. There would of course be gloating as soon as she was alone with her family. Malriel was not included in that term, she had lost any claim to that. If that trial did turn out the way Eryn hoped, soon even the official legal connection between them would be severed for good. Which was the interesting part for Ram'an, as according to her cousin it would allow him to be in charge of his House despite taking her as his companion. Which would of course not be happening anytime soon and which once more brought her back to the question of whatever in the world had made him think that he could convince her otherwise. Somehow her thoughts kept returning to that one imponderable.

The senate building came into view when they turned the next corner and she ascended the stairs with the two men next to her.

"You will not be sitting with us this time," Vran'el instructed her when they stood before the large doors. "You will stand before the podium where the triarchy sits and turn to whoever addresses you. Your answers to all questions will be addressed to the senate as a whole, so be sure to make eye contact with as many people as possible there. Do also include Malriel. You need to be seen not to be afraid of her, however unpleasant that might be for you. It is a demonstration of strength, and that is pretty much what is expected of an Aren woman."

Perfect, she thought sourly. It meant she was expected to more or less represent the character traits of a House she had every intention of leaving behind her as soon as she was able. But currently she was officially still a member, so she would heed Vran'el's advice as best she could.

Her cousin waited for her to nod before he opened one of the large double doors for her to enter. The senate was almost completely assembled already, with only a few seats remaining unfilled.

"Am I expected to walk to the front right now and wait there until everybody is present?" she whispered.

"No," Vran'el said equally quietly, "wait until everybody is here and is seated. Also, it would look rather strange if you stood there rigidly. And it would hardly serve to calm your nerves, would it?"

"Not really, no," she admitted and let her eyes wander over the assembled representatives of the Houses until she spotted a familiar blonde head at the other end of the room. Narrowed blue eyes were focused on her hand that was still linked with Ram'an's, and she hastily pulled it away and smiled at Enric apologetically.

She saw his shoulders rise and sink again in a resigned sigh. Then he straightened and gave her a reassuring smile and winked at her. Biting her lip, she forced her feet to remain still instead of racing over to him and hugging him, telling him everything about yesterday, about learning how to remove the barrier inside his head and making Sarol agree to travelling to Anyueel in the near future. However, Ram'an would not be content just to watch but would hold her back. Aside from keeping her away from Enric as best he could for personal reasons, he would surely not want to be seen to be too lenient with her.

Time passed with exaggerated slowness. They waited another three minutes for the last senators to arrive and take their seats. Then the triarchy took their elevated seats and Torke'na motioned for Eryn to step in front of the assembled senators.

"Maltheá of House Aren," she spoke, her tone formal, "this hearing today has been called to give you the chance of allowing us to hear your side of this story. You will be asked to answer questions to give us a clearer view of the case you are the accused in."

Eryn slowly walked down the few steps that lead to the subjacent circle in front of the curved tables, careful to hold her head high and keep her expression calm and neutral. Today would *not* be another occasion for people to witness what was known as the Aren temper, no matter what provocations there might be. Strength, she reminded herself. Strength meant control, and control always started with oneself. She remembered Vran'el's words from the last hearing three days ago about appearing superior, confident and unperturbed, like Enric.

"You were already asked to point out any... inaccuracies in Malriel's story last time," Torke'na said when Eryn was standing in front of her. "At that time you did not wish to correct any flaws in her account. You now have, once more, the opportunity to rectify any inaccuracies. I would therefore ask you to tell us your story again in your own words."

Eryn nodded and turned to the senate, forcing herself also to look at Malriel in the first row to her right. She had this time, again, opted for a slightly older appearance than in her everyday life. Eryn closed her eyes for a moment, then told her story afresh, for the third time now. Unfortunately, Malriel had been accurate enough, so there were no obvious inconsistencies with her daughter's version that would make her seem dishonest or eager to deceive her fellow senators in order to achieve her goal.

There was silence once Eryn finished the tale with the lynching of the baker, just as the last time, when Malriel had told them about it.

"You did this for reasons of revenge, if I understood you correctly?"

She scanned the rows of seats until her gaze fell on a face she remembered as belonging to Legara of House Finran. A House allied with Malriel.

"Yes," she answered carefully, not volunteering any more information than necessary. Vran'el had been adamant about this yesterday when he had sat down with her to instruct her how best to handle this hearing.

"I see. Having been trained by a man we know was a healer and very strict about the preservation of life, I assume that you were aware of the rules against using magic, healing magic in particular, against defenceless non-magicians?"

Her cousin had warned her to expect that question, and she was glad, as it might otherwise have thrown her off track.

She lifted her chin. "I had been told about it, yes."

"What induced you to disregard your father's instructions and break this rule nevertheless?" Legara continued.

"Youthful thoughtlessness," Eryn said calmly, looking the woman straight in the eye. "Anger at having been treated unfairly with no chance of getting even with the boy. Bad judgement, obviously," she added dryly, which earned her a few smirks from other senators.

"Since this incident," a man from the row of senators asked, "have you ever again used your healing skills to take revenge on or cause harm to another person, be they magician or non-magician?"

"No," Eryn replied with emphasis. "Never."

"That is rather difficult to believe," Legara all but snorted. "Many of our young magicians do not even refrain from doing so again after being punished by the Council for juvenile offences."

"Yes, Legara," Valrad threw in testily from the row behind her, "but then not many of them lose their father as a consequence of disobeying the rule the first time, do they? I imagine that this is an infinitely more powerful demonstration of what can go wrong than any reprimand or punishment from the Council."

Eryn saw several sympathetic looks directed towards her uncle. They were talking about his brother's death, after all.

"I see that this is a painful subject for you, Valrad," Legara replied gently. "The reason your niece needs to face this trial is because of your brother's death. This cannot be easy for you. Yet we need to make sure that she is no longer a danger to the people around her, especially as she intends to continue working as a healer."

Eryn held her breath when she saw Enric slowly getting up from his chair at the back of the room. "I request permission to speak."

Torke'na cast a quick look at her colleagues to make sure there were no objections from their side, then nodded. "Yes, Ambassador. Permission is granted."

"I think I am in a position to assist the senate in dealing with the doubts that have arisen by confirming that... Maltheá of House Aren has not resorted to using her healing skills to her advantage, even under the most extreme circumstances," he spoke earnestly, his clear, strong voice reverberating around the circular room.

"And what circumstances would that have been, Ambassador?" Abrak asked with a raised brow.

Enric looked up at the triarch, a faint smile playing around his lips. "The circumstances that consisted of her having been kept prisoner for several months."

That caused murmuring among the senators and more than one face showed surprise at this revelation. It had not been made public knowledge, Eryn mused. Only Valrad, Ram'an and Malriel had known about it so far. She wondered exactly why he had revealed it. It would hardly make much of a difference for the trial, would it?

"I would," Enric added, "be willing to testify under the influence of what is in my country referred to as a *truth block*."

The murmuring then increased in volume and Torke'na lifted her hands to silence the senators. "Senators, your vote by show of hands if you wish to take the Ambassador up on the offer he has just made."

Eryn saw several hands raised, more than half from what she could see at first glance.

"That makes eight votes against four," Torke'na announced and nodded to Enric. "If you would care to step down, Ambassador. Golir as the only one stronger than you will administer what we refer to as *lie filter*."

Both Enric and Golir stepped down to the space Eryn had until then occupied by herself. Enric stood close enough that she could touch him if she stretched out her hand. She caught Ram'an's warning look and balled her hand into a fist to prevent it from reaching out and resorted to watching the questioning that was about to take place.

Golir clasped his hand around Enric's forearm and looked straight into his eyes.

"I will start with my questions and if there is any other information the senate requires, you may ask them when I am done," he announced. "Ambassador, you just stated that Maltheá was kept prisoner by you. I would ask you to elaborate on the circumstances that led to her captivity and the exact nature of this captivity." His tone was not exactly a friendly one, Eryn noted worriedly. Maybe it had not been such a smart move on Enric's side to bring it up in order to establish that she had spoken the truth.

Enric nodded. "As you are aware thanks to Malriel's reports, Maltheá was captured after an injury to her head when she was on her way to gather herbs. The villagers were afraid of being punished for harbouring a spy and surrendered her to the King. She was then taken to the city of Anyueel and questioned by the Order of

Magicians. At that time we were not aware of her magical abilities, nor had we even considered the possibility of a female magician for obvious reasons."

Eryn suppressed a shiver. Hearing him repeatedly call her by the name that had been given to her here as a girl felt unreal and wrong. Then she remembered Vran'el's words about the wisdom of her not seeming too foreign today and she felt proud and relieved that Enric, too, had obviously reached that same conclusion and demonstrated to the senators by using her former name that she really was one of them. And judging one of their own for an action that would under normal circumstances have been dealt with in a less threatening way was just a fraction more difficult than doing it with a stranger, a foreigner.

"How did you find out about her abilities, in that case?" Golir enquired.

"It was in the course of the interrogation. When one of my colleagues used a truth bl... a lie filter on her, it became clear to them that her father had been a magician. When she attempted to resist any further questions, they tried to stun her, but Maltheá managed to shield herself against them. She then tried to leave the building as none of their strikes managed to penetrate her shield."

"How then were you able to stop her?"

"One of the magicians summoned me from my quarters and I finally managed to stop her by paralysing her with one very strong bolt. It was my first encounter with her," he added and looked at her with a faint smile.

Golir nodded slowly. "Why was Maltheá being kept prisoner? From what I have gathered she had not broken any of your laws, or am I mistaken?"

Enric shook his head. "No, you are not. There were concerns about the chances of her being a spy. The memories about your people, you see, were faint, but we still associated female magicians and brown hair with the Western Territories. So we were virtually confident that is was where she came from. Unfortunately, her memories were not much help as she was very young when she was taken away from here."

Eryn noted gladly that he didn't mention the reason for this: the memory block her father had put on her.

"The Order discarded these concerns quickly," he continued, "and soon agreed that having her join us would be of immense benefit. As it turned out, however, her father, Ved'al, had not been a great friend of the Order due to its exclusive purpose of training warriors for reasons of defence. Maltheá was not exactly eager to join us, as you may imagine. We thus decided to keep her with us and start training her in the skills that were required for membership in the Order."

"How did Maltheá react to her confinement?" Golir asked calmly but with disapproval clear in his eyes.

"Not very favourably," Enric admitted. "It was after only a few days that she made her first attempt to flee from the city. We used golden manacles to keep her powers blocked and she managed to persuade her combat trainer to remove them when her wrists underneath them were chafed open and bloody. She tried to flee through the city gates, but I managed to apprehend her. This was the first time I unconsciously provided her with an opportunity to use her healing powers adversely on me without any chance of my counteracting them."

"How was this?" Golir asked, obviously curious despite his disapproval.

"I cornered her in a turret. I assume she had counted on finding steps inside that would lead up the city wall, but instead found herself caught in a dead end. I pushed her into a corner and secured both her wrists with my hands to look at the undamaged skin where wounds had been before. It was the first time that I had seen actual healing with my own eyes, and I was fascinated. This skin contact, you see, would have enabled her to harm me. She had no feelings other than fear and hate for me at that time, so concerns for me were clearly not what held her back and stopped her from making use of that chance to free herself."

Eryn let her eyes wander over the faces of the senators, catching several sympathetic glances, even from representatives of Houses on Malriel's side. Malriel herself kept a menacing stare trained on Enric.

Golir nodded slowly. "I see. That is an impressive example of Maltheá's restraint when it would have been easy and to a certain degree understandable if she had used her powers for her defence. I can confirm to the senate that this narrative is in accordance with what Ambassador Enric believes to be the truth. Are there any more questions you wish to ask at this time?"

"Yes!" Eryn heard a familiar throaty female voice call out and closed her eyes.

"I wish to know what you would have done with my daughter had she not given in and joined your Order," Malriel's angry voice boomed through the senate hall. Even though she had known about her daughter's captivity, it now seemed that its extent seemed to considerably exceed what Malriel had imagined.

Enric turned his head to her and regarded her calmly. "We would not have given up. *I* would not have given up."

"Would you not?" she smiled cruelly. "What would have made you persist, if I may ask?"

"I started falling in love with her only a few months after she had been brought to the city," he replied simply. "I was determined not to lose her. I still am." The warning implicit in the last sentence, aimed at Malriel, was plain enough for everyone to hear.

"Was Maltheá falling in love with you as well?" she demanded sharply. "Or did you take advantage of her status as a prisoner as she was too compliant to her father's rules to free herself?"

Eryn felt a pause before Enric's reply when she saw the angry spark in his eyes at this insinuation. He was surely not about to lose his temper when everybody around her kept impressing on her how important it was for her to keep her own under control, was he?

"No to both," he replied with calm steel in his voice. "She had not started developing more than tolerance for me until after we were joined. And I did not take advantage of a helpless prisoner to make her compliant."

"Really? So it was her own voluntary decision to let herself be joined to a man you just told us she had at that time felt no more than *tolerance* for?" Malriel's fury was clearly visible in her posture, her balled fists and the daggers her eyes beamed at him.

Golir cleared his throat. "Malriel, these questions are clearly not pertaining to the case at hand. Whatever personal matters you wish to clarify with your daughter's companion will have to wait until the hearing is over. You are welcome to join the Ambassador and myself for dinner tonight if you so wish."

Eryn's head snapped to Golir. Dinner? With Enric and Malriel? She didn't like the idea, not one bit.

"No," she heard herself say. "I do not think that this is necessary. Malriel may rest assured that I am happy enough in the situation I am now, apart from being accused by my own mother of causing my father's death, that is." She flashed Malriel a cold glance. "I do not see any need for my companion to justify his actions to *you* of all people."

Golir looked at the blonde magician. "What is your decision? I will bow to your wishes in this matter as it is a personal one."

"I will see her in the evening if she wishes to talk about this. I do not wish to leave her in any doubt that her daughter is in good hands and will continue to be," Enric replied calmly.

Eryn swallowed the groan that wanted to escape her mouth with an effort and glowered at her companion.

"Are there any more questions as to the clarification of Maltheá's resolve in not misusing her healing abilities on people around her?" the triarch asked loudly.

Heads around them shook and Golir finally released Enric's forearm, then stepped back. "Good. Legara? As you did not wish to ask any more questions I assume this cleared up your doubts."

Legara nodded reluctantly.

"I would like to hear Malriel state her reasons behind accusing her own daughter while she is subjected to a lie filter," Eryn heard Uvel of House Tokmar, the one who had asked Malriel inconvenient questions at the first hearing already, say.

Torke'na fixed him with a warning glare. "Malriel is not the one facing charges here, Uvel. There is no legal precedent for justifying such a course of action - unless you yourself wish to make an accusation?"

Uvel shook his head. "No, I do not wish to accuse her. Alas, wasting the senate's time and effort in trying to keep her daughter from leaving here again is not against the law. It is interesting, however, that she seems to be angry about her daughter having been kept prisoner when she herself seems to have planned the very same." He turned to Malriel. "Or is it something different, if *you* are the one doing it, Malriel? No one to force an Aren but another Aren?"

Malriel glowered at him, all colour draining from her face. Eryn watched in fascinated horror how her breathing got more agitated and her eyes seemed about to spit fire.

"One more word from you, Uvel, and you will regret it," she hissed quietly, but the senators had all ceased talking, so every single pair of ears in the hall caught her words.

"This hearing is adjourned," Golir announced urgently. "We will meet again in five days from now for the votes to be cast in this case. Should there be any more questions for which you require answers in order to cast your vote with clear consciences, you may contact any member of the triarchy you choose and we will arrange for you to receive the information you desire." He then stepped, to the collective relief of most people in the room, in front of Malriel and started speaking to her in a low voice about something which seemed to be about procedure or etiquette.

Eryn felt Vran'el's hand close around her upper arm and tug her with him. "Come on, time to leave. No, do not look back. Just keep walking on. We do not want to provoke her any further." A second hand gripped her other arm. Ram'an.

"He is right," he added. "Let us get out of here before things get ugly. You do not want to be here in case she loses control of that vicious temper of hers. Uvel may decide to stay and taunt her even further judging from that mischievous look he has in his eyes. He really is in an unusually self-destructive mood today, it seems."

Eryn turned one last time to catch a glimpse of Enric, who was watching her being all but frog-marched from the senate hall and raked a hand through his blonde hair wearily.

CHAPTER 49

Warning Malriel

Enric sighed when he heard a knock at the door to the guest room he was staying in. That very likely meant that Golir had finished his dinner preparations.

"Come in," he called and Golir opened the door.

"I have finished cooking and was wondering if you would care to join me for a drink before your guest arrives."

Your guest, Enric thought darkly. So Golir wanted to impress on him that he himself had to deal with whatever trouble might arise from his decision to receive Malriel tonight. Fair enough, he thought. And it was not as if he wasn't able to hold off Eryn's mother if need be. He was stronger than her, after all. And he had only recently stepped between three angry Aren women, so dealing with only one of them would hardly prove to be that much of a challenge compared to that scene at the Aren estate. Had it really been no more than a week ago?

He nodded to his host who was still waiting for his answer. "That would be delightful."

Golir proceeded him into the spacious main room and stepped towards a dark wooden drink cabinet while Enric walked towards the sitting arrangement and sank down onto a cushion.

"I admit I was rather surprised at your willingness to admit to Malthea's captivity today at the hearing," the older man said conversationally when he joined Enric. "A rather bold manoeuvre to prove the truth of Malthea's claim never to have used her powers that way again after her father's death."

Enric smiled. "Bold moves work best in my experience, especially when they are unanticipated."

Golir regarded him thoughtfully. "That would depend on what your goal is, I would assume. Your little story has very likely served to make the senators more sympathetic to Malthea's situation. But I wonder how your own reputation will be affected by this. Although I cannot really believe it will suffer so very greatly from the revelations today. People have come to know you as a man made of steel, as it were. A hard, but decent negotiator, seemingly dauntless when it comes to facing dangers such as an Aren clash, and a man who delights in having a wild prey animal as his personal pet. Added to that you kept an Aren woman captive for months and still managed to make her join you somehow. That will probably make people hold you in even greater esteem." He took a sip from his glass. "Malriel was on the brink of giving us an impressive demonstration of the legendary Aren temper today thanks to your narrative. I had wondered if Maltheá would treat us to one, but *she* kept her calm wonderfully."

Enric nodded proudly. "That she did, yes."

"I was wondering whether provoking Malriel was one of your intentions today," Golir said reflectively and chuckled when Enric didn't answer. "But of course you would not admit this to me, would you? A little word of caution, though: be very, very careful when irritating an Aren woman. Then again, you should already know about this, having experienced the effects of such temper as you decided to live with one yourself. Interesting women. One of my grandmothers was an Aren. I was terrified of her. A boy once stole a piece of fruit from her garden. Nobody knows what exactly she did to him, but it is said that he could not bear to look at this type of fruit for more than two decades." His eyes took on a distant look at the memory. "They do get more frightening with age, you know."

Enric swallowed and raised a brow. "They do?"

"Oh yes," Golir smirked. "Scary bunch, the lot of them. The older, the worse. But at least there is one burden you will never have to bear in your relationship: boredom."

They both looked up when they heard the chimes from the entrance door announcing a visitor.

"Ah yes, speaking of scary women... Would you mind admitting her, Enric? Then I will serve the food. I am sure she is eager to get to the point and will not want to spend more time with eating than necessary. I am not ashamed to admit that I dread somewhat the thought of an impatient Aren woman in my close proximity. Especially in a confined space," he added crisply.

Enric remembered the story about Eryn's grandmother making a wine storage explode and chuckled while he rose to answer the door.

Malriel had seemingly returned her appearance back to the age she preferred to reflect when she was not currently trying to look more distinguished. She again looked about Enric's own age, just a few years older than him, and not the older woman better suited to accusing her daughter at a trial.

Her smile did not reach her eyes. He took both her hands to pull her close and kiss her on both cheeks, noting the annoyed flicker in her eyes with satisfaction.

"Welcome, Malriel. So glad you could join us," he purred and held out to her the customary bowl with cool, damp towels so she could refresh herself. She gave him another nonchalant look and, after dropping the used towel back into the bowl, preceded him up the stairs to the main room. So far she had not spoken a single word.

Enric followed her with a grim smile playing around his lips.

"Golir," she said politely when he emerged from the adjoining kitchen with three bowls in one hand.

"Malriel," he replied and placed the vessels on the table before turning to her and kissing her hand. "Have a seat, please. Dinner is ready, we can eat at once."

She nodded appreciatively and sank onto the cushions elegantly.

"Wine, as usual?" Golir asked and fetched her a glass when she nodded.

While they were washing their hands, he filled their bowls and then waited for them to start eating before doing so himself.

"I was just recounting a story of my grandmother to Enric," he said conversationally.

Malriel nodded. "My great-aunt Malhedre. Very skilled baker, she was. Known for her mean fruit cakes."

"Not the only mean thing about her from what I remember," Golir smiled. "Gave me a good beating with her steel-cored cooking spoon more than once. I remember how much I loathed visiting her. When I was older I pretended to have too many exercises to finish and so no time for a visit. From that time on my grades improved immensely as I kept doing a lot of extra work so I could stay at home."

"Yes, Aren grandmothers tend to have that effect on children," she said with a pasty smile. "But from what my daughter told me this is never going to be a problem in *our* family as she does not intend to have any children herself."

So much for casual dinner conversation, Enric thought, and raised an eyebrow at her.

"Indeed. But do not let this upset you, Malriel. Even if we had some children, they would be too far away for you to see, if that is any consolation," he stated calmly and noted the dangerous spark in her eyes. So she had not yet recovered completely from their encounter in the morning, it seemed.

Malriel stared at him with narrowed eyes. "Thank you *so* much, Enric," she growled.

They continued eating in silence, Golir clearly not too comfortable with the two of them.

Enric was the first to finish his meal and put his bowl aside, openly observing Malriel while she continued eating. He caught Golir's occasional frown at his behaviour, but decided to ignore it for now.

Toying with Malriel was different, he mused. Eryn was used to it already, but her mother had clearly not encountered resistance of any kind for quite some time. It was plain enough to see that it irritated her.

When she finally put her empty bowl aside, she lifted her eyes to Enric's.

"Well then, my *friend*," she said pointedly with a dispassionate glare aimed at him, "it seems you have some explaining to do."

"Gladly. It is why I agreed to meeting you, after all," he nodded, making it clear that the only reason she was here was his voluntary compliance that could be withdrawn at any time. "Ask away."

Malriel breathed out slowly as if finding it hard to maintain calm. "Very well. Tell me how you convinced my daughter to let herself become trained as a fighter. I assume she was not too keen on being made to adhere to a training schedule drawn up by her captors."

"You are right, not only was she not keen, but refused outright. Or tried to." He smiled when he remembered watching from his window in his old study how Orrin had hauled her to the training ground over his shoulder on their very first day together. "We entrusted our chief combat trainer with the task of turning her into a halfway decent fighter. He is not only the most skilled fighter we have, but also a man we knew would not be cruel to her and not let himself be fooled, charmed, bribed or blackmailed. I am not saying that he was always gentle with her, but the two of them have eventually become friends. Today she is his superior in the Order. She has even resumed her combat lessons with him, voluntarily this time."

Malriel considered him with pursed lips. "Would you mind repeating this under the influence of a lie filter?"

He smiled. "Not at all."

She nodded. "That is good to know. I will not insist on your subjecting yourself to it right now, but I might decide to have a thing or two verified that way later."

"And if you are fortunate, my dear, then you may still find me in the mood to comply with your little request *later*," he smiled thinly and enjoyed how her jaw muscles clenched at his words.

Aren power, he thought, it only works to its full advantage if people believe in it, my dear woman.

"How did you fall in love with her?" she asked sternly.

"I found her intriguing from the beginning, but it started as not much more than fascination for the unknown species of a female magician with a unique set of skills and no respect for the Order whatsoever. We have a custom in our country called *Freedom Night*," he started and stopped when she raised her hand.

"I know about your Freedom Nights," she told him. "It was mentioned in the reports from several of the search parties. A night of carefree sexual couplings to escape the rigid rules of your everyday life where everyone involved resorts to wearing masks so as to remain incognito."

He nodded. "That is one way of putting it, yes. Anyway, Eryn was persuaded to attend the one in our city by a woman she had

620

befriended. As she did at that time not possess the ability to transform her hair colour at will, she was easily recognisable among the others. I was surprised at seeing her there and watched her for a while, realising how quickly she adapted to the magical dances. I decided to experiment with a song or two where we had not yet worked out the underlying purpose and ended up dancing a seduction dance with her. We spent the night together, and from then on I found it very hard to keep my distance from her."

"Was she aware of your identity when you and she had carnal relations?" Malriel asked but seemed to have a good idea about what the answer would be.

"No, she was not. It was only a few months later that she found out," he replied.

"How?" she demanded.

"When I tricked her into fighting me after she turned out to be advanced enough to defeat her former trainer."

"That was before she had entered into that state of tolerance towards you that you mentioned before, I assume?"

He nodded. "Yes. I had decided to take over her training and she was anything but thrilled about it and refused to fight me."

"So you decided to reveal to her that it was you who had spent the night with her to encourage her to attack you?" Malriel enquired.

"No. I defeated her publicly after provoking her with a very powerful illusion. When I then claimed a kiss for my prize as retribution for insulting me, she realised that she had been held in such a way before."

Malriel looked at him for several moments. "You decided to punish her by *kissing* her? That is certainly no very flattering assessment of your skills in that area," she remarked.

He smiled quietly. "Oh, but it is. The punishment was that she enjoyed it despite fighting it." As had he himself, more than he had anticipated.

"So this was what united you, then? A reluctant kiss she could not help but enjoy so much that she ended up in your bed again?"

"No, it was not quite that simple. She tried to flee from the city once more, and this time she almost managed it. Only the fact that we had maintained a continual watch over her and that my own superior and myself were strong enough jointly to collapse a thick stone wall enabled us to stop her. As everybody was shocked enough by her unexpected resourcefulness, they agreed to my suggestion to put her under my constant supervision in my quarters. This was where I finally managed to break her resistance and became her lover. With that we reached the status of her tolerating me that you have been so eager to learn about," he concluded his little narrative.

She nodded thoughtfully. "I remember our little conversation at the teahouse some time ago, about your pride and how a man like yourself would not demean himself to taking a woman to bed against her will. I will therefore spare you from confirming that little detail to me. But what I would like to learn about is how she came to be joined with you. You were reluctant to talk about it back then, but I think the time has come now for you to tell me."

"Eryn and I had started getting to know each other, which was of course a lot easier with her being confined to my quarters. The King and the Order had started negotiating with her about her joining us, but at that point she was still reluctant to bind herself to the Kingdom. The King decided to speed things along by binding her to me and then as a logical consequence to the Order."

Malriel raised a brow. "You agreed to a plan like that? I admit I find it a little disappointing that you would sell your own principles to your King like that."

"I didn't," he dissented. "But I am afraid that the truth is hardly any more flattering. The King tricked us both into the commitment, though I was not nearly as reluctant as your daughter to comply with his wishes. King Folrin made her chose between making love with himself one time or entering into a commitment with me. I managed to persuade her that the latter option was the more attractive one."

"Only persuaded? Not convinced?" she asked with a lifted brow.

"Yes. At that time she was still under the impression that we were having an affair."

"While you had decided that you were having a relationship?"

He smiled. "Indeed."

"And her own perception has changed since then, I assume?"

"That it has, yes," he agreed.

"And yet she has not consented to entering into a third level commitment bond with you, even though she has the option here and would at the same time be free of Ram'an's attempts at winning her for himself," she mused. "I told you before that I can see that you love her, but I cannot help but wonder whether she reciprocates your feelings."

"She does; you may depend on that," Enric stated with serene confidence, "she has yet to admit it to herself." Then he leaned forward. "And now there is something I want to know from you. What exactly is it you think you can accomplish with your attempt at stopping her from leaving here? Even if you were to succeed, she would hate you for it."

She opened her mouth, doubtlessly to put him in his place, judging from her expression. But she reconsidered and sighed.

"Two years is a long time to try and stay away from somebody in the same city who is determined to see her, especially when confined to one house. She might leave here soon, maybe never to return, considering what has transpired between us in these last few weeks. She would be gone from here already without the trial. She is my only child, Enric. This is not how I can allow this to end."

He nodded slowly. "I see. And yet your attempts at getting to know her better have not been amiable ones. I understand that the daughter you met at the pier on the day of our arrival here was not the woman you were expecting or hoping for, which cannot have been easy for you. But I urge you to reconsider your course of action. Right now you are about to lose her, and locking her up here in Takhan for two years will not change that. Quite the opposite."

She smiled. "I see. So you think that your chances of winning this trial are not worth considering. It is good to see that you do not overestimate them."

"No, Malriel," he replied mildly, "you misunderstood me. I am very confident that we will walk away from here soon enough. I just wanted to illustrate that you will lose her, no matter what the outcome of this trial is. The best thing you could hope for is to observe her from a distance over those two years. That is the most you can win from this."

She rose abruptly. "This may be your opinion, Enric. We will see about that soon enough. I thank you for answering my questions. I am not happy with how Maltheá has been treated since her capture, but I can see that she has done well enough considering the circumstances. If you will excuse me now, I should be getting back."

She nodded at Golir and descended the stairs. They heard the entrance door close firmly behind her a few moments later.

"An interesting story," the older man said slowly. "Though probably none that will ease Malriel's mind so much. I was surprised, though, that she has accepted the way you treated her. I wonder if your reputation has managed to impress even *that* woman."

Enric sighed. "Not enough, as it seems. She is still determined to go through with her scheme."

CHAPTER 50

Ram'an's Plans

Valrad looked up in surprise when he saw Eryn sitting on the stairs to the garden, Ram'an leaning against the house wall behind her, yawning and looking anything but well rested.

"You are up early. That is unexpected. Normally I am the first one up," he commented and looked at Ram'an as if to ask him why he had woken her so early.

"It was not my doing," the younger man explained tiredly. "I would have preferred staying in bed for another hour, but she kept tapping on my wall until I rose to remove the shield from her door and let her out."

She snorted. "That puts me in the same category as Enric describing when the cat scratches at the door to be let into the yard."

"I imagine the situation was not much different in this case," Ram'an remarked with a raised brow.

"You should be thankful that I had no access to your bedroom, or I would have taken revenge for your waking me the way you have these last few days."

A lazy smile grew on his face. "We can change that, my dear. If your uncle gives us two rooms that are connected by a door, you may access my bedroom whenever you feel like it."

"I don't really see it being likely this side of the end of time, but nice try," she replied with a smirk and turned back to look over the garden before her. "I think this was the first time I have watched the sun rising here. What a beautiful sight. Extremely colourful. At home it is no more than shades of blue increasing in brightness most of the time. Though I admit I generally try to avoid getting up that early."

"Is there something that prevents you from sleeping, my girl?" Valrad enquired gently and took a seat next to her, putting a companionable arm around her shoulders.

She leaned against him and nodded. "Yes. I keep thinking about Malriel and what Enric might have shared with her yesterday evening. I still don't understand why he had to bring up the matter

624

of my captivity during the hearing. What could he possibly hope to accomplish with it? It will very likely not change anything."

Her uncle thought for a moment, then shrugged. "I would not be too sure about that. There might be the odd senator or triarch who has not made up his or her mind yet. Enric's openness, Malriel's behaviour and Uvel's remarks did not cast your mother in a very favourable light. It might be down to one single vote tipping the balance - you never know."

"Uvel," she mused. "He made quite a few very daring remarks both times, considering that people are supposed to fear the legendary Aren temper."

"Yes," Ram'an remarked dryly from behind them. "There is always one fool with complete disregard for his own safety and that of people around him."

Eryn half turned to him, shooting him an annoyed glare. "I don't really see *you* cowering in terror before me whenever you provoke me. Or is there too much Vel'kim in me for you to fear the Aren woman that is supposedly embedded somewhere inside me?"

"Hardly embedded," he smirked. "With you and me it is different, Theá. I can hardly afford to be afraid of the woman I intend to make my companion, can I? A man willing to win an Aren woman is usually very well aware of what he is about to get himself into." His smile grew wider. "And so far I think I have done a pretty good job in keeping you under control, if you forgive me my lack of modesty."

Eryn just rolled her eyes and turned back to her view of the greenery before her.

"Sarol contacted me yesterday to inform me that you will be working on cosmetic corrections today," her uncle cut in.

She grimaced, taken aback. "He has? Without even asking for *my* consent? I thought I had made it pretty clear yesterday that this is not exactly my preferred line of work."

"True," Ram'an commented. "But then he pointed out that he does not consider your arguments against improving your skills in that area valid. It seems he has taken it upon himself to have you trained to the standards he sees as appropriate." She sensed him crouching behind her, and then suddenly his hand reached around her to lift her chin and tilt her head back. His face was close to hers when he smiled down at her. "I would not refuse his attempts at educating you, my dear Theá. I dare say you will ultimately profit from them." A moment later she felt his lips on hers and drew in a sharp breath. He released her again and rose, narrowly avoiding her fist.

Eryn jumped to her feet, and before she was even standing straight, a bolt flew from her palm towards him and hit him full in his chest. He staggered back several paces, cursing and leaning against the house wall for support to remain upright. She was breathing deeply, staring daggers at him.

"Consider this a warning. Don't you ever dare do that again! Our little agreement from that one evening is no longer valid," she hissed and turned to storm inside the house, as far away from him as was possible under the circumstances.

She had made only a few quick steps, before a strong hand circled her wrist and jerked her backwards against a chest that was definitely not Valrad's.

"Ram'an," she heard her uncle's stern voice saying from behind them, "Stop this! Taking advantage of her confinement like this is beneath you."

Eryn felt an arm encircle her waist.

"Forgive me, Theá," Ram'an murmured close to her ear. "Being so close to you all the time truly is a test for my restraint." She felt his breath on the back of her neck as he released a tense sigh. "Has there never been a single moment when you were tempted simply to let me kiss you, to see what it would be like? Are you not at all attracted to me, not even a tiny bit? I sometimes think I am about to go crazy when I feel the warmth of your hand in mine without being allowed to do anything more. I dream of the smell of your hair, the taste of your lips, how my name sounds when you say it." His voice sounded strained and distraught. Slowly and deliberately, Eryn shook her head. Hurting him now would be kinder than doing it later.

"No, Ram'an," she replied as calmly as she could manage while still being pressed against him. "That temptation was never there. I am sorry that you are suffering, but you have brought this upon yourself. You should never have agreed to guard me. Stop this now and start getting over it." Her last words were spoken harshly.

He turned her around so they stood face to face. Before she could step away, he cupped her chin with his hand and let his thumb glide over her lips while he looked into her eyes. "Not yet, Theá, not yet. There are still a few moves to be made in that game."

"This is not a game, Ram'an. This is my happiness you are trying to destroy in order to nurture your own. Whatever you think this is, it is surely no regard for me."

"Your happiness?" he laughed bitterly. "Then tell me, Theá, do you love Lord Enric?" He kept staring down at her when she didn't answer and held her in place when she attempted to retreat. "Do you?" Warm magic flowed from his hand still at her chin to stop her from lying.

"Stop that," she snarled and tried to push him away.

"How happy can you be with him if you cannot even tell me in earnest that you love him?" he growled. "I do not see that I am destroying any great, blissful felicity of yours in taking you away from him."

"That is enough," Valrad said quietly and placed a warning hand on Ram'an's upper arm. "Release her. At once. If you want to continue your stay at my house, you will have to show my niece the respect she deserves instead of harassing her."

Ram'an stared at her a moment longer before he finally removed his hands and let her step out of his reach. He closed his eyes for a moment, obviously fighting for composure. When he opened them again, nothing was visible from the tempest that had been there only a few moments ago.

"Of course," he nodded. "Theá, I will exercise more restraint and refrain from pressuring you from now on as long as I am acting as your guard. I do not wish to make you feel like a helpless prisoner, especially as you seem to have had your share of that in Anyueel already. I do not want to make the situation even more difficult for you than it is already. Or for your uncle."

Eryn rubbed her face in exhaustion, wondering how she was to get through the next three days until the vote at the senate was taken. A few more days under his supervision, then she would either be free of him or, if things went really, really badly, be placed under his care for two interminable years. She shivered at the thought despite the warm morning air.

*   *   *

Eryn yawned loudly and let herself sink onto the cushions in her uncle's main room. That had certainly been an exhausting day. Dealing with wrinkles in places she hadn't even realised they could occur - or even be noticed, for that matter - had at times been immensely trying. Sarol had paired her with one of his colleagues - fortunately a woman considerably less grumpy than himself.

She had to admit that there were quite a few things she had learned today. Finally she was in possession of the secret of how to make herself and others appear younger, a trick Malriel had obviously mastered for both directions. Or she at least had somebody at her disposal who had. Yet again, she would probably not want to depend on anybody else for that little trick when it was a skill every magician could learn with a little time and effort.

She had experimented on her own face for a few minutes, which had earned her the healer's mirth. Obviously one needed to first *have* wrinkles in order to be able to remove them. That was why there had not been much of a difference before and after her efforts. Even so, there would be more than one opportunity to practice it soon enough, the woman had promised her with a cruel wink, as Eryn was not getting any younger.

Ram'an poured himself a drink and held the bottle up with a questioning expression. She declined the offer with a shake of her head. There was still tension between them due to what had happened in the morning. They had not spoken much during the day. Of course she had mostly been with patients to magic away the vicissitudes of ageing, while he had, just as the day before, been working at a table in front of the treatment room on whatever a lawyer was supposed to do all day long.

She looked up when she heard the door downstairs closing with an assertive thud and moments later a rather flustered looking Vran'el appeared at the top of the stairs. Without a word he took Ram'an's glass from his hand and emptied it in one go.

"May I ask you for a little quality time alone with my charming cousin?" he then asked her guardian, who considered him for a few moments with a raised eyebrow before nodding reluctantly.

"You may. I will be on the terrace."

Both of them watched him leave through the terrace door and Vran'el then took a seat next to her. His posture seemed relaxed, but his voice was low and urgent.

"I need you to stay calm now, even though you will not appreciate what I am about to tell you. That Aren temper may cost us an advantage if you do not keep it under control for now. Do you understand me?"

She looked concerned, but nodded. That did not sound promising at all.

"Soundproof barrier?" she only asked with a meaningful glance towards the terrace.

Her cousin nodded and a moment later the world around them went silent.

"There is trouble, isn't there?" she asked nervously.

"Let us say there is the potential for trouble, but thanks to your brilliant legal advisor, it might yet be averted. I cannot even remember how many books I have read through since Ram'an's offer to help you with your votes. I knew there had to be something in it for him, or it would be very foolish of him to count on your staying with him just like that when so far you have not shown any inclination in that direction. And there might be a few things one might say about Ram'an, but surely not that he is a fool. Quite the opposite."

"What have you found out, then?" Eryn urged him on impatiently.

"Relax, Eryn! He may not be able to hear us, but he can still *see* that you are agitated. Lean back and listen. Please stay calm." He waited for her to release the breath from her tightened chest and nod before he went on, his tone serious. "I found a law that is considered outdated and has not been applied in I do not know how many years, but longer than anybody still alive can remember. And yet it was never formally repealed and so officially is still in force. It pertains to arranged companionships and how they are affected if one child decides to renounce the family connection before the commitment has been carried out."

"How are they affected, then? Out with it!" His lawyer-like demeanour flustered her. That was not carefree, funny Vran'el, but troubled legal advisor Vran'el, little by little edging his way towards giving her bad news.

"If one of the parties of the intended commitment willingly gives up the connection to his or her birth House, the other party's House is entitled to claim the so-called *Right of substitution*. This means that after you are free of House Aren, he will be able to claim you for his own House. I would bet he will take over his father's position within the next few days. You would then be subject to his directives."

She didn't feel rage, like Vran'el had obviously expected, but instead cold fear gripping her stomach.

"So I am chained forever either to Malriel or to Ram'an? Can he prevent me from leaving Takhan?"

He nodded. "Yes. As your new Head of House he can order you to stay."

"But not to enter into a commitment with him, though? He told me that the commitment itself was voluntary."

"That is correct, he cannot make you join him against your will, but his new status would make it possible for him to stop you from joining anybody else," Vran'el explained. "While Malriel's punishment would have taken a mere two years, Ram'an could keep you close to himself even without your joining him for a lot longer than that."

Eryn closed her eyes and forced herself to remain calm. This was turning out to be a nightmare. And if Vran'el hadn't found out about the new complication, she would have walked right into the trap.

"I can renounce House Aren - that surely means I could do the same with Ram'an's House in case he really claimed me as a member?"

Vran'el grimaced. "Sweetness, that would hardly make sense, would it? A law that provides for the opportunity to force somebody into a House will hardly allow for the chance to leave it again quite that easily."

"Does that mean I can't leave House Aren and am stuck with Malriel until the end of her days? Or mine, if she is faster and kills *me* first?" she moaned.

Her eyes focused on the faint smile that appeared on her cousin's lips. That had to mean that there was still hope of some kind.

"Not necessarily. I have found a way around that without your being stuck with either House Aren or Arbil."

She leaned forward, taking his hand and squeezing it hard. "Which way?" she whispered despite the soundproof barrier.

"By getting you stuck with another House that would be more than happy to have you. Ours."

She frowned and shook her head in incomprehension. "What? How can you demand a right of substitution? Your House was not involved in the agreement. And being from my father's side, you do not really have any power, or did I misunderstand that?"

"Our weapon of choice would not be a substitution, but instead an adoption," he said quietly. "If you are a member of another House, the right of substitution cannot be claimed as there is no need for it any longer."

"And you think Valrad would do it? Adopt me, I mean? Malriel might not be very happy about that, and neither would Ram'an, for that matter."

He shrugged. "Malriel must be aware that this is for your protection and I hope that means she will not make us pay for it. As for Ram'an... I do not worry about him. He is not exactly the vengeful type. And as I assume that he will soon have both hands full with his new position as Head of House Arbil, I imagine that making enemies is not among his priorities. As for father, I went at the clinic to talk to him before I came here. He is more than willing to do it."

Eryn clasped her hands tightly and forced herself to continue to breathe evenly. Good news, finally! "So, what do I need to do now? Where I come from, people of age cannot be adopted at all. What is the procedure here? Do you even have one or is it just about making it known that I have changed Houses?"

"It is not quite that simple, I am afraid. Adoptions are usually made in order to ensure succession – or escape it, in your case. It needs to be documented in the form of an agreement, signed and finally approved by the triarchy to become effective. I will work on the adoption papers so you and father can sign them tomorrow. I will deliver them personally to have them approved. We need to make sure that Ram'an does not learn about any of this, do you understand me? He might dig up another law that allows him to counteract our plans, and we do not want him to start looking. Try to act as naturally as possible around him. Whatever that may mean in the case of the two of you," he added.

Eryn nodded slowly, then frowned. "How sure are you that this really is in his plan?"

"Pretty sure, sweetness. He is a very good lawyer and an expert in historical law, too. I seriously doubt that he will fail to employ this very helpful statute to his advantage when it caters to his plans so beautifully. It almost seems to have been tailor-made for his situation. Count on it - this is what he will try. I am willing to bet everything I have. Only then does his willingness to vote for you make sense."

Finally she felt the anger that Vran'el had expected earlier. "He even made me spend that evening with him in payment for his favour! He touched me, kissed me... And that was just what he insisted on after I refused what he wanted at the beginning!"

"As I told you, he is anything but stupid," Vran'el retorted mildly. "But console yourself; you are about to thwart his plans. That will surely hit him hard enough to be considered ample retribution for his trickery, I think. What is more, it will earn you your freedom from both him and Malriel. But only," he repeated his earlier warning, "if you manage to keep this to yourself, do you hear? Do not take any risks here. I know that you are not very good at keeping things to yourself, but a slip of the tongue could in this case be immensely problematic."

She swallowed her first impulse to deny his imputation, but she had to admit that there had been more than one opportunity in this last half year when the thinking had not managed to keep up with the speaking.

"How about Enric? I think he should know about this."

Vran'el nodded. "Yes, I agree. I will visit him tomorrow morning at Golir's place and tell him about this. Unless he has anything to add to the contract or any other objections, I will then come to the clinic and let you and father sign the papers - provided Ram'an consents to let you out of his sight long enough."

Nodding, she removed the barrier from around them, greedily inhaling the fresh air. Acting, she thought. She had never liked it very much, but as she had spent the greater part of her life pretending to be a non-magician born and raised in the Kingdom, fooling Ram'an into thinking she was unaware of his plans had to be something she could do.

Vran'el rose. "I am in my study. There are documents I need to prepare for tomorrow," he said when Ram'an returned to the main room and sat next to Eryn.

Ram'an looked at her questioningly once her cousin had left. "What was that about, then?"

"Family matters," she replied curtly. "None of your business. And there is no need to sit that close to me. If you overstep any more boundaries while I am subjected to your diligence, my next strike will be strong enough to send you off to sleep for a few hours." That was good, she decided. Genuine anger that could be released by making him believe she was still angry about the kiss in the morning while she had in the meantime discovered more profound reasons.

He shook his head with a sigh. "And there I thought you are getting used to having me close."

"Well, I would have thought that you had got used to my not appreciating the kind of closeness you want. It seems we were both mistaken."

He took her hand and held on to it when she tried to pull it from his grip. "There are only three more days left until the vote. Three more days that I have you to myself."

She smiled without humour. "It wouldn't matter if it were three hundred or even three thousand days. I am Enric's, and nothing will change that. Now, I would like to have my hand back, if you please. I want to go through the notes I had to take today. Sarol threatened to grill me on what I learned today. So if you would excuse me, or rather accompany me to my room and raise your shields to hold me there, that is."

"I do not like it when you are angry at me, Theá," he said gently without releasing her hand.

She lifted a brow at him. "You are not supposed to like it. That would defeat the purpose, don't you think?"

"Probably, yes," he admitted. "Why do we not get your notes from your room and I will help you go through them, test you?"

Eryn swallowed and felt her anger draining away. Another sweet gesture she would repay by crushing his hopes. No, she reminded herself, he was the one who intended to trick her. She just protected her own interests.

"Sure - why not. And then I might even permit you to act as my test object later. There is nothing like a little practical exercise," she said and smiled at his slightly worried expression.

CHAPTER 51

Adoptions

Enric put aside his book on the customs of nomadic tribes in the northern areas when Vran'el entered the main room at the Partém residence.

"Good morning, my friend," Vran'el said and chuckled when he caught a glance of the book title upside down. "Interesting choice of lecture. Last time you were reading something about magical music, were you not? There does not seem to be much in which you do not take an interest, does there?"

Enric shrugged. "You never know what you might stumble upon. And it does give me rather interesting insights into your culture. I wonder of how much of it you are still aware of here in the city. Did you know, for example, that your tradition of presenting gifts to a host stems from a system of exchanging favours and started more or less as a way of repaying debts? People used to visit members of their own or other tribes to thank them for their help when in need or for favours bestowed, and brought a gift to balance the score."

"No, I admit I did not know that. You know, I find it somewhat strange that *you* do, to be honest. But it will make me smile next time I have to choose a gift for an invitation."

"But you have not come here to talk about ancient customs and their influence on what we consider modern society, I think. As today you are visiting rather earlier than usually, I assume there is something important you wish to impart to me."

"There is, yes," Vran'el confirmed and took a seat. "I am confident that I have figured out what Ram'an has planned following Eryn's renunciation of House Aren. It explains why he suggested it to her in the first place and is assisting her in obtaining the votes she needs. We have an archaic law here which enables him to claim her as a member of his own House as there is still a pending companionship arrangement in place." He lifted his hand when Enric drew in a deep breath and was about to rise. "Wait, there is a way to prevent this, so let me finish before you rush off to damage him physically. Father has agreed to adopt her into House Vel'kim, ensuring she is safe from any unwanted associations with House Arbil."

Enric lifted his brow. "Adopt her? That is possible with a grown person here? Back home we can only do it with children."

"That is not a problem here, no. I prepared the papers last night and need her and father to sign them before I can get them to the triarchy for their approval."

"The triarchy pronounces on that?" the blonde magician frowned. "That means that Malriel will very likely learn of Eryn's plans to break with House Aren. Is there anything she can do against it? She does have good connections to one of the triarchs, Abrak, doesn't she?"

Vran'el nodded. "That is probably what will happen, yes. It depends very much on the other two triarchs. I hope that they will see that being accused by one's own mother really is a valid reason to leave a House. Although they might be reluctant to rob Malriel of her heir to the House. Everything is open to their decision, basically."

"What if they reject the request? I hope Eryn is aware that she cannot renounce House Aren if it leaves her defenceless against Ram'an and whatever legal hold he would then have on her? Am I to assume that he has taken over his father's position already?"

"Probably. I expect he has or will do so within the next day or two before the vote so that he can announce it at the senate. My next step is to go to the clinic to have father and Eryn sign the papers. That should be done as quickly as possible and without arousing Ram'an's suspicion. I want this to be a nasty surprise for him. I do not want to risk giving him time to prepare another of his convoluted old regulations that nobody except him is still aware of. It took me long enough to work out this one. This is his terrain - I am no match for him if he throws another one at us, I am afraid."

Enric nodded grimly. "Then we had better make sure he does not learn about it before the deed is done. Is there anything I can help with? How can you let Eryn sign the papers without his being around? From what I have seen he does not leave her out of his sight for very long."

The lawyer pursed his lips. "True. That is one of the challenges here. But fortunately she is working at the clinic today, and he cannot be in the treatment room with her, only waits outside guarding her door. So if I manage to get the papers in there with her somehow, that should not be a problem. Maybe father can take them to her after he has signed them. It should not look too suspicious if one healer carries papers to a colleague. They might be patient reports or whatever other documents healers push around."

Enric sighed. "I wish I could assist you in some way, but I am afraid persuading Golir to accompany me to the clinic so I can distract Ram'an would not serve to keep the matter quiet."

"True enough, my friend. I will return here after I have the signatures and hand the papers over to Golir personally. Let us hope that the triarchy will decide quickly. They will be aware that this needs to be settled before the vote on Eryn's situation."

"Thank you, Vran'el. Thank you for everything you are doing for her. Doing for us. Since our arrival here you and Valrad have shown us nothing but support and kindness. You have given Eryn and me a new idea of what family can be. Neither of us has exactly been blessed in that regard. Until now."

Vran'el gave him a warm smile and reached out to pull him into an affectionate hug.

"Believe me, Enric, the blessing is ours. Now I should be leaving. There are papers to be signed, a colleague to be tricked…" He got to his feet. "If everything goes the way it should, I will be back in about one hour with the papers."

Enric nodded and watched him turn and leave.

Golir entered the main room from the terrace door, holding a mixed bundle of herbs in one hand. "Was that Vran'el just now? That was a very short visit."

The younger man considered his host for a few moments, then opted for openness. He would learn about the adoption plans anyway in what he hoped was no more than one hour. The trouble was that there was no telling if he would treat the matter with the confidentially it required. He might as well inform his nephew. Maybe it was time to find out now.

"I expect him back again in a short while. There is a little matter he needs to take care of. A planned adoption, to be more precise."

The triarch lifted both eyebrows. "I see. I assume we are talking about Maltheá and House Vel'kim here?" Upon Enric's nod he continued, "So she is about to renounce House Aren. Malriel is not going to be happy about that. But after being accused by her own mother in such a way, it is to be expected. I wonder why Valrad is adopting her, though. He is asking for trouble with that. I dare say his shaky alliance with House Aren will suffer considerably after a move like this."

Enric shrugged noncommittally. Telling him that they suspected his nephew of trying to take advantage of the situation was probably not a gambit right now. Even if it later turned out to be correct, mentioning it now might enrage Golir. And if they found out later that this had never been Ram'an's plan, Golir's anger at finding his own nephew accused of such a devious plot would then be quite justified.

"Vran'el found it advisable for her to be subject to the protection of a House, and as he and his father are both very fond of her, it is also a symbolic gesture to welcome her into their family when she no longer officially belongs to the one she was born to." He then hesitated. "We would appreciate if this remained unknown to anyone beyond these walls for now. At least until there is an official decision on the adoption proposal."

The older man smiled faintly. "You may rest assured that I will not inform my nephew of this matter. I am of the opinion that confidentiality is a sign of professionalism when it comes to a position like mine. I feel I should warn you, though, that this is a sentiment not all of my colleagues share."

"Yes, I trust that Malriel will learn of this fairly quickly. I admit I am worried about her choices in preventing the adoption."

"She has none, apart from trying to convince the members of the triarchy to vote against it, that is. You are surely aware that Abrak will adhere to her wishes here. It is not a great secret that he is in league with her."

Enric nodded, but remained silent.

"I acknowledge that you must have concerns about my position in this matter, especially when it comes to what consequences this may turn out to have for Ram'an. But let me assure you that my decision in this will not be influenced by my own personal alliances." He lifted an eyebrow. "Have I answered the question you have been so careful not to ask me just now to your satisfaction?"

The younger man couldn't help but smile at that. "I admit it is a relief to hear you say it, though I had good reason not to ask."

"Such as not insulting me by implying that my family connections may lead me to favour my nephew instead of following a more objective course of action?" Golir asked with an amused twinkle in his eyes. "A wise decision, Enric. But then your King would not have despatched a fool to us. If you will excuse me now, I should be getting started with lunch."

Enric nodded and picked up the book he had put aside when Vran'el had arrived. Reading, however, was not possible right now. His thoughts refused to be diverted and kept dwelling on how Vran'el would at this moment be trying to secrete the agreement into the treatment room with Eryn without Ram'an's noticing anything was amiss - or rather have Valrad do it. This was only the first hurdle to overcome, the final one being the triarchy's approval. He rose from his seat after a few minutes once he had given up the attempts of distracting himself and let his body get rid of some of the nervous energy by pacing the room restlessly to and fro.

* * *

Enric was cursing under his breath when, more than one and a half hours later, there was still no sign of Vran'el. His hair stood out from his head at odd angles due to having been raked through by impatient fingers every few minutes. He froze in mid-step every time he heard a faint noise that could somehow be related to somebody approaching the entrance door, only to resume his pacing after each disappointment. Golir had retired to his study after a rather awkward meal with Enric, clearly not too eager to spend more time than necessary with his house-guest in his current mood.

Just when Enric had decided to summon a messenger and contact Valrad, he heard the noise he was so eagerly expecting: a knock.

A servant who was about to leave after finishing his cleaning work for that day started to descend the stairs to admit the visitor, but pressed against the wall when a tall, blonde figure rushed past him to open the door with such force that it almost became unhinged.

Vran'el looked up in surprise and raised both brows. "Oh my word, you are a little tense, are you not?"

Enric forced himself to remain calm instead of shaking the other man. "Talk."

"You might at least do me the courtesy of letting me in first. It is considered polite, you know," the lawyer retorted.

"Do not make me break any of your bones."

"Alright, alright! Everything worked out just fine." Vran'el lifted one hand holding a flat leather file. "May I come in now? This happens to be the hottest time of the day, and I would appreciate some shade and a wet towel right now."

Enric stepped aside, closing his eyes in relief for a short moment before shutting the door behind his visitor.

"So they have both signed the papers? And Ram'an did not notice anything?" he enquired.

Vran'el rolled his eyes while he rubbed the cool towel over his forearms. "That was what I meant when I said that everything worked out fine, yes."

"What took you so long? I was about to go up the wall here," Enric complained. "You said one hour!"

"How nice to see that even high and mighty *you* do not always manage to maintain that stoic calm you are known for. It took a little longer as Eryn was in the middle of a treatment session. They do not look kindly upon interruptions there, you know. Not even - or especially not - when another healer is attempting them, as they should know better. So we had to wait until she had finished bestowing an abundant crop of hair to a bald man or something like that. Then Sarol arrived and insisted on testing her right there and then on what he called basic aesthetic treatment principles. Thankfully father managed to persuade him to allow him a few minutes with her first."

They climbed the stairs into the main room.

"What about Ram'an? No trouble there?"

"Nothing major. When father was about to walk into the treatment room, I distracted Ram'an. Let me tell you that he does not appreciate being called a *spare time doorman*. But it kept his attention off the papers under father's arm. He hid them among a few medical reports in case Ram'an tried to check them. Though they would hardly have withstood any closer scrutiny. Anyway, his trying that was very unlikely as he has no right whatsoever to look at patient reports, but one likes to be prepared for all eventualities. Especially with that man. Are you about to offer me something to drink or not? It really is rather warm out there, you know."

Enric raised his brow at him. "You are still carrying those papers under your arm. Get them to Golir, *then* we can talk about sustaining you."

"Right," Vran'el muttered and shot the other man a dark look. "So much for coercing dehydrated people who are trying to help you to hold on to your companion."

Enric laughed, feeling the tension fall off him bit by bit. "You go on and make the next step in that noble endeavour, then I will get you as much to drink as you want. Golir's study is to the right, first corridor, third door to the left."

He watched the lawyer walking in the direction he had indicated and leaned against a wall with closed eyes, enjoying the coolness on his forehead. First obstacle cleared, one more to overcome. But the second one would not be something they could influence with cunning, this one required nothing more than patience. That was probably the harder part. Not being able to do anything to influence or speed things along but be forced to wait for others to decide on something that would have a major impact on his and Eryn's life was not a comforting thought. Two more days until the vote at the senate. At least he could be fairly certain the triarchy would decide on the adoption before that.

Vran'el returned with Golir only a few moments later.

"Done. I have delivered the papers according to your instructions." He turned to the triarch. "May I ask you for a glass of water, Golir? Enric refused to quench my thirst until I had handed over the papers to you."

Golir raised his brow in rebuke. "Enric, in our country withholding water from somebody who is thirsty is not looked upon kindly."

Enric nodded. "I know. Nowadays it is considered a matter of hospitality and politeness, but the practice originally stems from the punishment western mountain tribes bestowed on..."

"Come on!" Vran'el called out, "Nobody wants a foreigner around who keeps impressing on you that he knows more about the history of your own country than yourself!"

Golir blinked a few times, then smiled while stepping towards the refreshments cabinet. "Well, at least you did not violate our customs unthinkingly but with genuine malicious intent," he remarked dryly. "Thoughtlessness is so common nowadays that a little wickedness is to be preferred every now and then as it is more inventive."

Vran'el took the glass he was offered and swiftly emptied it in greedy gulps. "Not in my profession. Wickedness is my daily business; I would very much prefer a few thoughtless people every now and then who may just reconsider because the error of their ways was pointed out to them."

Enric smirked. "You should have stuck with your family traditions, then. That is surely not a problem healers have to deal with."

"Are you joking? Patients are probably the worst kind of people. I have heard stories…" He stopped and shivered.

"Is there a rough time estimate you can give me on how long it will take you and your colleagues to decide on this adoption issue?" Enric enquired of Golir.

Golir nodded. "It will not take longer than one or two days as this is a rather urgent matter. We do wish to conclude this whole mess soon one way or the other due to political fallout that might result. Even an unfavourable outcome is preferable to continuing uncertainty."

Yes, Enric thought wryly, and preferably it would be unfavourable for Malriel instead of himself.

* * *

Golir got up off the cushions to accept the message that had just been delivered. He looked at the paper, then held it out for Enric to take.

"It is addressed to you."

Enric took the message and unfolded the paper. It was from Valrad. His eyes followed the untidy handwriting he had by now come to associate with healers.

Golir raised his eyebrows questioningly when Enric let the letter sink in his fingers a short while later. "Bad news?"

"Probably. Though not entirely unexpected. Malriel has insisted on seeing me tomorrow at the Vel'kim residence while Eryn is at the clinic. It seems she wants to have a little chat - doubtlessly to talk about the adoption."

"That is a valid assumption, yes. A word of advice to you: Malriel is not at her most dangerous when she is displaying signs of the legendary Aren temper, but when she has it under control – which she has in ninety-nine out of a hundred cases. She certainly does not want to meet you to merely complain or cry on your shoulder. Showing a weakness in such a way is not like her at all. If she wants to meet you, there is something she has to tell you, and knowing Malriel it might not necessarily be something you will be pleased to hear. She does not make empty threats. She does not need to as she is in a position to carry out virtually anything she feels like threatening you with," Golir warned him.

Enric nodded slowly. "Thank you, I will keep that in mind. Anything else that will make dealing with her any easier? Last time she was here we did not exactly part on amiable terms."

"She is an Aren woman. I dare say you have had a fair bit of time to determine how to deal with them: show them strength and respect. That will secure you their attention for a while at least. Last time you displayed strength alright, but you were rather... economical when it came to showing respect. This time you will not have that luxury as she will surely not come to the table empty-handed, as it were. She will have something either to threaten, blackmail or bribe you with to strengthen her hand in whatever she plans to demand of you."

That much he had worked out already, but it was good to hear his own assessment confirmed by an experienced politician who happened to know Malriel quite well.

"Thank you, Golir. If you would excuse me now, I think I should consider a thing or two to offer her in order to at least show some goodwill if I cannot comply with whatever she wants."

The triarch chuckled. "You do that if it makes you feel better. However, be prepared for your attempts at distracting her from getting what she really wants to fail. I have always wondered why people kept associating temper with Aren women when it is no more than an entertaining display of the underlying strength that is so much more dangerous when they use it to get what they want instead of getting rid of their frustration."

Enric thought of Eryn and how she had somehow managed to be granted not only the permission for her healing services back home, but also the funding. She had not done it by making houses collapse or threatening people, but by refusing any cooperation until the terms in her negotiations with the Order and the King became more appealing. It seemed to be in the Aren nature, true enough. And this was what Eryn had accomplished only by following her instincts. Malriel not only had those instincts, but compared with her daughter several decades of political experience at her disposal as well. What a disturbing prospect, he thought grimly.

* * *

Valrad handed Enric and Malriel a warm drink before taking a seat beside Vran'el. He had just returned after accompanying Eryn and Ram'an to the clinic. They were not aware of this meeting, just as Malriel had instructed.

"Let me get straight to the point," Malriel said and looked at Valrad. "I was informed of your request to be granted permission to adopt Maltheá. *My* daughter." She took a sip to calm her nerves. "It does not take a genius to figure out what is going to happen as soon as it is granted. She obviously plans to renounce House Aren. And in doing so, renounce me." She then looked at Vran'el. "I have no doubt whatsoever that it was you who came up with the idea of adopting her into your House. An ingenious one, I have to say.

Another daughter for House Vel'kim. How very advantageous for you."

The three men remained silent without correcting her assumption regarding the reasons for the adoption. They were waiting to hear why she had asked them to meet her.

"You must, of course, be aware of what this means for House Aren. As long as she was lost in the Old Kingdom without our knowing if she was dead or alive, this was unresolved. Now, with her coming here - looking so very much like myself, a constant reminder for people that House Aren now has a daughter again, moreover a magically gifted one, too - expectations have changed. People look at her, and they see my heiress. But you are about to change that irrevocably. This is a heavy blow, as I have no other children."

"It was something you brought on yourself, Malriel," Valrad said calmly. "Your actions were what made her decide to reject you. Even if she had not, what makes you think she would ever have remained to take over your House? She has a life, a companion in a place far from here which she considers her home. What exactly is it you want, Malriel? You have not asked us to meet you to share your grief with us. You have never been one for unnecessary emotional displays."

Malriel smiled thinly. "No, I never was, was I? I sometimes forget how well you know me. I am here to tell you that House Vel'kim will suffer a number of disadvantages for taking away my daughter."

Vran'el leaned forward. "We are not taking her away! She would have renounced your House with or without our adopting her instead. There is no sense in threatening or punishing *us* for it!"

"Oh, my dear boy, but this is not what everybody else will see," she replied. "They will see your House taking away my House's heir. Do not misunderstand me. I am very well aware of your situation here and I appreciate that you are willing to take her in, considering that it is still in dispute whether she is subject to our laws, and I would not want her to be unprotected. Yet I must be seen to receive some form of compensation." Her gaze fell on Enric and stayed there.

He raised his brows. "Me? As compensation?" Then his eyes widened. "You can't be serious! I would never leave her or otherwise risk my relationship with..."

She laughed. "No, you misunderstand me. You are a very attractive man, my young friend, but I am after a little more than your body."

Valrad exhaled loudly, obviously well aware of what she was talking about. "I do not even know if you can do this. He is a foreigner, after all. The laws might not apply in this case."

"They can be made to if Enric agrees and a man of the law emphasises the rightfulness of the proposal," she smiled and looked at Vran'el.

"Pardon me?" Enric ventured. "I am still rather lost here. What exactly are we talking about?"

"I want you to join my House, Enric. Become my son, let yourself become adopted by me."

"Adopted?" He stared at her. "I am not even sure I *can* be adopted according to the rules in my own country; we have an age limit for this."

"Minor considerations," Malriel waved him off. "I am quite sure that your King will be more than happy to comply in this matter. It would ensure him a very valuable connection to our political circles, after all. What do you say, Enric? Will you join my House as my son and save House Vel'kim from the damage it will otherwise endure? They do have a daughter, but she is nowhere close to taking a companion and producing any children to secure power for the House. They are vulnerable - almost as much as House Aren will be. I would not hesitate to exploit that. Not for one moment."

Enric stared into her eyes, absolutely sure that she was uttering the truth. She would inflict harm upon Eryn's family, her new official House. Would make them pay for taking her in, even though she had openly acknowledged that they were not to blame for Eryn's leaving House Aren. They would serve as an example to others not to take what belonged to Malriel. He then looked at Valrad, who had gone pale. Vran'el stared at her angrily.

"Alright," Enric said slowly. "You win. I will do it. I will join House Aren. But do not expect this to mend anything between you and Eryn. You may from a legal point of view return to a status of a family member as her companion's mother, but no more than the *legal* connection it will be."

She bent over and kissed him on the forehead, her smile satisfied. "Which will be more than I would have otherwise." She drained her cup and couldn't quite hide the triumphant gleam in her eyes when she stood up. "I leave the documents here for you to look through." She pressed a leather file into Enric's hands. "I dare say Vran'el will be more than happy to advise you in case you have any questions or objections. House Vel'kim owes you a great debt now, after all. Send them back to me if there are no objections. Signed, of course. I will make sure to have them forwarded to the triarchy immediately. I am sure that I do not need to tell you that time is of the essence here in your own interest, so you might want to be snappy with it."

"I will accept the adoption only after Eryn's own has gone through, however," he pointed out. "Only when she is a member of House Vel'kim will I join yours."

"Of course," she smiled. "We could not have you being your own sister's lover, could we? It would appear rather awkward to casual observers. I bid you good-bye, then. I am sure I will be hearing from you in due course." She then nodded to the men, turned and left.

The three of them sat together for several minutes, not saying a word. Then Valrad shook his head.

"Incredible. I would have put my bets on her to trying and make them reject the adoption proposal, but I have once again underestimated her. She is masterful. A politician through and through. She has really managed to turn this whole thing to her own and her House's advantage. Not being able to keep her daughter from renouncing her has not prevented her from acquiring an even more powerful and influential son instead. And all this by not acting on impulse, by not letting her emotions do the thinking but playing the game with her head."

"I find your admiration of her rather disturbing, considering the circumstances," Vran'el growled. "She has successfully blackmailed Enric into becoming her son, after all! Let us try not to forget that, if you do not mind."

Valrad nodded. "Yes, there is that. And she is right, we are greatly indebted to you for accepting her condition for not harming House Vel'kim even more than Ved'al's escape and Eryn's abduction have done already. How will Eryn react to it?"

Enric closed his eyes. "Not favourably, not at all. I would request you not to tell her for now. I don't want her to change her mind about leaving House Aren because she feels she needs to protect me. I think her and Malriel being in separate Houses will be quite an improvement after everything that has taken place."

"You think you will be better able to handle Malriel's games than Eryn was?" Vran'el asked.

"Yes. I have a lot more experience with politicians, and I don't have this emotional connection, these unresolved issues with Malriel standing in my way and clouding my judgement," he replied confidently. "The idea of adopting me is not such a bad one, also not for Eryn and me. I can take dealing with House Aren out of her hands without treating her like a child, as it will officially be *my* House soon. In addition," he smiled, "it will reinforce your connection with House Aren. Your soon-to-be daughter will be connected to a man of their House, after all. This should carry some weight, as it also implies that House Aren has forgiven you for your brother's actions all those years ago."

"But the consequences for yourself!" Vran'el exclaimed and added urgently, "There are legal strings attached to this, Enric! She is the Head of the House and you will be her only son. This makes you the heir of the House! Unless you have any plans to move here anyway, I would not discard this consequence without ample consideration. Eryn would not have assumed her place as Head of the House, I am sure of it. Owing to the fact that she is able to claim that she is no longer a citizen of our country, they might not have forced her to, either. It would have depended on the composition of the triarchy at that time, but it would have been shaky legal ground in any case. Now *you* will enter into this voluntarily, however. This means that you will subject yourself to our laws willingly and be bound by them. If you do not, she can make the triarchy despatch people to your country and drag you here, which would maybe even spark a war, if you refuse to comply!"

"Calm down, Vran'el," Enric sighed. "I have no intention of violating your laws and causing a war. Malriel will be in power at House Aren for quite some time yet, I imagine. Decades. A lot may change in that time, planning ahead how to avoid taking over the House in who knows how many years is futile for now. Let us concentrate on the here and how."

"Yes, I agree," Valrad nodded. "For now, she profits more from your not staying here but returning to your homeland. You are a businessman in addition to your high rank as a warrior, are you not? So she will very likely aim to profit from that to increase her House's wealth and standing. And of course there is her connection to your country's governing institution of magic - the Order - of which you are second in command. I would not worry about her trying to chain you here for the moment."

Enric nodded. "I know. I wouldn't have expected her to. How likely is it that one or both adoption applications are granted?"

Vran'el sighed. "Likely enough now as I dare say she will be advocating both of them. Do not forget she has a very good connection to one of the triarchy's members. I have a feeling that both of them will be granted. What is more, granted soon."

CHAPTER 52

Insights

Ram'an carefully opened the door to Eryn's bedroom and widened his eyes in surprise when he saw her sitting on her bed, knees pulled towards her face.

"You are awake already." He smiled and closed the door behind him. "Good. We will make an early riser of you yet."

"I don't think I will be going to the clinic today," she said quietly. "I don't feel like I am in any shape for dealing with patients presently."

He sat down next to her on the bed, laying one hand on hers and squeezing it. "That is completely understandable. Tomorrow is a big day for you, and of course you are nervous."

"A day that will decide whether I am to be marooned here, more or less locked up for two years," she whispered and closed her eyes.

"Theá, look at me." She let him turn her head so he could look into her eyes. "Being made to stay here for a while longer would not be the collapse of your world. Of course you would miss your friends, but they are free to visit you here. Think of all the things you could learn here - the knowledge you could send to your trainees back home. There would be communication, trade, exchange. Staying here would not cut you off."

She looked away. "You are softening me up to accept a verdict that has not yet been issued. So little confidence that I might be released from here despite the four votes you promised me?"

There was a short silence before he replied, "It always pays to be prepared, Theá. I was trying to ease your heart by pointing out that what might at this moment seem to you the worst possible outcome has its merits as well."

"It would for you, wouldn't it?" she remarked bitterly.

He nodded earnestly. "Yes. Denying that would not make much sense, would it?"

She shook her head. "Hardly. Yet you have given away your best chance of keeping me here by agreeing to vote in my favour." Bracing herself, she met his thoughtful gaze. "In exchange for that one evening. I wonder if you are regretting that deal now. My resolve to stay with Enric has not changed, after all."

The flicker in his eyes was faint and she wouldn't have noticed it had she not waited for it. His expression was a little too jaunty. Without Vran'el's suspicions she might have considered it mere cockiness, but then this was a character trait Ram'an had not shown so far. So he clearly thought that he had valid reasons for his optimism.

"This evening gave me the chance to taste your lips several times, my dear. How could I regret it?" he said and lifted her hand to his lips to kiss it.

Smooth, she thought, and forced herself to smile. "At least you are bearing the prospect of your impending loss with dignity. I appreciate that in a man."

"That sounds as if you are a little more certain of your chances at winning now than a few moments ago," he noted.

"Yes. I think I have to convince myself that I am. Otherwise I will probably go awry today. The thought of being a prisoner once again fills me with dread."

She saw him swallow uncomfortably. Good. That should at least make him feel bad about planning to force her to stay here, at least to some extent.

"There are worse prisons than the city of Takhan, my dear Theá," he said quietly.

"There are worse prisons than Anyueel as well. That didn't cause me to enjoy it more," she countered. "Now get out, if you don't mind. I would like to get dressed."

He got to his feet and looked down at her. "I would do everything in my power to make your stay here as pleasant as possible."

"I know." She smiled without humour. "But you would not exactly be doing it for unselfish reasons, would you?"

"I would not, no," he admitted. "But that does not mean that we cannot both benefit."

She sighed. "Yes, that is exactly what it would mean, Ram'an. Because I want to be with Enric."

"A man who, both times I asked, you were not able to tell me you loved," he remarked sharply. "Why does this not make you wonder, Theá?"

"Out, now!" she barked with a stern look, before leaning back onto her cushions once he had left. It did make her wonder.

* * *

Valrad smiled when she stepped out onto the terrace.

"Good morning, my dear girl. Ram'an told me that you want to stay at home today. Are you sure about that? I imagine that working would be a welcome distraction. And Sarol would be devastated if you were not available for his torments today. He may lose you soon enough."

"Yes," she sighed and took a bowl to fill it with fruit. "You are probably right. I suppose it is preferable to staying here and tormenting myself instead. I am currently so much better at it than Sarol. At least that will keep my mind occupied. All the same, I should not work with patients today."

"I am glad to see that you put the patients' wellbeing before your own need to distract yourself. I wish more of my colleagues would make that decision sometimes," her uncle smiled and squeezed her shoulder. "It would reduce the number of mistakes. Sarol can keep you occupied without patients just as well. Why do we both not leave the clinic after lunch so we can at least spend the afternoon together at home?"

Eryn nodded. As long as there was somebody besides Ram'an here to keep her company, it was fine.

Ram'an cleared his throat. "There is a little family matter at my House I need to take care of this afternoon."

Eryn kept her expression carefully neutral. She had no doubt that it had to do with his taking over his father's position. "That means I will need to spend the afternoon at your place?"

"No," he said slowly, "that will not be necessary. You would only become bored. Considering your day tomorrow, I am sure that you would prefer to spend your day here in more familiar surroundings."

"You are leaving me here? Unsupervised?" she looked slightly surprised yet didn't quite manage to hide the smile completely.

"In so many words, yes. Nonetheless, in order to be able to do so I will have to ask you for a binding promise to avoid any visits to Lord Enric or invitations for him here." He cast a look at Valrad. "Unfortunately I cannot make your uncle promise me the same, so it is not really a safe way to keep the two of you apart. Not visiting Lord Enric is also a matter of interpretation. You might feel the sudden urge to go and visit Golir instead and just *happen* to encounter Enric there."

She smiled. "Then why bother with this promise at all? Why don't you indulge me and let me spend an hour with him? As you are about to neglect your duties as my guardian today, you could grant me a little time with Enric in exchange for my not telling on you."

Ram'an's expression darkened. "Are you blackmailing me?"

She nodded earnestly. "Absolutely. But I appreciate that you are a man of great personal integrity and will probably not want to put up with that sort of thing. I am sure that family matter of yours could easily wait until after the vote tomorrow so that you are better able to deal with it once I am released from your tender guardianship."

"Unfortunately, this particular family matter cannot wait," he replied, conflicting emotions clear on his face. "Very well - one hour, no longer. For this one hour you will stay here at the Vel'kim residence."

She grinned broadly. "No objections to that from my side." Meeting Enric, being with him for an entire hour! How absurd that this prospect seemed like pure luxury when they had been living together for several months now. What a pity that it was so much easier to appreciate things when they were rationed instead of when they were available in abundance, such as time spent with Enric.

Putting aside her empty bowl, she got up quickly. The prospect of that one hour with Enric in the afternoon had lifted her spirits enormously.

"I will be ready to leave in a few minutes."

* * *

Eryn looked around the garden with its splendour of blooming herbs, flowers, trees and bushes.

"I will miss this place, you know," she said reflectively and smiled when she felt her uncle's warm hand on her shoulder. "Looking at your garden, the thought of returning to a place where the main consideration for planting something is whether it can be used for food is somewhat depressing."

"And yet you are eager to return to Anyueel. You radiate impatience - literally," Valrad remarked with an amused undertone.

She nodded. "True enough. As much as I have come to enjoy being here for this time, I feel a strong pull to return. Apart from returning to my friends and my work, there is also the magical bond the Order placed on me to remind me that I am supposed to return. I started feeling its effect from the day of the first hearing, though I have only recently realised that. I wonder how Enric is being affected."

"You will have the opportunity to ask him that yourself soon, my child."

Her smiled broadened. "Yes, indeed. Luckily Golir is not as strict as Ram'an when it comes to keeping us apart, so I will not have to be content with just looking at him this time."

Valrad let himself sink down onto the warm grass with a contented sigh. "No, that you will not." He looked at her for a few moments, shading his eyes with one hand. "I wonder if you really are not sensitive to the degree of your attachment to him, Eryn."

She half turned to frown at him. "What is that supposed to mean? Of course I am attached to him. Very much."

"Why could you not answer Ram'an when he asked you if you loved Enric?"

Oh no, she groaned inwardly. Not that, not now. As if she didn't have enough to worry about right now without an analysis of her inability, unwillingness - or whatever else - to bestow romantic love on a man.

"I don't know!" she sighed exhaustedly and sank down to the ground next to him. "Why is everybody so concerned with my feelings for Enric? Isn't this meant to be a private matter between two people?"

Her uncle shook his head at her indulgently. "Not in your case, my dear Eryn. You have two men who are very attached to you, and one of them is demanding proof of your love for the other so he may renounce you finally. And that proof you are, for some reason or other, not able to furnish. I wonder why. It would have made things with Ram'an so much easier. But he has employed a lie filter on you, so the reason for your inability to confirm your feelings for Enric is either that you do not love him or that you are not aware of it."

She closed her eyes. "I don't know, I really don't. Love is a concept we use to tie two people together, no matter what harm comes of doing it. I believe that some things can only thrive when they are free, not shackled or confined."

"Do not tell me you have not forgiven him for keeping you shackled when you were a prisoner?"

"No, of course not, that would be nonsense."

"And yet you used that very expression to describe your perception of love. I realise that your own parents' story is not a very encouraging one - neither is my own, for that matter. Or Pe'tala's unreciprocated feelings for Ram'an. But then there are a lot of people who find great happiness with each other without experiencing any feeling of being tied or chained," he explained patiently. "Judging from your impatience at the mere thought of seeing Enric for one hour, I would not have assumed that you feel shackled in your relationship."

"I don't. Well, there are situations every now and then when I feel like hitting him with something heavy."

"That is natural, I am told," Valrad smirked and then turned serious again. "So you fear that admitting to yourself that you may indeed love him could cause you to find yourself in that prison you are so eager to avoid?"

"That sounds insane. Surely not," she protested.

"When we love somebody, we often realise it when we consider the deeds that have been done for us by that very person. If they have somehow managed to touch our heart one way or the other. I have seen Enric look at you, and there is no doubt whatsoever in my mind that he loves you very much. I would imagine that there must have been quite a few actions to speak of that."

Eryn stared ahead unseeingly, thinking back. He was right, there had been a few things that had spoken of great affection. She smiled when she remembered when he had learned healing in secrecy to induce the other magicians to apply for open trainee positions with her. Or when he had stopped her from disobeying the King during the execution of the apothecaries that one time that would have been one too many. And then he had bought these two houses with the street in between that could be turned into a yard for the wild cat she had brought back home. He had let Plia move in with them to keep her happy. And changed Vern's teaching schedule so that he could better focus on his healing training. There had been many things, great and small ones, she mused. Each of them touching in its own way. And then she didn't even count his everyday attempts at caring for her in the way of making sure that she was properly clothed and did not spend her nights at the healing place after falling asleep on her desk.

"There were a few events I can think of, yes," she admitted. "But these might as well have been tokens of affection and duty. Not to say that there is anything wrong with affection and duty. They are a combination worth striving for in any relationship, I think."

Valrad shook his head at her and started to rise.

"Where are you going? First you open this weighty conversation with me and now you are leaving just like that? Seriously?" she complained.

"You stay here. I will be back in a moment."

She watched him walk back to the terrace door and disappear into the house. True to his word, he reappeared not long after, holding something small and white in one hand.

"You may remember that we packed a few of our messenger birds for you to take back to Anyueel and breed them on your roof. Your King has used one of them to send a message here to our residence, as Enric requested the matter to be treated confidentially."

"For what matter?" she frowned. "I didn't even know that he was sending messages to Anyueel!"

"Here. Look for yourself. This is the King's message." He handed her the thin slip of paper that was filled with very small and crowded words.

She took the message and narrowed her eyes to better focus on the tiny scribbles. Her heart started beating faster after the first sentence and when she had reached the end, the world around her swam out of focus when tears started collecting between her lids.

"He has requested to be recognised as the permanent ambassador to Takhan for the next two years if the voting is not in my favour and I am stuck here." She swallowed hard and felt the first tear running over her cheek. "He told me that he wouldn't leave here without me, but I had rather counted on his stealing me away from here and fleeing across the seas."

"He would not have done that to you," Valrad said quietly. "Not again. You have only now got in contact with your roots, met your family, discovered all this knowledge you had been yearning for. He would never take that away from you. He would instead give up his own freedom for as long as you may be ordered to remain here. Whatever you think of the things he has done for you in the past, whether you see them as proof of love or duty, there cannot be any doubt as to what *this* here is." He pointed at the slip of paper in her hands, then lifted a questioning eyebrow. "And, my little Eryn, does this gesture touch your heart?" When she didn't answer, but continued staring at the message, he continued, "You said before that the feelings in a relationship are what concern the two people in it, not those around it. I wonder if you have ever thought of how Enric experiences that last defence you still have in place."

Another tear rolled down her cheek when she thought back to the evening of the hunting trip at the Aren estate when he had asked her to join with him in a third level commitment bond, and how she had refused him. He was not even angry about it, just resigned.

"Enric will soon be here. I will leave you alone until then. I have the feeling that you need a little time for yourself."

* * *

Enric saw her enter the main room through the terrace door and crossed the room in but a few lengthy strides to pull her into his arms and press her close. He lifted her chin to press kisses on her lips, her cheeks and her forehead before burying his face in her hair and inhaling deeply.

She wrapped her arms around him and squeezed as hard as she could, breathing in his scent and desperately welcoming his warmth, in spite of the still baking outside temperatures.

When they released each other again after what had probably been an eternity to Valrad and Golir but which seemed no more than a fleeting moment to her, he gave a troubled expression as he scrutinised her face more closely.

"Your eyes… Why have you been crying, my love?"

She smiled at him. "What a preposterous thing to say to a mighty Aren woman. An Aren woman does not cry, we just use the tear fluids to clean our lacrimal ducts from time to time. Basic maintenance from a healing point of view. Not that we really need to keep them functional, mind you."

He shook his head at her jokes. "Mighty Aren woman indeed."

She took his hand into hers and looked to Golir. "Golir, would you grant me a walk in the garden with Enric? I am willing to give to you a binding promise that we will not attempt anything that will get you into trouble, such as trying to flee or similar."

The triarch smiled. "I expect you will behave even without a first level bond. Anything else would almost certainly destroy your chances for tomorrow, after all. Nevertheless, please be so obliging as to remain within sight of the terrace."

Eryn nodded and pulled Enric along with her when she stepped outside. Only when they had put enough distance between them and the terrace to still be in view but out of earshot, did she stop and turn to him.

He raised his brow at her questioningly. "What are you up to?"

"Shut up now, will you?" she said quietly and closed her eyes for a moment, then she took a deep breath and exhaled slowly before looking up at him with a determined and slightly intense expression.

"Enric," she said with her chin raised, her tone formal, "there is something I wish to tell you. I love you."

He looked down at her, taking in her slightly too rapid breathing, her widened pupils and the large pulsating blood vessel at her throat. A slow smile began to spread over his lips.

"I am aware of that, my love. But I can tell you that finally hearing you say it makes me truly and deeply regret that we are under supervision right now."

Eryn closed her eyes for a moment, and when she opened them again, there was this usual defiant spark he knew so well. "What a completely bastard thing to say to me right now. What do you mean, you are aware of it? *I* myself realised it only a short while ago!"

He laughed and pulled her into his arms. "Depend on you somehow to manage to include the word *bastard* into your first declaration of love to me. You know, I am constantly working on being at least one step ahead of you, so I knew well enough that you love me. Your catching up was just a matter of time."

She frowned and tried to push him away in annoyance, but he held on to her. "This is not how I imagined this would go. I expected you to sink to the ground in relief, awe, gratitude - or some other emotion which makes your knees go weak - and repeat the words back to me. Fervently. Desperately."

Enric leaned his forehead against hers. "*You* are what makes my knees go weak," he murmured. "And my heart whenever you pull another stunt that makes me want to lock you up in a soft and safe place without pointed or flammable objects. But it is my pleasure to oblige you with that last thing. I have been wanting to say it to you for some time now, waiting for you to be ready to hear it. Whatever the outcome tomorrow of this entire mess, this here will have been worth it as it served to make you realise your feelings for me. I love you, Eryn."

She closed her eyes, smiling at the sensation of the hairs on her arms prickling at his words. When she felt him move his head so he could reach her lips, she lifted her arms around his neck to welcome the kiss. Funny, she thought through a haze, how telling him had not made her feel vulnerable as she had expected.

When he straightened again, she smiled at him and only then thought about the other little issue she wanted to address.

"Well, your reaction to my confession was not exactly what I had expected, but you managed to placate me."

"I am glad to hear it," he chuckled. "Being a high-ranking diplomat, I should at least manage not to turn my own companion against me after the first time she tells me she loves me."

"You *should* be glad. There is one more thing. Enric, I am asking you if you are willing to join with me into a third level commitment bond. With all that entails."

This time she was the one to grin when his eyes widened and he took a quick breath. "Look at *that*! It seems I finally managed to surprise you. That was clearly something you were *not* expecting. It seems now you are struggling to keep up right now instead of staying one step ahead."

Enric let out a shaky laugh and raked a hand through his hair. "You most definitely have. Only this time I have truly enjoyed being surprised by you. This is not the most affectionate proposal, but one that matches your personality, I admit."

She smiled. "Am I to assume that you just accepted it?"

"You may safely assume that, yes." He looked dazed. "So I finally managed to wear you down enough to yield to my request."

"Delusions," she laughed, "you waited nervously until I finally considered you worthy."

"Then each of us will stick to our version of the truth when we relate the story to our friends and family," he smiled.

"The trouble is that people here in Takhan are more likely to believe *me*, associating me with the famous Aren temper. But at home it will be the other way round, as your reputation creates more deference there than mine."

He pulled her close once more. "Come. Let us return back inside and share the news with Valrad. We require his help for arranging the ceremony. If the voting tomorrow is indeed in our favour, we should do it soon and then finally return home before somebody else comes up with another way to stop us from leaving."

She grimaced. "I swear to you, the next time I see a number of official looking men in uniforms approach me, I will start running in the opposite direction as fast as I can."

"I am inclined to agree with you there."

She feigned shock. "How very undiplomatic of you, Ambassador."

He nodded slowly. "Yes, I know. But somehow I am starting to become rather weary of diplomacy."

"Then let's hope that you do not get stuck in that position for another two years, eh?"

Enric looked at her in surprise. "You know about that?"

"Yes. Valrad told me only today." She pulled the King's message out of her pocket. "It was what jolted me into realising what you meant to me."

He took the slip of paper out of her hand and folded it carefully before putting it in his own pocket. "Remind me of this next time I roll my eyes when I receive a message from the King."

She grinned. "That it was a message from him that earned you my undying love?"

"I had your undying love before that, it just made you admit it to yourself."

653

"Still cocky," she sighed in mock resignation. "But as you will soon be mine in whatever country we happen to reside, I can start disciplining you properly and teach you some manners." She laughed when he lifted her up to carry her back to the house.

Enric saw Golir frowning sceptically, but didn't care about his possible disapproval of his conduct in this perfect moment of pure, raw joy that had brought him the fulfilment of a goal he had already given up on before this moment.

* * *

Eryn drummed her fingers on her knees impatiently. Ram'an should have been back long ago. She was waiting for him finally to put an end to this whole sorry charade by telling him that she had come to realise that she loved Enric, doing so even under the influence of a truth block, if he wished. That simply had to put an end to his wooing and would stop him from trying out a manoeuvre that would in any case backfire as she and Enric were more than prepared for it.

Vran'el arrived shortly after Enric and Golir had left and brought the good news that her adoption proposal had been granted and now nothing stood in the way of renouncing House Aren tomorrow, whether she won her freedom to leave or not.

"Where is he? He said he just needed a few hours to take care of some alleged family matter. He has been gone for more than five hours now, and I should go to bed soon to be rested for tomorrow," she complained.

"Who would have thought that I would live to see the day that you eagerly await Ram'an's return," Vran'el smirked.

"Shut up, idiot! You know well enough why I am waiting for him," she growled back.

"I do, yes. But snapping at me will not make him return any earlier so you may disillusion him. Better use the time for memorising the formal renouncement of House Aren. If you get the words wrong, Malriel may contest its validity, and that we do not want, do we?"

Eryn sighed and picked up the sheet Vran'el had prepared for her for what had to be the hundredth time in these last two hours. "I know them by heart, believe me. There is no way of my messing this up tomorrow - you can depend on that. If you must, you can test me again tomorrow over breakfast or on our way to the senate. Or both."

He rolled his eyes. "Right. Because testing you in the morning will be such a hazard-free undertaking when merely talking to you almost gets people's heads bitten off."

They both froze at the knock at the entrance door. Vran'el jumped up and descended the stairs only to return with a message a few moments later.

"It is from Ram'an, saying that he is not able to return here tonight. He writes that his family business has been a little more time-consuming than he anticipated. Good. It is nice to see that even smart Ram'an at times underestimates tiny matters such as taking on a position as Head of a House."

Eryn frowned in dismay. "Wait - this is bad news! It means I can't tell him about my impending commitment to Enric and stop him from making a fool of himself tomorrow!"

Her cousin shrugged. "He is neglecting his duties as your guard right now from a legal point of view, so I would say this is a more than adequate way to pay for it. Nobody forced him to play his little games, after all. He should have returned here as he was supposed to. Now it is for him to bear the consequences."

"I find this rather heartless of you," she frowned.

Vran'el smiled thinly. "I am a lawyer, sweetness. We are not exactly known for benevolence when it would be appropriate, let alone when it is not. Let us not forget that he broke my sister's heart and plans to force my cousin to stay here, shall we?"

Eryn furrowed her brow in incomprehension. "Why would he do that? He has been appointed as my guard to make sure I'm not doing anything the senate wouldn't approve of - how can he just neglect this apparently so important duty? What if the triarchy learns of this? Won't there be any consequences for him?"

"He certainly would have to do some explaining. Yet considering that it is of great importance for him that he takes over his House today, this is a calculated risk." He looked at the message in his hand thoughtfully. "If you would excuse me for a moment, I have to talk to father." Thus he turned and walked towards Valrad's study.

Eryn closed her eyes and once again repeated the ceremonial words of renouncement in her head, silently moving her lips along.

She then saw Vran'el and his father emerge from one of the corridors.

"Eryn," Valrad spoke while Vran'el determinedly walked towards the entrance door and slipped out a few moments later. "As Ram'an will not be returning here tonight, we have decided to inform Pe'tala of your adoption. Vran'el is on his way to collect her. This will not be pleasant for her to learn, and as you know she is not one to keep her anger to herself. You may wish to retire before she arrives."

"No, I think I should face her. There is no way I will be able to avoid her forever, and she is entitled to express her dissatisfaction with the current development from where I stand. I will get it over with now instead of having her throw rocks or bolts at me at my commitment ceremony." She smirked. "Unless the Head of my new House has any objections to the commitment as such? I am told I need his approval for it."

"None, my child, be sure of that," her uncle assured her with a tired smile. "You might want to start writing your vows. Many people find them very hard to put together and need quite some time for them."

"Writing my vows? There is no general wording I need to learn? I really have to write them myself?" she enquired with a slightly panicky expression.

"Yes, that is how we do it here. A third level bond is a serious covenant that needs to be considered carefully before being entered into. A standard formula to be learned by heart would hardly do the occasion justice," he told her.

She rubbed her eyes. "Alright. How long is it supposed to be?"

"No more than a minute. It is not meant to contain the history of your relationship or a tally of his unique qualities, but your reasons for entering into the bond with him. There are collections of books that have been published on the art of phrasing commitment vows, though I have always found simple but authentic phrases more appealing than literary works of art crafted by paid writers."

"Are you trying to tell me that however inexpertly written and unspectacular my vow turns out to be, it will at least be authentic? How charming."

"No, my dear girl," her uncle sighed, "I am trying to tell you that what comes from your heart and appeals to your companion will be what is ultimately acceptable and in accordance with the initial reason why couples were made to compose their own vows in the first place."

She got up to fetch a few sheets of paper and a pen from her bedroom. She could as well use the time for a first draft while they were waiting for Pe'tala to arrive.

*   *   *

Eryn took the third sheet of paper, containing drafts of snippets that had been cast aside as unsuitable and would never find their way into her vow, crumpling it up, as the entrance door opened and a few moments later Pe'tala and Vran'el appeared at the top of the stairs. Pe'tala's welcome was to twist her face into a grimace of pure disgust at the sight of her cousin.

"Still enjoying my family's hospitality, I see," Pe'tala scoffed and went to the drinks cabinet to pour herself a glass of wine. "Where have you left your enthusiastic admirer? Did he finally get fed up with you? Took him long enough if you ask me."

"I am not," Eryn said calmly.

"You are not what? Enjoying my family's hospitality?"

"Asking you," she replied curtly.

"Girls, stop this now," Valrad reprimanded them mildly. "Tala, my heart, there is something we need to tell you and I am afraid you will not be happy about it. We have applied for the permission to adopt Eryn into House Vel'kim, and it has been granted. She will from tomorrow legally belong to our family."

656

Pe'tala stared at her father, slack-jawed, for several seconds. Vran'el swiftly caught the wine glass her fingers were about to release.

"You did *WHAT*?" she then shouted. "Why? Why would you do this to me? You have a daughter for House Vel'kim!" Her voice had transformed from a scream into a wail and became a sob on the last, sustained, word: "Me."

Eryn watched her uncle step towards his now trembling daughter to wrap both arms around her. "Tala, this is not to replace or hurt you, it is to help Eryn."

"That is right, she needs every help she can get," Vran'el added softly.

"And everybody is so bloody eager to jump whenever *she* needs something," Pe'tala cried and covered her face with both hands. "For her every man suddenly turns into a shining beacon of chivalry! She comes here, takes away my companion to be, imposes herself onto my colleagues, steals my family and is now even adopted into my House!" Her glare landed on Eryn, who sat rigidly, awaiting the attack that was inevitable. "You! I hope they vote for you to be slammed into the darkest, dirtiest, most vermin-infested foul dungeon they can find and lock you up for the rest of your life with blocked powers!"

"Now, do not say anything you will regret later," Valrad warned her in a soft voice.

Eryn seriously doubted that her cousin would ever regret anything she said right now.

"Yes," Pe'tala spat and vigorously wiped the tears from her cheeks, "we would not want to bruise that precious flower with unkind words, would we?"

"I understand that you are unhappy, but I am sure that you would not want to see any real harm come to her, no matter how unfavourable the circumstances between the two of you are," her father tried again.

"You are damn right, I am unhappy!" she exclaimed and pushed him away. "And I do not care whatever harm comes to her, not in the least!"

Eryn exhaled, then rose slowly and started walking towards her cousin, who stared at her with an expression of pure hatred.

"Stay away from…"

"Shut up," Eryn said calmly and to her surprise, Pe'tala complied, probably surprised by the command. "Let me tell you the options here. Option one, I am adopted by your family and will I hope leave here in no more than a few days should the vote be in my favour tomorrow. Option two is that I am not adopted and so will be unprotected when I renounce House Aren tomorrow. This will enable Ram'an to keep me here for who knows how long. During this time I will visit your family regularly, work at the clinic with your colleagues, your patients, be part of your everyday life. We will have lunch together regularly, because Sarol likes me. What is it to be, dear cousin? Adoption and getting rid of me in a matter of days, or no adoption and as a consequence ample opportunity to really get to know each other, become bosom friends?"

That seemed to work. Pe'tala straightened and smoothed back her hair.

"Option one, then. It looks to be the lesser evil here." She turned to her father. "Adopt her if you must. Just make sure to get rid of her. The very sight of her makes me sick." With this she turned and stomped down the stairs and out the door, closing it behind her with a loud crash.

Vran'el sighed and emptied his sister's glass in one gulp. "Well, that went better than I thought. She even gave us her blessing."

CHAPTER 53

End of Trial

"Vran'el!" she whispered frantically and felt her way towards his bed. It was still dark outside and she let out a pained groan when she hit her toe against what felt like a heavy wardrobe.

"Go away, Tala, there are no strangers trying to abduct you," her cousin murmured sleepily from his bed. "Even if there were, they would bring you back in no time because you would drive them mad quickly enough."

Eryn followed his voice and felt soft sheets under her searching fingers.

"Vran'el, wake up," she implored him. "I am not Pe'tala, this is Eryn."

"Eryn? What are you doing here? It is still dark outside, go back to bed!" he moaned and made to turn away again.

"I can't! I can't sleep. I need your help, I have forgotten everything! *Everything*!"

The panicked edge in her voice made him stop in mid-turn and sigh. "You are not having a nervous breakdown, are you?"

"I don't know! I've never had one, it's something that happens to others, not me!"

"What have you forgotten, sweetness? The words for renouncing House Aren?"

"Yes! They are gone, just like that! Everything is blank, wiped clean!" She started sobbing. "I will be stuck with that woman until the end of my life! And they will vote against me, so I will be stuck here for two entire years and also take Enric's freedom away! That's what he gets for being stuck with me! Nothing but strife!"

She felt two warm hands on her shoulders that started shaking her a moment later. "Shut up, you idiot! You will *not* be stuck with her, because you will be able to remember the wording as soon as you have calmed down again. This is a stress reaction. You know about this - healers generally do. High levels of stress cut off rational thinking, and that is what is happening to you right now. Let me do a little thinking for you. I will paint you a picture of what the day today will bring. We will go to the senate, wait for them to vote on your case and then, regardless of the outcome, you will renounce Malriel and her House for good. Then we shall see if Ram'an really will try what I think he will and watch his attempt founder. Last but not least you will officially ask the triarchy for permission to be joined with Enric in a third level commitment bond. That is what is going to happen. I promise you."

Eryn nodded in the dark and took a few calming breaths. "You have not mentioned that they will vote in my favour."

"Because I cannot promise you *that*. I will not lie to you, there is the chance that you have to stay here for quite a while longer, but it will not be on Malriel's terms. She will have lost all and any rights to even seeing you if you do not wish it. And neither will Ram'an have any hold on you. If you really have to spend two years here, it will be as a member of House Vel'kim, and your status as Enric's companion will be indisputable after the ceremony. I know that you would use your time here well enough and take back who knows how many shiploads of books and papers and a head filled with inconvenient ideas your people will want to hide from."

She could hear the smile in his voice at the last few words.

"I am sorry I woke you, Vran'el. Thank you. Really. I will try to catch another few hours' sleep." Sighing, she started to rise again, but felt his hands press her down again.

"Come here." He pulled her under his light blanket with him. "If you feel the need for more gentle, comforting words, at least you do not have to walk so far."

"Gentle? You called me an idiot," she grumbled but lay down beside him.

"You keep calling people that. I have come to think of it as your favourite term of endearment. I now consider it proof of your affection, as it were. Now be quiet and let me sleep. And I hope you do not have the habit of stealing your bed partner's blankets. You might otherwise find yourself ejected from the cosiness of my warm bed to the cold, hard reality of the floor."

* * *

"Children, get up. It is time to get yourselves ready," Valrad called out jauntily and removed the blanket that covered both of them with an energetic swish before either of them had fully opened their eyes.

"What the...?" Eryn murmured sleepily while Vran'el gripped his pillow to toss at his father.

"Really now! I am thirty-four years old, one would think that this is old enough not to be woken in this manner any longer! Go away, evil old man!"

"Yes, and considering your advanced age, my boy, we would also assume that you would not need anybody to wake you anymore. Yet you are on the verge of being late. Up you get, or I will resort to less gentle measures," the older man threatened.

Eryn yawned loudly and scratched her head. "You have a very twisted notion of gentleness in this family. Others call that open warfare."

"Better get used to it. You are about to join us. Anyway, from what I have seen, your own way of dealing with your loved ones does not diverge so much from ours," Vran'el countered and swung his legs out of bed and then glared at his father. "For your information, the reason why I am so tired is that a certain person woke me in the middle of the night to have me soothe her nerves."

"Spare me your petty excuses. Get dressed, both of you. Breakfast is waiting for you on the terrace," Valrad instructed, then held out his hand towards Eryn with something silver on his palm. "This is a little something you may wish to wear for today, my dear girl."

She curiously took the item from his hand and saw that it was a silver pendant on a chain. Very much like the one Ram'an had given to her several months ago, only this time it comprised no more than a single large crest instead of two differently sized ones. She smiled broadly and let her thumb glide over the symbols that formed the official insignia of House Vel'kim.

"That I do very much, thank you! Really!" She pressed it close to her heart for a moment before slipping the chain around her neck. "Come, cousin. You promised to test me on this wording for renouncing Malriel over breakfast. I'll await you on the terrace in five minutes."

* * *

Since the senate building had loomed into view Eryn felt her palms getting sweaty, despite the pleasantly cool morning air. They climbed the stairs to the wide-open double doors and entered. The large hall was filled with people and their murmurs reverberated through the circular room.

"What are all these people doing here?" she whispered to her uncle. "Don't tell me they have come for the show?"

"I am afraid that is pretty much the case, yes. This is a case of considerable political interest and has also raised a lot of personal curiosity. Senate votings are open to public observers, after all. This one here is no exception," he explained quietly.

She let her gaze wander over the assembled senators seated in the first two rows. Ram'an did not sit at the same place as he had twice previously. He looked up at her and gave her a nod and a tense little smile. Vran'el took her arm to lead her down to the seats they had occupied before while Valrad moved to his own. It seemed Golir and Enric had not arrived yet as there was no blonde head visible anywhere.

"How much longer? I am getting more nervous by the minute," she whispered.

Her cousin shrugged. "No more than a few minutes, I should think. From what I see Golir is the last one to arrive... and there he is!"

The voices fell silent when the three triarchs approached the podium to take up their elevated seats.

As before, Torke'na was the one to address the senators. "Representatives of the Houses, this is now your last opportunity to seek answers to any unanswered questions that may have an influence on your decision." She waited for several moments and nodded when nobody gave any reaction to the offer. "Then let us delay the vote no longer. Malriel of House Aren, step before the senate." All eyes turned when the addressed rose and made her way to stand tall and proud before the assembled crowd.

"Maltheá of House Aren, step before the senate."

Eryn got to her feet as well, feeling her heart give a sudden race, to step next to her mother as instructed, though not too close. She glanced as benignly as possible at the many assembled faces. When her gaze first landed on Enric at the back of the room, his expression looked tense and serious. He smiled reassuringly when he noticed her looking at him.

"Senators," Torke'na prompted, "it is time for you to cast your vote. House Ordel?"

"Guilty," Voreld, the Head of House Ordel announced.

"House Finran?"

"Guilty," Legara stated.

Eryn gulped. That was not a promising start. However, both Houses were known to be associated with Malriel, so it was no great surprise. Yet the sequence in which the Houses were requested to report their votes did not make this sound very encouraging so far.

"House Vel'kim?"

"Not guilty," Valrad's calm voice stated.

"House Turbar?"

"Not guilty."

"House Tokmar?"

"Not guilty."

Three out of the ten votes she needed.

"House Feral?"

"Guilty."

"House Roal?"

"Not guilty."

"House Arbil?"

She held her breath when Ram'an lifted his head. "Not guilty." And released it again.

"House Landred?"

"Guilty."

Five votes in her favour, she counted, her heart beating much too fast. She needed five more and there were another nine votes to be cast, three by the Houses, six by the triarchs.

"House Partém?" Torke'na enquired.

"Not guilty."

"House Ulverd?"

"Not guilty."

Seven votes for her, another three required.

"House Aren?"

Malriel stared straight ahead. "Guilty."

"The Houses have voted with seven votes for *not guilty* and five for *guilty*," the triarch summarised the result. "Now the triarchs will cast their votes each of which will count for two. I vote with not guilty."

Abrak looked down at Eryn. "I vote with guilty."

Eryn closed her eyes. That made seven votes for Malriel and nine for herself. If Golir was on the side of House Aren, they had an equal number of votes. She had not even considered that possibility. What did they do here to break a tie in the senate?

All eyes were on Golir, who seemed calm and unfazed despite the fact that his vote was about to decide if this whole case was to be settled here and now. He cleared his throat.

"I vote for not guilty."

Eryn closed her eyes, the breath she had been holding escaping her lungs in a violent burst that made her bend forward and brace her hands on her knees. Over. It was over! She had won. She would leave here with Enric instead of being made to stay. She would see her friends again, return to her work, her home.

Yet it was not yet completely over, was it? She opened her eyes again, straightened and felt strength coursing through her body where before there had been apprehension and dread.

Torke'na raised her voice and the murmuring that had started died down immediately. "The senate and triarchy have jointly voted for *not guilty* with eleven votes against seven. Maltheá of House Aren, you are free to leave this country as you please or remain if this is what you prefer. Do you accept this judgement?"

Eryn nodded. "I do, yes. In addition, there is something more I would like to say." She let her eyes wander over the audience, seeking out Enric, whose smile was wide and triumphant. "I would like to thank the senate and the triarchy for handling this matter in such an efficient and expeditious way. I understand that procedures of that kind usually tend to take longer. I am grateful and relieved that the result is in my favour."

Then she turned to Malriel, who stood rigidly, her pale face a calm mask while her eyes bespoke the turmoil inside her. "Malriel of House Aren, I herewith officially renounce your House and will thus no longer consider myself or be considered by others a member thereof. I renounce you as my mother and will thus no longer be subject to your authority in this function or the one as Head of House Aren. I renounce my position as heiress of your House and will not be at your disposal when your position becomes vacant. My children will not be members of your House nor have any other official or legal connection to you or your family." She reached into her pocket and pulled out the pendant that combined the larger crest of House Aren with the smaller one of House Vel'kim and threw it to the floor, where it skittered on the smooth marble until it came to rest in front of Malriel's feet.

The older woman nodded slowly, bent down and carefully retrieved the pendant, looking at it for several moments before putting it into her own pocket.

"So be it then, Maltheá," she spoke with a voice curiously stripped of emotion. They stared at each other for some time, the people in the hall quiet as if afraid to break the silence.

Then there was one sound, which would under normal circumstances not have stood out, but seemed almost painfully loud in the calm: a chair being pushed back and scraping over the floor as a man slowly rose from his seat.

Ram'an raised his voice and the eyes that had been glued to the two women in front swerved instead towards him.

"I wish to inform the senate and the triarchy that I have assumed my father's position as Head of House Arbil as of yesterday evening."

Abrak nodded. "Congratulations. Your new position is herewith officially acknowledged, Ram'an, Head of House Arbil. May you serve your House in honour and dignity and provide well for it."

"Thank you." He raised his head. "As Head of House Arbil I herewith claim the Right of Substitution for Maltheá. This claim is in accordance with the rules as laid down in the book of family law. I have a copy here in case you wish to verify its validity."

Eryn's jaws clenched and she exchanged a look with Vran'el, who smiled grimly and raised his brow as if to say *What did I tell you?*

"The Right of substitution is an ancient law that has not been imposed for more than one hundred and fifty years as it is no longer in accordance with the values and customs of our society," Golir pointed out with a frown at his nephew.

"Yet it has never been rescinded and so is still in effect and executable," Ram'an countered. "Unless there are relevant circumstances in place to prevent this claim from being executed, the still valid companionship agreement between House Aren and House Arbil puts me in a position to claim Maltheá as member of my House and thus subject her to my authority."

Golir nodded slowly. "I see. Then I am afraid it is my duty to inform you, Head of House Arbil, that there are indeed circumstances that prevent your claim from being legal. The Right of Substitution can only be claimed if the person in question is not a member of a House. Maltheá has been officially adopted into House Vel'kim. This adoption became effective from the moment of her renunciation of House Aren."

Ram'an's head snapped towards Vran'el and he stared at his colleague open-mouthed. Vran'el coldly braved the devastating glare with his chin held high. Ram'an slowly sank back into his chair, his face a pale stony mask of disbelief and misery. Eryn swallowed and had to remind herself that seeing him seemingly broken and forlorn at this moment was far better than the alternative that would have meant he was victorious. Nonetheless, his grief touched her on a human level and she forced herself to look away from him. There was one more thing she needed to address.

"Honoured members of the triarchy, I wish to make a request and would be very grateful if you saw it in your powers to grant it. I wish to ask for your permission to enter into a third level commitment bond with Enric, Ambassador to Takhan," she announced. She saw from the corners of her eyes that Ram'an's head had jerked up, then he noisily shoved his chair back and fled the senate hall.

The triarchs watched him until the heavy door had closed behind him, then exchanged a few looks and nods. Torke'na was again the one to speak. "The permission is granted, Maltheá of House Vel'kim. You are, of course, aware that our permission is not the only one required to carry out the ceremony?"

Eryn smiled and nodded. "That I am, yes. The Head of my new House has granted his permission already."

"I have not granted mine, though, have I?" Malriel spoke in a clear voice with a cool smile and arms folded.

Eryn turned to look at her. She saw Enric and Valrad hurry down the stairs, wondering at their tense expressions as if they expected sudden doom to befall them.

"That is because you are no longer my Head of House, Malriel. I do not require your acquiescence for anything I do ever again," she said slowly and wondered if it was possible that Malriel had somehow lost touch with reality and just opted to ignore what was happening around her, caught in her own world where things were just the way she wanted them. Was there perhaps a history of mental instability in her family? Eryn hoped it was nothing that could be passed on through the maternal line.

The smile grew wider as if she was laughing at a private joke. "There is not only *your* House to be considered, my dear girl, but Enric's House as well."

Eryn stared at the other women in utter confusion. "Enric's House? What nonsense is that? Enric has no House."

"He does now," Malriel replied. "Though it seems he has chosen not to inform you of that little detail as yet."

The younger woman swallowed when realisation dawned on her. Oh no. *That* was surely not true. Impossible. She slowly turned to Enric, who had come to stand behind her and looked as if prepared to brave a thunderstorm.

"Please tell me that you have *not* let yourself be adopted into House Aren." She lifted her hand to silence him when he made to speak. "Let me be very clear about the answer I want to hear from you. It has to be some variation on *No*. You may put a little more emphasis on it, such as *No, never in my life* or *No, how could you even ask?* This I'll leave to your own discretion. But I am very adamant about the *No*-part."

Enric closed his eyes for a moment. This was definitely not how he had planned for her to learn of this. He had wanted to introduce this detail gently to her, not have it done by her mother, or his mother or whoever's mother she officially was at the moment, in a room full of politicians and strangers.

"I am sorry, my love," he murmured.

"You see, Theá," Malriel purred, "It seems your connection with me did not exactly end by your renouncing me. The moment you did, not only did your adoption become effective, but also Enric's. Enric of House Aren," she said with relish. "I like the sound of it."

Eryn balled her hands into fists and spun on her heel.

"You have not asked me for my permission to be joined to my son, Maltheá," she heard Malriel's sharp voice. "Am I to assume that you no longer wish to enter into a third level bond with him?"

One bolt - one well aimed, painful bolt - would shut her up in no more than a second, Eryn mused, heat flushing her cheeks red. Enric stepped in her way and lifted his hands to put them on her upper arms to stop her from leaving.

"Eryn," he said in a low voice, his eyes imploring. "Ask her."

"I am so furious at you that I am wondering whether joining you is a good idea anyway right now," she growled.

"Trust me. Trust that I would not have done this if avoiding the consequences of not doing it were not worth angering you," he insisted, his grip getting stronger. "Ask her. I am not letting you leave here without Malriel's permission. I am not willing to give this up." He leaned his forehead against hers. "Please. Please don't do this to me."

She drew in a deep breath. "You are going to explain this to me, and it better be good."

"Everything you want. I promise."

Eryn straightened and turned to face Malriel once more, forcing herself not to avoid the intense brown eyes directed at her.

"Head of House Aren, I herewith request your permission to join into a third level commitment bond with," she paused for a moment before making herself say, "Enric of House Aren."

"I herewith grant my permission. I very much look forward to the ceremony," Malriel replied with a satisfied smile.

Eryn nodded once, then grabbed Enric's sleeve and pulled him along when she made for the doors. "*Enric of House Aren*," she spat quietly enough for only him to hear. "I think I have to clean my mouth with soap and water! I am very much looking forward to that explanation of yours. I wonder if it will make me stop wanting to hurt you so badly."

CHAPTER 54

Chat Among Guys

Eryn closed the entrance door to the Vel'kim residence, folded her arms and glared at him. She had more or less dragged him along with her all the way from the senate. They had walked together wordlessly.

"Now talk," she instructed with eyes narrowed.

Enric sighed. "Let's go upstairs and sit down, shall we? I do not find it particularly comfortable here in the hallway."

She nodded briefly and preceded him up the stairs. He followed her, resigned to justifying himself to her when he instead felt the urge to celebrate the outcome of the trial and all it entailed.

He let himself sink next to her on the cushions on which she had flopped down inelegantly.

"Why?" she just demanded with a hurt expression.

"Because she would have made the Vel'kim family pay for it otherwise," he replied.

"Are you telling me that she blackmailed you?" Eryn exclaimed with a horrified expression.

Enric smiled faintly. "It is probably what she likes to think, yes."

"What is that supposed to mean now? Did she blackmail you or not?"

"She made it very clear that there would be sanctions against House Vel'kim if I did not agree to being adopted in compensation for the loss of her only daughter. But in demanding that she has aided House Vel'kim far more than her own House, or *our* own House, as I should call it now. She has given everyone to understand that there is no longer a grudge between the Houses due to what your father did so many years ago. This was the final step to redeem House Vel'kim. And the alliance is re-established and strengthened by a new generation. House Vel'kim will profit from the renewal of this bond with a very powerful House such as Aren."

"But you are her heir now, aren't you? I thought I had managed to escape the danger of being summoned here and made to take over the House - and it turns out that it makes no difference at all as you are the one now at her beck and call!" she groaned. "How could you, the great strategy player in the political game, fall for a trap like that?"

Enric took her hands in his. "This is now the part I am rather reluctant to talk about as it does not make me as selfless as I would like to appear in order to placate you."

"Out with it," she sighed. "I will not think less of you if you somehow manage to profit from it yourself. It will just make me point out to you how very surprising your decision to keep this from me was, as you made it very clear, on more than one occasion in the past, what you think about *my* hiding things from *you*."

"Very well, let's start with how I will benefit from this situation, shall we? Then I will tell you my reasons for concealing my plans and you may scold me."

Eryn rolled her eyes. "I don't need your permission to scold you!"

"No, but I hope to get you into a more lenient frame of mind if I accept it willingly." He linked his fingers with hers. "My connection with a powerful House here in Takhan will increase my influence back home considerably. This will also be in your interest, my love, as I imagine that there are quite a few fundamental changes which will happen once we return. Malriel has very good connections to the triarchy and may thereby influence them to a certain degree or, if not that, at least have them listen very closely to what she has to say. Malriel and I are both politicians, and we know that a successful relationship depends on working together for mutual benefit. Whatever strengthens Malriel, will as a consequence have the same effect on my position and vice versa."

"Which changes?" Eryn frowned.

"Changes in the structure of the Order, for example. They may decide that being the heir to a foreign dynasty, I may not be as reliable in my position as second in command any more, that this may constitute a conflict of interests."

She paused before speaking. "You think they may decide to, erm… release you from your position?"

"Not as such, no. That would not be very wise as whatever they from now on do to me, they do to a family member of House Aren and such things may cause diplomatic tension. So they will doubtlessly be more careful with me after we return. There is you to consider as well. Before we left, nobody knew of your own importance. You are still connected to an important family here, even though not one that is keen on wielding its power. So you, too, return as a more influential person than you left, politically speaking. You and I are now both more daunting to tackle, but also very much assets to our Kingdom. Due to this we may find ourselves in a position every now and then where our loyalty is questioned."

"Wait, what?" she frowned in dismay. "I am about to slither even more deeply into that damned political turmoil?"

"That is the beauty about it: being part of House Aren is an advantage back home in Anyueel, though the one playing the game will not be you, but me. Vel'kim is a very good House for you to be in, as it is not only a family of healers to cater to your personal preferences, but important enough to be respected without being too formidable. Aren, on the other hand, is a family that tends to breed leaders that rise as high as triarchs."

"So you are telling me that your being the formidable one of us two due to being in House Aren is better because you like playing the game? Also that it would have been a pity to lose the advantage of having House Aren behind one of us?" She shook her head at him. "You are probably as devious as she! It seems the two of you really should belong in the same House. I look forward to seeing you disagreeing for the first time. You will very likely turn out to deserve each other well enough."

He raised a brow at her bitter tone. "I do not like the idea of your putting me in the same category as the woman you hate enough to renounce. My abilities when it comes to playing this game may match hers, but I think what distinguishes us is the reason why we play it and what we are willing to sacrifice." He lifted her chin and kissed her. "I am not going to let any harm come to you. Not ever. I will do whatever it takes to protect you. And freeing you from her influence and taking your place instead is something that will serve this purpose well enough." He smiled. "She has not made her own life easier by connecting herself to me, that much I can tell you."

Eryn rubbed her face. "I am not sure if that answer is better or worse than I expected. Better probably, because you didn't do it primarily for selfish reasons, though worse because I feel as if we are going to be marooned in a political swamp worse than before. But be that as it may, consider the first part of your explanation over and done with. Let's move on to why you think that your concealing all this is a lot less objectionable than my doing it."

"I was worried that you would refrain from renouncing House Aren if you knew what the consequences are. I wanted you to do this, to free yourself from Malriel. I don't think anything the two of you do - or do not do - in the future to deal with the acrimony between you will work if she has some legal hold on you. Now you can act freely - or not at all."

She rolled her eyes. "The man who used to keep me shackled and stopped me from fleeing the city both times is now fighting to preserve my freedom? That is paradoxical, isn't it?"

He smiled. "Not as much as you think. I am only attempting to preserve your freedom from others. I resent the idea of freedom when it comes to the two of us. If there turns out to be an even stronger magical bond than third level to forge us together, you may depend on my somehow making you consent to that as well."

Pulling her closer, he noted with satisfaction how her eyes darted to his lips and lingered there. "Did I tell you how much I have missed you since they separated us?" he murmured.

She swallowed. "You are lucky that your proximity flusters me enough right now to not give you the beating that *freedom* remark would otherwise have earned you."

He leaned closer to kiss her throat. "Vran'el and Valrad are not yet back. They were surrounded by senators when we left. I imagine they will be busy answering questions for quite a while yet. Why don't you show me that comfy room of yours and I will in turn show you what's been going through my head over these past days?"

* * *

Eryn lifted her head drowsily from the pillow when she felt Enric's weight on the bed shifting. First signs of the impending dusk were visible in the quality of the light outside.

"Where are you going?"

"I am sorry if I woke you, my love," Enric smiled and bent down to kiss the crown of her head. "There is something I would like to take care of."

She frowned. "This does not happen to have anything to do with Ram'an, does it? You are not going to carry out the threat of making him pay for touching me up while he was standing guard over me, are you?"

Enric's face remained suspiciously blank.

"Come on, didn't you see him at the senate today? He was devastated! Don't kick a man when he is down already, it is beneath you!"

He picked up his clothes from the floor and slipped into them. "Do not waste too much of your sympathy on him, Eryn," he remarked evenly. "He is not a victim of circumstances and you are not doing him a favour by considering him as one instead of as a man who took fate into his own hands and lost."

"Wait!" she called across when he opened the door to the corridor. "Promise me that you will not injure him!"

"I promise. I am not meeting him to inflict pain, but to give him closure on the one hand while making everybody else see that I am not to be trifled with. If he complies and carries out the task with dignity, he will profit from it as well."

"What task?" she said, but by then he had already closed the door behind him and was gone.

* * *

Golir smiled when he opened the door and saw Enric standing in front of it.

"Enric. I was wondering when I would be seeing you again. Your cat is starting to become rather restless." He stepped aside to let his guest enter. "I assume you will be staying at the Vel'kim residence with Maltheá now?"

"I will, yes."

The older man nodded. "So she has forgiven you for joining the House she was so eager to leave behind. She did appear a little... agitated when you left the senate hall."

"I had some explaining to do, I admit," Enric smiled.

Golir chuckled. "I imagine you did. Though a man is willing to bow to greater authority in situations like that, is he not? Do not stand here in the doorway, Enric, come in."

"I am afraid I don't have much time. There is another visit I need to make. I have come to take Urban with me and also something from my personal belongings. The rest I will have taken to the Vel'kim residence tomorrow morning." He paused for a moment before he continued. "Golir, I wanted to thank you. For everything you have done. Your willingness to take me in and guard me for the duration of the trial enabled me to remain here in Takhan. I will not forget that."

"I expect you would have fought with tooth and claw against being sent away without Maltheá, so I dare say I did both sides a favour," he remarked dryly. "Come in and get what you have come to pick up. Oh, and Enric?"

"Yes?"

"I am sure that I do not need to tell you that I would not look kindly upon any harm coming to my nephew." The smile on his face did not conceal the fact that the warning was meant in earnest.

Enric sighed. "These were pretty much Eryn's parting words. She made me promise not to hurt him."

"Did she now. What a remarkable woman. Clearly a streak of Vel'kim in her."

Enric smiled. "She would have liked to hear that. All she ever hears is how much she resembles Malriel and how typical her temper is for Aren."

"People like to concentrate on the obvious. Looking a bit deeper requires so much more effort," Golir said mildly.

"But not you. You like to take a closer look, don't you?"

"I must. In my position doing so is a matter of survival. Also in yours, I imagine. It was instrumental in making the decision to let you stay with me. Had the picture the general public has of you been accurate, it would have been a great risk for me to do so. Possessive, demanding, dangerous. That is what people see when they look at you. The man who tamed an Aren women into joining him after he kept her prisoner. An unthinkable feat. The man who stepped between three Aren women when they were about to remind the world what a true clash is – and lived to walk away. But then it was you who were captured by Maltheá first. To see that you are connected to her in love and do not see her as a valuable and politically useful possession is what convinced me to let you stay."

Enric nodded slowly. There were not many people who managed to look behind his façade that thoroughly. Aside from Tyront there was probably only the King. And now Golir could be added to these men.

"However, do not worry, Enric of House Aren, I will not make it known to the public that you are a flesh-and-bone man instead of that invincible figure people like to see you as."

The younger man laughed. "Invincible figure indeed!"

"Dealing with Malriel on a regular basis may yet cause you to turn into one," Golir said solemnly.

*   *   *

Enric knocked at the door to the Arbil residence and waited with the compact but heavy wooden chest under his arm. It had turned completely dark by now and Urban's ears flicked this way and that, anxious to capture the sounds around her. She had welcomed him eagerly, rubbing against his legs and flopping down in front of him to have her soft, slightly lighter belly fur rubbed. Golir had stood behind him with folded arms, shaking his head at this display of affection from such a fearsomely wild-looking animal.

The door was opened by a man who had to be his junior by several years. He raised both eyebrows at the newcomer after taking in the blonde hair.

"Oh dear," the man said slowly. "Enric of House Aren."

"You have me at an advantage. I have no idea who *you* are," Enric replied, waiting to be admitted.

"Myself? Forgive me. I am Ram'kel of House Arbil. I assume you have come to visit my brother Ram'an."

Brother. He remembered hearing about a younger brother. There was not much similarity in their features. This man looked less solemn; a more easy-going and mischievous man in comparison to the new Head of House Arbil.

"That I have, yes." He waited for another few moments before adding, "Will you admit me if I promise not to injure him? It would be the third time this evening I have assured people of that."

Ram'kel nodded. "I admit that was a concern, yes. We have had our new Head for only one day now and would first like to see how he does before offering him as a target for violent retribution."

Enric lifted one eyebrow. Humorous despite the dire situation.

"I will then refrain from taking his life for the time being. Will you be so kind as to tell him that I am here to talk to him?"

The younger man nodded and then his gaze fell on the cat peering around Enric's legs, which then lifted its nose into the air to sample the new scents from inside the open door.

"Oh my, I heard about that one - though seeing it directly in front of you there at night is something else."

"Don't worry about her. As long as I am with her she is not dangerous. And for a magician who is able to shield himself in time, she poses no problem at all."

Ram'kel swallowed. "Then I better make sure to protect my back while you are here." He stepped aside and let the unusual pair of visitors enter, handing Enric the customary bowl with a cool towel to refresh himself.

"Does your cat need anything? Water? A small horse to snack on?"

"No," Enric replied dryly, "she has been fed already. And we try not to let her acquire any bad habits. It wouldn't do to have her snatching horses away from under their riders whenever she feels like it."

That made the other man smile. "I do agree. Follow me." He walked up the stairs into a main room that Enric remembered from the dinner he had attended here once. It looked completely different from any other Enric had seen since his arrival in Takhan. Pleasantly different, he mused. Books and dark wood, which seemed oddly exotic here.

"If you would wait here for a moment, I will see if my brother can see you." Ram'kel turned into one of four corridors and Enric counted the doors to see behind which one Ram'an's study was.

The young man returned only a few moments later and nodded. "He will receive you now."

Enric followed him to the door he had disappeared through only moments ago and stepped inside a large, luxuriously furnished room that reminded him a lot of Tyront's study. Ram'an sat behind an extensive dark desk, looking somewhat tired and less than happy about seeing this particular face.

The door was closed gently behind them and the two men stared at each other for several long seconds, before Ram'an sighed and rubbed his chin.

"What do you want, Lord Enric? Have you come to gloat? I did not think you were the type for it. Or am I now to be punished for taking liberties with Maltheá?"

"First of all, stop addressing me with *Lord*, will you? You mean to demonstrate more distance by using the title, but it rather conveys the impression of high esteem, which is clearly not what you intend."

Ram'an just stared at him.

"And no, I am not here to gloat. Though your second guess is fairly close to the truth, I must say," Enric said calmly. "There is still a score to settle between the two of us."

The other man shook his head with a bitter smile. "Of course. And being who you are, you cannot be seen to have let that slide, can you? Even less after joining House Aren now. Alright, mighty heir of House Aren, let me hear what you consider an apt punishment for me. I assume it is nothing physical, as you are playing the political game on two sides now, after all. You are still an ambassador for the Old Kingdom, and at the same time your actions have an impact on House Aren."

"All true. I am not seeking to harm you or your House, Ram'an. I have also taken into account that you showed rather more restraint than I did back in a similar situation when I was her guard. All the same, at that time there was no other man claiming her for himself." He leaned forward and placed the chest on the large desk, making sure Ram'an was looking at it before lifting the lid and revealing its contents. It was filled with the slim gold slips of the local currency.

"What do you think you are doing, *Enric*?" Ram'an spat. "Malriel's attempts at buying Theá free from the agreement were rejected before. Do you think I will accept this gesture of pity from you now?"

Enric smiled thinly. "This is not a gift. It is meant to cover the expenses for the commitment ceremony you will be hosting here at the Arbil residence in four days."

"*What*?"

"You will arrange for the ceremony and the subsequent celebration to take place here at your residence. And in addition to that, you will be the one to offer me Eryn's hand. I am told it is customary to have a female relative do it, but as there is nobody but Pe'tala who would fit that description, I think we will overlook that tradition and instead use the opportunity to show the world how civilised each of us is in handling this sticky business."

"What makes you think that I would agree to a thing like that? Why would I agree to assisting you so eagerly in humiliating myself for everyone to see?" Ram'an hissed, then abruptly rose from his chair. "Take your damned money and leave my house!"

"Now you listen to me, *Head of House Arbil*," Enric replied. His voice had taken on a slightly threatening quality. "I do not think that you can afford to lose an ally in the form of House Aren just after taking over your new responsibilities. From what I have heard your father has let things slide over the last few years, so making powerful enemies is not what you want right now. It is for now in Malriel's interest to keep me happy, so if I insist on breaking off her agreements with House Arbil, I am fairly positive that she will oblige me, especially as I am in a position to compensate her for any disadvantages that may arise for House Aren quite easily." He closed the chest's lid and pushed it towards Ram'an. "How much of a humiliation this is depends on nobody but yourself. For all I care, you may as well turn it into a demonstration of good sportsmanship; you throw a party for us, and in doing so generously acknowledge my victory by demonstrating how well you can deal with it. Show the world that a minor thing such as this cannot throw the new Head of House Arbil off track - that a woman is not reason enough for you to endanger your alliance with House Aren. I don't care how you decide to handle it, but make no mistake that you will go through with it. Or bear the consequences. I have signed trade agreements with most of the Houses, many of them including my own goods. House Aren would not be the only House that might be reluctant to do business with you in the future if you do not comply with my... let's call it *humble request*, shall we?"

Ram'an stepped away from his desk and turned towards the window, pressing his forehead against the cool glass, staring ahead with eyes unfocussed.

"So it is, Enric. A celebration it shall be. You win. Again. I will do as you command to protect my House." He chuckled without humour. "Who would have thought that I have to learn the lesson that personal pride has to stand back behind the House's interests quite so soon after taking over the position?"

"When I came here, I was confident that you would make that decision, just as any other honourable man in your position would," Enric remarked. "Make it a day for her that she will remember fondly. Should you need more gold to accomplish this, inform me by messenger. Consider it your parting gift to her. I should also mention that, for her sake and your own, make sure you keep your anguish inside. It would only make people pity you. Show strength; it will earn you respect." With this he turned and left, the cat trotting along lazily behind.

* * *

Eryn jumped up from the cushions in the main room when she heard the entrance door. Vran'el sighed when Enric appeared at the top of the stairs.

"Good, you are back. It was quite an effort to stop Eryn from going after you to protect poor, crushed Ram'an from your wrath." He grimaced when he spotted Urban. "Oh, excellent. The long-toothed, sharp-clawed brute is back as well. Life does so quickly become boring when I do not have to be on my guard against being sprung at from any direction."

The cat spotted Vran'el and sauntered over to him, gingerly sniffing his feet and then laying down right next to him. He shook his head in exasperation.

"I swear to you, she does this on purpose!"

Eryn gave her companion a questioning look. "So what?"

Enric took her hand and pulled her back to the cushions with him. "Rest assured that Ram'an is still in the best of health."

"Did he require any healing to reach that very desirable state?" Valrad asked dryly.

"No. I didn't even touch him. Why does everybody seem to think that I make a habit of hitting people whenever a convenient occasion presents itself?"

"That, my dear friend, might have something to do with a certain evening that involved first dancing, then your hitting a certain face with a well-aimed punch," Vran'el retorted.

"You mentioned a task you wanted him to carry out," Eryn prompted.

"Yes. I am happy to report that he has decided to comply. He will host the ceremony and celebration for our commitment bond," Enric announced.

Vran'el whistled through his teeth, while Valrad nodded appreciatively.

"He will *what*?" Eryn exclaimed wide-eyed, then shook her head. "Oh dear. Don't think that I can't see the cruel beauty of your little scheme here, but I can't help but empathising with Ram'an."

Her uncle sighed. "Your compassion does you credit, my girl, especially under these circumstances. But consider that this solution meets a lot of requirements without hurting anything except Ram'an's pride. His House is now more vulnerable than ever, and it would therefore have been easy to harm it even further. This event, however, connects him to House Aren as it will be seen as a gesture of forgiveness on both sides. By House Arbil because they are the ones offering it and by House Aren because they accepted it. Well, as long as the real reason behind it all does not become known publicly, that is."

"I know," she said with a sad expression. "Still I can't help feeling sorry for him. When he wasn't overstepping any boundaries, he still was a friend to me."

Enric squeezed her shoulders. "I am aware of that. This is what made me show him rather more leniency than I would have otherwise."

"So, when is the happy day?" Vran'el asked. "There are still a few things to be taken care of until then."

"In four days. Golir has offered to officiate at the ceremony. I am glad about that. I have come to admire and respect him in the time I have spent with him."

Valrad nodded. "Level-headed man, yes. People tend to underestimate him because he is the quiet type. That does usually end in a rude awakening. He was not made a triarch for being harmless."

"Four days," Eryn murmured. "Well, as you have so elegantly delegated the planning for the festivities to somebody else, this leaves only a few minor issues like having a dress made and writing the vows."

"I will assist you with the dress, sweetness," Vran'el said immediately. "I will not have you put my House to shame at the first opportunity. The vows - well, that is something you will have to put together on your own. But there is another little thing you need to take care of: your symbols."

"Symbols? Like the House pendants or something?" Eryn frowned in confusion.

"No," Valrad shook his head, "not quite. The symbols are not a piece of jewellery, but will be painted onto your skin around your wrists. During the ceremony the colour will be made to seep into the skin completely with magic. When you are apart, the symbols will be invisible. The closer you get to each other physically, the darker and more vivid they become."

"Really?" she leaned forward in fascination. "Why have I never seen this before in these last few weeks here?"

"I would assume that most magicians you have met that are joined in a third level bond have not had their companions with them at that time. And then we wear long sleeves here to protect our skin from the sun, so seeing the symbols unless you are looking for them is rather unlikely."

"What kind of symbol will it be? Is there a selection to pick from or how does this work?" she enquired.

"It is the same as with the vows, Eryn. You are expected to provide your own designs," Valrad smiled sympathetically.

"Damn," she murmured, "where is Vern when I happen to need an artist? What kind of things do people normally put in their symbols?"

"Well, some opt to include their family crests or insignias in some form," Vran'el shrugged.

Eryn flashed Enric a look. "If you try to sneak the Aren one in there somewhere, I am going to throttle you."

He lifted both hands in front of him. "No danger there, my love. Being part of the House for one day has not yet awakened the urge in me to permanently brand myself with their crest."

"Others add little things that were instrumental in finding each other," her cousin went on.

"Shackles and swords do seem a little out of place, I would think," Enric said mockingly.

"A Royal message delivered by a bird," Eryn said quietly. "It made me realise that... you know."

He smiled at her reluctance to repeat it and wondered if it was the words in general or the audience that made her feel uneasy. "I like it. We could use a bird carrying a rolled-up message with a crown above. I have another one. A broken branch. Without it I might never have met you."

She laughed. "I am not sure if the reason for my head injury is an appropriate image to use here."

"What is appropriate or not is to your own discretion," Valrad explained. "Just consider that you will have to look at the symbols for years, so pick ones that will not embarrass or irk you with the passage of time."

"A mask," Enric grinned. "I would very much like to use that one."

Eryn nodded. "I agree with it if you give up the broken branch. It seems a little strange."

"No, I want both," he shook his head. "They were instrumental in our relationship. You get the messenger bird and may choose another one you like."

She stared at the ceiling for a while, then shook her head. "I can't think of another one. Do we need to have four or will three do as well?"

"As I said, how you design them is up to you entirely," Valrad shrugged. "Some couples decide on one single symbol, others use as many as they can fit on their wrists."

She smiled suddenly. "I have something! My second symbol will be a shield to represent your ever-present need to protect me from the entire world, myself included."

Enric nodded in approval. "I like that. It will serve as a reminder to me not to let you out of my sight for too long in case you fall prey to trouble again."

Ignoring his last remark, she nodded. "That was remarkably easy. What's next? I don't have to draw them as well, do I? Pictures I drew would not be something I would want to have on my arm for the rest of my life."

"No, sweetness, that task you can safely delegate to an artist. We have two or three that specialise in this kind of work and a few more who do it as a side-line," Vran'el grinned. "What you might want to take care of next is working on your vows, though. Theoretically you could choose to hire an artist for that as well, but it is frowned upon."

"Yes, your father told me as much yesterday," she sighed. "I started making a few notes while you were fetching Pe'tala, but so far I have not really come up with anything useful. Do our vows have to match or complement each other somehow?"

"Not necessarily, no," Valrad replied. "Ideally, each of your vows reflects your own personality."

"Oh, dear, I hope not. Sarcastic and rebellious would hardly do the occasion justice," Vran'el chuckled.

"Shut up, *brother*," she scoffed at him.

That made him swallow. "You know, the thought of having Pe'tala and you not only in the same House but also as my sisters does make me a touch uneasy."

"No sympathy there, Vran'el," Enric quipped. "You yourself drew up the adoption agreement. And came up with the idea before. Now it's too late for second thoughts."

"I know," he sighed theatrically, "but then I could hardly leave my poor, mistreated, accused cousin who even had to spend time in captivity be subject to the evil designs of her unhappy admirer, could I?"

Eryn straightened and turned to her companion. "Speaking of captivity, that is something I wanted to ask you about. What made you offer that bit of information up at the senate hearing? There was little to no chance of influencing the loyalties of the Houses, so what did you hope to accomplish by doing so?"

"The Houses knew what to vote even before the first hearing had started, you are right. But not the triarchs. Abrak was the only one of them to be known to be slightly more attached to House Aren than he should be, but the other two had not shown any inclination towards one side or the other. It was them I wanted to convince," Enric explained.

"And Uvel's remarks at both hearings surely helped as well," Vran'el added with a broad grin.

"Yes," Eryn nodded, "good thing he is rather defiant and not shy when it comes to putting words to his thoughts, isn't it?"

Valrad shook his head. "He is not normally, no."

She watched Enric and Vran'el exchange a knowing smile. "What do you know that I don't? House Tokmar *is* allied with Vel'kim, isn't it?"

Her cousin nodded. "It is, yes. But Uvel is not exactly known for speaking up like that. That is why his making certain remarks carried even more weight than in the case of most other senators."

"Are you telling me that you *arranged* for him to say those things?" she asked incredulously. "How did you induce him to do it if he is not normally the accusing kind? We are talking about challenging Malriel here, after all."

"Let us say we have an inside man at House Tokmar," Vran'el told her. "Uvel of House Tokmar is Neval's father."

Eryn stared at him for a moment, then started laughing. "Devious, manipulative bunch, all of you!"

"That's how you play the game, my love. Always be a little more devious than those who try to harm you," Enric stated with a half-smile and a gleam in his eyes that clearly showed that he was not joking.

CHAPTER 55

Committing

Eryn beamed without opening her eyes when she felt an arm encircling her waist, a warm body pressing against her back. Another arm carefully eased itself under her head.

"Morning," she murmured sleepily.

"Morning, my love," he replied and kissed her shoulder. "We don't have to get up yet, so you may go back to sleep for another hour, if you want."

Opening her eyes, she saw dazzling daylight streaming in through the two large windows.

"That is something I have hardly ever heard you say," she remarked. "Normally you drag me out of bed instead of telling me that I can lie for a bit longer."

"Well, today I am aiming to please. There are still a few more hours left until you deliver the vow, so I don't want to risk angering you beforehand," he grinned.

"Then I suppose tomorrow will be a rude awakening for me, when I realise that you have turned grouchy, dull and lazy?" she chuckled.

"That is a risk you are taking, of course. But you never know, it might be preferable to demanding, possessive and relentless," he countered.

"No, I doubt that. I have adapted to the latter ones fairly well, I think." She stretched lazily and turned to face him. He looked relaxed and happy, probably for the first time in many days.

She thought back to the day before when Valrad had tentatively hinted at the custom of not spending the night before giving the vows under the same roof. Enric had rejected that suggestion immediately and explained that from his position, those numerous nights alone before at Golir's place were a more than ample compensation for sidestepping that tradition.

The gown she would be wearing in the afternoon hung on a hook at the back of the door, protected by a layer of cloth to keep dust and dirt away from it. She remembered thinking that the fabric would hardly likely withstand cat claws, and there was probably not a single tailor on this side of the sea or the other who was prepared to be asked to fashion the kind of garment bag that had to be forged by a blacksmith. Well, Junar possibly. But she would very likely just lift her eyes and repeat the need to keep wardrobe doors closed all the time.

The last three days had been packed with preparation work. Vran'el had taken her to the tailor and as much as told her to keep quiet and do no more than lift her arms and turn around whenever she was told to. When he'd had a generous few seconds every now and then, he had held up two or three carefully selected fabric samples and allowed her to express her preference. Which in two cases he had discarded instantly with a sour look, though in one case he had accepted as her taste seemed for once to have coincided with what he himself would have chosen.

She had been to the tailor's shop every single day, yesterday even twice to ease into the gown in its different stages of completion.

Yesterday afternoon had been the final fitting, and how lucky it was the last one, as everything clung where it was supposed to and flowed where it wasn't.

Enric had not yet seen the gown. Another tradition, though he was less averse to obeying that as long as it did not require him to keep her at a distance.

"How about your vow?" he asked into her thoughts. "Is it to your satisfaction yet?"

She scowled. "Probably as much as it is ever going to be. What about yours? I could have a look at it, if you like?" she added expectantly.

He smiled at her crafty ruse for getting a premature glance at the wording. "That is too kind, but I don't think that is necessary. Thank you for the offer, though."

"There is just no pleasing some people," she sighed. "In that case, I will get up now. I am hungry and it is going to be a long day today. Will you join me or stay in bed a bit longer?"

"Join you," he said at once. "I don't want to risk letting you out of my sight when it is not necessary. I intend to keep you as close as I am able until we finally leave here."

Eryn rose and slipped on some tunic and trousers. "There shouldn't be anybody else to try and detain us here now."

"We didn't expect such a thing last time, either," he countered and pulled trousers and a shirt out of a nearby chest.

"Come on - how likely is that to happen twice to the same people?"

He followed her out into the corridor and to the terrace where Vran'el was perched with a bowl of fruit on his lap.

"Where is Valrad?" Eryn enquired.

"Taking a walk through the garden. Probably to relax a little and calm his nerves. It has been quite a while since we last had a third level commitment ceremony in the family."

"Really? So you and Intrea are not...?"

Vran'el laughed. "What? No! This is not meant for commitments such as ours, politically convenient ones intended to merely strengthen alliances and provide heirs, but for real commitments as yours will be. This is serious old magic. Binding yourself to somebody you do not love is not advisable, you would not want the side effects."

Eryn frowned and Enric flashed her cousin a warning look. "Shut up. It has taken me long enough to get her to agree to this. If you scare her off going through with it, I am going to be very, *very* annoyed."

"I remember what your father told me about it," Eryn said, thinking back to the day shortly after their arrival in Takhan when they had talked in the garden. "He said something about being pulled back together if there were longer absences of one partner. And that hiding things from each other would not be easy any longer."

Enric smiled thinly. "Sounds like just what I have been looking for."

She looked askance at him. "That cuts both ways, my dearest. Or need I remind you of which one of us kept a secret that really should have been shared instead?"

He cleared his throat. "Let's not speak of things like that today."

Rolling her eyes at him she returned her attention to Vran'el. "Anything else I should know? Any other side effects?"

He thought for a moment, then shrugged. "Some couples develop a kind of *mind connection*, but I am told it is rather rare, so no need to be concerned about that for now."

"What would that mind connection entail?" Enric asked curiously.

She glared. "Don't be too eager to learn about it. I have no intention of letting you into my head as well. There are boundaries, you know. Abusing you in the privacy of my head when doing it publicly would get me punished is something I will *not* give up. Should we happen to be among the few *lucky* couples which develop such a connection, you may rest assured that the very first thing I would learn is how to block you out."

"It is not that kind of connection, sweetness," Vran'el waved her off. "It is not as concrete as words - more like feelings, moods, desires that are conveyed, and then not all the time but just when they reach a certain intensity. It does not happen often enough to have allowed conclusive research on it. So relax for now, will you?"

She breathed out and nodded.

He then picked up a sheet of paper from the cushions and pushed it into her hands. "Here. This is your schedule for today. You are up a little earlier than I expected, so the start is in one hour."

Taking a bath, massage, snack, having her finger- and toenails done, getting dressed, hair, painting of the symbols onto her wrist, practising the oath one last time and finally the ceremony. She blinked.

"This looks like a lot of people are going to have a lot of work to do today. Judging from your list I do not really seem to be among them, either.

"That is the idea, sweetheart. This is yours and Enric's day, and it is meant to be unforgettable and free of strife. Indeed, as this conversation almost qualifies as unpleasant, we will from now on only talk about nice things. I will be with you the whole time, reassure you when you feel jittery, listen to your complaints and make sure that you are in each place you are supposed to be at the right time," he smiled.

"What about Enric?"

"He will spend some quality time with my father as there is no close male relative from his new side of the family available."

"Is his schedule as involving as mine?"

Her cousin shook his head. "No. My father is more the unhurried, slow-paced type. He does not enjoy dashing from one appointment to the next."

"But you do, it seems," she sighed with an air of resignation.

"I will admit I appreciate a more dynamic approach, yes. Please do not worry, though - all these people on the list will come to you, not you to them. You will just have to walk from one room to the next."

She looked inside the empty main room. "Alright, that does sound better. Though I would have expected a little more activity happening here already from your plans." She waved the sheet.

"Sweetness," he sighed and shook his head, "how much of our efforts do you think would still be visible if I dragged you through the city after you were bathed, massaged and dressed? All of this will of course be happening at the Arbil residence." He lifted a placatory hand. "But do not concern yourself; Ram'an will not be there, at least not visibly. He has been instructed not to disturb you, and to be completely honest, men generally tend to steer clear of the female preparation rites anyway."

They saw Valrad walk up the stairs from the garden to the terrace, carrying a basket with a variety of plants, mostly herbs, from what Eryn could see.

"Have you been doing some early morning gardening, uncle?" she smiled.

"You might want to stop calling me that, dear girl," he said mildly. "If people heard you, they might think that you do not acknowledge my new legal status as your father. Better get used to calling me Valrad." Then he smiled. "And there is quite a difference in what I consider early morning compared to you. I have been up for more than two hours." He put a hand on Enric's shoulder. "Come, my friend, eat your breakfast up and then we will talk about my ideas on how to keep you entertained until you are due for the ceremony. Let me assure you, though, that your day will be a lot less filled than Eryn's."

Enric smiled in relief and took a bowl to fill it with fruit. "Good. I was starting to get worried."

* * *

Valrad leaned back with a sigh of contentment and a glass of hot tea in his hand.

"I am glad we have this opportunity to talk and spend some time together, my friend. So much has happened and there never seems to be enough time to just sit down and chat in private for a little while."

Enric smiled. "True enough, these last two weeks have been anything but relaxing, though I preferred the bustle of the last four days to the ten days preceding. Can I ask you something?"

"Of course."

"Is Vran'el very disappointed that he will not be the one to be giving Eryn away? Or you, for that matter?"

The older man chuckled. "A little maybe. But to be honest I should tell you that his gleeful delight at watching Ram'an being forced to do that will counterbalance any honour lost. Also, do not worry about me; all I want to see is the two of you getting through this without anything to ruin this day."

"I wonder what people here are making of this entire situation, especially those with political influence. How much contact have you had with your fellow senators in these last few days since the voting?"

"Frequent contact, to put it mildly. I had quite a few visitors at the clinic and somehow people have managed to bump into me by chance wherever I go. There are several theories in circulation. For example that Malriel actually planned on losing the voting or at least banked on it to make you agree to being adopted by her as compensation. Others believe this whole thing was arranged between Malriel and myself, though they wonder why it is I have not adopted *you* instead of Eryn, as I already have a daughter. But then some say that Malriel insisted on binding you to her House as this is the only way her pride can deal with having been made to step back that one evening at the Aren estate when you faced up to her and her mother: by making you one of them so that she can claim that the one man to brave three Aren women was an Aren man."

"They think she willingly gave up her only daughter and heiress to bolster her pride?" Enric asked in confusion.

"People never really know exactly where they stand with Malriel. One thing they do seem reluctant or even unable to accept, though, is the mere possibility that she has actually lost. This seems so unlikely to most, that they construct theories that explain the events without seeing her as somebody who was defeated. You know, looking at how things have turned out I see why she does not seem to have lost very much."

"What do you think? How much does Eryn's renunciation really hurt her? I have the impression that you know her quite well."

Valrad looked serious. "It hurts her a lot. Did you see how pale she was at the vote when Eryn delivered the words? She was shaken, even though she had expected them and came prepared. Of course her influence over both Eryn and you has increased considerably due to your adoptions. You have both willingly subjected yourselves to our laws, while before they were not binding for yourself after your departure here and in Eryn's case they would at best have been open to interpretation. Now however she can summon you here, and thanks to the third level bond Eryn as well, who will follow wherever you go."

Enric nodded. "I know. But I count on her being very careful with that. If she does it too often, I will not be happy about it and I make a much more useful ally if I am well-disposed towards her, after all."

"True enough. But you have probably heard about our troubles up north with Pirinkar, our neighbouring country. I imagine being the only House boasting a high-ranking Order magician cum fighting expert as a member is an advantage she will sooner or later decide to make use of," Valrad mused. "This might be in an advisory role from across the sea, but you never know with Malriel. It is hard to predict what she might or might not do."

"What do people feel about Ram'an's hosting the celebration today?"

"That he has decided to put his own pride second to the needs of a badly shaken House and is doing it to placate Houses Aren and Vel'kim. Though my father's lack of action two decades ago caused House Arbil to be angry with us, his more recent decision to step back from the agreement to commit to Pe'tala has reversed the situation, as he has more or less decided not to go through with the peace offering it basically was. Following today our three Houses will be considered allies again. A good thing for all of us, I would think. There were quite a number of wrongs we had to forgive each other." Valrad shook his head. "Amazing, is it not, how one reckless action such a long time ago left each of the three Houses angry at the other two for twenty-three years. And now the two of you will reconcile all of us, or at least lay the foundations for it."

"I would not expect too much eagerness in this regard on Ram'an's side - he is not exactly going through with it all voluntarily," Enric objected.

"He is doing it to protect his House, which is exactly as it should be. And he is a smart man, whatever else you may think of him. He will see clearly enough that he has lost all and any claim to Eryn after the bonding ceremony, and that all that remains for him to do is to profit from this new tentative alliance as best he can. Especially as you and Eryn will soon leave here and he will have time to heal in the time following. At least he has new responsibilities that will occupy him and keep him busy."

Enric nodded thoughtfully. "As long as he does not fall prey to vindictiveness."

"No, he is not the type for that. Calm, collected, gentle Ram'an," Valrad sighed, sympathy clearly audible in his voice. "They viewed him as the ideal mate for a temperamental Aren girl."

"Malriel once told me she thought him too weak to handle Eryn," Enric pointed out as if trying to justify himself for thwarting those plans. Was he?

"Did she?" The older man looked puzzled. "She was wrong there, trust me. Weak he is not, he just has a more quiet strength than most. He subjected Eryn to his boundaries well enough during his stay here without ever resorting to violence, even though he used his superior strength on her occasionally."

Enric's expression darkened. That sounded dangerously similar to his own way of dealing with her after he had taken over her training and especially after he had bedded her that second time. Did that mean that Ram'an might in time have succeeded in winning her, as he had adopted the very strategy Enric himself had found helpful?

Valrad smiled knowingly. "Are you mulling that the two of you have things in common you do not care to acknowledge? Are you wondering if Eryn would have chosen him over you had the timing been only a little different? For example if he had arrived in Anyueel before the King would have made her join you?"

Enric gave him an irate glare. "Not the kind of food for thought a man might wish for a few hours before his commitment."

"Enric," Valrad spoke softly and bent forward, looking into his eyes, "I was not the one putting these thoughts in your head in the first place, was I? Do not be mad at *me* for saying out loud what you do not want to hear but cannot help pondering. There is no point in worrying about what might have been if circumstances had been different in the past. Destiny, if you choose to believe in the notion, has favoured you. If you prefer the idea of luck, it, too has dealt you a winning hand. This does seem rather untypical for you, though. We are not dealing with nervousness on the verge of being joined right now, are we?"

"No," Enric replied calmly, "not really. Rather with impatience and concern for anything going wrong today. I have been waiting for this for quite some time."

"Then you will surely survive another three hours. Lean back and relax, my young friend. Do tell me about your plans to bring Eryn back here to visit us regularly in the future. And if you had none so far, let this be the occasion to make some," he added with a soft smile that did not hide the fact that it had been an instruction.

* * *

Eryn stood straight and stiff in front of the tall mirror and looked at herself fully dressed and prepared for the ceremony. The artist who had painted the symbols on her wrist had just gone.

Pale, despite the tan she had acquired these last few weeks. Nervous, she decided. Definitely. But the good kind, not the panicky. Binding herself to Enric would this time not cause so many changes in her life compared to the last. Though the thought about the physical effects the third level bond did make her a little uneasy.

She didn't turn when she heard the knock at the guest room door. Vran'el, very likely.

"Come in," she called and raised her brow in surprise when Ram'an instead of her cousin walked in and closed the door behind him.

"May I have a few a few minutes of your time, Theá? I promise I will not detain you for very long," he spoke unusually awkwardly.

She nodded, then turned away from the mirror, looking perturbed at his tired and crestfallen expression. He stood at the door and let his eyes wander, starting with the artful hairstyle and following the flowing lines of the dark red dress.

Stepping towards him, she held out both her hands for him to take and smiled with relief when he did.

"Theá," he murmured hoarsely, "we have not seen each other since the day of the voting. I was thinking of you, wondering how angry at me you must be."

Eryn squeezed his cool hands gently. "I am not angry at you. Not any more. I'll admit I was not very happy when Vran'el told me of his suspicions about your plans, but that was no more than a move in the game, wasn't it?"

"A game I would have lost either way, so it now seems," Ram'an said quietly. "So you have realised that you truly love him? You were not aware of it only a few days ago when I used the lie filter on you."

"I am sorry. I wish I had not been such a coward and instead dared to admit it to myself sooner. It would have spared us so much trouble. Not to mention pain."

He shook his head with a sad smile. "It would have been painful for me, no matter what. It would just have saved me from making a little less than a complete and utter fool of myself."

She lifted his hand to her cheek and pressed her lips into his palm. "I never thought you were a fool," she said gently. "Stubborn, unreasonable, devious, but never a fool. Under different circumstances I would have appreciated having a man like you going to such great lengths to win me over. The woman to capture your eye one day will be a very lucky one indeed."

He was not consoled. "Do not try to comfort me, Theá. It does somehow not sound convincing when it comes from the woman who has chosen another man over me."

She smiled apologetically. "Alright - no more attempts to cheer you up. I am sorry you have to go through this today, that Enric made you host all of this. And that he is making you give me away."

Ram'an rubbed his face. "Yes, he is very good at exacting his revenge, is he not?"

"Yes, he is. Fortunately, he does not often have the opportunity to put that particular skill to use. People generally tend to avoid angering him and back down when he brings that cold stare of his to bear. Not you, though."

He chuckled. "No, growing up as a magician with such a level of power makes you less susceptible to fear, I suppose, when you realise that others are more afraid of *you*, however unjustified." He let go of her hands and pulled a small leather pouch from his pocket. "There is a little something I wanted to give you." His fingers pulled the opening apart and he pulled out a thin, fragile looking silver bracelet. "A parting gift, as it were. I will not be there to send you on your way the day after tomorrow. Today is the last time we shall see each other before you leave Takhan. I hope you understand why."

She nodded slowly. Of course she did. After all that had happened in these last days, his plans going so very wrong, his hopes of ever winning her in tatters, being forced to plan the ceremony and everything around it, she imagined that getting rid of her and Enric rather sooner than later would be something of a relief to him.

"I do, yes." She looked down at the piece of jewellery in his hand. "It looks pretty. What is that little sign in the middle here?"

He lifted it for her to look at. "It is the crest of House Arbil," he explained. "As Head of the House I am now in a position to give away tokens of friendship to people I consider close to my House. They are a visible sign of the high esteem my House holds you in. When you next come to Takhan, you will find it easier to get a good table at certain places, a better price in some shops and easy admittance into places that are allied with House Arbil. But even though you will soon be leaving here, I hope that you will do me the honour of wearing it and let it remind you that I would rather be your friend than have no place at all in your life. Will you accept it, Theá? No obligation is attached to this, I promise."

Without speaking, she lifted her unpainted wrist for him to fasten it on. There was torment inside him, that was plain to see. Or was that because she had come to get to know his features so well in these last few weeks? Would others be able to spot it that easily as well? She observed his concentrated expression while his fingers fumbled with the tiny clasp. There were dark rings under his eyes and he looked worn down and exhausted.

When he had finally secured the bracelet, he beheld her thoughtful expression and smiled. "No pity for me, Theá," he said mildly. "It is a way of looking down on somebody."

She gingerly touched the cool silver and felt the uneven surface of the small crest. "Thank you, Ram'an. I feel no pity for you, I promise. It is astonishment at your generosity after all that has happened." She lifted her arms and waited for him to step into the embrace, relieved when he did.

Pressing her cheek against his warm face, she closed her eyes, holding him close for a while before releasing him again.

"Thank you, my friend. I am honoured and will wear your gift proudly. Now I think you should see that makeup artist of mine to take care of these dark circles under your eyes." She took hold of his arm when he made to retreat. "No, I insist. Or people will think I have caused you sleepless nights."

"But you have!" he protested.

"Well, that's not for the others to see but only for us to know," she insisted.

He smiled slowly. "You know, Enric said something about my better showing strength today. It seems with you next to me I do not have another choice, do I?"

"I wouldn't want to associate myself with a weak House, would I?" she said haughtily and winked at him.

The door opened and Vran'el stepped in, surprised at seeing the two of them alone.

"Is everything in order?" he asked carefully and raised a questioning eyebrow at Eryn.

She nodded. "Yes, perfectly in order. Apart from the man who is about to give me away. The rings under his eyes need some attention."

Her cousin sighed. "Well, that is obvious." He held out his hand to Ram'an and rolled his eyes when he didn't take it but frowned in confusion. "It will be quicker if I just heal them away instead of putting masking cream over them. That way, if you rub your face or start crying, nothing will smudge."

Eryn watched Ram'an take Vran'el's hand and moments later the dark circles started to recede until they were gone completely.

"I cannot do anything about the haggard expression, though. You obviously have not been taking very good care of yourself in the past few days. Not enough food and water, I would say, and probably a little too much wine."

Ram'an's jaw muscles tightened, but he didn't object. "Thank you," he said stiffly, "for removing the circles, though not for the assessment of my recent lifestyle."

Vran'el smirked. "I aim to please." He turned to Eryn. "Come. The guests have all arrived, been provided with wine and are waiting eagerly for the ceremony to start. Now that Ram'an looks halfway presentable, we can go on with it."

His gaze fell on the bracelet and he lifted her hand to take a closer look. He nodded appreciatively at Ram'an. "Very nice. And a sign of true greatness that you can bestow friendship where love was not meant. I bow my head to you."

The words seemed to please Ram'an and he nodded. "Thank you." He turned to Eryn and lifted his hand for her to take. "Then let us get you committed. Unless you have changed your mind because you suddenly realised that Enric has too many serious shortcomings for you to accept?"

She laughed tensely. "No, I am afraid there is no escaping it now."

* * *

Enric was standing next to the seating cushions on the grass where he and Eryn would sit with Golir, Ram'an and Malriel for the ceremony. From what he could see, the arrangements around him must have taken quite a lot of effort and time to create. The extensive garden was decorated subtly and elegantly. Ribbons in the two shades he suspected would be the ones on Eryn's dress danced lazily in the light breeze, lanterns and candles were placed for when it became darker. Malriel stepped next to him, looking beautiful and confident in a copper-coloured dress that accentuated her curvaceous figure to its best advantage.

"You look strangely calm. You are either not nervous at all or I have yet to learn to see through your façade," she smiled and raised a perfectly trimmed and curved eyebrow at him questioningly.

"Nervous?" He pondered this option for a moment, then replied, "I would think that only somebody who is not sure about doing the right thing would be nervous now. I have no doubts whatsoever about this."

"Your confidence is impressive. I wonder if all of it is as genuine as you want me to believe."

Enric looked down at her and held out his hand. "Why don't you check for yourself?"

She took his hand immediately and a moment later he felt a warm surge of magic pass from her skin through his.

"Your heart rate is a bit low, but they say that this is normal for well-trained, healthy people," she said. "No unusual activity in your sweat glands, no overproduction of secretions in the stomach. You really *are* relaxed. I stand corrected."

They both looked up when Eryn and Ram'an stepped out of the main room onto the terrace. Enric smiled at the sight of Eryn, the dark red dress with the white elements at the sleeves and waist clinging to her figure. His guess about the colour of the ribbons everywhere around him had been right. They really were her colours. Her neck looked long and elegant, as it did every time she wore her hair pinned up. He saw the other guests drawing closer to look at her and compliment her. Then Valrad stepped in front of her, holding what looked like a curious bunch of flowers out to her. The breeze carried her delighted laugh to him.

Malriel smiled next to him. "Valrad has made her a bouquet of medical herbs from his garden. Do you see the dark red ones that almost exactly match her dress? They are for increased stamina."

Enric frowned at her. "Is this an implication that he suspects my performance in that department to be deficient?"

"No, Enric, I rather think it was meant as a joke. And they have just the right colour, after all. Unless I am very much mistaken, I can also see a herb that makes you sleepy, so there is no need to fear for your reputation," she smirked.

"You do know rather more about medical herbs and physical reactions than I would expect in a non-healer."

"I was joined with a healer for a few years. One tries to take an interest in what one's partner does - especially if it is a life's purpose - a vocation, as it was in Ved'al's case." She rolled her eyes at his surprised expression. "I was young and in love, of course I made an effort. I find your surprise at that something of an insult, to be honest."

"I did not mean to offend you," he assured her hurriedly and returned his attention to Eryn, who was holding on to Ram'an's arm. Something silver glinted at her right wrist. Ram'an, he noted, looked better than one hour ago when he had last spotted him. The rings from under his eyes were gone. His posture was still tense, though. That, however, was not unexpected, considering the role he was being compelled to play.

"I like the little touch of doing it here at the Arbil residence and making Ram'an give her away," she said conversationally. "Some might consider it a bit cruel, but I think it is ingenious. Also, the beauty of it is that everyone will have their own favourite theory about it. Some will think Ram'an offered it himself to acknowledge your victory, others will be convinced that you forced him to do it instead of harming his House or even him. But whatever they think, you stand as the glorious, but beneficent victor. Well done. A deed worthy of an Aren."

He decided to take it as the compliment it was meant as, glad that Eryn was still far enough away not to have heard it.

Golir approached and put his half full wine glass down on the small table in the centre of the sitting arrangement.

"Ah yes, there they are. I must say I am pleasantly surprised. I had expected something a little more modest considering the short time span available for planning, but Ram'an has done well, I have to say." He nodded appreciatively.

"He has indeed," Malriel agreed. "Four days are not exactly a long time to prepare what other couples have weeks or months to organise."

Golir chuckled. "Well, *your* considering the arrangement worthy of a member of House Aren is high praise indeed."

"Are you saying I am finicky, Golir?" she enquired good-naturedly.

"I would never be so foolish as to say a thing like that out loud, Malriel, dearest," he smiled.

Eryn and Ram'an took the last few steps towards them and the guests with the wine glasses in their hands stepped closer as well.

Enric remembered that the guests would remain standing while the five of them who were directly involved in the ceremony sat down. He watched Malriel step towards her daughter to kiss her on both cheeks and saw Eryn's expression darken for a moment before she mastered her control. Golir sat down first, indicating to Eryn and Ram'an to take a seat on his left side and to Malriel and Enric on his right.

"Before we start, there is a question I need to ask in order to be sure that we may carry out this ceremony," Golir raised his voice and his eyes sought Valrad among the guests. "Head of House Vel'kim, do you agree with this procedure? Does your," he paused for a moment and sent a quick apologetic glance at Malriel, "*daughter* have your permission to enter into this bond?"

Valrad nodded. "I agree. She does have my permission."

"Head of House Aren, do you agree with this procedure? Does your... son have your permission to enter into this bond?"

Malriel lifted her head. "I agree. He does have my permission."

"Good. Then we will now join the two of them in accordance with their own wishes and those of their families'," the triarch continued. "We have learned that your story of finding each other was an unusual one, that you had to overcome a number of obstacles, both back in Anyueel and here in Takhan." He flashed both Malriel and Ram'an a short glance. "But overcome them you did, and now we are here to reward you for it by joining you in a third level commitment bond, the strongest magical connection that is known to us. Be warned, though, not to enter into it unaware or carelessly, for it is a bond that can be a blessing for those who are devoted to each other in love, but a burden to those who are not. Do you willingly and voluntarily wish to bind yourselves to each other by magic and accept all the consequences, whatever they may turn out to be? Maltheá?"

Eryn gulped. Why did the way he had phrased that sound so ominous?

"Yes," she replied, less timidly than she felt like doing.

"Enric?"

"Yes," he smiled, amused about how she had paused only for a moment before answering.

"Then let it be so. Ram'an, you will give Maltheá away. Do so now."

Ram'an raised his eyes to Enric's and for a long moment nobody spoke. It seemed as if even the guests were holding their breath.

"Enric," he finally said to Eryn's great relief and lifted her hand, "I give to you Maltheá, a woman with qualities as rare as water in the desert, as magic in a woman where you come from. Treat her well, whatever may come. Be to her the companion she deserves. And be prepared to answer to me if you are not."

Enric nodded once to Ram'an, slowly.

"Malriel, you will give Enric away. Do so now."

She took Enric's hand and lifted it as well. "Maltheá, I give to you Enric, a man with strength, intelligence, willpower, providence, honour and great love for you. Though you have until now always been the one to be courted by him, do not take this for granted and always remember that appreciation must flow both ways."

Both Malriel and Ram'an removed their hands and Enric took Eryn's in his.

Golir continued, "I understand that in the Kingdom of Anyueel there is a general vow that is customary for this occasion. In our country, however, we prefer to create our own, very personal ones instead. Have you each prepared a vow you wish to make to your companion today?" He waited for the two of them to nod. "Then we will have the woman speak first, as is tradition. Join your hands like this and let a small amount of magic flow while you speak. Maltheá, your vow now if you please."

Eryn straightened and breathed out slowly. She had practised it in her head only minutes ago. Leaning forward and taking Enric's hands the way she had been shown just now, she cleared her throat.

"Enric, I have asked you to join me in a powerful bond. As you know, binding myself is not easy for me, though with you the prospect does not seem as frightening anymore. We have come a long way from prisoner and warden to being companions, and despite the fact that our path was not exactly a smooth one, looking back I am glad we walked it together. I am willing to work on complying with the aspects that are important to you, and I know you will do the same, even if our positions in the Order and now in different Houses make that something of a challenge. Yet whatever troubles we will have to face in the years to come, I will treat you with the respect and honour you deserve. Always."

Golir nodded and then looked at Enric. "Enric, your vow."

She felt warmth now from his hands when he started speaking:

"I bound you with shackles, but that was not enough.
Thus I bind you with magic, I bind you with love.
You broke my restraint and took over my heart,
Of which you're in charge now, of which you are part.
Whatever I own is for you there to take,
If only you're there every morning I wake.

I won't clip your wings but instead help you fly,
As long as you don't leave behind our tie.
There will be no hiding, no running from me,
I would get you back, brave each mountain or sea.
That I am a swordsman with unerring aim
Will help me protect you from danger or claim.
I will be your teacher, your lover, your friend
And everything else on which you may depend.
This bond that we forge between my heart and yours
Shall never be broken by *whatever* force."

She stared up at him questioningly. "Have I just been warned?" she asked quietly.

"Not only you, Theá, all three of us have been," Malriel stated with a smile of dark delight.

Golir spoke up again. "The vows have been given and will now be reinforced with the magic of myself and the two people you have chosen to stand by you. This is in order to make sure that it cannot carelessly be dissolved again."

He waited until both Malriel and Ram'an joined their hands with the couple's and then placed his own on top. The magic flowed through them, pulsing like a living entity, sending warm waves through their bodies. Eryn watched in fascination how the artfully painted symbols on her wrist slowly faded, became paler until they were gone completely. A quick glance at Enric showed the same had happened.

When after a few moments the warm flow ebbed away and their hands separated again, Eryn gingerly touched her skin where the symbols had been. Without a warning they suddenly reappeared, although they did not look like paintings any more but instead seemed to glow faintly not on her skin, but beneath it.

"The third level commitment bond is complete," Golir announced and the guests raised their glasses as one. Eryn took the glass that had been placed on the low table before them for her and lifted it together with the other four people around her.

"Happiness to Malthea and Enric," the triarch said and the guests repeated it before taking a sip from their glass.

"I liked your vow, Enric," Malriel said when the noise level had risen around them. "Warnings, threats, promises and a declaration of love, protection and support all in one neat package. You do have a way with words, I must say."

Eryn looked thoughtful. That evil masterpiece of his had even rhymed.

CHAPTER 56

Returning Home

Enric looked out the window, reluctant to get up yet even though it had to be late morning already, and judging from the sun probably close to noon. His first impulse after waking was to check if she was still beside him in bed. He wondered if the time they had been forced to stay at different places had increased the fear of losing her to such an extent. All the same, the bond they had entered into the day before made that more unlikely than ever, didn't it? Unbidden thoughts of her parents and how their bond more or less had ended came to his mind and he pushed them aside in annoyance.

He thought of the ceremony and how smoothly it had gone. There had been this one moment when Ram'an had been asked to give her away where Enric had felt slightly uneasy, where he had wondered for a few seconds if it had been too risky to push him that far. But Ram'an had done what had been expected of him. Enric did not mind the little warning he had added, it had lent the whole situation more credibility.

The silver bracelet with the Arbil crest had been an interesting gesture, he mused. A token of friendship, Vran'el had explained to him in a quiet minute, one to be bestowed only by the Head of a House. A great honour that would also leave observers in no doubt as to how they all would part: as friends.

He wondered if Eryn was aware of the full implication of this gift yet. That it served not only to assure her of his regard, but also demonstrated that House Arbil was not at loggerheads with the House that was now Eryn's official family. A signal to the other Houses that a new generation had taken over the family business, that fences were being mended, alliances renewed or newly forged.

He would not point that out to her, he decided. Not yet. It would make her feel better to consider it as no more than a proof of friendship for now.

He smiled when he remembered Eryn asking Ram'an who all the people around them were. He had explained to her that he had invited representatives of all Houses, friends and business partners of Houses Aren, Arbil and Vel'kim and of course the people she would have missed sorely, like the friends she had made here and the people she had worked with at the clinic.

She stirred on the bed next to him and yawned loudly without covering her mouth but stretching both arms over her head instead. Blinking sleepily, she smiled at him.

"Good morning, handsome. Have you experienced any scary side effects of the bond yet?" she asked.

"No, not yet." He lifted his wrist and looked at the faintly glowing symbols. Being so close to her, they were at their darkest.

She followed his gaze and touched her index fingers to his skin. It did not feel any different from the area around it.

"Amazing, isn't it? The things people come up with in these foreign parts. I think we should experiment a bit on that today, what do you think? I wonder how far away from you I need to go to make them disappear completely. Or how quickly they react when we are getting closer to each other again. Or if they are visible at night. That glow is obviously magical, so that might appear really scary in the dark."

Chuckling, he shook his head at her. "The explorer is back in action, it seems."

"Don't laugh at me. I am told it is a vocation. A valued one, at least here. A country would have to be open for new things in order to appreciate people who are trying to discover or make them."

"Well, what can I say?" he remarked dryly, "You have obviously been dragged to a country full of backward barbarians."

"My sentiments exactly!" she beamed and swung her legs out of bed. Then she halted, frowned and turned back to him. "There was a little something I wanted to say to you. About your vow. Yesterday did not really seem a good time, but now there are no witnesses, so I think I can safely ask you *what came over you to write a thing like that?*"

Ah yes, that one he had expected. "Alright, let's talk about it, shall we? What exactly about it bothered you?"

"I suppose telling you what about it *didn't* would be quicker," she shot back. "You implied that I have no intention of honouring the commitment, that my fleeing and running here cannot be dismissed and that you will in that case more or less throw me over your shoulder and drag me back to Anyueel!"

He pretended to think for a moment, then nodded earnestly. "Good. I was concerned that my message had not come across, but I see I needn't have worried. You *do* have a propensity to run, so don't act so indignant. Or do I need to remind you of your plans to come here alone? I hope you see now what a disaster that would have been. There's more," he lifted a finger to stop her when she started to open her mouth, "I did not want to imply that you do not plan to honour the bond, but you have your own way of interpreting what *honouring* it means. Don't think I haven't noticed that little sting in your own vow, my love."

She pursed her lips. "I have no idea what you are talking about."

"Of course not," he smiled wryly. "Let me be more specific, then. The aspects that are so important to me, the ones you know that I will work on as well. Which was a clear hint at my keeping my adoption from you. And what about saying that you will always treat me with the respect I deserve? Everybody who knows you at least a little bit knows exactly what that meant. Should you decide that I do not deserve any respect at all, you will treat me accordingly. Judging from the past, I dare say there will be quite a few occasions for that."

"So what? Compared to your vow that was mild, and above all, more subtle than your blunt threats. I don't mind your threatening Malriel - she even seemed to enjoy it. But Ram'an? After everything he has been through?"

"You seem to forget that he warned me as well when he gave you away. You don't see me complaining about it," he said simply.

"Well, why would you? You got what you wanted. Everything. It seems Kilan was right. There is no defeating you in the long run," she sighed.

Enric grinned smugly. "Kilan said that? Smart guy, always has been."

"Right, depend on you to home in on what is important here," she growled.

"Why don't we agree that we each got what we deserved? Actually, your warnings were not as subtle as you thought. Vran'el had to work hard at covering his sniggering. I think Intrea trod on his foot quite heavily once or twice, judging from his pained expression afterwards." He smiled at the memory. "Obal found that great. She went to his other foot and stamped on it as well. Though it was of course with considerably less force. I liked the gesture, though."

He pulled her back into bed when she began to rise. "Let's not start our last day here with an argument but with what you so rudely opted out of last night simply by falling asleep, or rather collapsing from exhaustion."

That made her laugh. "Is there anything that cannot be mended to your satisfaction through sex?"

"That is a very good question," he replied seriously and let his hands wander under her nightgown. "I will need some time to think about it. I will inform you as soon as I have found the answer. It will very probably be *No*, though."

* * *

Valrad smiled when they strolled into the main room hand in hand.

"Good morning to the two of you. I trust you had a pleasant night, and well, half day?"

Eryn nodded. "Yes, that we had. And now I am ravenous." She lifted her nose and sniffed the air. "But it seems we are about to be fed soon enough."

"True enough. Vran'el should be done any moment. Come, sit with me. How did you like your commitment day?"

"I was more than happy with it," Eryn smiled. "Everything was perfect, really. I liked that it was all in all very unceremonious compared to our rituals at home. Though I suppose not letting people write their own vows would save a bit of trouble afterwards," she added with a sideways glance to Enric.

Her uncle smiled. "Ah yes... your vows. Unusual ones, I have to say. Not with the focus on declarations of love people generally prefer. Although the more entertaining because of it. I would think your guests will not forget that ceremony anytime soon, especially the group of those who gave you away. Enric, by the mother you repudiated, you, Eryn, by the man who was until a few days ago attempting to bind you to himself instead. A real drama that has finally come to an end."

Vran'el entered the main room from the kitchen, Neval close behind him.

"Good morning, you two!" Neval chirped and hugged Eryn.

Enric lifted an eyebrow at the very ruffled looking Vran'el. For once not every strand of his hair was relentlessly tugged into submission by whatever means the locals used for that purpose.

"Long night, my friend?" he enquired.

Vran'el nodded. "Yes. I had a brief but disastrous liaison with some very fine wine they say you produce somewhere in that country of yours," he croaked.

"Why don't you just heal away the after-effects?" Eryn chuckled.

"Because this would require cleaning my blood and removing all the poison from all organs, and I am not in any shape to do this without endangering their functionality. Into the bargain, my loving father has denied me any help. Heartless. He delights in seeing me suffer," he added with a malevolent look at the healer.

Valrad smiled. "You know full well that I do not support overindulgence. If you drink, you should also bear the consequences. No sympathy, my son. That is how I handled it when you were a boy and I will not change that now that you are a grown man who should know better anyway. How about the food that I can smell? Any chance that we can eat soon? I assume that our freshly conjoined couple here could use some sustenance."

"We are waiting for Intrea and Obal. It seems I invited them some time yesterday evening, according to Neval. I have no memory of that, but then I suppose we have to be grateful that I did not also invite a large number of other people," Vran'el groaned. "I bet I made quite an impression yesterday."

Neval shrugged. "It was not too bad. When you started repeating yourself I dragged you off to a quieter place and only permitted a select few to approach you. Around midnight, Ram'an and I took you to his study to lie down and sleep for about two hours before we brought you back here."

They heard the entrance door open and Obal's loud voice shouted, "Cat!"

Vran'el winced. "Dear me, I have never before noticed how loud her voice is! Must be from her mother's side of the family."

Neval gave him a wicked smile. "How very appropriate that you were the one to invite them so you will now have a lot of fun with a lively little girl who will surely not show much consideration for your current state."

Eryn stood and held out her hand to her cousin. "Come, I will assist you with the food. It seems everybody is here now who dares to eat whatever you have put together in there. You use a free hand with spices when you are not drunk or suffering from the after effects, so I am rather curious what you will bestow on us."

He took her hand and let her draw him with her to the kitchen. "No need to worry - Neval did most of the cooking. I just instructed him and took care of the less dangerous tasks that did not involve knives or spices."

"That is a comfort indeed," she murmured.

When they had left the main room, Eryn turned to him and took his other hand as well before she released a stream of healing magic into his body, flushing out the poison from most of his organs and his blood. His relief was evident on his suddenly relaxed face, the colour slowly returning.

"I love you. I really do. Whatever mean and evil things I said to you in the past, forgive me. I will never, ever, forget what you just did for me. I am greatly in debt to you. I love you," he repeated and then threw his arms around her and hugged her close.

"That is delightful," she grinned. "I will remind you of this next time you insult or scold me when you dislike my clothes. Or hair. Or whatever else you tend to find objectionable about me."

"Did I tell you that I love you?" he repeated blissfully.

"A time or two, yes," she confirmed. "And now let's feed those people out there. Your daughter is exhausting enough even when she is *not* hungry."

Neval narrowed his eyes at them when they returned from the kitchen, carrying the food and bowls.

"You healed him, did you not?"

Eryn opened her eyes wide, apparently taken aback by the imputation. "I am sure I have no idea what you mean!"

"Oh, do stop it! The colour has returned to his face, his forehead is not creased in a constant agonised frown anymore and," he paused to clap his hands twice, "he does not flinch when he hears a loud noise now!"

Valrad rolled his eyes. "So much for my educational methods."

"I have outgrown them anyway," Vran'el smiled and put down the large food bowl to pick up his daughter instead. "Obal, my sweet girl, how did you like your aunt Eryn's dress yesterday?"

She shrugged. "Fine."

Eryn raised a brow. "Fine? I looked radiant, just so you know. Your father picked it." Then she turned to Intrea. "Hello. Why does that child of yours not like me?"

The girl's mother shrugged. "Do not take it personally. There are not many people she does like. Neither her cousins or aunts, nor most of my friends or others."

They both watched Vran'el set Obal down on the floor again and hand her an empty bowl.

"Take this and sit down, then I will fill it for you."

Obal nodded eagerly and climbed onto the cushions next to Enric, giving him a toothy grin. The magician smiled back at her and accepted another bowl for himself.

"She is very taken with Enric, though," Intrea smirked. "I admit she does seem to have a preference for men at the moment. She is also crazy about Neval. He is one of the few people still willing to look after her when I have an appointment. I hope she will become a bit more subtle as she grows up. This rather direct approach may now be endearing, but will earn her quite a reputation when she is older. And not a good one."

"Well, luckily Enric will be much too old to be of any interest for her by then," Eryn said dryly.

Neval waved her concerns off. "Nonsense. She is fine the way she is." He squeezed the girl's cheek. "You are perfect, my little princess! Do not change one bit, do you hear me?"

Obal laughed and batted her long lashes at him.

"Oh dear," Eryn rolled her eyes. "She knows her flirting is working alright."

"Then she might be able to teach her aunt Eryn a bit in that area, I suppose," Vran'el smirked.

"That is very considerate, but will not be necessary as she no longer has any need for that particular skill," Enric smiled thinly.

"Why not? She might use it on you, after all," Intrea shrugged.

"Hardly. Too nuanced for her," he objected and opened his mouth obediently when Obal insisted on sharing her food with him.

"I very much liked the celebration yesterday," Neval said, opening a new direction. "My father was enormously pleased when you thanked him for his help in the senate, Eryn. He appreciated the wine you gave him as a gift as well. There is quite a demand for it, especially since trading in it basically means doing business with House Aren now."

"I think we still have three or four bottles stored somewhere. Why don't you deliver them to him with our best wishes? It would hardly make much sense to carry them back home again," she offered.

"That I am more than willing to do. I admit that I myself have developed quite a liking for it."

Intrea leaned back with her bowl. "I was surprised to see Sarol there. He is not usually to be seen at occasions with a purely magical background, such as a third level commitment bond. He must be really fond of you, Eryn. That does not tend to happen very often with magicians from what I have heard. As far as I know Pe'tala is pretty much the only one he has befriended so far. And now you, of course. It seems he has a fondness for Vel'kim women."

"But she was still Aren when he befriended her, so that is not really a valid reason," Neval countered.

"He might have realised right away that she is more Vel'kim than Aren in her heart, if obviously not in looks," Intrea waved him off.

"Change the topic, the two of you," Eryn scowled at them and turned to Vran'el. "Is there a chance for me to have my name changed here officially? I mean, people keep referring to me as Maltheá, but I don't consider it my name. I find it rather tedious that I have to respond to it."

Her cousin thought for a moment, the slowly shook his head. "Not much chance with that, I am afraid. There is official documentation here bearing your birth name, and as you will hardly have anything similar back at your home, the triarchy will very likely not grant it. Even if you had any other birth documents with your new name on them, they would obviously be considered invalid as you were born here in Takhan. Then there is Malriel. From the triarchy's point of view she has had to give up rather a lot recently and they will not wish to deal her another blow. No, shut up - I know exactly what you want to say. We all here know that everything she lost was of her own making. But I am trying to tell you why you have to accept being stuck with the name whenever you come here. Considering all that has happened in these last few weeks, I think this is something you should be able to endure. You can always ask your friends here to call you *Eryn* anyway."

She nodded reluctantly. Well, it had been worth a try.

Valrad cleared his throat. "There is something I would like to tell you that will surely be of interest to the two of you. The triarchy has officially granted me permission to instruct you on how to remove the barrier inside Enric's head. So instead of only reading about it, you can now actually see how it is done before you leave."

Eryn grinned broadly. "Excellent news!"

So she would not have to experiment on people and hope that she had understood everything correctly. Splendid! And then there was also the matter of the female magicians who would doubtlessly be born soon enough back home, and the triarchy and senate here would be able to discover who it was that had passed along that knowledge without permission. But fortunately that was no longer an issue.

"So the two of you will be playing around inside my head again?" Enric sighed and assisted Obal in climbing onto his lap so she could play with his blonde hair.

"I would have thought you enjoyed her playing around with you," Intrea smiled and winked at him.

He nodded and replied with a lopsided grin, "I do. But usually not inside my head or with other people present."

"I agree with the head thing, but there are people who would say that more than one partner can be very stimulating at times," Vran'el grinned.

Enric smiled back. "I know. But with advancing age I have found it to be more rewarding to instead concentrate on one partner completely."

Eryn stared at him open-mouthed. "I did not just hear you say that, did I? Are you telling me that you..." She gestured helplessly for want of words that could be said in the presence of a child.

He chuckled at her disbelief. "I have not always been *Lord* Enric, my love. I was once young and wild and my attentions were well-received by the ladies. I may not be an explorer like yourself, but I admit I did some experimenting in my time."

She stared at him. That really did not fit into her picture of him. But then, why would it not? She had heard about his lazy and carefree youth, hadn't she?

"It seems there is a thing or two I may yet have to learn about you," she said slowly.

"It would seem so, yes," he nodded. "Added to that, I am in no doubt at all that I will experience a fair few surprises with *you* in the years to come."

She snorted. "After your... eventful past I find that hard to believe. I rather wonder how I am supposed to keep you from getting bored with me."

That made him laugh and he shifted the girl on his lap so he could pull her closer and press a kiss on her forehead. "Trust me, that is something you will surely not have to worry about. Since you entered my life, I have not had any cause to complain about a lack of diversion."

Vran'el chuckled and looked at them both with indulgent delight. "How very tickling. The conservative Order magician actually has an interesting past. Who would have thought?"

"Not as interesting as the present, though," Enric said and kissed his companion once again, this time on her lips. "And I have great expectations for the future to be at least as interesting."

"Cat!" Obal screamed when Urban strolled into the room. "Come here! Here!"

The mountain cat froze in mid-step, then turned around in a liquid movement quickly to slink back to the corridor she had emerged from.

"Another one who will be glad when she can return to the peace and quiet of Anyueel tomorrow, I imagine," Valrad laughed. "The mighty beast, put to flight by a four-year-old girl."

*   *   *

Eryn felt a lump in her throat as the harbour came into sight. The last time they had attempted to board the ship, they had been apprehended by guards sent by the triarchy to escort her to the senate. She felt Enric's hand give hers a reassuring squeeze.

"Don't worry, my love. This time we are going to leave here," he said quietly.

"I hope you are right. Malriel now has even more options to keep us here as your Head of House," she replied.

Just as the last time, a group of people were assembled to see them off. Obal started hopping up and down excitedly when she spotted Enric, and Intrea held on to her arm when she tried to dash off towards him.

"Stay here, Obal - no running next to the water! You might slip and fall into the river," they heard her mother caution her. "You wait until he has come closer, then you may approach him."

When they were only a few steps away, Obal was unleashed and all but sprinted into Enric's arms. He lifted her up and placed her on his hip.

"You know that he is *mine*, right?" Eryn clarified.

Obal frowned at her and slung both arms around his neck possessively, daring her to intervene.

Vran'el behind her rolled his eyes. "And there you wonder why she does not like you."

She swallowed her reply when she spotted Malriel to one side of the small crowd. "I suppose this is a good sign, isn't it? She wouldn't have taken the trouble of showing up if she had any other nefarious plans to keep us here?" she whispered.

"That is a valid supposition, yes," Enric nodded.

"Good. Then I suppose it does make sense to say goodbye to people this time as it is not likely that I shall bump into them again tomorrow."

"Nervous about being stranded here once again? I share that sentiment, believe me," she heard a familiar voice at her side and grimaced before she turned to Pe'tala.

"You here? To what do I owe the... honour?" Eryn asked sweetly.

"I want to make sure that ship really has you on board this time when it leaves."

"How very considerate of you, *sister*," Eryn replied and watched with satisfaction when Pe'tala cringed slightly at the address.

Valrad shook his head. "I think it is about time to separate the two of you now. Although, as you are now members of the same

House, I expect you both to work on your attitude and be more civil to each other when you next meet."

"How very sweet," Eryn sighed. "My first fatherly admonishment since the adoption."

"Knowing father, it will not be the last one, however far away you live. There are messenger birds, after all," Vran'el sneered.

"Cat!" Obal called out in sudden recollection that something important was missing here.

"She is asleep in that large box over there, the one the three men are carrying onto the ship right now," Enric explained. The girl's face dropped.

"She really has become attached to that beast," Vran'el said, in wonder.

"Makes you look like a great coward next to her, doesn't it?" Eryn sniggered. "I will never forget the hunting trip, when you thought she was about to spring up onto you. Your face - priceless!"

He frowned and pretended to be listening for something. "There, I think the captain was calling for you. It seems he is about to hoist anchor. Hurry!"

"Very funny," she smiled. "You will miss me soon enough, you just wait."

They exchanged kisses and formal farewells with representatives of the Houses and the healers who had come to see them off.

When only the two men she considered her family were left, Eryn noticed Malriel, who was standing off to one side, making it clear that she intended to be the last one to bid her goodbyes.

Valrad cupped her face in both his palms and planted a firm kiss on her forehead. "My child, I have to admit that despite all the troubles you had to overcome to reach this point, I cannot help but feel smug at having you wear that pendant around your neck that marks you as one of mine. Be aware, though, that this adoption was by no means just a political manoeuvre as far as I am concerned. I expect you to keep in contact with your family here, do you understand me?"

She smiled and nodded. "I will. I promise. You will be getting so many messages from me that you will soon wish you had not made that demand."

"Hardly likely," he objected and pulled her into a firm hug.

"Now release her, there are others who want to say goodbye as well," Vran'el demanded. "Eryn, you were a nuisance, a trial for my poor nerves and you caused a lot more trouble than you are probably worth. Good riddance."

She grinned when she spotted the giveaway glint of wetness in the corner of his eye. "I love you, too, you idiot. Be more careful with the wine as long as I am not here to restore your sad carcass afterwards."

They hugged each other. Eryn felt a pang of sorrow at leaving the two of them behind. It was as if she had started missing them already.

When she looked up, she saw Enric in an embrace with Valrad, who then patted his shoulders. "You take good care of my girl, Enric. And of yourself. Remember that you promised me to bring her back here regularly. Do not make me have to board a ship and come over to your city to tell you off about it in front of all your important friends."

Enric laughed. "I wouldn't dare ignore that order."

Then he turned to Vran'el. "Thank you, my friend. Your persistence and foresight have brought this whole imbroglio to a good ending. I will not forget what you have done for us."

Vran'el waved him away. "It was my pleasure. This is what family is for, after all - to get you out of trouble. Or into it," he added with a quick glance at Malriel who lifted her chin in a surly manner at him.

They, too, hugged and then both Enric and Eryn stepped before the Head of House Aren. Malriel's smile became slightly frayed around the edges.

"So you will leave here, finally. I admit I would have preferred the other option, which had you remaining here for a longer time."

Eryn gave her a considered look. "Yes, I feel sure you would have. A pity it hasn't worked out to your satisfaction."

The older woman shrugged. "One has to make do with what one is dealt, I always say. Provided one has made sure to get enough in the first place, that is," she added as an afterthought.

"Like your getting a son when you put your daughter to flight?" Eryn asked icily.

"Something like that, yes," Malriel replied good-naturedly. "You are angry at me. I can see that plainly enough, Theá. I want to assure you that I never intended to hurt you or bring harm to you or Enric. I am proud of what you have become, and happy to see that you have found a companion worthy of you. We may no longer be mother and daughter from the legal standpoint, but blood is a stronger bond than law. I will *always* be your mother, no matter what the papers say." Then she turned to Enric. "I have enjoyed getting to know you immensely. You are strong, and strength is something Aren women respect and admire. Not only are you worthy of my daughter, but also of my House. I am sure I do not need to remind you that you are bound to it. Through it, you are bound to me."

He smiled back wanly. "Yet you cannot help pointing it out to me."

She shrugged. "A habit. I have come to realise that saying things explicitly at times is more efficient than relying on people to decipher inferences. Subtlety gets in the way a lot of time."

Enric chuckled. "A trait I would have failed to associate with House Aren anyway."

"Good. At least you know what you got yourself into," she laughed and pulled him close into an embrace. "Travel back safely, Enric. And write to me occasionally to tell me about what is going on in your life." She then turned to Eryn.

"Theá. I think a little distance will do each of us good. But do not make the mistake of thinking that this is final. We will meet again soon enough. I have a stake in your companion, after all." Before the younger woman had a chance to react, she pulled her into an embrace as well. "Good bye, my child." She stepped back again. "Who knows? I may even come to visit you to see where you live."

Eryn smiled coldly. "You shouldn't go to that much trouble." Her stare became intense. "Really. I mean it. Don't."

She heard Malriel's low laugh as she turned and stepped onto the gangplank finally to leave this place behind her and return home.

www.ingramcontent.com/pod-product-compliance
Lightning Source LLC
Chambersburg PA
CBHW070534030726
47505CB00001B/35